AZIMUTH

AZIMUTH

Jack Sanger

chronometer publications

chronometer publications, 94 Glebe Road, Norwich,
Norfolk, England NR2 3JQ

Azimuth first published by chronometer publications in 2012
Copyright   Jack Sanger

ISBN 978-0-9571471-0-2

For Joseph and Luke

Book 1

Chapter One

To know oneself is a journey that requires a beginning

If a man could be said to be constructed from the tools of his work, then Kamil was just such a man. He laboured with pen and paper and from them he built history. His flesh was as dry and pale as bleached parchment, his blood so dark it could have been extracted from crushed beetles and yet his intelligence was as sharp as the knife he used to give edge to his quills. If in total he could be thought of as a book, it would be a thick, learned, heavily annotated leather-bound tome, with a simple modest title and his name in small letters beneath. And it would gather dust, rarely read except by other scholars, in the Great Library.

Yet this literary hermit, this fugitive from commercial bustle, from adventure and risk and the intoxication of brushing up against strangers, was chosen by fate to play a formidable role in the affairs of the empire, a role which would affect the outcome of future battles, uncover deadly intrigues and determine generations of royal lineage!

This unforeseen and at times terrifying course of events was set properly in motion when Kamil wrote the following letter to the Princess Sabiya, daughter of the great Emperor Haidar:

It has been my privilege, as his Majesty's servant, to have collected together these events from the life of the Magus, in accordance with the wishes of your blessed father, Emperor Haidar. There were so many stories that it would seem impossible for one, even so great, to have been at the heart of them all. Yet...

What I have done is concentrate on those tales upon which everyone seems to agree. Imagine, as you read this, that so much else could be written here for his journeyings were long and the changes in him greater than I can possibly record. For that, my humble apologies. Upon the events of his life after the first Great Journey, I have hardly touched, just as one might dip a hand into a stream. So there is no account here of that one great event that led to his lasting fame as a peacemaker, the one we all grew up hearing about at school and from our tutors. The settling of the Great War. This will be the work of another period of incarceration with my pen!

One final word. I have written in a manner that combines fact with the elaborations of a poet. Sometimes I have written about acts and events which may not be appropriate for the ear of a princess. I know not about these matters. If anything here embarrasses or upsets you, I apologise unreservedly, though your father told me to hold nothing back on any matter. He says you combine a son's vulgarity with a daughter's imagination! I have conjured what I could not know. I have entered the thoughts of the Magus and reported his conversations. It is to make the tale engage with You, its audience, My Lady. Yet I feel it is not an excess. Rather, it is poor clothing for one of his stature. But one such as he deserves some clothing, do you not think?

The book had taken him three years to write in his painstaking hand. He had consulted what existed in the Great Library. He had laid it, finally, thick sheet divided from thick sheet by the finest, smokily translucent paper, in a specially constructed simple wooden box lined with velvet. The cover sheet was stamped with his name and bore the title:

Tales of the Magus
The First Great Journey

And now before him sat the royal tutor, staring at him with a hostile, compelling gaze, a man who knew that this work had been commissioned for Princess Sabiya's personal education into matters moral and spiritual - a challenge to his own role and status within the court!

-You say she has read it? Kamil asked the tutor at last.

-Reading is not understanding. Some read from letter to letter, some from page to page. Who knows what they understand?

-Did she like it?

-It is not my privilege or place to divine her royal feelings. As I have just told you, I am to bring you to the palace immediately, provide you with a servant and two rooms, one for sleeping and the other to receive her Highness, with a lamp that burns well for reading, two comfortable chairs and a small table for the book which will rest between you. Now!

-Other than the Great Library, I have hardly left my house and garden in ten years, Kamil groaned.

-That is of no interest.

*

Hours later he was ensconced in his palace rooms comfortably rested and fed. As the hour reached six there was a rap at the door.

-Come in! he ventured.

The door swung open, an enormous armed guard peered at him and then stood aside to allow the Princess to enter. She was too slim to be beautiful to Kamil's eye and too tall for all but a royal family member. Her black skin revealed her father's predilection for Ethiopia. Her eyes were a glittering blue set wide apart above the family's long shallow nose. Her rich plump red lips pouted at him.

-Does it take so long to come from the sea to my palace?

-I am sorry your Highness, he said falling to his knees, -I came as soon as the packing and the carriage would allow.

-Get up! You couldn't have much to pack, looking at you. Enough! I am anxious to start. Wait outside, she commanded the guard and thrust the door shut after him, -Good, you have your book. It sat in a tall pile on the table between them, -Let us sit. We can begin. The first Tale. Why is it called The Fool? I could see no fool in it.

He stroked his beard nervously, -After the tarot, Princess.

-What is that? I will have the royal tutor banished to hell. I seem to know nothing of this world!

He could see that stories of her impetuousness and disregard for protocol were not misplaced. He said softly, dropping his voice, -The cards of mystery. They plumb the heart and mind, the past, the present and in some hands, the future.

-I must see them! You have them?

-I do your Highness. He reached to the floor by his side and lifted into sight a small, rectangular block, wrapped in purple silk. He undid the wrapping and placed it beside the book so that a deck of ornate cards sat face down upon it. He picked them up, turned them and fanned their faces before her. The bright reds, yellows, blues and greens flashed in the lamp light. She saw courtiers, swords, coins, cups and batons. She pulled back.

-I am not sure I like them.

-It is too early. In time. They may be suspicious of you, too. He placed them back as he had found them, -I have arranged the major Arcana according to our needs. These are the powerful ones that speak of the cycles within our lives. Let us begin, one card at a time. Every tale begins with a card in sequence because I have collected stories from the first thirty years of the Magus's life. Would you like to turn the first one over?

With a degree of hesitancy rarely experienced by her, she did so.

-So it is The Fool, she said, -I can see that. Look, he carries all his possessions over his shoulder and marches along with hounds snapping at his tails. Tell me Kamil, what does this mean?

-Let me read the Tale with that title first, replied the man relaxing a little, -Then we may talk of such things. May I suggest also that we have no conversation until a Tale is read? Interruptions break a tale's flow as surely as a weir does the river.

She yawned, -If it must be so. You are a boring teacher. The young woman sank back and closed her eyes...

He is dancing in the smallest space where red merges with black, doing cartwheels, his irises huge in the velvet light. Baby in the womb of his mother. She is on a horse, side-saddle. In a scrubland. Dust rolling from the hooves. In a country where solitary women are hunted like game.

The mother keeps to the lee of the low hills, eyes alight, burning, boring into the heat mists and shadowy concealments, searching for sudden silhouettes or light flashes. Her roan horse canters easily and skilfully across the rough terrain. Signals from her hands and heels point it in the direction of the falling sun but it decides on the detail.

The baby bounces, jiggles, opens and closes its eyes, clenches its fingers and toes. The baby smiles. She already knows his name. She had sat staring at the fire and as she made fantastical creatures from the flames, smoke and sticks there was a crackle and a whisper from the chimney. It mouthed his name. A name she would never tell another.

The mother is a fierce warrior. Whether she fights on her horse, legs each side like a man, or as now, to give the child some comfort, she is feared in battle. Beneath her purple brocaded travel robe hangs a cross belt from her shoulder, down between her breasts to her hip. A dagger in its pouch is secured to it. Her two handed sword is scabbarded behind her on a carved cross belt harness. Her black hair is coiled and held by a bone needle whose point has been dipped in the venom of a water snake. In the curling toes of her shoes are sachets of plant extract to inflame the senses, produce coma or instil forbearance in the very face of death. Her handsome face is impassive, brown skin darkened by sun and wind.

The roan suddenly slows and turns into a thicket of scrub, which is also home to some small trees. It snickers to calm her and pushes its way into the green clearing. Water bubbles and coils in a small pool, only to sink a few strides further back into the underground stream. The water has a pinkish hue, dyed by the roots of a plant she recognises. She slips from the horse's back. It stands and waits until she has drunk. She fills the leather bottles from the saddle and makes a clicking noise with her tongue. The horse drops his head and whinnies softly and begins to drink. Inside, the mother feels the boy's renewed swimming motions. The cold water entering her stomach excites him.

She takes compressed fruit biscuits from the saddlebag and squats by the water. She feels the baby press into her pelvis and knows it won't be long. The baby stands on his head, as though practising to be born. When the horse has drunk and chewed some grass, it raises its head to the breeze. It listens for some time. She waits for it. It drops its head and walks back to the passage through the bushes that had admitted them. It stops and paws the ground. She rises, returns the water bottles and climbs up. It waits for her to take loose hold of the reins and then edges out of the thicket.

Some distance on, with the sun down and a sky spiked by steely stars, she is curled up in a blanket. There is no fire, nothing to give signal to this sleeping place. She is lying against the back of a rock which still radiates the heat of the day. The roan stands nearby, sleeping too. One of its ears remains cocked. Inside her, the boy dozes, his eyes shut and dreaming of other journeys, other times.

It is still dark and has become chill when the horse's nose nudges her awake. Despite the child's added weight she is standing in one instant motion. The horse's head is cocked, its eyes wide. She picks up the perturbation in the air. Several riders, perhaps half an hour behind.

The horse is watered while she eats in the saddle. Her stomach is heavy but she tells the child to rest a little more. This day should see them both safe. Behind, a fine skein of light suggests the coming of the day. The ground is rising towards a high ridge and the horse picks its way through a cold cut in the sandstone.

When her father came to know that she would take this journey so that the boy might grow up in a place where the tide of clan war had not yet lapped, he entrusted her to this animal. He told her that the beast had been born with both sun and moon full in the sky. Its mother had died at the birth but the foal had sniffed her body and then walked to her father to be fed. Since the horse's mother had made this journey many times, her father said that the stallion would know its way? It had

14

demonstrated this on other missions, following the paths its mother had discovered and used. Her father had held the horse's mane and talked softly to it, telling it what was now expected of it. The roan, with its distinctive red blotches, pressed its ear to his cheek, tipping its head in small nods of acknowledgement. Her father said that the roan was unique, one in an entire generation.

They reach a high point, just below the ridge. There is a little foliage, mostly dry bushes and grass. She is able to rest for a moment and scan the land below. There is some new cloud, enough to mask the opening sun. She picks out the three riders, still some distance away. They ride with very straight backs, their legs straight and thrust out before them. Men from the north. All three horses are black, taken and broken from the wild, small but stocky and at home in these foothills.

She considers her next step. She can outrun them but at a possible cost to her child. She can hide but if one is a tracker, they will find her. Soon. She can fight. Then the child would need protecting. Fight and flight threaten her life equally. Her one advantage is that of surprise. She looks round and makes her decision.

The three riders are in single file. At the front is an old man with one arm. He is bent over his horse's neck, watching the ground. He carries only a small, one-handed, hunting bow, tied to his saddle. Behind him are two fighting men. They are fully armed. One's eyes sweep the land to the left, the other's the land to the right. Neither holds reins. Their hands are free to rest on sheathed swords and grip the blunt knobs of their holstered throwing knives. They are garbed in leather battle-wear. Their stiff hide hats are pointed and have chain-flaps. One of them asks a question of the tracker. He shrugs. She can hear him tell them that the roan leaves little sign of its passing or the time that has elapsed since it travelled that way. She remembers how her horse slipped away to leave its business in a hidden place. She is satisfied that she has only two real adversaries. The old man does not fight.

The trio push their horses up on to a tiny plateau, little more than a ledge. The old man raises his head and mutters to the others. They draw alongside. They stare at the small fire and suspended above it a flat stone supported by rocks. On top are a number of small cakes, baking. The smell of the cakes suddenly rushes over them. It is like a string of memories; of being a child again, holding their mothers' hands in the village kitchen, the sweetmeats at funeral parties and weddings, the little trifles they exchanged with their brides on the first night of their nuptials, the rich foods they had eaten when they plundered the houses of their enemies, the scent of the young girls they had taken for their pleasure. Even the old man's eyes water in dim reminiscence.

They form into a triangle around the oven, facing away from it. Their eyes scour the hillside. There is no sign of their quarry. But she can only be a few strides away, concealed. The cakes have reached maturity. She must have been startled by them and had to move quickly. They know she has to be watched carefully. She has killed men in hand to hand fighting. There are stories of her ambushing a troop of fighting men with just three comrades. Legend has it that lightning jumps from her eyes and the power of winter avalanches is in her wrists. This they do not believe for she is a mortal woman, carrying a child who must die. The blood heir. Heir for heir.

One drops from his horse and walks to the fire, -Why do we not eat her breakfast and gain strength for what lies ahead, he suggests. He pokes a cake and juggles it off the stone, throwing it from hand to hand. The spinning cake gives extra scent to the nose, even as it cools.

-Be careful of her food for she is a sorceress, warns the old man but the teeth have bitten and the tongue is aflame with desire. He turns and smiles, wolfing it down.

-You must eat! he insists, suddenly snarling to his companions, - Come! Eat!

☥

He turns on them. He has changed. His eyes are wide and protruding. Flecks of pink saliva dribble down his jaw. He waves his sword at them as if to force them. Their horses rear and back away. He follows them jerkily, now slashing at the legs of the old man. There is a whisper through the air and a throwing knife penetrates his larynx.

Silently, he slumps to the ground. His dark blood joins with the pink liquid and crumbs of the cake oozing from his mouth. His comrade pulls out the throwing blade, cleans it and returns it to its holster. His killer's eyes meet those of the old man, -And now there are two of us. Still enough do you not think?

-I am no fighting man, says the gnarled tracker, -I have one arm and I am too old. I was paid by the clan to lead you to her. Not to fight her. I would advise you to go back. She is too strong for you.

-I cannot do so. I am pledged to them. They have paid the first half of my bounty. It is my honour. It is for this I live. The child must die. It is said that if he lives he might one day take from them their very name and the stories of their fathers. You may go. He draws out a leather pouch with a tied neck and passes it to him. The old man turns his horse and it picks its way back down the hillside. The remaining mercenary walks over to the oven and kicks the stone and cakes across the earth.

From where she sits among the rocks he appears calm and almost leisurely as he remounts. He has the posture of one who cares not to lose his life in the mission to take hers and that of her child. His current masters are from a clan that had once been content possessing the lands adjacent to her family's valleys. They had cohabited in peace. There was even some intermarriage but last year the eldest son was killed while out on his own, riding. His body was found on her father's land. A knife with the characteristic horse head markings of her family was found in his back. The dead man's brother vowed vengeance. A life for a life. She was the only child of her father. There have been several attempts to kill her. Now this.

She feels the baby move again. He is kicking and pummelling her with his little fists as though asking her whether her body will open for him. She presses her hand against her stomach and whispers that he should wait. The activity stops.

She stretches. Unwinds. She is directly above him on a ledge. He is

17

half aware of her. But the distance is too far for her to jump. He presents too foreshortened a target for her knife. She can only see the point of his cap and his shoulders which have metal strips to protect against the force of a slashing sword blow. He rides slowly out of sight and will emerge a few seconds later, level with where she is crouched. He will see the roan and stop before he is in full view. He will know she is waiting there. It will be a life and a death. Her throwing knife is gripped, point upwards, in her palm. She takes a position where she cannot be seen once he comes onto the ledge, and waits.

-You are there, Witch Princess? She does not answer. Her mind is like the coldest night of winter, a blackness so deep and icy that emotion cannot seed itself. She reaches out her senses towards him and against the mental backdrop the warmth of his presence becomes palpable. He has dismounted and is flattened against the rock wall that bends to where she waits. She pictures his sword held above his head in both hands. -Come out and do battle. I know of your fame. It will give me pleasure to end the life of such a one. She sees his fingers tighten on the sword's handle. He moves slowly around the wall. Such is the man's stupidity.

Suddenly with the speed of a striking snake, she launches herself away from the wall. Almost at the same moment his sword flashes down catching only a tuft of wool padding from her heel. As it rings on the ground her wrists thrust the knife upwards. It judders in her palm as it enters his chest, deflecting off a rib and then sinking deep. He falls beside her gasping. She stands over him.

-You have killed me, Witch. I am dishonoured.

-You are misled, she says, -I have saved your honour. He stares at her through clouding eyes. She squats by his ear, -Your paymaster's son caught me bathing. He roped me like a wild pony and took his pleasure in my body. As he fell off me and lay spent I broke free and ran for my knife. He turned to flee but my aim was true. I cleaned his manhood and retied his trousers so no-one would know he had taken me. It is his child you would have killed. The child of those who paid you.

The man smiles. He is dead.

☥

She gives birth to the boy on the down slopes of the next valley. She is strong and cuts the umbilical cord and ties it at each end. She spends the next day and night suckling him and then places him in a travelling basket on the roan. She takes its mane and whispers instructions. Its head nods acknowledgement and it trots away down the slope. It is a soft night. She takes her enemies' horses and rides back the way she has come.

The Princess eventually opened her eyes. It is better to listen to you than to read it myself. I understand much more. This time I like the mother. All I could think the first time I read it was that she abandoned her child.

-She is strong.

-I would like to be like her. I will ask my father to find someone to teach me the sword and bow! Are they not still the symbols of a true warrior? It is more romantic than the pistol. I am an expert with the pistol! She settled again, -I have a question. In all the Tales there are hardly any names for people or places and few of animals and plants. As well as this, the Magus' life story remains mostly a mystery except what everyone is taught in school about his two great claims to fame.

Kamil pondered for a while, -It is true. In the records, actually, the Magus went by a number of names. Many tribes have claimed descent from him. It was such a long time ago. Scholars argue about the place and time of his history. Some feel that many of the tales about him were carried along the silk route from the east and storytellers added them to his exploits, others that he was a great warrior from the ice and sand of the far north. I decided to portray him without a name, from boyhood to Magus. At the beginning he is The Fool for he knows nothing and is beginning the great journey of life. He is a cipher for the reader to interpret how he or she wishes. And just so with the unnamed lands and the people he meets upon them. Such a mystery houses the reader in a tent of mirrors reflecting the eyes back into the self.

She nodded as if satisfied, -It is so. The baby is born. It has no mother to nurture it. It is left in the care of a magical horse. That is enough for one day. Tomorrow, at the same time, you will read the second tale, Kamil. It is the tale of The Magician. I remember him, although the further names I have forgotten.

-I will be pleased to obey you, Princess Sabiya.

Chapter Two

Believing what is seen is a form of blindness

When she had plumped the cushions, twisted and turned and finally settled herself, Princess Sabiya smiled expectantly, -In a moment I will turn over the second card! He gave a short bow. The pack had not been touched since the previous night. The yellow light showed their faces. She trusted his somewhat unused features. She liked his shy earnestness, while Kamil was warming a little to her direct ways and wilful character. He did not believe that royal blood was divine but he believed in a special family of rulers, born to keep an empire together. How else were the myriad ways of tribes to be kept in check? They had to believe in something greater than themselves, divine or not. There were always troubles in the further flung parts and those within who would crack the world like an egg.

-But I have a second question about the tale of the Fool. She plunged on, -Why is it named The Fool? We have several fools in the court. They each have their place. All but one are clowns. But the court fool rises above the others. No matter how ill-conceived, churlish, defamatory or vengeful his remarks - the royal tutor is his current victim - as long as he is funny then he is allowed licence to bait and hook one and all. There is no such person in the opening tale!

He explained again, patiently, as he had done the previous evening, - No Princess Sabiya, it is not thus in the tarot. Here The Fool is the innocent, starting out on a cycle of life's great adventure. He has no history. He has nothing to light his mind. Yet within him are the seeds of knowing. His life will be fertile ground and many of these seeds will germinate and flower.

Her face brightened as she reviewed the first Tale in her thoughts, - The Fool is the baby! It is the Magus himself! He bowed again, smiling at her enthusiasm, -Good! She clapped her hands, -I see it! She bent forward so that her perfume enveloped him. It was almost too rich for his senses. Her long, dark fingers took the second card and turned it face up, then placed it on top of The Fool, -I see The Magician. He has a table full of tricks. I remember this chapter…but read it to me before my prattling takes up all our time. And I agree - it is better that I do not interrupt. It is my nature but it would do little for your telling.

He took the fine film away that covered the page and began.

-How did I enter the world? asked the boy, quizzically. He was sitting by a fire, cross-legged. The moon was low and young. The night was cool but not yet cold enough to wear skins. Today the strawberry roan had fathered an identical foal. It had then disappeared as though he had never been. The boy felt both grief and happiness. The roan had looked after him like a guard dog. It had shown little interest in a mare until earlier in the year and it had surprised everyone. He couldn't think of a single day when it had not been there. He had learned to ride its broad back, first in a saddle and then bare. The horse had kept him balanced by counteracting his every slide towards a fall. He would make up stories and whisper them into the roan's ear and the horse would stare gravely at him as though every word was understood. He had slept against the heat of its supine flanks, sheltered from the winter winds. When he first walked the roan would step gingerly beside him, its head bowed, offering its mane to hold. It was as though the roan was a conduit to another world.

So when he asked the question it was precipitated by the foal's birth and the shock that comes when there is a momentous ending to a stage of life. The roan had gone for good. But was not the foal also the roan?

Opposite him, also sitting cross-legged, was the Merchant whom he called father. The firelight jigged across the man's face revealing dark features, almost black eyes, large hooked nose and the deep carved sandstone skin of a distance traveller. His father was not from here. He had been born far south in a different world of markets, traders, clay houses and the sea. Once he had been dressed in silks with his head wrapped in cloth. He was the best horseman anyone could ever remember but he had never ridden the roan. No-one but the boy had rested on its back. The voice of his father was deep and had a lilt which set him apart.

-I cannot say for I was not there. You entered my world a day or so after you were born. Late in the evening when the moon was still a stripling I heard a pawing at my tent. There you were in a baby basket, tied to his saddle. It was a wonderful and strange thing. I, who have no wife nor children, who had rarely considered such possibilities, became both father and mother to you the moment I set my eyes upon yours.

-I must have had a mother?

-Of course.

-She loved me but she abandoned me.

-She left you with a fierce guardian. The horse stayed with you until now. It felt you were ready to face life without it.

-I am.

-I believe the horse wanted to be sure I could look after you, too.

-But it is still here.

-Yes, in the foal. You are an ancient sometimes in your thinking.

☥

Another night on one of the many journeys he took with his father, he lay in a blanket of animal fur by the fire and asked, -Is death the end of all things?

-What do you think little man?

-It feels so. But it also feels not so.

-Very good. I think this…The boy waited for his father to compose his thought for he had learned that these deeper moments could never be hurried. The Merchant continued, -At the very moment you understand life, death will come with its assassin's knife. For what else is there for you when such knowledge is yours?

There was silence between them, the Merchant considering his words and how they might be made more precise, the younger man weighing each syllable.

-I will seek to understand what it is to be alive. One day I will understand everything and then die! It will be a glorious last thought.

-That is a just ambition my son. You have an old spirit and therefore it may be possible.

-For you too, Father?

-Not in this cycle. But I have important things to do nevertheless. I am like a ewe who has lost her offspring, I have to bring up someone

24

else's lamb.

-And what was the pelt that so deceived you? The boy laughed.

-We have nobler spirits than sheep. You were dressed in mystery and portent. How could I resist?

The boy was becoming agitated by the analogy, -And the orphan lamb has lost its mother. Some say it kills its mother at birth.

-Do you feel you killed your mother?

He concentrated his brows, -No, she is not dead. But I brought her great sorrow.

He learned many things from his father. How to eat and drink in the desert where the land stretches forever under harsh sun and nightly frost. How to sew and clothe himself. How soils and plants give colour to cotton and leather. How to make bread from wild grasses. How to throw a knife. How to tune the wild horse's spirit to his own. Which creatures needed his eye to subordinate them and which required him to be still and look away. The smell of coming rain. The tracks left by all living things, including men. How birds' flight patterns told of the unfolding events below them. How to smell what is good for the body and what might poison it.

But even greater than the gifts of survival, including that of the sword, was the gift of second sight. That is, to know what lies beyond the visible. He learned that all things that exist speak also of other things. But few master this language.

With other boys he was at ease but somehow apart. He was popular but they fell away from him at certain times as though too close to an unforgiving truth. He did not share their ignorant waste of life or food or others' respect. He was taught by his father that all should be conserved unless his very existence was balanced on a thread.

With girls he was less at ease. His father was not willing, consciously or unconsciously, to teach him the words and gestures, the quality of gaze, to make them comfortable in his presence.

When he was twelve he attended the circumcision ceremony of a boy who was as close a friend as any. He joined the file of witnesses through the tent to observe and congratulate the youth on his purple and swollen manhood. His father asked him that evening about his feelings in the ceremony.

-For some, such events are as important to them as the sun or the moon, he said, -For myself, I see no need for it. Pain must be chosen sparingly and as a means to knowing something that is worth such an effort, -But, he smiled, -It is not normally a matter of choice.

His father nodded in agreement and said nothing for a while.

By the age of fourteen he was as tall as many men. His shoulders had begun to broaden and he was the equal of most with horse and sword. His roan had taken the place of its father and he fully believed by now that it was the same creature. It was uninterested in mares at their time of desire and always slept standing and untethered near the entrance to his tent. It seemed to possess understanding beyond its own life and experience.

From time to time travellers came by to talk with his father. They kept him aware of what was happening in his own land. The boy showed little interest in the ways of merchants.

One day he was following the trail of a wolf which had taken a sheep from the family of the circumcised boy. It was not to exact retribution. He wished to know more of why the wolf would dare to come so close to the tents. Wolves never attacked men no matter how they maltreated them unless it was to protect their young. It was a day-old trail but he and the roan between them found scents, scuff-marks and droppings which might have defeated others less aware. Eventually he was looking down at the family of cubs and their mother enjoying play. The mother was thin from giving milk but still bestowed her full attention.

-They will give you no respite, he murmured, -If you cannot provide for them they will suck you to death. This is why you will abandon them soon.

26

He turned the roan back. Seconds later he sensed his father riding towards him. He pushed the roan into a canter. They met some minutes later.

The two horses stood facing each other. Man and boy gazed at one another. The man made a gesture with his hand indicating that words were difficult.

-We must leave? the boy asked, reading his father's face.

-You are ready?

-I want to see the land of your elders. I have dreamt that this would be my destiny.

The man marvelled, as he so often did, at the boy's prescience, -The journey will take us much of your youth.

-It is the path. The throwing knife cannot stay in its holster forever.

The man smiled sadly, -I was grooming my horse and had a waking dream. My mother spoke to me.

-She is alive?

-For a little while.

They left without goodbyes when it was still dark. All they needed for sleep and survival was packed on their horses, his father's tall black stallion and the strong roan. They were a mile from the village before they cantered. When they reached the far ridge of the valley the youth motioned them to stop and indicated to his father to look back. Although it was no small distance away they could just discern fires breaking out and hear the cries of battle.

-We should go back, growled his father, unsheathing his sword.

-It is not our destiny, replied the youth, -It is not our pain. He looked steadily at his father with eyes that revealed no remorse for the death and suffering. The man looked back and said nothing but the wild anger drained from his face.

They rode on with the sun for a while and then took a rarely used trail south. Skirting isolated tents and settlements it was several weeks before they came to a slow moving river. The scrubland had given way to a carpet of green. The boy gathered knowledge of new birds and animals, of insects and plants. His father introduced him to the thread and hook, the stealthy hand in water and ways to prepare and cook fish. They camped by the river for three days, resting the horses and recovering their strength. They practised with their swords and the boy now made his father sweat.

He also learned a new art. His father sat with a piece of cloth laid on a flat rock and with three large seed cups set upon it. He would manipulate a bean beneath them so that the watcher was deceived as to which cup sheltered it. He learned also how to draw an egg from his ear, how to change water to wine by the sweep of his hand and how to make a bird break from the opened thongs of his shirt. He could order cut rope to join itself, slack rope to stand as stiff as a wand and he could remove a pebble from a hand, substituting one of another colour in the act of greeting.

It was a great amusement to them both. Then one day as they journeyed, the boy said solemnly, -Is life just a play of cups and beans?

-For many, most perhaps. But for us? There is more. To learn such deceptions helps us to uncover certain truths. Few that you will meet will let you see the furthest depths in their eyes. Most would keep you at their surface. As a practised conjurer you will see this clearly. You will know the hearts of those that appear to offer you gifts. You will see what they have hidden. The skills that you have learned are as nothing compared to the ability to weigh another's spirit. This happens without words and without the play of hands. It is a gift beyond my present life. But not yours. You have the sight. Not being able to measure such things led me mistakenly from that which I desired most. But from my ignorance eventually arose my journey to the north and my guardianship of you.

A month later his father led them into a city.

The court historian laid down the final sheet of the Tale of the Magician and waited for Princess Sabiya to begin her questions. Her eyes were closed and her breasts rose and fell slowly under her white cotton robe. Her hands were clasped on her lap. When she did speak she did not open her eyes and it was not a question.

-I have already had my first day's practice with sword and bow. They waken an ancient familiarity in me. My father is pleased. He has yet to procure a son from his wives. I am the alternative! I told him I was ready to be a warrior empress! He said that you must be a good teacher. You are lighting my path.

-None can underestimate the power of stories, he said humbly.

-My father is away from court so much, he is not like the Merchant to me. I must gather round me the best teachers to enable me to rule wisely; soldiers, ambassadors, cooks, gardeners, builders, sailors, spiritual leaders from other lands...our own Sufi Masters...she opened her eyes at last, -I will try not to ask too many questions each time you read to me. Over time everything can be discussed. It will be a discipline for me to ask one question after each tale and reflect upon your response.

Kamil was flattered though he tried not to show it, -I hope I find answers that satisfy your curiosity, your Highness.

-You will Kamil. I feel myself at an opened door when once there seemed no exit from the room I have occupied all my life. There are twenty two tales in your book are there not? He nodded, -A little over three weeks if I come to hear and discuss a tale each night. It will bring us to a crossroads in my life! How opportune! Perhaps our meetings will help me face events which could change the course of the empire's history! Kamil felt a nervous tic start under his left lid. His book might have such influence? He tried to concentrate on what she was saying though her words seemed to carry from a long distance, -And it is nearly time for me to be elsewhere. Here is my question! Already the boy-magus has shown that he is without sentimentality. His emotions are ruled by his head. He will not go back to try to save his neighbours and friends, the people with whom he has grown up. Is this aspect of character essential for a great spirit?

Kamil dropped his eyes and assembled his thoughts carefully, -I do not wish to talk of what is to come in the story and I have no knowledge of what you remember from your own reading but I have tried to portray a boy at a certain point in his life. He is still only the fool and not yet a magician figure like his father. But he has been born different from others. His mind is not ensnared by emotion in the same way. It is a spare mind. For the moment the world only consists of his father, his absent mother, his horse and nature itself. We will see how he grows. Perhaps a sign of a magus is the skill of detachment in even the most desperate of circumstances, of weighing all things, of forecasting how ends can only be reached by employing certain means.

-He is a model for good rule. Always the emperor must weigh the good of the whole against the desires of the few on the royal scales. Kingdoms are not havens of equality in all things. She looked at the stacked cards, -Well, the boy is growing. He is a quick learner. Let us see tomorrow where his journey takes him next.

Chapter Three

To find one's Purpose one must step beyond belief

Princess Sabiya swept into his room in haste and obvious anticipation. No sooner had she sat herself, this time perched on the edge of her chair, than she turned over the third card, -Ah, our first woman! The High Priestess. She seems austere. She seems not concerned with the kitchen, the herbs in the garden, with being a seamstress and the duties of motherhood!

-You are right. Though it would be mistaken to imagine any tarot card as having a fixed gender. She does not signify a woman's earthly needs. Her thoughts are higher. Their elevation concerns the search for the essence of meaning in life. She encourages the spiritual quest, the glories of art, all paths to enlightenment. She is a philosopher. The truest. In each tale the card might represent the Magus himself or someone he meets who will influence the growth of his being, Kamil sat back and waited for a response from his protégée.

-Hah! I know none like her whether man or woman. The acolytes of the oracle seem unable to do more than seek self-advantage from their temple lives, though the High Priestess is an exception. She raises in me some wonder and a little fear. The court philosopher speaks gibberish and his admirers smile knowingly though it is doubtful whether they understand one word in ten that gushes from his mouth. Enough! Read me the next tale.

LA·PAPESSE·8

There were canvass and hide tents as far as the eye could see. At the heart of the brown conglomeration were tall ochre buildings, clustered together, with narrow streets that barely allowed horses to pass each other. The youth drew it all in, in silence. He had never seen such constructions and felt they could topple at any time upon him and the roan, engulfing them. His father led their way down the cool shadowy alleyways, taking instructions from passers-by, speaking in a dialect which, though generally understood by the youth, contained words and inflections which he could not comprehend.

He sensed the strain in the older man. Cities such as these were not safe places. He noted the way the horses were the focus of attention and discussion, particularly the black stallion. They were going to meet a woman with whom his father had stayed on his journey north. He had said little more. The youth observed that his father kept his free hand on his throwing knife and had loosened the ties that secured his sword in its scabbard on his back. He followed suit. Their horses eased through bustling human traffic. Finally, they stood outside a metal-bossed wooden door, taller than a man on horseback and wide enough to allow three riders to enter. His father beat a tattoo on it with the heel of his knife. After a few moments a wooden slat was pushed to one side and a face appeared at the grill which had been revealed.

His father announced them to the mistress of the house. The slat of wood was returned to its place. They waited several minutes. Again the wood slid back. Again they were observed suspiciously. Finally the door opened on to a courtyard and they rode in and dismounted. A servant came to take their horses to be fed and watered. Another retrieved their saddle-bags. A third led them through a door up marble stairs and into a set of rooms. In one there were several beds with padded cotton mattresses and sheepskins. In another the floor was covered with cushions. A third small room contained a table with water jug and bowl for washing, a curtained section with a pot for their bodily needs and a mirror. A servant stood ready to help them wash, cut hair and the older man's beard, offer them perfumes, which they declined, and remove the pot to be emptied and returned. They were given clean shirts and drawstring trousers. His father strapped his knife to his chest under his shirt and so the boy followed suit.

When they were ready a servant came for them and led them down corridors that took them round and above the courtyard to the main part of the house. They reached the door. A wiry dark-skinned fighting man stood with his back to it, a sword unsheathed and laid at arms, point to his left ear, handle to his left hip.

-Remove your knives.

His father locked eyes with him. Moments passed. Their brooding silence was interrupted by the door swinging open. A tall grey-haired woman stood there.

-Let them pass.

She smiled and accepted his father's bow. The youth felt a warmth wash through him as she took his eyes with her own.

-I see much has happened in your life since last we met, she said to his father without taking her eyes off the young man, -Come, food is prepared.

They sat on cushions covered with pictures and patterns of birds and flowers. The youth felt that only with magical fingers could such things be created; the exquisite threads, the gold and silver tracery. Her robes were white but were trimmed in a thin edging of blue velvet. Her face was serene yet her eyes opened up to depths he had only encountered in his father and the roan.

Food was brought to them on plates that allowed light to pass, so much finer than the fire baked pots he had known until now. He nibbled at it, finding it too rich and sweetly overcooked. However the fruit was satisfying and the goat's cheese was like that of the countryside, though creamier. While they ate his father told her of their life together, from the moment of his arrival at the tent on the roan to this moment. Now and then she fixed her eyes on him and he felt as though she was probing, looking for a certain knowledge in him. He was being gently drained of thoughts and memories he regarded as his own, even those that he had never shared with his father. When the Merchant had finished she clapped her hands solemnly.

-It is a good story. You have done well by the boy and in turn you have gained much..

-He is as my own.

-He is your own. We do not need to limit our sense of such things to blood kinship. Tomorrow I will spend some time with him for he has an essence which offers much. I will instruct my men to equip you for the next part of your journey - which you will need to oversee. I would also like to add a further burden. You must deliver something for me.

-It will not be a burden.

-Perhaps not. But anything bearing my crest can be so. Speak not of it to anyone. Tell no-one that you have stayed here.

-It will be as you say.

-And promise me something.

-I will.

-You must hear the request first.

He smiled.

-I foresee that there will be a separation for you both. It will be sad but each of you will accept its inevitability. I hope it will follow the achievement of your quest but I am not privy to all things. May you find your mother alive. Perhaps your son will be a gift to ease her from this life. My request is this. You will discover your existence is a lonely one once your son takes his own road. Come back and be of service to me for I have other work for you. There are few men of your quality and we would both benefit from such an arrangement.

The father rose and bowed, -It would be a great honour.

The boy followed suit. Already he was casting his mind forward to the next day.

-Eat in your room when you wake, she said to him, -But ensure you are here before the streets are alive.

-I will be here, answered the youth.

☥

They were lying on their beds. The night candle spluttered, offering

34

an intermittent yellow light.

-What is she?

-The wisest, noblest woman you will ever meet. A true shaman.

-What does she...? He couldn't think what he was asking.

-It is best to think of her as a high priestess but one who has no god of her own. She offers wisdom to those who come to her. For many she is the difference between joy and despair. But for others she is someone to hate. It is only because she is protected by the ruler of this territory that they have not moved against her.

-How can anyone hate her?

-They have their gods.

-For that?

-For her all true gods are of the same essence. She says that a true god is a conduit for love. Some choose gods of war, some vengeance and some the oppression of the poor. These are many kinds of gods. Not all are true.

-This is obvious.

- It is. But men who seek to have power over others choose their gods carefully. She says that they make gods out of their own tribal histories to justify their futures.

-I have no sense of any god, said the youth.

☥

They ate goat's cheese and bread. The youth drank a juice of an unknown fruit and liked it. His father bid him fair fortune and left to oversee their departure. A little later he was ushered into her private chamber, past the guard. She wore a plain oatmeal robe but round her head was a thin ribbon of gold gauze. Two cushions were placed on either side of a low table. Painted on its top surface was a splendid bird with enormous fanned feathers. He assumed this creature was the dream of an artist's mind. Glasses were placed in front of them. They were small, green and opaque, the colour of gourds from his own land. A little liquid nestled at the bottom of each. She motioned him to sit.

-You slept?

-Very well. And this morning the food was how I like it.

-Simple food for a complex spirit.

He looked at her unswervingly. She smiled.

-I wish you to breathe from a glass with me.

-Breathe? What is this liquid?

-It is a preparation of fruits and herbs.

-What is it for?

-It will create a channel without words between us.

He nodded and said decisively, -I will try it. He breathed a fragment of the scent into his body. There was no poison here but there was something he found disturbing. It affected him as though soft cloth was massaging the back of his thoughts, making him drowsy. He put it down and sat with his elbows on his crossed knees, supporting his head. He was aware that she had done the same with her glass.

After what seemed an eternity, she said, -This is your mother.

He was a bird. He felt the air rushing and his wings straining, his feathers spread to rise higher and higher. He swooped low across a desert. A woman rode bareback, armed like a warrior. She pulled her horse to a rearing stop and scanned the sky. He flew closer and memorised her handsome desert-hardened face. Her eyes linked with his. A recognition passed between them. She lifted an arm in salute, then was gone. In her place was his hostess.

-She saw me. She knew.

-She saw a hawk.

He cried. She did nothing to intervene but allowed the tears to pour until his convulsions stopped.

-Close your eyes.

He did. He found himself inside a place for small children in a room with walls and ceiling. He was on a sofa and several women were sitting round watching the small ones play. He became aware of his body and realised without surprise that he, too, was a woman. The difference was startling. His body was warmer, softer and more open, as though floating in the air. His heart caressed the world. Even his sight provided subtle differences, embracing colours he had not perceived before and dimming ones that usually dominated his vision. In his arms was a baby. He raised it to his breast and suckled it. The peace of giving nurture flooded him. He felt a completeness he had never felt, even in his dreams.

He was in the room for an endless time, talking, listening, cleaning his baby and growing familiar with his new being.

☥

It wasn't like waking but more like becoming slowly aware again of his male body, as though it belonged to a stranger. This flesh and blood which he had never questioned was now a curiosity to him. The sharp edge between it and the air. The constant tension in the muscled frame. The coiled spring at the heart of it which made it ready, perpetually, to leap to action.

-I have changed.

-That is why you came here, is it not? It is the beginning of knowing yourself.

-I did not know the substance.

-We have only faint pictures of what will be, you and I. Our dreams are never whole pictures. Call up to your mind this experience whenever you feel anger or hatred and you will find an understanding which will subdue such weakness. When you fight you must do so from a cool judgment of the need for battle. If there are alternatives, only a clear mind may see them. A mind which is both male and female. The words of the priestess struck deep. He would not forget them.

-I can sense it.

-It will take time. You are at the beginning. Only old spirits like ours can comprehend. We will meet again, many years from now but it will be different. Supplicants will come to you as now they come to me. I, too, will make my pilgrimage. Then there will be much I will learn from you, in my turn.

Once again he found himself unsurprised. So much of his life felt as though he was living through what once he may have dreamed but forgotten.

-**This is, indeed**, a strange and prophetic meeting. She seems to have great power yet she exercises it only to release his mind from his physical body. She paused, lost for a while, -Do you know Kamil, my step-mother Malika, the Emperor's first wife, has plans to kill me?

Kamil was shocked at the unexpected turn, -I am sure, my Princess, this can not –

She raised an eyebrow haughtily and stopped him, -I say it. It is so. She gave my father his first male child but it died soon after birth. Then he had two more wives. The first was my mother who gave him me, and after me there are two sisters, both baby girls to his third wife. Kamil knew this, as did every citizen and nodded sympathetically, -But did you know this Kamil? She leant forward conspiratorially, -Malika is supposedly with child!

-I had no idea! This was indeed a palace secret.

-The ageing one has been taking efficacious drugs brought to her secretly, hidden in spices from the east. Extracts from tusked beasts and monkeys. Perhaps she will produce a horned baboon for her trouble! She laughed coldly, -If she breeds a boy then the throne will be hers for the male supersedes any female. If she breeds a girl, then the empire will be mine. She plots to have me and my sisters killed and take the throne for herself if the latter course comes to pass. She will then present the throne to her favoured nephew, Muez, that snake of wet grasses. Whatever the course of destiny, if she is victorious, the royal line will not contain my mother's blood. All this will happen the more quickly should my father die suddenly and unexpectedly.

-The great Emperor will not die …

-Ah Kamil. Are you going to save my father? Hah! Of course not. It is all a web. Father knows he is always in danger and takes steps to guard himself. That is the life of any emperor. Yet he would never believe that she is the greatest source of danger to his throat! They have been together for too long. He is overjoyed at her news of the child to be. He feels certain a boy will be the issue and lives for the outcome. But one disloyal bodyguard, one dish that slips unnoticed past the lips of his taster….She smiled at him bitterly, -Do not worry, the knowledge has been with me for as long as I have known her. I too have stratagems! But it all comes to the knife point in the next three weeks.

Kamil looked at her, helplessly, his lips pursed and his eyes constricted by a frown, -What can I do to serve your Highness?

-No more than you are doing. Fate may some day conspire a role for my doddery historian but not yet. She laughed.

Kamil recoiled inside. It was not true, he was not a doddery old historian. He had just entered middle age. He only seemed that way, more at home among dusty shelves and documents bound in silence than among people. What did he know of this world except what had been laid down by writers from other times?

-I will rely upon your Tales of the Magus, Kamil, for inspiration and illumination, said the Princess, -They must release in me the power to see. When I was a child one of the royal clowns made me puppets of all the senior courtiers. He taught me to speak through their mouths and imagine what each might think. It was a basic but telling apprenticeship! Her words had begun to lose their immediacy as she became preoccupied again, -So what is my question? First, though, I have had another idea. It came to me as I meditated on what I should ask you that you too must ask a question at each of our meetings.

-What about, Princess? He was stunned. This crossed a certain boundary.

-Anything that might lead my mind into new knowing. Do you know no-one asks me anything? I am above enquiry! You are privileged. Princess Sabiya smiled a particularly seductive smile and agitated his heart, -Don't worry, you can ask your first question at our next meeting. You can spend all day thinking about it! Now! She scratched the calf of her left leg with her right toe, -The High Priestess drugs the young man and he flies like a bird and also experiences motherhood. Is this yours, the writer's fantasy? Did the Magus ever do such a thing?

Kamil clasped his hands together gripping them until they hurt, - There are many tales of the Magus speaking to women as though he was one of them. He seemed to know all that they endure and what truly fulfils them. For him men and women are equal but each must follow a different path to enlightenment; a woman's through the nature of her being and a man's through his toil. But he has said that women live shallow lives if they do not reflect upon the great gift that life has conferred upon them and men may toil and never seek or find enlightenment. As a magus he could discern both paths in his own being. Such a prophet cannot be a representation of but one side of humanity! What wisdom would derive from that? He stopped abruptly,

39

feeling he had begun a sermon but she was nodding,

-Thank you Kamil. A very good answer, if I might offer a judgment! Till tomorrow! And she was gone.

Chapter Four

The spirit has need of its own medicines

All that night and the next day Kamil worried about the question he would ask the Princess. Her discussions with him were not those expected of a normal girl not yet seventeen. They were intelligent and carefully considered. They made him think and say what had not come to his mind before. His own questions could not be too intrusive for that would overstep the bounds of etiquette and he was not the court fool! But neither could he be superficial. Her request was specific and pointed. He must make her think in new ways about her life. Yet such an existence was beyond his limited experience. This was the first occasion that he had been called to court since his youthful appointment as royal historian ten years before and the later command from the Emperor to write these Tales. He knew nothing of the ways of high-spirited royal princesses.

The revelation that she felt her life was under threat would be something for a later question but not now. And what did she say about all being resolved in three weeks? She tantalised. But a princess need not tell what she wished not to tell. He asked himself how the Magus might resolve his dilemma. His thoughts flew forward to one of the Tales he would eventually read to her about the little kidnapped girl. It was a chapter of which he was very proud. He had based the personality of the girl upon his niece. He had even shed a tear when he wrote it! Then he thought about what Princess Sabiya had said about her childhood puppets. Again, this might be helpful later. But what was emerging as a scheme in his mind was to tie particular lines of questioning to particular Arcana cards in the book. Would not this help to further the Emperor's desire to give her a wider education?

*

He was eating a bowl of couscous, covered with a delicate sauce of sweet and sour vegetables and fruit when he finally realised how he might begin. He held the question in the air like a newly finished carving, examining it from all sides. It was not too intimate, no. It was not patronising. It was not a question which revealed how out-of-touch with modern life he actually was. There was a challenge to it but he was sure it would not be a new departure for her to think upon it. He put his airy carving down and swallowed the last mouthful, finishing by cleansing his palate with mint tea.

An hour later and punctual to the second, Princess Sabiya entered. She was a picture from paradise. Her hair was laced with blooms and her robes shimmered in a mix of blues and greens. Kamil found breathing difficult.

-May I remark on how beautiful you look, Princess? he found himself saying to his horror. So intimate! What a fool! -Oh ....I'm sorry, I should not have-

She laughed, a little coquettishly, -There is no better compliment than one that arises from the lips without the steadying influence of a cautious brain. Still, I would never have thought you capable, Kamil. No, this is not for you, she laughed mockingly, -I am dressed for a musical performance later this evening in the gardens. Candles. Travelling musicians from the dark south. Royal duty though the drums thrill me. They rouse in me my family blood. She arranged her silk robes and settled back asking sternly, -Have you worked hard on your question? Kamil nodded, flustered by what had just happened and aware that her tone was not so different from his mother's when he was a child, -Then we will see how hard! Her laughter was full of attractive tones, deeper than those found in most women. -Ask!

Kamil swallowed and touched his fingertips together forming a pyramid, -Would you put the empire before love?

The Princess affected dramatic surprise by slamming her palms down on her thighs, drawing in her breath and giving her upper body a shake as though ridding herself of the question. Her eyes sparkled with mischief, -Very good Old Kamil! Very good! You have surprised me. The relieved Kamil had been deceived by her acting and for one brief moment had seen his head in a basket, separate from his body. He tried to ease the stiffness in his shoulders.

-Of course, she said, -I have had to think about this many times. There is not a week goes by without some noble boy with pox scars or watery eyes arriving at court to test my interest. There are three possible answers. If the empire depended upon it then I would marry. If the empire did not depend upon it then I would dig my heels in and not be pulled by any rope. There! She became silent and eyed him amusedly.

-Those are just two answers, if I may –

-I know! I was just testing you. The third answer involves the first. Just because I might surrender my body for the good of the empire does not mean that my heart would not search for what it desires. Royal courts have tolerated such tensions throughout time as you must know only too well!

-Indeed Princess.

She sat straighter, -But let me rephrase my second answer. I would not in fact marry for love if it meant I must give up one thimbleful of power! I will be Empress! That is my destiny. Her words were imperious and her eyes sharp and cut deep into his own. She allowed the silence to lengthen for a while as he squirmed, -Enough! Let us see the colours of the next card. She flicked it over, -Appropriate. It says The Empress. She studied it, -She is not like the High Priestess. Is she all the things that that woman was not? Tell me.

-Indeed your Highness. The Empress has concerns for the material world, for family, for running the household. She has great interest in what makes the world work. But she has enormous power and will exercise it.

-Am I she?

-You will always be all the cards but at different times in your life different cards will dominate.

-Then let us hear the tale of this earth woman for in truth I cannot remember what happens next. I think I read it like an impetuous child and lost interest after the first few chapters! She pressed herself into the cushions, rested her chin on a braced upturned palm and closed her eyes, opening them for one final comment, -I look forward to his meeting with Love. I remember a little of that.

His father never asked him what passed between them. However he seemed buoyant again, particularly once they were clear of the city. Although they followed the main caravan trail south they avoided any groups of travellers and were wary of others. Their horses were also rejuvenated. His father said that her stable had given them nothing other than the best nourishment to restore them to full strength.

One evening they camped in a recess in a cliff some distance from the trail. There had been no sign of travellers for a night and a day. The horses seemed worried however, particularly the roan. It raised its head and drew back its lips, its ears twitching. It kept snuffling loudly. His father ignored it and settled for a sleep which seemed almost instantaneous. The youth sat on his blanket, undecided, then lay back, his eyes searching for patterns in the stars. He slipped immediately into a drowsy half-dream. He saw an owl fly overhead, flapping awkwardly as though its wing was injured and hooting as if in need of help. He stood up, strapped a saddlebag and throwing knife to his waist and walked over to the roan. He put his cheek to that of the beast and spoke softly to it to quieten it. There was a cool sweat on the horse's flanks. It had turned and was facing the darkness away from the fire. He took a lighted branch and walked into the shadows. Perhaps twenty steps further he stopped. His nose had found something. It was a heady blend of danger and something else. A plea. The owl had communicated that a wild creature lurked nearby, something large. His scent would have known if it was a predator he had met before. This was not what the owl had conveyed. In feigning an injury it was trying to lead an enemy away from its young.

A rustle above him drew his gaze. The flames caught and reflected in the eyes of an enormous cat. He knew this although she was a beast he had never encountered except in his father's stories. He sensed her

44

female nature as he had with the she-wolf. She was crouched on a low branch, her talons glinting as they gripped it. He found her eyes. This was not an animal before which he should pretend indifference. She rose and dropped silently to the ground a few strides away, then, without turning her head, walked slowly away from him, impelling him to follow.

They maintained the distance between them for some time, trees giving way to moonlit rock. The torch was no longer needed and he propped it between stones. Her cave was high on a steep slope, once an outlet for a stream. He followed her inside. The mouth was lit by the risen moon and a faint phosphorescence in the walls. Three cubs were curled in a corner but dominating the space was her great male, his head lowered and wet, his body shaking with the effort to breathe.

The youth dropped to his knees. It was not light enough to distinguish more than the crude shape of the beast and its half-closed eyes. The female hunched on the other side of it and began licking. Without fear the youth slipped his hand under her tongue and felt the broken end of a wooden shaft in the muscular shoulder. Seeping from it was the clammy thickness of dissipating poison. He laid a hand on the beast's side and spoke to it softly. Then he spread the fingers of one hand on either side of the wound, teasing it apart and with his knife removed the arrowhead. The cat growled feebly but did not move. Blood seeped between his fingers. The lioness licked fiercely, exposing the hole. From his bag he took dried moss. He gently edged her head to one side, chewed the moss and pressed it into the wound. The wounded beast protested with a deep whimper and closed its eyes. Within a few minutes its breathing eased to that of natural sleep.

The youth stood up and took his things to the mouth of the cave. The moon was now so full he had to adjust his eyes. With the softness of all predators she padded beside him and rubbed against his leg. He allowed his fingers momentarily to touch her head. Then he left her and found his way back to the camp.

Sleep took him immediately into another vivid dream. In it he met a rich woman who had three children and a husband who seemed mortally wounded in battle. The youth was now an elderly, respected, robed doctor and he had been called to cure the man. He did so. The woman, who was of royal blood, was so grateful that she offered him a high position in her court. But he refused because destiny had other callings.

☥

A captain of a roving advance guard stood listening to his chief scout. The fellow was from those parts and was known to be a man without a shadow. He said that he had trailed two riders for half a day. Their horses were fine beasts, well cared for and strong. The men wore clothes from the north, a lawless area far beyond the king's lands. They were staying clear of the merchant traffic, following a parallel trail some way off.

The captain detailed three men to bring them in for questioning. He could see the avarice in the scout's eyes. Good horses were at a premium but the King's law was merciless on such theft, even from those outside his provenance. The scout set off, leading his well-armed companions. When they were out of sight the captain returned to his tent. The hundred or so men in his command were weary and he was happy to let them feed and groom their horses and prepare to camp for the night. His tent had been erected, the bed laid and some dried fruit was soaking nearby. There was fresh water in a bowl. Smoke from a small fire was finding its way through the hole at its apex. He took a long draught, removed his leggings and his leather boots and lay down to rest. Then he dozed. Perhaps a half hour later his orderly shook him roughly by the shoulder. The man was holding a small cylinder with the unmistakable symbol of the court stamped upon it. The captain flipped the cord to release the lid and tipped out the contents. He ran a practised eye over the message. It was a command from the queen for all troops to return immediately to the city. At the bottom was the queen's stamp and beside it the smaller but unmistakable symbol of a broken sword. The king had been injured! He leapt from his bed and shouted for his sergeant, -Tell the men we must ride hard to the court. The king is in danger and needs us! Very little time had passed before the troop were at a strong gallop, driving their horses towards a ford in the river the way they had just come. Their tents were left to the slower pack ponies and a platoon guard.

☥

-I think we should camp away from the river down there. There are signs of too much traffic on its banks, said his father.

-Perhaps in that wood?

-I think so. Of what strangeness did you dream last night? The young man showed no surprise at the question. He would have been much more surprised if his father had not been aware of his dreaming.

-I was answering a plea for help.

-No human request I think, said his father dryly.

-No, smiled the youth, -It was a large cat. She led me to her lair and requested I minister to her mate who was wounded with an arrow.

-Oh did she? murmured his father, leaning forward and resting a forearm on his horses neck, -And what language did she use?

-The kind that speaks inside your head so that your body obeys and your mind catches up later.

-What of the arrow?

The youth described it and the father thought a moment before pronouncing. -This was army weaponry. It is a sign. We had better be vigilant. Take turns on watch. Soldiers don't hunt just for food at night. I now have second thoughts about the wood. If they have seen us they will come looking. The wood could then become our prison. This is a land of constant suspicion. Every soldier from whatever side will think us the enemy.

-The dream tells you all this?

His father nodded, -I can decipher the meaning sometimes. Tis a pity I am no great dreamer myself! It is a quality you have. One day you will learn to slip from your body at will like a spirit. Until you become truly adept it seems much like a dream I am told. He looked up into the sky, -The horses are still strong. Let them chew a little more grass and drink. What do you think?

His son followed the line of his pointing finger, -I have been watching them too, on and off. They have broken formation and scatter across the sky. There are many men not far from here and they are camped. The birds would have stayed true had they been on horse.

-Let us move on.

They ushered the horses into a canter, keeping just below the line of the wood. Under him the youth could feel the sudden tension in the roan. It stopped and turned its head back towards the lower slopes. Even in the failing light they picked out four riders, one leading by a small distance. They watched as the scout turned his horse uphill in their direction.

-He can follow a trail, his father said admiringly.

-Shall we outrun them or wait here? The youth's hand strayed to his knife.

-We'll wait. Their horses are more tired. We can escape if we have to. But now that I can make out their colours it may be that they are more friend than foe.

They stood still, their horses turned towards the oncoming group. The scout and the soldiers had slowed and were now riding together having seen them waiting. Within a few minutes they drew up to them. The youth noted the dirt on their horses' flanks and the battered clothes of the riders. They had been on the trail for too long.

-We have come to take you to our camp. My captain wishes to speak with you, ordered one of them.

-That may not be our inclination, said his father, amused.

-You have no choice. The leader of the three was belligerent. He was tired of being given these extra duties, his horse was fatigued and he was hungry.

-In the face of fate, no. In the face of three soldiers and a scout, yes.

-Then we will have to take you by force. The man grew red-faced.

-You would need many more men for that.

-You are but a man and a boy.

-My boy would not need my help to deal with you. But this wastes time and energy. Give me your weapons and we will ride back to your camp with you. No-one will suffer. You can explain your loss of pride to your captain.

The soldier stared at him, -You are foolish and deranged! He went for his sword, -Take them!

What happened next passed too quickly for the tired brains of the soldiers. One moment they were on horseback and the next they were spread-eagled on the ground, their would-be captives standing over them and their weapons removed. They looked up bemusedly as the roan rounded up their horses and drove them to a point nearby.

-You may get up. Neither the man nor the youth held a weapon in his hand although each had a knife and a sword at his disposal. The men groaned and gradually got to their feet, -Your horses are waiting. With complete unconcern, the victors ignored the vanquished men and prepared for their own departure. The man tied their weapons to his saddle. But the youth was examining the sky and then staring into the gloom.

-The rest of your troop is leaving, he indicated.

The scout followed his gaze and nodded a grudging affirmation. He said, -They are headed back to the river. They have been recalled. The four men stared glumly at each other.

-You wear the colours of the king of the City of White Stones.

-It is true, said the leader of the group, wonderingly.

-We are going there ourselves although we had thought to make it a trip of leisure in the morning. Now we will escort you there. It seems our destinies must be entwined for a little longer.

The city commanded a view over the fertile plain on all sides. In the early light of day it looked even more fearsome. It was built on a great collection of boulders placed there by giants of a bygone time. Only a narrow gap in the rearing white rocks allowed access to it. This was guarded constantly. Visitors had to prove the authenticity of their business and wait outside until it was verified. When the troop and their escorts arrived there was much amusement from the sentry post. The humiliated quartet tried to raise the guard against their escorts but to no avail. A brief conversation resulted in the soldiers entering and the man and the youth waiting behind. The Merchant passed the bundle of weapons over.

-I have something for the Queen, he said, -From her royal sister in the north.

-Give it to me and I will have it taken to her.

-It is upon my life to hand it over personally.

-That cannot be. My orders forbid it. I will be swift. The man touched his heart with a hand.

The youth watched as his father pulled out a small sack and carefully detached a metal disc that had been pinned to it. It bore a crest, -Take this to the Queen. We have arrived at a time of great need. If we are

49

not with her within the half hour we will come for you and no man will stand between our knives and your throat. The man's face whitened and he took the disc and hurried off. Soldiers stood by watching them fretfully. The queue of traders and visitors wound past them, each having to wait patiently for the order to enter.

A short while later the man reappeared. He gestured to the guards to let them pass and led them and their horses up the narrow defile. Taking them by side alleys he avoided much of the bustle and soon they were admitted through an enormous gate and into the palace courtyard. Their horses were escorted to stable and they themselves were ushered into the inner rooms. His father clasped the sack while the youth held his pouch of healing mosses and potions that he had dreamed he had used on cat and king. The palace was exactly as his dream had foretold. When the queen arrived he recognised her also, her beautiful face lined with anxiety, her hands shaking, fingers twisting round each other. He could also see, which had not been obvious from his dream that she was full sister to the priestess who had invoked the presence of his mother.

She took the gift sack from his father, distractedly, -My husband is dying. An assassin shot him through a window while he prayed to the statue of the Great One. She opened the sack. Inside was a leather cosmetic bag with small pouches that held a variety of phials and sachets. There was also a note, written on a square of thin, gilded calfskin. She read it and looked up sharply, her eyes focused on the youth, -You are a healer?

He bowed, -Both my father and I..

-My son has gifts beyond my own, interrupted his father quickly.

-Come with me both of you! She led them up stone stairs, her long embroidered house coat swinging to the floor with its intricate decoration of pairs of strange beasts and plants dancing in front of their eyes. She beckoned them into a darkened room lit only by a candle. A physician was ministering to the wounded king. He was attaching marsh suckers and muttering healing verses in a slow dirge.

The youth stepped up but the physician maintained his crouched protection of his patient.

-May I see the King? he ventured politely.

-No visitors! He is sick, growled the doctor authoritatively.

-Let him near! The queen intervened. The physician still did not move.

-I am afraid my Queen that I know best at this time. I cannot allow even you-

He did not finish his sentence for the youth's father crossed to him in an instant and lifted him out of the way. The youth undid bandages revealing a wound whose septic edges were blackening. He took out thin flat sticks cut from the plant that could draw enough water into its stems to survive a year of drought and dipped them in a slim vessel of alcohol. He created with them a pressure lattice which clamped the wound open. Removing a long needle from his pouch he held it over the flame. Quickly dousing its heat in the spirit he inserted it slowly into the wound and felt for the source of the poison. The needle contacted something small and hard. He withdrew it and inserted a pair of bone tongs which he had also sterilised in the vessel. By turning and drawing them this way and that he pulled the object to the surface. It was an arrow tip broken cleanly from the head. He smelled it and nodded, -This poison works slowly if left in contact with flesh. Hunters use it so that a wounded beast does not die immediately but will take them, weakened, back to the rest of its kind. Hold the doctor, he must not be allowed to leave! he muttered to his father. The physician rose abruptly but his father's sword was instantly at his throat. The youth made his compress of leaves by chewing them and in a repeat of the ritual of his dream, pressed them into the wound. -Where are your maggots? he asked the doctor, his eyes flashing. The physician opened a clay jar with a perforated lid. The youth sniffed it and then turned it upside down on the wound. After a few minutes he bound the wound lightly with gauze to hold the maggots in place. The king's face had already lost some of its pallor and he was breathing more easily.

-We are in time, he said to the queen.

-I did not realise that there was still an arrow tip in the wound, cried the physician.

-You did. For who else could have put it there!

-The boy is mad. What can he be saying? I have been the royal physician for as long -

The youth stopped him with a raised hand, -Where is the shaft that was taken from the wound? The doctor's eyes filled with alarm. The queen stepped to the door and called a servant. Seconds later he arrived with the broken arrow, bloodied at its fractured end. The youth placed it on the bed with the poisoned point beside it.

-The tip in your husband's body has been sawn from a poisoned hunting arrow, he told the queen, -The kind of arrow which is used to slow the death of wild beasts. The shaft you can see here has no clean break. The royal physician removed its metal head and then inserted the tip of a corrupted hunting arrow in its place. Your husband would have recovered quickly enough from his wound had it not been for the introduction of the poison. This man chose his venom carefully to allay suspicion. The shaft would have been thrown away and no-one would have suspected him by the time the king died. If another physician had investigated his body it would have been unlikely that he would find such a small tip. If he did then it would have been seen as an understandable oversight on the part of the doctor.

-Take him away and see that he tells all. But he shall not live beyond the sun's full height, cried the queen, her face drained by fury and remorse.

-It is too late, murmured the youth's father. They watched as the royal physician subsided slowly to the floor clutching his throat, his eyes staring and the muscles in his face and neck bulging and rigid, a tiny broken pilule gripped between his teeth.

-He takes the names of his plotters with him, murmured the queen coldly, -Have his body dragged through the city and burned in the square.

As the king recovered and the queen became less anxious she was able to take the young man under her wing. All that his father had been unable to offer him about the ways of the female, she taught him intuitively. But he had to become used to her constant strokes and kisses. She showed him how to be courteous to women, to praise them and to make them feel special amongst their friends. She taught him how a woman complements a man in the body and in the heart and mind. He had no previous notion of it, his view of women being born of the experience of those of the valleys, fighting women who would be as self-conscious in these surroundings as he was. In all things she was frank and open. On one occasion she asked him whether he had had an intimate experience with a girl. He shook his head soberly.

Then would he wish her to arrange it? Again the shake of the head. He told her that he was as yet young and such things, if they were to happen, would happen in their own good time. It made her laugh. She introduced him to the ways of colour, of shape and form and took him to the arena for mime, for singing and dancing. He learned how to spin for hours whilst maintaining his balance and with a complete dark stillness of the mind.

Whilst the youth absorbed everything with an ease and apparent unconcern, his father noted how his learning was an investment against future need but that he was not enamoured of them. Despite all the subtleties and fineries of the queen's court, his son remained subtly separate, focused only upon his father's mission.

It was not the queen, as in his dream, who asked him to stay on at court as its royal physician. It was the king. The queen's sister, the noble priestess, had warned him that prescient dreams might differ from what may then ensue in life. The king knew in his heart that he would refuse, even as he asked. The young man and his father were preparing for the next stage of their journey. When all was ready the king sent for the captain whose men they had vanquished and gave him orders to safeguard their journey to the boundaries of his land. There was much sadness upon their leaving but the youth felt relief as they reached the road outside the city. He had fulfilled the dream and at once it ceased to scratch at his thoughts. Parting was not a burden.

-**It is a tale** that demonstrates his shamanic qualities! she said without opening her eyes, -A dreamer of futures and a healer. Later is he not also the master of other domains? I see now that one such as he is born rarely, if at all.

-There must have been a unique man behind the legends, said the historian, -All the tales told about him, demonstrate it. What was magic in his life and what was real, who can say now?

-Smoke and fire? Princess Sabiya opened her eyes at last, -So now it is the time for our questions. What have you for me? Or should I begin and give your ageing brain a little time to compose itself? She laughed, -I jest. The story is as fresh as fruit still on the bough so I will begin.

-I await your pleasure, your Highness, mumbled Kamil, his heart fluttering again with anxiety, fearing her question would be unanswerable or that in answering it, he would betray something terrible in himself of which he was presently ignorant.

-My question is this...she lapsed into silence her eyes sharply focused on his own..., -The gifts he had, who has such qualities today? I know of none such. Have we lost what we once had in those days? For even the people he meets seem more...substantial ...than anyone in the court! Can another come with such supernatural powers? Or did he ever have them? Is it the speculation and embellishment of later times that have built him into this figure?

-I sense the heart of your questioning Princess, he replied, glossing over her lack of focus, -Some would say he is just a myth but a myth which helps to illuminate our times. A potent collection of tales. I think this is why your father asked me to write this history. For stories are what we use to bring us closer to truth. It is like night sight. With a story we are enabled to see from the corners of our eyes what cannot be apprehended directly. Kamil had huddled himself into a tight knot, - Can such gifts be witnessed in this age? I believe so! The curse of humanity is not its lack of superhuman effort but its lack of desire to unleash its power. Its unwillingness to risk what it has for what it might know. But history shows us that the unpredictable occurs and beings arrive among us who bring us colour and new perceptions and change. Today it might be a philosopher, musician or writer. At the time of the Magus his gifts were attuned to that savage world with its tribes and clans, its city kingdoms and princes, its law of the sword and the inhuman treatment of all who stand in the way of a man's desire.

-Have times changed? I think not.

Kamil chose to ignore her, -To make his mark the Magus had to excel in all things that men admired at the time.

-And all that women admired for he learns much from them! What man today is taught the way to a woman's heart? They blunder, deaf and blind at the entrance. I know this already and I have been a woman but three years!

-Whatever genius we possess, it is honed by those we meet, our teachers and guides, our sages.

Kamil smiled, perhaps a little too smugly, because Princess Sabiya immediately retorted in her most waspish tone, -Do not overestimate your own kind, old man. I am sure genius is capable of its own destiny without too many intrusions brought to it by lesser minds. He was suitably chastened and could think of no reply. Princess Sabiya was sensitive and headstrong. She reacted in ways he could not foretell, - Now it is your turn, she commanded, -Let us see what question my honourable teacher can ask with a day's grace in its construction!

Kamil's mind whirled. He had pondered on a number of possibilities during the day but none now seemed fitted to the present mood. He was of course titillated by being able to ask direct questions of the Princess but there was a tacit line that he mustn't cross. Should his question be broad and more philosophical or narrow and more material?

-Princess, he spoke through pursed serious lips, -If I may return to a conversation of another day concerning threats to your sacred skin -

-Hah! your old-fashioned charm. Sacred skin? Hah! But why not, though many might wish to despoil it with a blade or bullet. Or their ever hopeful manhood. Go on with you silver tongue.

Kamil blinked, blushed and straightened his sleeves, -In our discussion a few moments ago, about gifts that seem beyond human understanding–

-Yes?

-Have you an instinct for who is a threat to you and who is not? Can you read character?

-How do you know this? she asked softly, -You are cleverer than I thought! Or has someone told you? Her voice was dangerously calm and her eyes narrow. He became flustered immediately and sweated and mopped his face.

-Princess, I know nothing...I was only trying to frame a question. I live in seclusion. I talk to no-one of such things!

-I see it, she said and her gaze softened, -It is true. I was born with this gift. I am unsure how rare it is. As a baby I screamed at a new nursemaid. My mother had her stripped and a poisoned needle was found in the hem of her dress. When I began to walk I could tell by the hand of someone supporting me who I could trust. I would squeal like a stuck pig if it felt wrong. She laughed, -But because of this my mother was able to clear the court of much danger. She called me her little spy! When my mother died I lost more than my closest love, I lost her secret web of royal spiders for she had told me nothing of the protection she had build around me. My father married again and yet his first wife Malika whom I have cursed already in your hearing, made many changes in the court. She was fearful of my mother but once she had died, Malika grew again in strength. She is clever and plays the loving mother to me and my half sisters as well as the loving friend to my father's other wife. There is no evidence to take to my father who has always been loyal to her. But my own little web is growing and I am old enough to keep my own counsel. It is a game of chess. You know it? A game from the east with two courts at battle on a chequer board? He nodded his head, -Know your enemies' strengths and stay silent for you will come to know their weaknesses too. She who understands the long game wins though she may have to give up a hostage or two on the way. At the end there may be just one queen on the board! She nodded for emphasis. -What card is it to be tomorrow, faithful man of history?

-The Emperor.

-Ah, he around whom we continually position ourselves for battle!

Chapter Five

There is no journey longer or more arduous than the journey to enlightenment

The door was flung open and with flaring nostrils and diamond eyes the Princess strode into the room. One of her two guards softly and tentatively closed the door behind her. She circled Kamil twice and he could hear her ferocious breathing though he was too assailed to look up. He just folded his hands on his lap and stared at them.

-You see me at my most angry, she shouted at the ceiling, -Most most angry. Sometimes examples must be made. If it means the death of a servant then so be it. No-one, she turned to point at Kamil, -No-one betrays my trust and lives. Do you hear me?

-Yes your Highness, he croaked.

-Yes, indeed. She sat down sinuously, her body tight, -She is the first of many if such things happen! Do you know why she is dead? Kamil shook his head, -She stole my mother's signet ring! Can you imagine? A ring which invokes a royal decree? There are only two. My father's and mine, passed on to me by my mother. Not even my stepmother can wear the ring of highest power. By chance I went for it to engrave the wax on a letter. It was gone. Stolen moments before no doubt. The guards searched everyone and my maid had it hidden, couched between her legs. Vile creature. She shouted and screamed for mercy. I could hear her through the walls. Hah! No mercy! What do you say, Magus-lover?

Kamil pulled himself together, -It must be part of a plot your Royal Highness.

-Yes? He had made her stop abruptly in her pacing and she looked at him with angry interest.

-A ring with the royal crest. Why not some other easily missed article of jewellery? Such a ring is too...too...significant. He watched as sense began to replace anger on her face.

-I see your reasoning. She walked about, her eyes half closed, reflecting, -I am stupid! All I could think was that she had defiled the ring of my mother and put it in that place. And for once my instinct let me down. I was so fond of her. I believed utterly in her loyalty. A plot. Not greed and stupidity. My enemies would sign something on my behalf, something to bring me down. And immediately, before the ring had been noticed as gone. If I had had you with me I could have torn from her the names, the plans... One name would have led to another. And so on. A bloody line of corpses all the way to my stepmother!

-I am not versed in those arts, but Kamil was pleased his words had struck home.

-Exactly! You are an innocent and see it all from your bookish intellect. You think I was cruel, having her killed? He gestured opaquely with his hands, -You do! Good! All should know the future empress's capacity for extreme cruelty. It comes with the blood. As court historian you have an intimate knowledge of the lengths we have gone to protect our interests have you not?

-Yes, your –

-How many have died? Countless, eh? It is the way of things. The empire is generally at peace but has often been kept in its equilibrium by immediate and savage justice. Until my father became emperor. Hah! No mercy. No ambivalence. She was calming down as she talked. A hand that had been beating a chair arm for emphasis, stopped. She laid her head back and closed her eyes, -What a fool, she said quietly, - Will I ever learn? You read me the Tale about the king's physician only yesterday. And did I listen? No, I had my source of intrigue executed. I must learn to ponder in order to see clearly. I must also learn to listen carefully to your Tales. It may be, she opened one eye suspiciously, -That your stories are closely chained to events, as they happen around me.

-Oh, I'm sure that can not –

-Stop flustering Kamil, she interjected abruptly, -I will have no more about the servant now. Read. Bring me relief.

Their journey to the borders of the territory was uneventful. The captain was a quiet man and tended to hold his own counsel. If he was piqued by their treatment of his soldiers he did not show it. From the few comments he made it seemed that his mind was focused on other things, particularly the network of conspirators who had nearly murdered the King.

-May God be with you, he intoned as they prepared to go their own way.

-It will have to be a new god, said the youth, -The King's god stops here at the border. His powers give way to a holy family in the land before us, so my father tells me.

-You are cynical. An unbeliever. How is it that God has spared you for so many years? The captain showed bemusement.

-Perhaps the gods fight over which one will send a life-taker for me and therefore I escape while they are occupied in their argument.

The captain shook his head sadly, -I have not met anyone like you. Nevertheless, I still pray that the one and true God will keep you safe.

Ignoring him, the youth replied, -Doubly protect your king. Have the guards themselves watched by a small number you would trust with your life. Have his food and drink double-tasted. Be suspicious even of women and children.

-You are right. It is wise counsel.

-Only the queen herself is above such necessary consideration. It seems to my inner eye that this state of concern will last for at least one more year. Maintain caution and all will be well with your royal family, your god and your lands. They parted with these words still echoing in the captain's ears.

☥

-What is it Father?

-What do you mean?

-You have been silent since we left the city.

The Merchant said heavily, -There is less for me to teach as you become a man. I have fewer wise words as you have more.

-This is not true. I value your every word. I am your son.

-You are and you are not. You have thoughts of a rare kind.. From what loins they can have sprung I may only guess. The bold way you disparage people's gods, he shook his head and there was frustration and sadness in his voice.

The youth laughed, -It is not intended. People need their gods. They cannot trust themselves and so put their trust in beings that cannot be perceived through any physical sense. Each tribe has its own. As we travel south the skins of men and women become darker. So do the images of their gods. In lands where people are dwarfish I would venture that their gods are of the same build. It was you who told me that beyond this border a single god gives up his dominion to a holy family!

-You do not believe in any god.

The youth laughed again, -It is partly your legacy, Father. You taught me to think, to weigh evidence, to take no man's word without due consideration. When have you taught me to worship a god? Never! This is our first discussion of gods. Until now I have had only fairytale conversations with boys and girls and what I have overheard among adults, to inform me.

-I did not know what to teach you. He sounded contrite.

-You forget. You taught me that this world is the mother of all things and that they are connected in invisible ways; animals, plants, the earth, the air...you began telling me this in stories when I was not yet able to speak many words.

-You remember? the Merchant was astounded.

-As if it were this morning. My heart opened to it. It is in accord with every second of my experience of life. Therefore, how can I worship? I cannot worship the mother world. She is impervious to such acts! I would be worshipping myself as I am as much part of her as any living thing.

-It is true, his father said slowly, -But it will lead you into trouble.

My advice is to keep these thoughts to yourself, show no amusement or disdain at others' need for gods and in your very actions seek to conceal yourself in the religion of the people you are travelling among. Just as I taught you to leave no tracks in the sand and to hunt without a shadow.

-You see Father! Wise words! You will always be my teacher! I will remember!

The place to which they were heading was a full week's travelling. It was a graceful and extensive city containing every conceivable adventurous and innovative race of people, owing to its position by the sea. For hundreds of years it had been a commercial centre, having the best port facilities in the trading world. Whilst it had fallen in battle many times its conquerors had never spoiled it. It was a jewel. To own it was to own a priceless asset to a kingdom. You can never own this city, a powerful but wise king had once written to a friend, you can only be fortunate enough to be its caretaker. It was also a rich haven of every known craft from those connected with architecture to those allied to shipping, from agriculture on its alluvial plains to medicine, art, and astronomy. It boasted cotton and silk manufacture, weaving and dyeing, furniture, pottery, jewellery and glass making. Consequently its people had developed a casual indifference to whomsoever they owed liege. They paid their taxes and continued to maintain and amass their fortunes, passing them down through blood-lines of secret, specialist expertise. They showed little interest in the hue of the city's foreign administrations providing taxes were not too high and they could go about their business without much interference.

Its society was open and relaxed. It was as though all who traded there had undertaken an unwritten agreement when they left their arms at the portals to forget any instinct to plot and connive for change in the city's way of life. Tradition for hundreds of years had it that all strangers were welcome and should be shown hospitality. There were many from lands far afield or across oceans who kept a proportion of their wealth in the city for it was regarded as impervious to insecurity and the ideal refuge should your own territory succumb to an invader.

✟

The ruler at this time was famed for his fairness and good temper but was also known for his firm leadership and for the well-equipped army and navy he kept in extensive barracks along the edges of the bay between the main city and the sea. It was a time of relative peace along the great trade routes. The only blemishes to this were beyond the borders, far to the north, where the warlord of the Ice Lands was building a great empire which was spreading east and south. Travellers from the north were subject to strong surveillance, therefore, but having proven their benign intent were given the same freedoms as those from other parts.

✟

-Can you smell it? His father breathed in blissfully and looked as though he had received a much desired gift.

-For some time, said his son, -There is a thickness in the air. Salt and something I do not know. It must be your sea!

-You are right. The sun and the water combine to forge a different air which gives strength to all things. There are birds who are bred in this air and never need to land except to make their young. They are as large as eagles and fly the skies both night and day. There are creatures in the sea greater in size than a barracks' tent who sing strange songs to each other and throw up fountains through holes in their heads, high into the sky. There are trackers and killers in the water, bigger than horses. There are all manner of strange creatures that you can see right through yet have poisons you cannot detect. There are fish who fly, fish whose flesh is more delicious than the sweetest meat, creatures whose skin is armoured like a fighting man's and who walk on the bottom of the ocean looking for drowned sailors in order to gnaw their bones. You have to learn to survive on the seas in new ways. The laws are different to those on the land.

-You were for a time, a sailor? The boy knew this to be true from some tales he remembered being told when he was very young although his father had stopped telling him stories of the oceans as he grew older. His focus had been on teaching his son survival in the hills, valleys and deserts.

-When I was no older than you, I travelled to a great sea with young men and women from many related families. I belong to a clan that is adventurous unlike some of the other clans of our tribe. As many as half of each generation toil on this sea as traders. Most of the others barter across the lands on either side. Thus they manage a fruitful business between them of moving goods from one land to another over the water. Anyway, we undertook this family journey perhaps every two years. It was two days travel and we put our tents up on a green pasture overlooking the salt water. Below the small cliff was a stretch of fine beach sand and we could play and swim there. People came from other clans and the few men who travelled with each family joined together to form an armed unit to protect us all. The sea enables much ease in swimming. Your body is lighter. Those who could not swim in the river learned very quickly. They were dream days. I learned many things.

-What did you play at?

-The usual games. Archery, swords, knives. But also we played at bouncing stones across the waves and we made fragile rafts and learned to hold our breaths long enough to see into the eyes of creatures under the water.

It was at this moment that they came over the high point of a ridge and could see a thin strip of blue diffusing into the sky in the distance.

-There! shouted his father, -I have thought sometimes I would never again see it. It is the most precious gift of the Mother of all things. Some say that our world is as much ocean as it is land and that there are races of men who live within it as happy with the water as we are with the air!

-How can they do that? Do they breathe water?

-They have slits in their necks like fish, it is believed. And mouths for the air.

-Have you seen one?

-No and in truth probably no one has. But the sea has that effect upon you. Tales are more fantastical and you would rather believe them than not. He guffawed and slapped his horse ecstatically. The animals took to his playfulness and set off at a gallop towards the waiting surf.

☥

63

Wherever they went his father always seemed to have a contact. When they had arrived at the city and had given up their arms - although one knife was permitted to each man - he had mentioned two names and was soon led to a merchant's house. This merchant was the son of the man who had given his father work when he was young and desired adventure on the waves. This fellow was maintaining the success of his father, having a number of boats of various sizes which were so organised as to be arriving and leaving from port at intervals throughout the year. His ships brought in raw cargo and took away finished goods. Although rich his house was not opulent. He offered them a room at the back on the ground floor next to the stables where he quartered their horses. They rested for a while enjoying the table of the merchant and exchanging stories of their travels with his tales of trade and strange lands.

Mid way through one long and entertaining meal they were interrupted by a servant carrying a rolled manifest, -Ha! One of my boats is arrived. When it is light we will unload her. Would you like to see the treasures of other countries? The silks, the silver and gold, the hardest woods and the sweetest smells? And there are wild creatures for the royal zoo. They agreed but the son felt a strange twinge as though destiny was accelerating towards him.

☥

As soon as the dark sky started to turn to grey the large boat began being unloaded. A number of roped plank bridges joined her to the wooden pier. Sailors carried cargo at high speed down them with great dexterity. There was much shouting and oathing and the sound of ropes twanging and the flapping of furled sails. Carts were waiting with teams of horses to take their loads to the merchant's storage cellars. It was noisier than anything the youth had ever encountered. He could not tell the characters of the mariners at first glance as they were so unlike men he had met. Their faces were pitted and bent and blistered as much as the wood that made up the boat's sides. Mostly they were heavily bearded with yellow teeth from root and leaf chewing. They were hard-eyed strong and ferocious. Since they snarled and spat constantly it was also difficult for the youth to discern any sense of hierarchy among them yet each obviously knew his business and the boat's hold was unloaded rapidly.

☥

Their host led them up a swaying bridge where at first the youth had to be conscious of his balance and touch the side ropes for security. Neither his father nor the merchant required such assistance. Once on board the youth became fully aware of the smells of the vessel. His nose wrinkled at the stale animal stench which issued up from below. There was the smell of pitch and wet ropes, stewed meat and bread from the galley, human sweat as sailors brushed past with their loads, seaweed and soaking wood. Cotton wrapped bundles passed him that carried their own scented world of herbs and spices.

-We are bringing the animals up now, said the merchant trader, - They are our prize cargo. We have had a difficult time with them. They would like to die rather than be incarcerated in the dark. To keep their spirits up my men had to take each one on to the deck in turn in its cage. And the men themselves have to be disciplined to stop them enraging the beasts with rough treatment. For sailors are no different from wild creatures and their own animal spirits become stirred at the sight of their captives and they would wish to kill them all as if they were still out in the wilderness.

The line of animals was pushed and dragged past them down a ramp. They were all thin and ill-looking. There were around a dozen in all. Two bears and their young, a bull, stallions, camels, a snake as thick as a man's waist and wound up in a truss carried by three men and some birds in metal cages. The final exhibit was a great dark cat, lying in its prison, its jaws muzzled. The young man's eyes and the cat's caught and held. Images flickered through the youth's mind as he entered the cat's thought, mostly the degradation it felt in this cage among these human jailors. The youth bent under the anger and shame as it bubbled in his stomach and his arms and legs stiffened. But he straightened and kept his face impassive when the creature was taken past him and down to a cart below.

-Now that is a beauty is he not? He was bought from a travelling circus before he had ever been shown the whip and will grace the court this very week. A diet of red meat and exercise and he will be prowling round the royal pit drawing cries of alarm from the ladies and the raised fists of respect from the men.

-Where will you keep him? asked the youth.

-I have separate stables for such creatures on the far side of the house. They must be held away from the horses for the smell agitates them. When the cat is recovered he will grace the royal zoo.

☥

That night, long after the last reveller was asleep, the youth left his bed and made his way past dozing guards to the stables. He had visited the creatures briefly during the day, his eyes noting all the particulars of the building, the way the cages were constructed and barred, windows, exits and the guard's vantage post. Staying within shadow he came to the latter. The portly fellow was dreaming. He had jammed himself in a standing position between supporting poles so that he could maintain the appearance of being awake. The youth took a small clay bottle from his leather pouch and poured a few drops on to a torn scrap of cloth. Holding his own breath he proffered it to the guard's nose. Instantly the sleep deepened and the man's head lolled forward on to his chest. He hooked the cotton ball on to a fastening at the throat of the guard's clothing and left him there.

☥

The cat's cage was nearest. The animal was standing, his tail stiff and stretched behind him, his eyes fixed on the young man. The door was held by several hook and eye leather and wood fastenings. Within seconds they were loosed and the door swung open. The cat stepped out to him and he undid the muzzle. He could feel the heat and coiled energy of the creature. He retied the door and led the animal past the guard, retrieving his piece of cotton. He placed the muzzle over the man's head. With one hand on the beast's thick mane they made their way through the shadows. All entrances to the city were heavily guarded but the youth on his arrival had noted where the roof of a nearby building afforded an acceptable drop to the external grounds. With the practised stealth of a burglar he took the cat to that spot. It was easy to slip the bar of the door and like spectres they flowed up the stairs and past the noise of heavy sleepers in bedrooms and on to the roof. A series of drops of a few feet from roof to roof took them to the last one and a larger fall to the ground outside.

The young man gripped his companion's mane and began whispering and making thought pictures for him. The great head pressed against his neck. He described the journey the cat must take, the position of the stars and sun against the lie of the land by night and day, -Stay in the forests and hills away from men. There are many hunters. With care and good fortune you will become the emperor of a new land. We will meet once more. I have it in my memory-to-be. The creature's rough tongue licked his hand and then it sprang away into the darkness. For a few moments the youth could see a black shape moving at speed away from the city walls and in the direction from whence he himself had come.

His father woke him, -It's time for breakfast and then there are decisions we must make. I hear turbulence in the household. They ate fruit and yoghurt left for them by a servant. Hot green tea, sweetened and strong, arrived. They watched as the servant poured a few drops three times into a vessel, returning it each time to the pot before filling their cups. As the man was leaving the merchant entered, brushing past him roughly and wrathfully.

-My lion has gone!

They looked at him quizzically. They did not reply. His anger forbade it.

-An altogether strange event. At the change of watch before dawn, my guard was found in a trance-like sleep. He could not be wakened. He had the restraints of the cat upon his head as if the one had been changed into the other! The cage was empty but all its fastenings were still in place. Early intelligence suggests that no-one entered or left my compound. But late night travellers swear an immense beast with yellow-green eyes passed them travelling at great speed heading north. I feel this is not my cat. Why should a creature brought from the east across the sea, flee in that direction? These animals have a natural ability to travel home even over hundreds of leagues. My cat would have held to the shoreline, due east. Because such is the case, I have soldiers alerted to catch him. What do you say master traveller, you who have seen all manner of things both strange and absurd?

The Merchant looked expressionlessly at his son before turning to his fellow trader, -It is a puzzle. It is as though the beast has magical powers. What thief would have left everything as was? His first inclination would have been to remove himself and the cat as quickly as possible. And the restraint placed on the head of the guard? No thief would do such a thing. And what human would be able to leave silently with a cat of such a size and so dangerous? I have heard that there are those malignant djinn who are able to change shape at will - and one shape chosen by some of them is that of a great black cat.

-Then it is as well that the cat has gone! Our ruler will be disappointed but not as much as if the creature had used its evil powers when inside the court. In God's name it could have taken one of the royal females in a single leap from the pit floor to the gallery! The merchant's angry red face was fast becoming pale and anxious, -I thought the creature was exceptional. Too big! Too cunning! Too intelligent! He said the last word with a fearful look around the room as though he expected the cat to materialise there. -Hah! there are more hunters out there and wild cats to spare. He poured himself some green tea and subsided on the bench beside the youth. He changed the subject.

-Your father says that you might like a trip on one of my boats!

-He did? His father was still able to surprise him.

-I have not mentioned it to him yet, said the older man looking slightly rueful, -Too much has been happening.

-There is a short trip planned for tomorrow. It will take perhaps three days. We must collect fruit from an island south of here and rare plants with red domed heads that appear in the woods and grasses during the night and are used by the apothecaries. Plants for stews and to adorn meats but also to put your mind in a stew, eh? He laughed at his joke, - Does this intrigue you, young Master? No gold and silver. No silk and jewels. Merely fruit and vegetables as our bounty?

-For the starving man such goods would be rated more highly than gold and jewels. I would enjoy such a trip.

-Wise words, young one. It is arranged then. You leave at dawn tomorrow. The still moody merchant left them.

☥

They stood at the prow of the boat. It was sunny but a warm breeze pushed them quickly south. Once they had loaded their cargo the return would be made over night for the wind shifted with predictable regularity. The moment that land could not be sighted had had a profound effect upon the youth. To look on all sides and see nothing but a green swell without markers, filled him with a novel contentment. The movement of the boat had brought him a distant memory of being inside his mother. Then he had fallen into a reverie, his mind emptied as though washed clean of its thoughts by the waves on the great waters around him. He was nothing but a speck among billions of specks that made up the world and the sky. He had been formed from these specks and would disintegrate into specks once again. His life was a moment of mysterious light which would be extinguished all too soon. There was no remorse in this, merely acceptance and understanding. A life was just this. A momentary illumination. It was up to each being to decide what it should illuminate. The merchant, the ruler of this city and the great cat all exhibited the desire to be masters of their worlds. Their thoughts went no further and they could not be criticised for it. Each man had the power to shape his destiny if he so wished. Yet most did not harbour thoughts such as captivated the youth. They clung to the baseless hope that this illumination could be made to flare forever through the gift of a god or that their children and children's children would continue to carry some flickering of themselves within the great perpetual cycle of existence.. This was never going to be. There was no god powerful enough to warrant it. Whilst he had the deepest desire to discover his mother and he saw that he would one day father children, these were merely the rungs of the ladder of his brief life. But it was nevertheless a paradox how his mind could accept unconditionally the emptiness of existence and yet, simultaneously, suffer the seemingly eternal emotions of being human...

He thought that she was asleep for she did not stir for some time. Then in a little girl's, honeyed voice she murmured, -I like this gift of his. To enter the mind of an animal. It would be wonderful! Do they see what we see? Is everything simpler for them? Food, fight, sleep and sex? Kamil shut his eyes. It was shocking to hear a woman being so unfettered, -No stories Kamil! No science, art, music, religion, political intrigue, trade, war...stupid maidservants turned by greed and promises...

Kamil said slowly, -I was thinking of this as I read. If your gift to know who is friend and foe is so strong then perhaps she was not evil. Perhaps she was forced against her love for you to steal the ring. It might have happened many times without you knowing. As you said, the ring was needed for royal seals.

-What? She stole under threat?

-Who made her? That is our question. This may be your best line of interrogation. Who has she been with recently? What unusual events have occurred affecting her family and friends? For whom or what did she risk death?

She stood up, her face lit with determination and excitement, -Didn't I tell you, Kamil, there is something in you that I need? You have an intelligence....I must go and do as you say, immediately. Let loose the inquisitors! There will be no questions between us this night.

Kamil smiled inwardly in relief as she left, almost as violently as she had entered.

Chapter Six

Knowing the true isolation of being marks the beginning of love for others

She was brooding and private. Her eyes were hooded. Once again her hand was tapping the arm of her chair. She had been like this for several minutes. Her dark blue robes merely added to her forbidding air. She had not once looked at the two piles of cards, untouched since their last meeting.

-All the threads pass through many hands back to Malika. But they are finer than a newborn's hair. Grasp them and they break. It is a gossamer web indeed. They provide no tension to drag her off her feet. I must thank you old historian for without you I would not have my eyes and ears attuned to the threat she has become. I knew the danger yes but not that it was so close to me, living and breathing in my own apartment. My investigators are everywhere the maid is known to have been. Asking, cajoling, persuading. It is slow and very painful for some but there is nothing yet except innuendo and self-truths.

-Let us hope that something emerges, he murmured hesitantly.

-Indeed! Indeed! So, there is naught else to do while my men dredge their way through the capital. Let us return to the staple fare, eh? I need my mind diverting. Read to me and I will uncork a question which melds the two chapters in one. And you may do the same. I will be hypnotised by your tongue. She turned over the next card, -The Hierophant, eh?

-It is, your Highness.

-With two priests kneeling before him. Typical. She splayed her palms, face up, -Heads of temples behave like kings these days, they hardly differentiate between the material and the spiritual. But we need them my father has often told me. Always appear to be subservient to the god of your lands even if it means little to you. The people then see you feathered like an angel in shining glory and your every act ordained by divine authority.

Kamil did not raise an eyebrow. This mercurial young creature, barely a woman, talked like a heretical philosopher. Too much indeed like the early Magus of the tales he was reading to her! Would that she might change for the better as the young man did, yet he doubted it. Life for her was a calculated campaign where values were so many coins to be used in barter for political ends. He had an uneasy thought that the Emperor had engaged him in this task precisely to educate his daughter in understanding the motives and ways of men, the better to control them!

-Let us discover the hidden message in what you have written concerning this high priest, Kamil.

-I am grateful your Highness. I chose not to depict him traditionally as the lynchpin of a temple but rather as someone whose embrace of spirituality led him into contemplation and meditation.

-Ah, an ascetic, she muttered rancorously, -Hah! even so I will control my tongue and listen. She lay back and folded her arms.

The captain slowed the boat by drawing in sail and she drifted into the main bay of the island. Anchors were dropped so that she became stilled a few hundred oar pulls from the sand, -It will take from the high sun until dark to load, the captain told them. -These people are good at their word and all will be gathered ready but it must be carried down to the shore from different points. You have the opportunity to walk across the island. It is a perfect little jewel. No creatures that poison and no animals with an intent to cause harm. Nothing but strange and bountiful plants and a few farming families to tend for them. Oh - and, of course, the man of prayer. Why not visit him? I did so once myself. He is very isolated here in his cave. The farmers leave food for him. His life is devoted to meditation. He put me at my peace merely by pressing his palm on my forehead. But what good is peacefulness when you have to captain men such as these? They only respect my discontent. Perhaps I will come back when my sea voyaging is over! He smiled ruefully.

⚸

The walk across the island was eventful, particularly to the nose and eye. There were flowers the older man had never seen, blossoms on trees and shrubs, bright lichens and sinewy creepers, flashing birds and gaudy insects. On top of this the air was thick with heady fragrances, - Is this that place where life began? murmured the Merchant. -It is often mentioned by priests, no matter what the religion. Either we have come from it at our birth because it is the home of our oldest ancestor or we go to it because all life ends blissfully here.

-If the latter be true, then our days of travelling are over! grinned his son.

The Merchant ruckled his nose, -You find humour where few others dare. My son, I despair of you. You have the eyes of a priest and the tongue of a travelling clown!

-And the hands of a magician and the ears of a wolf and the legs of a deer and the nose of a bear seeking honey. What a strange creature I am! You charge me with many anomalies, father. They were both amused.

-It is true. You are blessed. You are hardly aware of how blessed. It takes your father to remind you how extraordinary you are. He touched his temple with a finger.

-Yet I will live the same cycle as the next man and my gifts will prove as substantial as a spring bird's hoot.

-The bird returns every year as the snows leave your valley. You will not be forgotten, though you may be known by many names.

The path, beaten by the hooves of horses and the bare feet of men, took them out of the trees and down an incline to a small inlet. The sea was flat calm and reflected the deep blue of the sky. It lapped the beach in regular whispers. They undid their boots and stepped into shallows. Here they became immobilised by the stretching horizon, the boundless water and the unchanging sky. They felt as though they were intrusions in an otherwise unparalleled sweep of perfection.

A voice shook them suddenly from their vigil.

-Welcome.

It was so rare for the son to be startled by another that he instinctively went for his knife. His senses had been muted by the smell and sound of the sea.. But even as he turned swiftly his ear had sifted through the notes of the stranger's voice and found no hint of danger in them. The tone was deep and melodious with a simple directness and an obvious warmth. His hand dropped by his side.

-You are the priest? Our captain spoke of you and suggested we should visit you, said the older man. His son stared into the priest's eyes.

-I dreamed you would visit. A boy about to be a man and his father, not by blood.

-You dreamed about us? The Merchant's voice showed only a little surprise.

-You learn to cast your mind into the sea and catch strange fish when you spend so much time in solitude! The priest's face was darkened by exposure to the weather, his nose a hook and his eyes large, brown and tranquil. His mouth was creased at the corners with the lines of laughter. Otherwise there were no marks of age and it was difficult for his visitors to ascertain his years. He wore only a cloth tied around his waist. His body was thin but not painfully so and his skin seemed almost translucent.

-Come, eat with me. They were led to the mouth of a cave in the sloping cliffs. It was barely deep enough to shelter a man. A mattress of dried grasses served as a bed, a spread cloth as a table and fruit gourds, stacked by the entrance, as containers for food and water. He motioned them to sit and they rested their backs against cool heaped sand, all three looking at the line between sea and sky. Finally, breaking their shared silence, the priest passed them each a small cup heaped with nuts and berries and another with water. The youth observed how the colours of the fruit vibrated by being next to each other. They ate slowly, relishing the range of flavours.

-What purpose has this life of yours? asked the youth after a while.

-No reason that would satisfy you. You are still waking. When your sun has passed its highest point, answers will have more meaning. Until then you must take your journey as the only road. You will experience enough in your life to fill the memories of many men.

-Still, I would have an answer from you, teacher.

-I am here so that I can do no harm to any living thing. My friends in the village leave food for me. Occasionally someone from the boat is inquisitive enough to visit. Otherwise I live alone, think alone, feel alone.

-What do you gain from this? What reward?

-A sieve of emptiness through which all that I am, drains away.

-Is that a reward?

-It is only by relieving your life of all knowledge and belief in this way that ultimately you become aware of your own existence.

The young man pondered for some time, -What led you to make this change in your life?

-I will tell you. The priest gathered himself, -It is the story of a former life, a dream to me now. I tell it as though it happened to another for it has little meaning for me other than that.

♀

The priest told his story as he said he would, describing the events of his life as if recounting a tale of another, a third person, told by firelight.

-He was born into a rich family. Everything he wanted was provided for him. He did not even have to ask. He assumed the world was his to plunder for he came from a long line of armed merchants. He had neither conscience nor awareness of the effects of his behaviour upon others. As a pillaging raider he travelled far. He added to the riches of his family name. At his word a man could be imprisoned or put to the sword. He had power over the turn of events. He took women for his pleasure and no-one had enough significance for him ever to cause him to question his acts. Then, at the height of his tyranny, he abducted a woman against her will and made her join his tent of wives. She refused him her favours telling him that if he forced himself upon her she would die. He tried to entice her to desire him because she was different from all others he had met and for the first time he wanted to be given to freely. He became besotted by this. He sought unusual gifts for her wherever he travelled and made her his only interest, freeing all the others from his power. She resisted him even so. The more she resisted the more he wanted her to offer herself in an act of voluntary desire.

One night he came home from an arduous campaign. During the time he was away he could think of nothing but how it would be when he returned. He had imagined she had changed in her feelings for him. She would greet him with warmth, a smile of excitement, her arms around his neck, her soft kisses on his lips.

When he arrived, certain that she would be waiting as he had dreamed (and as he had ordered), it was only to be told by a loyal servant that she was being visited by her young lover from the clan from which he had abducted her! In a terrible anger he went to her chamber only to find her lying dead upon her bed. She and her lover had taken a poison knowing that he would be informed of her infidelity. Their eyes were fixed in loving smiles upon each other.

He had held her hand and beseeched her to return to life, lowering his head to break the awful intimacy of their gaze, trying to capture the last meaning in her eyes for himself.

He sat beside her body from moon to sun to moon again. During this passage of time he realised that all desire is suffering. He resolved to rid himself of it, to cast himself free of his family line. He took simple clothes and left his home that night telling no-one. He tried to act in every way in contradiction to his past. He discovered what it was like to be treated as one with no name, to be beaten and humiliated yet also learned to have no feeling of vengeance for what was done to him. As he became strong in his ability to renounce all worldly things he found he never wanted for food and drink. He sought merely to reward the world with acts of kindness for the very fact of his being alive within it. He learned that by adopting silence and the purity of thought he would be given everything he needed. He became certain that once he had cleansed his being of all desire then he could achieve what had eluded him throughout his early life, an awareness of his very existence, of the place he filled in the world, of his skin and blood and flesh and bones, of the living earth and its plants and creatures and of life-giving air and water. Finally his journey brought him to this island and here he would remain until such time as his body was set alight on a raft of fire, pulled out to sea and left to drift on the tides by the people of the village, which was their way with the dead. Only then would he have atoned for those acts in his early life against all those to whom he had caused harm.

They listened to the priest's tale in silence. Every word hung upon the air. Finally the older listener said, -This is not our path, I fear. I too have done harm, sometimes beyond the law of reason but I have no desire to embrace such privations.

-Nor I but I respect your path to redemption, said the youth. His eyes became tied to those of the priest.

The priest's face settled into a focused intensity, -I see that you will cause the sun and moon to illuminate much that is good in your time on earth but, as in all things, you will also be forced to cast shadows. Though you have no great regard for the spiritual journey as yet, open your heart to those that do so, whether they be priests or hermits, women or children, horses or dogs. Each one that you meet may donate you something you cannot see or touch but which will add to your strength of purpose and inform your decisions when there is no time for reflection.

-I will try.

They made their farewells, adopting the priest's ritual of a solemn bow with one hand spread upon the heart and the fingers of the other touching the forehead. They set off across the island. The young man's mind contained little else but their audience with the recluse, turning it over, viewing it from different standpoints, seeking greater meanings. To do what the priest had done was to accept no obstacles to death, it seemed. It was an act of partial entombment in a place of calm and beauty. He felt he had begun a journey full of events and people which would bring him enlightenment whereas the priest had chosen to end his journey here, mostly in silence, seeking the same ends by an abstinence from such things.

It did not escape him however that the priest had taken much from life first.

-**Just as I** thought! she cried as the last word left his lips, -A perfectly successful king becomes a perfectly unsuccessful hermit! She laughed, -Don't look so put out, old man!

-Your Highness, I don't think he –

-Forgive me, I know I jest about subjects some feel should be insulated from the barbs of humour. It is idyllic, I agree. A picture of paradise. The simple, savage life of the holy fool. Indeed I admit that there are lessons in this story. There must be a balance between the exercise of power and the exercise of compassion - or guilt will corrode the spirit. Thus lies the road to torment and the abjuring of profound royal responsibilities, don't you think? She stared at him, levelly.

-It must be so, he said, inclining his head humbly.

-Do you believe in God? I know I am asking the obvious!

Kamil smiled. It was spontaneous and Princess Sabiya saw no smugness in it, -I do, your Highness!

-What is God? I am expanding my question, she added sweetly.

-The One who made all. All we see. Everything that there is. All we think and feel. The worlds that exist inside and outside our eyes. He touched his heart with his hand and bowed, meekly.

-May I ask further questions for clarification? He bowed again. He could not, of course, refuse, -Where is God now? When He made all things did He stay or go?

-Some believe he is always here in all things. Some believe he has withdrawn but observes his creation rather like an alchemist experimenting in a laboratory. There are some who believe He has sent His son –

She sighed, -I know. I am well versed in the major religions. My father insisted upon it saying that a ruler must know what drives all men, for on such details wars can be avoided – or won!

-He is wise!

-Yet religious observances may only win the respect of an emperor if they do not conflict with the laws of the empire. In this matter the emperor stands above all religions. Do you follow? Kamil did not hesitate but bowed, -Thus it is that religion may speak of the sanctity of life yet at times it is necessary to kill. In the complex business of ruling an empire much can be achieved by overruling God's commandments. Her eyes clouded. Kamil realised that the death of her

79

servant still caused her unusual disquiet. Yet he was also dismayed by her unremitting ambition to be Empress, no matter what cold-blooded act this might entail. He did not feel safe with her no matter what other feelings stirred in him.

-So, dear old man, who is so patient with his student, what is your question in return? She smiled her smile of honey and wine.

Kamil looked down at his clasped hands for a moment. He had no question. All was suddenly blank. His mind was unoccupied because this extraordinary set of events, this daily twilight contest of wills with the heir to the empire had never existed within even his most extreme fantasy. Now he could not remember the question he had already asked! Yet he could easily remember the panic he had felt before asking because a familiar twitching was breaking out all over his body.

-Have you gone dumb?

-It is an ...an...anxiety, your Highness. I feel so unworthy of honouring you with a question. To his further panic and embarrassment tears coursed down his cheeks. He made an effort to wipe them away, feeling utterly abject.

-Poor old historian, here! She pressed a perfumed ball of linen onto Kamil's face. He held it against his cheek and wiped his eyes aware that the using of it was in some deep sense profane while at the same time being unutterably honoured by her gesture. The alluring odours that caught and stayed in his nostrils made him dizzy.

-It is perfectly normal Kamil. Perfectly. To be intimate with your Princess should bring tears. I expect no less.

-Thank you your Highness. I understand my muteness but not my tears! Why? How does this happen?

-Hah! she laughed and her rising notes fell attractively upon his ears, -I have dragged a question from you! Why do I have this effect upon an old man whose life is circumscribed by the mouldy leaves of ancient texts? A perfectly acceptable question. He stared at her dumbly. -I should say that though I have witnessed similar events so many times I have not questioned them before this moment. Men, women and children can become unpredictably emotional in the presence of a princess! More so than in the presence of an emperor! It is the divine they seek in me I would venture. I am still a virgin. I am pure. Great blood flows through me. My regal eyes are believed to see as no others see, deep into the souls of men. It is the blessing of birth and all who stand before me know it. They have not had your close knowledge of this patchy gift! To be so close to me is often too affecting for my subjects who might hope to see me at best passing in a procession and surrounded by my noble guard. None would think to share the close confines of a softly furnished anteroom with me as you do my most favoured historian! There, is that not a good answer? Good enough for the moment anyway. She stood up, -Perhaps your questions are irrelevant now that you are proving of more use to me as a spymaster! Concentrate on strategies by which I can defeat my enemies. Yes?

*

When she had gone, Kamil pressed the linen to his nose and closed his eyes. He knew why the tears had fallen. It was not as she had thought. Each crystal drop was blessed by love, complete in itself. Each tear contained reverence, loyalty, obedience, exaltation and something more base that he refused to allow into his thoughts and all of this was mixed with pain and resentment that she saw him as an old man, completely unworthy of even tracing the footprints she might leave in the sand.

Chapter Seven

Your life changes every moment so learn to breathe it in

Kamil had worked intensively throughout the day. He had reviewed the Tale he was to recount that evening. He had also spent much of the time in the Emperor's private reading rooms adjoining the Great Library. A rectangle of warmth lay over his heart where the linen handkerchief was pinned inside his vest. Now and then he tugged the tunic around his neck and a warm up rush of air brought the smell of her perfume to his nose. He tried to organise all he had read into clear advice. The books he had chosen covered tactics in battle, historical discourses on how great wars had been won or lost, biographies of dynasties, court intrigue, plotting and the dark business of assassination. All things seemed possible in the bitter rivalry that attended most royal lines. Patricide, matricide, infanticide, fratricide, sororicide, ensuring that babies were still-born, or worse, with awful mutations of mind or limb. The desire to be sole ruler seemed bred into the very flesh of would-be kings and queens. He thought of the toothed fish that ate everything in the pool, even its own kind, to become sole arbiter of life in the shadowy depths. What advice could he offer such a creature? And would it listen?

*

She arrived early dressed in white, a shimmering red paper flower in her hair and gold sandals on her feet. Her black skin was as polished as a mirror. She exuded none of the edgy truculence that he associated with her, none of the harsh impetuosity. When she was comfortable she said, -I expect you wish to be brought up to date with my news? She gazed at him serenely.
-Of course, Princess.
-We have three suspects. They will be molested tomorrow by the army's chief interrogator. None has been known to withstand him. What do you say to that? Pleasing?
-Indeed, your Highness. A book came to his mind in which there was

a debate between a philosopher and a general about the value of torture. He preferred the philosopher's arguments. He began to marshal them now.

-Then try to look a little happier for me! She employed a poor-little-girl face to engage his support, -It is good news isn't it? Come, tell me what is going through your mind. I can see that you think to the contrary.

-Well -

-Ah. You do. I was right! And you will unsettle me again I have no doubt. And I may get angry! Her face became stiff and unyielding, suddenly.

He stared at her helplessly, -I do not know how to proceed, your –

-I know, I know. Get on with it! Tell me what I must hear. I am two people. One wants to punish and the other wants to learn. You know that, Kamil. Have little fear that the learner will triumph in the end. She sat forward like a pupil, her head slightly bowed, her hands folded on her lap, her eyes staring up through their lashes and her face earnest.

-There are two aspects to your news that we must question, Princess.

- Only two! she snorted sarcastically.

-The first concerns how the three suspects came to light. On what evidence? It may be sound of course. On the other hand it is a precipitous culmination to the search, do you not think? In which case it may be the work of those who would seek to direct attention away from the true enemy and throw us minnows to satisfy our lust for blood. He tried to keep the image of the predatory fish from his mind.

-So what should I do? Let them go? She laughed harshly.

-Perhaps.

-What…! She reflected for a few moments, -Ah! I must not repeat the mistake I made with my servant girl. We can let them go so that we can keep them under surveillance...

-That is one course of action. And it would obviate the second of my concerns. She said nothing but stared at him, -I have been examining many a mouldy leaf in your father's library. She caught his coy look and pouted in amusement but he continued quickly, -And what they seem to show is that torture rarely uncovers anything worthwhile. Under the extremes exacted by the interrogator, for example, they may say anything to stop the abominable pain.. They could well have been schooled in what to say. They will have been primed with more names, always leading further from the truth. Also they may have been chosen because they have absolutely no direct or even indirect connection with your enemies. This will lead to more interrogations, more false trails and more unnecessary deaths perhaps.

She nodded appreciatively, -Show a historian a pile of mouldy leaves and he returns with an illuminated manuscript! You are a clever man. I have much to think about but I will be good and hear my story first. It would be a mistake not to, I feel. Somehow the Tales embellish truth. What have we now? Oh, The Lovers. I did read this. The Magus discovers his one true love! And she as young as I! All is possible it seems. Read it to me.

After their short voyage to the island there was only time to prepare for a greater trip across the sea. On the boat he made his father sleep in the dormitory with the seamen while he slept with the two horses in the hold. It was a five day journey and even the youth's roan which was innately wise to what was happening, fretted a little because of the creaks and moans and the smells of wet timber and the scurrying of rats. With the installation of a ramp they could take the horses up for air during the day. The sea was calm and there was a continuous hazy sun. At night he lay on a pallet covered with straw. He could just discern the heads of the two beasts above him. Occasionally one of them would sway a little too far with the roll of the boat and wake, adjust itself and drop its head to snuffle him and he would open his eyes a little and caress its velvet nostrils. In this pleasant drift from sleep to waking to sleep again he had plenty of time to reflect upon their journey. By taking the merchant's boat they were saving weeks of travel around the shore.

When his father, as a young man, had initially succumbed to his wanderlust and travelled north and west he had encountered mountains and rivers, land where there were few trails and tribal areas that had sentries to prevent passage. While there were always risks in a boat such as storms, pirates or concealed rocks, this speeding of their quest more than compensated for any disquiet they might have felt. And they were being rewarded by a peaceful journey.

As his father went about his business with a steadiness of hand and eye and his characteristic purposeful stillness, the youth could sense the growing blaze of concern within him as he continually checked the heavens for signs of their progress.

-We will be in time I think, he once muttered aloud and then, hearing his own words in the air, he smiled quickly and added, -You will meet the woman who bore me!

-We will be in time, he had responded, -For is she not attached to the same thread with which fate binds us to its reasoning?

-You know it? asked his father anxiously.

-I am sure! His father had put both arms around him and patted his back with his hands in a rare gesture of their intimacy.

It made him picture his own mother and the meeting they would have when he returned to his tribal land. He had memorised the look in her proud eyes as he swooped towards her. Her face had become familiar because of it; the bent nose and the weather darkened skin, the man's hard mouth that had softened for a moment as she caught sight of him, the clearly etched black eyebrows the shape of young moons above her pale grey eyes, eyes she had given him. In that moment of contact much had passed between them, a concentrated burst of knowledge, an intensity of complex feelings of belonging, possession and love. Yet in her gaze resided something else, some painful memory or hidden secret relating to his very flesh and blood.

He sensed that it concerned his father. He opened his mind like a fan to try to contact her. But it was futile. She had learned to block both her past and her present from such communication as a defence against those who would seek to destroy her by these very same means. Her son must try to find her in his own time and in his own way.

He tried to bring to life images of his real father but there was nothing. It could only be that he was dead and this was why it felt as though one person's blood flowed in his body. The probability that this was so grew stronger and made a place for itself in his thoughts. Then the roan's tongue began licking the back of his hand. He placed a palm on the long bone of its forehead and it nuzzled his ear. The other horse joined in, rubbing itself gently on the other side of his head. They quietened him and he lay back and began to slide towards sleep. He was aware that his mother's visage which had been so clear, now began to soften and change. As he reached the point where sleep would take him, it had become the golden-skinned face of an unknown young woman. A small smile settled on his sleeping features.

☥

The shore that greeted them was more savage than any he had yet encountered. Within a day's travel of their anchorage they were met by sandy wastes engulfing the plains between random outcrops of misshapen rock. They each now carried several water bags and his father made them stop and drink at regular intervals. They wore white cotton drapes around the head and neck, kept in place by sturdy black ribbons and long, loose fitting shirts and trousers. The backs of the horses were similarly protected with shallow hoods running up their necks, through which their ears protruded. Wherever they found a watering place his father soaked the sheets to give the horses relief from the effects of the sand and sun.

When his roan whinnied and stopped his father nodded to his son's mount, -I was expecting them.

-They have been watching us since high sun.

-Yes, they are dangerous if crossed but will invite us to travel with them for that is their way. Once they are certain of our character we will be safe.

-Desert people?

-It is so. They have stamina to live in these wildernesses, always moving, trading between two worlds of plenty to the north and south like ants carrying great burdens on their backs. They are in demand because no other travellers would wish to cross this burning earth without guides and if they did they would have no desire to come face to face with these warriors. It was they who taught me how to ride. I owe much to them.

-And through you, me, said the youth nodding.

-It is true. They will be aware of it. They ride both camel and horse and can tell a tribesman's place of origin from his seat on either just as you do in the north. He stood in his stirrups and raised a sword arm in greeting, holding it there for several seconds, motioning his son to follow suit. There was an immediate response from the group clustered on the distant ridge of the white sloped dune. With arms held high they pressed their camels down the incline.

The five ungainly beasts stood in a line facing the two horses whose nostrils quivered in the air trying to make sense of the new scent. The camels' lips drew back in response. On their backs, legs hooked round their humps, were five sets of eyes swathed in dark material. His father and the leader of the group pulled to one side and engaged in a whispered interchange which the youth could not hear. It lasted for some time and then the leader of the group turned a hand over, palm upwards and followed that by placing it over his heart. The camels dropped into single line followed by the two horses walking abreast.

The Merchant whispered softly, -We are fortunate indeed. The clan chief is the man who gave me succour on my journey this way all those years ago. They know of me. He has enjoyed sixty summers but still fights alongside his men. He has recently taken another wife who has delivered him of a son so his prowess remains undiminished.

-How many sons has he?

-Numerous. And daughters too. When I passed this way he had ten sons and only two wives. Who knows now? His first sons and daughters will have produced their own children. It is good for the clan. It is a harsh life and many die.

The young man said reflectively, -We only accept one wife unless she dies.

-It is not true of all people as you see.

-How is it justified?

-Is there need to justify a tradition? Does the two-hoot bird justify laying its egg in another's nest? Does a fish count out its eggs and stop at a number? Does a she-dog ask if its mate is a brother or from another pack?

-Is it the god we choose that lets us define our taking of women then? Or just our nature? The youth grimaced in amusement.

-Enough. You are too attracted by such notions. Ask the clan chief but do so in an indirect way. Such discussions might see your head on a pole.

All the while the youth assumed they could not be understood by those in front. Their conversation was conducted quietly enough but carried easily across the windless sands. He was therefore surprised when the leader halted his camel and waited for them to come abreast.

-It would be best not to ask him at all. Such questioning is not permitted. The youth was stunned. He turned to his father.

-You did not tell me this was a woman? His father smiled at him amusedly.

The woman said in a prickly tone, -I am the first daughter of the first son. I have seen sixteen summers. You are surprised at a woman leading a patrol?

-No, my mother is a warrior too. It was his father's turn to look surprised. The youth had not told him of his dream, -I mistook your -, the youth made a vague gesture with his hands, -Shape for that of a man.

-There should be so great a difference?

-Perhaps it is the beast you ride. He looked embarrassed.

-It may be so. She laughed, -These creatures allow no elegant display. She pushed on abruptly to the head of the column.

After a few minutes the youth turned to his father and said, -I saw my mother in a dream. The priestess gave me a changeling potion. I became a hawk. They settled into silence again.

☥

The trail took them due south across a peninsula of desert waste with the sun an ever descending companion to their right. By the time they were leaving the soft silence it had become a great deep ball taking up much of the horizon.

She hadn't returned for more conversation but kept them moving at a steady pace and with an experienced regard for the terrain. They reached the encampment as the last cooling rim of red dropped from sight. The two strangers pulled jerkins from their bags as the temperature fell and led their horses to the pool that had been made next to the well. No-one spoke to them.

-The horses will be safe here?

-As safe as the chief himself. It is the law. A head for a horse. He drew a finger across his throat and smiled at his son. As soon as they had unsaddled and watered their beasts a child ran up to lead them off for feeding. Neither horse would move until its master whispered a command in its ear.

-Intelligence of that kind is rare! She had returned for them and was watching the horses move away. The young man felt a shiver run through him. It was a new sensation. She had changed her riding cloth to a less dense cream weave. A length of pale pink silk hid her hair but allowed them to see her face. Like forest honey, thought the youth. Her black eyes regarded them minutely, her lips drawn into a half-smile, showing the evenness of her white teeth. She was exactly as he had dreamed, the same oval face, the same sturdy build.

-They are like brothers, horse and man, she had noted to his father, as they watched him with the roan.

-It must be possible. It is said that a man can die and return as such a creature to protect the blood line, replied the Merchant.

The youth smiled as he heard his father's words. The Merchant waited for the acid remark he usually got from his son.

But the youth spoke softly, aware that he must make a good impression, -There are mysteries for which we have no real explanation. This conciliatory remark drew a slight nod of approval from his father. His son seemed to be learning at last. True, it took a young beauty to drive home the need to defer to another's beliefs but it was a small sign of growing up.

She swept an arm in the direction of the main tents, -My Grandfather invites you to eat with him. He apologises for the delay in greeting you but he has been at barter with men from the south. It has been concluded to everyone's advantage. First I will take you to your sleeping quarters for this night. Your faces have a thicker carpet of dust than the desert, itself. Would your mothers know you? She laughed and motioned them to follow. As soon as her back was turned the youth scraped his fingers frantically across his cheeks, dislodging the sand that had collected there. Beside him his father smiled to himself.

-You have returned as promised my friend, said the chief, after the ceremonial bows with hands on hearts.

-It was my duty and my pleasure, O Father. And here is my son.

-You are welcome, Grandson.

-My gratitude, Grandfather,

The tent was spacious enough for twenty people to sit cross-legged in a circle to eat but there were just five of them present apart from the tasters who were busy sampling food and drink.

-A necessary blight on today's life, the chief told them as he recounted a century of deaths by poisoning among the various desert families, -I trust my cook with my life but the journey from his fire to my lips is never guaranteed. Even among those in whom my blood flows there are some whose eyes are like standing water.

-Blood is polluted by greed, said the girl coldly.

-It is true, her grandfather replied, -Sometimes the true child contains no blood from the father and yet the love is greater for it has had to be earned. He looked at the two of them with an arch of his eyebrows.

-Such is my experience, agreed the youth and laid a hand momentarily on the shoulder of his father whose eyes glinted with a fierce pride.

The chief sat with the older man next to him opposite the youth and the young woman. The fifth member of the group was the captain of the guard, a man who said very little, had not greeted them and who sat slightly to one side. The young man eyed him curiously with an unabashed directness that had often made people drop their gaze because of the intensity of his regard. His eyes can pierce another, thought his father, who resolved to mention it so that his son would camouflage himself better when with strangers.

The captain seemed to the young man to be clearly trustworthy. He obviously loved the chief's granddaughter for his eyes flickered her way constantly and the expressions on his face, though barely perceptible, tended to mirror hers. He was tall and heavily muscled. His fighting hand rarely strayed far from his sheathed knife, eating, as was a soldier's custom, with the other.

-I too am blessed in this way, continued the chief in his deliberations on blood line and loyalty. He indicated the captain, -From orphan to son and now my army commander, I trust him with my life. The captain smiled and bowed. The youth caught a cloud of anxiety flitting across the young woman's face, -You have arrived at an auspicious time. Tomorrow those who wish to take my grand-daughter as their woman, will fight for the privilege! The girl and the youth turned instinctively towards each other and something other than surprise passed between them. It was not unnoticed by the captain.

-They will fight for me with horse and weapon, she murmured laying a hand on his arm..

-How many have declared themselves? He wanted more of her warm touch.

-Only tomorrow will reveal that. Not many.

-But your beauty will make men of boys and those with wives, seek replenishment, he said with well-intentioned flattery.

She replied sadly, -By law I must be a man's first wife. All know that the captain is my grandfather's choice. Few will oppose him. Men are fearful of him because he is already their victor in all trials of strength. There must be at least two other suitors because that is the tradition. These are not serious competitors. They volunteer to ensure that the triumphant one is able to demonstrate his mettle.

-As in the wild, murmured the youth, -The pretence of stalking the leader of the pack by the young males.

-It is like that.

-I see the way he looks at you.

She said to him sharply, -He is not my desire but the union will benefit the clan.

-Refuse him, he said softly.

-This would dishonour him and my grandfather.

-This is a complex puzzle of opposites! He said, quietly, -Accept this man for the benefit of your clan and your heart will endure an eternal centre of darkness and your children may also carry that shadow. Refuse this man and your personal happiness will be at a cost to your-

-I cannot refuse him, she interrupted, -It must be concluded tomorrow. I will become his first woman or the woman of the man who defeats him.

-I can defeat him.

-This must yet be demonstrated. She gazed at him frankly but there was hope in her words.

He held her stare, perplexed. It had not occurred to him that what he had been secretly thinking was now to be tested, -I have a journey to make which is fixed in the blood of my father.

-If it is written then so must it be.

-Yet I will return, that is certain.

-And you will not find another! she said. It was not a question.

-No, you appeared to me in a dream before I reached your side. There can be no other.

She closed the flap of his tent and they were in darkness, -Then I believe you will find a way, she whispered, -You and your father.

92

The calm of the previous day had given way to a sand-wind that half-obscured the morning sun. It came in whistling blasts and scoured the skin and filled the pouches under the eyes. Between the gusts there were minutes of silence and calm. The men of the clan had formed a great circle, sitting bareback on camel and horse. On command, the captain and two others rode into the circle. They drew their horses beside a pole that had been erected at its centre. It had a cross-beam supporting a hanging wooden disc on which the emblem of the chief had been painted. Each horseman touched the disc in turn and swore allegiance to him.

In truth, the youth felt, the skirmishes that followed were such as you would see among men practising their arms together in any army. There was some dust and a little dramatic flailing of limbs and weaponry but it was as with a passing circus. The captain was not extended and his opponents were allowed an honourable retreat.

-Is there any other who would shed blood for this woman? asked the chief pointing to his granddaughter who sat astride a camel watching, her face nearly covered by silk. Eyes turned to fix on the young man. Suspicion and anger fuelled those stares. Their time in the tent was common knowledge to all.

-What about the young stranger? asked the captain.

-A man could travel all the lands that there are and not find such a woman, called out the youth in a clear strong voice. To his mind came the teaching of the priestess. He need not fight if there was another way. Yet he must seek her hand.

-Will you compete for her? The captain's voice had lost a little of its confidence. He had hoped that the youth would have respected the courtesies expected of a guest and declined.

-Competing in this way is not my way.

-And what is your custom? asked the captain angrily.

-A woman is free to choose. She is the equal of a man. It is only right that she chooses the father of her children.

-It is so here too, smiled the chief, -We are not savages! Even after battle she may refuse the victor. But all could see that his smile was but a politeness.

-And when was the last such event? asked the youth.

The chief's face went sombre, -My very own mother was the last. She refused. Later, when more men fought for her, my father was strongest and accepted by her even though he was her junior by many years.

-And what fate befell the first victor?

-He became as a dog who brings death with its frothing jaws. He cut off his manhood with his eating knife and sent it by servant to my mother wrapped in his bloody undergarment. Afterwards he took his last ride into the desert. My mother carried his spirit with honour for the rest of her days. My father accepted the shadow that she had to carry.

-Sometimes we are chosen for burdens that are not of our own making, intervened the Merchant, -We are innocent but must live as though guilt has been proven. There was general nodding of heads but the youth cut it short with a direct question to the captain.

-If you are refused will you follow such a course? There was a long silence. The fine dusts were whipped up around them so that an answer would have to wait. But in the heads of the clansmen similar thoughts were being entertained. Until this youth and his father had arrived destiny seemed to be following a certain path. This had petered out in the sandstorm and now it was as though something different seemed possible.

-She will not refuse me, said the captain grimly, trying to give scaffold to his own confidence. All stared first at one and then the other, -And you are not in your tribe you are here. We have our ways. It would be my pleasure to try my skills against yours.

-I have already witnessed your prowess, said the youth, -I cannot fight you for a woman I have only just met but I will match my skill with yours - on one condition...

-It is? The captain's face betrayed uncertainty, already these events were moving beyond his prescience. The occult confidence of the youth was unlike any he had encountered.

-If I am victor, the youth continued inexorably, -The girl will choose what man she will take. My father and I will leave in peace and you will continue to honour your chief and command his army.

-There would be shame in such an outcome, unlikely as it may be.

-That is not so. Who can lose honour in a battle against such as I? He raised his voice dramatically and stared round the watching clan, -I tell you, I am not as other men. He strode forward into the centre of the circle of eyes. His voice lowered and became softly emphatic, -I arrived in this world alone, a new born on horseback at the tent of my father. No-one knows from whence. My mother, whomever she may be, passed on certain gifts of arm and eye to my blood and my father here gave me others. They are not those of a normal being. One of these gifts I will now demonstrate to you all. The youth reached inside his robe and took from it a large pale green egg, -You see this egg? I have blown it. It is as delicate as the lids on this woman's eyes, he pointed at the chief's granddaughter, -Watch! He placed the egg in his mouth which forced his cheeks to bulge. Suddenly he slapped them. The bulge disappeared. He opened his mouth and stuck out his tongue. There was no egg, -Look in your pouch, he ordered the captain but an angry stubbornness prevented the man from doing so. The chief broke the stillness by reaching over and undoing the catch of the pouch. He turned it upside down and an egg rolled out into his palm.

-It is the very same egg! he called, turning it lightly in his hand. The shocked murmurings from the circle of incredulous faces were silenced as the youth took the egg from the chief, held it aloft and squeezed it in his hand. As they watched, the handle of a throwing knife emerged magically from the youth's coaxing fingers like a snake being cajoled from its hole. No shards of green shell fell. Slowly, with his thumb and forefinger easing it, the knife ended its movement with its blade held by its point. He turned suddenly on one foot and with a smooth whirl his arm released the weapon. It arced across the circle and embedded itself in the centre of the battle disc some twenty strides away. His father followed it swiftly and pulled it out holding it high in the air. There was another shocked gasp. Impaled on the knife was a green egg, intact except for the incision of the blade and clear liquid with droplets of yellow dripped from it.

-It is as if the sun itself is being drained from a clear sky, muttered the chief inspecting the egg closely.

-Only a great shaman can reverse nature, called the Merchant to everyone in a loud and stern voice, -He has made the egg whole again! And you saw it here in this desert place!

☥

The two strangers left the clan that evening to travel by the cool of the night over what remained of the wastes. The captain had declined to fight on the order of the chief. There was no shame for him not to face such a half-djinn his men had reassured him but his eyes had remained hooded and all who watched sensed his desolation at his shattered hopes. The clan had then kept a wary distance from the pair who had brought such climactic and unsought events into their lives.

☥

The roan stopped suddenly, his father's horse following suit immediately. From the darkness on her camel, emerged the first daughter of the first son.

-I wished to bid you return quickly to my tent.

-I will waste no time, said the youth. He pushed the roan alongside the camel and stared up at her small figure on the tall beast.

-That pleases me. And do not forget your honour, she said without smiling, -You have much to return to. Their eyes held for several moments, then they each raised a fist aloft and beat their hearts with the other. Not speaking another word she turned her mount back into the darkness.

-She is like her mother I believe, said his father.

-And my own, said the youth. He stared after her into the shadows.

As he finished reading the Tale she clapped her hands, stood up and did a short, swirling dance around her chair. She stopped suddenly to look down at his surprised face, -You write well. There are not too many words so the reader must add her own! Yet how can you portray love? Love is pounding blood and mad thoughts and the desire for oblivion in the arms of a beloved. You have never taken a lover never mind a wife! Yes I know everything about you old historian, do not look shocked! You do not think the Emperor would allow you private meetings with his daughter without a thorough vetting of your entire life, do you? She dropped her voice and asked, -How old are you? I forget, if ever I knew that detail.

-I am approaching my forty first year Princess. He shrank slightly, expecting yet another jibe from her. Instead it was her turn to look bemused.

-You are full of surprises Kamil. I was unaware. I thought you to be a decade older at least! She sat down and demurely tidied her over-skirt. -I must be more careful what I say and do in your presence. It is natural to play the coquettish little girl with a man old enough to be my grandfather but this is not now the case. I cannot have you thinking base thoughts about your Princess. No! Kamil bowed and half covered his reddening face. Yet the irony hurt. Had he not wished her to see him as a younger man? Now she did she would draw a curtain between them and he might never again see the girlish excesses that stirred his heart.

-Let us to business, she said sternly, -I have learned something from the lovers' Tale, Kamil, if only because it confirms the good advice you offer me. It is that there may be other ways of achieving ends than first meet a warrior's eye and sword! Cunning requires a supple and creative intelligence, eh?

-Your Highness, he said and dropped his head.

-Now, Spymaster, I have digested your earlier suggestions and will follow them. But you know the vicious kitten I like to be. I need more exercise for my claws. How else should we proceed?

Kamil had prepared well for this meeting. His words were respectful yet firm and decisive with no hint of his normal obsequiousness.

-Our strategy, as I have said, must be to ignore the arrow slits in the wall with their limited viewpoints and take our vantage from the highest battlements of the tower so that all is within our vision. We must ask again the question as to why were you mistaken over your maid? Perhaps you were not. If she loved you and would have died for you, which I am sure must have been the case, what made her betray you? I think she may have had no choice.

-No choice? Princess Sabiya peered curiously at him but said no more.

Kamil continued, -The threat to someone she loved was too great perhaps. Was she to marry? Have your men seek audience with her family and friends and her intended's relatives, if such is the case. Seek out their fears. Seek connections no matter how seemingly innocent. Somehow pressure was placed upon her. She may have been promised that no harm would ever come to you and that the ring would only ever be needed for a moment. I am sure she was a simple enough child and had no idea of the depth of the intrigue against you. Have your men do this work through third parties carefully chosen for their good nature and winning ways and with no obvious connection to the court.. The sight of royal spies in their midst will terrify people into silence and further warn our enemies. Only if we can gain trust will we learn anything of value. My second suggestion is this. Have one of your retinue who is loyal beyond measure, look into how the three suspects were discovered. What were the circumstances? Who told whom what? If we can trace the events of their capture to a source then we may have real enemies to interrogate. His argument made her pause.

-Excellent, Kamil, my old historian, -Though you make me feel even more pain at my untimely act against the girl! We shall pursue matters as you propose. She smiled capriciously at him as though suddenly seeing something comical beyond his knowing, -In return I will send the royal dresser to measure you and have you attired more appropriately for a forty year old spymaster! And the Emperor's barber will find plenty to occupy him! If I must look at you every day then we must make the experience more entertaining!

Chapter Eight

The stilled spirit is not rent apart by opposing forces

Both men sent by the Princess felt that this work was below them. They shared that cold disdain servants develop for everyone other than royalty once they have become used to their life of privilege. Kamil could see it simmering beneath their eyelids but they dared not show it in public. The Princess's temperamental fits were all too well known to them. And the Emperor doted on his favourite daughter.

He was instructed to bathe before they deigned to lay their plump fingers upon him. A large marble tub was rolled laboriously in on a wheeled platform and then filled by a queue of servants carrying great jugs, in pairs. The water was infused with oils and fragrances. Nor was there any privacy. They stood watching him and instructing him as though he was a baby. He was told to wash here and there, to duck his head thoroughly and then have it soaped by a servant, to clean between his toes and between his legs. After a thorough scrubbing a servant appeared pushing a swing mirror. He stood up and began to dry himself before the glass keeping his emotions in check by pretending there was no-one else in the room. He was not too displeased by what he saw. Whilst his body did not compare with that of a career soldier, neither was he too bulbous in the midriff. True there was a paunch and true there was graspable flesh on his hips marking the passing of youth but his skin had no wrinkles, vein-blemishes, spots or scales.

The dresser said coldly, -Dress in these, throwing undergarments over the mirror. Kamil put on the silk vest and soft trousers. Concealing the act, he slid the square of linen into place and pinned it there.

The barber stepped forward nonchalantly, his attendant following with a tray of combs, razors, scissors, brushes, oils and hot water. Kamil sat while a towel was placed around his shoulders. The man was quick and sure. His face moved round Kamil's, close enough for him to see the coarse skin filled to smoothness with stiff cream and smell the unguents that had been massaged into the cheeks. Following the cutting and shaving, similar fragrant oils were applied to him. Then the pair left.

Servants carrying robes entered at the clapped hands of the royal dresser. Kamil was soon clothed in a white tunic and skirt, partially covered by a dark green coat that hung to his shoes. Other sets of clothes were hooked on wire along one wall and his dowdy rags removed. He never saw them again.

Within moments all the evidence of the barber and dresser was gone and Kamil was left alone to prepare for the Princess's arrival. He walked tentatively over to the wall mirror, coming to it from one side so as to maximise the impact of his new image. The sight of himself was mesmerising in its abruptness. He looked like a younger brother, one who had obviously achieved much in the world, a rich, cultured younger man with shining neck length hair and neatly pointed beard and sculpted eyebrows that set off perfectly his long hooked nose and full sensual lips.

-I could be the Magus! he said involuntarily but immediately reprimanded himself, remembering how the great shaman would not have allowed himself such pretentiousness. Nevertheless, though it may never be repeated in his entire life, he could not restrain a wide smile of pleasure at what stared back at him from the glass.

*

-You are not such a withered old desert thorn after all, exclaimed Princess Sabiya, clapping her hands heartily, -Some woman would be proud to have you walk before her! Unless you have instincts of another sort!

-Not at all your Highness, he flushed. Today she was dressed in white damask, embroidered with thin gold stripes. Pale blue trousers could just be seen above her gold sandals. Her hair was coiled on her head and pinned with gold brooches. Her skin was slightly rouged giving her eyes a startling whiteness around her pupils.

-Hm, I hope you were not offended by those jesters! They are pompous fools but not without skill.

-They hardly overstayed their welcome. She ignored him.

-Stand up. Turn round. Rather impressive. A silk purse from a camel's rear as father would say and with the overpowering scent of a thousand rose petals! Much improved on that disgusting mustiness from old libraries. Again he coloured. He had not known that he had smelled of anything, -Good. Sit down. To business. I shall inform you of developments after my Tale is read this time if only to curtail my impulsiveness. What card have we? She turned the card over and stared at the picture of a man riding a chariot and maintaining valiant control over two wilful galloping horses. She sat down.

The horses made their way at a slow trot on the sand. Their hooves were muffled and a growing moon showed the trail quite clearly. Both the roan's rider and his following companion accepted its instinct for the path they had to take. The father would point out the direction and his son's mount would take control. When they camped at a small spring-fed pool it was late at night. There had been no travellers this way recently to churn up its banks and the water was clear and slightly sweet. When they were settled in their blankets his father was the first to speak.

-Your desert woman is but the first. There could be many others.

-There can only be one. I cannot change what is. She ensures that no others may precede her in my heart. Why else would I have dreamt of her?

-You may be like a bow that has never been stretched.

-A well made bow needs but one arrow's flight!

-That is true! his father chuckled, -As I am your father I have a duty to point out the obvious.

-As I am your son it is my duty to listen and then decide for myself! They both laughed. After a few moments the young man spoke again, - I have to say my Father that you surprised even your sharp-eyed son when you lifted the skewered, unblown egg into the air!

-It was nothing more than we have practised, a full egg is more robust to handle and yet tells a greater tale.

-It was the perfect dessert for a rich meal and yet I worry that trickery is not best suited to such a serious event.

-In the eyes of the magician there should always be such doubt but in the eyes of the clan there were no such question. Sometimes the circus impresses more than the temple. In the circus the magician demands that the audience accepts a magic that they can see. In the temple the priests demand that their audience accepts a magic they cannot see.

-Even so it does not feel good here. The youth placed a hand on his heart, -If I had defeated him in battle it would have been a just ending in accordance with the traditions of his clan.

His father said feelingly, -Yet the pain would have been greater and more would have suffered it. We must live by the light of the moon as well as the sun. Perhaps the clan needs to escape from its history. They wanted their captain to maintain his nobility. The chief wanted the happiness of his granddaughter and his not-of-blood son. The daughter wanted her young fool. The young fool must travel before his fate with her is sealed. All gained something though no-one gained everything. All doors remain open. This could not be bettered. Be careful however when you return. The passing of many suns gives men time to think again about what they have experienced. Stories are never fixed.

The desert gave way to scrub and then dried grassland. His father talked now and then of his last solitary journey north through this landscape. It was as though he was preparing himself for his return to his mother. He was travelling back along the same path. The youth contemplated how it was possible to know a person during one phase of the moon and not at another. He had an almost blood-shared knowledge of his father's heart and much of his thinking but this entailed only that time they had spent together as he was growing up. His father's life before then was but a collection of carefully chosen stories, stories selected to educate him. How his father had carried himself in the world beyond the light of their camp fire was hidden in darkness. This trek was a path to enlightenment. He marvelled at the ease with which the man had led them through tribes, the clans that comprised them, their customs, courts and their nobility, their merchants and traders, the old, the young and the poor. He was touched by how people remembered him with honour and friendship and took them both into their homes, how they provided him with everything that he might need. Knowing how he had travelled north determined by some instinct and affinity with fate to be there when his son arrived carried by an occult steed, was in itself a miracle. And this was not the end. The man had then devoted much of his life to the growing youth.

He had sacrificed all these friendships, his needs and desires, his power and influence for a youth not of his blood. What was stranger still was that he himself had not questioned the selflessness of his father! He had grown up through all these years never thinking to ask what events had set his father on this path rather than any other? He, the boy who questioned everything! He had been a child so engrossed in his own importance in the world that he had not wondered what might have impelled the sacrifice and blind love of this man.

His father had taught him more than a whole tribe's skills in that time and had done it in a quiet, simple way so that his son was almost unaware of it. He had drunk from this inexhaustible cup and still did so. He had watched and copied by instinct. He had asked and been shown. Now and then he had been told directly as though his father knew that such occasional acts would stir the boy to passion and the lesson would be the greater for it.

He glanced sideways at the older man and saw him suddenly with the clarity that a stranger might enjoy. How proud, erect and contained within himself the man seemed to be. Such coordination of strength and movement. Such dark features, curved nose, black eyes and strong hard lips. Yet above all there was a purpose in his gaze and movement. Never once had he sensed his father being anxious about what was about to befall him in the next moment, the next sun or the next summer. Except today and his fear that they might not reach his mother before her death and his need to be reassured from his son's visionary lips that they would reach her in time.

-Father?

-Such a tone to a question suggests the answer may be a long one, the older man smiled good-humouredly.

-It is true, Father, -You know me too well.

-I know your history but you are a seed from which many branches grow. I do not know all their shapes but what I have is enough to give me fulfilment.

His young companion nodded, softened and made emotional by his reflections, -What led you to your journey north? Each day you add more pictures to that long quest but its beginnings are hidden in a mist.

-You never asked me this before. It was as close to an admonishment that his father would ever come.

-I have been selfish.

-Never that! Does each fly question the air or each fish the water? Does the roan question its destiny to carry its master? The child does not either. But as he becomes a man then he can begin to look upon his journey as though it were contained in a valley below him, seeing patterns, possible purposes and directions. You are still between youth and manhood although you have always had a curiosity beyond your age, except in this.

-Except in this! Perhaps we should pause here and eat.

Once the horses had been cared for they settled on blankets and began eating while his father started his tale.

☥

-Your whole lifetime and two summers ago I lived in a town which is our present destination and destiny. My father was killed in a battle when I was young and the only child. He was a humble guard to the lord of my land. I grew up in poverty. My mother worked as a washerwoman in exchange for our food and clothes. Our house was a single room of clay and straw with little more than two pallets for comfort. When I was as tall as the belly of a horse I ran errands for shopkeepers. Later I looked after their shops when they were away on business or were ill. I met many merchants and traders who brought goods to the stores. Eventually I went on trips with these men and gradually understood how the market works. They made enough from their travels to build comfortable homes for their families and employ servants and guards to keep them secure. After a while they would employ their own traders whose homes then dotted the great routes. Travelling became my way also. It was a hard path and there are many who are not fitted to trade but who would rather lie in wait to separate the hard working traveller from his bounty. I learned to fight like a paid warrior. For a while I wandered with circus people and learned their arts with animals and with trickery and balance. I learned the true value of everything that men might fight for and prize and pay for. I learned enough of the secret desires of women and how sometimes to tell these from the movement of their hands, the inclination of their

105

bodies, the depths of their eyes and the placing of their tongues on their lips, though I am not confident even now, in their wiles. So much so that I felt unable to teach you their ways. Even as I knew it I did not know whether my knowledge was universal or of interest only to my own breast. I learned to read the emptiest face and foresee any danger hidden there.

In time I built a home. My mother lives there and she has two servants who guard her and help her. She is old and tired now. She wants to see her son before her last summer is ended.

One day I was sitting in my courtyard sharing a pipe with my men. A latecomer rushed in to tell me that he had saved a trader from robbers. The fellow had been travelling from the far north but he had been slashed by knives and was close to death. He knew of my skills in effecting a cure - considerable, though not as great as your own.

-I was taught by you!

-I introduced you to the first steps of the discipline. You have already marched further than it is my fate to journey. No matter, I went immediately with him to the wounded victim. The stricken trader was in the hut of one of my men. He had no knowledge of where he lay as he was flirting with his final sleep. I administered potions and when his fever subsided I left him like a corpse. The next day he had grasped the handle of his life again. That evening I talked with him. He had been far to the north along paths I myself had travelled to trade for the life-like carvings made there from wood and bone which have high value here. There is great demand for these sculptures of trees and flowers and animals and birds that are not found anywhere under the hot sun of my homeland. The craftsmen of the north are also rightly famous for their intricate likenesses of people which cannot be told apart from the living original. They can even create imaginary forms as strange and beautiful as a man might find anywhere in this world or the next!.

-Like those of my own village. The youth was suddenly nostalgic.

-That is hardly surprising since it was from your own valley and neighbouring ones that the trader had been bartering for these beautiful adornments.

-Ah! the youth was pleased.

-While in your lands the ancient mother of one of the clans sent word for him to visit her. She told the trader that she had some sight of the future. Her eldest granddaughter was to come by a child through a bitter circumstance and she would by fate's hands have to abandon it to the care of another. This other would be a powerful merchant from the south who would bring the child up as his very own. She told the trader that he would be saved from death by this same merchant and that he must carry a gift for him once their destinies became entangled. Together with this gift he should give the merchant directions on how to find a certain valley and to be there four summers later at a particular moment early in the moon's journey.

-Where the father of my roan brought me!

-The same.

-And you left your own home and merchant interests on the word of this man?

-Not only his word. He had the gift from your grandmother with him. This carving. The Merchant went to his saddle and brought out something wrapped in velvet. He undid it and handed it to his son. It was sculpted to fit the palm of a man's hand. It was cut in such a way that the figures depicted upon it stood out from the bone of the background.

-This is you! cried the youth, -And this is the mother-of-my-dreams! And this?

-Do you not recognise yourself?

-I do. But-

-It is how you will be upon your return to her. Older. A man. Look, your eyes are the same as hers. The pale grey of her valley people. Your ugly straight nose! Not a beautiful bend in view! See how many summers are on my skin, too! They smiled but were silent for a long period pondering upon how fate had intertwined many paths through life. It was the youth who spoke first.

-Was it difficult to make this choice?

The man shook his head, -The choice was not difficult because it was my destiny. The difficulty was in enacting this destiny. No-one among my people could understand my decision to leave except my mother and she did not speak of it. So many depended upon me. I was their king as much as a man. But I was fortunate to have a young son as close to me as you are. Also, like you, not-of-blood. I had trusted him with more and more of the management of my affairs. I now entrusted him with all my business and the care of my mother whom he loved as his own. Once I had established among all my alliances that his word was my word and his mark was my mark, I was able to leave.

-Your mother must have shed many tears.

-Not so. Do not confuse a mother with a woman. A mother may understand in her heart the destiny of her son and her eyes remain dry - while she will cry copious tears over the child of another.

The youth stared at the carving, -Why does this carving show all three of us together?

-That question has long played its games in my mind.

-**We are beset** by choice, the Princess said, -And each decision we take leads us on a different path. Sometimes it is hard to distinguish the consequences of choosing one direction from another and at other times they seem vast and we know our lives have been utterly altered. What is most unsettling is that much of the time we make these choices without really knowing it. Something drives us of which we are unaware. Fate? Blood? Dreams? The sorcery of another?

-Only God knows.

-How predictable of you! she laughed, -But it gives you comfort I am sure Kamil. And what is a god for if not for that? Aye? I am sure that somewhere in your Tales the Magus says that it is much harder to be a non-believer and wrestle with the meaning of existence all alone. It is true. Oh don't look so dismayed we can talk freely here. The priests can't hear us and God if He is watching and listening, I'm sure looks kindly upon inquisitiveness. Princess Sabiya lay back in her chair comfortably relaxed. She focused on the upturned card, -I like the father, he is the magician card in your book. He is noble and true. He does not question his destiny as the son does. I am very like the son. They are just like you and I, Kamil. You accept. I question, if only in matters of faith! Yet in the affairs of man you have a hidden talent of which even you were unaware. Let us see what you have to say about my latest news. Kamil had managed an impassive face while she was talking. He bowed.

-Just as with this card, she pointed at it, -You have introduced choice into my life Kamil, choice where once I would have had none because it never occurred to me to do anything but act as the occasion took me. Now I know I must be rational and considered. She paused dramatically, -I chose a close friend, a man who loves me and would have me if he could, to further our search for truth. While others among my retinue were casting their apparently benign nets over those who knew my maid and those connected in any way with the three suspects, he sought the informant whose word led to their arrest.

He has traced him and he will be brought to you tomorrow. Her eyes sparkled as she watched Kamil's expression turn from incredulity to dismay, -Yes, to you! Who better to interrogate but my spymaster, my wily historian. You have a fox's cunning. You have wisdom distilled from a whole library. Tomorrow the man will be brought here to this room. I will be hidden with my guard in your sleeping quarters, able to hear and see everything. It will be an education indeed. As yet there are no connections to take us to the truth but I am certain you will discover them for us, Kamil!

Chapter Nine

True justice brings enlightenment to both the accuser and the accused

Kamil had woken up early and agitated. He had had a night of bad dreams. In them he had suffered a range of executions at the hands of the royal guards; burning, beheading, boiling and bursting. Princess Sabiya herself had suggested the four bs and in each case he was aware of her looking on, a quizzical expression on her face as though she found the whole experience novel and illuminating. He washed, dressed and prayed. He ate his hot flat bread and drank his green tea abstractedly. He endured the new regime of barber's and dresser's assistants with irritation, the finicky cutting of individual hairs and the careful placement of folds ate up his time. Then he went to the Great Library.

The Emperor's personal books were kept in an almost airless, circular room in what was effectively a dungeon at the base of a tower. It was lit by smokeless oil lamps to protect scripts against yellowing. Those that could be rolled were stored in tubes with wax seals. As court historian Kamil himself together with one assistant had arranged it thus. He knew the room as if it were an extension of himself and had always felt a peace descend upon him when he entered it. The waft of dry fusty air would slide over him in welcome. Yet this time, hearing the Princess's sharp words about his odour echoing in his ears, his nose wrinkled. The place was redolent of ageing, mortality and the lingering thoughts of the deceased. There was not a writer represented here who had been alive during his own lifetime!

With his apprentice he had developed a new classification system. The books most likely to interest the Emperor were immediately on the right and thus it continued in diminishing significance around the circle to those to the left of the entrance. War, politics, court life, faith, philosophy, medicine, tribal customs, languages, living creatures, farming - all the way round until there was a final section devoted to single texts of prose or verse on subjects of extraordinarily little consequence to anyone beyond the author. It astonished him sometimes to consider why a writer would wish to spend his time making a public copy of his ponderings on a subject such as the efficacy of moonlight upon the mind or gaining the affection of mothers-in-law or why clouds have shape and colour.

Despite a long and intricate search the futility that had attended him when he woke up, returned. There was no help here. He could not locate one paragraph in one text which even alluded to the kind of interrogation he envisaged. Interrogation was synonymous with torture in the works of these writers. He put the last script down, an illustrated catalogue of parts of the human anatomy, their vulnerability to pain and the shades of truth that could be extracted from them and sighed loudly. He sat for a while and considered. What was he searching for? It was a form of questioning which drew from a subject useful information. Yes. What would make the man talk openly as though to God? Fear? Yes. The fellow's fear of those who had drawn him into this conspiracy would need to be surpassed by careful forethought and some degree of trickery. He must introduce a fear that would subordinate all other fears. And yet the man should leave, all fear washed from him with freedom lighting his path. Slowly the beginnings of a plan began to form in his mind.

*

He stood before her, his body resolute but his head hung low and waited for the explosion of words. She was remarkably controlled!

-Kamil! You call on your Princess and it is only morning. I hope you have something important for me. I will be late for my sword practice. You see, I take the Tales seriously.

-I beg your pardon your Highness but I wish to embellish our arrangements for this evening.

-Indeed? she muttered haughtily.

-Not the substance of it.

-Well? She arched her eyebrows in mimicry of her mother when she was displeased.

Kamil talked slowly and in meticulous detail.

*

It hadn't taken long to prepare the room. The antechamber where he met with the Princess was unchanged save for a clear polished table top with a rosewood box at its centre. Kamil's bedchamber was now screened by a heavy arras. Princess Sabiya and her guard sat behind it. She had a pillow clasped on her lap ready to stifle any sound she might make. It was her own idea. Meanwhile Kamil had taken up his position in his chair with the table and box before him. He was dressed in a black hooded robe and his face was masked by a black veil with holes for his eyes. The hissing torch above him on the wall added flickering shadows and an ominous silhouette to his bearing.

Upon his signal the door opened and two similarly robed guards carried a long bundle into the room. It was laid a little roughly on the floor and quickly unrolled revealing a gagged and frightened man blinking at the flames and the half shadow above him. The guards helped the prisoner to his feet, removed the cloth from his mouth and put him in the empty chair. Kamil ushered them to stand at the door. There ensued a silence only broken by the man's guttural breathing and the rustle of his clothing as he stared agitatedly about.

-Calm yourself, said Kamil in a low, deathly tone, -No harm will come to you unless you bring it upon yourself.

-Where is this place? Is it hell? Who are you? ventured the prisoner's querulous voice. Kamil studied him. It was what he expected. Poor. A thin wasted body. A wispy beard. A dirty robe. Easy to buy or terrify.

-I control your destiny, be it life or death. Please me and I will let you and your family go free. The abject creature looked behind him at the guards, -Anger me and I will reach inside you and wrench out your living spirit with these very hands and after that everyone who shares your blood. You will then exist without desire or reason. Your eyes will be empty orbs that look upon a meaningless world. It will be thus until your body dies and decays. Even then you will continue as a shadow tied forever to a world you have ceased to comprehend, unable to reunite with your soul. The man was terrified. He understood the import of Kamil's words if not their exact meaning. He wrapped his arms around himself to stifle the shaking. Kamil allowed the minutes to pass.

-What must I do Master? asked his victim shuddering, his mind made up.

-Open that box, Kamil pointed. The man did so with trembling

113

hands, -Take out the cards. He did so, -See that the full complement of seventy eight is present. The man counted them clumsily, -Now turn the pack over so the faces are concealed. It was done, -Shuffle them. Again the man's fingers found it a difficult task, -Cut them! He obeyed. Kamil picked up the deck and turned over the top card and threw it down on the table in front of his prisoner. It was a picture of Death, its scythe beheading a field of corpses, -This is the card of indication, intoned Kamil, -It tells me that you are faced with choice. Choose wrongly and it goes ill for you. Shuffle the cards again. There was a heavy sweat on the man's brow and his fingers were clammy, -Cut again! Once more Kamil turned over the top card. It showed an image of resurrection, -This is the card of prediction, he murmured, -The card of opportunity. Rebirth. Yet only if the querent shows virtue and truth is told without blemish.

-There is sorcery here! croaked the prisoner, -What mean you by rebirth?

Kamil pronounced his next words quietly, for emphasis, -It means a release from your petty pilfering and the attentions of the palace guard, a life reborn in another place where none know you. Now tell me why I have brought you here, do you think? Kamil levelled his eyes at the man so that they flashed behind his mask.

-I cannot say. They came in the night, the monks, and wrapped me in that blanket and took me to a cell, then brought me here blind to the world. For what reason I know not.

-I ask you once more. Why you? What have you done?

The man's eyes were downcast. He still shook spasmodically, -I had thought all my debts were paid and now it is as if I have done naught..

-What debts?

-For stealing from the soldiers' kitchen. It was wrong but my wife and child were without-

-And?

-A palace guard was spying on me. It must be so because I was too careful for it to be happenchance. He gave me a choice. He would cut off my right hand unless I did a certain thing about which I must say nothing.

-He gave you three names and told you to go to the captain of the guard with them. You were to say that you saw them meet the Princess's maid.

The prisoner looked bemused and blurted out, -In the palace garden. You knew this already?

-There are some things I do not know. What was this soldier's name?

-I do not know and was too feared to ask. Yet I do know where a woman of his lives. I followed him when he left me. He is easy to pursue for he is tall above other heads and his hair is grey though he is young. She is paid for her favours. He seems not a soldier but he dresses as one.

-Ah! What is he then?

-It is my thought that he is a noble. He affects a soldier's ways but a hare cannot become a rabbit.

-And where is the brothel?

-It is the finest, to the left of the city's south gate as you enter. The harlot he visits is called Aidah. You cannot mistake her. She is much celebrated. She has red hair.

-Good. You have done well. The guards will take you to where your family wait on a boat. Take this money and start your new life. Do not speak to anyone of these events. You will have to leave the way you arrived. Kamil took a small bag of coins from inside his robe and placed it in the man's hands.

The sad creature mumbled his thanks with tears of gratitude on his cheeks. Kamil nodded to the guards and they gagged and rolled their unresisting victim in the blanket again. As soon as the door had closed behind them Princess Sabiya came out, her face alive with excitement. Kamil removed his mask and hood and wiped sweat from his brow.

-What a performance royal historian! You frightened even me! We have our next step in this intrigue.

-And with luck the enemy has no knowledge of it. He and his family will have vanished. In any case he has nothing to tell other than an unbelievable tale concerning a meeting with Death.

-It is true, no-one would expect such subterfuge from the royal princess. Without you my royal spymaster I would have blundered on destroying every shred of evidence presented to me. She turned to him with a naughty smile on her face, -How long is it since you visited a brothel?

-Never your Highness, he blushed not realising immediately the import of her question. Then it broke upon his consciousness and his face displayed his terror.

-This very night then!

-Your Highness, he stammered anxiously, -I am a scholar -

-And this will extend your studies. Now I am ready for my story for there is something in the rhythm of these Tales that infuses our adventures don't you think? It will calm you before your...ordeal! She waved the guard outside and sank into the chair, -Read, you harbinger of the void.

The roan was nudging him awake insistently. Still he tried to stay within his dream but the velvet nose scattered the dream into fragments which in turn became motes of dust and then disappeared altogether. He wondered why he could have vivid, lucid dreams while both sleeping and awake which remained in his mind forever and then these other dreams which left barely a fingerprint on his thoughts.

-What do you want my fellow? he asked softly. His eyes sharpened. It was just daylight. He could hear a distant roaring. Someone's god is hammering on our door he thought with an amused smile. He shook his father, -Father, a storm is nearly upon us. The roan fears for our safety here.

His father leapt out of sleep in a way the youth still could not quite emulate.

-That's not thunder. Come, get to higher ground! They had been camped on a small grassy ledge half way up the bank of a dried river bed. It took them little time to ascend to safety. All the while the thundering increased until a roar erupted behind them. A deluge of water rushed down the channel they had left, sweeping over the ledge that they had occupied.

-It is strange, shouted the youth, -No rain and yet a wall of water!

-This river is known as the Water Assassin, shouted his father over the tumult, -It will be empty within an hour. The flood is the work of men and not of the sky. Water is collected inside that mountain, he pointed, -And released when either too dangerously full or in defence of the City in the Mountain. It seems it is the latter. This time he looked into the racing waves. Men and horses, armour and weapons were hurtling down in the torrent. There was no struggling. They tumbled lifelessly, sometimes dancing together, sometimes alone, hooves on sticks arcing in the air, helmets, leather covered arms, eyes open or closed. They had been drowned much further up the mountain slopes. After the last body passed, the waters began to recede, -Water gives life but it also takes it, said his father, -Let us fill our bags. Already the horses had scrambled back down to the ledge, their legs splayed out for security, drinking, -This mountain river is a storehouse of good medicaments. They sifted the water through fine muslin to remove the twigs, leaves and insects.

☥

-We will be in full sight of the City in the Mountain when we have crossed that arm of rock. But we must be careful. The battle may not be over.

-What is this place?

-The people live in caves and tunnels made by waters long ago. There are rows of them reaching ever higher as in an ants' nest. If they are attacked they pull the ladders and the walkways up and into their holes. Inside the mountain they store food and water against evil times. There are streams and fountains. There are strange columns and carvings they believe were made by their earth god. Sometimes they reach from ceilings to floors many times the height of a man.

-They live in fear of invasion?

-I thought not until I saw those drowned soldiers. When I last visited the deluge was merely a festival in memory of a great battle in which they lost half of their people. Each year they remember that sad time. It begins with a speedy removal of all their ladders, ramps and other approaches. Then some of the water is released. It ends with a feast and trials of courage in the cave pools. It is both a light-hearted and a serious day.

-We are to stay with them for some time?

-Not more than half a moon. There is a noble woman here to whom I promised my return. I have a gift for her from your lands.

-Another carving? the youth queried.

-Indeed. Their earth god has the form of a female snake. The carving she requested is of the snake eating its own tail and giving birth to the sun and moon. He crossed to his bag and took out a wrapped sculpture. The snake was formed from white bone. Its eyes were tiny green stones that caught the light. A red wooden tongue forked from its mouth and from its belly dropped a yellow sun and a mottled white moon.

-It is one of the ancient stories.

-For this tribe it is more than a tale. Their god lives beneath the earth. They carry this emblem on their shields and weapons, on their dress and even on their clay pots.

-It is beyond my wit to understand such worship.

-For those who believe it should be beyond wit. For them the snake eating its tail is the continuous cycle of the seasons, of life, of death.

-And yet, said the youth, -It all amounts to what? Another god. Our travelling net catches another tribe's beliefs. He spoke forcefully and there was such deprecation in the young man's eyes that his father eventually looked away. It was unsettling to be with one who appeared so untroubled by the notion of a world without a god. The Merchant was certain that he himself believed in something. A great force of spirit. There was a power that was both of the world and beyond the world and which kept all things in its pattern. Further than that he could not say.

At least the youth appeared to have started to heed his advice and keep his own counsel on such matters when with strangers.

Even the roan showed some anxiety. There was the smell of ash and blood in the air. By staying high on the mountain's slopes and walking their horses cautiously, they moved over the spur of land. The roan kept to the shadows of boulders and rock faces, occasionally stopping and rubbing its neck against the rough stone, as if seeking solace. Just reaching their ears were the sounds of drums and pipes in a shrill but unmistakably triumphal rhythm.

-It seems the city is the victor again.

-The power of water.

-That is only one of their weapons. It is their art to drive their enemies into the Water Assassin. They roll boulders down wooden channels so that they drop from the sky, they pour boiling oils, they fire arrows. It is done with discipline and is a formidable defence.

They reached the top of the spur, still at some distance from the scene of battle but they could make out the caves in the cliff. Ladders were being pushed out like tongues and reassembled. Walkways were being reconstructed between them. Ropes were being hung as handrails. The youth eyed the muddy trail of the extinguished torrent as it rose right to the base of the cliff below the caves. It disappeared along a small gorge and into a wide, dark mouth. The biggest bridge was being resurrected, straddling the little gorge and just above the mouth. The ladders were fixed to it. Steps cut into the rocks led down from each end of the bridge into the river bed. It was the only visible approach to the city.

-The design of craftsmen, nodded the youth approvingly, -There is good reason for their feast day.

-It requires the whole tribe to act as one.

Further down the incline on the banks of the river there was a funeral pyre. Even as they watched, bodies were being thrown on to it. Men on horses were returning dragging corpses on litters. The wailing pipes and insistent drums continued from the higher caves, resounding and echoing among the rocks.

-How do they take their horses into the mountain?

-There is a tunnel, always well guarded, on the side of the mountain which receives the sun's last rays. This will also be our approach. It can be closed to entry on the clap of a hand for there is only room for one horse to pass, yet inside it is like the main thoroughfare of a great city.

-Might they think we are the enemy? They have been watching us.

-Not so. His father had taken a folded cloth from a bag and began to unroll it, -We will each hold a corner of this. It is their battle flag. Roughly painted on the near black material was a great white serpent, its tail in its mouth, its eyes glittering greenly and with a prominent red tongue, -The noble woman of whom I spoke gave me this for safe passage into the city. And this! He took a seal from a pouch in his belt and a small vessel of white powder. He spat on the seal, pressing it into the powder and stamped it on both of their foreheads. The snakes stood out clearly.

-How easily we become part of a tribe and its odd beliefs, said the youth.

-It must be our way. Respect all we meet. Never speak ill. What is important to others must be so for us while we are in their company.

☥

They were met by a large cohort of well-armed horsemen who, though cautious, did not relieve them of their weapons but led them single file into the tunnel. His father conversed with them in a form of the tongue he had been using since they reached these more southern lands. The youth could see that they were well-drilled, disciplined and confident. Each had the serpent on his forehead. The tunnel's narrow entrance led immediately into a spacious chamber. From it issued three major passageways. The roof had a large number of holes. Any aggressor having reached this far would be subjected to rocks, hot oil and arrows, too.

The tunnels were lit by torches fed by animal fats. Both horses had become settled and walked obediently in line with their hosts on floors covered by a mix of dried leaves and earth, muffling their hooves and allowing for conversation.

-Look, pointed his father. Large formations of wet, glistening rock lined their path. Some hung heavy and pointed from the roof, some speared up from the floor, some joined together in massive pillars and others formed sheets that were like hanging drapes. They caught the torchlight and shimmered, -It is a true temple to their earth mother. These jewels grow over eternity.

-Are the people of this city traders in such things?

-They are miners but not of this magic. The hills in this land are known for their metals and stones. They spend time in small gangs under the earth and return here to have their crude treasure traded with merchants for refinement into jewellery and other objects of great worth.

-They have no artists?

-No, it is not the tribe's way. To live much of a life in the dark does not prepare a man to fashion beauty for those who live their lives in the light.

The passageway took them into a great central hall. The sounds of pipes and drums drifted down from above. Hundreds of torches burned round the walls and the air was heavy with the fumes. Their horses were led away to be fed and watered while they were taken to a chamber in a side passage. There were straw litters on the floor and the customary urn of water and a roll of cloth for drying themselves.

-The great hall is to the mountain as the blown egg to our trick!

-It is. It would be a miracle if men ever learned how to make such structures! replied the Merchant.

-The lights, the reflections on the stone pillars, the darkness above - I can see no ceiling. It is like the darkest night when even the stars are masked.

-It is true yet still I find it oppressive and wish for clean air and a breeze on my face.

-What did you learn from the soldiers?

-They would not talk of the battle. I think that privilege belongs to our noble friend. She commands the tribe now that her father is old and close to his last sleep. She will give him the sculpture of the snake god to accompany him.

-She foretold this. It was a statement rather than a question.

-Of course. A few in every tribe may have this gift. You have it. My mother has it and I, in my turn, although in a lowlier form. The noble priestess, the empress, the spiritual man on the island. It is uncommon but not so very rare.

-Ah.

-There are those with this gift who live within a tribe and protect its beliefs and rituals while at the same time also knowing them to be primitive and even without substance.

-What is their reasoning? Is this not hypocrisy?

-No! his father said fervently, -Such people are older spirits and it is their fate to shepherd men and women with younger spirits to seek gods who might display the qualities to which all should aspire. Those who are devoted to merciless gods become a scourge on everyone and must be countermanded.

-Yet I am without a god. The youth faced him.

-I know. For you perhaps fate has some other purpose. It is beyond my knowing. In time you will find it.

☥

The strong-boned woman smiled pensively, -It is very beautiful, just as I dreamed. She turned it this way and that in the light of a torch, -So many colours!

-It is the best of their art, murmured the Merchant.

-You are happy with our agreement for this trade? she asked.

-It is my bond, he replied with a bow.

-I could increase it, said the noble woman.

-It is enough.

-I will have a saddlebag made up for you. One more to add to the many.

-As we travel so the load becomes heavier and then lighter. It is the way of merchants. The use of the plural made her look keenly at the youth but he knew that she had been examining him throughout the exchange. He could see a harsh wisdom in her features. Many lines were etched there though she was not much older than his father. She stood, feet firmly planted apart like a fighting man, seeking constant balance. She carried the short sword of the tribe half hidden in the cloth of her robes. These were yellow with many white snakes in different postures decorating it.

-He is not much more than a boy!

-And carries the wisdom of the ancients - when he bothers to listen to himself. To the youth it felt as though he was being presented for sale in a slave market though he could only understand a smattering of their words.

-He has the bones of a fighting man but not yet the full-grown body.

-There is no-one who could lay a knife upon him, even now.

-He has a face that will make a girl forget her vows to her parents or her lover.

-A bridge which he has crossed within this very moon.

- He has the gift of seeing! Her gaze plunged into the youth's eyes. He did not flinch but allowed her in, drawing her down like a swimmer vanquishing an enemy by holding him and allowing his own body to become heavy and sinking.

She laughed and withdrew her eyes, -Yes, the art is there. Have you trained him?

-Not I. He needed no help from me.

-He has come as I foresaw. He will leave a line of blood in my clan.

The father shrugged, -I cannot speak for him. He is already promised to a nomad woman. He may have shown her his favour.

-I will send the girl to him tonight. There is no other way. My men will assign you separate rooms.

They bowed.

☥

-You are sleeping elsewhere? You have a woman here? Not the noble woman herself? His voice was not incredulous but had a touch of humour.

-She has plans for you as you can tell.

-She is too old for me. They laughed.

-A young one is being prepared for you, barely freed from her childhood.

-And you would have me do this? Father!

-There are no options.

-My roan will not sire until he is ready.

-He has other duties. He is your servant.

-And what is the duty here?

-Her people need your second sight. Her tragedy is that she has not borne children of her own and hers is the only gift in the clan. They need this more than most.

-All tribes walk to the end of their line.

-Not without a struggle. This clan is unlike others of the south lands. They are not aggressors. They are not broken into families. The people are as one and merely defend their own. The clan is fair in its trade. It keeps no slaves. It renews its blood lines through arrangements with surrounding clans of their tribe. It shows leniency even towards its greatest foes. We are to be witness to its court later. Reserve your judgment until you have observed its laws.

☥

In the centre of the great cavern two sickle moons of benches had been positioned. The outer one was higher than the inner one by a man's head. Two stools faced them. Men and women were filing in, talking loudly and taking seats when the youth and his father arrived.

-They have been chosen by lot to represent all the interests of the clan. Other than these jurors the youth could see no interested watchers. Everyone else continued to undertake those duties that were essential to the community's health. Finally the prisoner was brought forward to one of the two stools and the noblewoman took the other one. His father translated for him. Men and women asked questions, listened to answers and sometimes disputed them. The prisoner was give time to think. He had been told that this was a trial. If he answered questions with truth then the sentence would be more lenient than if he did not answer or answered with deceit. The most severe sentence would be his beheading. Others included the removal of his tongue, eyes, limbs and branding.

-Branding?

-The sign of the snake is burned into his forehead and he is free to leave. But all will know in the lands beyond this place that he has been captured and released by this clan. It is a common verdict of its court on ordinary fighting men. I do not know about a captain.

The youth thought it over, -That would be lenient indeed. Yet those who are released in this way will carry a warning to others like the hung corpse of a bird may protect crops from its kind.

-It is their reasoning.

-You make no mention of imprisonment.

-It is too costly. Food is stored only for the tribe. Prisoners need their guards. Men and women here have only three possible roles. They may be miners, they may be soldiers and they may care for the children.

The court progressed with passion. The jurors argued among themselves, called out questions or went into protracted silences as they listened to the prisoner's explanations. Finally the noble woman raised a hand and asked the prisoner to make one last statement. This was lengthy but was respectfully received. When he had finished, the court was disbanded.

-He has acknowledged his wrongdoing in every detail, said the Merchant, -He was but an honourable captain of the force sent here by a warlord with whom the clan have done some trade. It appears his lord felt he could take the clan's treasures without the need for barter.

-What will be the verdict? asked the youth.

-What would you decide?

-In our lands he would be punished by death though not by beheading - our clans respect the whole corpse of our enemy even in death - and then he would be tied to his horse and the body released at the borders of his clan's territory. I see that by cutting off his sword arm he may be punished and might not fight again. Perhaps the same with a leg. It is no defence for him to say that his orders were given by another. Soldiers train for this. I can see the merit of branding. It is a new thought.

-Yet what would happen to him on his return to his tribe?

-It is true. His chief would have him killed for dishonouring his tribe and returning alive with the mark of the snake on his forehead.

-Justice is no easy matter.

Later that evening the court gathered again. The prisoner was asked if he had anything new to say and he said no. Their chief, the noblewoman, listed the possible punishments and asked him which of these in his opinion was the most just for his crime. The man showed courage. He thought for a while. The Merchant translated.

-I have a wife and children. I would not like the thought of them being taken by another man should I die at your sword. Nor could I protect them without my fighting arm. If I am branded it is also a death warrant for I would forever remind my tribe of the men and horses I lost in this conflict. There is no going back. Even release without punishment would leave me with no choice other than to travel to another land and hope to begin anew. I would not see my family again.

-So what must we do? she asked.

-Kill me or let me join your clan. If the latter, I will wear the mark of the snake with pride. Perhaps there may be a way for my family to join me here.

-Thank you, she said, showing no sign of her own thinking, -The council will decide your fate.

The youth had prepared himself for bed and waited. He felt embarrassed but intrigued. Customs in this mountain vault were very different. The people here used alien measures for assessing men. The noblewoman encouraged their snake god beliefs and yet his father inferred that she may not believe them herself. She seemed wise in the matter of judgment. Her true reasons for doing as she did were unlikely ever to be revealed.

☥

That night a girl pulled back the curtain and entered his chamber, an opaque white veil over her face. She was swathed in a length of white cotton, bright and starched. He could not make out any feature of her person. She knew enough of his tongue to converse a little.

-I here at command of chief.

-I did not ask for this.

-We need gift of your blood.

-I promised my line to another. I have never broken vows.

She was silent for a moment, -Here you give to clan not woman. You do not know me now and after.

-I am a man not a beast. I am unsure that I can do this even without pain and prejudice and as a gift to your clan.

-I am promised also.

-What does he say?

-My duty is to city but duty not enjoyment! Her remark made them both laugh.

-Then we will try to complete this labour quickly, he said sternly.

She moved to his litter and lay upon it with her legs apart pulling her shift up to her stomach. She had bandaged her legs loosely. The only skin that was visible to him was that covered by a small mound of curling black hair. She had creamed herself in preparation. He went to his knees between her legs and tried to urge himself to be ready. But his will was lacking. She took him in her fingers and slowly caressed him. Still the response was not sufficient.

-This your child, she whispered, -It will know you and your blood. My husband agree to this. The words enlivened him. He grew hard in her fingers, -It will be brother or sister in blood to your own. The way man takes woman makes child. Be bold warrior but soft. Force deep and far so seed reach the far doorway. He was aroused and thrust deep inside her. It was over quickly. She waited until he recovered and then slid from him. He washed the blood from himself.

As he lay there with the scent of her fluids still on his body, his eyes closed and he drifted into a half-dream. He became the body of his woman of the desert. It was as it had been when he had dreamt under the influence of the priestess' potion. His belly was big and about to split like a fruit. The baby was struggling inside him, forcing its head towards the air and the light. Pain wracked him in convulsions. It reached a great obliterating climax and then the girl jerked free of him. He had a momentary glimpse of her wailing face.

While he read the Tale named The Chariot, perfectly, he was also able to allow his mind to think of what lay ahead. He had absolutely no notion of what a brothel looked like, what its rules for conduct were, what was permitted and how much it would cost. He had led a private, academic and devoutly religious life and, apart from the conversations he had had with other youths when he was young there had been no occasion to talk of such things. Of the varieties of sex itself he had only a knowledge gained from the library. Painted scenes of congress brought from the east had left him more horrified than stimulated. At some deep level he had opted to estrange himself from coarse interchanges with his fellow men and women and sink into the vicarious pleasures of paper and vellum. Here he could pick and choose and it led him to tracts that rarely contained even obscure references to sexual behaviour. Other passions were raised and lowered in him. Passions for the lives of kings and heroes, of myths and legends, of spiritual leaders. Now the Princess wished that he enter the very world that he had eschewed and to have adventures there written in his own blood!

As the Tale came to its strangely affecting conclusion he became aware of the growing distance between himself and his voice. He began to squirm inwardly. He had written this at the Emperor's behest. His audience, barely yet a woman, was seated before him and the Emperor had said to treat her like a male. But he floundered in his embarrassment. He had chosen the poetic style to make the work accessible. The Emperor hated arid expanses of explanation and description. He was a man of action. Nevertheless he had not indicated to Kamil that he would have to read it, face to face, to the impressionable and highly volatile Princess! He steeled himself again and his voice soared impressively through the last few paragraphs until it stopped. He dared not raise his eyes to hers.

Even as he was writing it he had realised that the work had taken him as its prisoner and that he had little control over its wild course. The bare events of the Magus' life had become malleable clay in his hands. Yet these very hands had been directed by a strange force beyond himself. The Tales had written themselves through him. There were details that he had included which he would swear were not within his experience. Yet upon checking they proved to be authentic. The Princess knew little of this. She would assume that he knew far more than he pretended. She would think him capable of the acts that any coarse soldier might perpetrate. After all he had written knowingly about sexual acts. And more than that he was a man. It was expected.

-You are embarrassed for me historian? He nodded but could not speak, -Have no fear, royal children are well educated in the realities of life. The events in your Tale do not soil me. Far from it. Women talk together of the most shameful acts yet present faces of piety to their men. You have given this Tale a dream-like flavour. It is remarkable is it not that the young Magus was able to fulfil the needs of that tribe without prejudice to his love? Even he is but a man. Women are born with fingers that string the fates of men and bring them to destinations of their choosing. I will go now. Calm yourself. Tomorrow I will hear of your exploits in the boudoir of the harlot.

Chapter Ten

The greatest journeys may be fashioned in the mind's eye

Kamil paced the floor waiting for the Princess to arrive. His face was tinted by a pink flush, his eyes were watering and his hands acted out an interior drama. He was rehearsing his tale. His own Tale. The extraordinary adventures of Kamil the historian. As he heard the sounds of her arrival outside his door he sat and stilled himself. She entered following a bodyguard and he rose and bowed. The bodyguard was ushered out and the door closed by the Princess herself.

-Well, you look healthy enough, Kamil. Not ravaged by the pox yet! she added jocularly. He fluttered his hands at her intentional coarseness and followed her in seating himself, -Now I want to hear everything. Everything! As if you were talking to a brother in an inn after a bout of heavy drinking. I am a Princess, not one of lesser birth. All things that men do are my province. I think I have made that clear!

Kamil nodded, licked his lips briefly and began the story of the previous evening, -I found the brothel with little difficulty, your Highness.

-How were you dressed? Like some fine noble? Surely not?

-No, your Highness,

-Detail Kamil, detail!

-I covered my least flamboyant clothes - those kindly given to me by your Highness - with my black robe of death, yet in such a way as to reveal a little of what lay beneath. I had no wish to create the vision of a visiting spectre but I wanted to project a desire for anonymity befitting my apparent rank.

-Cunning historian! How does the brothel present itself?

-The door is lit all round by red glass jars containing candles. All else is dark and shrouded. The door itself is large but nondescript save for its great thickness. I knocked and a small shutter was drawn to reveal a pair of eyes. "Stand away from the door, so I can see you!" said a female voice. I walked away for a few steps and allowed my cloak to open a little, invitingly and then drew it back round me. I made sure she could see that I carried no obvious weapon, though later I discovered that this was not a house rule. "You may enter," she called and opened the door. It was curious, from the street no sound issued from the building. When she opened the first door there were only faint notes of music. She closed that door and we stood in a vestibule between it and the next. She then said, "It is a silver piece for entry. After that you pay in advance for what you desire." I gave her a coin and she pulled a cord presumably to a bell and the inner door opened. Instantly the sound cascaded over me. A band of four magicians were playing a fast tune for a dancer who whirled about, scantily covered. Men and women sat in pairs and groups drinking or smoking opium from communal hookahs. Some men wore hoods like me. Some wore masks. I was placed at a table and a girl of no more than nine or ten years came to serve me. I chose opium, the easier to feign imbibing. I parted with another coin for that and was left for a while to watch the room and smoke my pipe.

-Was it full? The room - not the pipe! she giggled.

-It seemed so. There were few empty seats but this changed as men went off with women to the many private chambers at the back of the building and on the two floors above. Then my hostess, the mistress of the establishment, arrived.

-Detail!

-I was pleasantly surprised - as I had been since I entered. The brothel seemed a well mannered and courteous place. There was no shouting and swearing. I understood why when I met her. She was elegant and from a noble caste from the look of her though not from our empire. She wore no veil or head dress. Her skin was perfectly white and her hair blonde but greying though she is some years younger than I. She seemed to me to be from the far north. She tied her hair above her head with pins and clasps. She wore a long loose house coat of embroidered cotton, mostly white but with tiny flowers of many colours. It was strung with a jewelled belt and had an ornamental dagger hilted on it. Her shoes were silver, pointed and turned up at the toes.

-Her face? I must picture her!

-Wise but firm and strong. A long nose which barely rose from her face. Intelligent eyes that penetrated my own as if seeking truth from lies.

-You were much taken with her! murmured the Princess, piqued, -I can picture her well.

-Only as with any other. Male or female.

-Hah!

-She sat opposite me and smiled a warm welcome. "What is your pleasure?" she asked. I looked back from beneath the shade of my hood, "I seek a particular beauty whose grace and sensuality are known among nobles in courts here and elsewhere." She replied, "All I have here are befitting that accolade. This is the most distinguished of all the palaces of the senses in the empire. Our ladies are chosen for these qualities and they are trained for the utmost refinement."

-Palaces of the senses! How exotic! murmured Princess Sabiya.

-"Yet there is one I would enjoy," I said to her, "She has red hair and is known as Aidah." "How is she known to you?" "It would be indiscrete of me to say," I replied. She pursed her lips, "She allows few to share her chamber. And an audience is costly. You will have to pay for an interview. If a union should follow then there will be a further charge." I nodded and looked resolute. "How much?" I asked, remembering my role. "Five to meet. Ten should she entertain you beyond that. If you come in future it will be ten at each visit - though you are always welcome to offer more if the spirit takes you." "From all I hear she is worth every gram of silver!" I said fervently. Then she stood up saying, "Your table girl will come for you shortly."

-You handled that well. You were born to be a spymaster, historian. Continue!

-I sat pretending to smoke. In truth, despite myself, breathing the odour that essayed from the pipe was affecting my brain which was already exhilarated by the circumstances. Finally, at the moment when I began to feel uncomfortable sitting on my own, the young girl was standing at my elbow. "Follow," she said and led me through an arch to the back stairs. We climbed two flights which led to corridors and many rooms and then up a narrow staircase to a small landing and a door at either side. She knocked on one, waited, then obviously reacting to a signal I could not hear, opened the door and stood aside. I entered and the door closed behind me. The woman, Aidah –

-Detail! The room! The Princess was stimulated by the tale. Her fingers clasped each other and her neck was taut, forcing her head slightly forward. Her eyes were wide and unblinking.

-It was like the interior of a nomad tent. Swathes of cotton and silk were everywhere. Beautiful camel hair rugs were spread on the floor and littered with embroidered cushions. The bed was only slightly raised from this sea of colour. It was white. Pillows. Sheets. She had strewn a handful of yellow flower petals upon it. The air was hung with delicate perfumes rising from candles floating in water in silver bowls on a low table. Either side of it were two large cushions. Aidah bade me sit with a motion of her arm. I did so.

-Detail! Aidah?

-I am still surprised, my Princess, for she was not young as I had imagined. Somehow I had expected - I don't know but –

-Age? Thirty? No older surely!

-Perhaps between forty and fifty.

-She was so old! The Princess stared at him in shock tinged with horror.

-Indeed, the lines on her face and neck were well concealed as they were on the backs of her hands and her hair was expertly dyed. But her essence…

-I did not know you were capable of 'essences' Kamil!

-The historian works all his life with palimpsests your Highness. It becomes second nature.

She nodded in praise, -So what said you to this ancient seductress?

-Well -

-Wait! How can she?

-Your Highness? he was puzzled.

-Seduce! Attract! Charge such high prices! I have always thought that that must be the province of the recently deflowered.

-It is said that men will pay highly for those experienced in the multifarious arts of the bedchamber. Some to lose themselves in the arms of a true mistress, some to learn so that they might teach willing wives, some, in relief from wives who will not or cannot learn to offer such variety. Anyway she was beautiful in her way. A regal posture. Grey eyes. Delicate features -

-Hah, enough! Go on. Who spoke first?

-Me. I said that I was honoured to be allowed into her holy of holies.

-Ha ha! You did not!

-I did! She smiled and said, "You are merely in my bedchamber! From here to my holy of holies is another matter."

-Ha ha ha, I thought as much. Very good. I like the harlot!

-Then she asked me what was the thing that I desired most of her. I said that the answer would surprise her. I took thirty pieces from my purse and laid them on the table. "There are limits to what I may do for a man," she murmured. "I want something from your mind not your body," I replied. This confused her. "What?" she asked. "Information," I said severely. "About one of your regular visitors." "I never divulge confidences," she said. I said nothing but stared at her coldly. She stood up, agitated. "At a word from me our guards will come and take your body to the river."

-Vicious vixen. I admire her!

-"You dare not!" I said quietly. "Why not?" she asked. "You do not know who I represent. My death would bring an end to this brothel, this palace of the senses. And you would be dragged to dungeons to perform your acts for the depraved."

-Well said historian! You were right! I would not rest until your death was avenged, snorted the Princess virtuously.

-So she sat down again. "Who are you?" she demanded. "Someone and no-one, I responded but better me than a cohort of troops and a torturer." "I swear secrecy to all my visitors," she said plaintively. I pressed forward my advantage. "And no-one will know that this night you betrayed their trust. For none will trace you to me. As I said I am someone and no-one." "What is it you want," she asked, frightened now. "The name of a noble who visits you every week I believe. A tall man for this country. Greying early for one of his age. He came but two days or so ago dressed as a royal guard." "Ah," she said, "I thought it might be him that you pursue. It could be no other. He has a secretive nature and at times he tries to press me to acts I never contemplate. There is something of the animal in him. He owes me payment but I dare not force the issue for I fear the consequences." "Then we shall both be beneficiaries at his downfall," I said softly. "His name?" "I do not know his real name. He calls himself Rafi when he is with me." She spat, "Huh, the name is too noble for him." I stared at her angrily, "You must know something more." She looked down and then said, "No man can hide everything when with me. He has slipped once in the midst of his ardour. He is married. On this one occasion he cried, " I wish that wet slug of a wife of mine, Iffat, could see me now, she might learn a man's true desires." I pretended not to notice.

-Iffat. Excellent my spymaster. Princess Sabiya was almost beside herself with excitement.

-I asked her if there was more. She said not. I told her that if she had lied to me or if she warned this Rafi - then she knew she would not be long in this life. I made to leave but she stayed me by the door. Her fingers pulled back my cloak. "You have wealth and looks," she said, "Return to me." I bowed and said I would - when this business was concluded.

-Historian! Would you return?

-Of course not your Highness. Nothing would have me venture back. I merely wished to live up to the picture of my character who definitely would have gone back!

-You are a strange man. Perhaps you have looks too! But what a spymaster! What shall we do next?

-More innocent enquiries from your network of spies now that you have a name. But next I will read you a very short Tale for the crux of the Magus' life is symbolised in it. She smiled sweetly and turned the next card revealing The Hermit.

Two sunsets later the young man had a waking dream. He was growing tired of the place and wanted to leave but his father was absent for hours meeting tribe members about trade. The ways of the merchant did not interest the youth. He had become used to the rhythm of their journey. New skylines, the change in the earth and its plants. The breathless atmosphere of the city intensified his discomfort. He spent time each day with the horses, talking to them and listening for the snickers of encouragement from the roan. They looked healthy and had a shine and plumpness that augured well.

He was stroking the roan's neck when the desire came to him. From an observer's view, nothing would have changed but for him everything did. With an act of will he closed his eyes and again took the shape of a bird but this time no hawk. He became a great winged creature which lived its life on high winds that followed the moon and crossed the sun. He could feel the air under his movement like his roan's hooves felt the ground. He soared above mountain peaks. There seemed to be only himself in all existence. It was a passage of great loneliness and yet great fulfilment for it was as though he was at the beginning of life itself waiting for the time when it would spread its many forms upon the earth. He flew higher and higher until he found a majestic current of wind travelling at great speed. His wings curved in hard arcs and he glided on and on. Below him the world unrolled like an illustrated carpet and it seemed as though he could see, simultaneously, everything that was, everything that had been and much that would one day take place. Some threads from the cloth were thick and strong, others were hardly defined and petered into faintness or invisibility. He could map his own past life until this moment in the weft and also many events that might one day unfold.

He realised that he was being carried from youth to manhood. Had he not just taken on the responsibility of a man by placing his seed in

137

young women? All his actions now were his own. He would be judged in the same light as his father. His very presence would change the course of the lives of those he would meet. He would have a forbidding space around him which would impose itself upon the world. He carried a destiny upon his brow as obvious as the mountain city's serpent and all would be able to sense it.

He had set out thinking that this great journey was in support of his father's destiny but now he knew that it was to be his own, too, separate and alone. Their two fates had coiled round each other like the plaited threads of rope and now would divide into strands only to come together again as they saw in the sculptured bone. Below his arcing flight the baby that had been him became a boy, a youth and then a man. The man had made an oath that must be kept and had also essayed upon a path which could not be foretold. This part of the rug would be woven not only by his but also by other fingers.

-I am glad it was brief, more of a heroic poem than a story, she said, -It was as if I had already had my Tale with your exploits of last evening.

-But essential in understanding the Magus, said Kamil, earnestly, -It is at this point that he truly realises his destiny. The Hermit looks back and reflects on what has been, in preparation for what is to come.

They sat for a few moments in silence. Princess Sabiya showed no eagerness to go. Then she said thoughtfully, -You are a religious man as we know. Did you find it difficult to write the Tales? Such a man? An unbeliever. He is not like you, is he?

-I feel closer in spirit to his father the Merchant, it is true. Yes, he was never what we think of as a religious man but his life has affected every generation that has followed him until this very day! His ideas have been absorbed into different religious faiths by the prophets who were told these stories when they were children. There are even those tribes who have no god as such who owe everything to him and the great sages who followed him and who breathed in his words and incorporated them into their own paths to enlightenment. It was not difficult for me to write about him. I am a historian. Within the true calling of my craft it is a given that you enter history through the eyes of the time and not through those of your own otherwise you merely turn history into myths that cosset you in your present beliefs. And where would be the learning in that?

Chapter Eleven

To an open mind, success and failure teach equally

Kamil received the message as he was having lunch in his outer room. No sooner had the simple selection of fruits, nuts, goat's cheese and breads arrived than one of the Princess's bodyguards followed. He handed Kamil an ornate tube, sealed at one end and stamped. Inside Kamil found a rolled sheet of thick paper in a flowery hand;

This evening is now impossible. Tortuous affairs of the empire. No progress with R and I. Will miss my Tale. Tomorrow you must read two!

The note was stamped, as the wax had been, with her seal. He handed the tube back to the guard who left immediately. The letter he placed with the square of linen in his fortified little box of personal things.

*

That evening Kamil left the palace for a walk. His papers of authentification took him past the various checkpoints and out on to the streets. He had persuaded himself that his head needed clearing. The palace and his rooms were suffocating him. In truth he felt a touch of misery that the Princess would not be visiting. He realised that she had begun to wage a great influence over him. His feelings towards her were noble and pure even though her beauty and growing womanliness could not be gainsaid. It was a strange paradox that she had raised in him a physical need whilst still retaining her separateness and unassailability. The physical stirrings in his body were not now directed at her but had become a generalised ache.

He pondered this enigma as he walked, seemingly oblivious of his surroundings and he would later reflect that there had been no motivation in his thoughts to visit the brothel again. Yet he started from his reverie to find himself stood in front of the same expressionless door. This time he did not need to knock for the door opened even though he was several paces away.

The same female stood there beckoning. At first in panic he made to leave, his irresolution obvious but his limbs would not offer him escape and moments later he was settled at the same table with his hookah, watching the same scenes and listening to the same racing melodies, his heart thumping in time. The young girl stood before him, -You wish Madame Aidah to entertain you? He shook his head, asked her to bring him iced water and mopped his brow. He would have liked to throw off his cloak such was the heat in the room. She brought it, - You want another lady? Young? Older? Connoisseur? Her accent was from further to the east.

-I would like to speak with the mistress.

-She not for sale.

-I do not wish to buy her ... her services. I need to talk with her. The girl stared at him unmoving, -Go! She turned perplexed as though she felt she had misunderstood his request. Time passed.

Finally the greying mistress glided gracefully between the tables and sat opposite him. She eyed him thoughtfully, -It is the first occasion that a man does not seek to return to Aidah! You were dissatisfied? I do not know whether this is an insult to the house or a compliment to its owner!

-The latter, Mistress.

-Thank you. No words were spoken for a while. -And so?

-I would like to hear your story.

-My story? My life, you mean?

-Yes.

She was pensive but he could see that she was intrigued by him, -It is too long to tell. Here I must work. My eyes are never still. It is too easy to lose what has been gained. One such as I is always prey to thievery and deception - if my guard is dropped! Kamil's face showed his disappointment, -Why do you want this? she asked.

-I do not know. You are the first woman I have ever asked such a question. It is surprising to me too. He laughed awkwardly.

-So another compliment. A great compliment! Perhaps we could meet somewhere else? Tomorrow? Perhaps in the gardens around the great temple? By its entrance? Let us say at eleven? She touched his arm lightly and slipped away.

Kamil left immediately in a state nearing ecstasy. He had inhaled a little more of the drug inadvertently which fanned the growing heat in his chest and increased the turbulence of the spinning thoughts in his brain.

*

He entered the garden much too early for the assignation even though he had tried to mop up time with the sponge of scholarly reading. Nothing he read stayed in his brain. Pages slipped by his eyes with the script little more than drifting spidery patterns. He had had to check the title of the pamphlet twice before he put it down in dismay. At another time the intricacies of different forms of poisoning would have captivated the man who had become the secret spymaster to a princess. But not now.

Now he was forced to pay attention to his senses. Was not the blossom extraordinarily powerful today? His nostrils quivered to the range of scents from the pungent to the cloyingly sweet. Were not the colours scintillatingly alive, vibrating in the morning sun? Were not the temperatures between light and shade dramatic? How could such a nondescript little bird sing a song of such entrancing complexity?

He sat on a well worn stone bench and watched people as they thronged by. Soldiers wandered among them, their scabbards swaying at their waists and their long barrelled guns holstered to their backs. Occasionally they stopped men and women and demanded to see their passes. No-one challenged Kamil, the inoffensive scholar, for he had his royal pass tied like a beacon to his belt. He closed his eyes and meditated. It was as though he was bathing in the very waters of paradise. He had never felt this strange aliveness before. It was as though his soul had left his body and now hung in the perfect air.

*

-I have to say, said a resplendent Princess Sabiya, settling her silken self in her chair that I feel like an addict who has been denied his drug.

142

My uncle grew to like the combination of pipe and wine to such an extent that he could not face a day without it. Just so with my Tales and your advice. She lies back somewhat indolently, thought Kamil, like a sinuous green snake. He wondered whether such an analogy was disloyal, -Also I am the carrier of a compliment, continued the Princess, -My father has noted that I am more 'self-possessed'. His words! He asked the reason and I said that it was your teaching. Stop! Think! Stop! Think! Only act if the evidence says so. He was very pleased. He has an even higher opinion of you now!

-I am flattered indeed, said Kamil, almost unctuously.

-You should be. Now, as to news. Nothing as yet. I decided not to discount the possibility that our man might be from the royal guard. It is bizarre is it not that generals have no knowledge of those who serve under them? Even the captains of the guard only seem to know half the names of the fifty men that they command. We have two thousand soldiers at the palace. It takes time to discover who they all are! In the court itself there are perhaps a thousand or so from noble families coming and going. There are half that number in servants and officers. It is a slow and delicate task for we do not want to frighten our prey. She preened herself, pleased with her carefully executed strategy, -So I have no news. And what of you? she looked at him through her lashes, -I hear that you visited the brothel again and then met the next morning with the mistress of the senses. She laughed convulsively on seeing his expression, the subsequent blood in his cheeks and the opaque drops of sweat on his brow.

He mopped himself, -I … I…did as you described, your Highness.

-What prompted you? she asked, plainly enjoying his discomfit.

-I know not. In truth I arrived at the brothel by chance or some deep reason beyond my conscious awareness.

-The latter! she chuckled, -And not so deep.

-There I met the mistress again and asked if we could talk. I thought that she might know more of our suspect.

-Good! I see the changes in you just as my father sees mine, old historian. From the library to the brothel. From the brothel to a public park, there to meet an infamous courtesan. Such risk! Such danger! Such adventure! Her tone was lightly mocking.

He dropped his head, -All true, your Highness. Yet she is not perhaps as she is painted.

-Come Kamil. It is she who has chosen to paint herself. A painted woman. How else?

He was silent, abashed. Finally she forced him to speak, -Come. Do not fall silent at my tongue. She has redeeming qualities, yes? He nodded, flushing again, -And you find yourself a little susceptible to her charms? Once more he nodded and wiped his brow. Salty sweat had entered his eyes and he blinked furiously. Princess Sabiya disturbed him. How could she see through him so clearly? Barely yet a woman and with the wisdom of a temple crone. Her voice grew harder, -Come Kamil, spit! She has stirred your heart a little yes?

-Yes, he answered, mortified.

-Good! Again she shook with laughter, -Good good good! You are turning from a dry old stick into a human being. The years are dropping off you. And you will be a better spymaster because of it. As long as - her voice dropped slowly and dangerously, -You retain your first loyalty to your Princess.

He leapt from his chair and fell on to his knees, -O your Highness as God is my guide it could not be otherwise. I would give it all up, my family, my few friends, my very life rather than betray your trust in me!

-I know it. Silly man. But it is good to hear it in words. On your feet! Now tell me of your conversation with her.

Kamil sat slowly and pursed his lips. His thoughts would not order themselves. How much should he tell? -I was sitting in the garden dreaming a delightful dream when words woke me.... "I hope I am not disturbing you," said a low woman's voice.

-Describe it!

-It was like cedar honey. Sweet, yet dark-

-Enough! On!

-I opened my eyes and had to squint in the sudden brightness. It was the mistress silhouetted against the sun. I said, "No, of course not!" and stood up. She smiled and sat on the bench where I joined her.

-What was she wearing? Was her face painted in the crude colours of the night?

-Neither then nor when I met her before. Her face was unadorned yet she had a natural beauty, a handsome quality which I mentioned before. She wore a simple grey robe trimmed with purple velvet.

-Huh, she deceives you. No woman goes out into the day without philtres and creams.

Kamil ignored her, -I did not know what to say. We sat for some time in silence watching families and soldiers. Then she turned to me and said, "You wish to hear my tale?" I nodded and found her eyes holding mine in an unbreakable stare. She spoke of being born in the north in the land of the black bears, the daughter of a noble. They had a palace on an island in a great river and he was rich from trade in timber. But her family was massacred by an unknown hand and she and her young brother were thrust on a raft at night by servants to escape the death of so many others. Upon this they floated away from the bloodshed. She was much as you are in age. Days later, desperate from hunger, they were rescued by village folk. Her brother was taken as a son by a kind, childless couple while she was placed in the women's compound to await a man who might choose her as his wife. She could not accept such a fate for she could read and write, paint and do many other things of which these illiterate people knew nothing. When she was strong she slipped away in the darkness after kissing her dear brother goodbye and took to a canoe, throwing herself once again on the mercy of the great water.

She had many adventures which she could not relate for they concerned the bestiality of men and the savage jealousy of women. Finally, on the edge of this empire, a violent man captured her and forced her into the brothel that his wife oversaw. She endured days of unimaginable molestation but a visitor, himself a noble, sensed her lineage. He insisted she relate her story. She told him I think in a detail far beyond her retelling to me. Promptly he brought his men and executed the husband and made her the mistress of that place. The dead man's wife became a harlot in her place. She transformed the crude horrors of the brothel into a place where men could go with a free heart and little guilt. At a point when she had accumulated some wealth her lover and benefactor was killed in battle. Knowing how every tide must turn she left with her wealth and travelled, finally to the capital of the empire. This very city. She bought the old brothel by the main gate and transformed it as she had the last, into a palace of the senses.

-A courageous tale!

-I felt so too.

-Is that all? How did you part?

-I wished that I might see her again and she agreed. The day following tomorrow. Again in the garden.

-Did you ask about our subject?

-I did. She felt that he was an impostor, not a royal guard. He reminded her of the man who had imprisoned her in the brothel all those years before. She said that there was something of the killer about him. She warned Aidah to be careful. She said she would enquire further but without raising suspicion.

-You trust her?

-Absolutely.

-You are no judge of women however. Go carefully. Enjoy your entrancing harlot but never ever forget that you work for my ends as well as your own. Let there be no competition between the two. She stared at him sternly and he nodded dumbly, fumbling for the page that began the next Tale.

-So your bow has twice shot its arrows to perfection within the last moon, said his father amusedly.

The young man was sober, -In truth, the second occasion was no test of its worthiness. The arrow was drawn by the target. It had little of my intention in it.

-The needs of fate sometimes overrule our strength of purpose. It matters not what we desire. Sure footed creatures may injure themselves or die falling from rocks they have known since they were born. The mad dog chooses not its victims and its victims do not themselves choose their agony and death. There are visible patterns and there are sometimes patterns which can only be traced at a later time.

-Then perhaps later it will be clear to me why we have joined this circus! laughed the youth.

They were helping to clear out a wooden cage of one of the larger animals. The circus was camped in a valley by water. For its people it was a time of regeneration and maintenance. Two full moon cycles would be spent here. Both men felt at home in the physical work, the smells, the calling of the beasts to each other, the bonds between men and creatures, the tightness of the loyalties. About them men and women were daubing new colours on to wood. Harnesses were being patched and sewn and the great tent was laid out like a giant's skirts on the earth so that plant juices could be applied to help it withstand the rain.

Although it was not the same circus with which his father had travelled, the folk here knew of that one. The world of travelling people was a small one with much intermarriage. The belief in skilled blood lines was strong, acrobats marrying acrobats, animal trainers seeking out their own kind and the same with magicians and clowns.

147

The best among them could move from circus to circus spending a season with each and then accepting a greater reward for moving elsewhere. His father did not have the same trust in these people as he had with some they had met on their journey. He ensured that their valuable possessions were always within sight and their horses standing nearby. It made each day a little more tiring than it should have been.

-We will leave soon, said the Merchant, -But our horses needed time to recover. It has been a long trek from the City in the Mountain. And what lies ahead is treacherous. We at least have the pattern of travel and rest to comfort us!

-Not much rest when you are watching for stealing fingers every moment of the day.

☥

As well as their labour in the cages they also spent time teaching new tricks to the circus magician. He was young with hair like straw and bright blue eyes. He was about the same age as the youth. His main work other than in the circus show was to be first to the small towns and villages to drum up excitement and interest. Supporting him in this activity was a young acrobat with large black eyes and pale skin. Her dark hair fell almost to her knees and she tied it up when parading her skills. The blond boy would make silk ribbons stream from her mouth or ears or a snake slither from between her breasts. In turn she would tie his hands and feet in intricate knots and then ask men in the crowd to hang him on a rope from which he would miraculously free himself. Some tricks the two visitors could not teach him however for he had not the necessary throwing arm. The Merchant and his son learned the art of mind reading from them. The mind reader would be blindfolded. By developing subtle prompts they could communicate to each other the object which was being held aloft by someone in the audience and at other times this was all prearranged according to an agreed pattern and the mind reader would know in advance what object would be chosen next.

They swapped their knowledge of knots.

The four of them were talking by the visitors' fire, their horses standing nearby and a great quiet in the camp. His father translated for him now and then although he was becoming better tuned to their dialect. Many words had different endings or were sounded in different ways. They spoke in low voices about illusions and illusionists, escapes and contortions. They discussed how a man could free himself from bondage when under water, how another might walk across a single, roped gorge with only a long pole for balance, how a bird might appear from a mouth, how jewels would fall suddenly from the sky, how a clairvoyant could tell a stranger's name and that of her husband or children. While they were talking the roan moved slightly then turned and lashed out with its rear hooves at the tent wall. There was the sound of a muffled blow followed by the impact on the ground of a falling weight. The four were immediately on their feet. Lying behind their tent was a clown and beside him was his knife and one of the Merchant's bags. A hole had been cut in the canvass.

The straw-headed youth ran for the circus master while the others examined the clown. He was unconscious from the impact to his skull. The roan was stroked and praised by everyone.

The circus master arrived. He was angry at being woken. He was a small man who could be irascible for most of a day if extremely displeased. He had bright eyes which flashed to signal his violent temper. Yet he was also full of wit with a clever use of a phrase. He was a shrewd business man and performers liked to work for him because he had no time for bad characters. He was fair and they were properly rewarded for their work. The animals were treated as though they were people. He would go round the camp each day and whisper to every one of them, touching and stroking, sometimes singing. He wore his hair uncut but greased into two long tails. He kicked the clown.

-He will be gone tomorrow. Those are the rules. My best clown! No matter. No good circus will have him after this. Only a zoo will have him! As he was speaking and cursing, the blond magician arrived with a blanket tied into a bundle. He undid it and tipped it on to the ground. In the firelight objects flickered. There were ornaments, a knife, jewellery and some fine cloth.

-This was on his horse. It was saddled. He was leaving after he had cut into all our tents.

The circus master screamed a curse, took up the stolen knife and with a brief and expertly executed movement, severed the clown's hand. He skewered it with the knife, enlarged the bloody hole and drew through it a piece of the cloth, finally tying it round the clown's neck. Then he stumped away without another word leaving a tent rigger to tie cord to stop the spouting blood.

☥

The following day the pair left the circus early. The events had hastened their desire to depart. The acrobat had embraced both of them with her arms encircling them. Neither knew what to do except stand and smile at her. She seemed just a child. They had then exchanged the more traditional ritual of parting with the blond man.

After some travelling at walking pace they rested the horses in the shade of some wizened trees. The father collected small fruit from them among their furry leaves which they chewed. They were not sweet and yet they nourished them. They ate dried meat and some black bread given them by the girl. Their solitude and peace was interrupted by the roan's snickering. He was looking back down the trail. A horse and rider was trotting towards them. Eventually they could see it was the clown. He had been tied to the horse's back.

He was dwarfish, thickset and strongly shouldered and was barely conscious. His face was contorted. His handless wrist was bandaged but bleeding. The hand still swung beneath his chin as though trying to reach and strangle him.

-Help me, he moaned as he tipped this way and that on his saddle. The ropes barely held him. His body was shaking.

-I will treat him, said the young man. The Merchant nodded and started to cut him loose. He was heavy and they had trouble easing him to the ground. The Merchant then went for his son's medicine and some water. He watched as the boy mixed a compress of leaves and mulched it. The blood was beginning to flow more freely but his son ignored it, cleaning around the wound until he was satisfied, then pressing in the compress and tying it there. He placed a hand on the man's heart and shut his eyes.

-It will heal now, he said getting up, -Make him a drink of the desert plant you showed me. Better to have bad dreams than such pain. The Merchant nodded and did so. He dripped the mixture into the man's throat holding his neck in such a way as to make him swallow. The groaning stopped. In its place the face began to twitch and the eyes rolled inside their lids.

-What next? asked the older man, -You are his doctor.

-We do not need his company if as you say the next part of the journey is the most dangerous. His spirit is clouded by poison, a burden too great for us. Our need is to make our way without such impediments.

-Then we will leave him

The youth acquiesced, -With food and water under this shade. His horse is tied. It is his embrace with fate which will decide his future.

They left the hand where it was. A punishment was a punishment whether in a circus or in the City in the Mountain.

☥

While they were riding the Merchant's son took out a ring from his belt and studied it closely. The band was rich metal and there was a large uneven polished blue stone. There were symbols on the inside of the band, -Can you read these marks?

His father stared at them, -They are familiar. The marks come from territories close by, nearer to my own. It is the ring of a trading family. She gave it to you? Have you made two oaths to keep now?

-No, laughed the young man, -I took it in exchange. When she embraced me I felt her hand in my belt. She stole a small rock-jewel from the City in the Mountain I was carrying for you. I did not want her to be wearing her hand on a necklace like the clown.

-Her punishment is more just. It is the ring of her family. It should leave the finger only on the death of the wearer or in marriage when it is exchanged with that of the man. To lose it is a disgrace. Hers must be a strange tale. She left home to be with that young trickster.

-Such is the lure of a magician!

-She cannot return without the ring. The bond is broken. Her life is with the circus now.

-It is a reversal. Losing her ring has bound her into a different marriage.

☥

They travelled on avoiding too much contact with nomads and traders and vigilant for any sign of bandits. The Merchant regarded the last stretch of the journey with great caution. He had lost many men trying to cross this territory. To take another route added weeks to travel - without any guarantee of greater safety. The path would take them down through a narrow and long gorge. Despite the heat the river would still be flowing. The waters were difficult to enter and as difficult to leave. The track followed it at a higher level still walled in by the gorge cliffs. Finding security for their camp would be almost as great a problem. There were few pieces of level ground off the track. It was more than two days travel from one end of the gorge to the other. The terrain made it too dangerous to sleep by day or ride by night.

They chose to walk their horses slowly, well into the dark and then sleep on the track with their horses saddled until the sun rose.

It was before its first rays that they both awoke suddenly. Something had disturbed them. A premonition. A threat. A danger. The horses had gone with most of their belongings on their backs! They looked in desperation. The horses had left some time before. There were no signs of any other visitor, man or animal. For the Merchant's son it felt as though his being had been sundered. The roan had been an extension of him since he was young. The horses had gone back along the trail. It seemed inconceivable that they had not been woken. Only the roan was capable of that stealth.

-It seems not possible, said his father.

-Yet it is so.

-No-one has taken them.

-They have taken themselves. There must be reason in what they do. Look, the young man pointed at the ground, -There is no fear in their prints. They show slow careful steps. Later they move more freely. They did not wish to waken us. My horse shut out his thoughts for I would have heard them even in sleep. He closed his eyes and tried to reach out to the roan, -He is not captured but other than that I cannot say.

-Shall we follow them?

-No, said his son, -It is for our safety that they have taken this decision.

They stood perplexed. Both men had developed such a confidence born of the habits of their journey that they could not assimilate immediately this change in their fortunes. As their trek lengthened they had grown accustomed to their mastery over people and events. They had grown to feel that they were shaping the world to fulfil their destiny. Now they were on foot. There was water. Food for perhaps two days. Not enough without the horses. Progress would be slow. It meant that they must hope to meet strangers rather than avoid them. There was nowhere to hide and they had little means of protecting themselves.

Collecting their blankets, water and food, they began walking along the path above the gorge. They sensed that danger lay just ahead. As they began a descent through the narrowest of passages they heard the scrape of metal on rock above them. Moments later, as they rounded a blind bend, they came face to face with bandits. There were many and they were in wait.

-Let us see what they intend before we act, whispered the Merchant.

Bound by rope they were dragged in front of the bandits' chief. His men had a wild and menacing air. Their locks were uncut and tied by thongs into single tails. They wore head and shoulder metal protection. On their wrists were wide bands. Hanging over their skirts were short swords sheathed in leather. Their faces were burned by countless suns and their eyes stared with an insolent hardness at their prisoners. To the son they were like wild dogs ready to tear them to shreds should the pack leader order it. This chief was as tall as his father and broader. He had the features of the desert nomad. They reminded him of his girl.

-Where are your horses?

-They ran off in the night. Something disturbed them.

-I have sent men to look for them. They can't be far. Where do you travel?

-To the great port where this river is at its widest.

The man laughed grimly, -They do not welcome me there. Who are you? he stared at the youth.

-He does not understand this tongue. He is my son-not-of-blood.

-He is from the north?

-He is. I brought him up as my own.

-What do you carry?

-Ornaments, carvings, rich metals, jewels.

-And these are on your horses. It was not a question.

-Yes.

-We will have them soon. What importance have you in your city?

-I am wealthy with many traders.

-How many?

-They arrive with each sun.

-I could ransom you.

-True.

-I might send them an ear. It will be a test of how much they love you.

-That is true too. The two men stood and stared into each other's eyes, one violent and murderous, the other still and wary.

-I will think this over. Give them food and water and secure them. The leader stalked away.

They ate and drank under armed guard, their knives having long been removed. Then their hands and feet were tied again and they were staked to a post driven into the earth. A guard sat in the shade of the cliff with his sword across his knees. The sun beat down on the pair. Each drew into himself and became very calm, conserving strength. They did not speak or move to draw attention to themselves. As the light gave way and the shadows spread across them the guard changed. More food and drink was provided. They returned to their unmoving meditation. Small bands of men came and went. Gradually the camp quietened. Night fell. There had been no sign of their horses. The chief had not returned.

When all was silent and the guard was drooping over his sword they slipped off their ropes as if they were gossamer threads and then waited for the blood to run freely around their limbs. Cloud drifting across the moon favoured them. The guard stood up and sat down at intervals to stay awake. The Merchant murmured audibly to his son in the northern tongue, "He will come over if I now speak."

Cumbersomely the guard got up. He rubbed his eyes and came close. He didn't see the fallen rope hidden behind them but he bent to check and was struck on the side of the head by the rock in the son's hand. They caught his falling body and lowered it to the ground. A quick whispered plan was outlined between them. The father moved to the tents. The son glided towards the horses standing in a group with a sleeping guard beside them. There was a call of a night bird from the direction of the beasts. Immediately a torch flared at the fire. It sped from tent to tent. Oil was splashed and flames started. In moments all the tents were like candles, fire spurting through their roof holes. The Merchant ran to where the horses were gathered and he and his son mounted. In an instant they set the animals charging down the trail.

Behind them there were screams as the fires raged. Men ran blindly in the smoke seeking safety. Others perished in the fires. The horses, used to staying compact in fight or flight galloped into the night driven by calls from the two riders, through the long gorge and out into the widening valley below. There was no stopping. They might still be open to an attack from a roaming band who had no yet rejoined the camp. The horses were forced on and on until the hills were just a thin black line in the night sky. Finally the riders relented and watered them. The trail had stayed close to the river and had grown flatter and easier.

They kept the band of animals moving through the next day without sleep. As evening approached the Merchant led them off the trail and up a winding path and into a village. He answered the lookout's challenge and they were allowed entry. Rapid conversation resulted in an armed group setting off for the gorge to complete the destruction of the bandit camp. They gave the horses to the village in exchange for food, keeping two for themselves. These they began to pack.

-We lost everything under the sun and regained a little under the moon, said the younger man.

-Our lives are not little to us!

-It is so. We live to journey on. We have regained a lot.

-More than you think. Look! the Merchant pointed. Hardly discernible yet, two shapes were moving down the trail, almost silent and very careful. The son whistled. The two shapes broke into a fast trot, bags still on their backs, swords sheathed, their ears pricked and issuing many whinnies of greeting.

There is yet another lesson in this for me! exclaimed the Princess after a suitable pause at the end of Kamil's reading, -And I am tired. I will postpone a second story. I have enough teaching in this circus adventure. Kamil wondered what she would say. She might extol the virtues of dismembering the hand, the perfect punishment for the crime. This is what she should have done with her handmaid, perhaps. But he was wrong, -I like the way the Magus taught the circus girl a lesson! She would only discover her loss later and yet it would have an irrevocable effect upon her destiny. She did not realise it at the time but the moment she stole the precious stone from him she was entering a contract with a shaman. She was bartering the one possible route back to her family for an uncertain future with nomads.

-Sometimes we are so drawn to our desire not knowing that its bright illumination is blinding us to all risk, replied Kamil, a sudden image of a silhouetted woman springing into mind.

-For one such as I, retribution is in every act of ruling. But I see that revenge need not be obvious. One can exact punishment upon the offender whilst appearing always to be a wise, just and humane leader.

-It is a subtle point.

-I never knew it before. But I will not forget it ever. Subjects who warm to their Empress are less likely to bear murderous progeny who would seek to shorten her life!

-I am sure your Highness will conquer the hearts of all.

-Perhaps I will, historian, spymaster and teacher! Perhaps I will. Now I must go. Tomorrow there will be another Tale. And news, likely.

Kamil bowed, -I await our meeting with great impatience, your Highness.

-Of course! Ah, one thing you have not told me! He knew what she would ask next for he had struggled whether to tell her when recounting his adventure in the park. It was as though he had wanted to keep that one gem of information a secret for as long as possible, until the inquisitiveness of the Princess drew it into the open, -What is her name, this harlot of yours?

-Baligha.

-Ah. Her father chose well.

Chapter Twelve

For life to have meaning death must be present

Kamil sat at his table writing. He had occupied himself during the day as usual, searching through the records in the library. The machinations of royal courts had proven to be an unending source of fascination. It had become evident to him that intrigue, deceit, imprisonment and assassination were ever recurring patterns. In most cases the perpetrators of plots did little to hide their handiwork but when their schemes were hatched against a ruler loved by his people and they were but few against the many or when their actions might be regarded as sacrilegious, unjust or evil, then they would establish the most elaborate ruses to remain beyond suspicion. These were the particular cases that he sought out and studied in the hope that something might be learned which could be of use to his Princess.

He was currently copying wise words from a Chinese emperor. This man had ruled successfully from late childhood to old age. In that time there were many uprisings in the empire and many plots within his own court, some from within his own family led by nephews who wished to switch the blood line in their favour. Kamil transcribed with his steady clear hand thus:

The wise emperor restricts his progeny to one source. Take more than one wife and he breeds nought but vipers contesting for his throne.

There is no blood hotter, nor ears so deaf, nor eyes so blind as those of the offspring of subsequent wives.

A court is a deep pool. To avoid the poison of stagnation, fresh water must enter and leave it. By this I mean it must seem ever open to people with their religions, philosophies, inventions, arts and trades.

The emperor must keep his own calendar-map of his court and let none see it. He must inhabit it with names and ambitions, loyalties and enmities, events and conversations, projections and reflections. Mine own is ornate and colourful. I use reds for those I suspect, blues for those who would follow any ruler no matter whom, greens for those new to the court and its ways and who have not yet declared themselves, gold for those who would die for me. Further subtleties are wrought with other colours. Sometimes the map seems redolent of danger and at others benign. Such a map needs the constant attention of an observant eye. It meanders on across many rolls of parchment and changes with the days

He considered and wrote further notes, these for his own clarification. Princess Sabiya was heir to an empire, the eldest daughter. There were no sons. Her stepmother hoped any day to produce a boy child and thereby usurp the Princess yet meanwhile remained publicly dutiful and loving to the Emperor. All this would come to a conclusion following the birth. Meanwhile a stratagem to use the signature ring of Sabiya's mother, the old Empress, seemed to have been foiled by chance. The poor victim of the deception, the maidservant had been killed before it could be established who had seduced or forced her into the plot against her mistress. Suspects had been rounded up - too quickly to be believable. There was a false royal guard apparently called Rafi who had a wife named Iffat.

Perhaps he could persuade the Princess to make a map as advised by the Chinese emperor. Doing so might draw out more strands of connection than were at first obvious to her.

*

When she entered he was almost blinded by the glorious shimmering pink silk of her over-garment with its flashing embroidered sequins.

158

Her dark skin shone in contrast. He told her about the map and her eyes brightened, -I will do it! she exclaimed, -It will be a pleasurable task though serious in its import. I will take time tomorrow with my stepsister's box of colours and a sheet of bleached paper. I will be a child again and you my tutor! Kamil started to mumble something about how useful it would actually be to gain a picture of the court but she stopped his words with a flourish of a flowery sleeve, -I must tell you the latest news from my spies when you have read to me! Do you like my coat?

-It is a thing of unsurpassable beauty, he replied fervently.

-Baligha would look well in it? She laughed at his blushes, -I am deliberately naughty! It is the way of women to test men's feelings and gain satisfaction from drawing them to the surface otherwise how else would they know that they have them? Come on, compose yourself and read. She turned over the next card, -Hah! Fortitude. Somewhat lacking in my case my teacher?

There was much fussing, stroking and embracing for the two horses. The Merchant remarked that animals sometimes received from their riders the kind of affection that women yearned. Though the roan was hardly a normal creature its arrival with its black fellow was still a cause for amazement. Where had they been? How had they got here? Why did they leave in the first place?

The son looked for evidence. He examined their legs and their bellies. On the legs there were traces of recent red soil. On the bellies was caked mud. In the hair on their withers and tails there were twigs and leaves. He discussed it with his father who thought for a moment and then said, -There is little doubt that they plunged into the gorge and passed below us. It is a long and dangerous route even when the waters are not turbulent. We could not have ridden them. They must have climbed out at the end of the gorge and walked up to the ridge where the soil is exposed. They probably followed our trail after that keeping to trees for cover when they reached the valley.

-The roan would have tried to rescue us had we not found our own escape, said the youth.

-If you so believe! grinned his father.

-I have no doubt. He did not need to. He was protecting our riches! See, the bags are discoloured with the river but everything is intact though some of the food has been spoiled. It seems to me that he became aware suddenly of the ambush. Perhaps we were being followed so the trail behind was also blocked. They must have slid into the gorge and swam. The roan may have felt that they endangered all our salvations and so it was better to leave us as decoys and meet us later! The bandits would look for the horses only having dealt with us first.

-It is a pleasing argument! The roan is an occult beast. The soul inside him has knowledge beyond a horse's life. He might well think these things, as was the way of his father, the one who delivered you to me.

-My mother's horse. He thought for a moment, -Nor is she an ordinary woman.

For much of the time now their journey was uneventful. They were in a less lawless land. There was cultivation of crops by the broad river and signs of wealth. They had word that the bandits had been found and killed, including their leader. News of the exploits of the two travellers had already spread along the trade routes. They were now heroes to all who had suffered years of pillage from the brigands. The pass through the gorge would be safe for some time. There were talks between neighbouring tribes and the City in the Mountain about charging a tax for passage through the gorge. This would support a constant guard to guarantee safety.

-It will not be so many days now before you see my home, said his father.

His son spoke softly and reassuringly, -We will be in time. I sense her struggle. She waits for you. She is tired but will not enter the final sleep until she has her son beside her again.

-It is a burden. I bring the present of her death with me. Her welcome will also be her farewell. I will have cut the threads that tie her to this world.

-But not the threads that she has spread through your body. These will not leave you.

The last two days were a long homecoming. Already they had been greeted by travelling merchants some of whom worked for his father's business. It was always a source of marvel how intelligence can precede the arrival of its subject despite the relentless pace of their journeying. This was a product of the day and night traffic of horsemen and their incessant bartering of the latest news. In this land the Merchant was already a legend. All knew the story of his sudden departure to the north at the very height of his success. Yet in his absence his business had trebled under the stewardship of his not-of-blood son. By the time they reached the port there was a small cavalcade following them of well-wishers and business associates.

Though it was nearly twenty years since his leaving many traders had been visiting the lands of the north, enough to keep him informed of all the changes that were taking place in his own land. He was even able to send advice to his merchant son though his counselling might take a season or more to reach him. The people who had joined them on the Merchant's return to his city were keen to know about this new son riding beside him but he waved away their questions with a smile and said that all would be made public later. His son glanced at him. His father's face was often difficult to read but here he could see the pride and the emotion at the welcome.

Their horses clattered down the main street. Stones had been laid there since the Merchant's departure. People gathered and waved pretty cloths as they passed by.

-Are you a king? asked his son, mystified.

-I left as an ordinary man like any other and that is how I return, said the Merchant, a little too seriously.

-Then the extraordinary ones must be a miracle to behold! quipped his companion.

As they rode up to the Merchant's home, a simply dressed man was waiting for them. He was close to forty years old with a strong open face and cropped hair. The older traveller jumped from his horse and embraced him.

-My Father!

-My Son! Meet your young brother. Dropping from his horse the youth was embraced by his new brother. Then the Merchant without any further word strode into the house. It was built of stone and clay and the floors now boasted polished tiles. A staircase led to a circular balcony from which rooms radiated. He disappeared into his mother's bedroom. The two men below heard crying and the Merchant's reassuring voice. They retreated to the kitchen to drink and talk. After some time their father came out of the room and called to them. They had been exchanging stories of their lives and sharing their knowledge of their father. The youth had learned of the success of the business and the growth of the family's trade and its acquisition of ships. His new found brother had built himself a house nearby and had married and already had a daughter. His own tales of bandits, powerful leaders, eccentrics and desperate challenges had drawn consternation from his brother.

His final question of this merchant sibling was, -He has no woman here then?

-None. No children except me - and now you! They had laughed and embraced again. However, his brother said that it was whispered that he was pledged to someone far away though he had never spoken of it with him.

It was at this point that their father's voice drew them upstairs.

She was propped up on white silk pillows, her son beside her. Across her bed was a counterpane with images the young man remembered from the dress of the priestess they had met near the beginning of their journey. It had been one of many gifts from her son following a long journey to the east. Her face was as white as her pillows and her eyes were deep sunk though still a clear dark brown. Her skin was fine with only a few lines but these were heavily etched and gave her face a powerful beauty. He went to her and held a hand and touched her forehead with his lips, a gesture only seen within families.

-It is good to meet my grandson.

-And you, Grandmother.

-You have been a good son to him I hear.

-He is the best father therefore it was not difficult.

-Of course, you see his mother taught him everything though only through her actions as he would never take lessons directly. The Merchant smiled. Hadn't his son-not of-blood been just the same? -He has been away from my side for too long.

-I am to blame.

She shook her head, -No. He was called by fate. It is a matter of pride as much as pain to me. His other son here was more than a substitute and has been as much a grandson to me as if he were of my blood. The Merchant smiled in appreciation at her words, -So I am a lucky woman though one who has had to endure too much separation. My son and my grandson raised me from poverty to this ... she waved a frail hand around her but you must never forget the earth in which you began and to which you will return.

-It is a house of great beauty.

She changed the subject, -You arrived in a saddlebag!

-Yes Grandmother.

-Too young to have memories.

-But a few days only.

-Your mother must have been stricken to have given you up to another. There must have been terrible reasons.

-One day I will know.

She pointed a wavering finger, -A mother must be forbearing with her men children, they have much to face. Many die before their time. If they do not they may be travelling much of their lives, coming back to make a child and then be gone again. It is hard for women. Their children grow without a man to discipline them. A woman learns to do it but it tears her heart. She would rather be the gentle one.

-You have been both, said the Merchant, -A father and a mother. I have not wanted for anything.

-You have learned a silver tongue on your travels my son! She laughed and said to the two merchants, -Leave me with my new grandson for a little while. I should know him before I die. They bowed to her and left.

The Merchant shook his head as he descended the stairs with his other son, casting his mind back over his adventures with the youth and thought that even his own mother had been touched by the young man's presence and must see him on her own.

When they were alone, she asked, -He has been a good father?

-Always. I would not have wanted any other life.

-I feel content in that. She paused and looked at him gravely, -I have not much time left.

-It is true. He could sense the fragility of her hold on the world. It was as though most of her had slipped out of sight and what remained was a fading reflection of her spirit only.

-My son said you were born with gifts.

-I have some.

-Tell me.

He drew a deep breath. He did not like talking about himself. Sometimes he wondered what a gift was. He only knew that what he possessed was unusual because others remarked on it. He knew no different. He just did these things, -They do not make themselves available at will, he said.

-That comes later.

-When I am forced to fight I see it all before it happens. I can hear the thoughts of my enemy.

-It is essential for one such as you. Many will be jealous, angry or possessive of you and these talents. Always there will be those who wish you ill. Most will fear you.

-I can heal.

-Like my son your father but greater. You have his skills but your touch reaches out to the will of the other. Take my hand. He took it and was instantly aware of the faltering beat, the slow journey of the blood, the seeping away of liquids from their life-long channels, the disintegration of the organs. He shut his eyes but he could do nothing more than steady her pulse.

-As you can feel, I am old. But your power calms me. She still held his hand, -What else have you?

-I have dreamt myself to be a bird. I can travel in this form.

-A bird. Only?

-Sometimes there is no shape. He remembered the great cat coming for his help, -It is like only being spirit, free of flesh.

-Train yourself! This is the greatest gift of all. With it you can guide destinies. You are indeed a shaman. She tightened her grip on his hand, -Yet you are naïve, still a foolish young man. Later you could command whole peoples. You will bring together the empires of east and west and stay the advances from the north. You can do anything you wish.

-It does not interest me.

-What interests you?

-There is no true answer. Until now I have lived in the shadow of my father. I have not thought further. I must find what it is that I must do.

-Ha! He would say the same about you. He has lived in the shadow of preparing you for life.

-I only realised this not long ago. I was so ignorant! He thought about it and then continued, -I must return to my mother so that I might know her. I have given my oath to a girl of the desert. And perhaps there is more I must do. I would still serve my father. Is there anything beyond these things?

-Your service to your father has ended. You are nearly a man. It is your fate alone that must be addressed. I will not die with you here - and yet it is my time. I wish you not to prolong it, do you understand? He nodded. She wanted her son back and her son could not be hers until he left. Becoming master of his own destiny would release his father from the responsibility that began when he departed her home all that time ago.

-I will leave tomorrow.

Her head gave a small bow, -He will understand but it will take some time before he is at peace with it.

-We are to meet again.

-A dream?

-Yes. She closed her eyes with a satisfied smile.

Kamil looked up from his text quizzically. She was staring fixedly at the card as though it held the secret of life itself.

-Like the Merchant I returned home from a visit to the mountains to reach my mother before she died. A messenger brought the news that she had succumbed to a fever. I rode like a warrior though I was just twelve years old. She died in my arms and those of my father. It was a noble parting for she too, smiled to the last. Much as my father sought the reason for the fever none could be found. Was it a plague that struck but one person or a poison secretly administered? Tears erupted from Sabiya's eyes but she seemed unaware of them. Kamil rose silently and took a square of cotton which he proffered to her unseeing face. He pressed it between her clutching fingers. She dried herself and became composed.

-What are you now Kamil? First my historian, then my spymaster and now my confessor and comforter. I have not shed tears since my mother died except before my father alone, until this moment. None must see me so weak.

Kamil sat again and leaned forward, -It is not a sign of weakness, my Princess but the natural expression of the heart. It is endearing, fear not. Do not deny the human in yourself. It will draw the loyalty of the masses as much as feats in battle and the just exercise of power.

She nodded but rose and left the room without a word. It was some time before she reappeared, more at ease but sombre. She sat upright with her hands clasped upon her lap, studious but, thought Kamil, vulnerable and with a truer reflection of her age.

-This is what my spies tell me. It is not much but perhaps it takes us a little further in our quest. My maid came from a loving family. She had been promised to the son of a fruit farmer. Then a short while ago a new man entered her life and turned her head. He was from better stock it seems but no-one has yet been able to paint his history. Her family was much distressed by this turn of events and threatened her life for it flew against generations of union between two clans. Upon her death at my hands the mysterious stranger vanished. There is no news of him. Nothing to pin him. He appears not to be the tall man who calls himself Rafi. It is little to go on.

-Yet we have conjecture and surmise at our disposal. Kamil furrowed his brow, -She must have met this man in the palace for this is where she worked and lived. Her few journeys by foot to her home would not have provided much opportunity for such a liaison and if so it is likely her family would have known of it. I am sure her family was not involved in her theft. We now have the beginning of the shape of things. Three figures to place on your map. Your stepmother, the visitor to the brothel and this interloper in the maid's life. Have you a spy close to your stepmother, the Emperor's wife?

The Princess pursed her lips, -No, I have not been able to insinuate anyone into her private chambers.

-There is no-one who sees those that come and go?

-No, except-

-Except?

-There is one who slaves in the corridors that lead to the Empress's quarters. She is old now. She slaved also for my mother. Her tongue was removed when she was a child for it was the custom then so that she might join royal service and not speak of what she saw. But she never became a handmaiden. However, my mother treated her well and taught her the language of signs as she did me, as well as how to write. Few know of this and so assume that she is as unforthcoming as the walls. I have not communicated with her for years.

-Have her keep a list of all who come and go, particularly those who are alone and who visit at times that seem not to fit with the regular beat of court life.

-Why did I not think of this? Perhaps the mute was too low in my estimation of who might be useful to my cause. I see that even the smallest detail can aid the construction of my China-map!

-Build the broadest net but ensure the mesh is fine. Nothing of use to us must be allowed to slip through it.

Chapter Thirteen

Selfless service enlightens the self

Princess Sabiya sat in the hot water of her exquisitely painted tiled bath feeling curiously light headed and full of an excited optimism. It was, she reflected, the sense of being in charge of her destiny. Until the momentous (she had to accept this) meetings with Kamil, she had played political games with a blinkered sense of direction. She had kicked and bucked and galloped and returned like a headstrong yearling captive in a paddock. All had been wilful. Her attempts to uncover the plot against her had been crude, if determined. She might have got what she wanted but it would not have been through subtlety and would have had little consideration for the general effect it would have had on others. As her bath maid gently sponged her body with scented soap she conjectured how she might meet Khawlah, the mute, without raising suspicion in her stepmother's camp. She stopped the soaping, -Go to the minister of court affairs and ask him to bring me a list of all servants who worked for my mother. Who is still in the palace. Who has left. What they are doing and where.

-Yes, your Highness. The girl pattered out.

Sabiya was dressed and at work with her crayons when the girl reappeared, -The minister is here your Highness. She rolled up the map and tucked it under a cushion, hurriedly.

-He can enter now. She examined the minister with unfeigned cool detachment, allowing her eyes to cover his flushed, padded features and pendulous gizzard, his perfectly circular bald spot, his thick embroidered robes and his ringed fingers spread out on the floor, in kneeling supplication. She noted the removed, sequinned shoes with their preposterously curled toes neatly placed by the door. She had hardly met him before. Her guard stood impassively by him, eyes alert for every detail and every movement, apparently excluding those of her own. She had never caught the man looking directly at her yet if she raised an eyebrow in request he would act instantly.

-You may stand, Minister Ayaz. He clambered to his feet in a series of ungainly contortions and stood there, mouth agape, eyes down, before her. She could see his fear and uncertainty. He was rarely summoned by a royal personage, owing his position and status to the intricate politics of court bureaucracy and not patronage, -You have brought what I requested?

-Your Highness, his head bobbed repeatedly in affirmation, while pulling a small, ribboned roll from his pocket and proffering it. She took it and he took two steps back with a sideways, nervous glance at the guard.

-Is this true? she asked, indignation in her tone.

-Yes your Highness, he wheedled.

-One servant left in the inner court! After such a short time? Where are they all? She stared at the uncommunicative piece of paper.

His plump body shivered, -Those that were not transferred to your retinue, your Highness, at the passing of the Great Mother, have been moved on by order of the Empress.

-Moved on! Where?

-To the outer court, your Highness. To the retinues of ministers, generals and admirals. They are safe and protected, he added unctuously.

-Huh! And the one who is left?

-The Mute, your Highness. You may remember –

She expostulated with a dramatic stamp of her foot, -Of course I remember. Khawlah is her name. You may go. Return with the list I actually requested. This is opaque! Where are they all? Who are they serving? One hour. Before the midday meal. Summarily discharged he backed from the room, collecting his footwear on passing. The door closed and she was alone. Her stratagem for seeing Khawlah was much strengthened and she had more evidence of her stepmother's scheming. She pulled out her map again.

*

The list he had brought her later had a dozen or so names, spread across various political and military households, all in positions more menial than those enjoyed under her mother's benevolent charge, except for three who served in her own household. She had ordered him to make immediate arrangements for all of them to be brought to her grand chamber that afternoon, for a small reward for their past work. Food and drink would be prepared and they were requested not to dress in any special way for the occasion. Sabiya knew that her reputation for impetuosity would be veil enough to hide her intent. Khawlah would be lost in the crowd. Who would suspect her intention of seeing the mute and enlisting her help in such circumstances? She had insisted to Ayaz that every single servant be brought to the reception. She guessed correctly that all the current households of the servants would be panicking. Was the Princess checking up on their treatment? What stories would the servants tell? Sabiya imagined the mix of threats and bribes from those they served as they prepared to come to her gathering.

*

The food was simple. She didn't want to exhibit a sudden show of opulence. It would have been out of keeping with the nature of the occasion. The wine was coarse and from the region. Despite her request the servants' appearance spoke of sudden attention to apparel and cleanliness. Only the mute remained in her daily stained garb. Sabiya made a pretty speech apologising for taking so long to thank them for what they had done for her mother, that she had suffered so much from her loss and that this had constrained her faculties. She hoped, too, that each and every one was being cared for properly as befitted those that had worked so loyally for their Empress. If not she would like to hear of it. Now she would come round and talk to them individually to hear their stories.

Kamil had been right. Show your emotions and you take the people with you. Your display of sadness at your loss and gratitude for their service was a potent combination. Their eyes showed it. As she moved among their bowing heads, a sliver of gold, her black skin strikingly different from theirs, she heard their tales and instructed a lady-in-waiting to make a note of this or that. In the middle of her procession around the room she came across the mute. She had practised during the afternoon for this moment. It must not take long. Her hands played in the air. Delight and devotion shone in Khawlah's eyes.

-How is my mother's speechless favourite?

-I survive, Royal Daughter.

-How does the Empress treat you?

-I am but a shadow on her wall.

-I wish you to serve me. To be my spy. Sabiya made a small aperture with her forefinger and thumb framing Khawlah with it.

-It would give my life meaning.

-Keep account of all who privately visit her royal chambers. Times. Names if possible. Descriptions. There is a plot against me. Think back, too, over what has occurred. We will arrange for someone to contact you. Khawlah, the dumb one, smiled and turned away to a table of food while Princess Sabiya moved on.

*

The park was thronged as usual. He waited for Baligha, a little more at ease in his fine clothes. His heart trembled as it had done yesterday but he was steadier. Yesterday he had not known if she would appear. Today he knew that only the unforeseen would prevent it. The novelty of Baligha's occupation of his heart entranced him. She had carved out a teeming space inside him where none had been. Until he had become tutor to the Princess he would not have recognised that such a space could exist. It was her Highness who had prized open the portal and Baligha who had entered and created the unknown territory within. Where once, not long ago, he had been a well-meaning, diligent, scholarly dough of a man, the bearer of few of the burdens that beset the hearts and minds of his fellows, now he had a full kernel of purpose, desire and expectation. And these would lead no doubt to similarly strange and unexpected problems! The thought was greatly cheering.

This time he was able to watch Baligha approach. Her long, slow, swaying stride caught the eyes of passers-by. Her proud erect deportment seemed to cut a confident swathe through the crowded flow. From a distance their eyes caught and were held by a power foreign to him. Every detail around her diffused so that only she remained sharp and distinct, almost burning in his sight.

-You are dressed like a noble, she smiled.

-And you like a muse intent on unlocking the imagination of a poet. The words exhaled from his lips without the volition of his thoughts. He was as much an audience to them as she was.

-You know how to shape a compliment.

-It is you who shapes it within me. Shall we walk together? Challenging acceptable behaviour he offered his arm and she touched it. Then, separately, they teased their way to a less crowded path shaded by a tall hedge, cut as smoothly as a plastered wall.

-I counted the minutes until our meeting, he murmured,

-It dwelt upon my mind too.

-I know that there is much intelligence that I must glean from you for such an exchange is demanded of us yet I would delay it in order to prolong your presence. He had turned his head to observe the fine lines of her profile. A tenderness suffused him.

She looked ahead gravely, -When I was not yet known to you and those distant rulers of destiny for whom you work, I was free of serious concern save how to ensure the health of my affairs. Now I am caught in an intrigue beyond my awareness, my freedom suddenly curtailed. I cannot change it except by fleeing.

-Please do not consider …his voice had a desperate note of disquiet.

-No, I will not flee. For if I go I gain the small recompense of freedom and lose the great reward of my deepening awareness of you. I will see this through for good or ill. Her hand squeezed his arm and he pressed it against his side.

*

They were both seated, sharing an air of elation. Princess Sabiya had felt it all day, since bathing that morning and Kamil following his meeting with Baligha.

-Who shall start? she asked, -You or I? Then she interrupted herself, abruptly, -I shall! She explained how she had made contact with the mute, Khawlah and that the servant had gone back to her duties in the Empress's household and immediately made a list of all whom she could remember had recently passed down her corridors. Sabiya's mother 's foresight in teaching her to write had been a blessing, -Here! She produced a tiny rolled sheet.

-How did she pass it on?

-Simple! She rolled the scrap and placed it in a small hole, one of a thousand carved in a stone screen! It connects to an outer courtyard to allow air to circulate. Another servant of mine picked it up. Neither was observed in their actions.

He examined the list. The hand was difficult to read. Crude, child-like strokes and misspellings. He could not decipher all the names but there were simple descriptions of the same male visitor. Tall. Noble. Grey hair, -Here is our suspect. She has had repeated sightings of him. Although I cannot read her hand fully, others seem to have visited but once. There is no name, I think.

-There is not.

-And no pattern. He comes in the morning one day, evening the next, afternoon and so on. What does this say? He turned the sheet on the table and pointed.

Sabiya stared at it, -I think it says 'now in soldier's dress'. It must be our man. She stared at him with a strange smile, -I have already put him on my map. She drew the paper roll from her coat and spread it before him with the look of a wide-eyed child expecting praise.

Kamil explored the rich colours, symbols, words and names with his sharp, erudite gaze, -It is magnificent. You have an artist's hand, your Highness. The line is delicate and the colours perfectly chosen. There are none better in the archives of the Emperor of China!

-It is a thing of wonder is it not? It astonishes even the eye of its author.

-And what new insights does it hold?

She stared at it intently, -There is more dangerous red than I ever imagined. The Empress is less subtle than I believed. She has saturated the court with her followers, both those of her extended blood line and from her previous household. Note here that of the four generals of the compass two are now in her thrall. The palace guard and the people's ministry are half loyal to her. Only the exchequer and the admiralty are free from her stain.

-If your father was to die, God preserve him?

-I would flee to a port and fight my battles from there. It would be close run. I command no popular support whereas she, though not greatly liked, may have respect from the populace. I may not have time but I will use what you have taught me. I will seek the love of the people. Thus, in the event of war, there would be willing followers of my cause.

-It is essential! he declared adamantly.

-Other than this broad inference from my chart there is one point of note. Kamil smiled, acknowledging her furrowed concentration, -As you saw from Khawlah's message the man we seek has no pattern to his visitations. This is deliberate to avoid suspicions. The Empress, like myself, has a fixed round of public duty, arranged in advance. The opportunity for private, secret meetings is limited, even more so when my father is in court. It is easy for me to discover when she has time to herself. If Khawlah cannot inform me in time I can at least arrange the deployment of spies who might catch sight of him. But the key element that struck me is that such an outlandish visitor, by which I mean so tall, is virtually unknown to anyone. Why would that be?

-Your thoughts?

-He must be from her previous court. He is a secret assassin. He must live in another city. Like any traveller from a far away place with longing in his loins, he takes his sex from the nearest brothel. Whilst again shocked by her matter-of-factness, Kamil smiled warmly.

-You have done well! They both looked exultant, -You have a shrewd brain and deduce the correct interpretation from that which you see before you. This will only refine over time and become a great asset to you. Then their smiles faded and seriousness returned, -What news from your other spies?

-None yet. It is slow, the apparently innocent questioning, the masked surveillance. It takes many hours from my limited, trusted resources. Princess Sabiya leant back in her chair and dangled her arms over its arms. She gazed up at the ceiling for a while, her face serene, yet touched with a satisfied half smile. Then she raised her eyebrows, - Your turn my spymaster. What of your meeting with the Queen of Senses? You had more time together today. She walked close and once touched your arm! Rather shocking for such a conservative man. Even a step too far for your Princess.

Kamil looked disconcerted and scratched his head before saying, confidently, -What if we should have the reading first? Then our riches will be divided into three courses and the meal, therefore, will feed our investigations and our imaginations.

-Hah! You are becoming too bold by half! Go on miser. I am learning to trust your instinct.

175

They stood embracing for some time. The black and the roan rubbed their heads along each other's necks. His saddle bags were full of food. He had enough to barter with for a long journey however long that might be. He also had his father's seal should he ever need it.

-I have only one piece of advice to you, my son-

-Stay silent when in the presence of others' beliefs, interrupted the young man, laughing.

-Then I have no advice. I have no fear for you, I only regret …

-Your mother needs you to be here. And your other son.

-I know. I knew this throughout our long journey. But the passing of so many suns has not made it easier.

Finally they separated and he and the roan left. It was early and few of the servants were about. He had kissed his grandmother and brother farewell late the night before. Then he had taken his last sleep in the Merchant's house. The roan whinnied loudly and there came an answering call from the stables. The horses, too, sensed they had different fates to follow.

He had no clear idea of what course he would take now. It would not fulfil his urges to return immediately along the trail down which they had lately come. He was younger than the Merchant had been when he had begun his great adventure. But unlike him he had no sign, no dream, no-one's persuasion to press him forward. He realised how little choice was needed in life. People and events push, pull, exhort and invisibly force you in certain directions. Life for most of the time consisted of reaction. This was why the ascetic on the island had isolated himself. He wanted to live without such influences. But at what cost? How could he, a sole traveller, do this without such privations? What would be the rewards for the long time spent on that single-minded journey? Once he had become satiated with an aimless, deliberately pointless wandering he would take to his path again and face back towards the valleys of the north.

He resolved when he came to the crossroads outside the port to override choice by following the fortunes of chance. He took his knife from its sheath and flung it up into the air, spinning it, blade around shaft. Like the seed of a common tree it gyrated to the ground. The blade pointed north not east as he imagined it would. He had expected confirmation of an urge to go elsewhere to new land. Stilling the frustration he dismounted and took up the knife. He shut thoughts from his mind and remounted, setting off with the early sun over his right shoulder.

When it shone directly down on him he was still in a state of blankness and indifference to his journey. He only emerged from this empty reverie when the roan pulled up and walked into some shade and began drinking water. He assumed that this was part of the same river that they had followed to the port. A little tributary. He dismounted and took some food. The roan started foraging. As he ate a feeling of loneliness came over him. To be separate from his father was not a new sensation. The Merchant had often gone on trips lasting several weeks once he was old enough and could be left. It was the knowledge that this was for a great spread of time, that all events would stem solely from his thoughts and decisions and that he would be the only audience to their realisation or otherwise. The world had been reduced to one pair of eyes, one set of senses and one understanding.

☥

It was cooler here. It was silent. There was no bird song and the air was still. He threw down a blanket and lay on the earth and shut his eyes while the roan stood by, its ears moving this way and that. A little later he awoke refreshed. And the feeling of loneliness had gone to be replaced by a strange but pleasing emptiness, as though fears and expectations had been washed out of him. One short sleep. Everything had changed. He sat up and looked for the horse. It was standing partially out of the thicket and looking up the trail listening. Whatever it was interested in must have been a great distance away. It had a stiff concentration which suggested that whatever it was, was on the very edge of its senses. He ate and drank, occasionally looking at the creature. It didn't move. The roan was enigmatic. Sometimes it would seem as though it was listening to sounds from another world for no person or creature ever appeared. At others its senses would save his life.

When he had finished he gathered what needed returning to his saddlebags and walked over to pack and scratch the roan on its neck. It made a deep rumbling whinny and then returned to where it had been looking. After a while he caught it. A faint smudged line rising from a distant hill into the air. Smoke! Whoever it was had no concern about his or her presence being discovered. Unless of course that is exactly what was intended. It was either a confident group of fighting men which was unlikely as everyone was too schooled in caution, even this close to a city, or someone wanting help. The roan was not on edge, just curious.

It was some time before they were close enough to see anything. The smoke had all but vanished. It was a faint white mist now. It came from the side of a steep rocky bank. As they approached they could make out the dark shadow of the entrance to a cave or a fissure in the rock. Closer still and there was a body on the ground. A black horse was tethered nearby even bigger than his father's. He dismounted and stepped over to the body. There was drying blood over the entire cloth covering the chest. He walked towards the dark cut in the rock. He could hear sobbing, amplified by the empty recess. He stepped across the near dead fire and peered inside. A little girl was crouched against the back wall holding a sword in her two hands that was too heavy for her. She pointed it at him and its end kept drooping. He put a hand over his heart in universal greeting, spreading the fingers of his other hand and motioning her to follow. He took food and drink and laid it on a flat rock near the cave entrance. Then he looked more closely at the body. The warrior had been dead for more than a day. Opening the tunic he could see where a sword had slashed deeply into the stomach. From his dress he looked as though he came from lands to the south. His weapons and amour were of high quality. He was a paid fighter. Such men held no allegiance except to their current contract and their present paymaster. Behind his crouched back the young man could hear the girl eating and drinking. He turned and sat and watched her. She looked down at him. She seemed about six years old. She had fair hair like that of the young magician and a sallow skin and blue eyes.

When she had finished he indicated that there was more. She shook her head. He got up and went over to the tethered horse. The saddlebags were like those of a trader. He heard her move and turned round. She was holding the sword pointing at him. She didn't like him searching the bags. He growled at her suddenly and she dropped the sword and ran back into the shadows. He picked it up and moved to sheath it on the horse. He saw the blood on the blade. He looked from the blade to the dead man to the pair of eyes watching him from the darkness.

Gradually he gained her trust. He pretended that she had a choice to stay or go with him even though she didn't but she wanted to believe it. After a few minutes she indicated that she would travel with him. She couldn't ride the great horse. Its saddle was too broad. There was little food in any of the black stallion's bags. Through odd words and mime he gradually pieced together her story.

She had been taken while sleeping from her village by the dead man. He was a trader in girls. He found such girls for rich families. Blonde hair, blue eyes and her light skin were much sought after. She had been ordered by a rich family in a southern port and would be kept until old enough for the master's pleasure. She was able, laboriously, to convey all of this through word and mime. On the journey here they were caught in a trap by two men. Her kidnapper killed one with his sword and the other ran away not realising that her captor had been badly wounded. He became weaker as they travelled with her perched before him on the saddle. She showed her back which was matted with the man's blood. They had had to stop here. He started a fire to attract help. He lay and went to sleep. He did not wake up. She tried to keep the fire alight but there was little dry vegetation under the trees. She couldn't break enough dead branches.

He could not understand where she said she lived but she certainly did not want to go south to the port. She caught his arm and pulled him pointing up the trail. Somewhere up there, who knew how far away, was her home.

✝

She was a strange little creature. He had not had much experience of small girls and did not know what to do in response to her changing moods. And they changed as rapidly as the weather in the mountains. One moment she was pressed against him seeking warmth and comfort like an animal and the next she would pull away and look stern and scold everything and everyone around her like a displeased queen. She made him brush her hair after first cleaning his own brush for the purpose. She pointed mockingly at the loose hair and oil that was clogging it.

She sat sideways on his lap as they rode. The great stallion was roped to his saddle and followed obediently. It recognised the leadership of the roan. He had transferred many of his bags to lessen the weight on his own horse.

Gradually he learned some words from her. By listening he could catch the connections between her language and his own. She would repeat these words and stare at him as if he was deaf. She liked to control him. She didn't, for example, appreciate long rides without stops. Slapping his arm she would point to the ground. Then she would relieve herself or play games for a short while. He remembered most of them from his own childhood; rolling stones to be nearest a target, throwing them at rocks or trees, jumping and marking the distance, skipping, hide and seek. In some of these games he was required to take part, too. He did so with a smile but inside he questioned how he had come to be responsible for this little stranger. As soon as they encountered a suitable group of travellers he would pass her on.

Slowly he drew from her more of her journey with the child abductor. It clearly distressed her. She managed to convey that the man had touched her between her legs but had not penetrated her. That he had hit her and kept most food for himself. He tried to gauge from her how far they had travelled but she had lost sense of the number of nights. It seemed she did not count beyond her fingers. Her village appeared to be on the edge of a desert. They had camels as well as horses. It was a place for travellers to stop before or after crossing the great wastes. She was from a tribe not unlike the people of his desert woman. He drew his village in the sand with a stick and showed houses and the trail and the mountains. She drew her own village but he could only gather that it was a much bigger settlement.

Each night he wrapped her in blankets and waited until she slept. This could involve her singing a great number of songs. He liked her voice. It was melodious for one so small. Nevertheless he felt a weight, an unasked for burden. He had tried to free himself from his own desires by offering his fate to chance and chance had somehow tied him to the will of another. He mused. Perhaps he was wrong to think of his quest as a solitary trek which would lead to greater understanding. Perhaps it was always going to be a series of encounters, companionships and conflicts. Just as with his journey south. But something in him still yearned for isolation and meditation.

They were not now on the same trail down which he had come with his father. He couldn't remember leaving it but he knew that they must have done so. Perhaps the roan had decided for him. Perhaps the roan knew where the girl was from. He believed it was even possible that the roan would find their destination from the stallion. He had asked the girl about the gorge and the City in the Mountain. None of it resonated with her. He remembered hearing that there was another route from north to south which avoided the gorge. It was long, circuitous and arduous. Perhaps this was it.

He taught her some simple tricks which excited her. She practised every evening after they had eaten. He corrected her when she revealed too much to her audience which made her eyes flash in annoyance but did not stop her practising. She was an odd little hybrid.

They were riding. She turned to look at him. If she didn't think he was listening she would grasp his ears and pull his face down and stare up into his eyes. She did it now.

-Who mother?

-Not see never.

-Who Father?

-Not see.

-Who baby you? She made a nursing sign.

-Merchant. This was a word he had taught her. His father-not of-blood.

-Good merchant baby you, she nodded, -Trick you mother.

She returned to her thoughts. Then she looked and smiled, -My mother baby you. She was offering him her mother to care for him. He smiled and tightened an arm around her briefly. She leant back against him.

☥

Even he began to lose a sense of time on the journey. It was late one afternoon and they were travelling north east. She seemed to be familiar with landmarks on the trail because now and then she pointed at trees or outcrops of rock or an outline and muttered encouragingly. They were climbing gently but steadily. There was no vegetation except by the narrow rock stream. It was reduced to a single, thin flow now. The trail followed it up towards a hollow in the arm of a hill that later descended in a ridge towards the plain. When they reached it the stream's source could be seen higher up trickling from a hole in the ground.

His eyes swept across the terrain ahead and below them. It was one red. Again there appeared to be no vegetation other than that growing in and by the water. He decided that they must fill their leather bottles and allow the horses rest and have one last feed for some time. He and the girl chewed dried meat and hard black bread while the horses foraged by the stream. It had become a monotonous diet. She pulled a face when she saw it but ate hungrily. He realised that she was not as pale as he had thought. Now that the fear had gone her face had colour and was a golden brown. Yet it was still lighter than any he had seen except that of the circus girl. She was spirited and did gymnastics whenever she could find suitable ground. She would not exercise herself in this way unless she commanded his entire attention. He helped her to learn to walk on her hands by tipping her upside down against a rock face. Looking at her in this position he thought he was like her. Since he had been drawn to her fate he was upside down, walking on his hands painfully slowly so that he could not see where he was going. His life was almost at a halt whilst hers was in full cry. There was not even a puff of wind to move his spirit on.

He tried to ask her how long this red wasteland would continue. She appeared to understand the question but after a while shrugged.

-No know. Bad man stay closed eyes.

He was uneasy. Three days would be almost too far. They had food and water for themselves and their horses for two. But a desert like this, even so late in the year, was hot and inhospitable.

They prepared to set off again but the roan alerted him to movement behind them on the trail. A small cloud of dust. One or two riders travelling as slowly as they had done. He knew that they wouldn't see him and the girl for some time but they would know that they had travelled that way only a short time before. He looked at the roan who understood his enquiry. It stood calmly. They were not bandits. He decided to wait. Perhaps his desires were being met and the girl could be handed over.

When they came close enough he recognised them as Spice Merchants. Of all who plied their trade on these dangerous trails these were the least molested. They carried medicinal plants, ingredients for cooking and body powders and paints. For the price of a sedative, an analgesic, an aphrodisiac or something to disguise the taste of rotting meat, they were allowed to pass through bandit camps, settlements and warrior blockades alike. He and the girl permitted themselves to be seen at some distance. The richly coloured robes of the two caught and shimmered in the sun. They were both women as like each other as two fruit from the same branch. He tried to restrain the hope in his mind. They each rode a horse and towed a mule. The horses were wiry mountain beasts. The women themselves were tiny with facial features unlike any he had seen before; moon-like, angle eyed and with unblemished skin faintly greened by colouring powder and shaded by wide-brimmed hats. Their hands were gloved.

He bowed to them. The girl hid behind him, her eyes big with intrigue.

-From your dress you are from the north, said one, -A full year from here? He was amazed to hear his tongue spoken so well in this wild place.

-I am.

-And she is from the pale haired ones. We have visited them often. The village has many like her. They are much sought after for wives. You are a child trader? They eyed him incuriously, without judgment. Children, spice, weapons, carvings; all were merchandise on these routes.

-No. He explained his new-found responsibility.

They made it plain that they were not going to take the child. Their direction was elsewhere but it was only a two day journey to her village. They would draw a map in the sand after eating. He and the child were invited to join them and even though they had already eaten he welcomed the company and the lilt of his homeland tongue. Losing her fear the girl approached them and touched the finery of their robes as if she was encountering magic.

One merchant took out a slab of hard honey cake and broke a piece for her. She tasted it and ran off in shocked excitement to perch on a rock and suck it slowly.

-She is lucky you saved her. He realised that only one spoke while the other remained silent and watchful. The speaker's mouth had a redder hue.

-Doubly. The trader had not harmed her.

-He would not. Her value is in an unsullied body. We saw the trader's corpse. We met him once. No one will grieve his death. Even merchants such as ourselves need protection from his kind.

He decided to forego the plan to ride late into the evening and prepared to camp with them that night. There was no greater safety in numbers but a reassuring, temporary sense of community. The girl fell asleep quickly. The northern tongue excluded her and though the two knew her dialect they chose not to use it. He was intrigued by them. Whenever spice merchants had come to his village everyone behaved as though the circus had arrived. All had their needs and desires. It was common for villagers to believe that the very best products must come from far off lands. No-one haggled. Spice merchants had more buyers than goods. They had a keen sense of the value of what they sold or exchanged but generally they were fair.

These two were on a long journey to a distant city in the west. The city was a staging post on a route to lands so far away that people here knew of them only through myth and legend. Their exotic cargo was passed from hand to hand and from city to city in an unbroken chain. The further it had to travel the more valuable it became.

-If we travelled a month further west we might double its value for there would be fewer hands taking their cut. But we would double our risk and double our time travelling. Short journey, acceptable profit and low risk make a merchant happy. Their mouths moved in unison though the sound only issued from one. He had heard his father say much the same. It seemed to him that he himself was on the longest journey, taking the greatest risk for perhaps no profit at all. He said so.

They were seated around a screened fire. The women had blankets around their shoulders.

-What is your journey? they asked.

-To gain knowledge. To understand who I am. Why I am. What purpose directs my life. The clarity of his words surprised him. He was saying what he knew to be true but had never spoken aloud.

-Do not think that by travelling you will gain more understanding. If that were the truth of it merchants would be the wisest people in the world. It is more likely that merchants travel in order not to think about such questions. To escape them. After all there are those that stay alone in one place to become wise. They shun the world and other people.

-Indeed, I met one such, he replied.

-Purpose! You are right. That is the question, she intoned, -The more gods you have, the easier this question is to answer. This made her laugh and her two listeners follow suit silently, -But if you have no god –

-Have you no god? He leant forward, fixing them with his gaze.

-Not with us! But we trade gods wherever we travel. Giving one for another. We always accept the preferred god of each tribe along with the preferred food and drink.

-So what is your answer to the question of purpose?

-The more you search the less you find. Purpose will pay you a visit when you stop thinking about it. Be content with small victories. Serve others, such as returning this gold haired child to her tribe.

The following morning he gave them a little precious metal and they gave him medicines, herbs and spices, explaining the preparation and uses of each. He took more honey cake for the child and some colouring powders for her face and arms. Lastly he acquired a small hand mirror made from polished metal. With it they gave him a length of brown silk. It was so fine that it wrapped into a tiny bundle. It was sewn in the shape of a hermit's habit, -It will be your salvation, she said cryptically, -One day you will wear it to quell hordes from east and west before they shed the blood of thousands.

As they were preparing to leave the speaker said, -We spoke not in jest. Do not look beyond each succeeding purpose which befalls you. Be content to see each to a conclusion. Live for others with all your will and in this way the purpose of purposes will be revealed.

In the early morning light, watched intently by the girl, they coloured their faces with their green cream, highlighted their mouths with a dark red powder applied with tongue-wetted brushes and blackened their eyebrows and lashes with carbon sticks. When ready they bowed and took to their horses.

☥

The girl loved her gifts. He allowed her some time to paint flowers on her arms and then gestured that they must leave but she insisted that he attend to her face. He did it studiously and slowly with her disconcertingly wide eyes staring up into his unblinkingly. When he finished he realised he had made her look like a woman.

She rested against his chest as they rode, her hair brushing his mouth now and then. He felt a surge of protectiveness and wondered whether this was the same as purpose. He had only felt this once before with the nomad girl. But even then this was protectiveness of a new sort. It was immediate and limited. Perhaps the Spice Merchants were right. Nothing could now happen in his own story until this child's story was complete. He had strayed into her tale.

The women had given him good directions, mixing stars, sun and landmarks to orientate him. These he had repeated to his roan with the great stallion nodding its head nearby as if it knew what he was saying, too. Since it was only two days to the tribe, there was little fear of thirst. The journey might be even shorter if they met outriders and he could hand the girl over.

It proved an uneventful day. They had to conceal themselves on two occasions to allow travellers to pass. The roan had shown no concern but he had no wish for contact. That evening he painted the girl's face so that she looked like a third spice merchant. He showed her the decoration in the hand mirror. She had looked at herself soberly for some time, her eyes moving from detail to detail, then she smiled suddenly and stood up to do a small mime for him. He was entranced. Somehow she was able to convey in every mannerism the coquettish, abrupt little movements of the spice twins.

When sleep took her later he sat nearby and gazed into the stars as though they floated in deep water. The vast sparkling ocean failed to communicate any meaning.

As the sun reached its highest point the next day, they took shelter away from the trail under an arch of the pink rock. The girl took it upon herself to go through the food bag to see what he may have been given by the merchants. His eye was momentarily distracted by a movement close to her, accompanied by a quiet snort from the roan.

-Still! he commanded softly but with an adult's menace. She froze, recognising the imminence of danger. A snake was within striking range of her. The man was unarmed. He had given her his knife to cut the dried meat. The snake raised itself. All was still. The girl, the horses, the man. He focused on the snake's head, his mind reaching out, drawing its attention to him. It looked into his eyes. He held it there as though his mind was a gripping hand. Their eyes were tied by an invisible yet indestructible filament. Slowly he moved towards the creature as if reeling in a connecting thread. Time passed slowly. He came close enough for the creature to strike him. Gradually he bent on his knees. His eyes and the snake's were at the same level. The amber orbs were large. His own were inviting spheres of silvery grey.

Images came to him. Hunting men with long sticks and knives, pinning, cutting, decapitating. Fear and a slithering headlong flight to holes in the ground, in rocks. To be pursued relentlessly.

-We will not cause you any harm. We are not of that kind.

The oval head shivered and the eyes broke contact. It swayed, gazing from the girl to him and then it dropped to the ground and slipped away. Sensing the change the girl turned and watched its unhurried departure.

-Bad! She mimed being bitten and dying immediately. He nodded but mused on the experience. He had developed an affinity for the snake in the same way he had had with the big cat and which he had always had with the roan. He had the power of entry. So far this had always been at a point of crisis. Did it have to be?

187

☥

The roan communicated a warning. It stiffened as they walked through the wasteland. Then it turned and they hid in the rocks and waited. The sun had moved through half its falling when finally he could see them individually in their dust cloud. There was a scout leading bent over his horse's neck, looking left and right. The man seemed not to be focusing on the trail but where someone might have parted from it.

He was startled when the girl shouted and ran past him waving her arms. He drew his throwing knife and took a short sword from its scabbard. The men caught sight of her and yelled in response, quickening their horses down the trail. As they reached her, one bent and swept her on to his saddle. The horses stopped and jostled. He could see the jabbering man and the girl, the pointing fingers to where he waited, the constant signs of affection. He put his weapons back.

☥

He did not know how often he had to repeat to the girl via a clan interpreter that he couldn't stay with them and wait until she was old enough to be his woman. Her father and mother were amused but indulged her with serious expressions of support. He had to dance with her and she used her colours to look even more like a woman than as a result of his own crude handiwork. He was treated to a feast that night and slept well into the next day. He left their encampment after many speeches and signs of friendship. They made him a gift of a well balanced bow and arrows built from dovetailed woods and bone. The bow was powerful and took great strength to flex it. The arrows were tipped with metal. It was altogether an advance on his hunting bow.

Kamil laid down the final page of the chapter and allowed his gaze to meet that of the Princess. He felt much more at ease in her presence now though he would never be able or wish to eradicate the core of deference he felt towards her. The veneer of a headstrong, selfish young woman seemed to be peeling from her, revealing warmer empathic depths.

-Tell me the meaning of The Hanged Man?

-It is when you have no recourse but to suffer the current phase of your life though it may give you great pain. You are a victim of circumstance, even a noble victim.

-Ah, I see. The father must stay with his mother. The son must return the child. I know many like this. All are servants! Not for them the luxury of choice. Khawlah the Mute was stuck at this card once her tongue was removed. I am glad we no longer practise such obscenities. After this I will bring her into my service. Then she may move on. What is the next card?

-Death.

-Ayee!

-It is not as it appears.

She fell into deep thought.

-There are few that do not pass through all these phases, murmured Kamil.

-I am like the Magus. I must occupy myself with my own journey. My father loves me but he still dotes on my stepmother and is oblivious of the threat she carries. He is too familiar with her ways. He cannot see to my interests. It is not a journey saving pretty young girls but it is a fight with a usurper. Perhaps when all is done I will travel like the two women and understand the subtleties of trade. But for the moment the cards must be turned, one by one! Which leads me to your adventure of today. I will not embarrass you with jibes concerning your burgeoning desire for Baligha, the Harlot Queen. He winced, - Secretly however it pleases me, for just as I learn and change under your tutelage, so do you under mine!

Kamil could not suppress the red heat of his cheeks even though his voice was steady.

-My mind had come to that conclusion too your Highness. He continued after a pause, -Baligha had one further fibre to add to our cloth. Aidah received a note from our suspect. He said he was being followed and could not visit for the time being. His wife had sent spies out after him, he said.

-It does not lead back to us, his suspicion?

-Who knows, replied Kamil, thoughtfully, -Has he a wife far away? Could she do this? We know so little of him.

Chapter Fourteen

Celebrate your death and treat it as your last

The day had been spent in the Great Library. Kamil alternated between reviewing his assignations with Baligha and scripts relating to court intrigue. Whilst drowning himself in the scents and images of the former he managed a cool detachment regarding the latter. Could any life be better lived than enjoying the sweet foolishness of love and the cool surgical detachment of scholarship? Whilst his meeting with Baligha had been public and proper to a degree, notwithstanding the intimacy of their arms, perhaps even appearing to the undiscerning eye as sister and brother or even man and wife rather than aspiring lovers, their private words contained deeper feelings and delightful possibilities. He would take her for his wife as soon as he had discharged his duties to the Emperor's daughter. Then a cold tremor wracked him. The court was a labyrinth inhabited by the powerful from which it may be impossible to escape and Baligha had made it plain that she would not live within its confines. He hoped the Princess's spies would fasten their claws quickly upon the man they pursued so that he might soon be relieved of his service to live with Baligha outside the palace walls.

*

Princess Sabiya meanwhile met ambassadors, organised her diary with her Private Secretary and had enjoyed a steam bath with two close friends.

-What is the matter with you? one had asked.

-You have become so serious! had said the other.

-Education, she replied, -I am following the path of the Magus. They had stared at her and then each other, mystified.

*

Kamil read a gripping history of his own empire which in earlier times stretched from the northern deserts of Africa to the beginning of the ice plains, from the east of Russia to the rich Uzbek soils and whose court contained the royal families from all those conquered races. It was as though a golden village had been created of chosen people, where the variety of skin, face, height and shape was as great as could be imagined. Kamil explored further this history and came across an extract that chilled and thrilled him simultaneously:

Of all the families of great lineage present at the Court, the most prized young women for concubines to the Emperor are those unique daughters that issue from the warlords of Ethiopia. Their blue black skin recall the night, their piercing blue eyes, twin daggers, their tall long-limbed grace the deer of the plains and their fertility, legendary. Notwithstanding all these gifts, their intelligence in the ways of Man are unparalleled. Combining an acute and ruthless execution of justice with the wiles and charms that disarm even their greatest foes, they are formidable opponents. Be warned. To become close to them is to cohabit with Death.

*

It was a worried and crestfallen Princess Sabiya who entered the private rooms of Kamil. Without explanation she sank in her chair and turned over the next card. -Of course, it had to be Death! I remember. How apt. See the heads rolling under his scythe? But you say there is more comfort in this Tale than meets the eye. A mere crumb would give me solace! Read!

He left quietly without fuss. When the girl awoke she would find a ring he had carried for her from the Spice Merchants. They had told him that it was a ring of memories. It was made from beaten metal and small stones glittered from their settings in it. He hoped that she would remember him even when she became an old woman. For him these were new feelings, strange and beyond his power to control. He compared them to those he felt for his desert woman. These were for someone for whom he felt a fatherly kinship. The woman was his equal and a warrior and the prospective mother of his children. He did not need to protect. He just wanted to be with her. But their babies would make him swim again in these new feelings. Every day. Stronger. And what of the other one in the City in the Mountain? Again he felt a stirring.

☥

The ache of leaving the girl stayed with him, twitching at his stomach. He gripped the roan tightly with his heels and it responded by trotting, its knowing head held high and its ears bending to catch his thoughts. The new black stallion followed obediently, accepting the roan's lead as it had done from the beginning. Before the sun had cleared the low hills ahead of them they had moved far beyond the wider borders of the girl's tribe. He ignored a trail north when they came to a fork and continued to head into the source of the sun. It was a small decision but the first he had made which had not been forced upon him by person or circumstance.

Their direction was taking them away from the desert and the land of red rock and soil. The risen sun was still casting long fingers of shadow towards them. Sparse shrub and small crooked trees were scattered across the rolling landscape. Now and then birds rose shrieking and chattering into the air. These few sounds made him realise how silent the desert had been. Save for the wind. It was a harsh place for a tribe to live yet the girl's ancestors had been there for generations. Why did people make these choices? For desert people lush valleys and rivers and forest might seem too soft and cloying. For the valley people of the north the desert was a fearful place. Apart from tribal lords who wished to extend their territory, only merchants and traders moved across the changing terrain with a willingness to explore and even indulge in the qualities of both. A thought came to him. Why hadn't he considered it before? His woman of the desert, would she be happy to travel with him to the lands of the north, far away from the bare red rocks and the inhospitable earth?

His vision turned inward and he saw her in her tent again resting on his shoulder. Her animal strength had been stilled and her black eyes closed. She had known what to do and had taken him on their first journey to physical pleasure as if it was second nature to her even though her blood flowed and there were moments of pain. Then he remembered her lids opening. She had whispered, -When you come back for me it will be for us to truly know each other. You will leave me again but it is our fate and I can accept it. I will be at your side even though you may be far away. Her black eyes and her bronzed features were earnest and committed. They had kissed and kissed, sealing their vows.

He had not considered it then but it would be a heavy burden for her to leave the sands.

He woke up suddenly and was on his feet in a moment, something he had practised hard after experiencing how much faster his father could become alert. But it was nothing outside him that had awoken him. The two horses stood facing him, the roan curious. Had he been dreaming? It infuriated him that some dreams would remain elusive whilst others were as open as swinging doors. He walked forward and stroked the long foreheads. His back felt cold and clammy and his neck seemed locked. Then the dream burst back upon him and he was in it again.

His father the Merchant was murmuring a farewell to his dying mother. He was bent forward clasping her bird-like hands in his strong fingers. Her eyes were fixed on her son. They seemed to glow very brightly for an instant and then were emptied of light. Her eyes closed and her thin arms relaxed. His father stood up and said farewell with a gesture of love, his hand on his heart and then he turned to face his far distant, younger son-not-of-blood as though he knew that he was a witness.

-I will see to my mother's last journey and attend to our business matters. Then, when the time is ready, I will set out to meet you in the valleys where you rode to me as a baby.

☥

How long he stood stroking the horses' soft nostrils he did not know. The closeness with his father was as immediate and vibrant as though he was standing next to him. His sympathy and sadness had flowed into the older man, comforting him but also celebrating his being with his mother when she died.

He withdrew grudgingly from the dream and involuntarily rubbed his jaw. For the first time he was truly aware that the soft down on his chin had given way to the rougher bristle of manhood. His hair had not been cut since the beginning of the long journey. Increasingly, he had to tie it back in a tail with waxed string. He had continued to grow taller and broader so that few men would be able to look him levelly in the eye. With his darkened skin and pale eyes, none forgot him after a first meeting.

He saw to the horses but did not yet eat. First he practised with the sword and knife. He moved with speed in lunges and spins, somersaulting, rolling, leaping and falling. He repeated where he felt there was a better performance to be gained until finally he was satisfied. Only then did he sit down and take bread and dried meat. It seemed to him that he was slipping into a dream again yet this time it was not to see his father. Instead there was a blankness, a hazy curtain that swayed before his eyes. He seemed to move into it until he was submerged as though in a cloud on a mountain.

-A fine show! You are a man of great skill! He whirled round. He could see no-one. He concentrated and then slowly out of the mist appeared a shape. It was a long brown wraith.

-How did you creep into my mind? He was calm and his hand strayed towards his throwing knife.

-I am your death's attendant. It is my way. His eyes tried to probe beneath the stranger's hood but its eyes seemed to melt away as he was about to fasten on them. And the voice? Was it male or female? -I am always here if you practise the gift of seeing. There was something incorporeal about the shape. It stood, unmoving at its core but wavering at its edges, as one might see a desert figure in a heat vapour. Yet now it seemed certainly female. The young man sat down, beginning to doubt if this was a dream and the truth was that he was beside his horses and a real mist had fallen on him.

-Would you like to share some food?

-I have no need of it, the attendant mocked in a soft voice. Its head bowed so that it was totally obscured by the cowl. The young man rubbed his forehead. He knew he had been staring at the stranger's face, trying to meet her eyes but try as he might he had not been able to discern it.

Finally he asked, -Why are you here?

-You are fortunate we are able to converse. Only a few are born like you. A long life awaits. You will dance with death as though you have a charmed life. But every existence is at the cost of those not so fortunate, not so blessed. For every death you survive someone will die in your place. Death is unremitting. It is greedy. Lives are its fuel. The cloaked figure's head raised. The cowl slipped back to reveal momentarily a wild female countenance that changed rapidly under his stare, becoming featureless. Her voice repeated for emphasis, -As you enact the purpose of your life to become a magus, a man of knowledge, others must die.

-How many such deaths? he asked.

-You are unfearing. A man made of metal would have become molten at this meeting. You are made of the hardest crystal, able to cut through terror and withstand much that is of this earth. But beware, such crystal has a heart line, a fault that sunders if struck truly.

-This would not be a blow from a weapon.

-No. Of course. The blow will not pierce your body but will nevertheless mark your mortality.

-Those that must die in my place, will they be at my own sword? he asked, dispassionately.

-It is the way.

-How many? A coldness entered him. A sudden precognition of his destiny.

-This many. In a movement that could be comprehended and yet could not be seen, the spirit appeared behind him and took a handful of the end hairs from his tail and cut them. The wraith threw the hairs in the air and they floated away in the shimmering cloud.

-How many do you think?

-I could not count them.

-You will kill until you have reached the allotted number. Men, women and children. It matters not.

-Women and children? And if I do not?

The figure shook her head, -You have no choice. It is your path. You have the power of one who will know when it is done. When you were young did you not abandon the villagers of your childhood in the very tragedy of their massacre?

-Yes

-Have you mourned since?

-No. He was sombre.

-It is your destiny to be a man who balances all things.

-I would not kill -

-Except with justifiable cause. I know. You apply this belief to bird, fish, animal and man, alike. We will work well together.

-We?

-I am forever at your shoulder. When in battle wear the occult brown cloth that the handmaidens gave you. It will be your sign. All will come to know it. It will aid the writing of your legend.

The apparition vanished. There was silence. The mist lifted and he seemed to jerk awake.

He walked over to the roan and took the cloak from a bag under the saddle. He let it fall its full silken length. He smelled it and rubbed it between his thumb and fingers. There was no smell of spices, nothing to betray its original maker, its origins or its purpose. The wind blew gently. The earth was hot under the sun, the horses waited patiently and he held the length of material which now floated like a magician's cloak. He tried it on. Despite the heat and its colour, the dark material seemed perversely to create a cool shade, a detachment from the world. His mind became exaggeratedly focused as though stripped of all emotion. He saw one aspect of his journey with a strange clarity, a cycle of events from birth to death and for the sole purpose of extending his bloodline. It was blood that flowed unceasingly through time, coursing from parent to child to child's child. Each tribe sought to preserve and protect this flow even, when necessary, through the very spilling of it! And he knew he was no different. He slipped off the cloak and the sun's heat struck him. His thoughts turned immediately to his desert woman, his father, the girl, his own mother-of-the-dream and many others that he had met on his long journey south. He was swamped with a sense that they were all calling out to him, beseeching him to return to them. He slipped the cloak over his shoulders and he was a solitary man with a stilled mind again.

☥

It was late the same day with only a little riding ahead when the roan slowed to a walk, its nostrils twitching, its ears circling. It pulled off the trail and took them up a small, shrub covered hill and stopped in a clump of stunted grey trees. Finally, his eyes picked out what had concerned the horse. Tiny flashes of familiar bright colours caught his eye. There was dust from an encampment and smoke from fires being lit. The lack of discretion suggested a large group of fighting men. He left the horses and set off on foot, keeping to the shrubbery. He had both knife and sword. The brown cloak fluttered about him and helped him remain a little concealed in the shadows cast by the setting sun. He moved quickly, enjoying the extra exertion of staying silent on an earth littered with dry twigs and leaves. It was nearly dark when he lay at the edge of the firelight.

☥

A group of mercenaries were eating, unaware that their look-out was lying in a pool of his own blood, his fat throat opened like a ripe fruit. Tied in the firelight were the two Spice Merchants. They had torn, bloody underclothes. Their colourful dresses and coats were thrown over the branches of a tree. The youth's mind recoiled with the barbarity of what had been done to them. He experienced horrible flashes of empathy at his own body being torn, ravaged and brutally penetrated. All inside him became a raging red sea.

One of the men rose and walked up to the women. He stopped and laughed. He took out his thickened manhood and urinated on them, waving it to increase the spray. All they could do was turn away their heads in silence. The others looked on and laughed too. Another stood up and began undoing his breeches, in turn. The crash of his comrade's body stopped him. It lay before the twins, its legs twitching, a knife protruding from its back. The remaining men rose uncertainly and stared fearfully into the dark, their swords drawn.

He threw stones so that they clattered around them, first on one side and then on the other. Meanwhile he moved swiftly in the darkness around the fire until he was just behind the twins. With a quick slash of his knife he cut them free and pressed them behind him. One of the bandits shouted and they aligned themselves, facing him, aware of his brown cloaked strangeness. They were mercenaries. Their clothes were of fair quality and their swords were well crafted. It would have been hard for any normal man to withstand them and they would know this as any winged killer knows its defenceless prey. But, despite it they stood like statues. He could have taken the women and slipped away. They would not have followed for they seemed frozen with the suddenness of his intervention. He stepped into the full light of the fire, the brown cloak billowing around him, his face in shadow and then, as their eyes widened, he was among them like a fearsome cat in a domestic herd. There was a brief fury of crimson rain when he seemed to move faster than thought itself and their bodies lay, spilling blood, on the earth.. He cleaned his sword on their garments and turned to see the Spice Merchants pulling their clothes from the tree.

☥

They had set up camp some way from the dead. The roan and its companion had answered his whistle. Using water from the mercenaries' bags the two women cleaned themselves. He fed them. They would not think of sleep and hurried so that they might ride on through the night. Nor would they talk about their suffering but he could see the pain in their eyes, though he could also see that this was not the first time men had acted thus against them. Instead, he talked about the girl and her return to her tribe. Finally he told them of his dream of the brown cloaked female wraith and how he had been instructed to wear the robe they themselves had given him. They looked at him without fear or awe.

-You are a powerful warrior, they said, -Soon a magus. Only such a man may wear the cloth. We understood that this might be so. We carried that robe over the years knowing it would one day save us. It was written.

He considered this in silence. A magus? What powers did he have? The crude magic of the fairground. Skill with weapons. A certain bond with animals. An ungovernable ability to be awake in dreams. This did not make him a shaman even though he felt that he was becoming a man apart.

-We can do something for you, they said. He looked at their faces and saw how old they were for the first time. Perhaps fifty years. Yet when painted and with their soft grace, they could be any age.

-It is not much, they said, -Turn round. Your dream has left a faint white line across the hairs of your tail. It is like a stripe in a bird's feathers. They divided the waxed ends of his hair and began counting. When they had finished, the speaker said, -There were two hundred and six hairs. According to your vision, two hundred more will die. Exactly.

- So I will live beside death so much of my life? Can this be so?

-Yours will be a life worth witnessing! They painted each other's face in the firelight and then left taking the men's horses and their stuffed saddlebags for trade.

☥

The rain woke him. He had sensed it coming and had covered his blanket with a light skin. Spatters of raindrops fell on him from the branches above. The horses stood bowed enjoying the cool downpour. He rose and bound up his bedding. He remembered no dreams and felt properly refreshed. There were six corpses lying not too far away. How did he feel? He could not discern a twinge of guilt at what he had done. His father had taught him to kill only in defence or for food and to offer a prayer to the oneness of all things for those that died at his hands. Had he killed in defence? He thought that he had not. The men would have fled if he had given them time. Their fear of the cloak had made them defenceless.

-May you go on your last journey cleansed, he said, closing his eyes and with his hand on his heart. But he had no thought of burying them. In a world of oneness the deaths of six men could mean an extension of life for whatever fed upon them.

He touched his young beard. He had become a man as he lay between the thighs of the daughter of a desert chief. Older when he left his father. Older still having taken the lives of these kidnappers and rapists. Through these events he had become different. He had become a warrior.

He needed to talk further with his death's attendant. In many tribes under the full sweep of the sun such a creature was known as a life-taker. In his own valleys the life-taker was believed to be a man with a horse and cart. The horse was blind and the man was deaf so that he could not hear the cries of those wanting to cling on to existence. His father had told him of other life-takers. In some tribes it was a young woman who sang such sweet songs that she seduced the spirits of the dying so that they sought her company for eternity. There was a boatman on an underground lake who carried the dead to a world beyond. There was an inhaler in a cloud who settled around the dying and sucked out their spirits through their noses and mouths and holes drilled by priests for this purpose in their foreheads. For most tribes there was a further world beyond this one. For a few there was a world within this one that could not be seen. He knew of none like himself who needed proof that such worlds existed. It was more likely that, with death, the spirit tipped into a void so deep that it could never return. He had become used to not accepting any tribal story as truth. This had sometimes caused conflict with his father who believed that every individual died, rejoining the oneness only to return again as another life whether it be man, animal, plant, bird or fish. Why? he had asked. Why not? Had replied his father testily. When you find me a better explanation of how things are then we will talk further.

Were there many life-takers or was there only one who had a sorcerer's power to be everywhere, each time conjuring up a shape drawn from a tribe's imaginings? Would he be able to see the creature again through his own will or only when it wished him to do so? And how was it that this occult being seemed able to cast its mind across his life, from childhood to its eventual ending, just like a god?

⚥

Horses and man had been following the direction of the sun's rising position in steady rain. It was warm and hardly uncomfortable. The vegetation was becoming less sparse with some stretches of mixed grasses while the trees were straighter and taller with lighter leaves. They were able to stop at new pools for the horses to drink and graze and for the man to chew on dried fruit and his remaining meat.

That evening he resolved to set a trap. His body craved fresh flesh.. He took a length of leather strapping and made a running noose. Studying the ground for a trail he hung the noose from the branch of a bush. There were scattered droppings and faint paw prints, running through a narrow gap. He skirted this point in a wide circle until he was some distance behind it. He waited for a while, his ears tuned to all sounds and then he moved forward making some noise but not enough to scatter his prey in all directions. He heard scampering and calls of alarm among birds. When he got to the noose, it clung round a small writhing animal. A quick twist of his hands took its life. He touched his heart and then carried the game to his camp to skin and gut it. He had made bars of compressed fat and straw to start fires on wet days such as this. Searching, he found dry twigs under leaves beneath the trees and bushes. As they burned larger sticks and branches dried out above them, covered by a skin stretched to shelter them. It made a lot of smoke but the rain was clearing it as it rose. He turned the plump meat on a spit. The rain was unceasing but he had always had the capacity to separate himself from the elements.

The taste was good. He ate half the carcass and wrapped the rest for the next day. The horses were happy grazing and he stroked them both before settling in his blanket with the now-warm skin covering him. He felt at ease, pleasantly full and dropped instantly to sleep. At some point in the night the life-taker re-appeared.

-So, she said, -You have killed six and the merchants have told you how many more lives you must bring to an end! I said you would come to know it!

He viewed the featureless face, -Are you a god?

-Are there such things?

-I don't know. I think not.

-Then there cannot be gods.

-What are you?

-I am a part of you. My form has been chosen by you to lead you on your final journey. This is how you will want me to appear at the end. For some such as your father's mother, who left life a few suns ago there was a high priest in white robes. For a child it could have been a furry creature such as you have just eaten. For your six victims their attendant came as half-man, half-beast with horns and tail. For you I am the great She, risen from the earliest past. No, you are not one that seeks a god but one who wishes to collect the lessons of life and from them construct its great purpose.

-My purpose!

-Indeed, whispered the creature.

-Why must I kill to satisfy you?

-It is not for me. It is to satisfy yourself. Your destiny. It is laid out before you and you will know it in time. No-one will stop you from taking lives on your great quest except yourself. Now you must think about each event and act and understand its meaning. Life always dances within the embrace of death. To know this is now a part of your being.

-What is death?

-I cannot answer what you do not yet know. I am your inner companion only. What you find inside you is for us both to discover. It is from the unknown that you have emerged. It awaits your return with patience. The tree ends its cycle because of axe, fire, flood or age. The animal you killed for your night's meal may die at the hands of hunter or of disease or old age. At the moment of parting you cease to be and become other. You were other before life. You will be other after it.

-It is not to be feared! The youth said it with conviction.

-It is not. But many fear it as if it were their own shadow with its hand on their throats. The six men you killed feared it so much that their eyes were closed as they left on their final journey.

-You will be my attendant at death.

-I am your shadow. How could it be otherwise? I will be there when your assassin comes and you will not resist his thrust.

-My eyes will not be shut.

One thing that you have taught me Kamil is that I can no longer imagine that each day is a blank page to be written on as the whim takes me. I am not talking of my diary of duties but of life itself, the book I thought I made up as I went along. Now, I realise that life is also filled with instalments of a greater story that embraces my tale. I must attend continually to it so that in the few blank lines available to me, I may insinuate enough to affect the disposition of the next and succeeding pages. The Magus may embrace fate and death as an equal but not I. Yet your Tales of the Magus allows me my crumb. We dance with events and occasionally we are left still spinning, wiser, as they seat themselves for a while. We cannot control everything nor know everything. Just as news may drag us down, further news may lift us up again. That Wheel of Fortune! She held the latest card in her hand, - And here, Death. It is literally so, Kamil. Our suspect Rafi is dead. Murdered.

-It is so? Kamil's eyes betrayed his anxiety but he kept his voice steady and dispassionate, -Why does it not surprise me? There are layers of intrigue far below any we have so far seen. Come. Let us focus. Tell me all you know. His very death may point us forward if we can read the true nature of its importance. It is rare for any crime to leave no trace of the circumstances of its happening.

-His wife is travelling here, I am told. The body is in a holding chamber.

-How did she come to know?

-Information on his person. His actual name was Askari. Rafi was one he assumed when he was here. Her home is two days away. They sent for her. He was our road to truth. Her disappointment made her tone dull and expressionless.

He mused in a quiet voice, -Perhaps the body should be examined by a good doctor? As well as the place of its discovery.

She raised herself, -What are you thinking in that scholar's mind, historian?

-I have read in the many documents of China several treatises on the recovery of the last hours of life as imprinted on the body and its surroundings.

-I do not understand you. Are you talking of magic? Is a brown robed figure to appear and whisper truths to us? But she had begun to show signs of animation again, looking sharply upon his face.

-Just as the Magus retrieved the arrowhead and understood that there had been an attempt of a different kind on the life of the Emperor... Who knows? Have you a doctor you can trust? I will accompany him if so. Now.

She jumped to her feet, -You have become a man of action! I have. He is devoted and loyal. Even my father is jealous of him, saying that he would not reveal my secrets even to an emperor!

-Then shall we try this path?

-We shall historian. And now there is a second, bigger crumb of comfort. She was returning to her old self, -I will have my men seek out the information that rested on his body and what his wife said when she came to be informed. Perhaps she arranged his death. But the greater likelihood is that the Empress had reason to be anxious that he would lead us to her. My spirits are raised suddenly by the potential of his corpse. The offhand way she said this disturbed Kamil, as usual, but he suppressed his misgivings.

*

While he was waiting for the doctor to arrive Kamil pondered on his life's latest twists and turns. He felt entirely different. More alive. It was strange. Words, ideas, suggestions, hypotheses fell from his mouth in an increasing spate. His old one-paced studious path through the world had become a network of continual alternatives. As his Princess had said, blank parts in each day's page were now to be filled and he was freer than her to pursue them. Nor had he the great embracing story of the empire subordinating him, filling most of his pages. He was taking his lead from the Magus, putting the years of his investment in learning to the practical test.

He would examine the body. He was used to the sight of corpses. It was common enough for villagers to die from accidents, quarrels, disease. He had grown up with it. Even now in the city bodies floated in the river each day or lay, in the morning, outside the smoking dens. Yet, of course, he had never touched one. But the thought energised him. He was aware of a force that drew him forward into the unknown. The desire to act. To grasp the unpredictable. His senses raised their nerve endings in anticipation, his mind constantly flickered across a terrain of possibilities.

A discrete tap at his door announced the arrival of the doctor who introduced himself as Faqi. Within moments Kamil found that he liked and trusted him. He was a cultivated, grey haired man, some ten years older than himself, with gentle eyes and a soft voice.

-We have an interesting challenge from her Highness, Faqi ventured, soberly.

-I am sure we can meet it, replied Kamil confidently.

-I have the instruments of life - Faqi raised a leather bag - let us hope they reveal the picture of death.

-How was he killed?

-The report suggests he was knifed but said little else. Let us investigate. Mm? We have a guard outside who will lead us where we must go.

*

In a windowless room smelling acridly of lime wash and lit by lamps filled with oil laced with lemon extract, lay the long body of a man in the raiment of a palace guard. His eyes were open and creamily white. His face was abraded by dirt. A small patch of blood stained his midriff. At his head stood a guard with belted pistol and scabbarded sword.

-Where's the knife? asked Faqi.

-Taken by the killer we assume Doctor, replied the guard.

-Hm, let's cut off his clothes then. Kamil watched as the body was peeled like a fruit. It revealed an incision to the stomach. Faqi studied it, placed a thin taper of wood in it and pressed. It sank barely a thumbnail's depth. He examined the rest of what was visible and then they turned the body over. There were no further marks. The Doctor took an angled mirror, had a torch brought close and peered around the mouth. Finally, he stood up and nodded to the guard. -Put a cloth over him. His wife will collect him with clothes for his pyre.

*

Another city guard led them to the alleyway where the body had been found. Telling him to wait out of earshot, Faqi and Kamil entered the shadowy cleft between the two buildings.

-What did you discover? asked Kamil.

-His tongue was swollen and blackening. His teeth had a green powder along the gum line. His eyes were clouded. Poisoned. He was knifed later just after he had died. Why? What difference should that make? Mm?

-Someone felt that poison would raise a greater suspicion?

-Exactly. Knowledge of quick acting poisons is not given to everyone. Certain plants. Certain minerals. Certain subtle combinations. Some brought here from distant lands. There is only one merchant who can trade such substances by the Emperor's decree. To be in possession without authorisation is to lose one's hands.

They searched the alleyway. The dust had been trampled by the feet of guards collecting the body and searching for the knife. It was Kamil's fertile mind that led them to their next clue. A small stain showed where the body had lain face down, just inside the shadows. Hoof marks had churned a circle at the alleyway's entrance. He surmised that the body had been dumped hurriedly at this point which accounted for the marks on the man's face. He pictured a possible stain on a saddlecloth. He searched the ground along the edges of the churn marks. A tiny glimmer of colour caught his eye. It was a small feather, curled and dyed green.

*

Like lovers deferring the potent phase of intimacy, the Princess and the historian talked about the picture of death on the card she had turned. It was later that evening and he was seated in a small room leading to her chambers, -Did the card refer to the man's death, Kamil?

-To many things of which this would be the least important. Rather that there is an end in sight to part of the cycle that binds us. A new beginning perhaps. A new force to guide us.

-Appropriate, was all she would say.

-Death is an end and a beginning. Winter precedes spring. We end a phase in our lives and a new one emerges from the remnants of the old.

-It is hard to see anything positive in death but I will try. Come, we both have much to tell. Faqi my dear doctor, is much impressed with you!

-And I him. He would die for you of that there is no doubt. Kamil described the events of the day, corroborating all that she had already heard from Faqi. She picked the feather up from his open palm and turned it over in her fine, polished black fingers so that it seemed to dance with sudden life. Finally she gripped it between thumb and forefinger and held it up triumphantly.

-Muez! He wears a cloak embroidered with just such feathers.

-Have his saddle and saddle cloth checked for blood stains.

-That may be difficult, Muez is the Empress's nephew. His horse will be stabled with elite guards. But there are ways....

*

Sabiya told her news in turn. An outrider had met Iffat on her journey and questioned her. She knew little of the happenings in the court. She had not sent spies to follow her husband but he had been away for some time with only the occasional message. All she knew was that he was working for a very powerful person. One of the most powerful. What did her husband do? He was a mercenary soldier. She had always worried about his activities. Also she feared he still visited brothels even though he had promised her that this had ceased.

After relaying this, Sabiya smiled savagely at Kamil, And following Dr Faqi's report of your activities in the holding room, my cousin went straightway to the apothecary. A poison had been requisitioned yesterday by a guard named T'ariq. He bore an official stamp from the Emperor's household. No-one knows how. Another temporarily stolen seal I should guess. All the food tasters are in full employment. The Empress has now insisted upon it, fearing for the safety of her husband. It is a strange convergence, historian. My cousin is searching for this T'ariq. We appear to be living in times as dangerous and challenging as those of the Magus. The book entwines with us. And our card was Death!

Chapter Fifteen

The stilled spirit will choose the right path

It had been a fitful sort of day, the second day of abstinence from Baligha. Their relationship felt as though it was suspended from the ceiling of the high vaulted palace dome, a glittering ball of faceted glass, far beyond reach. She had arrested the dry decline of his life and suffused him with a coursing stream of hope. For the first time since those days of apprenticeship in the Emperor's library, he felt hope. Then, he had fantasised about the infinite adventures which lay before him in the written word only recently to realise that these were the words of other lives lived, not his own. Now there was Baligha.

For the moment however, the days, hours and minutes had to be lived with absolute and equal concentration or the future might be lost through blindness to dangerously evolving circumstances.

*

The only news I have, said Princess Sabiya, -Is that Doctor Faqi has confirmed that the poison requisitioned from the apothecary is the one that killed Askari, regal stamp and all. My adversary Muez has not been seen in the city for several days. A well-constructed alibi don't you think? It has been broadcast that he is on a trading trip to the southern continent. But there is no proof of course. It is more likely that he is hidden in his aunt's rooms. Nothing from Khawlah though she has orders to try to uncover him. Nothing from my silky net of spies. Everything is silent, waiting.

-Let us hope it does not presage a storm!

-A storm would mean action! she retorted severely. She laughed at him, -You fear the turmoil of events because you cannot order them and file them. You are drowned by them. I am a fighter! These are the conditions in which I prevail! It was a flash of the Princess he first knew.

-Your security is better served by order rather than chaos, he almost whispered, lamely.

She ignored him and turned a card, -Hah! I might have guessed, you have groomed me for the next card. Always the teacher. She sat back, - At least it appeals more than the card of death.

Kamil said sagely, -It is true that it is a card that symbolises our current state - but by accident or fate I could not hazard. We have to be patient and wait. Like the spider you once described your mother as being, we hold all the threads of the web and wait for the twitch of the enemy.

-It is purgatory!

He travelled into the sun's rays day after day at a speed which maintained the strength of his horses but covered much terrain. The muscles of man and beast were taut, glistening with the oil of health and pumped with energy. The land was bountiful and there were no obvious places for ambush. There were permanent villages with the surrounding land being farmed for crops or turned over to grazing. The local people showed no interest in him, their eyes sliding over him quickly and then returning to the focus of their chores. Instead of the robes of the south they wore woven jackets and tight leggings. The men covered their heads with black peaked hats with ear flaps.

He had begun to make camp in a circle of trees away from the trail when a deputation arrived. They were local men intent on peace. They spoke another variation of the dialect of these parts. He had picked up enough to communicate.

-Traveller come. Be the guest of our people, said a thickset farmer.

-You are kind. My gratitude. But I live alone. I need not the company of men. His hand covered his heart in thanks.

-Our people want man like you. We know you. Many stories, warrior man. You be our story too. Young people must join their blood. Boys must pass to men. A stranger must witness such things. Such man makes bonds strong.

It was not possible to refuse, -It will be my honour. He redid his saddle bags and led the two horses behind the group as they walked to their village. It was a collection of wood and clay dwellings each large enough to hold at least three generations. The octagonal roofs came to a central point and smoke emerged from each apex. He was taken to the largest. Before he entered he was asked to cover his head. He donned his brown cloak. Inside it was divided into rooms by hanging cloth.

Shortly after, the heavily built farmer came to lead him through two sets of curtains and into the tribal meeting space. A fire burned at its heart and a group of black-hatted men were seated around it on skins. The chief was a fat fellow whose shadowy eyes were largely hidden in folds of flesh. He wore the only red cap. He stepped forward and greeted him by placing one hand on his shoulder and the other on his own heart.

-You will eat in our home?

-It is my honour.

-And ours. Come. Sit. They sat together, separated from the rest of the conversation and were served flat grey bread and a wild fowl stew. While they ate the fat man quizzed him about his journey. He pretended not to know much of the language and told him as little as possible. He did mention the Spice Merchants and their attackers, assuming they had passed this way. They had.

-We hear. You kill many men. The man stared in trepidation.

-They were six.

-You and one sword.

-Yes.

-You, warrior for pay?

-No. Such were these men.

-You child trader?

-No. Traveller.

-What you trade?

-Nothing.

-What you seek? Revenge?

It was difficult to answer this in their language, -To know myself. To know the world. This was incomprehensible to his host whose own life was patterned by the ceaseless seasons and the demands of the earth.

-We know world from traders. You travel alone?

-Yes.

-You have no woman? You have no place?

-I have woman. I have no place.

-You live on trail?

-It is my home.

They sat in further silence. He declined alcohol but took a compressed bar of fruit and honey. There was good natured banter around the fire. Men glanced at him now and then but did not seem

overly interested.
-You will bless blood ties?
-I can stay not beyond one more sun.
-We are ready. We waited for you. Sleep now. After, you tie couples.
You also take the skins of boys. We have five soon to be man.

☥

The roles of doctor and shaman did not trouble him. In the village of his childhood there was such a man. His father respected him. He remembered vividly witnessing him conduct a circumcision. The foreskin stretched and cut and the honey and vinegar paste applied to heal the flesh quickly. The village shaman was methodical and precise. The boys did not cry for to do so would blight their first moments of manhood with an act of weakness. The shaman of his boyhood village also presided over the feasts of union. A woman could be taken for a bride if her family agreed, after her twelfth year. Wealthy men in some of the northern valleys might take three women in union, spacing them out so that there were perhaps five or ten summers between each of them. It was believed that this kept these men young and strong. But in his own clan, unlike the rest of the tribe, only one was permitted.

☥

He arranged his bed in his tent to his liking with his short sword by his side and his throwing knife under his pillow, the flap open so that the villagers could observe him. They showed no surprise at this open show of caution. They expected it of a warrior. For him it was now the way of things. One part of his being, his father had instructed him, must always reach out to the unforeseen. Perhaps because he was to be the binder of couples and the sunderer of childhoods the following day, he began to think of the night he had spent with his desert girl. It was easy for him to imagine slipping inside her waiting body. He forced himself to resist the ache of his hardening member. It came from a fear of losing touch with the sounds and movements of the world around his sleeping place that prevented him.

☥

He awoke with the first steps of a villager somewhere outside the tent. He whistled softly and heard the whinnying responses of the two horses standing on the other side of the canvass. Propping himself against a pole, he prepared for what was expected of him. For the herdsmen, their insulated way of life demanded the chance arrival of a stranger. This man would come and go like a warm wind. The couples who needed his presence would remember little detail save some almost magical scrap of their own myth-making. "We were conjoined by a tall warrior who rode two cunning horses into each day's sun for no other purpose than to journey into fate. He was a powerful man indeed. Not even six armed fighters could withstand his force. A man such as he will pass this way once in many generations. Our children will be blessed by his greatness."

Similarly, as his knife parted the foreskin of the boys, both children and their parents would build a story around the warrior and his skilled surgery. The growing boy would narrate to wide-eyed listeners by the evening fire, "The man who took my skin did so with the knife he used to slit the throat of his enemies. He has passed its power to me."

He took his short weapon from beneath his pillow and began to strop it on the inside of a belt. As he did so he thought about how stories drove tribal custom. From their special ways of making bread to their laws of living together and taking husbands or wives, to the way they would spend their time working through the ceaseless seasons and finally, to their very gods, they would invoke everything in stories passed from elders to children by the fireside and on the knee.

Of all the legends and myths recounted in the firelight, ones concerning the gods were the most perplexing for they bore such little relation to the daily round of earth and air. Why was it that empires and kingdoms dreamt up the divine nature of fantastical beings to whom they would then abase themselves as powerless slaves? It seemed to him that people would rather maintain this state of perpetual subordination to the unknowable than take courage and face the great mystery and unremitting uncertainty of a life without meaning.

A life without belief? Was that to be a summing up of his own existence? His father had once said to him that belief was like food and water, so natural that you could not separate it from life. If so what did he believe? It was hard to find any substance to fill the void in his mind on venturing the question. He believed....he was as other men in most things. Part of him existed in the same world as other men and women. Some other part existed in another realm that stayed stubbornly beyond his apprehension. Yet like a plant that might flower once in many seasons he would glimpse it momentarily. But the moment of his glimpsing would quickly become the moment the petals would fall and it would return again beneath the soil.

His life would follow the same course as any other living thing. He would grow old and die as his life-taker had said, returning to a state of not-being. What then was his purpose? He did not want wilfully to create meaning. He wanted meaning to arise out of the very stones, the plants, the air, the stars. He wanted meaning to infiltrate him from all that existed around him. Then he might come to know why. This could be the only way forward to uncovering purpose.

☥

As he placed his palm on the joined hands of each couple, he said in a priestly voice of invocation, the traditional words;

"Be true to each other and protect
Against those who would seek
The spilling of your blood
And that of your clan"

His voice had a power that led the watching tribesmen to drop their heads and clasp both hands on their hearts. When he stretched tight the tiny foreskins of the boys he looked deep into their eyes in the same way that he did when he took the life of a creature. It was a look of absolute respect for a kindred being.

"The knife cuts away the flesh of the child
Leaving him a man
He must protect the ways of the elders"

The boys stared back and heeded not the sudden pain, their eyes round and clear in awe of him.

He ate well at the feast. No-one approached him save to bring him food and drink. He sensed their desire for him to be gone. Once the tribe were merry and losing their senses he stole away and mounted the roan and with the black stallion following he rode from the village.

A little way down the trail one of the young boys waited, perched on a low branch. -Where do you go?

-I know not.

-Why always face the path of the sun?

-Because it is the way of the unknown.

-You run away?

-No. I chase what I do not know.

-Ah, you look for something?

-Yes.

The boy smiled, -I see. I will follow one day! He eased gingerly from the branch and patted the horses' necks, allowing the rider to lay a gentle hand on his new black cap. Then he set off stiffly, back to the village. Another destiny is altered, thought the mounted man. A seemingly chance encounter with a warrior and a youth comes to realise his fate may be different from other children in his tribe.

He had only travelled a little further when the roan alerted him to a pursuer. There was no danger. He tried to still the irritation in him. He had done his duty to the village people. He did not need more entanglement with them. He had not much affection for them despite his best intents. It was a woman. She was running. He had noticed her eyes following him everywhere during the morning. She was even-featured and had the bearing of someone who had not been bred for the fields. Her hair was red-black like the wing of the bird that steals. Her skin was pale and her eyes the luminous amber of a snake he had once encountered.

-Take me with you! It was an imperative.

-No. It cannot be so. He did not pretend to know little of her tongue.

-You have a spare mount. I am light enough for it. It is your duty to fate.

-How can that be so? I knew you not until this moment. I owe you nothing.

She cried distractedly, -You came not for the villagers' rituals. Fate chose you to take me away. It is written here! She touched a breast, -I was carried in flight by my mother as a girl to the village but she died leaving me there. They cared for me. I have repaid my debt to them.

-How did you do that? He studied her face. It was even less like those of the villagers than he had thought.

-My childhood saw an acquaintance with the needle. I made the men's hats. For some reason this made them both laugh, -But I have made enough hats for generations to come. It kept me out of the fields.

-How many red hats? he smiled.

-Five. Enough. Again they laughed.

-I understand your impatience to leave hat-making but where would you go?

-To a city to the east. It is the city of my kin.

☥

As they cantered along the grassy trail, the horses stretching out and relishing the exercise, he learned that she and her mother had been travelling with the sun protected by horsemen, when they had been attacked. All their guards were killed. She and her mother had fled during the battle, though her mother had been struck by a blade. They had been spared by fate but had neither food nor water. They had walked for a week, drinking from streams and gnawing on roots and berries until they reached the village, her mother exhausted and dying.

Because she was born of a woman of high birth she was allowed to undertake tasks in the village rather than the fields as was more customary. The villagers were fearful that some of her kind would come looking for her, so treated her well. Nevertheless, as her body ripened she had had to use all her wiles to keep males from her. Only the patronage of the chief saved her. But she knew that he was as desiring as the others and soon he began to threaten her with days in the fields exposed to the farming men unless he could come silently to her waiting bed. He was fearful that his wife would discover them but his fear was outweighed by his lust for her. She had a dream and in it a stranger came to the village for a great feast day as was the ancient custom. He rescued her. When she woke from it she felt her hopes rise. She promised her body to the chief during the night that would follow the festival of conjoining and manhood.

218

-What kind of dream? Sleeping or waking?

-Waking. As I sewed a hat. It was not like sleep. It was like seeing the fulfilment of destiny and as clear as though enacted beneath the high sun's rays.

He made a tent for them, tautening skins between branches and staking their edges close to the ground to protect them from a rising wind. A fire, concealed between stones, projected much of its warmth into their shelter. She had come with nothing save her feast clothes and so wore spare garments from his saddlebags. They slept back to back all night. Neither made any effort to touch the other.

Much of their time together was spent in silence. He gradually became used to her. In time he did not even feel inconvenienced. The black stallion visibly enjoyed having a rider after the labours of being a pack horse. The roan liked her and offered his muzzle for her long fingers to stroke. She proved a good cook for one so young and would make flat breads quickly in ovens dug beneath the evening fires. It occurred to him that they were as any couple, apart from the urge for procreation. Even when they came to a river and swam unclothed there was no show of desire between them. He raised this question one evening.

-We are almost like a conjoined couple.

-More like sister and brother. This was true, he admitted to himself.

-You do not desire me? he asked frankly.

-A sister only desires her brother before her twelfth summer and now I am fifteen. Anyway, you are too removed from my need.

-How?

-You are a warrior. All begin to know of you. You fight in a hermit's cloak. I am the virgin daughter of a queen. My life will be with her. I will meet a man of equal standing. He will not journey like you, nor kill, nor indeed live with the threat of being killed. He will give me children who will look after me when I am old. Your children will inherit your wandering lust. Always searching, never finding, forgetting who they are, lost inside themselves, until they become but shadows moving silently across the land, searching for their bodies.

-You think it must end like this for me?

-It is for you to define but it is likely.

-There is a woman.

-I felt it.

-When we met she was of an age like you. She is from a desert clan.

-You have chosen with your own needs foremost. She will accept your journeying. Tell me about her. What likeness has she?

-Dark like you but with a honey skin, the colour of sunset on sand. Strong and broad in the shoulder for a woman. Eyes too black for colour to be found in them.

-You were her first lover?

-Yes. There was blood at our first mating.

-It was short and painful for her?

-No. I was taught by a wise woman to be gentle.

-She did not cry at your penetration?

-Not with pain but sadness at my inevitable leaving.

-She clung to you?

-Through the dark. And me to her.

-And you vowed to return?

-I will.

-You see - this is why I am a sister to you! This woman took your heart and keeps it. I sensed its absence and then I lied about my feelings. I had to swallow my desire for you or I would have taken you into my body to be my first mating.

-This is true?

-It is true. Few women could travel with such as you and not feel desire but we are not fate's pairing. Sister and brother we must be. Warrior and maid. We must not break our taboo.

-It is undeniable.

-You see, even a motherless girl with little time spent in learning can offer wisdom to a famed warrior in some matters.

-In matters between male and female I am a novice.

-You know more than most men but that amounts to little enough! They laughed.

-Teach me the sword, she said.

-Teach me the ways of young women, he replied.

-It will be a fair exchange.

-And a great reward.

She learned quickly. They practised with sticks and she received many blows as she progressed but never remonstrated with him. After each lesson he bathed her bruises while she spoke of maturing women and the differences between needing and wanting. He discovered that to need was a feeling engendered by the heart and expressed through the body. To want was the body's sole call, disregarding its heart's permission. Her lessons revived what women on his journey had taught him. He told her of these teachers. Of a queen and a priestess. Of the noblewoman from the City in the Mountain. How he had once experienced giving birth. She told him more about the female body. Of places to touch and words to whisper, of the order of such touches and how to move inside a woman to give her most pleasure.

-How do you know such things when you have not yet been breached?

-I was companion to the chief's daughters. We practised on each other most evenings. We gained much pleasure from it. For one or two of them it will seem like a golden time for no man will attend to their bodies with such a devoted regard for instilling pleasure.

It was in close friendship that he eventually brought her to the city of her father. The tears that were shed, the celebrations, the heads of young noblemen that were turned by her moving among them, their fearful looks as they caught sight of the imposing stranger with pale grey eyes.

He had only been a vehicle for her return but much had passed between them that formed a link as firm as any. Finally he came to her to take his leave. She embraced him and cried even as she wished him joy.

-When I have a son I hope he will not be like you, she laughed.

-When I have a daughter, I hope she will have your flame, he replied. He did not mind the tears in his own eyes though he was unused to this expression of emotion.

Kamil found it easier to read out passages concerning the taboos of intimacy now. Something had changed. Perhaps it was that he had ceased being a hopeless single man in his middle years, inviting suspicion or derision from females. No longer did he look down upon himself and tremble at the inappropriateness of such material to someone who had barely entered womanhood. Baligha had given him authenticity. He was now promised to a woman.

-I see the temperance here. Most men would not have questioned it and taken her body, since she was offering it. Perhaps all normal men. Even you Kamil, eh?

He blustered, -I don't know if -

-Stop! I know. And that's an end to it. You have written it well but I sense you are being holier than thou in your words. They are the words of someone who has not access to the secret delights of a woman's body. Men are what they are. Civilised in public and beasts in private. Did you know that Muez tried to rape me when I was 12? Kamil shook his head and looked down, chastened. -He thought that since I was of age he would claim me and the throne in one act! He entered my bedroom with a key, no doubt obtained by his mother. But I was awake and my knife was ready. Share the steam baths with him and observe the scar on his thigh! Much blood and much pain but not deep enough or in the right place unfortunately. I had aimed to prevent him ever fathering a child.

He nodded, trying to shut the words out, not wanting to share the revelation.

-But very bloody and very painful, nevertheless, she smiled coldly, - So you have another reason why I hate him and his bloodline.

-Did you go to the Emperor?

-No. We were young. He would have been absolved. My father is a man after all. But it is stored here, she touched her head, -And can always be used against him should I need it, when the hour comes.

Chapter Sixteen

Enlightenment means knowing what you cannot give

She sat under a lemon tree, her grey hair coiled on her head, a long white burnoose to her ankles. He approached her with a radiant smile, excited flickerings in his chest and his breath short and barely controlled.

-You are here already, he half stammered, seating himself so that there was faint contact between their arms.

Baligha looked happy, -I wanted to see you approach just as you did me. In those moments before you could see me I hoped to have a picture of you as you are to yourself and not to others.

Kamil considered this carefully, -I am sure that your picture of me is unique but accepting that, what did you see?

She laughed in her low melodious way, -An honest man. A man not given to chasing the rainbows of a rich life. A loyal man. A man with a humble yet pleasing countenance. He flushed, -An innocent man, she added, -For only such a man would be so overcome by compliments.

-You make me very content.

-And you me. And now, before we lose ourselves in this endearing play of words, I have some news. She said softly, -Aidah has left me.

-What? Why? After the life she led I thought she felt safe with you?

Baligha turned her face away, -It is as you say and as I have told you. If my door was an arch of garlands under which men pass, she was its brightest bloom. Both harems and palaces of the senses need their Aidahs from which younger women can learn grace and our arts. She knew all that there is and yet still conveyed a strange mystery.

-How then? he asked, fretting.

-A man came to her last night. Cloaked and hooded. But all else about him advertised him to be a noble. She confessed to me that if Rafi could be thought of as evil, this man was the devil himself. He burnt a symbol on her arm. An ancient branding. A rose with petals falling. It marked the end of her noble calling. She is no longer a goddess of the senses. She has fallen to the lowest place for her kind.

She can be maltreated. She is nothing. No man can now come to her and be lost in her illusions. She is reduced to a plain whore. Her screams brought my guards but he had gone. He was her last visitor in my house. Whatever you are engaged in, sweet Kamil, has left honey in my home and the wasps, the flies, the rats and the ants are drawn to it. I cannot stop the infestation.

He took her hand, -Baligha, it distresses me so. What must I do? Shall we leave this city? But he knew that this was a futile suggestion.

-No. Finish the game. Perhaps in some ways I am safer now because of our association. We are watched but whoever does this must know by now that we enjoy the Princess's patronage. There should be no assault on the court historian and his beloved.

-One day soon we shall share our days, he protested fervently. Despite her news, it felt wonderful to him to be able to make such a declaration.

-Let us hope so.

*

Khawlah the Mute served her mistress well for the second time. Brushing the corridors of the Empress's rooms in her discoloured rags, her head bowed, her thin arms uncovered by her folded back sleeves, she peered now and then through the filigreed stone screens that allowed air into the Empress's chambers. After days of innocuous cleaning she happened upon movement in the Empress's bedroom. Furtively applying her eye to the bottom corner of the screen so that she left no silhouette she saw Muez and the Empress in conversation. They talked in low voices. All she heard was the name T'ariq and she saw Muez make the sign of a slit throat.

*

A male and a female body were reported later that same day to the city authorities. The male, who was not of the court, was dressed as a royal guard. His neck had been severed so badly his head was barely connected. The female was found floating close by. She had been strangled by a long leather thong, still attached to the wrist of the male. The angry mark of a decaying rose on her arm helped to identify the body.

*

They discussed events. It seemed obvious how the deaths had come to pass. Aidah had been caught in flight by Muez's henchman, the waiting T'ariq. It was likely that he himself was being shadowed by Muez. As soon as Aidah was throttled T'ariq was murdered and the two bodies pushed into the river.

-They are becoming crazed, said Kamil, -More and more desperate in their measures to silence even their own. They must feel your net tightening.

Princess Sabiya frowned, -Yet we are short of the proof I need to take to my father. He is too trusting of Malika. What we have is conjecture and coincidence. I know him. He will interpret the evidence differently. It is not enough to stop her. They debated for some time trying to tease from all that they knew what might be the next steps of a stratagem, only to be interrupted by a messenger with a rough note from Khawlah. She had witnessed the comings and goings of Muez at times that fitted the pattern of the macabre events by the river.

-Let us sleep on our knowledge, said Kamil, -We must not rush our tactics. I sense we have the upper hand as a result of what we now know, because they do not know that we know it.

-I believe you are right, she nodded, slowly, -Have no fear, I have men guarding Baligha and her prostitutes' palace. She ignored his wince, -We can allow ourselves the luxury of the next Tale for who knows we seem to be partly driven by these stories and gain succour from the truths that abide within them. She turned the next card and recoiled. A squatting, horned devil held two people in chains. It had breasts and a bared torso yet masculine features. -It is Satan!

-That may be one interpretation, said Kamil soothingly, -In truth it speaks mostly of change as often for the better as for the worse. It is the unpredictable that enters our orderly world and causes momentary crisis or catharsis.

-Not a special friend of yours then Kamil! She glared at the image, -Read.

Leaving proved not as easy as he had imagined. Knowledge of him had reached the king and queen of the city. Stories of his recent adventures had become magnified and more heroic with time and retelling. Words could fly like birds across the land quicker than the gallop of a resolute horseman. It was as though sleeping people, a distance apart, shared their dreams of him simultaneously. A circus had passed that way with tales of a merchant who could play the magician, his strangely gifted son and of a magical horse. Traders had brought stories from the City in the Mountain where a magical youth bestowed the blood of the shaman upon the tribe. Strange twin females who sold spice carried tales of a hooded warrior who avenged the breaching of their female sanctity. Enough seeds here for legends to grow.

He was leading his horses away from the nobleman's quarters when the queen's messenger accosted him from a side alley.

-The Queen requests your presence, the fellow called.

-I offer thanks to the Queen but I must journey on.

-She will not take kindly to your refusal.

-I seek not her kindness nor her displeasure.

-She will have me beaten and then send an armed force to take you to her. The man was almost whimpering.

-I am not the locksmith of your destiny nor that of her soldiers.

-Please, kind sir! wheedled the fellow.

The Warrior stopped. He looked at the envoy, -Why does she want to see me?

-She wishes to present you to her court and her many visitors from far away cities.

-Present? Her court is a zoo?

The envoy spoke persuasively, -No my Lord. It is a most civilised society. Rich and powerful men. Most beautiful ladies. Singers.

Musicians. Dancers. Actors. A golden palace with the finest silks and furniture.

-I have visited such courts. They hold no attraction for me. I am a man who seeks only his own company.

-She wishes to entertain you. You are a great warrior and have magical powers. A shaman. Such men are rare.

-Such men may not exist at all except in the minds of the gullible.

-Yet you are such. There are many tales about you. How you wield an invincible sword. How you can throw a knife with the deadly accuracy of God's blessing. How you can cure kings. How you speak with your horses as easily as with people. These stories are true?

-These are just stories. Is there a face in the moon?

-Some can see it.

-That is my point. Nevertheless he felt uncomfortable that so much seemed to be known about him, so much had been embroidered into the one garment. He made to move on. The envoy pulled back. From the shadows stepped another figure, cloaked and hooded but unmistakably a woman. A scent arose from her as though a bush of sweet blossom was suddenly flowering.

-I thought you would reject my request. Why should a wild savant endure the sophistication of the court? Her voice was honeyed and deep. She looked up at him, smiling. It was as if the girl child whom he had saved and returned to her village had mysteriously become a woman. The golden hair. The blue irises. The playful mouth. The intensity.

-There is no reason, he said quietly.

-There may be one. He did not answer but looked at her closely. Her eyes were whirlpools. His gaze spun deeper and deeper. It was an intoxication. He seemed to drift inside her. Eddies and currents of feeling coursed through him making him tremble. He found his sight misting and he had to blink to hold the perfect outline of her face. He looked past her with a great effort and spoke over her shoulder.

-I am not an exhibition for your court.

-No, I have other plans. Follow me. Please? It swayed him. He did as she bade him. A small band of soldiers flanked her as they made their way down the darkened side streets. There were few about and those that were withdrew quickly at the gleam of the soldiers' swords. Only the slow muffled clopping of his horses' hooves interrupted the evening's silence. Before him the armed men strode with the tall slim female at the centre of their protection. Their heads moved constantly like birds of carrion gauging the roofs of buildings, windows, doors and dark alleyways. She glided between them, her body swaying, her bearing erect and imperious. They turned into a courtyard and a heavy door was barred behind them.

-See to the horses and take their burdens to the guest chambers. This man and his beasts are honoured guests. Let no harm come to either. He followed her to her room. Rugs had been spread on the tiled floor, silk draped on the walls and hung in great billows from the ceiling. A curtained bed filled some of the space. Cushions were positioned round a low table. Candles flickered everywhere. A girl servant was replacing some that had burnt out but with a clap of hands she was shooed from the room. The queen dropped her cloak and hood on the floor and sank on a cushion indicating that he should do the same. When he was seated she poured them both a drink of mixed fruits. His sniff found it acceptable.

-What do you want of me?

-To hear your stories. To watch your mouth as you tell me of the lawless men you have slain, the strange people you have been among, the woman who has won your heart. I want to gaze into the eyes of a wild man from the north whose adventures are on all the lips of the compass.

-You are mocking me?

-You are a legend. A thousand tales are already told about you from child to man. Some I know are old stories which now bear your name to add lustre to your greatness. Some are new and likely to be true. Speak of these!

He acquiesced and despite himself he narrated his adventures in simple words and brief, unadorned descriptions, first when with his father and then alone. It took him some time. Certain events he did not elaborate concerning his prowess with arms, the hermit's cloak and his way with magic. When he had finished there was a long quiet pause. She had her hands twisted together on her lap and stared at them distantly. Finally she looked at him, -You are sworn to the woman of the desert?

-Yes.

-Yet you gave your seed to the bloodline of the City in the

Mountain?

-It was a troubling gift.

-You travelled last with my beautiful cousin and remained a brother to her?.

-Your cousin?

-She never said? I thought she was dead. She is a gift from God.

-She has become as you say, a sister to me.

-Nevertheless, I can see that her beauty would be hard to resist for any normal man.

-She forbade it -

-Aye, I thought so!

-And saved me from the need to struggle over my vows.

-Your desert girl is as beautiful as we?

-Yes, though to you she may appear strange and different. She rides a camel or horse as well as any man. She is broad and strong. Her face is dark. Her hair is black. She can throw a knife as well as I. She is a natural commander of men.

The queen's tone was seductive, -Whereas I am none of these things. I am soft where she is hard. My skin has the bloom of a flower petal while hers is more like soft leather. My flesh is as yielding as a ripe summer fruit and hers is as a man's. I am a woman who has drawn many men into this lair and they have left, their hearts drugged with love for me. Each places his lips at my disposal. Each would kill or die for me.

-You expect the same of me? His eyes explored her beauty, the way the fine black material clung to her slender figure, emphasising her breasts, the silver torque around her throat and the many glittering bangles and rings around her slim wrists and long fingers.

-I never expect what may not come to pass. You are not a man who can be softened inside by glances and touches so that all becomes clay for a woman to mould.

-It is a great power you have, he stated, matter of factly.

-It is simple. My beauty is but a small element of my strength. All my people know that my family has the One God's blood in its female line. Imagine the power that that brings?

He wondered whether she truly believed this, -It is true? Even as he asked he weighed her beauty and found it wanting. He longed for the simplicity of his desert woman, the grip of her thighs, the wildness of her body.

-I sometimes believe it. None disobeys me. Even my husband the King whose wealth is great indeed. For is it not I who am blessed by God's blood? And through me his daughter is, which is enough for him. He has married into divine blood. Our line stretches back beyond memory to a time when God descended to the earth and took the form of a woman among mortals. She was our first queen and conquered the clans and made them one tribe with one tongue. She was immortal whereas our people were born and died in their never-ending cycles. She took two husbands from our lands. One gave her a daughter and the other gave her a son. Neither child could take a mortal lover and therefore, with Her permission, they became one with each other. They are my ancestors. Like God their Mother they did not die. At a certain moment, known by them long before, they returned to the holy world that is above this one. Since that time all those carrying direct blood return to the holy place and do not embrace a mortal end. There are no graves or fires for us. There is no need.

-You know your moment? It is in your mind now? he asked, curiously.

-It is within me as a seed. I sense it. It will flower and I will know. To be able to think of it now would obscure my delights in this world. Her words made him think of the life-taker. Did this queen also have a death's attendant to take her, invisibly, from her people?

-Why did you want me to come here?

-As I have told you, to know your stories. Stories are all we have to mark the passage of lives. We may learn from them if we listen and then pass this knowledge on to our young in further tales. Thus it is that they themselves have a little more power over their destinies than do we. Such is the word of God. Was that not true of the Merchant, your father? Did he not prepare you better for the world because of his own life?

-He did. And I have told you all I have to tell. He maintained an impassive calm but he was aware of an uneasiness. There was something chaotic and forbidding about this woman. She was used to exercising her rule without thought of consequence. His mind flew back to the island and its hermit and his stories of unfettered power.

-I have not finished with you. There is something I wish you to do for me. She smiled that melting smile, -Do not worry, I have no wish for you to break again your vow to your desert girl, great though the pleasure would be. I have no desire to take such a dangerous man to my bed. He stared back at her quizzically. He had no desire to mount her but he was intrigued.

-My husband does not interfere with my occasional lust for a rich young lover. They are no threat to him providing I do not conceive. He has his mistresses. But you? You would threaten us all. He could fear your wild seed. He could imagine you taking his throne. He could imagine you plundering my love. You cannot be controlled. Your path cannot be predicted. Your strength may be limitless. How the people would love a true warrior king! Neither he nor I could countenance such risk. You would be a threat to my bloodline. You are godless. You might take my life and stifle the breath of my children and replace them with children of desert blood.

-It is not possible. Such a life has no interest for me.

-Many speak like you before they come to exercise power. Then they use this power to change history. Some do it for good, others for evil. All are seduced by the reins that suddenly twitch in their hands. No, I want you for your warrior qualities and not for your manhood. She looked at him intently.

He felt hemmed in. He sensed that he would be asked to stay in the city for some time. His spirit wished for the trail again, for nights on the earth, for fresh-caught food on the fire, for the sole company of his horses.

-It would be painful for me to stay in this city.

-I know. I am counting on it for you will complete the task that I will set for you quickly and thereby protect the king and I from treachery. Every day that passes the more dangerous it is becoming for us. She leant forward and said dramatically, -There is a hired killer in the court, ready to strike.

-From my knowledge of such things, he said, -There is always someone willing to kill a chief, be it in the mountains or within the comfort of a court. It is as though the power of one becomes the incentive to destroy in the other. The assassin remains asleep, blind to his future assassin's role, until one day he awakens to his fate. What makes these killers do so I know not.

-Words in their ears. Promises of great rewards. Jealousy. Love. Hate. Many things, even in a court where all are treated with love and honour. She turned to him, her eyes shining, -But more poisonous than all of these is faith. Faith can make a murderer out of the mildest man. He becomes bold and wages war on those who profess their love for another God.

-What I have witnessed supports such a view, he nodded, -There is much cruelty in the name of a chosen god. But is this not a city with one god?

-Would that it was. The scriptures of our people tell us that when the One God became queen she had a younger brother whom she loved greatly. But this brother became jealous and angry when She took to herself, two husbands. He felt rejected in favour of the two mortals! He vowed that the bloodlines from these matings would be cursed. Carriers of this blood would always live in fear of an unknown assassin and they would die from bloody acts. Despite the strength of his jealousy, our God loved him still and so did not remove the curse altogether. She left a small opening in a royal woman's life when she would be defenceless against a killer. God wanted the tribe to be vigilant about the sacred blood of its queens.

She paused and then continued, -The line might be severed one day and our tribe humbled and returned to shepherding in the hills and valleys. Her brother's vow is known to us all. The assassin can only strike when the female child commences her first ripening to conceive children. Thus it is within our noble line that after the first bleeding of womanhood the emerging woman is taken in marriage and sired immediately so that she becomes safe from attack.

He puzzled this over, -How does the assassin know?

-He does not. He is an unconscious puppet who acts within the edicts laid down by God. Assassins have mistakenly attacked too late but always God has intervened and the attack has failed. The assassin is allowed to go free - but not to live within the city.

-You free him? Such justice!

-Or her. When my time came to take my mate, it was a maid servant. We must free the would-be assassin, for such a person was chosen by God's brother and cannot be held to blame.

-You want me to find the assassin?

-No, for God's brother would merely choose another's body to enter. This is why we need your protection. You will act as a guard to our daughter.

-She has become a woman?

-Before her time. She is hardly twelve summers. It was expected three months hence. The man chosen to be her husband is trading some distance from here. A messenger has gone to him. It will take two days. It is a marriage for the glory of the tribe. Two old clans. His family joined with our blood many generations ago from the male side. Even so they have important wealth and influence.

-Why do you not surround her with your guard?

-There are guards everywhere but not in her room. Who can know the face of the unknown? I could place a killer to guard over her and not know until it is too late.

-What of me?

-You are godless. You are the new shaman of the wilds. God's brother has no power over you.

-I hope it is true.

-You will protect my daughter?

-It becomes my purpose. He said these words with a finality. A little while ago there would have been a tinge of resignation but now he was intent on subordinating himself to the needs of those around him.

☥

Immediately, he was shown to the daughter's quarters. While she was being bathed he studied the building. The room in which she would receive the chosen male was spacious. Barred windows let out above an inner courtyard. They could be shuttered from the inside but were open to allow the passage of air. His eye roved over the space below with its potted plants and fountains. On the other sides of the courtyard well there were further windows. These were repeated on every storey. Above were flat roofs where guards patrolled. He instructed the queen to have all shutters closed and all guards removed to the perimeter gardens of the building. Outside the daughter's room was an antechamber with a hastily installed pallet bed for him. A landing ran round the entire palace. The stairs to this were on the other side of the building. On the corridor outside the girl's room were barred windows that faced out to the streets. Each was securely shuttered. He tested all the hinges, bars and bolts throughout the building. Soldiers watched him nervously. They had heard the stories.

They did not see him rub a gritty cream into all the moving metal.

-Are you not increasing the danger by removing the guards? asked the queen, returning with her bathed daughter.

-In the desert you may hear the feet of a burrowing insect, he replied, -For there are no human beings to distract your ears. She smiled in satisfaction. She expected such an answer from a shaman.

The daughter was left in the room on her own and the announcement was made across the city that she was now a woman, according to custom. A fearful silence settled on homes and streets. All in the city prayed for her well-being. All except one.

And a warrior.

The queen came to him as night fell. A messenger had arrived indicating that the chosen male was already travelling back. Outgoing and incoming messengers had met a mere half day from the city. The royal daughter had only to suffer one night of guarded solitude and he, himself, could leave after the consummation.

He ordered the queen to her quarters. Every other room in the house had been vacated and searched. No servants. No soldiers. These were now deployed in a three deep ring around the house. They were ordered to keep watch on each other and not upon someone seeking entry. They were all armed but were not allowed metal protection. They were barefoot at the Warrior's orders. The king kept vigil in a house across the narrow street at the front. The queen had made no effort to introduce them. Apart from the slight whisper of the breeze and the occasional barking of a dog, the city was silent.

There was a tap at the door and the daughter whispered, -Can you come in here? I am frightened. He pushed the door open and stepped inside.

-I was waiting until you slept, he said softly, -Have no fear, no-one will harm you. She was still a child to his eye, her body only partly developed, her face not yet formed into the distinctive features of womanhood. She had her mother's hair and eyes, yet, unlike her mother, she had no resemblance to the little girl he had saved.

-Take to your bed, he advised, -I will remain in the room but you must be silent for my ears are our most powerful weapons at this time. She nodded and climbed obediently into the bed, pulling the woven fabric up to her nose so that only her eyes, forehead and hair were visible. For a moment she was just like any small child.

He sat cross-legged on the floor in the doorway to the anteroom and allowed his body to relax. His eyes closed and his hearing reached out into all the rooms around him. In his mind he could see whatever he could hear. He could see the stiff lines of soldiers. He could see into each room. He could see the empty roofs. In the midst of this many-layered visualisation of the building was something that he did not see at first but gradually it grew at the centre of his understanding. It was not moving. It had no shape. Yet it was there, as definite and threatening as any following day's battle.

Something was in the room, lurking and menacing. It was fearful of him and yet, at the same time, at ease with the girl and she with it. His mind puzzled and played with the possibilities. The girl was sleeping peacefully. The room contained no other but himself. He would have been aware of the smallest creature in the darkest corner. Yet the danger grew and her life was in the balance. Then he had it! He moved swiftly to her bed and took her wrist in one hand and pushed back her eyelids with the fingers of the other. The assassin was inside her! He smelled her breath and her skin and then crouched over her, nipping her nostrils with finger and thumb. Then he began to breathe for them both. As he did he expelled his own life force into her.

Finally he saw it. Her life-taker was a boy, dark-haired and brown-skinned. A nomad child. A shepherd. The Warrior spread himself between the boy and the girl in his brown hermit's garb, obscuring her. As he lay, the nomad slowly disappeared until there was no shimmer left in the air. The girl struggled beneath him and he took his mouth away to let her cough. Her eyes opened.

-Why did you stop me! she cried angrily.

-It was my purpose.

-You should have let me die.

-You are strong! Only the strong can bring death to themselves by will alone, he said approvingly.

-It would be death for me to take that man. I have nothing to live for.

-You are but a girl. There is much to be done in your life. Nothing is written beyond this night. I have a gift for knowing such things.

She said, through tears, -I will be shackled for life to a man three times my age and for whom I have no regard. It is the will of my mother. Neither she nor my father have ever shown love for me. I am the sacred bloodline. The female carrier of God's mark. I am the guarantee of the prosperity of the city. My body, given by them to this man, will be a symbol of the family's enduring power.

-Is it not a sin before your god to take your own life?

-God is in my blood. My flesh would not have been here by the light of the next day. It is written. I would have been the true enactment of the vow of God's brother and the city would have perished. You have interfered with my fate.

-I am your fate. It is now another path that you tread.

☦

He told the Queen none of the events of the night. For her, his very presence had ensured her daughter's safety. She congratulated herself on her presence of mind in employing him thus. Already the rich suitor was lying with her daughter in her room, sealing the bond between families and making his bride safe from any assassin. Meanwhile, the Warrior had left the city and was riding the roan and leading the black. He picturing in his mind the events taking place in the royal daughter's room. It was as clear as if he was present. He watched the queen and the king as they stood, smiling and laughing in the anteroom, waiting. Then the chosen male opened the door to them. There was something wrong. His face was sickly and white.

-I am cursed. My manhood remained sleeping. I could not take her. There was no entry. Then she...she...He leant and vomited against the door.

They rushed into the room, the Warrior's inner eye following them. The girl was lying in bed with a still smile upon her face, the chosen male's short knife in her womb where she had plunged it, the fingers of both hands holding it there as if it was a baby.

-How stupid! Sabiya muttered, -You see what blind faith does? How many go to death trusting that they cross the threshold to a god? They adore their divine beings and sentimentalise them, giving them the pretence of mortal flesh and bone and then they rush to embrace these badly constructed figments of fantasy as though their existence was irrefutable. If there is a god then He or She must be so much beyond what can be comprehended that there is no point to worship, for such a being would hardly be enamoured by it! Her eyes rested on Kamil's lowered head, -Ah, my historian, believer in the One God, as proclaimed by the beloved prophet, I see my words offend you.

-It is difficult for me, whispered Kamil, -There are no doubts in my soul.

-Which is why I will be Empress and you, always a servant of the court. I was born to bear the burden of the agnostic. How else can an Empress rule? I am like your Magus. No servant of God, though, by my very blood, many will find God through me, It is the role of royalty. We lead, we rule and we impose whatever is needed to keep an empire obedient. Look at your histories Kamil and see the emperors who have changed religion to keep an empire. It is our way. We decide which God satisfies our country's needs most. Or, if that is too crude for you, we decide which path people must take to appease God. For, of course, there can be but One God though there may be many religions with their many versions of Him. Emperors who fail this challenge lose their lands.

Kamil was silent.

Chapter Seventeen

Enlightenment does not come without moments of despair

Kamil had not seen Baligha that day. He had sent a message the previous evening explaining that she was being watched over and that he was staying away from her to ensure her safety while also relaying his sadness at Aidah's death. In truth he was glad that he did not have to see her for he had no sense of what he might say or do to support her in her distress.

He could not become used to Princess Sabiya's complete indifference to God. She treated the subject as though she belonged to a species of higher beings who had little need of faith or contemplation on the mysteries of existence. Whereas he often became anxious when his faith was tested because it had always buoyed him up in life, she showed no anxiety at having little faith at all. His strange, contradictory feelings about her had grown more measurable. He would give his life for her yet he distrusted her. How could that be? His head shook slowly and was doing so when she entered the room.

-Kamil! You look worried. Have you news?

-No Princess. I was merely reflecting on the task before us. He was aware of the imperious yet calm nature of her arrival. She had an expression of pensive determination but she was in no mood to talk before her next Tale.

-Read to me, Kamil and then we shall talk. I too am lost in our plots and plans.

Despite the comforts of the air and earth and the release into the solitude of his own being, his mind would not become a windless pool. It was not that he was besieged by ungovernable thoughts that had sometimes been the case when he was younger. It was the puzzle of the death of the young princess. He focussed this way and that upon the events in the city and his part in them. To take one's own life for a cause suggested a belief so strong that he wondered about his own lack of such faith. His mind mused over the people he had met for whom such decisions were so critical. The man who had walked into the desert and insanity rather than live without the mother of his desert girl. The captured soldier in the City in the Mountain who only wished the love of his family. The Physician who took poison rather than tell what he knew. And the princess. He had foreseen the girl's death but had not understood. He had misinterpreted his vision of her future thinking that the void he sensed ahead of her meant that she had choice in defining her forthcoming life. Perhaps she had. Perhaps that was it. Life or death. He had thought he had spared her by his intercession but he had merely delayed the companionship of her life-taker. The city was complicit in its slow destruction just as a flake of snow could begin an avalanche. She was the city. Her death would lead to its death.

Together with his lack of religious faith he found a lack of feeling in himself. Were faith and feeling like the sun and moon? How could he witness pain, suffering and death without his heart responding and becoming engulfed with sadness or remorse? His father's heart was more open and generous and his face often showed how he could be bound to the hurt and pleasure of others, how he showed feeling for plant, animal, bird or human and even the death of his enemy. Whereas for himself much that happened was separated from him by an invisible skin which protected him from extremes of emotion. He made his way, sought his purpose and became for a while an agent of fate in other people's lives without obligation or consequence.

The princess's death was to him a fragment of a shattering vessel. It drew his thoughts less than the sweep of the whole, the great pattern of disrupted fate, the complicated force of life that carried people in its tidal thrust. People were caught up in its flood and were flung hither and thither by it. Few could stay outside it like he did, observing, noting, meditating. If this was the result of his obsessive search for purpose, what did it mean? The Spice Merchants had told him to help others in order to help himself. Others' destinies would inform his own. Was it that his existence had no value except when it was plaited into others' lives?

His waking dreams told him that he was journeying in a great arc of experience, one that would eventually bring him back to the valleys of his childhood. He had had glimpses of the events unfolding around him but he found it easier to foresee the future of others than his own. It was because their desperate desire to know of these things lent him the power to see what might happen to them. He himself lacked such intensity. Maintaining a certain balance between past, present and future were an essential part of him. If he concentrated on illuminating his own future then the present would become a fog. Just so with history. The past must be allowed its journey into insignificance and its own death. There were stark borders between the past and now and between now and the future. To submerge himself in any state other than the now would mean joining the vast throng of sleepwalkers who had little control over their own lives. The death of the girl was in the past and the memory of it would have its own slow demise. Only the core of meaning would be extracted from it and taken in to himself. He must move on, casting off the husk of his experience of her. Between the present and that point on his journey where the final border presented itself and his brown robed life-taker joined him, was an endless river of nows in which he must become immersed like a fish swimming in its totality. There could be no coming up for the air of uninvolved detachment, for senseless melancholia about what had been or wasteful anticipation of the future.

These thoughts spoke to him of change. Another shift in whom he might become. It seemed possible that his purpose was more attainable. He must learn to live fully in the now, to learn to experience it with an intensity he had rarely felt other than at certain moments among those very close to him. Or at moments of utter aloneness. He must open his being to the rawness of feeling and emotion. And he must do so without any semblance of armour or shell.

☥

It was a high plateau frequented by herdsman to graze their long haired, brown beasts. They did not come near him. It was more than the usual instinctive distrust of strangers. It would take several days to cross it but the grasses made travel easy for the horses and he did not work them hard. They had the sheen of their summer coats, their ears were pricked and their muscles were full and toned. Yet even so the roan showed some concern. It paused now and then and eyed the sky as though expecting a storm. On its back the man applied himself to emptying his mind, harbouring no thoughts other than a sensual awareness of an air thick with scents and the dust of flowers. He watched birds rise and fall to their ground nests, their songs of praise ascending and descending with them. It was as though all ill had been banished from the world. Yet the roan could sense something else and alongside it so did the black. It trotted forward and nuzzled the neck of the roan now and then as though to comfort it. Their behaviour began to distract the rider.

Finally the peace was broken, not by a storm but by the beating wings of a pink feathered bird. As it dropped slowly towards them they halted and it came to rest on the bags that were tied to the black's back. Its claws clung to the rough cloth but the man could see that it was exhausted. He reached over and lifted it gently, stroking its neck with a finger. He dismounted, removing the white silk parcel tied to one of its legs and found it water. Soon it was preening itself and murmuring, showing signs of recovery. He spread out the small square of fine cloth on his knee. Painted on it in black ink was a tall column, seemingly ravaged by arrows and lances. A sun was crossed by two thick lines and beneath it were two blood stains as though pressed there by the tip of a finger. Further fine markings suggested dead bodies lying around the column. Along the edge of the picture was the profile of a soldier in a metal helmet. He did not recognise the design with its flap covering the nose and the spike on its crown. The dove fluttered to the earth and began pecking for seeds and insects. Then it took more water from him. He held it in cupped hands and stared into its eyes. At last he saw that the column was a tower on a crag, that the sun, moon and stars lay in a particular pattern and that the distance could be covered in two long days' travel. He reversed the silk, took a Spice Merchants' black stick from a bag and drew a sword upright in a fist with, below it, two horses and a single rider. Above these he drew two suns. Then he retied the silk to the bird's leg and lifted it into the air.

☥

They maintained a steady gallop for an entire day, camped without unpacking and were moving again quickly at dawn. Ahead, the plateau was giving way to low blue hills, beyond which he could pick out a further ribbon of mountains. Perfectly balanced, he was able to relax upon the steady rhythm of the roan and the even nature of the trail's surface. The horses exhilarated in this sudden test of their endurance and speed. Despite being bigger and faster, the black's head remained level with the shoulder of the roan. It was only when they reached rising ground that the man slowed the beasts to a walk. When the roan found a suitable, cool, rock-shaded pool, they stopped and rested as the sun dropped to the horizon. He chewed dried meat, mixing it with leaves of plants growing by the water. Their sharp taste reinvigorated him. Eyeing constellations, the moon and the path of the disappearing sun, he knew he was close to his destination. He donned the brown robe. It warmed him in the cool air. The track was increasingly rocky so he stopped and tied sacking to the horses hooves. They moved slowly now, careful not to dislodge stones, the sounds of battle reaching them.

He sensed it before he saw it. Breasting a rise through a rocky fissure he saw the column on the next ridge. It was a tower, its top lit by fires. Flaming liquids fell upon a besieging army. The tower was completely surrounded by wooden ladders and roughly tied tree platforms, most of which were burned and sagging. A hundred or so men were camped at a respectful distance from the tower's base. Now and then a cloud of arrows rose upwards from them, seeking the apertures and the open space of the turrets. He could tell that the battle had been waged for some time. There was none of the impetuosity of a new engagement. All was controlled and planned. The army was waiting because it could afford to.

He pondered on his next actions. In the past he would not have been drawn into such a turmoil. Wherever he found himself such things happened. There were always chiefs wanting to extend their domain by subjugating more and more villages and towns. There were wars waged between faiths or against those who interpreted faiths differently. There were battles to recover stolen girls taken for brides and fall-outs between royal children. But he was here because he was called. Someone in the tower had the power to call him, powers not unlike his own, entering the mind of a bird and sending it to find him. It intrigued him. He knew with a certainty that he must act in order that he might meet the sender and that the lives of many depended on it.

Once it was dark he left the black horse with orders to stay and prepared the roan by removing all except what he needed for battle. He checked the hooves to be certain that the sacking was secure and then took the trail down into the valley and up on to the next ridge.

There were no sentries, so certain was the army of its show of force. All eyes were on the tower with its high fires and the cascades of flaming tears whenever soldiers moved towards its base. As he approached he arranged his brown cloak and hood and took his bow, the gift from the desert. He notched an arrow. He and the roan climbed to a point above and behind the besieging troops. The air was thickened with the smell of burning oil, the shouts of soldiers, the clash of metal and the creaking of wood as two great catapults were being erected. On the turrets an occasional robed figure appeared, to be greeted by a further volley of missiles.

He and his mount were masked against a dark rock face. Before him were the backs of the small army. He examined the pattern of movement and noted who was giving the orders, who commanded the catapults and who was guiding the forward troops. When he was satisfied, his bowstring tautened and was released. There was the whipping of wind by his ear and he watched the arrow strike a thickset captain in the act of pointing. Another arrow was notched and released. The soldier overseeing the deployment of the catapults fell. Uncertainty spread rapidly among the army. Cries of fear and panic grew. He was emptying his quiver quickly, methodically. Twenty men lay dead or dying. There was no-one left to command now. Already those close to horses were mounted and fleeing. The rest were scrambling among rocks and down the slope from the ridge. Where the land was flattened around the tower, bodies lay on the burnt land among the machinery of war, the blackened scaffolds and the ladders. He housed his bow and the roan picked its way down from their vantage point. He collected his arrows from corpses. He heard the sound of soldiers' feet before he saw them come charging round the base of the tower. They were running wide to escape the dripping flames and seeing just one adversary felt certain of their advantage. He dropped to the ground lightly and stood between them and the roan. They stopped and spread in a half circle before him. His face was in dark shadow from the cowl of the robe. With the effortless movement of the trained warrior he coiled his body and held the sword's point towards them.

There was something about him that communicated a terrible strength. None dared begin the battle. They had suddenly become aware of the bodies and the awful silence. They were locked in a tableau like mesmerised creatures before a predator. Should they fight or flee? But it was too late. Their last images of him was of a swinging sword, in the act of launching an attack. They did not register the final movements that marked their chest with bloody crosses but the pain wakened their senses and they stumbled away. He wiped his sword and stood, surveying the scattered dead, put a hand on his breast and dropped his head to wish them well.

☥

As he raised his head from his meditation he saw a single soldier walking unarmed up the trail towards him. He was young and forlorn. His shoulders drooped and his legs were heavy. When near enough he called out, -Do not kill me! The Warrior remained silent, waiting, -You have killed my father and my brother.

-It is the way of war, he said gently.

-It is true. This was a battle for nothing. The priests in the tower should have been left to their own god. They harmed no-one. But soldiers must take their orders.

-And now?

-I seek forbearance from you for those that live, to come and take the bodies of the dead back to their homes.

-It is granted. The youth nodded in thanks, turned and made his way back from whence he came. The Warrior murmured to the roan and set to cleaning his arrows. While he did so the roan cantered along the ridge to a point where its whinny could carry to the next rise of land. There was an answering call and soon the great black beast could be seen, carrying its baggage towards them.

Later, he watched as they came for their dead. He sat impassively on horseback, an arrow notched in his bow. Men came with their horses and lifted the bodies to lie across their saddles or on rough litters. When they were ready to leave, one kicked his horse forward to where the Warrior and his horses stood.

-You have no men? He shook his head in response, -You, a single warrior, defeated us? He nodded, -What kind of man are you, in your monk's cloak? You are not as those who live in this tower. The man stared at him curiously, his brown eyes in slits, his lined face tight.

-I am a traveller. Nothing more.

-How did you come here?

-I was summoned by someone in the tower. They sent a bird.

-Birds and messages I know. But they fly to roost. It is magic beyond understanding for a bird to find a nomad. We should not have imagined that the tower would fall to us. Too great are the powers locked up in those walls. The priests are new to it but there have been others following other gods, other ways. Their fire god must be great indeed for he sent for you to save them from a whole cohort of soldiers. His face changed suddenly, -You must be the Warrior of whom people speak! The robes. I had not thought…

-I am he. The Magus smiled chillingly and the man dropped his gaze.

☥

When the bodies had been taken and the little plateau around the tower was silent again, he turned towards its great door. He and his two horses stood facing it for some time with that immobility that characterised his patience. He would have waited until another sun rose for the occupants to receive him. If not by then he would leave. All hung in the balance of his stilled mind.

The doors' bolts were drawn slowly, one by one, bringing him to alertness. He held his bow, arrow loosely strung. He disliked the silence of the building and the coldness in its stones. The final bolt groaned and the door swung inwards. Out of the shadowy arch stepped a black-robed figure, cowled like himself but slim and small. In its cupped hands was the pink dove.

-You will not need weapons, said a young voice. The cowl was pulled back revealing a boy with a pale face and shorn head. His eyes were haggard and dark from lack of sleep yet they shone with triumph at the tower's immediate salvation. The mounted man pushed back his own hood and gazed sternly into the boy's face. Unabashed, the youth's eyes travelled over his saviour's broad shoulders, muscled neck and arms.

-I am sorry to have made you wait. There are few of us and we were attending the fires and oil on the tower.

-How many are you?

-Five. More than twenty dead. Only boys remain. We were ordered to hide but as our older brothers died we could not creep into holes any more. Bring your horses inside. We have a little food and water left for them. His mounts walked into the shadows. Beyond the arch was a small, roofed courtyard. Another boy was waiting to take the horses. First the man carefully removed the bags from their hooves and packed them away, -You will spend the rest of the night here with us? He nodded. He was curious and there was much he did not know.

-Where are your dead? he asked.

-Burned in the perpetual fire, the boy sighed, raising his eyes towards the roof. Their ashes and bones will be scattered soon. We melted their flesh in the oils and so they helped to fight the enemy even after their spirits left them.

-You are now the leader?

246

-I am the eldest.

-You sent the bird for me?

The boy stroked the bird and nodded, -There were stories about you brought by traders. They said you were a warrior hermit. An assassin. He looked at the dove, -I can see through birds' eyes. I can talk with them. It was our last hope. Such power is frowned upon here but there was no other course. Those that might have stopped me were dead.

-Do not try to tie those horses, the Warrior called to the other boy, breaking off, -They do not take kindly to it. Feed them and leave them to their own will.

☥

They ate on the roof. A fire was burning in a great metal dish. The blackened bones and ashes of the dead were piled in rough sacks against the turret walls. The man and the boys were gathered round a simple meal of seeds and grains soaked in the juices of fruits stored in casks from the previous winter. He was aware of five pairs of eyes appraising him with a mixture of deference and gratitude. Stars glittered above and the moon had risen from her knees.

-Tell me your story, he said.

-The Order of the Fire God travelled here a generation ago, began the boy, -It was part of our great flowering. We received permission from the tribal chief as we had done elsewhere. The tower was a broken thing and needed many seasons of toil but with the help of labour from the villages it was made whole again. Here we lived within the laws of the one true God - He who sent the first fire that burst forth from the land and formed the sun in the heavens to relieve the world of the unending rule of the moon and stars.

The order flourished here as I said. It attracted the boys of the villages who did not want to live the life of their forbears. Sometimes families resisted. Most were tolerant because the order compensated them with food through the harsh times of the year. All here pay tax to a king though his court is far away. A group of families who still follow the old gods and whose sons wished to come here took their complaints to the king's court. He is also a believer in the old ways. They said that we were taking boys who would have become the king's soldiers! The king sent these men and demanded the Order release the boys to return to the villages. But no boy wanted to return and our superior said that all who were here were under no will other than their own and that of the God of Fire. We would all die for this belief. These words enraged the captain and he began the siege. Several days passed as the army built its scaffold towers. Our superior was struck fatally. As he was dying he asked me to seek the escape of the boys. And he gave me this. It was a flat, wooden casket with ornate carvings, set in it in metal, -It contains the ancient texts of our religion. He said that God would forgive my skill with birds. He drew the map with his failing fingers. He said you would come. I sent the bird but you were far away. One after another the brothers died. It was a sad turn of fate that the last remaining man was felled as your arrows took their leaders. But you saved us as our superior foretold. It is God's design that brings you to us.

-What convinces you that such a life is your destiny?

-We feel it in our very hearts. It is our faith. We are drawn to the One God, He who is formed of fire. His is the power that lights the land by day and nurtures all life, from the humble plant to man, himself.

-How came you to know this? By word? By books? By dreams?

-It is the way of the order to travel in this land and speak of the One God. Some are touched by His fire and believe. Some of these wish to give up their lives to join the Order. Our travelling monks teach reading and writing to those who have a receptive mind. Also they initiate them in the great dances and the fire rituals. Much that they do brings hope and strength to people. They learn that to feed and clothe even the poorest among them is the path to God. All must be shared when there is need.

-Do they instruct the people to refuse their tithes?

-No. They teach them that the world of men has its laws just as the world of God has its own. These need not conflict, for God's is the path of the soul and the king's is the path of the body. The Warrior nodded. He ran his gaze over the sacks of the dead and smelled the oily air. Despite its thickness he was aware of something that lingered here and stretched back to long gone ancestors.

-Who built this tower?

-It is not truly known but there were many bones here when we came and the local people would not approach it. Our Order burned continuous fires of purification in every room before we began to rebuild and heal the stone.

-And what will you do now?

-To stay will mean our death. We must leave for another place where our Order knows no enemy. They will return with the sun. They dare not retreat. The king's law is absolute. It is death to disobey.

-You have no wish to be with your families?

-The creature who becomes winged does not wish to return to its old nest. No, its desire is for the air. We would ask you to protect us on this journey until we are beyond the reach of our enemy.

He slept fitfully. A dark dream shook his body. He saw the tower as it had once been. It was not a place of rituals but the stronghold of a general. Part of a great empire that once held sway as far as any man could travel. His rule was cruel. He and his men took women at will, took all they wished from the villages and killed those who protested. Then, one night when the stars fell into a new conjunction, a raped girl slipped the bolts of the great door. The feasting and drinking revellers heard nothing as a band of men from the fields entered with curved knives. The butchery was without exception. In rejoicing they lit a vast fire in the courtyard and the flames leapt up through the tower to its very roof, burning timbers and bringing down its stonework. Then the door was barred with rocks so that none might enter.

When he awoke he expected the boys to be ready to leave immediately. Although they had prepared for departure with food and those essential holy relics they needed for their daily observance, he found that they had spent the night planning.

-We must cut off any pursuit by the enemy and if we gain vengeance upon those who killed our brothers, so much the better. It will require great bravery of you.

-Of me?

-And me, said the tall one, grimly.

The army reappeared before the sun had reached its zenith. The tower was silent, deceptively tranquil. Its door was open. The Warrior stood at the entrance. They saw him disappear inside.

-Let us destroy the home of these fire worshippers! shouted the new captain, -And take our revenge on the man who killed our brethren. The soldiers poured forward and into the tower. They charged into rooms, slashing at all that could be destroyed. One caught sight of the Warrior at the top of a flight of stairs and shouted to his fellows. At his call they rushed upwards.

Ever higher, he coaxed them, arrows glancing off the stone walls, oaths filling the air. In every room they searched and destroyed, spoiling sacks of corn, scattering the bones of the dead and a dark powder whose use they knew not. As they reached the final flight to the roof, the Warrior and the boy levered a great metal dish and fire began to roll on liquid waves of oil down the stairs. The men tried to retreat but were washed back and fell among themselves. Their screams were terrible to hear. The boy and the Warrior moved quickly to the rear of the roof and slid down the long, waiting rope to the roan and the black. As they galloped from the tower, a first explosion thundered across the ridge rolling into the valleys below. Another and then another, greater and more deafening followed, shaking the very clouds. Birds scattered and animals fled. Dark, thick smoke rose from the torn building and then with another immense blast the tower's walls crumbled and fell in.

-You have your vengeance, said the Warrior, calming the two beasts.

-It was the vengeance of the one true God, was the reply, -And the bones of the elders were there to witness it.

The Warrior stared at him for a few moments, then ordered, -Stay here. We will need more than these two beasts. He took his bow and notched an arrow to its string and galloped back to the ridge. There were a few men standing near the tower but they fled upon seeing him, screaming for their lives to be saved. He rounded up five rugged mountain horses and herded them back the way he had come.

♀

By the time they had camped, they had had several hours of contemplation. The journey had been slow as they were not

250

accustomed to riding. He prepared a meal with them. As they sat and stared into the flames, he said, -I have heard of powders that make fire and thunder and lightning. I thought they were mere fables.

-The order knows these secrets, said the eldest boy, -It is said that such knowledge comes from that far-off land where the sun begins its journey. We are taught to be masters of fire in all its manifestations as it is the greatest gift from God. It is entrusted to us by Him. As the Warrior watched the boy's face he had a vision of him in the future. He was not dressed in black robes but in warrior mail, with a feather plume on his metal helmet, a sword raised and a multitude shaking their weapons at him in tribute.

-**Oh that we** could put all my enemies in a tower and explode it thus! Everything gone in one go. Then we could live happily for a while, eh Kamil? Yet it is a sister to a plan I have been devising and wish you to hear, for it could mean the end to their plots and intrigues and their designs on a new dynasty. She stood and stared down at him with a calculating girlishness so that he felt as he had done at their first meeting, uncomprehendingly helpless, a mere history teacher at the whim of a girl's emotions. He bent under the weight of her authority as he always would and tried to still his fear before the naked metal of her will.

-What have you conceived, Princess? he asked humbly, for it quickly crossed his mind that Baligha's safety depended on her good offices and his acquiescence.

-We must draw Muez from his aunt's lair in such a way as to prove his guilt and thereby hers, too. For this we need a decoy. He must believe that his life is in extreme danger. That someone knows. She smiled at Kamil. His heart stopped and a coldness filtered through his body.

-Baligha. Her name leapt from his lips involuntarily.

-Of course. I once asked you Kamil, when it came to it, whom would you choose? Where would your loyalty lie?

*

He was crying the sobbing tears of a child, the tears that he had never shed in his own young years. He was in Baligha's palace and she was pressing his head to her bosom.

-How can she demand this of us? he wailed.

-It is simple. Her blood determines her loyalties and thus ours. We have no choice. She

stroked his head, -Have courage Kamil as you have shown in the past few days. We must believe we can prevail. She has promised no harm will come to either of us. Let us rehearse what must be done.

The plan was this. A note from Baligha, wrapped around the small green feather would be pushed through the stone screen into the Empress's chamber where Muez lay low. The message would say:

I know you killed Rafi, T'ariq and my dearest Aidah. Place a thousand gold coins at the door of the palace of the senses before cock crow and I will leave the city immediately, taking my secrets with me. Fail to do so and I will use my influence through Kamil, the court historian, to seek an audience with the Princess. He is in my power and will do ought for me.

It would be stamped with Baligha's mark.

*

In the early hours of the next morning a group of four horsemen drew up at the palace of the senses. One leant forward and beat a loud tattoo with the heel of his sword. The grille slid back and he dropped a heavy sack on the step.

-Take this to your mistress, he ordered, -On your life! And the four galloped away.

An hour later, Baligha, dressed in a black cloak, left by the same door and climbed into a curtained coach. It clattered through the south gate and on to the stone bridge that led out of the city. As it reached the midpoint, two hooded horsemen appeared before it and two behind. The carriage jolted to a halt. One of the horsemen forced his mount alongside and drew the curtain back. A shot rang out and he fell to the ground. His companions came to his aid from in front and from behind but as they reached him they became aware of the steely clatter of horses at either end of the bridge. Further shots were exchanged.

Not much later, four bodies floated down the river and through the centre of the city. One was being dragged along under a cape trimmed with green feathers.

Chapter Eighteen

Hope needs cupping like a candle

He had thought for a while about how much the Princess was changing. He even had deluded himself into thinking how much her time with him was helping change her. The readings from the Tales of the Magus, the signs that her famed, violent temper and impetuosity were giving way to a more considered sympathetic personality. But the happenings of the day and the night before had dispelled such illusions. He saw his Princess as she truly was, a construction of calculation and manipulation. He wondered, disloyally, who might be the greater monster, his Princess or the Empress? Fate had ordained that he follow the younger woman. He still loved her with that strange emotional thirst that sprang from a life of obedience and service but it tried his heart to find her so implacable, so blinkered, so willing for others to suffer or die so that she might achieve her ends.

She floated into his sight in a suffusion of soft pink silks, her hair decorated with little pink butterflies and gold sequins. She sat down. Her face was soft and content. She examined him through sweeping lashes, -All is well, my spymaster?

He bowed, -It is, your Highness.

-Baligha is at ease?

-With relief she is.

-Ah Kamil, have no fear. I would not allow even a hair on her head to suffer injury now that she is the wife-to-be of my old historian! Have I not played cupid to you both? You are one of the great successes of my short life! You shall live happily ever after. You, the favourite of my court and chief advisor and she, your faithful companion.

-You are most generous, your Highness. He bowed. In his heart Kamil felt intimidated and wondered whether he and Baligha would ever be free of her influence and needs.

She looked at him, perhaps sensing his internal disquiet but said nothing of it.

Instead she mused, -Perhaps. But we have one last obstacle, have we not? We must see through the final stages of our campaign and expose my stepmother before your happiness can be fully confirmed! We need do nothing for a day or two. As you say, I shall be a spider and test the threads. I am content. The end is in sight. I think I need to be read to, dear Kamil. She had adopted her little girl voice, her lips pouting yet her eyes sparkling as she turned over the next card, The Star of Hope.

-See! the cards fall into line more and more. Are we their puppets or are they little mirrors of our thoughts and acts? Whatever, it is a peaceful card after those we have recently seen. She smiled at the image of a maiden bathing in water with stars surrounding her, -Read!

The boys were slow to become used to the ways of their beasts. Their lower bodies ached and their legs were severely chapped. He was forced to give them frequent rests. However, they had been well educated by the monks and could, in the main, speak better than most adults on most subjects. Particularly the eldest. The entourage was a strange sight. Barefooted, black-robed boys and a broad shouldered Warrior with sword, knife and bow, his face hardened and darkened by travelling so that his grey eyes seemed even paler and more startling in contrast. He was forced to keep to well-travelled routes to avoid the hardship of rough land. The boys could not have endured those travails. But he realised how much he missed the wilderness and its privations, the harsh isolation from people, the limitless space and time for his mind to work over events or conversations and the never ending search for greater meaning.

Now and then he glanced at the boy riding beside him. He had thought about divulging his dream of the boy's future but rejected the impulse. Whereas he had determined he would be guided by the needs of others he would not knowingly intercede in their journeying to force them down a particular path. It would not help the boy to know his future. It would visit him soon enough and his fervent eyes would in time give way to the hard gaze of a fighting man, a general commanding armies, thrusting the boy from the certainties of a spiritual path to the uncertainties of armed life and politics.

-What do you think of us? asked the boy, as though reading his mind.

-You are unusual but brave boys. You leave your villages for a tower where life is hard, where few pleasures are allowed. Not for you the caresses of young women, the pride of fatherhood, the contentment of old age and being cared for by your children. You must have great faith in your god of sun and fire!

-It is so. Yet you are not so different. You travel alone, you have no great liking for cities. You live in your own tower though it be of your imagination and not of stone. Where will your life-taker accompany you when you die? We will rise like the white feathers of the dove to meet with the sun and join all those who have lived obediently under the One God.

-What shape is your life-taker? asked the Warrior, curious.

-A great golden bird, of course. It will plunge into the sun's fires with us in its beak and return ever again to repeat its ceaseless toil. What is yours?

-A female hermit somewhat like you though its cloak is brown.

-You have seen it? Is this why you wear the same? A woman - you are certain? The boy's eyes glistened.

-In dreams.

-What god does this hermit serve?

-None that I know. She is my death's attendant. She moves along the path of my history and walks with my future. Sometimes she pauses at that point we always call 'now' but so far she hasn't stopped there! He smiled, -If she stopped it would signify my death. For death is the final 'now' for each of us. She watches me to be there when my time is ready.

-Your life-taker is personal? Can this be true? It seems a servant to you! The boy asked questions like a court arbiter.

-Servant? Master? Part of me? Separate from me? I do not know. Yet she has more than my single fate to consider. He then told the boy of the outcome of his meeting with his attendant and how his own life was now balanced against two hundred others.

-You helped us kill many men in the tower.

-It is true - though I thought not of my strange contract at the time.

-It seems to me that there is no need to heed its terms. For if you live your desired fate to the full, men will surely die. You are powerless in this regard. The will of men appears to be made of choice and freedom but it is illusory. God, who is wise in all things, creates such illusions to develop in us a desire to follow Him. If we go to Him through choice then we are elevated. We come from Him and will return to Him when we are worthy. The Warrior guessed that the words were recited from schooling in the tower but said nothing for a while.

-It is an easier path for believers, he said finally.

-Why say you this? It is a hard and exacting path.

-But it is prepared for you. It is flattened in the grasses and the woods, across the streams and through the snow. It has signs and measured distances. All you must do is follow it and it leads to your God. For those who do not believe there is only the wilderness. To make a personal path, to make sense of it, will break many a man's will.

-I had not thought of it in this way, said the boy, reflecting, -I see why you are a mighty warrior and a shaman. You are neither a man of this time nor the creature of a god who has yet to be revealed to humankind. He looked over at the Warrior, feeling that his words made a new sense. -There is no-one like you. There will be many in every place who curse you silently, or worse. You will be hunted the moment your strength appears to wane for there are those who would gain prestige from taking your life. It is almost beyond thought to conceive of a man like you. You must be some special offspring of fate and impelled to take a journey which is beyond an ordinary man's comprehension.

-We shall see. If there is a fate then the pattern will eventually be seen in the cloth.

-You see? If! If! I have never thought other than that there IS fate! There must be fate! Even your attendant says so!

-My dreams are but dreams and my attendant walks in them.

-You wear the brown cloak in battle!

The older male said quietly, -It was given to me before my dream. Are the Spice Merchants fate-shapers? If there is fate then it seems to me, according to cold logic, that there must be a god. If there is no god then fate becomes fractured into a thousand flakes. Do you know that the strange twins trade a disc with the picture of a god on one side and a representation of fate on the other?

-You would stand the disc on its edge to discover what joins the two faces! His laughter made the older man smile such that eventually he took from a bag a small woven purse. In it was a disc of wood. On one side was a five pointed cross and on the other a circle. He handed it to the boy without explanation.

The boy examined it closely, -What is this? Is this the sun and this... I know not...perhaps a man?

-They are what you wish them to be. He took back the disc, -Watch!

Tell me which side will face up. He flicked the disc into the air so that it turned over and over, caught it with one hand and slapped it on to the back of the other, covering it.

-The sun!

-Correct! Again?

-The sun!

-Correct! Again?

-Ah! This time I will say the man!

-It is true.

-Again? For some time the boy sought to defeat the power of his own oracle but always the disc proved his guess correct.

-You are a magician.

-Or you. Or is it the work of your god?

-No, it is not. It cannot be.

-Why not?

-Why should God concern himself with such a game?

-I thought gods must concern themselves with all things, from the small to the great?

-Show me how it is done magician.

-If you answer me first. As he said this he spun the disc from one hand and caught it balanced on its edge on the back of the other.

The boy's eyes were round. He thought for a moment, -The trick is the work of God as all things are in His gift. He reveals Himself through you. And yet again it may not be so for how could he act through a godless man?.

-So it is possible to take your answer and fashion it thus. God is in all things and knows of them. In some things he has an interest and intervenes while in others he has no interest or leaves us to make our own choices. But then I might equally say that god is not in all things. God does not exist except in our fears and desires.

-He exists. He is of the Sun. You are the greatest blasphemer I have met. But the boy's expression showed an emerging amusement.

-For you and your kind. Remember, other tribes have a family of gods. Still others worship a female god. Some pray to their ancestors. He threw the disc into the air and caught it in a clenched fist. What say you? he enquired, tapping it.

-The sun!

He opened his fist and there lay a small white feather. He handed it to the boy, -May your god be good to you and your journey to him be as you desire.

♀

The journey stretched. The boys became horsemen. All questioned him about his life, his prowess and his beliefs. In the evenings they demanded lessons with sword and bow. He indulged them for it kept him honed. They had passed beyond the borders of their enemy and were now making steady progress towards their destination. The land was at peace here. Often villages gave them food on seeing the black robes though they kept their distance from the Warrior. His fame was here too. Sometimes his father's seal opened doors to houses that welcomed merchants. All showed interest in him, openly or otherwise. His face was stern and forbidding. His black hair was plaited to his waist and his unusual eyes glittered in their dusky skin. He was strongly built and taller by a head than the tallest in any clan.

♀

The end of their journey together came abruptly. It was as though the old fortification in front of them had materialised from the very sky. It had four towers and a great open arch as its entrance. They caught up with a returning monk who took the eldest boy's reins, questioning him with a sombre face and shedding tears at the news of the deaths of his brothers. As they reached the archway the boys dropped easily from their mounts and they all listened with nods and fixed gazes as the eldest told of their escape and the great deeds of their saviour. When he had done he turned to introduce the Warrior. But he and his two horses had gone. None had seen it happen. He could not be far away in such a short time, yet there was no trace. The monk led the other boys through the arch while the eldest stood for a moment. He gave a whistle and from the tower a dove fluttered into his waiting hands. He stroked it and whispered to it. Then he released it into the air.

♀

He knew that the bird was coming. The roan looked up as it had done once before. They halted and it dropped lightly on to his cupped palms. There was no message attached. It looked at him, cocking its head. It swelled its breast and murmured softly. Then, it dipped its beak and pulled out a tiny white breast feather and presented it to him. He smiled and took it, stroking its neck and back before whispering that it must return.

The sun was bright, though the air was cool and still. He took the feather and blew it from the palm of his hand. It rose on the air for a while but then gently descended to the earth. He had a brief image again of a general in a plumed helmet.

☥

-I need to learn from you!

-But I do not need you to learn from me. You should be with your brethren. The Warrior tried not to reveal his irritation.

-It cannot be. The superior said so. When he heard our story he asked me many times how I talked to birds. Then he said that it was God's work to talk thus and there was no place in the order for one such as I. Talking to birds is a heresy. He gave me this horse and I rode like the wind, day and night. I am sore.

-They are fools. But the Warrior smiled at the boy's determination.

The boy clapped his hands together, -It may be so! Therefore it must be written that I learn from you. It will not be forever.

-It will not be at all.

-It is your duty. You must follow my destiny now - until there is a natural parting.

-The parting was two sleeps ago.

-I entreat you! The boy's eyes filled with tears but he looked at the man with determination. So much so that the Warrior relented. In truth, he liked the boy's company. It might be better to accompany him in his destiny than that of another he might meet.

-Until the first flake of snow, he said at last.

-I will need clothes like yours, said the boy as though he had not heard, -This robe has served its purpose.

☥

-I look like you!

-Of course. They are my clothes.

-It is a compliment.

-You are a mere boy. In time you will look like no other.

-Will they fear me as they do you? The man said nothing though he knew that this indeed would be the case.

☥

-Where are we going?

-It has yet to be written.

-It is a strange thought. All I have met are roped to life more securely than you. Their days are full of what must be done. In the tower every part of the day was fixed for us. Just so with farmers and traders and soldiers. Some more fixed, perhaps. But all fixed.

-I am none of those.

-You are not. You are an earth wanderer. A solitary warrior. Do you know why we go this way? he repeated.

-I feel it.

-Will you wander until you die?

-It may be so. Who knows which sun will be the last to shine on my life.

-You may die of old age.

-Perhaps, but before that day I will return to the valleys of my childhood. There I will meet my father-not-of-blood. There I will embrace a mother I have never seen except in a dream, since I was but a few hours old. On my journey I will take to my side the woman to whom my body is sworn - and with her my first child, whom I have yet to meet.

-You know all this?

-These are my great desires and they are with me throughout my wandering. Much else may happen. Even I have my rope of attachment.

-If these are your great desires why do you not satisfy them now? Go immediately to your woman and then the valleys of your youth.

-It is not possible.

-Why? The boy had a way of challenging what was said which reminded him of his own stubbornness with his father.

-All is held together in a certain tension. My journey is balanced like a spice merchant's scales. To return is not quite the equal to further journeying. It is strong but does not yet outweigh the urge to discover more, to know more.

-You may end up at a point from which it is impossible to return. There might not be enough seasons left in your body for such a trek.

-My journey is an arc. It will lead me back though there will be branches and diversions. From some of these I will learn more, some will be like the plant that chokes the river and some will seem rich in possibility but afford little.

☥

The boy taught him how to attract a dove from the sky and also how to master the secrets of powders that the monks had had brought to them by their merchant brothers, to prepare the terrible thunder that could make a tower collapse. He trained the boy to foretell the fighting moves of an opponent even as a battle rages, not with the mind but with the freed instincts of the body, -Never question your body, he said, -For that will slow you down and you will be vulnerable. Let it do the fighting and allow your mind to be as a void.

-What do you feel at the death of an enemy, one that dies at your hand? Sorrow?

-I have not yet experienced any sadness. My father instructed me to feel thus. It is easier with a bird or animal I am to eat. With my enemy there is something which forestalls it. Perhaps if I became the cause of an innocent death, it may be so. All whom I have killed have sought to kill me - or other innocents that I have protected.

-Yet you are mightier than they. They are innocent of this knowledge. They fight you, expecting to kill you but have no chance of success against the fatal edges and points of your weapons.

-If I were to allow such thoughts to strangle my heart I would not be strong. In battle the heart cannot speak. All must be emptiness as I have said.

-Yet it would make my own heart tremble I know it. To take another man's life is no small thing. The man took these words in. They became a battleground for his thoughts.

☥

-How do you feel towards this desert woman?

-Certainty. We are locked in an embrace, though parted by many years' travel. There is no other, nor will there be.

-You have not lain with another?

-Not with my heart nor with the desire of my loins. He then recounted how he came to a congress with the girl whose name he never knew.

-Your blood and hers spoke to each other.

-It was so. The choice was made for me. It was none of my doing. My father has many pacts of friendship with powerful ones. He could not refuse my service at this time.

-And so you were not unfaithful to your camel rider?

-A person cannot be held guilty when he is but a blind instrument of others. A soldier obeying orders is not contaminated in the way that he who gives them is.

-If the act has no worth he is as guilty as his captain. Killing children and women can never be honourable. Nor the old and the defenceless. Nor, in your case, an enemy who has no chance against you.

There was a long silence. As the Warrior had suspected, the boy was worthy company, -You are right. All who kill must be guided by whether the act is a just one. Yet true justice can be like a patterned snake on its own land.

☥

The boy fought poorly but it gave him some exercise. He was at least learning to trust his body and so their bouts lasted a little longer although the outcome was always the same.

-You should let me win just once to save my pride and honour at this humiliation! panted the boy.

-Better honourable defeat than false victory. You will win too many battles in your later life to be concerned about the defeats of your apprenticeship. He smiled, -And if we are forced to fight at that time you will know in your heart that you have never beaten me which will be to my advantage.

-You think I will win battles? But I will never fight you even so, no matter how I fare as a soldier.

The man said nothing and began to prepare food.

☥

-If you do not rise into the sun when you die where do you go? asked the perplexed boy.

-We talked of this.

-You did not answer.

-I cannot speak of that which I know not. I have not met any who have been beyond this life so I know not what exists beyond it.

-Something divine must exist. What would be the point to life if it didn't? The boy laughed loudly at the very thought, -The prophets, the priests, the women who guard the sacred river, all speak of worlds we must enter after this one.

-I did not say that there was no such place, only that we know nothing of it from witnesses. It seems, according to those you mention, that it is a place where no physical body is allowed entry and where all stories end.

-If your life is a good one then such a place will be a reward. If your life is that of a dishonourable man then it will be denied you. Don't you not believe this? His young face was earnest.

-No, if I am left with just a belief to hold on to then I cannot accept it. If I am to experience proof of such a destination on my journey then I will willingly embrace the god who reveals this mystery to me.

-May the God of Fire do this for you! I will pray that it is so.

☥

-We have talked of love and death, said the boy.

-And right and wrong.

-I would like us to talk about fate.

-We have already mentioned it.

-We have. The boy halted his horse, -You say one thing and then another. Sometimes you are sun and sometimes moon.

-They can shine at the same time, without conflict. And their opposition can create a strange harmony.

-You stated that fate and God were two sides of the same coin.

-Did I?

-Yes, believe in one and you must believe in the other. If there is a god who concerns himself with our lives then that must be a kind of fate.

-That may be true.

-And you talk as though you believe in fate so you must believe in God. Hah!

-Or neither. Everywhere I travel there are gods. They change with the tribes and even clans within tribes. Could it be the same god who takes various forms or are there indeed many? Do gods allow us to choose our beliefs? To be free to do as we wish? Or do they decree that we be prisoners of the fate they have set for us? Most people I meet are hostages of what they think of as fate. They are as the beasts in the field. They follow the path you have described, each day being filled with acts that allow no choice. They do not even think that this is strange. Among them are a few who would be different. For them fate is a force which can be given new pathways just as a man might dig a channel from a river to divert it. The water can now flow another way. Some of the sages that I have met believe that gods are only needed to keep people content with their way of life. Through the sharing of the same beliefs and rituals, villages and towns can grow more easily in peace and prosperity. For me it is simple. It is better to be the writer than the one who reads.

-You are a fate-shaper.

-Sometimes it feels so. It seems possible to determine one's life. As I told you, the Spice Merchants insisted that my purpose would only be made visible to me if I helped others to fulfil their destinies. I must relinquish my will and be at the mercy of others' fates. It is a paradox!

They were silent for a while as they struggled with these thoughts. Then the man said, -It is the act of letting go that frees. When nothing is demanded of life then everything is possible and everything in turn has meaning and purpose. As soon as fate ceases its hold upon you, then it becomes a dog on your rope.

-You are a true teacher. None of the fathers was ever so clear in his thought.

☥

One evening they swam in a river. The horses, freed from their burdens, swam with
them, snickering and thrashing their tails. The Warrior felt a calm he rarely experienced, as though the water was washing through him like the waters in a woman's body preparing a child for life. Being made to answer questions by the boy was reshaping him. He found that he liked doing so whereas once he would never have offered an opinion of his own for fear of imposing it on another.

Though he was not really aware of it, he had reached the furthest point on his journey's arc.

-**It is an** interesting relationship, Sabiya shuffled for comfort, -A little like yours and mine, teacher! The novice learns much from the Magus and the poor Magus cannot be rid of him! You see Kamil, once you have proven your calibre your pupil begins to depend upon it. Soon she cannot see a world without such wisdom and advice. You become worth all other advisors added together. But the Warrior is right about fate. Persuade the people that in following God and Emperor they are following the fixed coordinates of fate. Their own fate and the fate of the empire are joined at the hip. Such unquestioning devotion makes ruling a good deal less exacting.

Chapter Nineteen

What would day be without night?

How portentous it is, thought Kamil, that as the Arcana of the tarot move towards the end of their cycle, the events of this world also move towards a conclusion. Her royal Highness was right, life and the tarot entwine so that it becomes difficult to see which might be the progenitor of the other.

For the moment, Baligha, despite her desires to the contrary was ensconced for her safety in one of the Princess's private chambers where Kamil was unable to visit her. Kamil felt a tiny flicker of guilt. He knew that Sabiya wanted her out of the way so that she could have his undivided attention but he had not resisted the decision. He was obliged to serve her while events and the cards came to their culmination. The Tales had to be completed, then there might be some peace for Baligha and her man. He turned over the next card knowing what it would be. He studied it. The Moon. It presided over a strange, divided world of life and illusion. Above, dogs bayed, below, strange creatures crawled and swam in a nether world. If the card spoke clearly, her Highness would be faced with further deceptions, ones of which they were as yet unaware.

*

-I have brought my new map, she exclaimed, -Look, I spent much time bringing it up to date. She spread the thick paper on the table, placing candle holder and bowl to stop it from rolling back.

-It is much bigger and more complex! he complimented her.

-It is now a triptych. See? I have made three sections. The past is here combining all up to the point when we had our first meeting. Then there is the period from then until now. And over there is the future. You see that the days to come are only outlined. But that green figure stands for me and that shaded yellow area for the palace and my empire. Here you are with Baligha. Who else will inhabit my world we shall see. Anyway, at the moment it is a mere affectation. The middle and greatest section is what preoccupies us.

Kamil could pick out in this central zone a series of events such as the deaths of the chamber maid, Muez, Askari and T'ariq outlined in black. The blue figure of the Emperor was in the middle. Beside him in violent red were the Empress and various of her courtiers. There was Sabiya in green again with, he assumed, himself in gold at her side. Baligha was speckled in all colours except red, in a room by herself.

-I made you gold, she said, following his intent gaze, -Because you are my alchemist. In your hands the base becomes pure.

-Who is this, he asked, covering his pleasure at the words and pointing at a bent figure in grey.

-That is Khawlah, the mute. See, in the final zone she is a lady in one of my chambers! She has been a surprising ally. In truth I find the act of talking with hands a boon. It calms me.

-You have talked with her?

-I have brought her to my apartments. Suspicion would eventually fall on all the servants after Baligha's message was delivered. Even her. Her last act of spying was to observe the Empress in a fit, screaming and wailing, running through corridors and tearing at her hair and clothes, my father following and swearing he would capture and kill those that had taken the lives of Muez and his men. She laughed, -If he but knew!

-What would he do?

-In truth I know not. She bit her bottom lip and narrowed her eyes, -Banish me to the country of my ancestors? Back to command a droplet whilst here I would rule an ocean. I cannot think of it. It upsets me. Let us have my story. Then we will conjure the final phase of our plans.

Their time together lasted more than three years though without danger. They passed through many encampments. Sometimes they helped villagers where such help was needed. The Warrior found sources of water by pacing the ground and swinging a stone attached to a fine leather string close to the earth. The boy showed how to improve crops by the careful choice of seed. They demonstrated better welfare of animals and fowl and different ways of trapping food. In the evenings, with firelight playing on his face, the boy told stories about the God of the Sun, so that many whom they met changed their beliefs. The Warrior listened to these tales and marvelled at the boy's prowess. If he disagreed he did not show it. It seemed to him a relatively benign path to follow for those who needed comfort and explanation.

One day the boy said suddenly, -My village is close. He had given no sign that they had been approaching it though he had made choices of direction for some time. The man had not objected for he was intent on following the advice of the Spice Merchants and the way that he was being led was, in any case, in harmony with his journey home. Instead he kept silent knowing that the boy would soon explain his secretive juggling of forks and turnings.

A little later the boy said, -I did not mention it because I did not know if I wanted to return. I will be a great disappointment to my parents for they hoped that I would become a monk, and even a superior. Then they would have been cared for by the order into their old age. But my desire to see them is strong. Now, because of you, I have become used to the ways of the fighting man. I can join the tribe's army and then make them proud of me when I become its captain.

-I will not come with you to meet them.

-I felt that this might be so.

-My obligation to you has run its course. See? He held up the sleeve of his jacket. A snowflake rested on it like the dove's breast feather.

The boy smiled, -I saw it descend. It is time.

-But I will give you something, said the man. He undid a pouch that hung from his neck and took out a watery pink stone, -This may buy your parents' forgiveness. Sell it to a rich trader. It is worth a hundred horses.

-You have been as a father to me.

-And you as a young brother.

-I owe you my life.

-If I need you to repay me I will send a dove!

-Even when I become a general, your request will outweigh all others. The man reached deep into the boy's mind and knew that he had begun to sense his destiny. As he rode away he saw the boy watching him. He had taken out the wooden casket containing the ancient texts of his faith. He raised it in the air.

☥

He was alone with his beasts. Though he would miss the boy he felt strongly the pleasure of solitude, the realisation that at last he had begun the long adventure home was pulsing within him. How it had happened could not be fathomed. Something beyond his grasp had led him to this point. He wondered at the way instinct commanded thought. Was it truly he who was writing his story?

Snow was falling. It would cover and cleanse the earth. The roan and its black companion were untroubled. Their coats had grown thick and warm. When he unburdened them each night they rolled in deep drifts like foals. He made a protection from a skin stretched against the wind, cleared the snow and they lay together, he between them, sharing their bodies' heat. He found these sleeps the most refreshing of his entire journey. It was warm within his fleeced skins, his cap drawn down over his face, the cold air in his lungs and the scent of the horses' bodies. It was as it had been when he was a child and he was taught by his father how to live off a land that seemed to promise nothing. Using the signs offered by trees and shrubs he dug beneath the white crust, uncovering roots, stores of nuts and the shoots of new growth. From tracks on the surface he knew what life made its way round him. He would sit motionless with his bow taut and his clothing thick with gathering flakes until the moment when his fingers could release an arrow. By a deep relaxation of his mind and body, he became neither cold nor stiff and was able to move swiftly within a single breath. When the nights were clear and the moon seemed a mirror to the white world, he lay and memorised new patterns of stars. From the untouchable canvass above he was able to map the tangible world around him.

All the while his thoughts played on the theme of purpose, sometimes directly but more often at the back of his mind, beyond his immediate grasp. The great paradoxes that enfolded him became more and more apparent. The less he was concerned to leave a mark on life the more he appeared to do so. When he had wished not to be involved in the lives of others, he had then been instructed to tend to their fate. The more he sought peace for contemplation the more he became drawn into battle and instinctive action. The more his thoughts had turned to his deep desire for his desert woman, the more he had extended the arc of his journey. Enough wealth came to him without request. Heroic deeds attached themselves to him without him lifting knife or sword. He authored his life only by following the prescription of the spice women. He had befriended a little desert child, a monkish boy and his young companions, a hermit, kings, queens and nobles, powerful women and countless villagers. Meanwhile men had died before his sword and bow and a princess had also died despite his attempts to protect her. He had become a magician like his father, a warrior with no equal, a shaman of the wilds who spoke few words but gained fame for wisdom. Yet, at the heart of him, he knew nothing! No great secret had been revealed. No thread in the great tapestry had been traced. The everyday detail of life that men took for granted caused his own thoughts to fly in a storm. Why the sun? Why the stars? Why this cold sorceress of a moon sipping life out of the world? Why killing? Why love? Why did the powerful and the weak equally see in him a man with answers when he had none? Why did they whisper 'shaman' as their eyes dwelt upon him?

He heard the hiss and thud as the arrow struck home before he realised that it was his own body that had been pierced. The roan and the stallion reared and galloped off with him as more arrows flew past. Despite the blood soaking his back and the terrible pain his mind stayed calm and clear. He took the agony and forced it into a dark far-off place in his mind and focused upon holding to the saddle. The beasts could smell his blood and their fear for him took them on an arduous marathon climb to a concealed clearing overgrown with heavy green foliage. He dropped to the ground and stumbled stiffly against his horse, the reins holding him upright. Then he embraced a stout tree like a lover with his good arm and legs and muttered a command to the roan. The horse drew air loudly through its teeth and took the arrow between them moving backwards slowly, step by step. He fought with the pain. Gradually the arrow eased free. Removing his jacket, wool shirt and cotton under-cloth, he stumbled into the snow and turned on to his back. He rubbed against it to remove much of the blood and then lay for a while, allowing the wound to go numb, the arrow hole tighten and the blood flow to slow.

Finally he stood up and took plants from his bags and chewed them before pressing them awkwardly into the hole, his hand stretching backwards over his injured shoulder. He pressed his mulched back against a tree trunk, holding it there. The roan stood unmoving against him, warming him. When he was satisfied that the blood had stopped flowing, he tore a strip from his under-cloth with teeth and hand. He laid it on the saddle and took out honey from his food pack, spreading it on the cloth. By backing against the saddle he was able to draw an end of the cloth over his shoulder and the other under his arm. The honey kept it stuck in place. He secured the ends together with two finely pointed wooden pins. Then he dressed slowly in a fresh cloth and shirt before replacing his jacket.

☥

He had heard a dog howl and then silence. He rested. His trail could be followed. Droplets of blood covered by snow. But he had some time. He slept.

☥

A long time before he was wounded a king had looked upon a group of harsh fighting men. These were the best dozen that his generals had been able to gather together, -Bring back this so-called immortal warrior, dead! I will reward you. The king had stood imperiously before them. The men had growled their accord and raised their arms before mounting their horses.

✞

After long years on his trail they had caught up with him during a storm. They knew his powers and so had stayed far behind him waiting for this moment. They had heard tale upon tale of his prowess from people in the villages. They heard of the hundred or more men who had died in the tower. Each succeeding story had made them more careful. Now, with the wind blowing from him to them and his horses' ears flattened against the wild storm, the most skilled archer fired his arrow. They saw it strike. The others fired their arrows as the injured man was carried high into the woods. None hit him or his mounts. Their leader raised an arm, -We will follow slowly. If he is sorely injured then he will be even weaker. If not then it will take our undivided strength. We must protect each other. Together we cannot be vanquished but if scattered we are easy prey for such a man. The dog will do our work for us. Put it down.

One of the troop dropped a tethered hound from his embrace. It barked and snarled. They showed it the bloodied snow. Almost immediately it bayed and pulled, tensing the rope. But its handler refused to let it run and muzzled it so that with the dog leading the ten fighting men could stay in a tight group.

✞

They found him face down in a sheltered clearing, among thick bushes. His clothes were stiffened with ice, his peaked cap, half off his head. The leader bade them stop.

-He is cunning. A dozen arrows will make his death certain. All the arrows struck the prone man. As their bowstrings vibrated, empty of their missiles, they were all assailed by the same thought. The sound the arrows made as they struck was wrong and the lack of substance to the body was unnatural. It was a trap! In that moment a cloth bag with a short burning cord flew through the air and dropped among them. They stared at it, unsure. It fizzed. Their mounts started to rear. Suddenly there was a clap of thunder and a flash of lightning. Flames erupted under them. Some horses fell. Others bolted. Men clutched at unseeing eyes and two who could still see started to chase their horses as a brown robed hermit appeared among them with a throwing knife. He took one man round the neck and held him in the crook of his good arm, like a child, blade at his neck. To the rest he said, calmly, -You owe your lives to a boy who will one day be your own general. It was he who persuaded me not to kill if I had the choice. Go! Wait for him. Your king will be the first to fall before his sword. Those who could stumbled away blindly, calling for their horses.

☥

As he rode slowly through the forest, the snow building on his outer jacket, he pondered on the badges worn by the men. They were from the city of the dead princess. He visualised her again lying with the knife held between her clutching fingers. Their failed attempt upon his life was only hastening the city's decay.

He would learn more from the prisoner who he had strapped across the saddle of the big stallion.

☥

-Why have you spared me? asked the man.
-I am thinking about this.
-I will tell you nothing.
-If I was your prisoner would I speak?
-If you were my prisoner you would speak.
-What would you do to make me?
-I would cut off pieces of your body until the pain was so great - the prisoner stopped, considering his foolishness.
-How much would you cut from me before I would be forced to answer you?
-It would be the equal of your courage.
-But I would speak?

-I have never known a man not speak - eventually…

-Where should I begin? The man stared at him fearfully, -Or will you tell me what I need to know? It will save your body so much pain.

-It is true. But if I return with no sign of ill upon me they will think I am a coward and have me killed.

The Warrior thought of the captain in the City in the Mountain. He said, -Once I would have killed you quickly and cleanly. Perhaps I would have left your head upon a sharpened pole. Your fate would decide whether you would be found before those living creatures that prefer carrion, stripped your face to the bone. But I have been in the company of a young monk who made me consider many things. The most important of these is not to kill. To try to be just. To offer compassion. To free your enemy. The prisoner was hunched on a fallen log, -If I was your prisoner you would make me speak by torture. And once I had spoken you would kill me anyway. That is the way of the army is it not? The tied man said nothing, -I will offer you this. Tell me what I do not know about the death of the princess and I will feed you and let you go free at the next village.

-You know where I am from?

-You wear the badge of that city, he said flatly and returned to his theme, -Tell me nothing and I will leave you here with your hands tied. You are a trained fighting man. You can take your chances. With this he turned his back and began a fire. The prisoner watched in amazement as even with a single hand the Warrior prepared for a meal. He stared as the man slipped away for a short time and returned with a small creature which he skinned and skewered. He wondered as he witnessed how the shaman found the roots which he simmered in a clay pot, how he shook special seasoning on to the turning meat. The snow fell around them and even with the protection of the trees, the prisoner was turning white. The Warrior sat close to the fire, his dark features lit by the sputtering flames. It was as though he had made a cave for himself in the icy night. Behind him his two horses stood, now and then reaching forward to nuzzle the nape of his neck.

The prisoner was very cold. His bonds had numbed his hands. The smell of the cooking meat tortured him and his mouth filled with the water of anticipation.

-If I tell you, you will feed me?

-It is my word.

-And let me loose at the next village?

-At its edge. They do not need to know that you have been my prisoner.

The Warrior began eating. He pierced a piece of flesh with his knife and put it to the lips of the tied man who took it and chewed.

-Ah, if my woman could only cook like this! he said, wanting more. But the Warrior ignored him and continued eating.

-I will tell you what I know, the tethered one said, breaking the silence, -For you already know where we come from. The Warrior waited, stripping lengths of meat from the bone with his teeth, -You had not long left the city when it was discovered that the princess was dead. The king and the queen and the one chosen to be father of the royal child said you should have saved her for your powers are so great - but you chose not to. You wanted to see the destruction of the city. The ancient curse says that when the royal line is sundered between the first showing in the royal maid -

-I know this. The city will fall into ruin.

-Yes. The King ordered the best dozen fighting men to be brought to his palace and then sent us to find and kill you. Your body would appease our God.

-I could not stay her death. My powers are not so great. She was sworn to fulfil the ancient curse. I merely delayed her self-execution for one night. Even so it stays with me. I feel responsible though in truth I cannot be.

-You cannot alter the fate of another unless Fate, itself, decrees it! proclaimed the man.

The Warrior smiled. For some, fate was the inescapable fifth element in their lives, -Your pursuit has been long!

-But no great challenge. You leave a trail of deeds that would please a god! Some villagers worship you and you are not yet dead. Everyone talks of you, farmers, merchants, traders, nobles, monks. Tales are told and songs are sung at every camp fire. Does this not fill your breast with pride?

-It is of no consequence to me. It is wild talk.

-I would have more meat - it is the work of a magus!

-Have you told me all?

-All that there is. I did not think you could withstand us. We were the most feared of all the king's fighting men. We could have laid a hundred soldiers to waste.

-You all but took my life. He motioned to his shoulder.

-But we did not. That is the mark of your prowess. We did not. How did you remove the arrow?

-My beast pulled it from me with its teeth.

-Ah, the horse of fable! And where did you learn to throw thunder and lightning? We knew of the fall of the tower from such god-given magic but never thought to be the victim of that sorcery ourselves.

-A boy showed me the secret.

-Another ungodly being!

-Not so. But he is closer to a god than most. He will use his powers to become the lord of all these lands. He will make one tribe of all tribes. All will bow to him.

-What God does he serve?

-The sun and its fire.

☥

-It is here that I will untie your bonds. He pointed to the smoke of a village. He placed the prisoner's sword on the ground, -In return for your life, do as I tell you. Do not use this weapon against any who are not trained for battle.

-I swear.

-Take a message to the queen. Tell her that I spared you so that the king would know the full story of his ten assassins. He pulled a long hair from his tail. She will see from this that you tell the truth. None other has a length such as this. Tell her that in a few years an army will mass and put her city to the sword and no man shall stand against it. No stone of her palace will remain standing. If she is wise she will leave for sanctuary elsewhere. The queen will protect you for she fears what I might do if she does not. And when the boy of whom I have spoken becomes a man and lord of all, go to him and tell him your story. Tell him that I spared you for I foresaw you that will serve him well. He undid the prisoner's hands, -Then, under his command, you will enter your own city in triumph and the great bloodline will be over.

The freed man was silent for some time as though digesting each word carefully before he bowed to him, -I shall do all as you say. I am in debt to you for sparing my life. He picked up his sword and trudged off through the deepening snow to the village, looking back now and then in wonder.

☥

As he rode on the Warrior reflected on these events. It felt good to let the prisoner go. It felt just. He thought about the shock of the arrow striking him. It had happened just as he was pondering on why people had begun to talk of him as a shaman.

It disturbed him deeply that he had not known that the arrow was coming.

Princess Sabiya was genuinely shocked at the twist in the Tale. It gave Kamil grim satisfaction that his storytelling prowess had drawn such a reaction before his eyes but he stayed silent. -How could this be? The Magus is deceived? First, he was unable to stop the death of that princess and now he is unable to stop the flight of an arrow? He is mortal. He could have died. You or I would have died. Is that not so? Kamil nodded, -Yet we have no magic horse and superhuman strength, she added plaintively, -Is this an omen? The card is the Moon. Are we being deceived, even when we think victory is in our hands?

There was a loud knock at the door. Her guard called to her. A shaken Sabiya half hid behind a grimly standing Kamil.

-Enter! she called in a strong, level voice, despite all. The guard stepped inside followed by a servant of the Emperor, hot and flushed from running. He bowed.

-Your Highness, your father commands your presence in the royal bedchamber. Her Majesty, the Empress, is sorely ill and no-one knows if she will survive -

Chapter Twenty

Ensure first that the enemy is not yourself!

For the first time Kamil took his cards and book to the Princess's apartments. He passed courtiers in black capes but with sidelong inquisitive looks. He passed bowing servants with eyes watching him under their lashes and finally, stern-faced guards who gazed at him stonily.

She was waiting for him in an internal garden. Water played a perpetual tinkling melody as it fell from a fountain into an artfully shaped copper bowl. The sun filtered through a grid of slatted canes. There was fragrance everywhere from climbing plants and more in large ceramic pots, from cut flowers in vases and from the grasses that grew between tiles. She was perched on one of two chairs, either side of a table, in a simple white gown. A black square of silk adorned her luxuriant hair which was tied high. He had overheard rumours of course, though being the perpetual outsider who spoke to no-one but the Princess, nothing had been said to him directly. But there were signs everywhere. The horn of grief had sounded close by and black weeded women had prostrated themselves beneath his very window.

-Sit master historian! He did so with a bow. She turned over the next card and looked briefly at The Sun, with a nod of recognition. She looked up, -You have heard the news? He made a non-committal grimace, -No, of course not. Who would tell you? It seems our campaign has found its closure. The map may be rolled away for another day. She poured him water from a slim crystal decanter encased in filigreed silver, -When I reached the royal bedroom she was nearly gone. Doctor Faqi administered antidotes for the tremors and jerks but her eyes were unseeing. The sheets were sodden by her cold, evil smelling, acid sweat. My father stood silent in angry helplessness. While we watched she went still. Faqi pulled the sheet over her head and motioned servants to carry her body away to the royal holding chamber. He bowed to my father who laid a hand on his shoulder. Then we were left alone, my father and I. Alone together at last - as it should have been for many long years.

We sat in an anteroom in silence, my fingers in his strong soldier's grasp. "It is too much to comprehend," he said. Then he told me what had happened. The death of Muez caused her great grief but it did not unhinge her mind. What caused the drama witnessed by Khawlah was the sudden death of the baby born to the host-mother secreted in her royal chambers. Princess Sabiya smiled savagely at Kamil.

Kamil looked uncomprehendingly at her.

-It was the final deception! She was never with child! Certain potions had helped to distend her stomach to make it appear so. Hearing of the death of the baby she swallowed a phial of a poison that gave her the semblance of the plague. It acted quickly - more quickly than it had done with my mother! Doctor Faqi recognised the symptoms, though he has no knowledge of the poison or its source. Kamil thought back to his readings in the Emperor's library. Poisons, mutated children, still births, miscarriages...

-The death of the substitute infant was the final blow for her, said Kamil softly. His eyes met hers. He saw something flickering in her pupils.

-Indeed, she said, -Indeed. She hugged herself and suddenly smiled sweetly, utterly changing her mood, -Now read to me The Sun for surely we have entered a time of warmth and security.

He had not known the arrow was coming! The ache in his shoulder brought repetitions of this thought to his mind. He had not known and therefore he was not in charge of his fate! He had not known therefore he was not in charge of his fate. The thought repeated itself over and over. Fate was not a dog on his leash. Was it that only a part of his life was at his behest and another part was not? Was the latter a hardly visible thread on the loom to which everything belonged?

He imagined fate then as an intricate pattern woven from all who had, did and would exist. Pull on a thread and the tension would be felt everywhere, even at the furthest edge. Even in the past. Perhaps his father was right after all. Everything was connected by this invisible tension. The king and the dozen men whom he had sent to kill him must be woven into the detail, together with their families and all that lived around them and even those who knew them not; all connected in the one tapestry. If there be fate then even the very rocks and soil played their part in destiny. Even the thoughts that passed through his mind like snow on warm earth must also affect the pattern and its ever changing shape. There was no act, no opening or closing of a single eye that did not have meaning or purpose for the whole.

To him this seemed to chime with an inner wisdom. It was not that fate was the other face of god, it was that fate was everything. A Warrior must choose and act knowing that there were no estranged events. No matter how alone, how distant from the nearest village, his passing thoughts would in some way have weight for the whole. Thus, the boy had been right and his father had been right. In all things it behoves a Warrior to be just and to live always with the desire for perfection. It was a path that must be followed.

☥

As he lay down between his horses for sleep that night, he prepared to dream of his attendant. His eyes closed and for a while he became without being.

The brown robed life-taker appeared before him. Snow fell around it but did not rest upon its hood or cloak.

-You have called me to you?

-Much has changed.

-Each moment everything changes. All that exists submits to this law. It is the perpetual cycle of creation and destruction.

The Warrior thought to ask the question that had led him to invoke the strange being but delayed and asked something else, -Are you subject to this law?

-It is the law that governs us. I am your shadow, your ghost, your guide, the one to whom you talk inside yourself. We are, together, what makes you.

-Then you change as I do?

-I am not as I was when last we talked.

-I thought you had knowledge of a place beyond this.

-None that you yourself do not possess. Though it may be hidden deep. Knowledge of all that has been and all that will be, is there. You have the key. In this, you are a magus.

-This is why I took the path, first with my father and then alone!

-Your purpose. There will be two further journeys. More is to be learned.

-I was blind to the reasoning. Now I understand a little more. This is why I called you to my sleep. The brown figure was without motion, attentive, -I have lived my life, unknowing, according to laws that lie within me. They guided me. In weighing the justness of my acts, most would have thought me a man of honour. Yet now what was hidden is clear. I know that what I have done even so has been forced upon me by the accepted ways of the world. My reactions, though considered, did not stem from the deepest meditation which might have offered truer value. There is, beyond my present understanding, a certain path, a path that is pure and just. It is this that I must follow and understand. What is as yet an untouched instinct can become my spoken word.

-You have come to maturity.

-I look back on all I have done and seen and heard and know that every breath was for this one purpose, to draw from me the certainty of a just way.

It seemed as though a long silence ensued in which he drifted again into not being. It was the attendant who reanimated him.

-You have yet to ask me your question.

The Warrior nodded and wrestled with what words to use, -You said that I must kill two hundred to weigh against my charmed life.

-That was so then.

-Is it not still so?

-No. It was so when you were a man who had still to understand the true nature of the act of killing. It was a measure of the value you placed upon another's life at that time. The greater the value, the fewer you would come to kill.

-Then I am not the prisoner of this number?

-You are but a prisoner of your own construction. It was not I who determined this number but you - who then used me as your mouthpiece. Each time you open further the door of understanding the less you will feel obligation to do anything but that which you know to be just.

It was true that he felt changed. The constant questioning in his mind had given way during that night to a decisive intent. Since his previous dream of the attendant he had begun the long route back to the desert. He was not carrying with him the old deference to the needs of others any more. There was a lightness in his being and a contented acceptance of what lay ahead. Instead of shunning villages, he moved from one to another. They greeted him as the great Warrior, sometimes the Shaman. Now, he did not demur but used it to enhance his teaching. As he had done with the boy he offered help where it was needed. He toiled on the land. He cooked with the women. He taught the use of the sword and bow. But the latter were no longer tied only to strict martial disciplines and formal skills, they were taught as part of a Warrior's code of conduct that he began to devise painstakingly.

He had stayed in one village for several nights. Villagers looked after his horses well. In exchange for lessons in simple magic, the boys brushed and combed the beasts until their coats glowed. When light promised to fail, the men gathered and with cut staves he taught them the rudiments of self-defence.

-A long stave may defeat a short sword, he emphasised. For such villagers, swords were foreign. They had a few bows but they were made from inferior wood and could not send an arrow half the flight of his desert bow.

-Let us ride to find a bow tree, he said, -It will take us a day. With three men and spare horses they rode back along the trail from whence he had come. He had seen a cluster of trees below a cliff face where trickling water and the partial sun they received gave balance to the strength and flexibility of their branches. They had many straight growths of a suitable length and the wood was grey and had a heavy spring to it, if the arm was strong enough. They ate in the shade and then harvested all that might be used. These were strapped to the black and their spare horses.

Their arrival at the village was greeted with some interest. Men and women left their work to gather round. Only one of the villagers had any skills with wood and this was in trussing roofs. The Warrior took out his bow and laid it so that all could see. He explained its construction, how thinly spliced wood and bone were combined for strength and how it was tapered from its centre to its tips to increase its power. He showed how to wind cord to take the weight of the pull and how to shape the grip for stable sighting. They would have started chopping the cut branches there and then had he not forestalled them.

-I do not expect anyone here to make a bow like mine. But these single branches can still become effective weapons. First, the wood must be well dried, he said, -Leave the sticks close to the fires for two complete moon cycles. While you wait, exercise your bow making skills on wood you have about the village. We will have a contest. Each of you must fashion a weapon. I shall choose the best and that bow maker will be rewarded with a gift. Tomorrow, before we eat at the fire, I shall choose.

It was like a festival in the village the following day. Bows were made studiously in private. Sounds of cutting and smoothing were heard everywhere. The Warrior disappeared for most of the day and returned dragging a large carcass on a rough litter. He had bled it and washed it mindful that no horse likes the scent of a dead creature near it. He helped the women skin and stake it over the fire on a spit. He painted it with honey, salt and spices, explaining the virtues of each of these in turn.

It came to the judging time. Strung weapons appeared from everywhere and were laid in a long line. With serious faces the villagers walked along, trying each string and passing comments on their quality. Two broke under such examination to their makers' dismay.

There was silence as the Warrior moved down the row, lifting, flexing, sighting and caressing each offering. Finally he took up a small, well-crafted weapon.

-Who made this? No-one stepped forward, -I repeat, who made this? It has a balance that sets it apart. A girl, new to womanhood, stepped forward. Some men allowed their indignation to show.

-I did not speak at first for I thought you were about to mock me.

He smiled at her, -It has a special quality. He took an arrow and notched it. When he released it, it flew over the heads of the circle of watchers and embedded itself in the centre of a tree. He spoke loudly, - She found wood such as we brought back for drying. She has cut it well so that the balance graces the hand. It is small but carries the power of many a larger weapon. He gave it back to her and offered her one of his arrows. She aimed at the same tree and the missile struck it just below his own. There was a shout of approval from the villagers so that her face reddened.

-You have a choice of reward, he said, -I have face colourings from alchemists far away in the east or a bow maker's knife, crafted by metal workers in the City in the Mountain.

-I will take the knife!

He spent some time with her, perfecting her skills.

☥

His horses were fully ready to travel again. The snow came and went for the land was lower here and the winds often blew from warmer parts. He wished the villagers well and before the light erased the stars he raised himself from sleep early and packed the animals. He was about to mount when a young herdsman ran up, his eyes frantic and his breath gasping.

-A band of soldiers are camped on the trail ahead. They have taken women and beasts from the next village. Soon it will be us!

-Bring the girl archer. Then gather the men where the trail rises to the village. Have them hide each side of the track with bows and staves. They may not be needed but it is best to be prepared.

The girl arrived shaking away sleep, her bow in her hand and arrows at her waist.

⚥

The lookout saw him coming down the beaten path. He walked barefoot, his brown robe concealing his sword.

-Stop! He stopped and was asked, -Who are you?

-A hermit.

-Where are you going.

-To the village in the next valley to offer work and prayer for food.

-Hah! You will find little there. They have fled and we have the pick of their women.

-Why have you done this?

Another voice answered him, as soldiers gathered, a voice of authority, -We are soldiers, far from home. We take our pleasures where we can. The leader laughed.

-What does your god say about such acts?

There was silence. Then, -It is of no weight.

-Let them go. He spoke softly and without aggression.

They laughed, -Let them go? Perhaps, after we have finished our need of them.

-Let them go. There was now a cold metal to his voice that stayed the laughter, -You will not be punished if they remain unharmed and the animals are returned.

-They are untouched but two beasts are feeding the fire already. Their captain gave a short laugh, -And who will punish us? This is far from any city and there are no laws here.

-There is the law of just action.

-And what, hermit, is that?

-A soldier may not use his prowess against those not trained to fight.

-Hah! That is new to me!

-He should respect the farmer for whom else feeds the people?

-Hah! Since when?

-He should strive to be just in all his acts and seek to follow the path to enlightenment.

-What does that signify? Enlightenment?

-A pure spirit.

-Where are these words from? What writing? What God?

-They are from my mouth alone. I am a fighting man like you. A warrior. But I do not seek battles now. Let the women and beasts go.

-I fear your death is close, hermit. The man raised his bow and began to string an arrow.

-His heart waits for your arrow! shouted another. The hermit's hood fell back and he pulled open his robe, revealing his sword.

-It is him! The bow faltered and pointed to the ground, -The Warrior! The Shaman!

-Put down your weapons. They did so, fearfully, -Bring me the women and the animals.

☥

The girl archer led the freed women and a small herd of domestic beasts to her own village. She had confessed to the Warrior that her hand shook as she trained the arrow on the bowman.

-It is a greater challenge to hit a man than a tree, he said, -Unless you empty your heart.

-But if I had missed, you might have died!

-I trusted in your skill. He stared at her, meaningfully, -It has been easy for a man such as I to kill but even for me it grows ever harder. He watched the soldiers break camp and mount their horses. He let them take their swords. Men arrived from the village to carry the cooked beasts.

-In matters of fighting, he said to them, -Be guided by the girl. She will make a wise captain.

☥

The trail dropped into lower land. He passed the sacked village and found people returning. He informed them that their women and beasts were safe and rode on, politely refusing their requests of hospitality. He was still a full season away from the deserts and the nights, though cold, now saw little snow. He had stowed his sword and bow in a pack on the black, feeling more at ease in the long brown cloak with its hood back on his shoulders. His powerful form still engendered respect but there was little fear in people's eyes as he passed through their villages. Some, who had heard of him, waylaid him and tried to buy the protection of his arms but he refused. Others sought his wisdom. He spoke always without reluctance, giving of his time and stressing the virtues of the just path. His message was of equal weight whether for women in the fields, fighting men or traders. Whilst at first people were suspicious that he acknowledged no deity, they were still drawn to his thoughtful words. He found it easier now to speak fluently and conjure lines that stayed within their minds. His prowess with arms and his wisdom in settling disputes with enticing phrases were becoming part of the lore of every tribe in that land. The stories that were exchanged between travellers, villagers and townspeople increased his renown. Long, long after his three great journeys, much of what he did and said were written down and influenced lawmakers, religious leaders and kings.

After the reading Kamil stood to take his leave. Nothing was said between them but at a signal Baligha was ushered to his side. They bowed and left their Princess there, reclining on a couch, a hand dangling in the bowl of fountain water, serenity in her face.

Chapter Twenty One

Be prepared to be judged at any moment

Again he found himself in the inner garden. Princess Sabiya was being the perfect hostess. Dressed in white once more as though she no longer needed the artifice of gorgeous allure or the temporary black weeds of mourning, she examined Kamil's face and saw that the worried, drawn look had left him. He sat smiling with his box of neatly scribed sheets and his silk-bound tarot pack.

-Now we can finish the Tales but no longer need to employ them in our plotting, eh Kamil?

-It seems so your Highness.

-What is this card? The Last Day! The Day of Judgment. She looked anxious, -It is not forecasting my end so soon? she laughed.

-No your Highness, merely the end of this stage of events and presaging that there is always another beginning, if we reflect keenly upon what has been.

-Whichever god I choose, He or She will surely have much to condemn me for.

-Surely not, your Highness, replied Kamil, expressionlessly.

-Hah, you're no fool, Kamil. You will save me come the day. Your loyalty will always stay any judgment on me. I will insist that we walk to the Gate of Heaven where such decisions are made, hand in hand, so that you may smuggle me through! She laughed loudly, -Let us return to how this all started. A question from me and a question from you. Is there anything you would wish to ask me, my rejuvenated historian?

-Perhaps, following the reading?

-I bow to my tutor's superior instincts.

He came across a caravan of traders and slowed his travel to follow them. They had had many generations of business with the desert people. Their journey would end at the edge of the wasteland within the encampment of the tribe of the Warrior's desert woman. Their goods would then be carried across the desert with two men from their caravan to oversee the trek. Another caravan would pick up these goods and take them onwards having exchanged them for merchandise from their own lands. Each caravan made its profit and the desert people also gained reward for their part in moving the goods across the wastes. The caravan that he followed carried silks, cotton, leather and spices which would be exchanged for precious stones, metals, carved woods and weapons. The route saved two months of travel through lands where the terrain was fiendishly tortuous to cross. Once they had met and were camped on the edge of the barren waste, the traders and the desert clan would feast together and exchange news and stories from distant lands. The chief subject of such tales in recent times, the Warrior, now travelled just behind them.

When he had first seen the convoy travelling below him in its cloud of dust, he had smiled. There was much about traders and circus people he liked. Their willingness to share all labour, their love of the detail of travel, their desire to meet the new and the strange. The very sounds of a moving company, the bellows and the bleats, the growls and the barks, the yelling of orders, the swearing and cursing, the eating around fires and the talking, all warmed his heart. There were perhaps thirty in the company of whom ten or so were guards. At last he approached and two of the armed fighters dropped back to appraise him. One recognised him and whispered something to the other. There were immediate changes of expression from suspicion to hand on heart greetings.

-It would be our honour if you were to join us, said one. The Warrior examined their bright waistcoats, circular black hats and wide trousers gathered at the ankles, then nodded.

-The honour is shared. Your journey is to the desert?

-We have much business there.

-I see from your garb that you are from the ports of the south.

-It is true.

-Then you know of my father? He began to describe his father's city but one stopped him.

-We know him. All traders know him - and you, his son!

-Everyone talks of you! exclaimed the other, -Your deeds are the talk of every camp fire from the snows of the north to the sea ports of the south. Each new adventure is told and retold. Men marvel at your prowess, women desire you - and some fear you may come among them.

-None need fear me.

-We mean those that seek to bring ill to their brothers and sisters.

-Then they are right to be fearful. He smiled inwardly as he watched their meaningful glances to each other.

☥

His acceptance within the caravan was instant. There was a great pride that he rode with them. He refused all requests to recount his adventures but mixed with his new acquaintances, working with them throughout each day, making and breaking camp, hunting, bartering for food, finding water. After the long trek it was a welcome return to comradeship. The leader of the caravan was an elderly merchant. A nobleman. He was tall and thin, with a white beard that clung to the edges of his face, no moustaches and still well able to withstand the rigours of these long journeys. When he met the Warrior he bowed with a flourish.

-It is my honour that I welcome the son of my great merchant friend to the protection of my caravan. May you travel many suns with us, though protection may be of little import to one such as you. He laughed, -In fact it is we who are the protected ones!

-I am grateful for your company. When did you last see my father?

-He left in a great hurry, before us. He received news from the northern valleys which prompted his sudden departure. He is a half month ahead of us.

-How was he? Does he travel alone?

-He was as always. Strong. Maintaining his own counsel. Alone. Two beasts. His own beast who is as much part of him as that great nose and a big pack animal. The Warrior controlled his jumping heart for a moment. Until now he had not allowed himself any thought that he might soon meet with his father though he had always known that instinct would lead him to the valleys at the chosen time.

-He must now be the wealthiest man who is not a king! His other son has his gift for trade. Whenever your father makes profit, your brother then doubles it. Their men are loyal to them for they are a fair family and distribute handsomely the rewards of their business. The man lowered his voice and looked at the Warrior searchingly, -It is curious, don't you think, that he has two sons not-of-blood yet none of his own line?

-He is as a true father-in-blood.

-That would be certain. Yet now and then there have been rumours of someone in the north. Perhaps it is to her that he travels? The man looked at him with a slight smile. The Warrior was used to the frank questioning of traders. It was born of their constant movement. To survive and be successful they developed bonds quickly and sought to impress people who may not be visited by them often.

He shrugged, -In all our time he has never revealed such an interest.

-Hah! The merchant did not believe him.

☥

Later he wondered about these exchanges. His father had never shown any attachment other than friendship to local women when he was a child, nor to others on their journey. He did not even know whether his father had ever met his mother though it now seemed suddenly strange that he had not asked him. His father had described how his long journey had come about and that had seemed enough for a young, self-centred youth but the words of the trader raised other possibilities. Perhaps their intertwined lives contained a yet more ingenious pattern than he had thought.

☥

They passed in single file through marshland led by a local guide. They had to cross it in time to set up camp far away from its noxious smells. Any man or animal that strayed off the path floundered quickly in a black stinking glue that made extraction an effort for the remaining men. Small flies floated as though on fire through the rising mists. All were spreading ointments on their exposed skin to ward off winged creatures that exchanged poison for blood

-They say that these sparks are all that remain when we die, said the leader humorously, -If this place of watery excrement is where we might end up in the life hereafter, it is designed to make us want to live as long as possible. I have told my sons to leave me for the great birds. Their beaks are as sharp as leather knives and they will make short work of my old flesh. Then I will ride them above the clouds. What is your wish?

The Warrior gave no indication of his flights of fancy. Since nothing had yet persuaded him of the permanence of anything beyond death, what would happen to his body seemed irrelevant. He was happy to end his days embracing the earth like those he had fought, killed and left for carrion eaters. Why should they not benefit from his remains?

-I see no point in special rituals, he said.

-No? I would see my family all together and watching me being taken by beak and claw. Then my eldest son would be given the hat of our ancestors to wear as I and all before me have done in our turn. There will be great feasting and many stories told about my life so that even my children's children's children would know of my times just as I do those of my forefathers. You think this is of no consequence?

-It is your way.

-And you? It is said that you are godless. You will fall to the ground one day on one of your wanderings. Soon, nothing will remain of you and no one will think more. If you were not the Warrior there would be no stories floating on your blood line.

-If descendents wish such things they will make them come to pass. The dead are beyond caring. Meanwhile, I am not driven to shape tales of my life for them.

The old man laughed, -In truth I jest. I think it is in the stars that your life will be remembered by more than those close to you. You are a legend. You are a warrior-shaman. A Magus. Who has ever seen such a man? People collect your words and tell of your deeds. The bands of robbers and killers who used to travel down these routes to take women, horses and whatever riches they could find, shun us now. They fear you and they fear the villagers who have become brave enough to protect themselves.

-This is not all my doing. It does not make me proud to hear people saying such things.

-In the south we have a saying, "If a man achieves the impossible then it becomes possible for all men."

For the first time since he was a child, the Warrior had found sleep difficult to encourage. They were a little more than a day's ride from the desert's boundary. For nights he had sat awake thinking of his woman. Their brief time together was now a tale that began, ended, began again in his mind, unchanging in its substance and more vivid with each repeat. He had no wish to arrive in the company of others. He left before light. The early dawn was cold and only when the sun was fully risen could he remove his outer garment. The familiarity of the harsh land with its aroma of herbs kicked up by his horses legs, comforted him.

While he was resting in the high sun, the roan whinnied, its eyes gazing down the trail ahead. It was not a warning, it was a greeting. It was letting him know that someone familiar was approaching. He shielded his face. A horse and rider, moving at a trot, an ever changing wraith in the heat haze, was rapidly closing the distance between them. He hesitated. Should he wait? Should he ride to meet her? He waited. It would be better to meet, to touch, to kiss and feel her against him in the cool shadows rather than in the full sun. He stood like a child, feeling more vulnerable than at any time in battle. Much as he might have wished it the meeting could not be truly foretold. Deep inside, he held the absolute conviction of her feelings for him. He had carried it through everything. She was proud and strong and, like him, she sought to impose her will on destiny. She had done what she wanted with him not from a sudden urge but from sensing that his path had merged forever with hers as inevitably as the river and the sea.

He stood silent, his arms by his side. Behind him his horses waited, unmoving, their heads dropped as though too abashed to witness this coming together. She rode into the shade, her face stern, her robes dusty, her black eyes unblinking on his face. With strength and suppleness she swung to the ground beside him. There was a full pace between them. Silently their gaze moved slowly down the lines of each other's shapes. Then he stepped across the space and cupped her face. In a moment they were embracing, instantly transported back to that time when they had made love. Each could feel the hard muscles of the other. He picked her up and carried her past the horses, pulling her tightly against him. With the harsh demanding desire that comes from so much separation, they dropped to the earth and fell upon each other.

-There will come a time, she said, when our bodies will learn that stealth also has its rewards. For now it is enough to know that you have begun our second child. His eyes asked a sudden question, -The first is well. She walks already like a tribal chief. Her words draw people to her. She fights and rides better than I did at that age. Every night of her life I have told her what I know of her father. What a man he has become. She fears meeting you I think.
-No more than I her!
-Had I not foreseen our separation I would not have borne it so well. And when she came out of me it was as though you were there.
He smiled, -I dreamed I was. I dreamed I had become you and felt her leaving me.
The woman stared at him and shook her head, -Much of you is beyond my knowing. Enough that you are back and she is but early in her woman years.
-It is everything.
-No, everything is yet to pass. We have had our coming together. Now we must ride. She rose to her feet, -At least what lies ahead is now a battle that we can share.

As they rode, she told him about his father-not-of-blood. He had stayed for one night only with her clan. He had been very serious and thought only about returning to the north. He had shown great love for their daughter, treating her as his grandchild. He had also shown his pride in his son's fame, "He has grown in virtue despite his becoming a man apart," he had said.

-I am honoured that he thinks so well of me.

-His love for you is in his face when he talks of you.

-What impelled him to take this hurried journey to our valleys?

-He would not say. I think it was a feeling for which words cannot account but we are to follow him with equal speed. Of that he was adamant. He is like you. He senses certain futures.

-He commands it better than I. The greater the need the less is my power.

-I have ordered the best fighting men to be ready to accompany us. There is one who knows the ancient paths on the other side. Something in her voice told him of a change in her clan.

-Your father has died?

She smiled, -Much time has passed, my wandering warrior. Even he could not span that age. I am now the clan's chief but it is for ceremony only. I do not lead them..

-Your brother-not-of-blood leads them?

-You understand well. When he lost me to you it was as though death sat at his tent's door. He rode into the desert to die. Yet he returned to honour my father's body. His act has brought about the end of such madness. He brought with him a woman whom he loves. And many children. But then he rarely leaves her for long! We have learned to honour each other again. He has been as a second father to our daughter too.

-I owe him much.

-You do. And you will show it.

It was as though his long journey had only been a means to delay this moment. He looked at her riding beside him and found his feelings for her spreading warm honey through his body. Every detail of her dark, hard beauty, her balance and her strength fed his opened heart.

The beauty of his daughter astonished him in much the same way as her mother's. Taller than her mother already and strong with black hair to her waist and eyes not quite as light as his own, she was already in her first year of womanhood. At first she was awkward and a little cold in his presence, resentful perhaps of her mother's warmth towards this stranger who had abandoned her. He too found it difficult to draw her to him but as they ate their eyes met more often and then there grew a little laughter. Soon he was able to show unclouded affection.

-When this last great business is done, he said to her, -I will be all I can as a father.

-Good, she replied, courteously, -It is everything I wish, though I know it will be difficult for one such as you, whom all regard as their own.

-**So the Magus** returns to his loved one as I knew he would. For some, paths will always conspire to come together again. It makes me happy for I feel that those I love will always return to me. Now, I have a question. Settle yourself. You have that stiff, anxious look again. Good! Much better. What have you become, my spymaster, in this strange liaison with your royal Princess? Tell me the truth, Honestly. Frankly.

Kamil blushed, -A more complete man. Happy. Fulfilled, your Highness, in ways that once were alien to me.

-That will do. No judge could wish for more. I am satisfied. But your first duty?

-Will always be to you your Highness. Kamil could say it with apparent conviction though he wondered otherwise.

-Ah! All is perfect. Your question? Have no fear, you are free to be as the Fool in the court. Ask me what you wish. She stared at him with a glint of challenge. Dare he ask the unaskable?

Kamil huddled into himself. He chose his words slowly, painstakingly, -I began to feel, not a puppet exactly but in a sideshow as though you were playing games and I was only a small part in them while other more important forces were at work. Is it true?

She allowed herself a haughty smile, -It must always be so. I entertain myself in many ways. My father bade you educate me so I set to the task of educating you, also. Yet, let me say this, I learned much from you even if most of it was impractical and intangible. Then, towards the end, you gave me the means to finally defeat Muez and his aunt. Without you and your beloved harlot queen, it would have been more difficult. Other paths would have been walked, perhaps even greater dangers faced. But the end was never in doubt. I have a will of steel, Kamil. Unshakeable. Unbreakable.

Chapter Twenty Two

Oneness stretches the imagination to its limits

Kamil began to read the final Tale of the first great cycle. Princess Sabiya listened as always, silent, accepting she must deny herself any intervention.

-Your talking horse is your guard dog still, his woman murmured as they cantered in the sand-scouring wind. They were followed by five bearded riders and pack horses carrying weapons. All were covered in white loose clothes, including the animals. They stopped regularly to water the beasts and soak the protective coverings, sometimes at wells and sometimes from leather sacks.

-He is as strong as ever. The Warrior patted his animal's neck.

-He does not age. He must enjoy the sacred blood line of the first of his kind.

-It is possible. His father was as he is. He became my mother's horse who in turn cared for me in my child years.

-What think you of our own blood line? she asked, teasing him.

-I love her. She is a miracle of you and me. I am sorry I missed so much of her life.

-Enough, she laughed, -It was in the thread of things. I accepted fate's law. Better this than a life without the man for whom I was born. He said nothing but nodded. It seemed to him of little importance that this woman's beliefs were different from his own. There was enough to hold them together. Her journey was different from his but their paths had come together to form a single one wide enough to satisfy each of them. She would never travel like him to test fate and belief. She seemed unaware of how much she shaped her own destiny. She was pure, a woman who was not born to question as he did. In all regards she was the equal of any, man or woman. His feelings for her were kindled at that first moment in the desert when he discovered that the camel rider was female. It was beyond the horizon of his sight to know how this attraction was conjured. It was not fate as she thought, it must be that their blood had talked, as the boy had suggested.

-She is like you in many ways, he said of their daughter, -Born with a knife, ready to throw.

-Hah, more like you. Nothing on life's wind blows past her without her questioning it.

-She has your beauty.

-It is true. Yet she has some of your shaman's sight that sees beyond.

-She has your laughter.

-True again Warrior but with age she laughs less and thinks more.

-I will work to make you both laugh.

-Three! You forget your son to be.

☥

As they travelled they learned of each other's lives. She listened gravely to his adventures. Occasionally she asked further but she did not pass comment except on hearing from his own lips that he had fathered another child. In telling it his conflict was obvious to her.

-I feel no dismay, she said, -The story had reached me. How could it not? Sometimes we are not able to withstand the desert wind and for us to survive we must turn with it until it has passed. The half-child will always be welcome.

Though he had expected her acceptance he realised he had held an anxiety about it. They did not discuss it further.

He listened to her time in her tribe after he had left. The joy that everyone felt in their child. How only the returned captain could match her on a camel. How she had fought and killed in battles to defend their desert paths. How she had kept all suitors at bay. When he offered her his rich jewels, she laughed, -I have no desire for these. They are stones from your travels. I will take only what we find when we are together.

☥

Each night they lay wrapped in skins. He was able to leave more and more of his aloneness with his clothing at the flap of the tent.

☥

She had never journeyed far beyond the sands. As the land became covered with greens, she was as a child surrounded by the gifts of the

305

unfamiliar. She ate strange flesh and plants, turning each new taste slowly in her mouth with her eyes shut to hold hard upon the flavours and textures. Now that their beasts could graze and drink they regained their weight and strength. Their five companions were sometimes as child-like as she. They treated the Warrior with due deference, even when practising against him with their swords. He taught them greater skills. When all five attacked him together they found him impossible to corner and contain. He would slip their net and feign the killing of each in turn. His woman never practised with them but learned through watching.

-I could not face you with a weapon even in play, she said. It surprised and pleased him.

♀

By being guided along the shortest routes, often along the narrowest cliff paths and across frothing streams, they travelled within one season to the valley of the Warrior's childhood. Whomever they met, the message was always the same. The Merchant had passed that way but they seemed to be gaining upon him.

-How do you feel? she asked, -Your valley is close now..

-I have no special feelings for the land. All earth has become dear to me now, even the great desert in which grew this, my flower, he touched her shoulder, -It is my father that fills my thoughts.

-And your mother?

-I do not allow it. Look at me. A man in his thirtieth year. I saw her once in a dream and she was riding a fighting man's horse. It seemed as though she was being pursued. It permits no firm belief in her present hold on life.

-Your father is of similar age. He shows no weakness.

-It is true but he is a merchant and avoids combat. Of her I know nothing. She would not let me die with her. It was a harsh act for a new mother. I was to begin my life with the Merchant. It does not augur well.

♀

He was wearing his long brown robe. But it did not protect him from

306

the impression that he was entering a dream as he rode down into the valley of his young years. It was the very point on the trail where once his father had sought to return to defend the villagers against marauders. He had refused. Let their fate determine the outcome he had said. No more. Now it pained him to recall it. They galloped down the side of the valley towards the same village. Beyond, on the sparsely grassed hillside, where the roan's father had once carried him safely on its back they could hear the faint sounds of fighting. Tying his reins to the pommel he urged the roan forward. A word commanded the black to drop back. Neither the woman nor the men could keep with the roan for it seemed to dance among stones. They galloped through the village and up the trail, all the while the noise of fighting increasing. As they slowed over the brow of the hill his eyes encompassed all, instantly.

Below two figures carrying bows were half-hidden in the shadow of a cave. The only approach to them was through a narrow passage in the rocks. Archers were trying to fire into the cave without themselves being hit. The bodies of those who had tried and failed were obstructing the attackers. There were as many as fifty fighting men in the force outside the slit, their backs to him. He could see from their clothing that they were local men and their armour was not the best.

He began the descent towards them, his brown robes billowing behind him, the roan gripped only with his thighs and his bow held cocked with an arrow. Instantly the shouting stopped, as the men all turned to face him. Their faces showed confusion and fear.

-Which of you wishes to die first at the hands of the Warrior? he called. At the same moment six white clad horsemen appeared on the ridge above and behind him. They, too, had bows strung and ready, - Put down your weapons and no more shall die. There was an immediate rattling and clanging of bows and swords being dropped, - Come away from them. They did so. At the same time the two figures, stepping over the dead, emerged from the passage and into view. They were a man and a woman. The Warrior's eyes did not acknowledge them but remained icy as he watched the now unarmed clansmen form a line, even though the beleaguered pair were his mother and his father-not-of-blood.

Two suns had risen and fallen before all the elders of the two clans had been able to gather. It was high on a plateau not claimed by any village. They were standing in a circle below the Warrior, his mother and father-not-of blood mounted in their saddles.

-My heart is yours, he said placing his hand there. They followed. It was courtesy. Some eyes looked suspicious, -You know who I am? Of course they did. Was he not the great Warrior all talked about? Who else would kill wearing the robe of a hermit? -What you do not know is that I am a child of these valleys like you. Surprise showed on their faces, -This woman that some of you have hunted through countless seasons is my mother. The man with her is my father-not-of-blood who protected me and nurtured me from childhood to manhood. There were some angry looks and murmurs.

-Many have been killed in these valleys. Those gathered here from my mother's clan have no homes in the valley of their ancestors now. They have returned at her word. They were scattered through the mountains like seeds in a high wind. Yet all the while you hunted her, your children learning the hatred of their fathers, for she had killed the eldest son of your clan chief. More murmurs and some raised fists, - When you heard that she had returned to this valley you gathered to hunt her down. Calm your thoughts and listen to what she will tell you. Then consider whether you can hold vengeance in your hearts.

Her voice was clear and her son felt pride at her commanding tones. She spoke in a man's way, imposing her will upon the gathering. As she uncovered the tale of rape and revenge, there was a grave silence. While most of the listeners seemed to accept her story some wondered whether a rape merited the death of the heir to their chief's blood line. After all, who had not taken a girl in his youth, protesting or not? And a chief's son could take what he wished. The custom was that a life should only be taken for a life.

-Does anyone doubt this tale, he called, when she finished. There had been no request for sympathy in her telling of it. It had been detailed but unemotional. There was silence. He raised his voice imperiously, - Then let me say more. I am the child of that unwanted union, the product of our two clans. There were looks of surprise and wonder. The Warrior was their own? It sank into their minds slowly, -Observe my face. Can you not see your own features in it? Of course they could. All wanted the Warrior to have their likeness. -What my mother

308

took from you with the death of the eldest son she has given back with my life.

-The Warrior will be our clan's chief! shouted one and fists of agreement were raised.

-The clans will once again be one tribe, the Warrior said, -I will be at its head though each will keep its own chief-in-blood.

Gradually, one after another placed a hand on his heart with the other offered towards the Warrior, palm stretched out and turned up. Except one. The Warrior saw him without moving his eyes. The man was standing at the edge of the circle, drawing a bow. Yet, even as he did so, there was a whistle of a knife, the sound as it struck the man's body and the sight of him falling to the ground. The bewilderment for all was that no-one could tell who had thrown the knife. The three on horseback had seemed not to move, nor had the six behind them and yet the knife had impaled the man's chest. One of them must have thrown it.

-Who was he? called the Warrior, eyes probing the crowd.

-The brother of the man who was your father, said his mother softly, -Your uncle. It was his desire for vengeance that has stalked me all these years.

-Then it is done, finally. He looked at them and there was a great authority in his face. The heads circling him showed their agreement.

Two men picked up the body and placed it over a horse to be led away. Then, one by one, the tribesmen lined up to receive his hand upon their foreheads. Each pledged allegiance. It was the first such pact any could remember.

Two days before this climactic end to the enmity between the valley clans, when those who had trapped his mother and father in the cave had been entrusted with their weapons again and allowed to depart, he had dropped from the roan to embrace the two waiting archers. His arms pulled them to him. Their heads pressed against his chest. When he at last released them his father's eyes were misted but his mother's remained inscrutable and dry.

-I foresaw your coming, said his father.

-I did not, said his mother, -But I trusted your father's word. Her face began to soften as she stared at him.

-You have become more than a man, nodded his father, -Everywhere they talk well of you.

-It was all your teaching, his son laughed, -I had not forgotten.

-Your father too is more than a man, said his mother, -Without him all would have ended long ago. I owe him my life and its long protection, just as you owe him yours. His father smiled humbly but said nothing. Then his desert woman came to stand with him and the women's eyes met for the first time. His mother said, after a moment, -You have chosen well.

That same evening, for the first time in their lives, they ate together, gradually fitting their stories into one picture. It was the first time, too, since the mother had placed her baby on the roan and directed it to the Merchant that she had returned to her home valley. The dwelling had been strengthened for permanence by her grandfather and looked over the village as was customary for the homes of clan leaders. It was made from split trees, tied by rope with a roof of thick straw. The hole in its centre allowed smoke from their fire to escape. They sat round it, finding occasion to touch and pass food to each other. The Warrior's tales were known to all and he was content to answer questions where detail was demanded. The Merchant recounted his headlong journey back to the valleys and then said more about his time with his son-not-of-blood - and his contact with the mother.

-Your mother lived a nomadic life, as she will tell you. I had news from her through messages she sent by traders even as I cared for you and as we journeyed together.

-You had intelligence of her? All that time?

-It was hard. The Merchant's face was shaped by sadness.

-I made him swear to silence, his mother interrupted quietly, -I feared you might look for me. This was not to be your fate. I hoped you would become a merchant like him, part of a prospering family.

-You could have travelled the roads to the deserts, said the younger woman to her, -There you would have been safe.

The older woman grimaced, -It may be true. All things may seem possible to you but for me there seemed no choice. My virgin body was taken against my will and I killed the man who planted the baby inside me, who is now this man. She placed a hand on the Warrior's head, -Your man. It felt as though bad blood had been seeded in me. I did not want to see my son grow and wonder what effect it might have on him. Again, a mother and child find fewer places to hide than a woman who can pass for a man. She paused but her son said nothing, - I had met your father here many times when he traded with the village. He was unlike any I had met.

-Nor she like any woman! interjected his father, emphatically, -She is a great warrior. She has a fine heart. No man would want another, having met her. Their son looked at them both. She, the greying, nomadic fugitive and he the wise, black haired merchant, she in simple village garb and he in leather and cotton.

-She made you swear to stay away, said the desert woman sadly to the Merchant.

-I did, said the Warrior's mother, -I did. The child needed him and not my accusing eyes nor the fear of an assassin stalking me during his waking and sleeping. As soon as I found that the child was growing in me I visited a wise friend and she drew him here.

-I came. I waited in the next valley. I expected mother and child. Instead I received a horse and child! There was muted laughter.

-And how do you feel now my mother? asked the Warrior laying a hand on her shoulder.

-You are all that is good from the blood of two people, with little as I have come to understand, of the bad. But whether that is your nature or owing to the care this man gave you I know not. My pride in you is as great as a mother's could be. I have the son of whom I have dreamed all these long years. Her son smiled at her. He sensed that the words were difficult for her. In her life she had learned to remain hidden in the dust of her own movement. Always with men. Always denying her womanhood.

-I feel no sadness in the way of things, he said, -You chose. Our lives took their course. Now we are united. Who is to say that a different choice would have brought more joy? I have father, mother, my woman, a daughter and now a son being made. Is that not enough to satisfy the desires of any man?

-What you say soothes my heart, said his mother, -My life, from abandoning you until this moment, has been a trial and filled with the close companionship of my life-taker. First I returned to this, my village but it seemed my future here was at an end. I hid in the hills, giving you to the world, my son. I took the horses I captured from the assassins and became invisible, travelling the ancient trails. Something in my heart kept me a half month's journey from here and from you and this most noble of men. Once I came by your village and the roan re-joined me to be my companion in the wilderness. I now ride a son of his, as you do.

I watched from the hills when the place of your childhood was burned as our enemies sought to find us. They knew not that you were their child, too. But as I travelled your father ensured enough bounty reached me to help buy safety when it was needed. I became braver and desired more the company of others. I joined the guards of a settlement. They thought me a man. These people sieved streams for the wealthiest of metals and made jewellery from it. Such as this. She tugged back the rough material of her trousers revealing yellow bands around her ankles. She pulled a pin and unlocked one, -This is for my son's wife, she said. The desert woman took it with a bow and circled her own ankle with it.

-It will protect us all, she said.

-I became a captain and no single man dared face me in battle but there were those still searching for me and I was forced to leave before the village was attacked. I harried my pursuers in the hills and took many lives. It then became my calling to trade between settlements. With your father the Merchant's help I could barter from one to the next making profit enough to survive. I fought off robbers and other men, alike, when I was dressed as a woman, for they thought I would satisfy their needs in all the usual ways. They did not know I carried a deadly sting. Many seasons passed thus and all the time I was sustained by news of you, first from your father and then it seemed from everyone who travels the trading routes. Recently I gleaned from merchants that you were returning. Only once, in all these years did I dream of you and saw that you were close to taking manhood upon yourself.

-I visited you in a dream. I know!

-The moment when the final droplets of poison left my heart was when I heard that you were returning. I knew I must face the dangers of discovery, even after such an absence. As I drew near, stories suddenly spread about my coming. Yet again, hunts were ordered. It was fated that we should come together in this way, she said, finally, - And thus, as your father here foresaw, the shadow of vengeance that hung over the clans was lifted at the moment when all our life-takers were gathered around us like birds of carrion.

-Hah, the Magus triumphs as I knew he would. He has drawn the tribe together. It was a good preparation for his later, greatest acts, don't you think? His father-not-of-blood was always the true love of his mother. And all through the Warrior remains beyond the grip of a god! This is the true lesson and it was why my father, the Emperor Haidar, asked you to write the Tales. All said, my historian, it is a pretty ending to the first great journey. The final battle that conjoins all. It appeals to the soldier in me. How else are tribes or empires held together? Through kind words only? No, I fear not.

Kamil continued her earlier words earnestly, -And it is only the ending of one cycle. The Magus' real work lies ahead. He will leave his warrior state behind. There awaits greater fulfilment and further renown of a different kind.

-I am intrigued. I will have to commission you to write the second book. How many years did the first take, did you say?

-I have lost count your Highness.

She appeared relieved, -Good, I can wait. A house is being prepared for you and your woman in the palace grounds. She will not like it, if I know her but she will accept because of her love for you.

Chapter Twenty Three

For the wise, ends and beginnings are one and the same

A month later, Kamil sat in his writing room and considered the additional chapter to the first book of his Tales of the Magus. It could also be thought of as the first chapter of the second book. He read it aloud to Baligha.

This was his place between the desert and the valleys. Here he thought he would teach and meditate. Around him his children would grow and their families prosper. His woman would be less a warrior, more the eyes and thoughts of her tribe, a chief who advised her husband wisely on all things when he so needed. His mother would stay in her village far to the north and gradually their kin would return and the clan rebuild. She was its chief. But all clans were now one tribe with the Warrior at its head. Each complete cycle of the seasons he intended to return with his growing son who would someday settle there and become its head in his grandmother's place. Now and then he hoped he and his son might camp in the woods of his own childhood and, lying there, they would watch as a family of great cats padded by, the male dropping its head and scratching the ground as if to acknowledge the man's gaze.

His mother meanwhile would rule wisely and the savage events of history, now stories by the fire, would cast her in a true light and she would win a place in the hearts of all. His father would travel to and from the southern ports as emissary for the priestess who had once transported his young man's mind with her sweet smelling potion. Somehow the Merchant would ensure that frequent journeys north to the valleys were in the nature of his business. Gifts and messages would always be in the tapestry of their lives.

At times the Warrior knew he would have to leave them all to ride the son of the roan into the land beyond the places of men and women and live the way he had always loved. There he would intensify his reflections on purpose.

☥

For a while it came to pass almost as he had imagined. He left and returned, his mind a little more enlightened each time. He delighted in visitors, eager to debate with him and seek his advice; the merchants, nobles, warriors and farmers. Sages. Even the noble priestess, herself.

Then one day as he rested in the wilds of the mountains, an event occurred that rudely interrupted the pulse of this pattern with a premonition of events to be. A dove dropped softly from the sky. A silk square had been rolled and attached to its leg. On it was a drawing. It showed a familiar face, that of a young general gazing sternly down from a hill. Below him a brown-robed figure sat in contemplation, surrounded by a circle of armed men. Written in a fair hand were the words:

Is it our mortal will or God's command that shall bring us together again?

Book 2

Chapter One

Within each moment we die and are reborn

Kamil the historian pressed his forehead against the intricately painted jasmine petals on the marble tile but its cool surface did not soothe him.

-She is telepathic! he cried, -I have not seen her for three years or more and the day following the book's completion, her servant arrives. He glanced furtively at the door as if to make sure the red-robed emissary had actually left.

-She is the Princess and of Ethiopian blood and will always hold you between thumb and forefinger, said his wife, -You are hers, even before me. It is better to be resolute and do her bidding without rancour. It will pass the more quickly. Read her the book well. It is a fine work and you are a great scholar. She placed her hands on his shoulders and drew him away from the wall.

-You know what it is that I fear? he asked.

She smiled and nodded, -Princess Sabiya wants the return of her spymaster.

-I am not equipped.

-You were not the first time. And see what you achieved!

-That is debatable in itself. I fear she could have manipulated the same conclusion without my help. But look at me. I am a soft-fleshed pear of a middle aged married man. I cannot fight and even my two babies look to you for discipline. It is your eye that they fear.

Baligha continued to smile. She kissed the raised lines on his forehead, -She does not want a swordsman, she wants the finest mind in her court. She has left you alone to write this second book knowing also that this time of immersion will whet the blade of your intelligence so that you are ready to serve her in her hours of need. The less that you visit the court the more detail will be open to you when you return for you will see it like a wide-eyed child from the countryside.

They looked down in unison at the sandalwood box with its gold hinges and clasps. Its lid was fully open, revealing the thick card of the cover-piece and Kamil's fine, ornate pen strokes:

Tales of the Magus
The Second Great Journey

And below the title in a plain, unobtrusive script, he had printed his name.

*

Kamil had collected his best clothes, neatly packed for him by Baligha and walked from their house in the compound reserved for the most favoured servants of the court, through the sweet scented gardens and up the marble steps of the palace. It was but a few minutes' walk but for three years it might have been another country. His Princess kept him close yet she sheared away from all actual contact with him. He could live the life of a married man but as Baligha said he was held at arm's length between thumb and forefinger. He wore the coloured scarf of the Princess's personal retinue pinned to his belt, flourishing it to each silent guard as he climbed, his wooden box held firmly under one arm, his bag of clothes under the other.

Nothing had changed. The corridors, with their intricate play of sunlight and shadow cast by the carved marble screens let into the outer walls, the heavy wooden doors with their iron bosses and fortifying bars and the fine gauzy silk drapes undulating on the breezes that entered through the screens. His rooms had been prepared. In front of his bedroom was the familiar antechamber with its table, two chairs and oil lamps. He imagined he could hear the whispering echoes of his voice, reading the first cycle of the Tales of the Magus to the Princess each evening three years before. Nor was it hard to visualise her draped lazily over her chair, rapping the chair arm with her palm as the tension in each Tale rose.

An hour later and he had been bathed, scented and groomed by palace servants and was standing nervously by the table waiting for Princess Sabiya to arrive. Finally, the door swung open noiselessly and the same great guard that had always been with her filled the void for a moment before retiring to the corridor. Kamil fell to his knees as she entered, only catching a glimpse of pink silk and the luxuriant tresses of oiled black hair before his nose pressed firmly against the white floor tiles. He listened as she settled herself in her chair.

-Enough Kamil. Raise yourself. Let me see for myself whether she is looking after you properly. He stood up in stages, bowing at each interval, -Mmm you look well. You are a plump fellow. Marriage and fatherhood have helped you prosper.

-Thank you Princess. She is a good wife.

-No matter. She stared at him and gestured for him to sit down. After a long pause she sighed, -Ah my dear old historian, it makes me feel good to have you back. I am somehow safe again like the child I was when we last used to meet. Just having you sitting here warms my heart and eases these fears that have been plaguing me. Kamil's chest filled as he heard her words. He allowed his eyes to see her properly for the first time. It was a shock but one that thrilled him. Even despite her tall, boyish shape which normally did not appeal to him, she had become the most beautiful creature that could be imagined. A goddess. The child-like impetuosity in her face and eyes had given way to a regal haughtiness and an uncanny, unwavering stare. Her smile was warm but hovered uncertainly on the brink of departure as though it had outstayed its welcome. Her cheekbones were high and sharply defined and her long nose lay straight and low above the full, red mouth. In some women, faces seemed so soft that their outlines blurred but his Princess's was cut out of the very air like blue-black metal.

-I see you are digesting the changes in me too, she said softly.

-Oh your Highness, he cried in embarrassment, striking his forehead with an open palm, -I didn't mean to stare-

-It is natural and not offensive to me. What do you see? She spread her silk robes and relaxed against the back of her chair, half closing her eyes just like a courtesan.

Kamil buried the thought but his embarrassment knew no bounds, -Your Highness, … he flustered… -You are…and suddenly it was as though a golden liquid flowed from his throat in a gush of what was, for Kamil, poetry, -You are the rarest flower among flowers, a star that dims both sun and moon, a beauty that blinds the eye and sears the heart … He fell back overcome by his sudden outpouring.

-Well Kamil, that was indeed prettily said, if not too original! But the heart is all. Having Baligha by your side has loosened your tongue among other things. She added the last coquettishly and he dropped his gaze. It was another reminder of how vulgar she could be, -Now historian, all is as it was before. You and I will meet each day at this hour for my reading and ... I have another task for you, as I had last time. You are my most secret, most valuable weapon. Even now your past service to me has gone unnoticed by my enemies and you will once again execute such duties as are necessary to keep mine what is rightfully my own. But before we enter these matters we must perform our private ritual and read the beginning of the second volume of your Tales. Tales that are virgin to me unlike last time. I shall listen like a devout acolyte of the High Priestess of the tombs. But I am being naughty. In truth I cannot wait to hear more of this Magus and his exploits. How will he react now to the act of killing? Will he find his god despite himself? What of his children? I would like more of his mother. Read to me Kamil. My questions are making me more impatient!

Kamil swallowed and wet his mouth, nodding, lifting the hand written pages, the translucent dividing sheets and the card frontispiece clear of the box and placing them beside him. Then he took from his pocket a silk-wrapped pack of tarot cards and placed them next to the loose-leaved book. The Princess's eyes widened and she gave a girlish giggle before leaning forward and turning the first card.

-It is The Fool, again!

-Of course. All the cards will be as they were in the first set of Tales and in the same order, for life contains cycles that are completed and begun again. If you remember I have divided the life of the Magus into volumes. This is the second which describes his middle years and leads to that final magnificent act that made him so legendary. And even then I have passed over many years because he did not begin his second great journey until he was nearly forty. He paused and then said, -The cards will not seem quite the same this time. Their auguries concern an older, wiser man, as well as casting light upon our own lives.

-I see. Clever historian. I am waiting.

And with that Kamil began the long labour of reading the second book of Tales about the Magus, beginning with The Fool.

The mountain was wreathed in mist as the sun raised the frost. At the mouth of his single tent, the man who had become known as the Warrior squatted by the fire and recollected his dream. He saw the beheading of a king in a city of wood and clay. He recognised the place. He had stayed there unwillingly once and failed in his task of saving a princess. It seemed to be one of many such executions. Kings, queens and their offspring either died or swore allegiance to the bloodline of a humble villager who had risen to power through force of arms and savage intelligence and who now controlled all the lands between the northern mountains of the empire of ice and the first sea to the south. This chief wore no crown or other regal symbol. He dressed simply in a black, cowled robe. Across his back he carried a short sword recovered from a mysterious source. With him always was a flat wooden box inlaid with metal patterns and the shapes of exotic creatures and containing the holiest words of his faith, fine-brushed in ink on rolled skins.

He was known by all as the General.

In a pouch in one of his roan's many saddle bags was the square of silk, brought to him by dove from this very man. The Warrior took it from its container and examined it. Time had passed since its arrival but it seemed to him that what it presaged was now upon him.

From the camp on the mountain's edge to the desert was a three day ride. The Warrior would often leave behind the daily round of trade, hard labour and those who would seek his counsel to be on his own. It was only when embraced by rock and plant that he could think with clarity. Here he could hunt and trap, search out roots and berries while his mind transformed his history so that it became a series of tales that may have happened to someone else. The three days of travel saw a translation of browns to greens, whirling sand to solid earth, moisture sucking winds to rain and matched these internal changes and even precipitated them. He could sit by his fire and lose his outward sight in its flames, utterly immobile, allowing a fathomless submergence in thought beyond experience. It was as if his mind and body became expanded until it changed completely as the wood turns to smoke and the smoke fades into the air. And in this state of non-being he sought to become all things, from the fragile petal of the smallest plant to the towering strength of the tallest tree, from insect to great horned beast, from dust speck to mountain, from raindrop to ocean.

As always his meditations would lead him back to the nature of his purpose. He was a man in full maturity. What should he do now with his strength, his strange gifts, his ability to change the hearts of those he met? Thus far in all his wanderings he had travelled only a little in his desire to know what might be his calling.

Everywhere, it appeared to him, among all the tribes, the nomads, the courts of kings and queens, there were few who asked the questions that he asked, as if purpose was beyond the comprehension of flesh and blood. He had come to accept that for most human beings there was a resignation towards the world into which they were born, with its repetitious ways, its demands on their labour and its suffering and occasional joy. In his life he had already been fortunate, through the wise office of his father-not-of-blood, to meet a dispersed few for whom there was no such veil of constraint. Each of them in his or her own way had intoxicated him with what might lie beyond mortal sight.

So it was on one such solitary day he was hunched by the fire in a favoured mountain camp. A carcass was roasting over it. Sweet roots were simmering in a pot in the ashes. Bread was baking in the earth under it. Then his young roan's nostrils twitched and quivered and it gave a sudden whinny of greeting. Birds made telltale swoops and cries. The breeze carried a scent of the unknown but not of danger. As he waited a rider pushed her horse into the clearing, imperious yet welcoming, despite her small stature. He shook his head and smiled.

-My Mother, he said softly as she dropped into his arms, holding to his body's warmth.

-My Son, she replied, her head pressed against his shoulder. They stood longer than most in such circumstances. It was at moments like these that they drew, gratefully, on the fortune that had brought them together again. He stroked her grey hair and she allowed a long breath to escape her.

-You would find me in the thickest forest, he said.

-I did not spend all those years, invisible to the eyes of my pursuers, yet also hunting them down and culling their strays without honing my scent for my quarry, she smiled, -And you were not hiding from me. If you wished to deceive me, it would be my greatest challenge. I have travelled without rest and I am hungry. You have enough meat for many people so I will enjoy a royal meal.

-My duty is my pleasure. He did not ask why she was there but sensed the trouble in her. She watched as he set about carving the meat. Most he put to one side for the next few days but, choosing the choicest cut he divided it up and took long hardwood needles and impaled the pieces. He placed the pot of cooked roots between them.

-Where did you come by the spit? It is ingenious.

-A recent gift from the City in the Mountain. They have a skill in the invention of tools and there is little they cannot make from metal.

-It folds for the saddle.

-Two hinges allow it.

They ate the skewered meat and flat bread together with the simmered roots.

-You are the equal of a king's cook but have greater speed.

-You know the demands of the trail. It is a pleasure to find that I have cooked for my queen. There was a silence as he waited to hear why she had come for him.

She allowed a few moments to pass, -I am unspeaking and yet there is need of haste. I come to you as my chief not as my son.

He sat cross-legged and intent, -There is not much the tribe needs from me except my name. He spoke quietly, -I hope you are not asking for my sword and bow. I now give my attention to vellum and brush. I counsel all who come to me to follow the way of the unarmed man, the path of peace.

-I know this.

-Then?

- I cannot ask you to foreswear that which rules your spirit, great warrior and son of mine. I can only tell you what I know and you must decide what is or what is not to be done. He bowed, -A half moon past, men came from the General's army on their usual hunt for conscripts, asking who would seek adventure with them. They laid out food and drink. They wanted only younger males for mind and body training. As must be, the heads of the various clans came together and we held a full tribal meeting. If too many of these young men were to leave at once we could not survive. Over the years there has been moderate conscription which took from us the boys with little desire to shepherd in the hills or work at our crafts. So we have maintained our grazing herds, our hunting, our wood carving which your father not-of-blood trades for us in the south and upon which we now depend. As always we decided we would release up to three youths but only if they were very desirous of such a life and were not taken rashly by thoughts of adventures such as your exploits have engendered everywhere. Yet when I set out as spokesman the next day to talk with their captain it was to discover that they had already gone. With them there were twenty or so of our best young blood.

He said judiciously, -It is hard but fair. The young must follow the spirit's path. They goad each other. One of them sees it as a short journey to another way of life and like sheep the others follow through the gap the first has made in the boundary.

-It will damage the stability of the tribes.

-Yet children flourish among us. Will they not take the place of those having left?

-It is a darker tale than you would understand, my son and chief. One youth of our blood struggled back to us, much cut, bruised and weak. He had wished to leave and they beat him and left him on the trail as a warning to the others. The soldiers had taken them all after plying them with root spirit. They have dishonoured us. Our tribes are not known for their way with arms as you well know. It is why assassins were hired to hunt me down through those long years. Even so the clansmen would have pursued them had I not counselled against it. I promised them my son's help. Is this not my right?

-As a mother and as a clan leader, it is your right. He closed his eyes for a moment, -The General would not countenance such criminal acts from his men.

-He may be your sworn friend, never to engage in arms against you but he is far away and does not oversee the further limits of his lands. He has not the eyes of a god. She stood up and stared down at him sternly. She made him feel that he was the child he had never been to her.

-How many soldiers? he asked.

-A full complement. All with spare beasts. They ride fast.

-Where will they take them?

-There is a hill camp, east of here and many days' hard ride. There, drink and daily training will ensure they forget their valleys. The soldiers are well groomed and disciplined. It seems they are successful at maintaining numbers for the General's needs. It is said that we escaped the worst of their sword's edge owing to your friendship with the General. But something has changed. She put a hand on his head and stroked it, -Only you can bring back the young, without recourse to loss of life.

His head bowed under her fingers, -They are my people. I cannot forsake them.

-The tribe will thank us.

He looked up sharply at her final word.

-I could not send a son where his mother would not herself go, she said, with a hard smile.

-What thoughts? she asked. They were continuing through a green gorge at the end of a tiring day's journey. A gauze of water filled the air from tiny waterfalls splattering off the rocks. It was refreshing. The passage brimmed with life of every sort. He halted them.

-This is a place where we must rest. There are plants…

-And food! she hooked an arrow and released it. The fish thrashed in the shallow pool and turned to reveal the shaft through its shiny side. She lifted it with an effort, -A gift for the royal cook! We can add it to yesterday's fare.

-It will fill us and more. I will smoke some and we can hang it from our saddles to complete its drying in the sun. As to my thoughts, he continued, answering her earlier question, -I was musing on our close company. For thirty years I live without a mother. Now-

-You cannot escape her! They laughed.

-It is a rich diet. I must guard myself or I will be like the greedy cow gorging itself on spring grass and become bloated.

-Of all men, you would be the last to lose control thus. There was something double edged in her words. He knew it. To lose himself completely happened rarely.

They ceased talking while she made a fire and he prepared the fish. When she had done she removed her clothes and entered the shallow water. It was scarcely deep enough to cover her. He glanced at her now and then, noting that she was still as strongly built and muscled as his desert woman, though she was two decades older and slighter. Her frame was taut, her breasts firm and small and her grey hair long and luxuriant.

-You have the muscles of a man.

-Not of one such as you my son but enough to deal with those that underestimate a woman. Are you to bathe?

-In turn. We would be open prey if both of us played like children in the water. She watched from the pool as he wrapped the fish in wet leaves and placed them in the glowing ashes. The fire spluttered and smoked. The rest he hung from his metal arch above the burning mix of dried and green twigs.

-It is a sweet smoke, she called.

-It is good for the fish. It flavours it in a novel way. As she dried herself he lifted the wrapped pieces of fish from the ashes using two small branches as tongs. He placed them on a flat stone. He disrobed and swam. Afterwards, they squatted either side of the flames. With a sharp knife he cut through the blackened and dried leaves so that they fell open in two crusts taking the skin with them, leaving soft pink flesh exposed to the light.

-It is a world upside down, she said, -A mother being taught the secret of a cook's fire by her son.

-Much comes from my father, the Merchant. He has the arts of the fire. The Warrior's thoughts flitted briefly over the times he had watched his father-not-of-blood cooking.

-He nurtured the early seeds in you but you have grown them far beyond what he and others have given you. How can this be? I did once think that all we can know must come from our elders and from the trials of our experience and curiosity.

-It is much of the picture.

-There is more. You have the instinct of the shaman who calls on knowledge beyond himself and his teachers. She regarded his face but it did not change at her words.

-What is natural to me seems not so strange. Perhaps it is to others.

-This is the mark of men such as you. You bring more wisdom into the world the less you try. Where does such knowledge come from? What is the ground in which these grains lie asleep until your feet stirs them into growth? It is as though you pass to another world and carry back what was unknown so that we all might know it.

-To cook is a small thing, he laughed.

-It is alchemy, she replied stubbornly.

-Perhaps so. It is as with sleep and dreams. Once I slept without reins in my hands. Where I went and what I did were determined by forces beyond my understanding. Now I have a few dreams that are mine to guide. It is as though I sense my destination and impel myself to that place. It is a place of natural treasures. He smiled as he cut himself some cold meat.

-All is open to you?

-It cannot be so. That would make life a worthless task! He laughed again.

-How? she asked, seriously.

-It is a condition of waking to find pleasure in the smallest pool of light cast on the mind. We live in shadows and delight in any illumination. For all to be bright under the sun would mark the end of our time in the body. He returned to another skewer of fish and chewed it slowly.

-Is that what we can expect when the final arrow strikes? Now her face was earnest, desiring an answer but she was to be disappointed.

-Who can tell? I cannot. Perhaps for the greatest among us who has forged such thoughts for the entirety of a lifetime. The Merchant, my father, believes that all there ever was and ever will be lies beyond the edge of this life. Death may be its name but to die is to wake from the sleep of living.

-And you?

-I cannot permit belief to guide my mind. It is only when I am convinced of something that I take a step towards knowing. And these steps have not yet made much of a journey.

-For a warrior-shaman no. For the rest of us it may already be too much to comprehend.

The meal he cooked on their next night excited the spittle of his mother equally. He had found a sleeping snake, its belly distended by its swallowed prey. That such a creature, no longer than his arm, could bloat itself to such a degree, defied the mind. He removed head and tail and allowed liquid to drain. He skinned it and hung the satin hide to dry. He would oil it later. The rest he coated in fats and then encased it in a bundle of tied twigs. He dropped it in the fire. Smoke billowed and tiny green and blue flashes were thrown from it, -By the time the wood has dried and begins to burn, it will be cooked, he said, -You know the tree, Mother. Its sap eases the joints of the aged. Meat cooked thus encourages the deepest sleep even among those wracked with such pains.

-You will be too numbed to guide your dream!

-All minds need rest.

Their four horses had gained upon their quarry, those who had conscripted the young men from the valleys. They were riding longer hours and at a greater pace. The two roans loped side by side, one the mirror of the other. They could not be told apart except by their riders and it was not through discrimination of colour or shape but some indefinable feel they had for the common bloodline of their beasts as living extensions of their bodies. Behind them galloped their pack horses. He was aware that his mother had no difficulty in matching his exertion. Like him she moulded effortlessly into the rhythms of headlong flight, balanced even on the roughest terrain. Neither roan felt the least resistance from its rider.

When the sun was at its highest they stopped to rest the horses. There was cold meat from the previous evening, -The snake chooses a tender morsel for its stomach, she said, -It is lucky we find it so, for it may have contained poison. She took a mouthful and chewed it appreciatively.

-This snake is singular in its prey like many creatures. Should its favoured food cease to roam the earth the snake would surely do the same.

-Then would not hunger drive it to seek another?

-Would it see another? he replied sagely, -Would another know it was the snake's new prey? All each knows is that they are bound together as killer and victim.

-It is their destiny, she nodded, thinking she had understood him.

But he responded, -It is only destiny for those who do not question. For those who train their eyes truly to see, the bond breaks. The illusion of fate parts beneath the opened eye as surely as a rope above a candle's flame.

Sometime later she questioned him, -You tell me that you do not believe in fate? It frightened her to make the query. It was almost inconceivable that anyone could deny fate's very being.

-Do you?

-I did not think of it until we talked of the snake. She shuddered.

-You chose to give me up to the care of another rather than risk my life at an assassin's hands. He said it gently. There was no accusation in his voice or eyes.

-I did not want our fates entwined. Your father-not-of blood seems to have a pact with fate. Better with him than a mother hunted like a wild dog. You would have slowed us down and been the cause of both our deaths. I do not believe we should give ourselves to fate like sacrifices. We should act as though we are in charge of our destinies. It is an illusion but it helps us live our lives.

-How? He watched the struggle in her face.

-It is like the snake and its prey. If we cease to act as though we make the future we should soon disappear too.

-Belief! he laughed, -That is all it is. We are back to that again.

-Son, she said, laying a hand on his arm, -I believe that you are here. You are real to me. It is my deepest belief. If I stopped believing, I might lose you forever.

☥

All the signs of the encampment were there ahead of them. Birds wheeling in the air. Smoke. Faint noises. With such a large company there was little need of lookouts. Was this land not the garden of the great General? The captain liked the way his men went about their duties. He had instilled this discipline in them. They were loyal to him and would fight to the very last to defend the honour of their calling. No one shirked his daily duty. The recruits, sitting in a large circle, were being fed. They looked miserable and confused. Discipline would put an end to that. A few more bruises. Some would be transformed from peasants to soldiers. Even at this distance he could pick out those who would embrace their new life and do well and those who would fall at the first arrow. All armies need early casualties, he thought. It spurred comrades on. Such deaths raised the blood for vengeance. Fate was greedy. It needed sacrifices too, otherwise it might take the good men. War was a fire that needed stoking with the daily dead. What did the General say on this matter? "Upon its death the body is relieved of its fire which returns to the Sun to add heat and lustre to Its magnificence." He imagined the sacred bird carrying the individual flames of the dead in Its fiery beak as it rose into the sky.

His thoughts were suddenly scattered at a cry from within the camp. Riders! He screened his eyes and saw two strangers and their spare horses, cantering towards them. His men continued their work with only the occasional curious glance at the approaching pair. Only his two lieutenants came to stand on either side of him, their hands resting on their sword handles. At this moment he recognised the woman and sensed the stir among the recruits. They had seen her, too.

He studied them. One was a man about his own age, broad-shouldered, with black hair, a trimmed beard and so big that he seemed almost too large for his mount. He was wearing a brown monk's habit yet he was armed like a mercenary. With him the man's mother looked slight, her grey hair emphasising her age. Yet she too was well armed. His thoughts were moving faster than he could follow.

-It is the Warrior, murmured the soldier to his left.

-And his mother, muttered the one to his right, -They are untouchables. The General has ordered it.

The four horses came to a halt before them. The two riders looked down at him. The woman spoke.

-Release the men from our villages. You took them by deception.

-I think not. They came without ropes.

-Save the bonds that spirits induce, she said. The tension between them communicated to his men and they gathered around them, hands on swords.

-Easy men! These two are guaranteed safe passage by the General. They must not be harmed.

-Nor any of our kin, said the woman. Her companion sat silently, his pale eyes fixed unblinkingly on the captain's own. The woman snapped angrily, -All the prisoners you have here are joined to us in blood. Release them!

The captain did not like her insistence. Women could irritate him. He was sure the General did not intend his forbearance to extend to receiving insults no matter who the woman. And these unbroken youths were not prisoners and hardly her blood, in the true sense of the word. He looked across at the circle and called, -Who among you wishes to return to his village with this man and this woman? All raised their arms. He thought for a moment, -I see that they are more fearful of you than the General! Let me take a small number that I have marked out as having the seed of the army life in them and you can return with the rest.

-All who wish to return will satisfy their desire, she said coldly, -It is the General's command.

-You know nothing of the General's command, he replied angrily, -The General is not here. I am the General in his absence. If you seek to further this debate I will withdraw my offer. No one shall return. Hands everywhere clutched their swords. The woman raised her fist.

-Stay your weapons. She dropped from her horse, -I will fight you for them. The victor will take all. She barely came to his shoulder, her face lined with age, her grey hair bound by a black ribbon at the neck. Not a woman to fear.

-We have sworn not to harm woman or child. My general made this decree.

-Except they be royal. Is this not so? The General has topped the tallest trees of powerful families across the land. All who oppose him. Male or female. He nodded grudgingly. It was true. She stared up at him, -My blood has ruled the valleys of these men since the first sun rose. Let us test our argument. She stepped back, slowly drawing her sword. The captain motioned his men away, following suit.

-What of him, your son? he asked, -All know of him. He is the great Warrior. Some say he cannot die by another's sword.

For the first time the Warrior spoke, -I will not interfere. However, should any man here seek to enter this dispute he will be dead at the moment such thought enters his head for I can read the minds of men. A shudder like the first breeze from the north, stirred the faces of the soldiers. All had heard of his occult powers. Yet he was but one and they were many. He may kill many of them - but not all! The captain would defeat the old woman, anyway, witch that she obviously was. The shaman would have to keep his word and carry her body to the Great Fire. The recruits would stay. There would be handsome rewards from the General.

The captain stepped away from the woman with his sword held point down. A circle formed. The Warrior had not moved. The woman began to rock lightly on her toes, her sword touching the ground. The captain flexed his shoulders and rolled his head on his neck to ease any tension. He bent and straightened at the knee and then raised his sword in front of his face, his eyes narrowed on either side of the blade.

She moved towards him, frail and female as though in a slow tribal dance, stepping first to one side and then to the other, her feet turning and raising little clouds of dust, her eyes cast down submissively. It was as though she understood him and his need to take her. She was offering her neck for his blow. He could not disappoint her. He raised his executioner's arms. In the time it took for his blade to reach its full height for a blow that would sever her head her dance transformed to a snake striking. So fast, so deadly that his eyes did not see what had entered his heart. None but his own ears heard the fatal hiss of flesh being sliced.

The Warrior said, -I will travel on. It is time to meet with the General. He must know what his men are doing in his name. They looked at each other, hands on saddles.

-I will come with you.

-No Mother, you must take the youths back to the valleys.

-We will detail one of the lieutenants to take them. I too have my reasons for going with you. She smiled at him winningly.

He laughed, -And what are they?

-To spend some time with my son. I still owe him many years of a mother's attention.

-I would not have accepted your decision to accompany me had I not seen you fight. He was proud of her and she could feel it.

She covered her pleasure by saying casually, -It is a fact, even among those of shared blood that we must prove ourselves to each other constantly.

-It will be a long journey. His castle is far to the east.

-Perhaps I will come to know you even more as my son through it. History has left us strangers still but come the end of our journey this will no longer cause me such pain.

She was not asleep. He knew that from old. He had to wait patiently for her to find her way out of her reverie. Her black eyelashes stroked her cheeks which had been slightly rouged so that the long fringes at the base of each lid stood out dramatically. She spoke without opening her eyes.

-Your voice transports me. At once I was back in that time of myth at the side of the Magus and his mother. How clever of you to satisfy my wishes in these Tales without a direct command. I want to know more about her. How came she to produce such a son? To which god did she make offerings? Were special unctions spread across her belly? Were secret incantations sung by the elder women? She opened her eyes with a gentle, innocent smile which sent Kamil near to swooning.

He smiled, a little tremulously, -There are some things that are beyond the stretch of my poetic intuition. These I must leave to the reader. I am sure Princess that you will embroider that which I have lacked in the telling.

-True, she murmured thoughtfully, -I think that in the terrible congress of her rape some divine force softened the brutish breeching of her body by doctoring the man's seed. It must have been so. Magic of the good kind. Which brings me, she lowered her voice as though the walls might be listening, -To the quest I have for you old historian. Kamil's head sank in response and he moved imperceptibly towards her, interlacing his fingers on his lap. He expected the worst but to his surprise he was also aware of something stirring in his stomach that seemed to be akin to excitement.

-My lord my father has become enamoured of someone. She stopped as she considered what she might say. Kamil's mind raced to conjecture. He had heard nothing of the Emperor's liaisons. Was this going to be a repeat of his last labours as spymaster for the Princess? Had the Emperor taken another consort who threatened the Princess's succession to the throne with the promise of a son? The Emperor was old. He had not much time and he was wont to bring daughters out of the loins of his wives. His one son had died on his journey into air and light.

He broke her silence by asking, -Has the Emperor taken a new wife?

-Hah no! It might even be worse than that. If it were a woman I would know what to do for it would be easier to enter the mind of my enemy. My father has become as beguiled and as hypnotised as a small

338

creature by a snake. She tidied her robes as though to protect herself against some imagined threat, -This man, she continued, -Comes with the reputation of a sorcerer. He says that he is the son of a shaman who withdrew from his family and friends to devote his life to meditation in the ice on a mountain top in these very territories. He was taken as a child on rivers to the far north to the empire of ice and snow, those lands where the sun and moon split the year into dark and light. There he was taught the shamanic arts. Now he sits at my father's foot like a poodle but his eyes betray him for they are full of an evil cunning, shrouded as they are by his long, red, uncombed hair and his wild red beard. Already he has performed miracles, clever subterfuges to spellbind the court. The ill have been cured, the faces of the disfigured have been returned to their earlier countenance. Prognostications concerning the outcomes of battles have borne fruit. Her lips were tightly pressed and her eyes focused on a midpoint between herself and her listener.

Kamil said, -But you feel he is evil?

-My heart is repulsed by him but I have no evidence. I have my spies sifting through the dunghill of his past but all they have carried back is rumour and conjecture. He covers his tracks well. But none has your intelligence nor your elliptical approach. She stood up and faced her palms from her as if to press away an unseen demon in the air, -I trust in your skills Kamil. We shall journey together you and I. You will be like the Magus and I will be like your mother! She laughed delightedly at the thought, her tones forming the tinkling bells of the child he had known and then her silken figure swept from the room.

Chapter Two

Even for the Ancient, on his last litter, there is much to be learned under the sun and moon

Between reading the first Tale and the second Kamil paid a brief visit to Baligha and his two children. While it was understood that he must live in the palace until his mission was complete the Princess had not expressly forbidden him from seeing his family. Once he had caressed the little ones' locks and covered their faces in kisses the nurse took them away to leave him with his wife. He was then able to tell her in lucid detail all that had transpired in his first meeting with the Princess.

-She has all the qualities of a future Empress, snorted Baligha darkly, -She is clever, beautiful, seductive, confident and also cold-hearted, manipulative and unscrupulous.

-Shh! cried Kamil, terrified, -Do not even think those thoughts. They will bring vengeance down upon our heads.

-I am sorry husband. It is what I think but I will say no more. In truth I hardly knew that I was speaking aloud! However, what I have said will always be true. The tiger cannot become a deer. I think anyway that you will be safe. Your good nature and my counsel will protect you from harm. She sat on a cushion at his feet and rested her head on his lap so that he could stroke her hair knowing how much this calmed him, -So Kamil, what plans have you to discredit the ice-shaman? I know him to be a fearsome foe.

-Know? Kamil asked, -You are better informed about the affairs of the court than I in that case.

-My dear husband, that would not be difficult! she laughed, -You spend all your time with your nose in books. Yes, I knew that he had been accepted into the inner circle of the Emperor though I have no knowledge of his acts there. I have never met him but in my long journey south I heard many tales.

-Tales? Tell me.

Baligha rose, using Kamil's thigh to lever herself and she sat opposite him. Her beauty never failed to startle him and remind him of how much she had changed his life from a reclusive historian into a flesh and blood family man. His heart fluttered in gratitude, for fate having brought her to him. -The ice-shaman, she went on, -Has the lives of a cat, according to all the stories. He has attended many courts but sooner or later he makes powerful enemies. A man such as he with his cunning at influencing nobility, inevitably becomes a threat to others who crave power and the throne.

-Princess Sabiya, muttered Kamil.

-Exactly, said Baligha fiercely, -She can see the potential for harm to her cause. Anyway, many have tried to kill him. From being thrust down through a hole in the ice of a frozen river to being buried in a coffin or burned alive in a wooden shack circled by soldiers. In none of these circumstances did anyone see the manner of his escape. He has been shot many times and poisoned at least twice but each time he rises again shaking off death like so much dust. Is this enough to give you a portrait of the beast?

Kamil replied after much thought, -It says in all the records of war that you must know your enemy. When meeting him in combat even the smallest, seemingly most insignificant detail, may help defeat him. While I may not face him with weaponry, our minds will be opposed on a great games board and we will move our pieces as though it were a mortal duel. It will not be long before he senses me sitting opposite him. He may even know it now if he has the occult power you talked of. He took her hand and kissed it, -What you say makes him inhuman.

-It is best to imagine so, whispered his wife, -But there is one thing more. She pulled his head to her abdomen and hugged it there.

-What have you for me now? asked Kamil's muffled voice.

-It is said that he was born a twin and that he tried to choke his sister to death even before he had formed his first word or could walk but their mother tore him from her. She was so terrified by his wickedness that she gave the boy into the keeping of a passing family of river folk who plied their trade on the waters of the great artery that runs from the furthest north to the furthest south of the world, even passing through this city. None knows where the twin girl went either. But he was taken to the northern lands where boats are stopped by frozen waters. And when he is drunk with spirits he swears he will kill his sister when he finds her, even as a man of your own age. That is the story. She pushed back gently and stood a few steps away from him.

-It is evidence, he said, -There is sometimes more truth in a fiction than in any fact. No more nor less than that. Who knows, it may make the difference between life and death.

*

Once Kamil was back in the palace he settled himself in the familiar surroundings of the Emperor's library and began to do his searches. There seemed to be nothing there that might immediately further his knowledge of the ice-shaman but then he began to realise that the arrival of such savage creatures was not unusual in the history of the great courts. He found a number of instances when uncanny shamans such as this had affected the course of events. Rulers had been deposed, lands had been pitched into civil war, princesses had been mesmerised and attempts made to take them as brides had resulted in lakes of blood. It was as though these wild men brought with them a pestilence which infected all that was natural. There seemed no common element to the pattern except that these creatures had all disappeared without trace. No bodies. Nothing.

But there was something else that gnawed with rodent's teeth at Kamil's brain. He returned to his research.

*

Later that afternoon, resting in his rooms with his pile of beautifully crafted notes, Kamil felt a tremor run through his body. He recognised it. All good historians would have recognised it. It happened when, while sifting through what had been gleaned from records, a previously unknown insight, extreme and implausible at first sight, suddenly exploded into conscious thought, laying to waste the ignorance that had preceded it.

*

He waited for his Princess, impatient, yet as still as a post. His face was aglow with the expectancy that everyone experiences when harbouring news that will astound their listeners. In the past he had become an accomplished reader of his Tales and knew how to elicit tension. He had no intention of revealing his discovery until after he had read the Tale. He laid down the next tarot card, ready for her to turn over. Although they had already worked through the cycle of major Arcana he knew she had not memorised its sequence, even if each card, once turned, was familiar to her.

When she entered she found him standing, head bowed, his wide-sleeved arms stiff by his side. He had resisted his habit of dropping to his knees although it was hard because she disliked it so much in these private audiences and had made fun of him when he did it. Here court rules did not apply.

-Hah good! You are ready. I hoped for a glimmer of light from my spymaster and I sense that you have already something to tell me. She arranged herself in her chair and Kamil allowed his eyelids to rise sufficiently to catch sight of her white kid shoes and white silk pantaloons as well as the hem of her rose over-gown, -Come on Kamil. Sit down. At least you are learning not to grovel like a pig when we are being so familiar.

He smiled to himself and sat down, at last allowing his meek eyes to meet her sharp stare. She shook her head at him as though he was a naughty child and reached forward and turned over the card, -The Magician eh? The merchant father of our hero.

-Not in this cycle, Princess, though the principle is as you might remember. The card represent the beginning of the journey through the next period of the life of the Magus. And also, as we shall see, as a magician of some power in his own right. Shall I start? She spread herself and closed her eyes, the way she preferred. It was a sight that always stirred Kamil's heart. Few, like him, could indulge in bold glances at her Highness.

-Did you know much of my true father? He didn't look at her but waited, intent.

Her face grew solemn, -Before I killed him I knew little. Afterwards I gathered crumbs yet not enough to make even a finger of bread. Like all stories people recount, some are lit by the sun and some by the moon.

-Was he loved by any? He did not disguise his desire to know.

She looked over at him, -Who knows. Loved or hated it does not matter. You are your own man. His blood has not disfigured you. If there was a stain flowing in you at birth, the Merchant washed it away in your boyish years. She sighed, -We are lucky to have that man in our lives.

-I sense your blood in me but not my true father's. Yet sometimes I wonder. When I have killed I have done so with the emptiest mind. It is only afterwards that I have shown respect for the corpse and this only because of my father-not-of-blood's teaching.

She said with a happy smile, -You are the Warrior. It is your way. It is what separates you from all else. I have killed, too, in anger and in hate because there was no other way. It is more difficult for one who has given birth to take a life. To kill is forced upon the unwilling hearts of women.

-I begin to think that to kill is but a reflection of our weakness of will and lack of imagination. A strong will and a developed imagination will find another path. It should be beyond anger or hate. His head bowed in contemplation and he interlaced his fingers around the reins.

-If the heart is strong enough, she said abruptly. He knew when she said this that his mother was thinking of the many men she had killed in her long journey to survival.

He said, -It is true. There is a time when to take life is all we have.

Yet we need not be like the beast who lusts for more victims despite having taken enough prey to feed itself many times over.

-Have you never done such a thing?

-I have. To avenge the rape of two women. Had I killed but one the others may have fled. Yet my anger knew no end.

She raised her voice in advocacy, -But their acts against the women would have gone unpunished. Did they not conspire together? Even though they may not have defiled their bodies themselves, did they voice their concern? Did they stop their fellows? Were they willing to die to protect the women?

-I think not.

-Yet you were willing to die to mete out justice. The balance is heavily on your side my son. She placed a reassuring hand on his arm.

-It seems like a natural law yet I must strive for other forms of justice. I am too easily a hound of death. Once released, none may prevail against me.

Their conversations were interspersed with long periods of privacy. Around them there were changes in colour and sound, in scent and in the tugging of the breeze at their sleeves. Always their gaze embraced the sky and land but this did not require their deeper thoughts. Their eyes were sentinels unto themselves leaving their minds to ponder and chew.

-I feel nothing for the man I have just killed. He was a soldier. He had sullied his command. He had taken our young men in greed and against his orders. Then he had tried to justify it by agreeing combat with a woman. It took no courage on his part. In truth, I enjoyed it.

Her son looked over at the animal look on her face. He replied, -He had no imagination. Therefore he was blind to his approaching death.

-His death gave freedom to twenty others, replied his mother stubbornly.

-True.

-You speak it but you mean it not! Her voice was touched with irritation.

He replied soothingly, -All you say brooks no argument. No one would judge you less than pure in motive. It is how justice is weighed.

Yet-

-Yet? Can there be any further debate?

-Yet his life is ended. He has no path left him now. His eyes no longer see. His mind no longer seeks to understand. He cannot touch, feel and hear. He cannot be forgiven. He cannot grow into another, better man. Our swords end much, Mother. Every time a man dies at our behest an understanding of the world dies with him. The world is diminished because there is one less pair of eyes to see it. The more who die before their natural span, the poorer the world.

-If this be so then if some great cataclysm took all that live from the face of the world, the world would cease with them. Like the snake and its prey.

-My thoughts have often come to think this.

They were following a well trodden trade passage along valley floors. Neither had travelled this far to the east though the Merchant had regaled him with many stories of the peoples and places on the road. Where it was crossed by wide water that stretched from north to south there was a fortified house belonging to a rich merchant and old friend. Furs, horses and wood floated slowly downstream on great rafts. Pottery, jewellery, carpets and blankets sailed, or were dragged by horses on the shores, north. Silk, spice and medicines came by caravan from the east and ore from the west. The man's house was a resting place for the wealthier travellers. Others camped under the night sky on the river banks. As they trotted down to the shore of the great reach of water his mother remarked, -I had heard it was a challenge for the bravest swimmer. Now I understand! She saw the silhouette of a boat without sails unmoving in the distance. Beyond it the far banks could not be seen. They stripped the four horses and led them down into the shallows where they rolled and splashed. She laughed, -They are like children.

Mother and son rested in the grass with their feet in the water, their eyes closed, each preoccupied with thought. Finally they were interrupted in their meditations by the beasts climbing out of the water and spraying them as they shook themselves before they began to crop plants at the river's edge.

-Where is the Merchant's home? she asked, looking up and down the coastline, -I do not see it yet.

-No? You are losing your keen sight.

-It is sharp enough, she scolded him but saw that he was jesting, -It is a riddle, Shaman, is it not?

-Perhaps, though a deep one. He emphasised 'deep'.

-It is not on this shore therefore, therefore...what? It cannot be under the water! She peered into the river in mock fear.

-That would be an adventure. No, not under the water. He stressed 'under'. She heard it, -Ah, an island!

-It is what my father described to me. I have seen it too in a dream. It is close. He looked across the water.

-Now I see what it is, she exclaimed, -I saw it before but took it for a boat. How shall we reach it?

-They will come for us. The merchant who lives there is a magician of sorts, too.

A passage across water can impel the mind on its own journey, he thought. The great current moved slowly under the raft pushing it downstream while the oarsmen aimed the leading edge north so that they would arrive after a long arc of effort. Now and then he saw dark shapes beneath the surface and bright flickering from underwater weed. All the while the water's colours changed from browns to greens to blues. Nothing stayed still enough to study. As with meditation. Sometimes the more he tried to rope a thought like a wild beast the more it careered away. Indeed his greatest understanding often came from having no expectation that there was any answer, thus creating a void into which novel thoughts swam, unannounced. Perfect emptiness could be the womb of discovery.

The raft rocked with the rhythm of the oars and the swell of the river. Their horses lay obediently on sacks not relishing the sway. He and his mother sat facing the island. It moved towards them slowly as though it was floating and they were still. It appeared to be a small hillock, bare save for grasses and small shrubs. At its centre was a standing ring of trussed tree trunks. This was too high for a man to scale without ladders. Their tops were defended further by thin, embedded spear heads. Inside this forbidding boundary they could just see the smooth, curved stone of the crown of a building.

It was only upon landing that they discovered that a deep dyke surrounded the stockade which was filled with water, -It seems that he has delight in fish, said his mother, staring down into the depths which were teeming with shoals.

-There is much guile in his defences. My father says there was no safer dwelling even when this route was infested with bandits. It is a haven for those who can pay.

-I saw! She had been surprised at the exchange on the shore. Her son had offered a small piece of shining ore the size of her thumb, to be ferried across.

-He is fair. If I gave too much we will be given a return.

A section built in to the standing timbers was lowered to make a bridge across the moat. They entered through the gap and were faced by a second ring of wood constructed exactly as the first. Each had ladders on the inside and a high walkway for those defending the house. They were led around this second fortification to its farther side, a gentle climb. Here, where the land was highest, they were admitted through the defence and into an earthen courtyard.

-What kind of place is this, muttered the woman, -It is the lair of a sorcerer. He lives inside the egg of a giant bird!

It was as she had said. Great cream stones had been smoothed and cut in curves and then locked tightly together so that the whole comprised a dome many times a man's height and offering the illusion that it continued beneath the ground to complete itself as an egg buried up to its middle. There were slits to allow light, high on its curving walls.

-It seems as though the egg is growing hair too, smiled the Warrior for at its summit tendrils of plants hung and flowers flashed colours at the evening sun. The man leading them offered to take their horses but the Warrior stayed him, -Let us meet with your lord first. Take him this. He took out his father-not-of-blood's seal and rubbed it with a soft red wax stick before pressing it on the back of the man's hand. The servant nodded and, after a knock and words was admitted into the dome. A short while later the door re-opened to reveal a tall, white-haired man in the silk robes of a merchant. His eyes glinted in his smiling face. He strode forward and embraced the Warrior heartily.

Then he turned and gave the woman a graceful bow.

-I was expecting you, Warrior and this woman.

-My Mother.

-Nay, she is too young and delicate to have birthed such a lion of a man! The Warrior smiled at his mother's confused pleasure at the traditional compliment. She was unable to reply, -Take their horses and look after them well - better than your own children, he instructed the servant. Then he turned back to them, -Enter the Vault of Heaven and the kingdom of your father's true friend, namely, myself.

His warmth and hospitality relaxed them immediately. A servant showed them to a room and left them to settle. Their saddlebags appeared shortly after.

-What is this my son? She was inspecting a smooth stone trough. Above it a wooden tube emerged from the wall. Let in to the pipe's top curve was a small handle of bone. The Warrior stared at it for a moment then bent and filled a hole in the trough with a tapered, leather-covered plug. He turned the bone and it screwed out of the pipe. Water gushed into the trough.

-It is for bathing! she laughed.

-It is Mother. Come. Feel. She did. The water was warm and becoming warmer.

-How is this done? Is it safe?

-We shall hear soon enough. This Merchant is proud of his strange egg, his Vault of Heaven.

They were greeted by their host, much as the Warrior had surmised, -I hear you needed no help to tap the waters of paradise, their host exclaimed. His voice was loud and enthusiastic at all times. They had joined him in his room and were sitting on cushions around a spread cloth covered in vessels with food and drink.

-My son has an eye for magic, she responded.

-Like all magic the explanation is without sorcery. I have

constructed perpetual flame in the roof beneath a stone tank that holds water for twenty troughs. My men keep it full from the currents of the river. Courses cut in the stone walls carry it to where it is needed, at any time.

-Any time? asked the woman wide-eyed.

-Any time, day or night. It is a simple device that directs the water to its destination, comprising little gates such as you might find in dykes in the fields. It is not my own magic, Mother of the Warrior. The means to do this were brought to me by a merchant from the east where fire has long been used for such purposes. It is but a small step from boiling soup to heat our bodies, to boiling our bodies themselves! They laughed. Meat, vegetables and fruit filled them. Then they soothed their stomachs with herbal infusions.

-Now for my own magic! called the Merchant. He clapped his hands and most of the candles were doused. They followed his eyes upwards. Gradually they became aware of the small points of light in the ceiling.

-It is the night! she murmured, -It has entered the egg! Here are the stars that govern us.

The Warrior studied the ceiling carefully, -Yet they are not of this moment. See? This pattern is for the time of snow in a few moons from now. The sky is ruled by the Hunter.

-It is so, said the Merchant approvingly, -You have studied the stars. He clapped his hands.

The Warrior stared upwards once more and then put his palms together in respect, bowed to his host and said incredulously, -The snow is gone and new life is everywhere! See, now we have the Cutting Blade! A further clap from their host followed, -Now the heat of the sun is at its height. Look, the bent back of the Prisoner. A final clap, -It is miraculous. The heaven is now how it is outside. The Circus Tent at rest! You are truly a magician like my father.

-A great compliment! I am honoured to be so described though I prefer the term, scientist, for we are different in our illusions. Your father brings magic to any moment of the day. He plays games with all we see and use. His hands are too quick for the eye. It makes us laugh. Sometimes we are made to fear our own footfalls. It is a skill he has developed to survive on his great travels. I do not travel. I run the Vault of Heaven for travellers. I stay in one place. I develop my own magic. It is an illusion too but it has a different purpose. It is to bring light into the dark world of ignorance. It is not the road to riches. It is the road to wisdom.

The self-proclaimed scientist showed them many strange creations. He had had two channels drilled into the walls of his dome that admitted sunlight on the longest day and the shortest day, beams of sunshine that would pass through fine discs of pink crystal. On those two days the beams lit the centre of a tiled mosaic on the floor. At its centre the great bird of the sun flew with outstretched wings and a flame in its beak, -The holy bird is white for all but two moments of the year and then it becomes red! For me it signifies that moment when we return to God!

He took them down steps that led to a cave in the rock. Again, candles were doused and gradually light filtered in from a window no bigger than a man's face, in one wall. It was constructed of thinly cut translucent shards of the same crystal that had been used in the dome. They were held in a stone network. By coming close to the crystal they caught glimpses of fish clustering to be fed from above.

The scientist's crafting of crystal had led him to make an eye which, he said, took the light of the sun and made it a pinprick which so intensified its heat that it could start a fire. The same kind of eye could be placed against silk or vellum so that the smallest area became large. He said, -Take a fine wood pin and dip it in the thinnest ink. It is possible to write a message or draw a picture too small for the eye to read. All you might see are dots. Thus, messages can be sent in confidence that the enemy will not decipher them! Or secrets handed down from one generation to the next. Only with an eye such as this can they be read again. The only failing is in the crystal itself. I have yet to find rock without faint flaws that disfigure the clarity. It is a slow process to make these instruments. Most rock breaks during their making.

-You said it is the road to wisdom. The Warrior took his eye away from the crystal.

-Is it not obvious to you, Shaman? These magic eyes open windows to what cannot be seen. We do not know what miracles may lie beyond the limits of our natural sight. See? He put the eye over a strip of decaying curd. On it there seemed to be creatures of strange shape and behaviour stumbling over a rough terrain.

-If I find the perfect crystal these creatures would be seen as clear as a dog! There is much in this world of which we have little knowledge. Perhaps with such an eye we can view God, himself. Not that bright chariot, the Sun, which brings us warmth and life, but He who cracks the chariot's whip!

☥

-So, you are journeying to see your friend, the General. For once the scientist's face was serious and his voice quiet.

-It is our mission, said his mother, -His army is losing discipline everywhere. The captains are snatching young men who have no desire to join them. Even the bond between the General and my son was broken by one them.

-He cannot be aware of these deeds, said the Warrior, -His heart is not stained in this way. He could not allow such acts.

-The purest water is defiled if left too long in pestilential air, remarked the scientist, -There are those around him who none could ever trust. He brought a time of peace to our lands. Travellers could journey freely and without molestation. But not so easily now. They are attacked frequently. None can be sure whether the robbers are lawless men or soldiers acting lawlessly. There is talk of plotting among the princes who swore allegiance to him to save their heads. It is also said that his heart is changing. It is the hardest task to carry the burden of a kingdom with naught but your own just sword.

They were talking late into the night. Above them the stars of spring shone optimistically. The merchant scientist's long robes shimmered, red upon blue, in the candlelight. The insistent strength of his gaze and upright body belied his white hair and lined face. He was the same age as the Merchant, his father-not-of-blood and shared the same nobility and sense of purpose. The mother and her son sat cross-legged, their backs as straight as his, their unblinking attention on his face.

-In what way has the General's heart changed? asked the Warrior.

-It is said that he retires for as much as a complete moon at a time to a bare cell. The land is governed by others who lack his fair and firm justice.

-Such time spent with his own thoughts represents no change in his ways. He was always thus. When he came to find me in my mountain camp it was to leave the noisy thoughts of men behind him. The loosening of the reins of command is not as I know him nor is his trust in men who lack his own soundness. But I have not seen him for many seasons.

-If any could ignite wisdom in his rule again, it is you.

As the Warrior had intimated, the scientist returned what was owed them after their stay. It took the form of dried food, jewellery that he pressed with great solicitation upon the mother and a disc of crystal set in a circle of finely carved wood. He entreated the mother to return to see him in a voice whose tones suggested far more than the entreaty of a family friend.

-He is a fine man, said his mother.

-Indeed. It should be expected. My father has a keen eye in choosing his friends. He was insistent that you should return to him. Your woman's ways are much to his liking!

She flicked the ends of her reins at him in a pretence at irritation but would not meet his gaze. The Warrior had never questioned her on the men that she had encountered in her life save his own true father. He was unsure whether she maintained any such interest. Though her relationship with his father-not-of-blood was as if they had but one heart, he had no notion what that may have meant for them as a man and a woman. He himself had not been entertained by the entreaties of other women. His desert nomad had reached into his body and taken his heart with her clenched fist.

Eventually she said, -If fate decrees it I shall return to his great egg! That made them both smile.

-A fine pair of chicks the two of you, her son laughed.

-So, the mother is not fixed in her affections? asked Princess Sabiya with a smile.

Kamil was confused, -Fixed?

-Upon the Magus's father-not-of-blood. It seemed to be so in your first collection of Tales. She continued to smile amusedly at him, -But then do times ever change? I think not. Men, being the primitive souls that they are will always take an extra helping if it is available so why should not a warrior woman like the Magus's mother? Don't bother to answer. I know you to be a virtuous man and that you would not dishonour Baligha, your wife, in word or deed.

-No, he replied fervently hoping that this would end the topic.

-I like the scientist, she continued, -He is a pragmatist as well as a genius. They do not often come combined. It is common that the brightest lights are extinguished by rulers for acts of heresy. She picked up the Magician card again, -I wonder Kamil, when it comes to my cycle of cards, whether you are my magician? We are at the beginning of an obscure adventure and you have the art of uncovering what did not seem to be there as the Magician does here with his trick of the three cups. She bent forward and pointed at the rest of the cards, -Spread them! she ordered abruptly. Kamil was surprised but did so. She tapped one, -Turn it over! It will be the card which represents this new evil in the Court, the ice-shaman who is our new enemy. Then she pulled back as if afraid of what she might have unleashed. Kamil slid the card from the fan-like spread and turned it over. Even he, despite his familiarity with the strange correspondences between cards and events in the world, looked shocked.

It was The Devil.

Princess Sabiya looked on grimly, -I knew it! This is why I tested it. Instinctively, she gave the spread cards an annoyed flick. Kamil was sure that she had not disturbed the order but vowed to check. -Return it to its brethren. We will speak no more of its import until its turn has come in the Tales. It points to the formidable nature of our enemy. She sat back abruptly and touched her lips with a forefinger, -What have you dug from the unwilling ground for me, historian?

Kamil had to tear his mind away from contemplating her feat in picking that card of all cards with its implications for plague, deceit and an end of a phase of harmony. He recounted to her what he had achieved during the day but stopped short of his main revelation.

-But is this news? she asked, staring at him, -I myself have heard many tales of these half wild men with strange powers. How can this help us?

The historian straightened, -Before you know more we must keep before us the one great truth. We cannot countenance assassination. All my evidence suggests that he will survive such an act and it will add lustre to his occult reputation and the consequences will rebound upon us. We must wring from evidence and whatever intelligence your agents might find, a more subtle, telling strategy, though there is no clue to it yet. His face became animated, -This afternoon I looked again through all my notes and found a strange pattern. Among these savage savants there is a sequence that did not spring to mind at first. I went back and checked only those with red hair and beard such as your interloper possesses.

-And? Her face mirrored his excitement.

-Each one appears in historic records exactly one century to the day from the last, no matter how long they remain in view. It is chilling. He wiped the cold sweat from his brow.

-I see the horror in your thought, she responded, her face paling, -The creature is not truly of the living. He comes and goes between this earth and the underworld. You are right, such creatures cannot be killed. It is good detection Kamil though your findings are not what I would have wished! It raises an even more formidable question. She had a look of barely disguised fear. Kamil trembled. This was his royal Princess. She normally controlled her emotions with a will of iron.

-Princess? He knew that her mind was capable of leaps to awful consequences much faster than his own.

-It is this. If he returns constantly what is it that impels him? What gratification does he receive from these dark visits? There must be a reward for him in the world of flesh and blood. This is what we must discover for in it may lie the way of hobbling him.

Princess Sabiya and her spymaster held each other's gaze for a long moment until she stood abruptly and left without another word. He asked himself whether he should have mentioned Baligha's tale of the ice-shaman's twin sister but it would add further terror to her fears and he felt relieved that he had kept it to himself. In truth, also, the thought of telling her had caused him more deep dread.

Chapter Three

Life and death are separated by more than the senses

The silence of the circular room, the scent of lemon from the preserving lamps and the perfect order of the serried shelves, left no distraction to the historian's work. Nevertheless it was difficult to clear his mind totally for the task he had set himself. The strange, oppressive feeling he had had when he wondered why he had not told the Princess of the ice-shaman's twin sister returned again in force. Images of awful events swirled through his mind, of blood and mayhem, of leprous diseases, of torture and wasting flesh, of women and babies snatched and mutilated in some perfidious design to end all blood-lines.

Kamil held to his discipline and began leafing through the papers, skins and books that his assistant was collecting. Progress was slow. The cross-referencing systems that he had devised had paid no attention to the likely search for writings on twins! Hours of investigation had not thrown up one treatise dealing directly with the subject. A biologist had ventured to suggest that the kind of twin which appeared from a woman's womb resulted from two distinct causes. In the first, where twins could not be told apart, it was felt that the female bearer, unnaturally, had two receiving sacs for the male seed as opposed to one in normal women. Each received the father's seed at the same astrological moment. In unalike twins the sacs were filled at successive moments and thus the stars had transited onwards in their heavenly paths between the fertilisation of first and second.

In myths twins could be wrought by divine intercession. Gods could enter the male and enjoy with him his act with the woman, thereby experiencing the pleasures of mortal flesh that were otherwise denied them.

In some lands twins were venerated, kept together in solitude for long periods, dressed in the same clothes and treated as two halves of the same being. There were tales of women encouraging the issue of such progeny by taking to a diet of all foods which fell into equal halves when removed from shell, rind, pod or the twin offspring from the womb of cow or sheep. Among other tribes the second born was killed immediately for it was feared it would taint the blood-line of the elder infant or damage its fate line through abnormal bifurcation.

As he was perusing these fragments of history Kamil tried to develop in his consciousness a sense of what it might be to be a twin. Know your enemy, he kept telling himself. The best initiation into this apprehension of human duality seemed to him to be found in the work of a scholar who had accumulated the dreams of ancient prophets. The academic recounted that a certain clairvoyant had meditated on his own birth with surprising and terrifying results so that when he emerged from his deep reverie he was chastened and wanted his fellow seers to know why all human beings are born with a certain guilt. All except twins:

And from nothingness I formed into a mote of life, floating in a black cavern. I felt beside me somewhere, another, exactly as I. It seemed that time fled past us in haste and our bodies multiplied in their size until we filled all the volume in the cavern and there was no space left for the two of us. So we fought and I vanquished my brother with the choke of my fingers and he became a speck again and then was gone. Thus it was that I had complete dominion in the cavern but I still grew. When there was again no space left for me to breathe I pressed the walls and breeched them and was suddenly thrust into the world.

The scholar's annotations suggested that it was his belief that this visionary episode confirmed that all are conceived as twins but only a few, subject to fate, survive the womb to birth. All others experience the womb as in the clairvoyant's dream, born with the blood of a twin on their hands.

Returning to the records of the recurring visits of the red haired creatures, Kamil could find no evidence that they may have been twins. All he had was Baligha's anecdote and her instinct for its importance.

But he knew her intuition and prized it above any historical fact. After more unprofitable sifting he left his assistant with the task of seeking all evidence of bitter conflict between twins and climbed the circular marble staircase out of the library. He had a vague desire to glimpse the red haired seducer of the Emperor but he had no immediate passport to the inner court and contented himself with a plan to talk with the servants who laboured in the kitchens, the corridors and the sleeping chambers.

It turned out that there was nothing much to be gleaned from the gossiping workers. Largely they were awestruck by the reputation of the newcomer who had quickly become known as the Red Man. Most wanted to stay out of his way for fear of his devilish gifts. Kamil heard variations on the stories his Princess had relayed to him, the tales becoming more ornate and exaggerated with each retelling. Finally he found himself sitting in the eating hall having declined food being brought to his rooms which was his normal practice. His high official's robes made him conspicuous and no-one at first sat near him at his end of one of the long tables. Eventually a rosy cheeked plump youth sat beside him, not registering his presence, being so preoccupied. Kamil could see that he was a trainee cook. Eventually their eyes met.

-You seem exhausted, said Kamil winningly.

The man looked down and then up again, -My Lord we are preparing a banquet for the Emperor. It is exotic and demanding. Much of the food is not normally eaten in this land. The preparation is very exacting. We are under orders from the Red Man. I would not like to be the royal taster. Who can tell whether the food contains poisons or pleasures? He went on eating his meal, thrusting lumps of food down his throat with his fat fingers, his mouth open and his eyes staring.

-You have seen him? asked Kamil casually, made conscious of his own measured and fastidious manners.

-Seen him? Have I seen him? How could I forget? He is a giant. My head would seem a mere lemon in one of his hands. His appearance is enough to transform your blood into devil's juice. His hair is redder than the best nut dye and leaves only his eyes and nose in view. He speaks quietly enough but his voice rumbles lower than a bull's. But those eyes! They cut as deep as any knife.

-I must meet him, smiled Kamil.

-Must? You are mad! Stay away, if you have choice. He finished his

358

meal by forcing down the last handful of clumped food and stood, -I must get back to business. There are snakes to be skinned, rats to be roasted, beetles to be baked and crows to be kebabbed. The Red Man calls it, 'The Devil's Dinner'. The name amuses everyone, it is said. Not me. Not me!

*

-Yes, said Princess Sabiya that evening, -It will be an incongruous meal. Your informant was right. We are to eat much that offends the natural law. Only in extremes of survival would I put such obnoxious food in my mouth.

They were back at the table and the next tarot card, The High Priestess, lay face-up at his elbow. He had spoken of the results of his earlier combing of the library records but made no mention of twins. He had convinced himself that he needed more evidence before he precipitated that conversation, trying to ignore his growing sense of guilt at his silence on the matter. Princess Sabiya was not in an impatient mood. She was pensive and relaxed, -I have sent, she said, -One of my agents on a long trek north. He goes by the great river and will pick up such information as he can, for just as all the streams help form and make up our great empire's artery, so gossip flows from the surrounding lands and ends in the ears of the river traders. Kamil nodded supportively though something suggested to him that whatever information her agent collected would be too late to aid them.

-Tell me about the meal, he said.

She smiled, -You think my agent is on a wasted hunt? We shall see. As I hear it, the Red Man told my father that he wanted to repay his kindness in taking him in at court by concocting a special meal of thanksgiving. It would also have the added potency of vanquishing all foes of the empire. She laughed, -As if eating beetles would do that. They are all so gullible. The richer in body, the poorer in mind. Even my father! Do you know Kamil, he has changed. His eyes have become clouded by inner thoughts and he remains closeted with the Red Man for hours each day. Her face hardened, -We must act soon or he will have bound my father to him like a vassal. She frowned, -The Red Man is powerful. Our eyes met once and I felt a tremor run through my limbs. It was not fear but an unwelcome stimulation. I felt his mind trying to enter mine and had to shut out his prying. She looked up suddenly, -Read me a Tale to take my thoughts off him. Even thinking about him brings his mind closer to me. It is as if he can reach across distance and time. Kamil nodded. He had felt the same oppression in his own skull. They looked down at the upturned card.

-So, what does The High Priestess represent? Let me remember? Ah...I think so. Her countenance suggests wise counsel and the search for meaning. Higher thoughts. She is an ascetic, perhaps. Is this not so? You see Kamil, I am a good pupil.

-You are your Highness. And you are in all matters correct. He stopped.

-So?

-When your hand disturbed the cards this card became unseated by fate and has ended up reversed in the pack.

She became anxious, -This is significant?

-It is. Perhaps I should read the Tale and then you can comment on her changed nature.

As they were carried away by the raft, the Warrior was thinking about the rituals of death. All tribes have ways of treating their dead. Those that are followers of the sun build a column of wood and lay the dead upon a nest of perfumed twigs at the top. The whole edifice is lit and the spirits leave their corpses to rise with the smoke towards the heavens. Those, including his father-not-of-blood, who feel they must nourish the world with their deaths, have their bodies left on high peaks for the claws and beaks of black winged scavengers. In this way their final gift is to the ceaseless cycle. Some seek the earth for their last clothing, feeding it with their decomposition. Mariners may wish for rest in their harbour's depths, having spent their lives defying and fearing the pull of the water. And all these multifarious ways of honouring the dead are attended by ceremonies and rituals. The chief desire among all who have religion - and that seemed to the Warrior to include all but himself - is to ensure secure and eternal rest for their loved ones, no matter where or how.

In the land immediately before them on the nearing bank of the great river lived a religious sect, with members drawn from many tribes who had the most mysterious rituals that his father, the Merchant, had ever encountered. He had described it to his son, thus.

"In a region east of the great river in line with the rising sun at it greatest there is a very strange settlement indeed. Clan is too ill-fitting a word. Sect is far better for many come from afar to join it. They are attracted by stories of everlasting life carried by traders. I know that you are deeply interested in such matters my son and thus this sect will be of fascination to you. They search for the secret of life and the deferment of death, of life-takers, of the release of the spirit. They conspire through arts and skills and wisdom collected and stored on ancient skins to change the relentless natural cycle. Not to die in the way we think of it. No sudden end. Only beginnings. I have yet to cross these people though I have heard many tales of their rituals."

The Warrior and his mother loaded their horses as the ferry slipped away from them back towards the island. He mulled over his father's words. He had not talked of this with his mother but he had discussed it with their host. The scientist had spoken carefully, -They are indeed a strange collection. Their clothing is from different lands. They have skins from white to black. Yet all their eyes shine wetly with the same belief. They are convinced of their mission. All who join will be freed from the death of the body. Eternal life.

-Is it possible?

-Who knows? A man such as I who dabbles daily with mystery would be happy to leave that question in the air. They are severe in their calling. They tolerate no acts against them of any kind. Their vengeance is extreme. No bandit would dare to anger them. It is a paradox is it not? They will shorten the life of another at the whisper of an ill word while they themselves hold life to be so precious. It is their custom to cut their enemies' corpses into pieces small enough for a stew pot and scatter them far and wide so that there is no complete body for a death ceremony. It makes their foes ponder. No body means no fulfilment in death. To which piece of flesh would a life-taker attend? For myself, they remain good customers. Stay on the sunlit side of them and they are very engaging.

-What of yourself? Your beliefs? Your windows give leave for the sun to visit the bird of death. The scientist was one of the few whom the Warrior had felt might enlighten him.

-I am too wild a horse to wear blinkers. Worship of the sun god is favoured here and so my designs impress those who visit my home. Sometimes I feel that all religions are but candles lit by the one great fire. He laughed, -I have not disputed this with the sect. It would be enough to have them sharpen their swords!

His mother's voice lifted him from his reverie, -What closes your face, my son? Deep thoughts? Some darkness that comes unexpectedly to your mind?

-No Mother, I am the willing victim of it. I was chasing it like a puppy a stick.

-You think too much of impractical things. Such thoughts are meat and drink for the old. The young must pursue what is immediately about them or no future can be carved from the pain of the present. Or am I ignorant of the ways of the shaman?

He considered her words, -But as we are journeying my eyes watch the world and my ears listen for the softest sounds. Our half-brother roans speak with their ears. I am in the world but am active in another realm too. And you? Do you not spend time with your mind slung into the void?

-It is true, if the past is the void! I watch the present and I seek the best of fate's paths into the future but these are not a shaman's thoughts.

-What are a shaman's thoughts? he smiled.

-They are like a prisoner's hands trying to claw a bandage from his eyes thinking that there are great secrets beyond the blindfold.

-It is a gift of your blood, Mother, like all else.

-Hah, now you say the fault if mine!

It was the third message he had sent his woman, the mother of his children, since they had begun their journey. Drawn on silk and rolled tight within a tiny, oiled leather snakeskin pouch, he attached it to the bird's leg. Then, whispering to it, as he felt its regular heart beat through the warm feathers in his cupped hands, he tossed it firmly into the air.

-Where did you learn this? asked his mother.

-The General taught me when he was a boy. I already had some of the skills but I still needed his tutoring.

-It is a sorcerer's gift to pluck a bird from the sky, to take it from its natural ways and make a messenger of it, to have it carry your thoughts across the land. It defies understanding. How is the bird to know its place of descent?

-You have to see through its eyes. I have done this. The dove sees the ground from above. It is like a rug. It has edges for it is limited to its daily flight for food and mates. I see its rug like a picture. On it I see my family. This I tell the bird is the place it must land. I am not as skilled as the General. He can show the face of the receiver to the bird and it will go to no other! This is the last message I will send for the distance is becoming too great and birds will soon have no knowledge of the land of my family. From now we must rely upon the slower progress of travellers.

-Ah, a world I understand.

☥

He led them up a stream for a while. The bed was sandy and the horses' legs were cooled by their splashing in it. He saw a storm was being raised over the plateau below them. The movement of birds told him it would be fierce and would be upon them soon. Both roans had laid back their ears in disapproval.

His mother saw it too.

-There is wrath in the heavens!

-We have a choice, he replied, -We may stop here and tie up a skin between meagre trees for a partial shelter against the storm or we can move on quickly and hope for a better camp among the rocks. They are soft and given to caves and tunnels.

-It is an ancient trail and we are three days only from the river. This is the first high ground. Are there no settlements here? Did not our host forewarn you? She looked at him questioningly.

-He did, my mother, as you know he must have done. He laughed, - There is a settlement nearby.

-Then we will seek their protection. She had always followed the ancient customs of hospitality towards strangers, give shelter even to your enemy.

-They are strange people I hear. He said it with a low, slightly foreboding voice.

-How, strange? The grey haired woman propped herself straight in the saddle but still had to crane her neck to watch his features.

-I only know a little so it would be remiss of me to say too much. I would have preferred it for us to have found a secure camp. Then I might have visited them alone, first.

-Ah, you are a secretive son and so male! You tell your mother only enough to keep her at peace with you. What is this settlement? If it be poison to the traveller, then it would be better we went together. I am the equal of any man in battle. She grimaced and slapped her scabbard.

-That is true - if it were as you describe. I think the danger is little. It is their way of life which may discomfort you. His mother knew little of the strange customs of other tribes.

She snorted angrily, -Now you are protecting me from you know not what! A way of life? What people are they? Are they monsters with tails and scales? Have they three eyes and horns? Do they breathe fire and cook their children with it for sustenance?

-They are as you and I.

-What then?

He pointed, -We are about to discover.

The stream had led them to a point where it fell as a short waterfall over a great boulder. Circling it they had ascended to a flat strip of grasses that formed a large ledge along a low, sheer cliff. Along its face was one continuous simple wood and straw dwelling supported by timbers angled between earth and rock.

-It is like one side of a great tent, she said, -There can be few longer buildings under the sun. Above them the sky was darkening by the moment.

They stopped their horses by what they took to be the largest door. All was silent. There was no movement. It was as if the place was deserted. The rising breeze blew chaff off the never ending roof.

-Perhaps it would be better to enter? We could sit here until the storm drowns us! she finally exclaimed.

-They have a pestilence. His eyes were narrowed, focusing on what existed beyond the door.

-What senses you to it? She sniffed the air, -I catch something like the rich rot of fallen fruit.

-You can smell medicinal pomanders.

-What are they?

-Fruit pricked all over with spices. It is believed by some that the scent may deny the spread of the plague.

-Ah! I remember as a child...

-It helps sleep but does little else.

-Plague you say? Then we cannot enter.

-No. He pushed his unwilling horse up to the door and leant forward to rap it with his fist. The roan jittered back quickly. They waited.

Finally the door opened. A tall woman in a frayed red silk gown stood there. She stared coldly at them. Tiredness gripped her features. She was somewhere between the Warrior's age and his mother's, they both judged. Her hair was trussed in a knot but its deep brown colouring showed no grey, yet it did not reflect light. Her noble face was dominated by a strong hooked nose which reminded the Warrior of people from the south, though her skin was as white as he had ever encountered.

-This is no place for you to rest the night. You are safer beneath the trees.

-What is the display of the disease? His sudden question shook her attempted calm.

-You can tell? From your horse's back? How is this?

-I am versed in such things. Tell me, where and how does it afflict the sufferer?

There was a deep groan of approaching thunder. Violent flashes lit the edges of the land.

The woman looked more closely at him, -I know you. I have heard. You are the Warrior, The shaman of the wilds! I would that I could entertain you but it is not possible. There are few of us left standing and those that are, look after the ill. We are preparing for everlasting life. It is complex. Many medicines are needed. Our stores are depleted. It was a poisoned hand that brushed across the backs of our people. Their skin bleeds. Their eyes become fixed and stare only ahead. Their limbs turn to stone. A raging fever covers all, its thick yellow excesses reddened by blood. Tongues distort and allow no passage of water. Then, a miracle, the body heals itself and is as smooth as a river stone. Thus it ends and they take up their lives in the place beyond, exact in all detail as here.

-How many dead?

-Three in four.

The first heavy drops of rain slapped the straw.

-There is but one path for you, he said. He was silent.

-There is? Have you a cure?

-A cure, no. An act that will save a few, yes.

-What is it? Her face betrayed her realisation at what he would say.

-Bring the living out and lay them in the storm. Set fire to your dwelling. It will warm them as the rain cleanses them. It will kill the pestilence within.

-It cannot be done. I have led these people with my visions. Years of labour made this our sanctuary.

-It is that labour that now pollutes you. The place is full of the dead. The air is thick with their decay. Each is a black shoot of the plague.

-No! They become preserved for ever. None of our dead show such signs.

-They are like the white stem that grows in the night. Eat it the next day and it gives nourishment. Soon all changes. Beneath the white grows a black dust. It will kill.

-I give them eternal life.

-You are their priestess. It is for you to decide. Bring out the living and some may survive. Continue as you do and you will be the last of your people standing. They will have left you and there will be no-one to prepare you for your final journey. Then you too will be overcome by the creeping plague.

She cried out, -Why should I fear this? I will sleep with my people. And awake anew.

-It is your wish. You have led them to this. It is right you do not forsake them on their final journey.

She stared at them defiantly, -Had we met at another time, I fear my men would have been forced to kill you, Warrior though you may be. This is as I once dreamed. That I would bring my people to salvation. Then she turned and re-entered the dwelling. They heard the wooden bar sliding to.

The rain began falling heavily.

Mother and son weathered the storm in a sentry's lookout shelter that overlooked the encampment. By adding skins to the roof they remained dry enough. The horses huddled in its lea. It was not cold but the rain stayed with them for several days. Meanwhile, they trapped food, maintained a fire and waited. Earlier he had said to his mother, -This must be ended. I have heard of this disease. It grows with confinement. Even an open door slows its progress. Yet they have sealed themselves within. It will be finished soon.

-Why do they follow this path?

-Because it is one they themselves created. They came to believe it was the one true way. This they told all who listened. They promised everlasting life. A living sleep. They took vengeance on all who slighted their beliefs. Now they have closed the doors on the world so none can see that all was for nothing.

-It is possible that people's faith may cause more death and suffering than even the desire to possess land and its people.

He put a hand on his mother's shoulder, -Truth weighs heavily in your words, Mother. All who carry their faith lightly and do not seek to burden others with it are free from such tyranny. They have learned to see the world through the eyes of another. It is a path that stems conflict.

Each day the Warrior went down to the dwelling house. One day he returned and they saddled their horses and loaded their pack beasts. They walked them slowly down to the long house. A haunting silence grasped the air. The main door was open. Lying across its threshold lay the priestess, her hand outstretched, palm to the air. The Warrior cut a stave from the roof and with it levered her back into the dwelling. They lit torches and turned their horses and commanded them to kick each door in. Where they found beasts they freed them, then they lit the undersides of the straw where it was still dry. A snake of fire burned along the dwelling, lighting up the cliff face. When they were sure that all would burn they urged their horses away.

-It is a strange turn of fate's wheel, said his mother.

-Mmm?

-The sect denied the God of Fire. Yet, at the end, His life-takers came to claim them, one and all.

Her son looked at her steadily for a few moments and thought to speak but in the end said nothing.

He finished the reading and looked up to see his Princess bent forward in her chair, her hands laced in her lap and her eyes staring at the card intently.

-So this is what happens when a wise counsellor is upturned! she cried, -A plague. The woman knew so much but in the most vital aspect she was lacking. Religious pride makes fools of us, Kamil. If the Gods were barricaded in their temples and shrines, then there would be none of this. Let your divine ones influence you however they wish from their seats of glory but never assume that you are wise enough to act upon their behalf. She thought for a moment and said, - Unless you are an emperor for then the people expect you to have a godly agency.

Her historian said nothing. He was not shocked now to hear her blaspheme against the gods. She had revealed her agnosticism during his reading of the first volume of the Tales. He had come to understand then how royalty occupied a strange vantage point over world affairs and saw all religions as yokes and harnesses to keep their peoples in thrall.

-I fear the Red Man will try to bring his own plague to us, do you? She was still stiff and bent.

-I do. Though it is early yet. In the histories he is not revealed as the fulcrum of evil for some time, even years. The pattern seems to be that he gradually ingratiates himself into the inner sanctum of the emperor or ruler by a series of exceptional acts and deeds and by foresight and critical advice so that he becomes accepted as a seer and answerable only to the highest authority in the land. Then he exerts his uncanny power. None can believe he is the source of evil for he appears to goad each and every one to battle against the rising tide of misfortune. Kamil dropped his voice, -Misfortune that he, himself, is orchestrating. It is a recipe for chaos and destruction.

She heard this, nodding throughout and finally sat back, her face determined, her eyes penetrating and bright with anger. Finally she folded and smoothed her garments around her, -What shall I do tonight at the banquet? For I will not eat. I cannot. I fear it is the first homoeopathic dose of his poison. No one will notice but inside each a trickle of evil will be released.

-I cannot say my Princess but you are wise to be so careful. We know little of what we seek. Watch him carefully but stay aside from his eyes. Who can tell whether or not greater poison travels along his gaze? Kamil nodded as though the warning he had given was equally meant for himself.

Chapter Four

A person is like a bush under the moon. Nothing is as it seems.

Even in the insulated silence of the library Kamil sensed that something was perturbing the normally tranquil yet busy ambience of the palace rooms above him. Putting down a scroll which contained painted illustrations of fables concerning gods and heroes, he focused on the sensation of unrest that seemed to be seeping through the ceiling. Once again, just below his level of self-awareness, he felt the soft intrusion of a mind stronger than his own. He recognised it now. It had the signature of the Red Man. He gave a physical jerk of his head and opened his eyes wide to stare at the scroll. It gave him an immediate sensation of relief as the invasion stopped. He listened acutely again and realised that what had disturbed him was not noise but too much silence. Where were the vibrations from above made by slippered feet or the movement of furniture? Even though it was just daybreak there should have been much servant activity. Then he caught the sound of someone coming down the circular stairs. He was unnerved but fought off the desire to hide and sat facing the bottom of the staircase where three steps were visible. First a pair of red slippers and then the hem of a robe became visible until finally his assistant turned the bend.

-Hah it is you! laughed Kamil almost hysterically.

-Master? replied the younger man, -Are you unwell?

-I am the better for seeing you.

The man raised his eyebrows, -I wondered Master whether you had been to the banquet and were sleeping off the after-effects like everyone else.

Kamil's stomach sank. What was this? So soon? Had the Red Man already branded the court with his curse? -Tell me! he demanded, sharply.

His assistant smiled nervously, -It is as though a sleeping sickness has swept through the palace. Only those servants who were not entitled to finish the leavings from the banquet are up and about this morning. The rest and all the courtiers are still asleep. Already a hunt has been cancelled while the would-be riders mount only their beds. He laughed.

-What of the Princess? asked Kamil, hesitantly, -Is she asleep too?

-How should I know? shrugged the librarian, -She has not been seen. Oh, the author of this dreaming, the Red Man, was in the kitchen early this morning demanding his breakfast. He was checking that all the pots and plates had been washed. Can you imagine? Then he ate heartily and drank enough fermented juice to lay down an army. The son of my cousin is a kitchen boy so what I tell you is the truth.

His assistant went off to his station to continue with his labours while Kamil sat pondering. He was in the middle of this reverie and considering whether to send a message to Princess Sabiya enquiring as to her health but fearful the note might fall into the wrong hands, thus implicating him with her, when another pair of feet began descending to the room. It was one of the Princess's chamber maids. Looking in terror at these strange surroundings lit by the spluttering wax candles, she lowered her eyes before Kamil and thrust a note into his proffered hand. She stood, silent and shaking slightly, her hands clasped to her stomach. He broke the seals and read:

I did not savour the drug and am in good health. I must stay and observe how things turn out. Will the world return to itself or will this great sleep lead to death? My men are armed. I will be with you at our appointed time, all the gods being willing!

He refolded the note and applied his imprint to three new seals. The girl raced away with it in relief. Kamil was instantly in a lighter frame of mind, heightened by expectancy. To quell his impatience he returned to the hand painted images that were beguiling him earlier.

*

Her cheeks were ripened by excited self-restraint. She had divulged nothing to anyone all day. Those that had happened to see her would have thought she was suffering a fever like the rest of the court who had attended the banquet and who had risen late, each head seemingly filled with fine sand.

-What is the card? she demanded and Kamil, though almost paralysed with frantic curiosity, was far too obedient to do other than turn it over. It was The Empress.

-This card is me, I know!

-All cards-, he began

-Yes yes the ceaseless cycle. All are aspects of the journey I am making. I remember it very well. Too well! she scolded, -But this card? She is the ruler. She cares less for great thoughts than practicalities. And she is strong, even within the extremes of suffering. Princess Sabiya smiled radiantly and looked at him, -How do I look? Truth historian? Look at the evidence and tell me.

Kamil stumbled on his words, -A trifle...

-Yes? Oh come Kamil, how long have we known each other? Speak! She regarded his portly shape and meekly bobbing head with amusement.

-Flushed, he whispered.

-Good. And -?

-Perspiring but only a little -

-Excellent. And my eyes? Are they pink where the white should be pure as a bleached sheet?

-Yes your Highness.

-Perfect. My deception is complete. I took nutmeg mixed with a harsh pepper and have done so each hour. No-one suspects that I did not eat at the banquet. I copied everyone's slow, dreamy talk with my eyes lidded. Even the Red Man could not tell for he gave me half a glance only when I went today to see whether my father had recovered. Kamil's narrow focus widened as he digested her account fully and he too smiled.

-Princess, you are a true spymaster!

-I am Kamil, I am! I feel light headed anyway because my concoction is not the most appetising of diets. But I am well enough to hear the next Tale and afterwards, should I still have some sense and energy, I will recount the strange events of yesterday evening. She watched as his face struggled to suppress his eagerness to hear more and laughed again, -You see I have learned a thing or two about storytelling from the master. He bowed at the flattery, -The best stories are those that are drawn out like flax on a twig. So you can twist first, old historian.

The mother was lost in her own thoughts. Her son was right. She was troubled deeply by their experience at the long dwelling house. And they had not entered it. They had not spoken except with the priestess. They had not seen what lay within. She imagined what might have been there. Preserved bodies lying in rows, their skins like stretched fine cotton, oiled and shining, their eyes closed and all in the everlasting sleep of eternal life. Yet inside each corpse, her son was convinced, grew a living black dust seeking to escape the waxen shell, to blow across the land where it might settle again on others like dirty rain bringing more wracking pain and death.

She shivered.

-My Mother. You are fearful?

-I have heard of these plagues it is true. Yet to meet one! It is an evil force. She turned to him her face blanching, -If you placed that disk the Merchant gave you over the black decay, would there be creatures eating the flesh?

-I know not. Perhaps so. The Merchant was sure that much life lies below our sight. Perhaps that small world is a replica of this one with wars, predators and saviours.

She shook herself, -I will not think of it further, my body is healthy and my mind will not pollute it with dark thoughts.

They rode on in silence. Eventually she spoke again, -If we had refused her command and set fire to the dwelling when we first encountered it then some might now be alive.

-It is true. It is what has been exercising my thoughts. His voice was troubled.

-Yet she was chief, chosen by her people and we had no authority over them.

-Except a moral authority.

374

She waited in silence for him to continue.

He said eventually, -It is possible that a greater good could be invoked in a code to which all people can appeal when there is doubt or they feel that whoever commands them is wrong.

-Of course the General sets out such laws for us all to obey.

-It is not the kind of law passed by rulers of which I speak. Those are the laws of possession and theft, of ownership of land and of people. It is true that we could have put a torch to the building when we arrived. We did not. Is it for each of us to decide and act according to our urges - or if we are law-abiding must we wait for the orders of our chiefs and kings? Neither seems to have true worth to me.

She pursed her lips into a grimace, -Had we saved some from the plague and the fire, would they have shown gratitude? I think not. They were all of one mind. It was not for us to determine their fate.

He replied reflectively, -Yet if you know that the thoughts of another are based on false understanding does it not behove you to stand between them and those thoughts? We do so with our children and the aged who have lost their minds. Where are lines drawn?

-All life is war, she exclaimed passionately, -Good and evil battle from birth to death. Yet in this pestilential conflict it is difficult to know which is which. It seems one is clothed more like the other. Sometimes I know not to whom I should offer my arms. She slapped the hilt of her sword emphatically in that familiar gesture, -As I said to you, you think too much. It is done. We did not intervene. Thus fate's path is now inscribed. Perhaps the next time we shall. And fate will bow at its inscription. To act or not may seem to us to be a choice. It is merely the spell that fate casts over us which determines.

-To think like that, he said to her softly, -Leaves not a hair's width between us and dumb beasts. It seems to me that we should act less because each circumstance affects us thus and thus and more because of a code of living and being that we have established after great thought and disputation. Such a code marks the direction of what I think of as the Right Path. It should shape all other laws.

As the light began to fade they made camp. As was their growing ritual, the mother saw to the horses and the fire while her son hunted for food. They were on the bank of a small lake in the hills. The water had a brackish taste and was discoloured. She made a cone of broad leaves stuffed with moss and poured the water through it to sweeten it. The horses drank from the water happily. The bond between the almost identical roans was as close as that between herself and her son. They rubbed necks and seemed forever to be snorting and whinnying softly to each other. The other horses seemed not offended but took occasion to join in.

Not long after the fire was lit and water bubbling in a pot over it, the Warrior returned with both fish and fowl. The fish he stripped to dry over the fire and the fowl he plucked and quartered before placing it in the water. He added salt and eastern herbs, fresh leaves and roots and covered it.

-It will take some time, he smiled.

-There is no forcing goodness into food. It must finds its way out no matter how long the cooking.

They reclined by the fire. The worst of the events of the long dwelling had eased from her mind. She had watched her son cook, following every detail of his movement, the expressions on his face and the concentration in his pale eyes. This was why she had come with him, why she had insisted. That great time of separation could never be healed completely but most could be regained. She observed him under her lashes as she lay back. She could see that his mind was occupied. No doubt he was finding the subtlest shades of meaning in what to her might appear black and white.

At this moment her son was also watching her while pretending not to. He was musing on the strange nature of this journey with a mother whom he was only just beginning to know and understand. There was so much within that great absence that was obscured. It may have been a time of hiding and fleeing but what else? What had she been forced to do to survive?

-Let us tell each other a tale from our time apart, he said suddenly. It threw her into a confusion.

-What?

-I will tell you of an adventure and you will reply with one of your own. This way the bird will be cooked and we shall know each other better.

She nodded at last, -I will tell you one. One that you know not. It will suit the ease of my storytelling to begin. I do not wish to have to compete with an exploit of the great Warrior.

-That could not be so, he said, showing a little embarrassment, - Begin. I will lie here, like a child as my mother tells me her story.

She arranged her thoughts and began:

-Several cycles of seasons after I gave you into the care of the Merchant, I was hiding in the hills near your valley. From time to time your father-not-of-blood sent me such goods that I could exchange for food and other needs. One day, unknown to you, he brought my roan back. You had his colt and it was growing beside you. It was a moment of great joy at a time of fear and danger to see them both! The great Merchant who had sacrificed his life for my son, a son I felt I would never see and the horse who was also a magician among his own kind.

Your father did not stay more than a half day. He would not leave you longer. It seems that in the time that I have known him, only a pinch of it has been spent in his presence. Yet he has been the only man...

She stopped herself and the Warrior was left with questions he felt unable to ask.

-To have my horse again gave me renewed strength and security. It was proof that with time all could change. I knew that you had ridden him and I imagined that I could smell you on him. Also, as you know, the roan's mysterious bloodline has its own power. Look into the eyes of these beasts and you feel hope in your heart. Their tongues calm your fears. Their ears signal all that is happening in the world around and ahead. They outlast any beast over distance, travelling days without much sustenance. And if it were possible, they would die for us, their masters.

So it was with great joy that we were reunited. He was older but still a fine beast for you cared for him well. This happened as I had news that yet more assassins were looking for me and offering rewards for sightings. So I put my trust in my creature and asked him to take me to safety. It is true. I wilfully denied myself and urged him not in any way. It was his instinct that took us farther from you than I was ever to go, my son.

One day - I remember it as if it is happening as I tell you this - we reached the very peak of a high mountain. It was the time just before the first snow in the valleys and there was already a white covering where the sun could not reach. Ahead I could see the countless ridges of that land where none can live, even the nomad shepherds. Behind lay the softer valleys that have given shelter to our tribe, for all of time. It was a bleak place, a place without nourishment or shelter. A place without any history that I know of. The wind entered my clothing at will, freezing me and the roan and the pack horse stood with bent backs, their noses touching the very rock. The sky was scratched with cold red lines.

Then I began to doubt him. I wondered if my trust in his cunning might have been misplaced. I tried to urge him on but he would not move. Slowly the cold entered my mind. The cruel wind stripped all thought away and with it all fear and pain.

Then, I know not what prompted it save it be the roan's sense of the absolute void that lay within me, he turned and we headed back from whence we came. It was as though he had understood that I must start again. That was why he had taken me there. I was emptied of the old. Something might grow in its place. We gained speed and warmth as the land eased and the wind ceased to blind us with its fury.

Somewhere we left the old trail and found ourselves at the edge of a sheltered upland vale, small and invisible to me until we forced our way through trees. At its centre was a crude dwelling made from piled rock. The roof was laid with thick timbers covered with grassy sods. Much of the building, it later transpired, was dug deep into the ground. Smoke issued from a tall pipe of stones and clay at the centre of the roof. A she-goat was tethered nearby and she bleated and bucked on her rope when she saw us. The door opened.

Who was more surprised to see the other? Me, a wild shred of a woman on horseback carrying sword and bow like some blown seed that could not find fertile earth. She, an ancient creature whose bony hands fluttered and dived like frantic birds. Yet our eyes met and fear and suspicion fled from our breasts.

It was there I stayed for several seasons. Safe. I had found another mother, different from my own and she had found a daughter different from her own. We learned each other's stories, cooked for each other, tended each other. It is strange but the presence of another leads to care for oneself. We combed each other's hair and mended clothes. I drew out some creams and face paints your Merchant father had sent long before. Each day we would wake and spend what time we wished preparing each other as though we might meet nobility. Gradually she added flesh to her bones, as did I. Her face grew a little younger.

Who was she? It is both a sad and noble tale. She had been the consort to a king in a city to the east. She was journeying to stay with her sister when a loyal servant caught up with her to tell of an uprising. Her husband was dead and her daughter had fled with what was left of the king's guard. Even now assassins were chasing her party. She took the best horse and left her servants and guard assuring them that they would be safer without her. She took to the hills far to the east of the little vale. Imagine, before this she had only ridden for show, as the king's favoured one. Her clothes were not fit for rough terrain. Her hands were soft from a life of creams and perfumes. Now the hard leathers of the reins and stirrups chafed and cut her skin. Yet all whom she met took pity upon her for her eyes melted all hearts and engendered love even among those with the least feeling.

Finally she fell among herdsmen who led her to this place in the high hills. They strengthened the shelter for her and they brought her food every few days. In return she gave them what jewellery she had and it was enough to feed their families many lives over. They swore to protect her with the last issue of their breath. When they found me there they did not question it. They ignored my battle sword, knife and bow. They complimented the old woman on her renewed health and good looks which pleased her greatly. It was a wondrous time. There was more love and peace there than a traveller might find in a lifetime of journeying.

Then one day a herdsman brought extraordinary news. The city had been returned to her family. Her daughter had taken it with a small army. She was queen and still hoped her mother might be alive for stories were told of a noble woman hiding somewhere in the hills. Servants were sent across the territory.

I prepared her well for this journey into her past. I gave her my pack horse and dressed her in the best clothes we had between us. Her hair shone and her skin was soft and alluring. We sat and ate our last meal together. She said it was beyond reason. She was leaving the greatest kingdom she had known for one for which she had little desire. She said that she must now leave this place of perfection. Here she had come to know the order of things. She understood the ways of plants and creatures, the place of earth and the stars, the different journeys of sun and moon. The winter winds had not blown her away. The snows had not engulfed her. The rains had not once dampened her floor. Even as her flesh had aged her spirit had grown stronger. This spirit would carry her to her daughter, no matter how feeble her bones. It was the call of blood only that made her leave. Here she had been an Empress, filled with love for all around her. In the city of her former life she was but an empty queen.

The herdsman took her with them, circling her horse as though they were a royal guard. That same day I left, too. I could not countenance being a subject in a land without an empress.

☥

As the pot threw forth the mouth wetting scents of cooked meat, he told her of his own adventures with the little, golden haired girl of the desert, of his learning concerning the face paints and creams that his mother had shared with her solitary friend and of how he had served her destiny.

-It is true, his mother said, -All women have a time of being an empress. For most it is fleeting. Its memory must be kept sacred for it feeds the female spirit.

-**Ah, I like** this mother of the Magus. She is a true empress as is the woman she found. It is a fact that we do not know what our bones are made of until we face the greatest extremes. She bent forward and stroked the face on the card, -I hope I am you, she intoned to it, -For I fear I face the extreme here in my court. She arranged her robe in her characteristic way, folding and smoothing as she composed herself. This evening she wore a pale lime silk robe, shot with blue thread which made it shimmer as she ruffled it, -So, dear spymaster, I will tell you my tale and a strange one it is too. Sit back and stop looking like a dog wanting to please, it is not appropriate. Be a child. Rest yourself. Kamil leant back stiffly and she shook her head despairingly, as if giving up trying to organise him.

-I made my entrance at the banquet as is customary for the heir to the throne. Only my father can enter after me. Everyone was standing by cushions which were arranged in horseshoes of seven facing the platform where my father would sit, like stars around the sun. The most powerful in the court, nearest. I wonder sometimes how the protocols are decided. There is bitter argument over seating as courtiers are advanced and regressed. The Red Man stood furthest away near the great entrance, yet he is so much a giant that all could see him standing there and there were many sly and half concealed glances at his savage countenance. When my father entered and bade everyone sit the Red Man remained standing like a statue. I could tell they were gazing at each other. Then, the Red Man sat, satisfied and my father welcomed everyone and said that this was a special meal created by the court's new friend and ally, to vanquish all enemies to the Emperor's rule, both in the court and far beyond. Then he asked the Red Man to perform a speech. The mountain stood and said in his foreign voice full of throat and gruffness that it was an honour to serve such a glorious court, renowned everywhere for its gracious elegance. The food might seem strange but we must see it as a return to times when people had an intimate knowledge of what can make you strong and resilient in mind and body. It would cleanse everyone of any weaknesses that undermined their courage. Afterwards they would sleep the sleep of battle weary soldiers but after a second night's sleep they would wake to find themselves truly alive in a way that they may never have experienced before. I could see that most found this statement mystifying. Then he offered a prayer which I can only recollect, partially:

O ye Ancient Gods
Gather at our shoulders
Give us leave to drink your blood
Give us leave to eat your flesh
Give us leave to breathe your breath
Let your thoughts enter us and make us your warriors
O Ancient Ones

There was a fearful silence in the room for it sounded almost as if he had conjured a curse! Then he clapped his hands. A servant entered with an enormous bowl filled with a liquid that suddenly sprang alight. Incense poured from the flames in a pale green smoke and it made us all feel merry. Even me, I admit.

It was difficult for me for I was facing the room of eyes in their horseshoes but I feigned eating and tried to copy the expressions on the faces around me. Course followed course and soon everyone was talking wildly and unguardedly. The Red Man walked among them, listening. As he came up to me my father tapped me on the shoulder and cried out, laughing, that this would all be mine when he was dead. I would sit in his place and all would obey me! I pretended to be like him and shouted, "I look forward to it, my Father but not until you reach a natural end to your noble life! I wish to have time for the irresponsibilities of youth first!" We laughed and the Red Man smiled also but it was cold and condescending and he passed on.

Soon the evening began to degenerate even more. The laughter gave way to shouting and jostling even though everyone seemed to be in a trance for their eyes were wide and unseeing. I told my father that I felt sick and would leave temporarily though I had no intention of returning. I left by the royal door and once outside I sped up the stairs to a small, curtained balcony where I could view the animalistic activity below. The courtiers had begun kissing and fondling each other regardless of whether it be male or female pressed against them and, as though to protect him from these excesses, the Red Man led my father away through the same door that I had exited. I stayed hidden with curtains before and behind.

He led my father to the royal chamber but did not try to follow him inside, there being two stern guards outside and two more within. However, I feel that he could easily have overcome all defence had he so wished. But it was obviously not the right time for such a breech within his grand plan. As he returned the way he had come he looked in the direction of my curtain and grinned, baring his great teeth but his stride did not falter. Moments later he was back in the struggling, licentious mob beneath me. I saw him signal with his hand and a servant bore in another vessel of fluid which again he ignited with his sorcery. Now a red fog spread through the hall, billowing and gathering into clouds. Instantly they breathed it the revellers stopped their wayward lechery and excesses of aggression. The Red Man clapped his hands during the lull in the tumult and told them, in a soft, insidious voice to return to their beds and to forget everything that had happened that evening. They trooped away like beaten curs. He left the hall last but with purposeful long strides and I hurried to my room in case he tried to waylay me. The rest of my story you know, Kamil. All day the court has been only half awake. No-one but me remembers what happened and I fear the Red Man suspects me. All I have talked to now speak of how warm they feel towards the giant stranger and how he will make the empire even greater with his otherworldly powers. I think he has achieved his first goal which is to eliminate opposition to him among those most powerful in the land. Sabiya shut her eyes and looked a young child suddenly and very vulnerable.

-All opposition save you, whispered Kamil, gently, -It is a hair-raising tale indeed for he is acting swiftly to build his power base here. He knows you are his enemy but something prevents him moving against you at the present time. We must be very careful and deduce his plans from what can be observed. I hope the Emperor and his court are not yet too much in his thrall for this intrigue to be reversed.

Chapter Five

Death attends the table of the true Warrior

A word which summoned up Kamil's plagued spirit during the early morning was dolefulness. Nothing had been progressed in his library searches which might illuminate the mission of the Red Man in his continuous reincarnations nor was there anything to chew on regarding the consequence of his being a twin. Nevertheless, it was to the enigma of twins that Kamil's mind returned, time and again. It plagued him, together with his stubborn reluctance to disclose this aspect of the Red Man's history to Princess Sabiya. Was he protecting her, intuitively, as if the knowledge would put her at greater risk? The Red Man seemed to have the power to enter minds so the less that was in them concerning him, the easier to keep his probing at bay. Or was his secrecy less altruistic? Did he like the sense of owning information of which the Princess was ignorant? Finally, it came to him that it was neither of these. Some burst of clarity struck him as he was reading abstractedly. It arrived as he experienced a sudden relief from the sense of the Red Man's overpowering presence. His mind was free to go where it pleased. He knew, as clear as could be, that the reason he had not yet told Princess Sabiya about Baligha's tale was that his thoughts were being shuttered by the occult mind-probing of the Red Man. He had been half-hypnotised by him even though they had never met. They were opponents, as he had told Baligha, set against each other on the board of chess, to which the Princess had alluded during the last readings. What then made his back shiver with hope was the sharp realisation that the Red Man was trying to stifle his preoccupation with his twin birth because he was fearful. Something in that part of his history might have made him vulnerable in some way.

This led him to consider his Princess's artful question. What was it that remained unrequited in each of the Red Man's returns to the living earth which forced him back into his perpetual cycle? The creature seemed doomed to relive his time among men, always bringing with

384

him the stain of unspeakable evil which spread from him among the people he contacted like blood in white cotton.

Kamil was a deeply religious man though he hid his zealous nature beneath the studious demeanour of the historian. He had had to catch his breath many times as Princess Sabiya vented her candid disregard for religious observance. It was, as she often told him, the right of royalty to see from a vantage point high above ordinary people. But being religious was not something he could alter. And being religious led him to ask a fundamental question. What kind of life form was the Red Man? Was he immortal? Had Satan conjured him up to challenge all that was good in God's creation? Or was he a djinn, fated to shuttle between a ghostly limbo and physical existence?

As he sat there, his chin resting on two sets of knuckles, his eyes closed, his mind turning over all he knew or could conjecture about the Red Man, the image of the said beast rushed into his mind, submerging it, framing it as if in a painting or as though being caught through an open window. The man's inhuman green eyes dilated and seemed to draw Kamil towards them. At the same time he could hear a barely discernible sound of drums, fast and furiously played by soft hands. Around the Red Man's head were swirling clouds of pastel colours. His beard and hair seemed to stretch out and from their very tips, tiny flashes of lightening erupted. Kamil knew he had to summon up resistance but hardly knew how. He was falling, falling. It was at this moment that a question fell loudly from his tongue as though it had been shaped by someone else.

-In the name of your sister, born your twin, what is it you want here?

With an alarming fragmentation the face of the Red Man dissolved giving way to a darkness which was itself dissipated as Kamil opened his eyes. His face and hands were prickly and clammy and his body was wracked in shivers at his near escape.

*

He was much calmer when she arrived, her guard sweeping his room with a raking glance before retiring. She was clothed in a simple hooded white robe, her feet in delicate, embroidered gold slippers and her face plain and unadorned. To Kamil she seemed even more beautiful though several years younger than her normal self. She sat and pushed back the cowl. Her face lacked its animated spark.

-Good evening my loyal historian.

-My Princess! he bowed formally.

She pursed her lips, -I have little to tell. What of you?

Kamil shifted uneasily, -Only a fragment, my Princess but who knows. Then at last he told her of Baligha's story of the Red Man having a twin sister and of his research and of the Red Man besieging his mind only to be thwarted by his own strange incantation invoking the man's sibling, words that had sprung from his mouth from nowhere. He left nothing out of his tale including his surmise that the Red Man had hypnotic power and had tried to prevent him telling the Princess about his birth.

She stared at him, frightened, -He is the most terrifying of enemies, Kamil, if he can insert his power between you and me in this way. I experience it too. He has stationed himself in some part of my own mind like a viper. I woke this morning and was convinced that I should send you from the court back to your wife. It seemed absolute. I had lost confidence in you. What use was a mere historian in my affairs? Then his power suddenly waned and I was able to think again. All that you have done for me in the past rushed to the forefront of my mind and I felt a surge of strength. Princess Sabiya allowed a laugh to roll from her lips, deep tinkling wooden bells to Kamil's ears rather than the silver he loved.

-We must find ways to give each other strength, he replied, trying to play down her compliment, -For surely he is focused on dividing us. I think he has sensed that we stand between him and the Empire.

She plucked at a white sleeve, -Will he wipe us from this world with his occult powers? What stops him, Kamil?

Kamil continued thinking aloud, turning the danger around in words, -He must not be able to act or he would have done so. Perhaps the Emperor is not yet absolutely under his influence and would deduce that our deaths might be connected to the interloper. When he moves against us it will be planned but indirect. If my research into his histories is correct he will act through others, seemingly unconnected to him, or through an apparent accident conjured up from the natural world. Drowning. Sickness. Fire.

-We will be doubly careful.

-We will. My other thoughts follow from your question yesterday. There may be some as yet unknown thread to his coming and going. It might be connected to his sister and it may be a source of weakness in him. If we find out what this is we may vanquish him.

She sat straight and ran her long fingers through her black hair, - Good! The very possibility of defeating him is succour is it not? Let us unpick the knot that is his ghostly sister and at the same time find ways of keeping him out of our minds. She added, jocularly, -And we can start by reading the next Tale for, truth be told, when your crafted storytelling fills my ears, no-one can intercede between you and I.

Kamil, energised and inflated equally by her words, began reading.

-How long will this trek take? The General may not be in his castle, grunted his mother, looking around at the sameness of the hills.

-If he is there, perhaps two seasons. If he is not then there is no answer.

-It is said that he moves constantly for fear of assassins.

-Fear or careful consideration? To rule a land it is better to be seen in every part of it. Then the people know who it is to whom they pay their dues. He is ruler of all the territories. It must also be that dark desires fill the hearts of those that would take his place. But he is a man who sees all and ponders even before his foot disturbs the sand. -Two seasons for you is nothing.

-Nor for my mother who hid for many summers and winters in the hills, he cajoled.

-I did not know it would be never ending. I hoped each day for relief but good fortune made no such haste.

-It is best to think likewise here. The General may be in his castle but even so we know not what diversions may thwart our journey. Are you tired of the quest? He smiled at her, knowing her likely response.

-No! Not so. It is just that much time has passed since we had what you call a diversion. The same rock. The same hills. Not so much as a herdsman to give us news. The world may know what we do not. The General could be dead! Or he could be sitting by a fire in the next valley. She sighed in exasperation.

-Long journeys into unknown lands test the patience of one such as you my mother. For me the slow rhythm of travel allows contemplation without distraction.

-That is it. For the shaman even a prison is a gift to the mind. It becomes a door to what lies within, if not without. Anyway, you have my jabbering as a distraction.

He patted his roan, -Fine words. All of them a product of this toil.

-Perhaps so. And it is true I would not exchange this for another adventure. Nor am I impatient to lay my eyes upon those of the General. But it would be nourishment if there was but a little change… As she spoke the ears of the roans flattened, signalling people ahead. She looked at her son and they both raised their eyebrows, -I am a shaman! Fate lends its ears to my wish.

-You are. Let us hope it is a gift that you have been granted and not a curse. They stopped and scanned the upland pasture ahead. The beasts' eyes had picked out something their riders could not see yet their ears remained flat.

-They do not think it is a gift, she murmured.

-Whoever is there probably has little knowledge of us, the roans' eyes are keener than any. Let us move into cover and wait. A glance around confirmed that the only concealed vantage point was behind them in a jumble of boulders and shrub. Once settled they waited. The horses remained intent, ears flicking. Then the Warrior's roan stepped cautiously from hiding followed by the others.

-It seems we can proceed.

-The danger has passed but something remains, replied her son.

They trotted along the rarely used track, eyes searching every horizon. First they came across two loose horses which followed them immediately. After some time they saw bodies. All were soldiers. The man and his mother walked among them.

-Swords have done their work, said the woman, examining the wounds, -Three fought like men and two were killed running, she continued, looking at the positions of the corpses on the ground.

The Warrior stood still. His eyes also took in the pattern of the bodies. He remembered their beasts' reactions. Gradually a picture grew in his mind. He nodded, -There is nothing to be done for them. We must travel on. He passed a hand through the air and wished them well on their last journeys. His mother stood silently watching him, forehead furrowed.

As they remounted she said, -There were few signs of their attackers. I could not say how many.

-They were not running but were caught from behind. There was but one assassin. He killed two before they could turn. The others tried to fight but he is skilled. Each was penetrated by one thrust. He took three horses but knew that we were nearby and did not chase the others.

-How is it you know this, Son?

-By what I saw before me. It draws the past into my mind. Her son touched his forehead above the bridge of his nose as if to emphasise his gift of clairvoyance.

-What kind of killer is this man?

-A warrior and mercenary but no shaman. I could not conjure his face but I touched his mind. It had but one desire in it. The death of another.

-Who?

-Me.

His mother was filled with anger against their unknown foe and indignation that anyone could seek to harm her cherished offspring, - Why should he want to kill you? Who rewards him? What enemies have you? Is it the General? Was it not said that he had changed? Perhaps he cannot face you? Or perhaps someone else wants to kill the General and fears that you will protect him.

-All is possible under the stars, he answered, looking up. The sun had slid from sight and the first pricks of brightness could be seen overhead.

-What think you? Can I be near the truth in my reasoning?

-I think he takes no reward. The mind I entered had only space for me. I could see myself in my brown robe, my sword across my back, a bow upon my knees notched with an arrow, astride my horse. Then I understood why the roans showed extra fear. He would kill the horses to bring us to the ground. He has heard of their mysterious senses but he does not covet them. He covets my death.

-For no payment? It is without reason!

The Warrior stared warmly at her. There was little fear in her. It was a gift she had passed to him through her blood. Her face was blank, eyes focused on the trail, thoughts crowding her mind and her hand resting upon her throwing knife.

-I think the picture comes to me too, she said slowly, -The mercenary killed those soldiers as a sign. He wishes you to know that he waits for you and that he is strong and skilled.

Her son smiled sadly and nodded, -It is a call to battle, of this I am sure.

-What badness eats at his heart to lay such a trail to his door?

-He is not one who would follow the Right Path. His mind is not able to see. He is a killer who seeks its prey. It is enough for him. Each death is food for his journey. It feeds his sense of purpose. When he has killed me then the world will acclaim him. Victor over the great Warrior! It is then that he will seek rewards from the richest courts.

-He is a blind man if he cannot see his own death. I hope it is a weapon of mine that calls for the presence of his life-taker!

-It cannot be. I will face him alone.

-I will not allow this my son. I swore I would never abandon you again. She halted her horse, -I will fight beside you.

-No. I have thought. He may use you as a weakness in me.

-Hah! She gripped her sword handle.

-No Mother! He leant over and his powerful hand pressed her sword back, -My mind needs emptiness in combat. I cannot fog it with thoughts of your protection, or that of my roan. He is a man who will use what is at his disposal. I will approach him on foot. Alone. I will leave you my bow for he carries none himself. His mind is fixed. The Warrior imperative imposes its will. He will defeat me with sword alone or die. He took his hand away and she dropped her arm. -He is close enough, look! The roans' eyes were large and troubled, their ears back against their heads.

He walked a little way. A brief turn of the head showed his mother sitting in shadowy stillness with the six horses. He cast his mind forward and a picture emerged of a starlit flattened circle of grass inside a ring of great old stones, some sunk into the earth and some fallen. It was an ancient place of worship erected there by a tribe now departed. The unknown warrior waited for him inside the circle, seated upon a stone. Was he the assassin his life-taker had forecast?

A little later he climbed a rounded hump of grassed earth, seeing the tops of the stones come into sight against the night sky. His adversary sat as he had imagined him, observing him entering the ring. Then he too sat on a stone and waited for his enemy to speak.

-All this I have dreamed! called the man across the circle. It was in an accent the Warrior remembered from his travels, -You see Shaman, I too can picture much that is to happen and prepare myself accordingly. Yet of this battle I know no outcome. Sometimes the future is not entrusted to us, eh?

-It seems not, said the Warrior. His long brown robe ruffled in the breeze. His opponent wore a dark red leather jerkin and heavy black cotton trousers. His boots were supple and well greased. But it was his face which was distinctive. It carried the Warrior's mind to the Spice Merchants he had met and saved from a band of murderers and rapists. The fellow shared the same half moon eyes and high-boned cheeks. Beyond these features, the man wore long, hanging moustaches that drooped to below his chin.

-Now you have so carefully observed me, what do you see?

-A man from the east. I have met people from your lands. I would notion that you travelled this way as a warrior guard to a spice caravan, a man whose sword is his reward, a man who seeks riches and fame. And, in truth, a man who is jealous of the reputation of another warrior and so creates a theatre of death to draw him to combat.

-Very fine! Very clever! Such is to be expected of a shaman. You are all I hoped for when I heard tales of you. I have killed many fighting men. Warriors I have always battled, face to face. It is our way is it not? Warrior before warrior? Of others I care not, they die facing me or running, asleep or awake. With each true warrior's death my spirit burns brighter. Yours will add such fuel to the flames that I will hardly be able to contain the blaze.

-Let us talk first, said the Warrior in his wind-stirred brown robe.

-We have talked enough, his opponent said in a hiss between his teeth, -The light is nearly lost.

-Not yet. There is much I must know before you fall before my sword. The Warrior issued the words quietly.

-Hah! It shall not be so. I see what you intend. What you say cannot undermine me. He got up and strode in small circles, his hand on his sword and his chest puffed out, his feet stamping purposefully.

-Do you remember the first man you killed? asked the Warrior, unaffected.

The mercenary stopped turning, -Of course. Hah! I knifed him. With the reward I bought a sword.

-The second?

-Hah! The reward was greater. As for the third and fourth, soon I had a sword made for me. This one, he tapped its handle, -With it I have travelled from east to west and countless have fallen to its immortal blade.

-Do you remember every death?

-No. Of course not, it has been a river of constant blood. What warrior does? There was silence from his audience, -You do, eh? Then you must have killed fewer than I supposed.

-I remember every one. And in each I sensed the reluctant leaving of their bodies, their spirits led by their life-takers.

The eastern swordsman sat down again, -Life-taker? What is this? A ghost? A god?

-Death is the destination for us all but people who live in these territories believe that we do not have to travel alone in that last journey. When a man dies at my sword I feel the ebbing of his spirit as though it is being gathered up and carried away.

-It is not so for me. Just another pair of dulled eyes. I feel nothing. It is not this warrior's way.

-Then you are no warrior! retorted the Warrior harshly. Their eyes gripped each other, -A true warrior feels all. He is not an animal who knows nothing else. Each time he takes a life, its death must be respected. Each spirit must be hurried on its way with a prayer. In this way the warrior gains knowledge. His own spirit is purified and sharpened just like his blade. His reputation spreads among the people. A reverence grows. In time few oppose him and a wise word from him is enough to settle dispute and conflict. Only the ignorant and the vain will now oppose him. He attends more to thought than to action. He seeks to attain wisdom and this wisdom is attuned to his sense of purpose. Why is he a warrior? Why is he set apart from others? What must he accomplish in his life? How can he make right choices? How well can he follow the Right Path?

-You think me empty and vain? You have ceased to be a warrior if you choose not to kill!

The Warrior looked at the man, calmly, -If there is no other way, I take life.

-I am not such a man as you! I gain no such solace from the dying. I feel no guilt. I kill because it pleases me. With each death I am raised higher in the eyes of men. I take pleasure in the fear I stir in people when I stride past them. I take what I will when I wish it. I have no spirit that endures beyond the death of my body. I may return again, it is true, as some base creature. This my mother taught me. Be kind and generous and you may return as a nobleman or even a king. Be not so and you will return as a creature whose belly never leaves the soil, to be trodden underfoot. Hah! My mother was squashed under the heel of her master all her life until he succumbed to my knife and I received my first reward from a man he had also dishonoured. Now my mother is freed from that yoke. He glared at the brown robed figure opposite him, -We are similar men, Shaman, though stoked by different fires. We both are wed to killing. You picture it in fancier garb that is all. He sat, his legs apart, defiant.

-Thank you.

-You thank me? For what?

-It is better to know who it is you must kill. It is better to know that your victim suffers no remorse.

-I have already said that your words have not the effect upon me you intend. I can see your plan. But I am a man of ice. Look, no nerves! No fear. Nothing. He held his sword out straight before him. It did not waver, -And now it is time! He stood and took his throwing knife. With a snap of the wrist he buried it in the ground between them, -I will come to my knife. Release yours.

The Warrior's blade stabbed the ground, a stride from the other. They caught and reflected a little light from the night sky.

-When our boots touch our stuck blades then our swords can speak for us. The two combatants walked slowly towards each other in the dimness, with unmoving gaze. Each sought perfect balance. Each carried his sword point down. They stopped short of their knives and each slid a foot slowly forward. As they touched, their swords swung left and then right, cutting and then thrusting, each chasing the silhouetted wraith before him, swords clashing and ringing. Their bodies ducked, leapt and danced backwards and forwards. It seemed as though the warrior from the east had greater strength for he pursued his opponent with a storm of blows yet he could not pierce his guard and find flesh. Slowly, a look of desperation began to form on his face as the brown-robed swordsman floated ever beyond his blade, staying its edge with his own. Time passed and they fought on. The eastern fighter had a growing realisation that his strength was diminishing as quickly now as the sweat gathered and blurred his blinking eyes. His feet lost their light tread and his breath came in ever shorter gasps.

The Warrior continued to move as he had begun, his face expressionless, his breathing calm, his soles making no sound on the beaten earth.

The last thoughts of the man from the east were of the measured, fluid dance of his robed opponent, of the man's hooked nose and pale eyes and his calm, untroubled features. His ears did not hear the crack as his sword splintered into pieces. His blurred eyes did not see the blade before it entered him. He felt its burning entry and then the numbness that followed as his death reached out for him.

-Shaman! he muttered. And fell.

The Warrior knelt beside him and gave a short prayer that his god would receive his spirit, before pulling his sword clear. He was startled by the sound of a knife thudding into the ground, mid way between the other two. He looked up. His mother stood, barely visible, her back to a standing stone.

-If he had…, her words were choked though her face showed no emotion. She turned and called the horses.

They lay under the stars. The fire was now a collection of dying embers. They were covered by fleecy hides. The horses were grouped a little way off, all standing and facing in the same direction, as though receiving a lesson from a teacher.

-It is good sometimes not to have meat, she said.

-It is cleansing. Yet I am a hunter. It is in my being. I take pleasure in eating what I capture.

-When I was pursued, I had little fresh meat. Herdsman gave me gifts of dried fowl. I ate grain and nuts and roots. Sometimes the wind lifted me from my saddle, I was so thin.

-You are strong now.

-As I have ever been, my Son. As are you. I am blessed to have given my blood to such a man. I was fearful when you fought. I crept close. It was the fear of a mother for her son. It seemed for a while too close.

-He was as skilled as any I have met but he had not the wisdom to defeat me. He knew the ways of battle but not the ways of the mind in battle. He could see only me, my body and my sword. I saw his life. Thus I knew his pattern of attack and defence. I saw them form in his mind and was always ready. Then, as he tired and came to know that I had not ventured a blade in attack, fear took his heart. It was at that moment I struck.

-You could have spared him?

-It would have ended the same. He could not have borne his defeat. He would have taken his own life without thought. This was nobler for him for he was a man who would never change. He killed for pleasure only. He did not deserve a place among us.

-It is well, then?

-If death can be so regarded. Yet among all whose lives I have taken, his was singular.

-How?

-He did not reach out his failing mind in the hope that a life-taker would come for him.

She said, reflectively, -For some, death is the very end. There can be no return inside the hide of another living thing.

It struck them both once more that there was a similar thread in the Tale to one in their lives, -The Tale heartens me Kamil, for is not the foe of the Magus like the Red Man? Is he not cold and evil and gaining strength and fulfilment from overcoming those standing against him? It is as if, in his own eyes, each death imparts a lustre to his reputation as a warrior. But he was no match for our Shaman!

-It is true, murmured Kamil, -And this is because, despite his power, the Magus is beginning to act according to a moral code which, if you recall, he names the Right Path. This guides him more and more from now on. He is the Emperor but his empire is men and women and what they must do to be noble and virtuous in their lives. Generations have learned from this. It is a lesson for us. We can defeat the Red Man because our cause leads to the greater good. We seek to save the empire from the chaos he will bring. Family will turn on family, man upon woman and child and all we have will disintegrate into evil until such time as another conquering king or general brings it all together again. We must keep close counsel and follow reason and instinct in our war against him.

-Well said, my general! These are optimistic thoughts. Thank Baligha for me for I have not forgotten her role in our knowledge. In fact, bring her to this room tomorrow evening before our reading. I would question her a little more, in case she has some hidden understandings, unbeknown to herself, for you are too much the lovelorn boy to draw it from her. Bringing her here will afford you a little time in the love nest, too! She took her leave, acting coy.

Chapter Six

Fear imprisons understanding

If yesterday had been a hangover from the previous evening's banquet, today seemed more like a celebration of a great victory. The court was noisy and light-spirited. Although some work was being done, servants and courtiers took every opportunity to gossip and tell stories. It was no surprise though to Kamil that there was no discussion of the banquet itself. It was as if no-one had been to it! The Red Man's strictures, delivered like an order in his foreign lilt, had mesmerised all who listened into erasing from their minds those turbulent and uncontrolled hours.

The gaiety was too much for Kamil, even down in the library and he left early to spend a few more hours with his beloved Baligha.

After they had taken time in bed for themselves they lay on the white cotton sheet, their limbs wrapped around each other. It was the union of two needy souls too long denied such tenderness. Each prayed that this blissful time would continue for the rest of their lives. Only then would it make up for Baligha's years of wandering and pain and Kamil's barren years of solitary toil.

-I have no anxiety over coming to the court and meeting with the Princess, she said softly, -She has kept her word to us and protected us. I cannot complain.

Kamil moaned, -I only fear that she will find a way of involving you as she did last time. I cannot have you put in danger again.

-She is hardly going to pit me against the Red Man! she giggled, -I am no David although I hear he makes a passable Goliath.

-Do not jest.

-Now now my cherub, calm yourself. I would like you to tell me everything that you have said between you, so that at least I will know where in your story I fit. Something in what you say might make me think. Who knows?

He lay back on the crook of her arm and ordered his thoughts. When he was composed he recounted what he knew in time order, crisply and without the frills of emotion. When he was done she kissed him, -Go and play with the little ones while I make myself ready.

*

Kamil felt proud as they waited by the table in his ante-room. Baligha gave his life completion. She was dressed in an oatmeal linen robe edged with cream embroidery. She had chosen it so that the Princess would outshine her for she knew of the young woman's fits of jealousy in such matters. Her hair was enclosed in a fine silk net revealing the grey hair that Kamil so adored. Her tribal shoes were soft, natural leather and turned up at the toe. She sat beside her husband holding his hand but ready to let it go as soon as there was noise on the other side of the door. Once more she glanced at him and was content. He had become rounded in personality as well as girth. He was a testament to her cooking and her daily care. She cut his nails, shaved him, washed his hair and oiled his body. It was not that he could not do these things but she could do it so much better and they both enjoyed the intimacy.

There was a sound outside and they stood, waiting. As the Princess strode in Kamil dropped to the floor on all fours and Baligha lowered herself to one knee. Princess Sabiya flicked her hand and the guard closed the door.

-Come now. Sit, both of you. I told you Kamil I will have us meet without the airs and graces of the court to slow us down. Baligha, you are a beautiful woman. And you turn out your husband as well as the chief groom his emperor's horse; well upholstered, clear eyed and ready for the parade! The women's eyes sparkled, enjoying the flattery and the jest. Baligha warmed to her. She recognised some of her own headstrong youth in her. Kamil meanwhile looked confused and abashed. Women sometimes talked about him as though he was a child whose head only reached their navels.

-You are very kind, your Highness, Baligha said, -It is thanks to your care for us that I can provide a wife's service to my husband.

-Good. Sit please. Finally they did so. She spread herself in the chair and watched them under her eyelids. Baligha had been right to dress soberly. The Princess glittered in a silver gown. There were gold bands around her ankles and wrists and her neck was roped with gold chains. Her hair was covered in circlets of tiny silver butterflies. There was no doubt as to who was the Princess and who was the historian's wife.

Baligha emphasised it, -Your Highness, if I may say so, looks divine. It is a boon to an empire when the Princess attracts every gaze and fulfils the needs of her people for a royal goddess.

Princess Sabiya relaxed and smiled happily, -I rarely listen to compliments. As soon as a courtier embarks upon one I hear all the words that are to follow and have heard them a hundred times. But you, Baligha, have a gift for praise.

-I am sincere your Highness.

-And I take it as such. Her face became more serious and she patted the arm of the chair, -Let us begin our conversation and then a servant will escort you back to your children where, despite all, I am sure you prefer to be. And then your husband can continue reading me his masterpiece. She looked at them both and then addressed Baligha, -How did you hear that the Red Man was … is … a twin?

-I heard it many times. It was a well-travelled tale along the banks of our river. Much of his early life was spent in the far north. Perhaps stories about him did not filter down to the south here.

-And nothing was spoken about the girl, his sister?

-Not much. She was given away by her mother when she found her son's little fingers squeezing the life out of her. It is said that she had to strike the baby boy with a broom handle to make him let go. She told no one which family took the child from her. They were passing river merchants and wanted a baby but had been unsuccessful. My guess would be that they were not poor. The Red Man's mother may have received some wealth for the act.

-Do you believe the tale?

-I do. It is not too exaggerated as many tales become. Its bare bones are appealing. It strikes me that she must have known the foster parents otherwise she could not have trusted them with her child. By all accounts she was a good mother. Even discovering that her son had evil blood in his veins did not stop her from offering him constant love. When he left her it must have been as much in sadness as in relief.

-The mother is dead now?

-I believe it must be so.

-And this is all we know about those early days?

-It is but it raises an interesting question.

-Which is? Kamil and the Princess glanced at each other. Both caught the unmistakeable significant note in Baligha's voice.

-It is this. We are looking for the twin sister of the Red Man. She emphasised the word 'twin'. She sat back with a teasing smile on her lips.

-Princess Sabiya gave a groan, -Ah Kamil we have been upstaged by your clever wife! I will have my river spies put out a description. We are looking for a redheaded woman aged about forty, do you think?

-I would think so, replied Kamil, eyeing his wife admiringly.

-There is one other thing, went on Baligha, relishing being the centre of their attention, though looking convincingly demure, -It is this. As Kamil tells it, both of you experienced a sudden withdrawal of the Red Man's intrusion into your thoughts.

-It is true.

-In the early part of the morning? Could it have been at exactly the same moment?

-I know not. I never check where we are according to the palace obelisk. That is for servants to deduce. It was light and the court was about its business. Perhaps we were three hours after sunrise.

Kamil?

-I think that it must have been at that hour.

-Kamil was immersed in his books, pondered Baligha, -And you Princess?

- I cannot recall doing anything. I woke with my mind convinced that I should send Kamil from the court and then, in a moment, I was clear to think again. So what do you make of it all Baligha?

-It seems we have some small steps towards staying the power of the Red Man. Or, at least, Kamil does. The first is to fill the mind with such substance that draws your focus. This acts as a curtain to stop his contagion entering. The second is to invoke his twin sister's presence. My simple suggestion is that when you feel his intrusion you adopt the former. My intuition tells me that invoking his sister should be withheld until events allow no other course of action. At the moment we do not know if the invocation will always ward him off or one day send him into a mindless rage.

*

401

Baligha had left with the Princess's understated compliment echoing in her ears and the possibility that she would be called to further meetings to discuss the campaign. The women had found that they respected each other more. The historian's wife felt that this was an important step forward and that she was not living in the palace grounds merely as a beneficiary of Kamil's past triumph on the Princess's behalf. It awakened in her the sense of destiny which, she had to confess to herself, she had been happy to relinquish in exchange for the peace of marriage and motherhood. It was surprisingly good to feel close to the centre of events again.

Meanwhile Kamil watched as Princess Sabiya turned over the waiting card, The Hierophant.

-More religion! she exclaimed with irony, -We need fighting cards to aid us not those that drive us into contemplation and inactivity? Kamil held his peace and began reading.

It was suddenly there, the change from the rock and grass plateau to a few strewn boulders, rolling woodland and the blue ribbon of mountains on the northern horizon.

-Ah, something to aim for, she grunted, looking into the distance. They had been travelling north for some days.

-We will not need to venture to the peaks, he replied, -But traverse the foothills only. Our way is to the east.

-Tell me what you know of the General's palace. She eased back in the saddle, slowing her roan to a gentle walk. The four beasts were happy to pick their own way around the occasional rock and between trees. It was cool and a recent local rain had left puddles on the clay soil. The clouds responsible for it had blown away to the south.

-From what I hear he stays in a tower much like the one in which I first found him. It is naturally fortified for it stands on a crag overlooking a river. It cannot be reached from the rear, except by foolhardy climbers as it is set into a cliff. Only a single path leads to it with rock face on one side and a deep chasm on the other. One cart at a time can pass. There are several bridges, all guarded and each can be dropped so that there is no way forward - or back. It may be his base but as I said, as often as not he is travelling his empire.

-It is enough of a picture. I like to have a vision of where my road may lead even though it takes forever.

-You are growing tired of this journey, Mother? he asked solicitously, though he knew her answer.

She hurried to quieten him, -No, no! I have told you, I am happy because I am with you but it seems a lifetime ago that we had our last adventure. I would like fate to throw us a crumb or two if only to pass our time with a diversion. Not that I wish for you to fight for your life again. Perhaps a puzzle such as was presented by the scientific merchant.

-Mm. You still have him in your thoughts, he cajoled. She ignored him, craning her neck and blinking her eyes and looking up into the hills.

-Am I mistaken or is that a settlement where we might stay the night?

-You are desperate for human company other than me? He grinned broadly and followed her line of sight, -It is away from our trail but there will be shelter if they are disposed to strangers.

-It is their duty. You can cook them the pieces of carcass you have on the black. He'll be glad to be rid of it. Raw flesh clogs the nose of a live animal even when bagged.

They arrived at the flattened circle of earth in the centre of an encampment of sod and timber dwellings as half the sun remained in sight, just as she had predicted. The villagers eyed them suspiciously and for a while no-one spoke, despite their hand on heart greetings. It was a small settlement for herders. They could see the pens for wintering the sheep and goats. A few old men were about and there were women and children at each hut. Evening bread was being baked and thick stew-pots had being placed in the ashes of a communal fire, away from the main blaze.

They dismounted and his mother attracted a few women to her. It seemed that they were less imposing to them on the ground. Their faces seemed cut from the same stock. They had large, bent noses, almost without chins. The dialect was similar to their own but had a singsong quality which demanded careful listening. His mother told them that they bore the gift of meat and her son would cook it for all. It was novel to them. He set to with his knives, offering the organs to the women who promptly chopped and dropped them in the various pots. Soon cuts of meat were on spits and being turned over the fire.

Until now conversation had been limited. The women and the old men appeared to have heard nothing of the Warrior and his exploits which delighted him. In fact they were much more interested in his mother. A woman who fights was beyond their experience. Not only was she a warrior mother but wasn't she too old to be travelling like this? She should be looking after grandchildren while the men were at work and their mothers were preparing food and growing vegetables. Why had she so little fat on her? All the women in the village were plump despite being hard working. They were like their beasts, fattening themselves up for the winter which, they inferred, could be profoundly cold. The Warrior stayed silent as they plied her with more questions.

-Why does he work while you stand by like a queen? You are his mother! Where is your land? Do all women bear arms there? Do your men stay with the children? Have you killed a man? Show us your marksmanship.

She entertained them with an exhibition of knife throwing and archery and tried to give them some understanding of life in her own village.

-You are a man-woman, exclaimed the clan chief, -This is not natural!

-Many people in my own valleys think as you do, she replied, -But they dare not say so to my face or they must say it also to my blade's point. She pulled it out for emphasis and swung it about. They backed away in mock fear.

As they feasted, the villagers turned their attention to the Warrior. They were intrigued by the meat. What was the beast that they were eating? What plants had he glued to its skin with honey? Had he brought the carcass from far away? They were incredulous that it was a local creature. None could picture it and they demanded detailed descriptions. Now they knew it but had only glimpsed it at night and, since it was shy, only very rarely. It made its hole under the earth and grubbed its food there.

-You are a giant, said another, -You are paid for your arms?

-I am not for hire.

-Where will your path take you? asked another.

-We go to see the General.

They were silent at this news and then one grandmother spat on the fire. She said disapprovingly, -His men come here every year and take the tithe. Too many goats and sheep are stolen from us. It makes the winters hard.

His mother asked whether they also took young men.

-What for?, was the reply, -To eat?

-No, she laughed, -To add to their army.

It was the woman's turn to guffaw, -It would greatly weaken their army to filch our men. They can trap and fish but not with great cunning. They are herders. We have always been this way. There are

405

few of us and if any left we would suffer. We live and die here in the embrace of our ancestors. She pointed across the circle of beaten soil to where a hut stood, different from all the others. It was constructed of logs, sloping to a central point where a clay chimney was perched.

The Warrior could tell that it was a burial chamber. His nose had picked up the smell of bones and the scent of the same perfumes used by the priestess in the long building that they had had to burn, -You keep your dead there? he asked.

-We take the head bones there, she replied, proudly, -After we have boiled them and a sweet spirit added. This we drink so that our forefathers enter us and become one with our flesh. The heads become clean to the bone and we paint them to keep flies and crawling things from them. They are filled with earth and we grow a medicine in them. The plant is sacred to the tribe and we dry it and the men take it with them into the mountains to eat and to protect them. Every night a woman in the village rests with the ancestors to give them the company of the living. There is someone there now for the sun has fallen. Would you visit with them? They would be honoured.

His mother declined instantly. Bodies should be buried or burned. Even the desire to be left for the birds to pick over, dismayed her. But her son was curious. There had been no mention of a god. He followed the speaker to the hut. A flap of hardened leather covered the doorway. He entered. A fire burned at the room's centre. Aromatic twigs threw out a strong scent and the incense was intensified by drying flowers hanging in bunches. The Watcher, as the night companion was called, sat on a sheepskin cushion, in a reverie. She appeared not to know that he was there. She did not lift her face to acknowledge him. The flap was closed behind him, leaving him with her and racks of skulls. From each grew white stalks surmounted by flat hats. He used these plants himself to flavour soups. They appeared magically in the woods and meadows of early morning. He sat cross-legged beside the fire and emptied his mind as well as he could. Nothing came to him. No images. No history. It was as if he had become a no-thing.

-What wish you here? The voice seemed both outside his head and inside it. He lifted his lids and stared into the flickering shadows at the rows of heads.

-To know the meaning of death, he responded calmly and quietly.

The Watcher's lips moved though her eyes remained closed, -You

406

are the Magus?

-It is new and not my choice of name.

-It will be used by all. She was silent for a long time before her mouth shaped words again, -We are dead but live on in our children. They bind to us each night and their spirits feed us. Thus we stay attached to the land of our forefathers. Our memories of the hills, of our flocks, of our families, stay with us.

The Warrior asked, -Is there ought beyond this being-in-skulls?

Again there was a long silence. The lips moved again and the voice seemed to come from elsewhere, -We do not know. If a Watcher is not with us each night then there is only darkness and no memories. If there were to be many such nights then we would become sundered from the present world. Where we might then be is not given to us to comprehend.

It was as the Warrior supposed. It seemed the clan here had a rich ritual but little else. The log tomb was a solace for the living and not the dead as they seemed to think. Like all others who devoted themselves to mystical practices it gave them hope for something beyond life. He touched his heart, -Thank you for your words.

-We are honoured that you came to us, Magus, the lips said, -And we have a warning for you. There was a pause. The Watcher's voice seemed to drop to a lower key, -Prepare yourself for the child, the sleeping man, the mistaken sword and the fire of a god, for they will gather together to take from you much that you love.

He left the burial place perplexed. When he reached his mother, seated in a ring of silent women, he sat himself beside her.

-What happened to you? she asked, -The fire is just a few embers. I thought to come for you but was told that the visit to their ancestors always took much of a night.

It gave him a slight spasm to find that she was right. Time had passed and yet it felt to him that he had been among the dead for only a short time, -It seemed to me but a handful of moments, he said levelly, -I do not understand it. He told his mother what had happened but not wishing to cause offence to the circle of listeners he did so without the embroidery of his thoughts and feelings.

-You are favoured, said a woman who had listened intently to his account, -It is not often that our forebears speak through a Watcher. It is the first time in my lifetime. They must have been gratified deeply by your visit.

-You must beware for what they say must come to pass, added another gravely.

☥

While her son was in the house of the skulls his mother had talked with some of the female elders. They told her the history of their small clan and how it became established. At one time they were part of a nomadic tribe that herded goats along the unending mountain ridges which ran from west to east and marked the furthest extremes of the empire now controlled by the General. The tribe would take years to wander this land of upland grazing with its ferocious winters and short, bountiful summers. All the while they had carried with them the skulls of their male forefathers, each family protecting its own. Upon their bone temples were inscribed maps of the territory which helped fathers tell sons of secret routes, passes, perils and the hidden delights of well stocked pastures. Then there was a winter that lasted too long. Many died. Disease struck. One tribal member, a young man, broke away and managed to reach the valley where the settlement now stood. At that time it was just a snow covered upland meadow. A farmer's daughter, bringing wood down to below the snow line, found him near dead and tended to him. She gave him milk and the white caps of plants she dried in the autumn and carried with her on winter treks. They descended to her village. They became conjoined. The following year they returned to the place where they had met and built the first hut of the settlement. Two more pairs joined them. A new clan was formed in which the women grew vegetables and wheat and the men herded during the spring and summer, returning to their womenfolk for the winter. The first woman of the settlement was strong and took from her husband some of his clan's ritual ways of caring for the dead. Men were buried upright and intact in ground next to the path from the village up the mountain. The graves were marked with small mounds of rocks. The women's bodies were buried lying, below the village but their heads were removed just as the Warrior's mother had been told.

These were kept in a house of the dead. There were no maps inscribed on their bones at that time as the herders stayed on their own mountain and it had become familiar to them. It was a new life for the clan. They had grown roots when previously they had wandered for lifetimes. It was the first ancestor too who envisioned that each skull should be a nursery for the sacred plant for it had saved the life of her husband.

-You have a god? asked the mother.

-The General's men exhort us to submit to the bird of fire but when they are gone we put away the images. We pray to our ancestors when we are Watchers and we drink of their minds. The sacred plant returns to us before each winter and it is harvested. This cycle keeps us safe.

The following morning early, as grey light spread from behind the mountains, making them loom, the four horses and their two riders continued their progress along the trail. His mother was pacified by an evening in the company of womenfolk. Her son had mixed feelings. It seemed that the house of the ancestors was part of yet another curious tribal religion with its idiosyncratic clan customs and observances. It fitted well with the limited lives of the peasants, constructed by them over generations to bring them comfort and meaning. There was little new in it that he wished to puzzle over.

The only aspect of it that did cause him to think was the oracle from the half-sleeping Watcher's lips. It was strangely affecting. Though he tried, he could not dismiss it for he sensed the palpable pull of future events in her cryptic words.

-Does your shaman's wisdom suggest to you that oracles can foretell what is to come? she asked.

He patted her lightly on the back as they cantered, -If you asked this of my father-not-of-blood, he would laugh and cry, "of course not!" He sees how every ruse comes about. We stayed with a circus on our way to his home where his mother was languishing and a quick witted pair of lovers taught us tricks even he didn't know. They could astonish audiences with their knowledge of some of them, though they had never before met. They also dressed as magicians do and sat within a tent and foretold the futures of their victims by reading the lines on their palms. They said that often people came back to them swearing that their foretellings had come about in all exactitude. People will believe anything if the magician impresses them enough with his gravity and staring eyes. He will tell them many things, most of which can be interpreted in a hundred different ways. His audience only remembers what actually comes to pass. The rest is forgotten. Our two young friends said that people who go to them want to believe what they are going to tell them and this makes their task easy.

-But this message was neither long nor complicated in this way. Did not the Watcher mention four things of which you should be aware; a young girl, a sleeping man, a fallen sword and a god of fire? These are plain words are they not? she frowned at him.

The Warrior pulled at his black beard, -Not so simple, dear Mother. Already your mind has played with the Watcher's words.

She was mystified, -How so?

-She said child not girl. She said the fire of a god, not the god of fire. She said a mistaken sword not a fallen sword. Only in the case of the sleeping man are you in agreement.

She was piqued, -Are they such different messages? Child, man, sword and fire.

-There is enough play in the words for much error. At some point on our journey we are bound to encounter all of these. Then we might look back and think we have remembered the Watcher's words. But were these the words used and was it the message intended? We can never really tell for our memories are notoriously playful.

-I begin to see. She thought for a long time and then announced, -It cuts two ways. If the four elements are dispersed throughout our travels it could be as you say, that we may be deluded. But if all four elements fall together in one brief snatch of time then there may be more truth to it.

He nodded, -I had come to that reasoning, too. We will remain vigilant. I must not let my lack of belief blind me to possibility. When we come across any of the four we will keep our eyes open for the others to see if they be nearby. You are too precious a gift for me to lose you as I have missed my entire childhood with you. I will take no chances in losing one whom I love so much.

-Me! She laughed but there was a mother's joy in it, -I can protect myself full well or do you think not?

-I would be too afraid to say otherwise! he laughed.

She slapped his shoulder, -You can be the child yourself, my son. I will soon prove it.

-You do not need to. There is no man I would have in your place in battle. This mollified her. Yet, while he said this, the Warrior's thoughts were musing on the Watcher's four elements and trying to cast his mind forward to discover a moment when all four would be in harness.

They pondered on the Tale. Each found a particular emphasis that seemed the more significant. For Kamil it was the proposition that the Warrior, even as he dismissed the death rituals of the clan, did not disregard the oracle that issued from the mouth of the Watcher. It was an indication of the shaman's openness. Kamil found that he was reading the book as though someone else had written it. On occasion it was as if he was reading it for the first time. He complimented himself silently on his skilful writing. The Magus was reaching out to the ineffable in human affairs and such reflection was an inevitable part of his search for spiritual meaning beyond this physical life.

Meanwhile Princess Sabiya was engrossed in the business of soothsaying and its effects on credulous audiences. Emperors invested fortunes in the prophesies of oracles. In her father's case the royal High Priestess had long guided his decisions in battle and in governing the empire, interpreting the mysterious moans and groans that rose from the depths of the Crying Caves beneath the palace. Only a high priestess could fashion messages from those sounds. That is, until the arrival of the Red Man and his many prognostications on the future. In contrast to the words of the High Priestess, which had always seemed cryptic and ambiguous, clothed in riddles, the Red Man's were direct and required no deep study. When Kamil and the Princess had discussed what each had gained from the Tale, they realised they had just been taught the same powerful lesson that the Warrior had given his mother.

-It has given me an idea! exclaimed the Princess excitedly but she wouldn't elaborate further for she had grown to like undressing a mystery for Kamil's benefit, just as he did when his researches threw up new illumination. It was particularly satisfying if the mysterious events she would later recount had been the result of her own instinct for what might further their cause and had not been the result of his counselling.

-We are desperate to know the future, she stated imperiously, -Even when there is little likelihood that soothsaying carries the truth to us. Human beings are gullible creatures. Their lives are usually dreary affairs at the beck and call of their lords and masters. They have little choice in what happens to them - unless they are of noble birth. They take their bribes to the oracle in the hope that it will prophesy that their future will be better. Slaves hope to be free. Peasants wish to be landowners. Servants wish to be courtiers. Siblings desire to leapfrog their sisters and brothers and become heirs to the throne. Kamil, I am surprised that the Magus is affected by the Watcher's words. He sees through everything. Why does he muse on this warning to him?

-I think it is because, if such a prophecy came to pass, then the Magus would have evidence that fate truly does affect life. If there is fate, then a God must exist to have designed every life in its fixed round. Kamil studied her face, -The Warrior leaves all portals open. He may be cynical about the religions he has encountered on his travels but it does not make him deaf or blind. If there is some plan that defines existence then he is driven to uncover it. He suspects that existence has no meaning beyond itself but will not allow this suspicion to interfere with his search for truth.

The Princess played with a wisp of hair. Her eyes shone brightly against the glossy black skin of her cheeks and temples, -Well, I look forward to discovering how the Magus faces the challenge of this mystery. It is one that vexes the philosophers among us even today. Is there a fate or are we free to do as we will? As I have said, the higher you are in the empire, the more freedom you have to decide your path. It is the privilege of power.

-Unless even that is an illusion. Emperors are often the prisoners of their thrones and all their acts can be seen to be fixed by the imperatives of high office rather than by untainted choice. Kamil spoke in the dry tones of the historian.

-It is a nice conundrum, replied the thoughtful young woman, -If there is a god then what freedom do we have since he has placed us in the meshes of fate? If there is no god then we have complete freedom to be what we will. But, because all around us people are fearful of such freedom, they prefer to believe in a deity, not aware that the security they desire from believing in such omniscience shackles them and starves their imaginations. She stuck out her chin provocatively and gave him a glinting smile. He nodded appreciatively. The Princess was well schooled in metaphysical argument and he would have liked to have proceeded in debate with her. But he knew she was about to leave and such discourse was in her gift, not his.

Their meeting ended with different images held in their thoughts. Her mind was following a route through the machinations of the court via underground passageways. His was exploring how to practise and

413

develop further a barrier against the incursion of the Red Man's probing.

Chapter Seven

Love's boundaries are in the mind not the heart

Kamil began his day in the Great Library. He arrived while it was still dark and gathered texts, making small piles on a square of black linen, trying to create clusters of like information. He was attempting to gain some grasp of the process of hypnosis and as usual found the domain full of overlapping tracts, none of which seemed in any way a complete authority. The miscellany covered such topics as how to subdue, subjugate or influence domestic animals, birds and fish. There were further pieces on gaining control over wild creatures and there were a number of idiosyncratic attempts to explain how to use the power of the hands to gain mastery over people. These ranged from healing the sick, expelling evil spirits and enforcing sleep states, wherein dreams could be precipitated for interpretation. There were no actual instructions in the writings despite each authority extolling the virtue of using a particular approach. He found several treatises on the use of plants and other sources in the pacification of violent dispositions, on extracting truth from stubborn prisoners and inducing coma-like states. By far the biggest volume of thought was on love potions.

By the time he was done he had only two worthwhile manuals in his main areas of enquiry. The first of these was a comprehensive guide to all those drugs which, when ingested, led the victim to a state of euphoria coupled with forgetfulness. The second involved the inculcation of hypnotic trances without the use of touch.

*

Kamil set off for his lunch in the refectory. He was seated at the same table as on his first visit. He could not detect the Red Man's presence in his thoughts and was soon eating ravenously, having missed his morning's meal. As he ate he cast his eyes around for the young man from the kitchens. In fact it was the assistant cook who found him, seating himself beside him and digging an elbow into his ribs in over-familiar fashion. Kamil decided it was expedient to ignore it but moved slightly away from the sweating bulk. He eyed the youth's pile of food, -You have a healthy appetite my boy, he said in admiration. The use of the term 'boy' alerted the cook to his earlier indiscretion. He dropped his gaze.

-Yes, Master, he concurred, -It is a strain on the body working in the kitchens all day. The ovens are likely to boil my blood. He swallowed water noisily from a pitcher.

-Is everyone recovered from the banquet?

-More or less.

-And has the Red Man left you in peace since then?

-He has. In fact it is said that he has gone hunting with the Emperor into the hills for wild deer. It will take a day's travel, a day for the hunt and a day to return. Everyone is calm again.

-Deer eh? A fine adventure I am sure. He drew closer to the fat young fellow, -Tell me, you said when we last met that the Red Man supervised the cleaning of all the pots and pans after the banquet.

-True enough. The young fellow's eyes peered up at Kamil from under their flour-flecked brows.

-Was anything left? Herbs? Spices?

-Not that I know of but I have not looked or asked. Why should I? I am the youngest cook. I will have my hands cut off for touching what is not mine. They would take an eye from me if I snooped, I am sure. He forced a prodigious handful of meat and couscous down his throat.

-Well, I am sure you can observe without appearing to be looking for something. Kamil patted his lumpen arm and eyed him appreciatively, -You seem a clever enough character.

-That is not what the head cook calls me, Master.

Kamil pressed home his interest, -Listen, my son, I have a job for you. Take this silver. He dropped the coin beside the cook's plate, -If you can discover for me the name of any ingredient that your head cook had not previously encountered, be it plant or meat, then I will double your money. If you can find a tiny sample of it then I will quadruple your reward. I will return tomorrow at this time. Kamil stood abruptly, -Tell no-one, on your life! The young cook stared at his food and gulped down another mouthful while covering the piece of silver with his free hand.

Later, Kamil could be found back in his beloved library making notes from the two sources that he had deemed useful for his further investigations. The parchment that listed the use of drugs in inducing transfixation was clearly structured. Kamil admired the taxonomy. It was titled 'Poisons both efficacious and malicious' and was divided onto three sections pertaining to plants, animals and minerals. Each section was graded according to the degree to which the drugs affected the senses, from slight euphoria to coma and finally to death. There were drugs to induce fevers of varying intensity, blindness, sleepwalking, vivid dreams of portent, bestial excess, skin eruptions, hysteria, amnesia, truthfulness, stupor, unrelieved coma and death - both peaceful and natural, as well as painful and drawn out. In fact he found more than he would have wished. But by eliminating all those that seemed irrelevant to the mass hypnosis at the banquet, Kamil was left with a small number of potential suspects. From the plant section there was a red capped toadstool and the leaves of a rare cactus and a strain of flower related to the opium poppy. The animal world provided a secretion from a spiny fish, a marsh toad and crushed larvae from the colony of a species of ant. Among the extractions of minerals by grinding, leaching, heating or chemically transforming, he found a small number of likely substances which in wine or water could produce effective potions.

It was a short enough list in the end and Kamil hoped that some clue, discovered by the fat young cook, would point to the medicine that the Red Man had concocted for the wild night in the palace. The efficaciousness of hypnosis by the imposition of thought on a willing or unwilling subject was another matter. It involved careful preparation and determined practice.

*

There was an air of mutually suppressed excitement in the room as they sat down opposite each other. Kamil was dressed in a loose white robe and capacious trousers. Princess Sabiya had her hair coiled on the top of her head and held there with ornamental silver daggers. Her pale blue damask robes contained lines of fine silver thread which caught the lamplight fetchingly.

-I have much to tell, she said, coyly smiling.

-I have a little too, he replied, -A small advance on our knowledge.

417

-Then let us remain silent until the Tale is told. It will add a formidable tension to our narrative.

Kamil raised his eyebrows, thought for a moment and then nodded, - You are right, if we tell all first then we will obscure the story with our jostling thoughts. If we save our information until afterwards then something of the Tale may be absorbed.

She preened, -I shall try to concentrate, I promise, O Master!

As they travelled further east the mountains to their left grew bluer and steeper and the path they were on undulated among the foothills. The air was thinner and they covered themselves with extra skins at night. Hunting was straight forward and the Warrior brought back a wide variety of game within minutes of leaving the fire. His ways with meat gave his mother the thrill of anticipation at the end of each day. There was always extra to provide a break in the following day's travel. The visit to the village of the Watchers had not dented her desire for intrigue and adventure. Rather, it raised in her a curiosity which had been stifled by the long years fleeing her pursuers. She had not dreamt that tribes and even the clans within them could differ so dramatically from each other. She had always imagined that she would have had to travel months before such differences were noticeable. Yet within days they had encountered people so unalike in their ways that they might have come from different ends of the earth. Meanwhile she now talked incessantly both to herself and to her son. Her words were so continuous that he rarely even tried to answer her questions or respond to her comments. Queries hung in the air to be replaced by further demands to know or reflections on the past and the present. He heard it all with patience and good nature for he understood that she needed to rid herself of the memories of so many blighted years.

He was preparing a meal one evening, the fire was dry and hot and she was pressing a mixture of fruits from nearby bushes into a thick, sweet mulch when from the darkness emerged a tall, elderly hunter. Neither they nor their horses had been aware of his approach. The roans snorted and stamped, moving backwards in surprise. The Warrior and his mother were stranded from their main weapons having only their throwing knives belted on them.

-Stay your hands, ordered the intruder in a deep, booming voice, -I could have killed you if I had wanted. This did not put them at their ease. The stealth with which he had arrived shocked them. The Warrior in particular had not experienced such craft since he was a young boy and his father-not-of-blood played games on him or the one occasion in adulthood when he had received a sudden arrow in his back from a cohort of pursuing fighting men during a snowstorm. But these incidents had resulted from his own preoccupations and distractions and the near fatal arrow had travelled a great distance. This aged warrior, for this is what he appeared to be, was only a few strides away when he had become visible. Mother and son eyed him up and down suspiciously. He wore a rimless leather cap with ear straps tied beneath his chin, a long, shaggy sheepskin coat pinned with wooden pegs and thick cotton leggings tied by crossed cords over strong leather boots. There was no sign of a weapon. As the silence grew between them they heard a swift, hurtling flap of feathers which seemed to stop mid air in a moment's silence before a large hawk landed on the man's raised forearm. The son reached out with his mind towards the bird's thoughts but found no hospitality there, just a veil of darkness.

-What do you want here? asked his mother.

-Food would be a fine offering.

-You are welcome, said her son quickly, sensing her rising indignation, -Seat yourself. The stranger bowed and came to the fire. As he sat his bird disengaged and flapped to a branch a few feet away.

-You live up there, indicated the Warrior to the stranger, -Judging by your apparel. It is not valley wear.

-You are correct, Shaman. High on a peak. Not alone, yet a solitary man. He took a short knife from his belt and cut himself some meat from the spit, slicing off skin and fat and throwing them on to the ground below his bird. It waited for its meal to cool and then dropped upon it, gripping it in a talon before returning to its branch to rend and tear.

-You have been following us?

-For longer than you might suspect. Years. When you reached my kingdom it was the result of my power of attraction. But everything has its own time and I was content that you would come eventually. The man gazed at him contentedly as though an obscure point had been proven.

-I have watched your bird for some time, remarked the Warrior, -It flies high but always within sight. We never left its vision. A fine creature. Wild but contained within your spell.

-As are all I meet, if I so choose. His voice rumbled with humour and his old eyes crinkled in a smile, -Though I may have to make an exception with you for are you not carved from the same unbreakable stone as I?

-Do not exclude me, muttered the Warrior's mother.

The stranger laughed louder, -Only courtesy forbids me taking up your challenge!

The Warrior caught her eye in an effort to quieten her but she had become irritated by the stranger's offhand manner, -Try me! she ordered.

-No. Pacify yourself. I have no argument with you. It is not my custom to demonstrate my powers except where evil shows itself and you, gracious queen, are the harbinger of all that is good. It felt as though he had brushed her neck with feather down, perfumed with the extract from the sweetest flower for she subsided instantly and her stern, lined features gave way to a maternal, beatific smile. Coyly, she passed the newcomer a gourd of pressed fruit. Her son smiled inwardly at the transformation. The intruder was subtle but effective in his powers.

-What wish you of us? he asked.

-To break your journey to the General by staying with me on the mountain. We have much to discuss. I would talk with you about beginnings and ends, about placing our positions among the stars, about grappling with the gods. What else? Is this not your affirmed purpose, too?

-You read me well.

-Your intent is not difficult to perceive. Even so, much of you remains hidden from me just as my bird's thoughts remain hidden from you.

-We will rest with you, agreed the Warrior, -Is it far?

-Let us sleep here. It is no journey to undertake at night. The Warrior's mother smiled happily.

When the Warrior awoke it was to discover that the stranger was up and about. The fire was replenished and the roasted meat was now mixed with vegetables in a stew. How he could have done this without the Warrior waking was further evidence of the man's powers. Bread was baking in the ashes and a black tea was simmering. He was unsure whether the old man had probed his mind in the night. Having seen how his mother had succumbed to the fellow's soft tongue he realised that if his mind had been similarly entered there would be no clue left of the intrusion.

They ate and packed the horses, extinguished the fire and buried it under sods, then began the climb. The old man's horse was a curious mix of shaggy hill pony and cart-puller. The man rode it bareback. From a simple broad leather strap, hung two bags. The rider held its mane in one hand and gripped easily with his knees. Soon they were strung out, the roans and the pack animals unable to match the creature's pace.

The path rose sharply and they had to dismount at times though the stranger was never so inconvenienced. Before long they were riding in clouds and the first flakes of snow clung to their garb. The greyness brought with it a silence that separated them even more. Wet and chilled, the Warrior and his mother reached a wide ledge where their guide waited for them. A small waterfall splashed down the rock face, fringed by icicles and they let the animals drink. Nothing was said but the Warrior observed the old man keenly. Although at an age when the joints seize up and the heart beats more fitfully, the man was agile and strong. His face was as marked by time as the ancient rocks beside them. They followed the ledge around a buttress and met with a narrow gap which ushered them above a tiny plateau. It had tilled fields, husbanded orchards and a well defended stone dwelling with an internal courtyard and a few slit openings on its exterior. Around the edges of the plateau were stakes with skulls stuck on their sharpened ends. Everything was carpeted in snow.

-Welcome to my home. May it refresh your bodies, cleanse your minds and open your spirits to new understanding. He led them down to the building. A narrow, heavy door opened and they entered the courtyard. Several women came out to greet them. There were no children or men.

It was his mother who first broached the subject. She did it in her usual frank and simple way, -Are all these women your wives? she asked, -And where are their offspring?

The old warrior studied her politely for a moment or two before embarking on a long tale. They were reclining on cushions following a satisfying meal. Roasted mountain birds and fresh bread filled their stomachs with warmth and comfort, the logs crackled and threw heat and flashes of intense light over them and the fragrant wine loosened their thoughts despite its low fermentation, -You see before you an ancient warrior, he began, decorously, -Not a man of these parts as you can easily tell, nor indeed of any land near here. I was born to a fisher family as far west as the pony can trek and where the great ocean reaches to the shore. My father had a sailing boat and he stretched nets to the bark of his brother. They were brave men for the climate was savage and changed on the whim of the wind. One day he returned to the village with an object of wonder, so strange and remarkable that it changed my life.

He had gutted a killer fish the size of a full grown cow and during the slicing his knife struck metal. Carefully, he drew out the object. It was a short sword, black and simply made, all of a piece. What added to the wonder of it were the bones of a hand still grasping it. There were no other remnants of the fighter who had last carried the blade. He disengaged the skeletal remains and put it down heavily in front of me and my sister. She was frightened but my whole body was pulled mysteriously towards it and I put my fingers around its handle. The effect was instantaneous. It was as though my body had become home to a fire. I lifted it like one of my hawk's tail feathers and all the flecks of fish entrails dropped from it and the dull surface slowly changed to a shiny lustre. Everyone, even my father, sat back in fear and alarm. But to me the sword was alive. It jumped and twisted in my hand but not to escape. Some strange reckoning told me that it was teaching me its essence. I had become its rightful owner.

I was twelve years old and on course for manhood. Until then I had been certain that I would follow my father on to the sea. But that moment changed everything and all who watched the sword dance in my fist could tell it. The following day my father was drowned in a violent storm along with most of the men of the village. Even as they were being burned on floating pyres, marauders landed their long-oared boats and snatched the women, killing any child or baby they could find. I escaped into a wood, my enchanted sword pulling me this way and that. One man chased me. He had me against a tree and raised his blade. My arm straightened with a speed that could not be gauged and the sword buried itself in his heart. I fled. They came looking for him and seeing his body, they ran in fear to their boats and left with their women prisoners. From a tree top I saw them driving the vessels out through the waves. I was alone. The past was being carried away over the ocean by rows of oars and dark sails. The future was a game to be played between me and fate.

I will not linger on my haphazard journey across land and water, the battles I fought, the strange skills I suddenly developed as though I had been born a new man. Yet, though I journeyed in those lands far to the west among different peoples with their own gods and demons, I followed a path so like your own, we may as well be two seeds from the same pod. I became a warrior too, feared by those with evil hearts, a threat to those who abused their power and a saviour to those who needed protection. I had no special horse, no father-not-of-blood to guide me but by luck and the force of the sword, I survived and grew strong. I was blown by the wind, a warrior with no destination, seeking justice for others and illumination for myself.

The young warrior listened to him, marvelling as this ancient man, like a ghost of himself come back from the future, recounted his adventures late into the night. The manner of its telling and the almost mystical nature of its subject matter seemed to sink and merge with his own memories as though the two men had become one.

Finally the old narrator said, as his mother slept beside them, -My journey came to an end in this place. I was aware that the sword had been fashioned by some power beyond human understanding and that it had found its way to me for a purpose that I know not, save joining the timeless battle between good and evil. I sensed that I was the latest in a line of owners, anointed by it to carry out its purpose and whom it had chosen to elevate to a warrior rank. I did my best by it and it taught me much that I will discuss with you after sleep. But I will conclude the pattern of my journeying first.

I saved the women you see here from a band of murderous outlaws. Their men were dead and their children sold on. I followed their trail to this hidden retreat where they would use the women for their pleasure before killing them too. In one night I butchered all thirty of them. They were primitive minded, crazed beasts, who, only at the ends of their lives came to know what real fear was as I moved among them. I saw their life-takers come, horned demons with tails and eyes of fire.

And here another mysterious change took place. The sword, so familiar to my hand, so comforting in its protection, went heavy and lifeless, just as it had been in my father's fingers. I could not stir it.

So here I was in this mountain refuge with so many women. None wanted to leave. They had been soiled by life. At first they thought they might set up a religious clan but I persuaded them otherwise. Believe in yourselves, I said. Make this retreat a place of delight, a sanctuary for your spirits. You will find god in other ways if that is what you need. We burned the robbers' wood and straw huts and built with stone. It took two years. We made the fields and the orchards. The women ornamented the borders with the skulls of their captors as a warning to all men who might come this way. The summer is short but we grow enough to store for the winter.

One day a man visited us, ignoring the symbols of doom on our poles. He was an individual of great strength of purpose and a clear mind. He came alone carrying weapons and a flat, ornate box, in which he kept his religious artefacts.

The younger man's eyes narrowed but he said nothing.

-He stayed two nights and drew from me the tales I have told you. As the birds sang the day's beginning, something woke me. My visitor had my sword in his hand. It glowed! I pretended sleep and watched as he slipped silently from the room with sword and box. Already the emperor of half these lands, with the sword on his belt he quickly gathered to himself the other half.

-The General? But the Warrior needed no confirmation from the storyteller, even though he asked the question.

The two men walked together in the mountains the next day, talking intensely, exchanging ideas, searching for joint understanding until by evening they were sated and there was nothing more to say.

The Warrior and his mother left the next day. The old fighting man seemed at peace. The women would tend to him and he would protect them and hunt for them. His journeying was over.

-I have not seen a man with so many wives, noted his mother distractedly as they descended through the clouds, -Is he lucky or is it a curse? She laughed loudly, -One thing is certain, every one of them loves him as deeply as any woman can love a man. She dismounted and led her roan and pack horse down a treacherous path, the Warrior following. When they reached a wider track and were able to ride abreast, she demanded, -Tell me all.

She listened as the Warrior recounted the exploits of their host, right up to the point of the General's departure.

-But how could he take the sword? Is it not fashioned for good alone?

-It seems not. Or perhaps for a good we do not yet ascertain. We know the General is accused of crimes and that his armies are losing their discipline and virtue. This would not have happened under the man I knew. Something has changed him. Perhaps the sword draws what is inside to the surface, be it for good or ill. He was pensive, -The old warrior told me that when the sword becomes separated from the General, the corruption of his men and the evil that is spreading across these lands, will end.

-**That cannot be** true! exclaimed Princess Sabiya indignantly.

-Your Highness, you are thinking about the wives? he asked, nonplussed.

-No, foolish man! That is common enough practice in some quarters of the empire and it is the privilege of royalty, is it not? The higher the rank the more wives, though I agree he did have rather a lot and all in one go. One of my father's first laws when he came to the throne was to make it illegal to coerce women into marriage, whether the culprits are related or suitors. Women must be free to choose. She glared at him under her heavy eyelashes.

Kamil hastened to appease her, saying unctuously, -Emperor Haidar is an exemplary ruler.

Sabiya grunted, -It was not his doing it was my mother's. Without her nothing would have changed. My father is like any man and needed much education from her. No, Kamil, the sword! The enchanted weapon. This cannot be fact. It is a myth, yes? A nursery tale for children.

Kamil tried to remain impassive but he felt a little pained, -It is recorded in most of the histories of that time. At the very least the sword was an emblem of great power as we shall see later in the Tales.

She sighed, -I will not persevere with my objection. It is a pretty notion, I suppose. I like the ancient one. He deserved his harem. Now, Kamil, to our own tales. I will trump whatever you have done with an adventure of my own. She flicked her hair and organised her flowing pale blue gown so that it completely covered her pantaloons.

It took Kamil a short while to recount his findings, the science behind the Red Man's powers of mesmerism and the possibilities that the young chef might find something useful. Neither Kamil nor the Princess had experienced any attempt at entry into their minds and assumed there was a distance beyond which the Red Man could not cast his thoughts.

-Your findings are fragments of the jigsaw, historian. Little building blocks in the house of the Red Man. You never know. She leaned forward and Kamil was entranced by the dusting of gold flecks on her throat and neck, -While we were talking yesterday, it came suddenly to my mind that we might have an ally, someone who has suffered most from the arrival of the Red Man. I realised I must pay a visit to this strange creature. Can you guess of whom I speak? She challenged him with a defiant jaw.

-No Princess. In truth he had no idea.

-The High Priestess of our palace!

-Ah!

-Ah, indeed. I have not been in her cave since I was introduced to her as a child. My father went every week until the interloper arrived at the court. I remember I was terrified by her underworld domain. I begged my father never to take me there again. She wiped her brow, -Do you know what terrified me? Not the hag.

Kamil shook his head.

-The smell. Imagine decomposing corpses and rotten eggs and putrefying fruit carried on gases from subterranean cracks and pits. It was branded on my memory. This time my guards carried thuribles with the strongest incense we possess in court, one before me and one after. I wore a fine veil over nose and mouth soaked in rose oil. It was barely enough to subdue the rancid rot. So, I was thus attired and protected as I made my way down the marble steps to her cave. It lies below your sacred library. Did you know that?

He shook his head, mutely.

-We keep it a secret. The stairs are hidden behind a concealed door. Anyway, I descended and gradually the steps turned green with scum from the fetid air issuing from the belly of the earth. It is a miracle that she thrives in such a dismal place and carries no warts and blotches nor the hanging skin of a leper, and she furnishes it with lanterns and drapes like a royal chamber. These are washed every other day or they would decompose into musty rags within a week.

So I entered. There is a difficult protocol involved. She is my servant as are all the subjects of the empire, apart from my father. Yet both he and I must show respect and obedience to her. This meant that I had to stand there between the swinging incense burners for a few moments, waiting for her grand entrance. What nonsense! However I bided my tongue and acted the good princess. Difficult to believe, eh, my historian? She giggled.

-In she came in her long black gown, her face painted white, her eyebrows and lashes touched with coal, the premature whitening of her hair in tresses to her calves. She looked ancient but I would calculate that she is younger than you. We bowed to each other as is required.

"Welcome Princess. It is many years since your first visit," she croaked at me, "It is sad that the threat of the Red Man is what has brought you here and not a prediction regarding your own affairs." Her voice was as dreary as the surroundings but what she said gave me a little tingle of shock. I had told no-one I was visiting her, not even the guards who accompanied me, nor had I made an appointment which had been the rule with my father. "You are truly far-seeing and wise!" I replied, to gain her approval. "I am a seer," she said. "But the Red Man is as powerful than I. The oracle must speak to you, not me." She led me to a tunnel that ran from her cave and thence down even danker steps to a dungeon, dimly lit by sputtering lamps. In the floor at its centre was a well, covered by a grill. There were two chairs set either side of it. We sat, just like you and I at this moment Kamil. I was nearly vomiting with the fumes, my face buried in my veil and my guards waving the censers above my head. "Ask your question," she wailed. "How shall I rid myself of the Red Man?" I asked. I waited for several minutes, watching her closely. Her face went into a spasm and her lips began to move but the voice issued not from her mouth but from the shaft at our feet. Her eyes were unseeing, rolling like white marbles in their sockets. The oracle spoke thus:

"Find the she-worm and feed his flesh to her as he sleeps the sleep of truth."

This was all it uttered and immediately the words were complete, the High Priestess swooned on the grill. Four acolytes came and carried her off, a white froth pouring from her mouth. I kept my self-control and left with befitting grace, my spirit quite undiminished.

-You are brave, your Highness. He bowed to her.

-I am, I think. It comes with the blood. An empress-to-be must never show fear, even in the face of the ungodly.

Chapter Eight

Be careful with life's candle. Blow on it and it may go out - or burn too quickly

The following evening found Kamil and his Princess closeted in his anteroom with the tarot pack as if they were sculpted from sandalwood and mahogany, delving deep into their personal thoughts, trying to find some meaning in the cryptic words of the oracle. Between them on a silver platter was a vivid green chicken leg.

A little time before, Kamil had begun their assignation by recounting his activities for the day. They could not bear the name of adventures. There had been little more gained from the library. The one author that attempted to convey the science of transfixation could only say that it was a power innate at birth and therefore no-one need suppose that it could come about by practice. This man also claimed that the majority of the population was vulnerable to 'mesmeric control' but that there were a few who could withstand the onslaught of even the most powerful hypnotist by an act of wilful repulsion or because they carried immunity in their very blood. Mesmerism was a contagion and passed from one person to another as an effluvium from the strong to the weak. Apart from gleaning this insubstantial knowledge Kamil had waited at the prescribed time for the young cook but he had not appeared, probably waylaid by orders in the kitchen. Kamil had dared not enquire as to his absence for fear of raising suspicion about his motives. Why would a senior official of the court want to consort with a lowly peasant being trained to cook?

On her part the Princess's enquiries had led her to understand that the Emperor would return on the evening of the next day with the Red Man at his side. Nothing was yet known of their exploits in the hills. No word had been brought by rider or dove.

-Then we have nothing substantial, Kamil had said in resignation.

-I did not say that, had replied the Princess slyly, a mocking crease around her mouth, -I have not been entirely futile in my investigations. Kamil had looked up quickly, recognising her childish pleasure at playing games with him. He would have smacked the table with his hand had it been any other person sitting before him and demanded to know what she had discovered but had clamped his tongue and restricted himself to a look of expectation. She had then surprised him yet again, -When the cat is away the mouse runs free. He had looked at her uncomprehendingly. Her eyes had had that familiar glitter which sparkled like her bejewelled red waistcoat, -In other words, she had continued, -Sabiya the imprisoned princess becomes Sabiya the spy! She had then made a theatrical gesture with her fists, -I decided to burgle the Red Man's quarters! It seemed the right course to take when a servant came to me and said that the Red Man had left orders that his rooms must not be cleaned in his absence and that a pestilence would befall anyone who made unlawful entry.

-Princess! was all he was able to say in a strangulated voice, so shocked and terrified had he been. His mind had recoiled from the worrying images that crowded his thoughts such as his Princess being observed by guards or worse, leaving behind evidence of her entry for the Red Man to discover when he returned.

-Don't be so lily-livered, Kamil, I have the most loyal and feared guards in the empire. I had them block the corridors so none would see me enter or leave. His rooms are just off the royal apartments so I raised no suspicion during my unforced penetration of his lair. Nor would it have caused any suspicion among servants had they observed the guards. They are bovine creatures and do and see as they are told. She had stood up and moved theatrically around him to ornament her tale, -I walked on soft toes to his door, expecting it to open at my touch for our rooms can only be locked by bars on the inside. There are strong boxes for valuables should a visitor require such security. It opened. I found difficulty in seeing because he had closed all the shutters and barred them. The room was very hot as you might guess. Now this is fantastical, historian, for one of your Tales from the first book came to me in a flash of inspiration. It was when the Magus was asked to protect the young princess before her marriage day and he went round all the bolts and put grit on them to make them squeak if an intruder tried to break in. So I had a torch brought and I studied the shutters.

-You are a born spy, your Highness!

-I know! There is much excitement in it. What I found was that every bolt had been sprinkled with tiny green crystals. A guard brought me a small jar and I brushed a fraction of the dust into it with a corner of a silk square. Then I returned to the door and checked it and there was a similar covering on the inside handle but not on the exterior. I have to admit that in the face of the Red Man's precautions I was becoming a little anxious that I would leave evidence of my intrusion. So I opened no drawers and touched no objects. Then my eyes spied a small casket on a stand next to his washing basin. It was very strange. I felt s forceful compulsion to open it and even stretched out my hand to do so. Then I jerked away as if coming awake and stopped myself.

-You have a great will, your Highness. Kamil had been stiff with anxiety as he watched her moving stealthily around him just as she had done in the Red Man's room, carrying her imaginary flame.

-Another shaft of illumination told me that the whole chamber was set up to trap and reveal the identity of an intruder. I could not chance my father discovering that I had broken the golden rule of hospitality and entered a guest's sanctuary. I took one last look round in case there was something I had missed. Tantalisingly, there seemed only to be the casket on the stand that was worth investigation. As I was leaving I brought the torch close to it and looked at the small key that locked its lid. It, too, was dusted in green crystals but this time I felt no compulsion to touch. I now knew that this was part of the larger trap of the room and that the Red Man had set it for - me!

-You! Kamil had blurted out, askance? -Surely not?

-Yes Kamil, I am now certain of it. I am his only real foe and he inveigled me to burgle his rooms by entry into my mind. Only I could arrange secret entry to his chamber for the guards would have stopped anyone else. I realised it at that frightening moment inside his quarters when I almost touched the casket. Can you imagine the awful spectacle of the Red Man revealing me as a common criminal to the entire court? My father's love for me might have been sundered. She had stopped and faced him, her features pale, -Do you know how I came to this understanding?

He had shaken his head dumbly.

She had pointed to the livid green chicken's leg, -I returned to my room full of suspicion, as though I was the Warrior in the Tales of the Magus. I knew that the green powder had some fiendish purpose and that if touched it would bestow on an unsuspecting intruder some terrible calamity. I had a chicken brought to me, alive. Its leg had been plucked of feathers. I dropped a tiny dusting of green crystals on the bare flesh and in moments the whole limb had turned green, as you see. I had the chicken killed and tried the powder on the other leg. Nothing occurred. The crystals work their evil potion only on the living! Being cautious I had the chicken burned but saved this leg for you as my evidence. The jar is buried too and the green powder leeched into the earth. No flesh of mine nor that of my guards have been touched by the crystals or by this leg.

She had stood and waved an imperious arm, -If I had drawn a bolt or tried to open his casket my entire body would have become green like this leg. How would I explain that? Perhaps the Red Man told my father while they were hunting that he suspected an intrusion and had set a green trap. My father might have seen it as unlikely since we treat our guests as if they are family. They may have struck a bet on whether or not a green thief would be exposed. And then the thief turns out to be his own daughter! It does not bear thinking about. She had clapped her hands and Kamil's door had opened instantly. The Princess's giant guard had stood there. He had carried a metal skewer and one hand had been gloved.

-You know what to do. He had nodded, pressed home the skewer into the leg to secure it and then carried the platter with gloved hand from the room, to be burned.

*

And now they were sitting either side of the tarot cards, pondering everything they knew and trying to assemble meaning from it. At the heart of it was the cryptic pronouncement of the oracle. It defied them and yet there was something about it that proclaimed that a mystery would be revealed if they could only resolve its meaning and that this might lead to the Red Man being defeated.

-Let us drop this painful exercise for the moment, the Princess finally said, -Read me the Tale of the Chariot, Kamil. Perhaps there will be a clue in its telling.

By the time they had reached land low enough to camp the snow had caught up with them. Billowing black clouds hid the mountain and gusts of high wind piled the snow in drifts against the leading edges of trees, bushes and rocks. The animals' heads dropped into the blizzard and they slowed, feeling their way with cautious feet through the blinding white curtain. It was impossible to talk as they followed each other in grim, single file. At last they entered a wood mostly filled with prickly, green-leaved trees, not high but so dense that the wind lost its fervour and only a little of the snow reached the ground, giving it a slight, patchy whiteness. The trees allowed no easy passage and they had to lead their horses, arms covering their faces against the lancing foliage. As soon as they arrived at a small clearing near its heart they set up camp. They made a fire which burned fiercely because of the oil in the dried leaves and branches. Very little smoke rose from the white flames. They were carrying food from the old warrior's encampment including goat's cheese, salted meat and stored fruit so the Warrior did not need to forage except for fuel. They let the horses scrape their way through the trees to seek what they could find and retired under their skin shelter, now warmed by the flames.

His mother was not for once keen on questioning him as she was exhausted from their descent and the driving snow. Having eaten and taken a little fruit she fell instantly to sleep. He put an extra fleece over her and patted her hair, causing her eyes to open momentarily and her lips to form a brief smile.

The night drifted slowly past and he entered that strange state of waking dreams. Across the fire from him materialised his brown cloaked life-taker, her face indistinct, wavering like smoke under her cowl.

-Have you come at my bidding? thought the Warrior.

-You are learning well how to materialise me from your deep thoughts. came her answer.

The Warrior asked, -My conversations with the old man yesterday. I would like to pursue them with you. He gathered from a movement of the brown hood that he could continue, -First, the sword. I cannot determine what to make of it. If it is indeed supernatural it would alter what I have so far understood about what is possible in this life. Until now I have always looked for the trick that lies behind the miraculous but what sleight of hand turns base metal into something alive?

-You have not seen or touched this weapon, yet! cajoled the life-taker.

-It is true but I trust that old warrior. He would not lie to me, I am certain.

-He may be lying to himself and thus imagines he speaks the truth.

The Warrior considered these words carefully. Then he said, -If a man believes the sword to be supernatural then he would believe that it is supernatural in its effect. Yes, this is possible. Some believe that strength is contained within the hair and if an enemy cuts it then a weakness spreads down through the body. Some hang a talisman around their necks. Some bathe in sacred waters to build their invincibility.

His life-taker remained silent as he pondered on the acts of men that he regarded as absurd and irrational. Finally she said, -If the General believes that ultimate power is vested in the unearthly nature of the sword then to remove it will deplete his strength and confidence. The Warrior nodded in agreement. Had his mother been awake at this moment she would have assumed that he was talking to himself. The life-taker was not so different from the sword. After all only he could see her and conjure her up. It did not mean that she existed other than in his own mind. She was a device for deepening his understanding. Yet she had a reality… Most tribes believed in life-takers. How else could you be led from this life to whatever lay beyond? Many had sworn that they had seen them just as he was doing now but none other than he supposed that they only existed as illusions of the mind.

More thoughts crowded in on him and he spoke out loud without realising it, -There is very little in existence that is not an illusion. The words woke his mother for a moment and she cast an anxious look at him but seeing his immobile form she fell back to sleep. He returned to speech inside his head, -My father-not-of-blood made me think of this. What is real? How is it we know what is and what is not?

-It is what separates you from others, replied his shimmering companion, -It is your life's task. When you are dead you will be remembered in tales around the fire as a great magus. You have already become a warrior myth and as potent a symbol to many tribes as the sword is to the General. They want to believe in you. You are a great illusion yourself.

This satisfied the Warrior regarding the unlikely occult properties of the sword. He would wait until he could touch it. He sank into a reverie for a time recounting to himself all the conversations he had had with the old warrior. The sword was only a small part of the greater questions of life which was really what his life-taker was implying. They had talked already about it. Each time they met he sensed a slight progress in his understanding.

He pushed on, -I have no knowledge of the time before I was born and I doubt I will know anything after I die. So what is the nature of this existence? Some believe it is but a shadow of some true world, some that is but one of an eternal cycle of birth and death and some that it is but a rehearsal for something greater than we can imagine. No-one I have met has an answer which is as substantial as this rock, he said, tapping it. The Spice Merchants offered me the best path to enlightenment. Remember?

-I remember all that has befallen you, she replied, -Exactly as you do. They said that you are the sum of all those you meet. Your purpose can only be revealed through your submergence in the lives of others, helping them to find meaning. To seek to force your knowledge of what life may mean leads to self-deception such as that suffered by those who died of the plague in the long house. You must free your mind to absorb all and judge little. Then an alchemy might take place in the essence of your being and revelation become possible.

-Might? the Warrior murmured aloud, dubiously but he affirmed his understanding of her message with a bow. His talks with the old warrior had led them to agreement on this very same point. He and the older man had argued fruitlessly over one issue only and that was the old warrior's certainty regarding the reality of good and evil. For him they existed in the world as substantial as mountains and seas whereas he, himself, found it harder to make moral judgments on people and events.

Nevertheless, they were as one when it came to religion. Neither believed in the existence of a god.

It seemed only moments later that he awoke with the first bird song. He was sitting in the mouth of the tent before a still warm fire with the conversations of the night clear in his mind.

He rose and began to prepare the early meal from what remained of their store of food. His mother woke and set to organising the horses for the day. A shrill whistle brought them bustling through the trees, heads down to protect their eyes and muzzles. She could see that they had fed themselves despite the constraints of branch and snow.

They ate. packed and then retraced their steps to the edge of the wood. It had stopped snowing but everywhere was white and the snow had a thick icy crust.

Two further days were spent trekking through the white landscape and then the trail dropped steeply into a more hospitable land of grass and pale warm sunshine. A further day's easy cantering took them to a river crossing guarded by a village and sentry post. The river was broad here and swollen from melting snows. They were greeted coolly but with respect, the villagers' eyes drawn to the weapons on their belts. As had become usual his mother drew more attention while they were mounted and he once they alighted when they could see how tall and strong he was.

They were invited to share food and ate their first fish for some time, giving their hosts the barest details of their journey and not revealing any indication of the Warrior's identity, their demeanours deflecting the most probing of questions. However the head man accosted them with a request.

It seemed that the clan mixed river fishing with the exacting of tolls on merchants. Half of them lived on this side of the river and half on the other. Sons and daughters married sons and daughters from either bank and all had been well. But a year before there was an argument and then a skirmish in which many were injured. The clan became split and neither side now talked to the other. The Warrior had to work hard to understand what he was being told because the local accent was laden with strange words and inflexions. His mother was only able to watch. It seemed that the head man wanted them to cross the bridge and fight, bringing the other half of the clan into submission.

-We pay. You fight!

-No I not. Not fight for pay.

-Fight?

-No.

The head man launched into the tale of the tribes again, this time adding that the clan was suffering because no-one crossed the bridge. Once, when merchants or drovers crossed, they paid an agreed sum at the sentry post and the bounty was shared between the two halves of the village. Since the clan had split there were now two posts and two tithes to be paid. So travellers had stopped crossing here, preferring to be rafted further downstream. Because they were in such conflict they would not agree to charge the visitors half on entering the bridge and half on leaving it. Each believed its own side should take the larger proportion of the tithe and had reasons for this which the Warrior could not comprehend. Families were split and boys fought each other on the bridge to prove their valour.

-Fight! said the head man, -You make them kneels on knees. Knock down their post. He lit a pipe and handed it to the Warrior. The circle of clan elders nodded eagerly. To inhale it would mean that he would do the head man's bidding so, instead of smoking it, the Warrior pulled the pipe into its two parts, the bowl and the stem and lay them before him.

-I sleep. Tomorrow, all will be good.

The head man and the elders smiled hopefully and led them to a hut to sleep, bowing gratefully all the way.

☥

In the early hours of the night when even the sentries at either end of the bridge were sleeping there was the noise of thunder and a great flash of lightning. None saw anything but all were woken in great fear.

The two halves of the clan carried torches to their ends of the bridge to find the central planks missing, the guard rails disappeared and the great supporting pillars of wood blackened and sticking out of the water like bad teeth. They smelled the air and in it found the scent of the devil. The head man rushed to fetch the Warrior and his mother.

But there was no sign of them.

Once all around them had gone to sleep in the half-village by the river, the Warrior and his mother had crept from their hut, gathered their horses silently, tied sacking over their hooves and led them at a muffled walk across the bridge. The Warrior, taking a bag from his saddle, then returned to its middle and prepared his sorcery. With agile strength he climbed over its edge and hung below it as he placed the bag on a heavy timber cross-piece. Lighting the fuse, he swung up and ran swiftly to where his mother and the horses waited. They were clear of the river and the other half-village when the great explosion broke the bridge in two.

They rode on looking for a place to continue their sleep, his mother now animated, -What a lesson for them, she laughed.

-I hope so,

-Now they must work together to rebuild their prize possession.

-It is in their hands, said the Warrior quietly, -They are fortunate. They are back at the beginning of a time in their history. If they can learn from it then they will make one bridge to serve both halves of the clan, equally. And they will not have paid mercenaries to settle their differences.

-I like the Tale!

Kamil beamed, -Thank you your Highness.

-He's clever, your Magus. I agree with his mother. Serves them right. I shall remember this lesson, Kamil. When miserable princes come to court and ask my father to settle a dispute over land or a prospective bride, I will consider how I might teach them a similar lesson.

Kamil continued to look beatific, -The Magus is changing from being a warrior whose weapons are the only solution to all the injustices he encounters. There is now the growth of the sage about him though this truly flowers later in his life and perhaps I will devote a third book to it.

-I hope you live to write it and I to read it, said the Princess soberly, -We have to remove the Red Man from his influential seat at my father's elbow first. Does this last Tale give us a handle against his threat to us all? He has no sword that we might capture to weaken him, nor can we cut his hair, nor bathe him in waters that might reduce his powers. At least I think not, she regarded Kamil enquiringly.

-Yet we must tease some weakness out of his circumstances, replied the historian, thoughtfully, -Let us gather our discoveries in one hand so that we may consider what might befall next. We know there are ways of preventing him from entering our thoughts and we must increase our barriers in this regard. We have the riddle of the oracle to solve and as yet we are befuddled as to its true meaning.

-And we must continue to search for his twin, she interjected, -There seems to be some hidden potency in our discovering who and where she might be. From your experience he may fear her. But, as Baligha suggested, we must husband this knowledge until we have no other weapon left.

-Kamil frowned, -Let us continue to gather evidence from his behaviour in the court. I will try the fat young cook again tomorrow.

-No Kamil!

-No? he asked in confusion.

-No. I think it is best I conduct a discreet enquiry within the kitchens first. She screwed up her eyes, -The less the Red Man knows of your role in my affairs the better. Think! If he enters the mind of the fat young cook he may discover a picture of you asking the boy to spy on him and offering silver. We are already at risk. All rests upon whether the Red Man can infiltrate our memories as easily as he can swim in our passing thoughts.

Kamil admired her deduction, -Your mind is as clear as crystal!

-By that I hope you mean that I am a high priestess of reason, she laughed, -And not that my mind is such that he can see all my thoughts at one glance. We must stop now. Although we have only progressed a little I think we have begun to place our army in a more redoubtable defensive position.

Chapter Nine

Happiness may be the wilful offspring of ignorance or the child of knowledge

She dispatched a loyal maid to the kitchens requesting a fruit paste made from wild mountain berries and a little honey. She liked the mix of colours, red and black and she liked the bitter sweet combination. She thought the delicacy was a little like herself in character. She also knew her maid had a cousin in the kitchen.

-When you see your cousin ask her what is the latest gossip. You know how I like to keep abreast of everything happening in the palace, from the highest nobles to the lowliest serving girls. She was careful not to mention the Red Man.

When the girl returned with a silver decanter full of pressed fruit she made her ladle some into a bowl. She sat with it balanced on the flat of one palm and a spoon with her own image adorning it, poised in the other hand. The maid stood obediently behind her.

Princess Sabiya first asked if the food tester had tried the concoction and then she tasted it, -Perfect! she exclaimed, -Who was responsible?

-The head cook himself, your Highness.

-Mmm. Good. How many cooks are there?

-I do not know. Many, your Highness.

-Guess.

-Perhaps thirty or more.

Princess Sabiya thought carefully about her next question, -So tell me, is the kitchen a happy place? Are all the thirty cooks smiling at work?

-Yes, your Highness. My cousin thinks it is a good place to work. The head cook is well liked as a master. Though he swears and shouts he is very fair to all. Why, he had to dismiss a young cook only yesterday for pilfering but he still took pity on him and gave him a week's wages.

Princess Sabiya did not change her posture but continued to spoon from the bowl, -What did he steal? Meat? she asked casually.

-Oh nothing really. He took a fancy to a spice the Red Man brought for the great banquet. The head cook was spitting fire. He had been keeping a little pot for his records as he does with all new ingredients. He is a master cook and that is his way. If it had been meat the man's hand would have been forfeited.

-What a strange theft! That won't feed his family.

-No your Highness.

Princess Sabiya scraped the last of the thick mixture onto her spoon and swallowed it, -Take this back to the head cook and commend him.

-Yes, your Highness. The girl took the bowl and spoon and curtsied.

-While you are doing that, send in the captain of my guard.

Moments later the man stood just inside the door, his enormous frame filling it. She raised her hand and gestured with her fingers, her rings flashing and her silver and gold bangles clinking. He bent beside her and she whispered instructions to him. He nodded and straightened, bowed from the waist and left the room.

*

Later that day Princess Sabiya received a messenger from the Emperor Haidar. Her father was returning that evening from the hunt but would arrive late. He hoped she would take the first meal of the day with him the following morning.

An hour or so after this another messenger arrived from the Emperor's hunting party. It was one of Sabiya's own retinue. He reported that the hunt had gone well. There were many more kills than usual because the Red Man seemed to have a nose for where creatures hid in the wild. Also the giant had led the carousing each evening and entertained everyone with wild tales of adventure and intrigue.

-Tell me one, demanded Sabiya, focusing upon the man's enlarged pupils.

He smiled and started to speak but then he became confused and his face went pink, sweat gathering on his brow, -In truth your Highness I cannot remember though I feel as if they are all in here! He tapped his head angrily.

She dismissed him kindly. When he was gone, a grim smile played around her tightened red lips.

Her final visitor was a young man in a simple cleric's robe who almost fell into the chamber. The bleached brown garment and its frayed waist cord, the worn and cracked leather sandals and the head, shaved to a clean line above the ears so that his hair appeared more like a skull cap, presented a picture of some poverty. He could have been a novice monk or a scribe. Yet Princess Sabiya rose and smiled at him, as only to a close friend.

-Raashid, my loyal brother.

-Your Highness! The voice was strong and had the pronounced inflections of noble lineage.

-Your counterfeit appearance is a masterpiece, she laughed.

-It appears so, your Highness. I have not been discovered by any I have met though in the palace I hid beneath a hood. Your guard dragged me here quite roughly. It would have been even more amusing if he had not taken his acting so seriously.

-My poor pet! I shall reprimand him.

-Not at all. We are men, both of us. I like him. The young man settled in a chair opposite her and told her what events had befallen him.

When he had finished she was pent up with excitement. Another tale to beguile her old historian.

*

Throughout his day Kamil, of course, was unaware of Princess Sabiya's meetings with messengers and her assignation with the noble Raashid. Yet he too had had an adventure of sorts.

Word had reached him from Baligha that he should return home for there might be news regarding the one whom they feared. When he arrived it was to find a riverboat cook sitting in his own chair, Baligha beside her. Kamil had watched women like this many times, either from the river bank or from a bridge. She was a handsome, mannish creature with long hair plaited all over and well-oiled such that he immediately thought of Medusa. She wore men's knee length boots and a velvet gown in dark green, the whole topped by a sacking jacket, waterproofed by wax.

-May I present Madam Lazim, queen of the galley, smiled his wife.

-I am pleased to meet you, said Kamil, gesturing that she should not rise, -I am sure my wife has seen to all your needs?

-She has, noble Master. She was always thus, even when I transported her as my fish-gutter all those years ago, supposedly as her mistress. That was a game. No man wanted her for the smell of fish innards on her body was such that a man's ardour would fall into his boots whenever he approached. They all laughed. Kamil had heard this tale from Baligha but it had a new resonance when recounted by another.

-What have you for me? he cut to the quick, -You look like you have many a tale at the beck and call of your tongue, though it is your knowledge of the ogre that should employ my time.

-True, Master. My tale shall be told this very moment if you will allow. She settled her strong frame in his chair and eyed his alert stance with mischievous eyes, -On one of my journeys south to this city our boat moored at a makeshift landing place in the wilds as we took on fruit and water and sought to trap a few small beasts for the pot to vary our diet of fish. Everyone was full of sloth after days of hard work when a deck boy shouted a warning that something odd approached. It turned out to be a strange vessel that none before had witnessed. It had flat planks like a raft but it also had sides built up from hollow gourds, somehow held together and the gaps between filled with resin. It was just long enough to take the sleeping body of a giant. And as I see you have already guessed, lying inside it was the Red Man. He was as if dead, for, though we tied his craft to our boat we could not wake him, nor lift him, such was his weight.

Lazim, queen of the galley, paused and showed her handsome teeth, -Someone tried forcing water between his lips and lo he drank. He also took food yet all the while he remained between this world and the next. We examined him but neither wound nor any marks could be seen. Only in his pocket did we find a clue to his strange predicament. There we discovered a thin slate and scratched on it a message. She stopped dramatically.

-And? asked Kamil, taking an animated step towards her.

-It was in an old script from the north. Only Lazim herself could make meaning from it, she declared with pride, -It said,

Brother, know that I have been and gone, causing you the sleep of the dead. Fear me, brother. Next time your eyes will remain closed.

-What did you then? asked Kamil, eyes alight.

-We were terrified so left him in his boat. During the night both giant and boat disappeared. One of the crew had cut the rope, I suspect, to be rid of the monster.

-It is a typical tale, Baligha whispered, -Not hard to believe.

-And it is true for here is the proof! Lazim drew from her pouch a thin grey slate, the size of a man's hand and placed it on the table before them. They stared at it in wonder tinged with a little apprehension.

Kamil bent over it, -The hand is fair though I cannot decipher it. Male or female author, I cannot tell. He stared at it curiously.

-Female, noble Lord. You see the "I" has a dot below it as does the "me." This is the female form. A man writing this would not adorn it with those marks.

Kamil was struck with a sudden thought, -He was gone you say before you could return it?

-He was.

-Then he knows nothing of this message?

-No, I think not, Master. It was left by his sister to distress his waking. It seems from the lips of Baligha your wife that he woke later and made his way to this city. All the while I kept the slate, I know not why. Some months afterwards I heard from river talk that the Princess was keen to hear of any adventures regarding the giant. I came, naturally, to my old friend first. I knew not whether the Princess was a friend of the river folk.

Kamil bowed to her, -You did well. The Princess will be pleased with you. And you will be rewarded. The slate is valuable indeed to us. Have no doubt.

*

That same evening Kamil and Princess Sabiya sat facing each other with the tarot card called Strength placed between them. They were both on edge with anticipation. As soon as the Princess had walked through the door it was obvious that both had something important to impart yet wanted to keep it unsaid until the last possible moment. It had become an amusing competition between them, growing ever more so as the Princess had forsaken her usual spectator distance from the

446

affairs of men and become an active participant.

-I have news of great import, she exclaimed.

-So have I Princess, so have I!

She banged the table, -Then who goes first? Or do we wait until after the Tale again.

-If your news is as critical to our campaign as mine is perhaps we should wait. The Tale must be read, for as you have often said, it is likely to infiltrate our minds with lessons that play out in our acts, either knowingly or unknowingly and all might be lost if we are drowning in new news.

-Read then Kamil!

It had seemed the perfect place to rest. The man and his mother had been accepted with great warmth and hospitality when they arrived, minds weary from travelling although otherwise healthy. The horses were happy to put on extra flesh and wander around the village being patted and feted almost as much as their owners. The village itself was set on a ridge where a fold of earth not too far from the main route east hid it sufficiently to avoid the traffic of merchants, drovers, mercenaries and soldiers. The people of the village all looked as though they were bred from the same father. They had wide, moon-like faces with small eyes and ruddy skins. The General's men did not seem to recruit there which caused the mother consternation.

-How is this possible? Our valleys are far to the west and yet they come to harvest our youth each year! Her son raised an eyebrow but said nothing. Despite their easy familiarity with the local people something about the encampment gnawed away at his thoughts.

They had been there for over a week and had become used to the daily rhythm of cattle herding, tending the crops and the occasional small hunt. He had been able, with extreme patience, to teach them to improve aspects of their labours just as he had done when travelling with the novice monk who was now a general. They were grateful for all that he offered. His mother, meanwhile, helped the women with cooking and their babies, moving from hut to hut and being received like a queen.

Yet it was his mother who first voiced an observation that set his mind in motion.

-Why, we have been here for over a week and it hardly seems more than a day! This is the first rest we have taken where you have not been impatient and wanting to push on with our journey.

-It seems so, he said, suddenly puzzled. He looked around them and saw happy villagers smiling and joking, waving when he caught their eyes and working in an easy rhythm with their hoes and rakes and driving their oxen, pulling carts with cut wood or stored winter feed. Apart from the blissful expressions on their uniform faces the only distinguishing feature of these people was their choice of god. The General's insistence on worshipping the god of fire seemed to have passed them by. Like the village of the Watchers they had their own clan religion. Although he knew that this was so, he had not witnessed any of their rituals. They took place at night when he and his mother lay for sleep. His keen ears had caught the tell-tale beat of religious chanting and shouts and cries, although they were not from a source within the village. All he had observed was that they pinned black feathers to their hats or jerkins and occasionally intoned a prayer, touching each feather with a fingertip. The words were from an older tongue that he did not know.

What half-surprised him was his lack of interest in what they believed. It seemed as if, just as he became intrigued, his curiosity died away and he more or less forgot to follow through his passage of thought. It was his mother's words that jarred him into questioning for the first time why they were still in the village long after they should have left.

-Let us hunt together, he whispered to her, -Now! She looked at him, surprised but started preparing the two roans without any further word.

As they rode out of the encampment and further along the ridge he told enquiring villagers that they would bring meat for them. There were puzzled nods and waves and comments that they were guests and did not need to trouble themselves. At length they left the last field behind them. For some reason both son and mother found their spirits, which until now had been light and joyful, descending into a heavy trough. It was as though they were approaching something deeply forbidding in the late morning sun. The Warrior turned his roan back in the direction from which they had come and the joy returned. He twisted in the saddle and faced away from the village and the heaviness descended immediately. He motioned his mother to do the same.

They stared at each other, puzzled.

-It is sorcery! she grimaced.

-It is an unusual power, he admitted, -Let us test its boundaries. He urged the roan gently with his heels and even it seemed to be walking through quicksand. They progressed slowly, seemingly growing heavier with each step. Both mother and son were visited by the same thought. If they were attacked now they would not be able to defend themselves.

Finally, the weight of their bodies and the lassitude in their limbs became so great that they stopped. The trail ahead changed here and became less distinct while a well beaten path forked off to the north, up an incline. When they turned in that direction the horses started to move again yet urging them to go straight on was met with complete resistance.

-We are being forced, murmured the Warrior softly.

-I feel it, she replied, -How can we combat it? Where is its source?

With a supreme effort the Warrior dismounted, almost falling from the roan. Below the branching path where they stood was a steep bank of grasses leading down to a stream. He teetered on its edge and then let himself fall, rolling over and over until he came to rest in rushes and shallow water. The brook was partially dammed by a fallen tree and a pool had formed deep enough to cover a man. As his mind absorbed the details his mother rolled against him. Instinct made him crawl deeper. He had not the strength to remove clothing. He submerged himself, followed moments later by her. It was as if the thick syrup that had trapped their thoughts was being washed out of them. Their minds were their own possessions again. They came up for air and submerged themselves time and again, unable to speak as they sought a way to salvation. Each time he emerged the Warrior tried to gauge the land around them. The stream flowed alongside, below the little used path and away from the village. He motioned to his mother and they pulled themselves underwater with its flow. They clambered over the fallen tree and now only their noses and mouths could be submerged, so shallow had the stream become. They drew in air and waited. All was clear. The torpor did not return. With water-filled boots and sodden clothes they climbed onto the stream's bank. They were fifty paces or so further away from and below the crossroad. Their horses still stood where they had left them, like statues, heads down and in discomfort.

-Let us walk up the hill on the safe side of the path that we were being forced to follow, he instructed her. The sound of his voice cheered them both. It even spurred the horses to lift their heads slowly and stare at them forlornly through glazed eyes. As they scrambled up through bushes and undergrowth the roans laboured to stay abreast on the well-used track.

It was an unnerving experience. There was a slight but discernable sensation of weight pressing down on them. The path followed by the sluggish horses began to wind back in the direction of the village again. Slowly mother and son edged forward through trees and bushes keeping the horses a safe distance away. When the thicket ended they found themselves on a flat area of white earth empty of any plant life. The Warrior bent down and scooped some up and smelled it.

-It is not natural, he said, -It has been spread to keep the land clear. It will not hurt us unless we stay on it for days. They moved on, the land rising slightly. Then, ahead, they saw the top of something protruding from a hidden dip in the earth. As they approached, cautiously, more of it was visible. In the centre of a shallow quarry was a round pillar of carved rock topped by flat, white stones locked together to make a platform. Around its edges was a fixed rail of metal only a hand's width high. But what caused them to stare were the birds of carrion that perched on this shallow rail and wheeled in the sky.

-It is for the dead! exclaimed his mother, -The body is placed there for the birds. The Warrior's memory harkened back to his father-not-of-blood for whom such a disposal was preferable to earth, fire or water.

There did not seem to be any villager nearby. In the quarry were ladders to reach the platform on the pillar, coiled ropes hung from staves hammered into the white rock walls and neatly arranged at their base, large earthen pots with wax-sealed lids.

The track that the horses had walked bent away from the quarry before straightening and continuing back to the village. The beasts stood a little less listlessly waiting for their masters to do something.

-Let us hunt and return, muttered the Warrior, -We know a little more of their ways and we are forewarned that they wish to hold us here by some mysterious persuasion.

-I like it not. Such ways make me fearful, murmured his mother, her fingers gripping his arm, -I am thankful I am with my son.

They joined their mounts and walked them closer to the village, marvelling at how their strength and vitality returned with each step. A short time later they had trapped two fat rooting animals, dragging them on makeshift litters to the village. Again they were greeted by friendly faces and gestures and also some frank questions about their soaking clothes. Their story that they had fallen in a pool while trying to tickle fish met with uproarious, innocent laughter.

That evening, as the beasts were being cooked on spits, the Warrior fought with the urge to relax and do little. For the first time he tried to note every detail of the villagers' behaviour, whatever they were doing. His mother did the same. She had become familiar with every family and their homes and entered each in turn assessing everything she saw inside.

When they settled for sleep they exchanged accounts of what they had witnessed. It amounted to little. The cause of their blissful lethargy did not seem to be in the food or drink. There were no special ingredients. Everything was familiar to them. The villagers were simple in their tastes and the Warrior could not find any wilful hiding of thought when he probed their minds.

He rose in the night, gesturing his mother to stay where she was. He had heard the faint sounds of a voice, rhythmically chanting. Avoiding the track to the pillar he set off on a long deviation. Again, disquiet and slothfulness descended upon him but he was more resilient than before and kept it banished to the edges of his being. He reached the white lip of the quarry from the other side, the voice now loud. In the light of a circle of burning torches on poles, he saw a figure in robes decorated with black feathers and a beaked mask moving around the pillar in a slow dance. In a pile on the ground was soldiers' armour bearing the insignia of the General. Two bodies had been hauled up onto the platform. The chant rose to a long, high crescendo and then there was silence. The feathered dancer stood with its hands stretched up towards the platform in supplication.

The end of the supplicant's hymn to its god was a signal for dark beating wings to descend and the great black birds of carrion dropped to their perches. As the Warrior watched the flesh was torn from the bones until just the skeletons lay there. The birds rose into the night air and as they ascended the worshipper began his chant and dance again.

The death ritual ended and the dancer's hands were raised once more. The birds returned to take the bones in their claws, rising with them in silence except for the beat of their flight. The platform was empty.

-It is not unusual to have the dead delivered to a god in this way, his mother told him, -I do not like it but I am not surprised. It was still dark after his return and description of events. They sat close together in their beds.

-Nor I but never at night. And the birds! It is as if they had been trained for this secret role. I have never encountered one bird of that size flying under the stars. And there were many.

-I do not know natural law as you do my son but now my question about the General's avoidance of this village is answered. The soldiers do come here for their young men but do not return. It cannot continue without the General becoming suspicious. She looked at him grimly, - Do you think this is to be our fate, too?

-It may be the intention. Yet the villagers seem as though they walk in a trance. Only the simplest details like our wet clothes draw any curiosity from them. They have asked nothing about our journey and intentions.

-You suppose they are being governed by others?

-It could be so. They behave as though they are being herded like their cattle. I sense that the masked worshipper was not of the village. There was a purposeful power and pattern to the ceremony.

-Let us leave! she exclaimed, -It is not our business. I shall not mourn the General's loss.

-Not all his men are as lawless as those who took the youths from our villages. We do not know if the two soldiers were innocent before they were caught and killed or guilty as you assume, or whether they died from an accident or disease. Once there is light we will walk the whole encampment.

She did not argue. She was a woman who preferred action to debate even if danger loomed, -There is nothing to be found in the huts so we must find answers elsewhere.

-It will narrow our search.

☥

They had wandered pretending innocence across the terrain, their faces wreathed with smiles and nodding to all around them. Almost ready to admit defeat in their quest they took the path back to the pillar and stood looking down at it. The column reared in the very centre of the white pit. Around the lip of the quarry where they stood there was a further white circle of powdered earth. There was no evidence of what had occurred the previous night. High above one black bird floated, watching them.

The Warrior tried opening his mind to it. At first there was no connection but slowly as he pressed and the bird circled lower, indistinct images came to his mind. He began to see the land below through the bird's eyes with the prominent platformed pillar and he and his mother standing overlooking the quarry. He nestled gently in the bird's mind and cooed softly to it so that it glided in rapture across the sky, its head down, its eyes traversing the scenery.

Suddenly, everything went dark and the Warrior was back in himself but not before he saw what he wanted.

-What is it? asked his mother.

-I know where our sorceror is. It is an hour from here along the trail we could not ride. Let us gather our things.

-He? There is but one?

It was almost as difficult to leave the village as before but their minds were better able to block the force that would drag them back. The roans and the packhorses were led down to the stream and onto its other bank. Although man and beast slowed to an exhausted walk, they pushed themselves through their fatigue until they found their energies returning. They crossed the stream again and mounted the bank to the little-trodden path. It was not long before they were cantering, the Warrior's eyes remembering details from his view through the bird's gaze.

As they approached the place he had seen they slowed to a walk. The roans, their sharp senses returned, flicked their ears and looked nervously ahead. Eventually he halted them and guided the horses into a thicket of small trees. They dismounted and organised their weapons, she her sword and knife and he, his sword, knife and desert bow, covering them all with his brown cowled robe.

-Do we need to conceal our approach?

-No. I wish no harm to come to our mounts while we are about this business. They will stay here and be safe. As for us, we are being watched. She followed his gaze. There were many scavenger birds floating high above.

He led the way through rough scrub and thin straggling trees. The sandy soil was poor and could not sustain more than sparse foliage. They climbed slowly towards a high, red cliff, dotted with black shapes. The nearer they approached the more the shapes became detailed and they could see that it was a vast colony of the flying carrion eaters occupying every available ledge. The rock face was pitted with their nest holes.

Below it, now in full view, was a large building built from gathered rocks balanced on each other, becoming smaller with height. The roof was constructed from heavy tree trunks, tied tight and covered in waxed skins.

There was no door.

They approached it warily, their eyes watching the cliff face in case of ambush, constantly being distracted by the shuffling black birds.

-Come out, you have guests! called the Warrior, his deep voice echoing along the cliff. Black flapping bodies moved uneasily on their perches.

They waited. Then, from a cave in the base of the cliff, a figure emerged. It was dressed in robes adorned with black feathers and it wore a beaked mask.

-Why have you sought me Warrior? called the feathered one, -I have done you no harm.

-No, that is true, placated the Warrior.

-Only those who seek to hurt the villagers need fear me. The creature raised his arms and the folds of feathers formed glossy wings on either side of him.

-Like the soldiers? asked the mother, her voice carrying a high echo.

-They were outlaws, once the General's soldiers, -They had become practised in their evil ways.

-You killed them? she asked.

-Not I, my army. He gestured upwards and there was another rustling and shuffling. His voice dropped, -They will not hurt you, mother of the Warrior, nor your son. Now you have seen me you need do nothing more. Leave.

The Warrior nodded, -We will depart in peace but I would wish to ask one thing.

-You are intrigued by a power you have not met before, one that keeps the villages from wandering beyond their fields. The feathered man made a circular sweep with his wings.

-I am intrigued.

-They are simple people and could not survive anywhere else. I protect them. They pass their simplicity from father to son, mother to daughter. It is their way. They were once just a handful of wandering, smiling fools and came across me, injured by mercenaries and all but dead. Somehow, I know not how for their minds do not fashion thoughts such as you or I, they nursed me back to life. In return I guard them. I give them a god to worship and land upon which to grow their crops and herd their cattle. You have taught them more than I was able, for which I am grateful.

The Warrior smiled, -It was a pleasure or so it seemed every second of our stay. We were entranced.

-You were, though not by me. There is something in the very soil which invades the grass, the crops, the fruit, the milk and the meat. It is so faint it cannot be discerned by the senses. It is intoxicating and grows stronger with time spent there. Even I do not enter their land without taking my guard. I eat and drink nothing there but on spring days when the flowers fill the fields, even the air intoxicates.

-And the power that prevented us from leaving?

-That is mine. Few have it. You command it too, Warrior but have not learned its use. I see through my army's eyes and cast my mind into those who would wander away from the village, drawing them back into the fold. Even you felt the strength of it but it was a game to draw you to me. I wished to see for a moment the Warrior who would one day be that Magus with whom all peoples will become familiar.

Then the feathered man lifted the mask from his head and revealed a face not unlike that of the old warrior, lined but alive, gentle but powerful. A moment later the mask was replaced and the moment after that he was gone.

-**What a strange** Tale. We have creatures just like these villagers but they are not allowed in the palace grounds. They are not quite imbeciles nor are they adept at labour but they do have good natures. Is it not more than co-incidence that the Tales mirror our own concerns? Occult hypnotic power! It is good. The feathered man keeps his people secure with their own god and territory. I wish that I had his agents, the great black birds that can kill a man and then eat him. On the face of it the feathered man is alarming but what he does is in a good cause.

-Perhaps we should measure acts only in their consequences, Kamil interjected, in his teacherly way, -We judge too readily people's intentions and not what happens as a consequence.

-Spoken like an emperor, Kamil, though there might be a limit on how long we might wait for an act to prove beneficial.

-Your acuity confounds me, Princess, he said humbly.

-Enough, flatterer! Who goes first? You, I think.

Kamil had known from the beginning that this would be the case so he re-told the story of Lazim, queen of the galley, finally flourishing the grey slate with its inscription before her rapt gaze.

She picked it up warily, -What strange female hand wrought these words, Kamil? If your legends be true then she may have survived as long as the Red Man, her twin brother. When he returns to life every hundred years, then, perhaps, so does she. And their enmity never ceases.

-Though the message she has left suggests an end, Kamil observed.

-An end only to his life among us but who knows? Future generations of royal courts may be visited in their turn.

Kamil bowed, -Of course your Highness you are right, but whatever the outcome the slate is a weapon we may one day use. To disclose it at our hour of need may throw the giant into turmoil. Such a thought fills me with excitement and fear, equally. They stared, not really seeing anything, as each followed a separate train of thought. It was Princess Sabiya who broke the deadlock.

-My story now, though in truth yours may well outshine it.

-Surely not your Highness, responded the historian. His unctuousness always irritated Princess Sabiya but she knew that it was so inbred that she would never change it, no matter how much she might rail against it.

-All right, she sighed, -Then begin I shall. I discovered through the

457

spying of my most favoured chamber maid that your fat young cook had been dismissed for, as you might have surmised, stealing one of the Red Man's secret ingredients.

-Ah, said Kamil despondently, -There ends another line of hope.

-Not so! I sought the aid of a noble brother - I grew up with him and he dotes on me - to chase down the fat one. My brother often plays at theatre, presenting small productions in the palace. He astonishes everyone for they do not recognise him when acting a character. He is a chameleon. So he departed from me like a novice monk, humble and serious, into that part of the city where the young cook was spawned. He was like a child born on those same rough streets. He passed himself off with a walk and a lisping voice so authentic that none would ever know his true identity.

-He sounds like someone we might keep at our side! exclaimed Kamil.

-Indeed! In short he quickly found the fellow and soon had him talking. The young man had no time for you, blaming his downfall squarely on your shoulders.

-He was not far wrong, said Kamil guiltily, -I feel to blame.

-Soon he had extracted from him the full story which we already know. He was caught with his fingers around the head cook's phial. But what was not discovered was this! Triumphantly she held up a tiny, cream, stoppered ceramic pot. Earlier in the day he had stolen yet another sample from the store and secreted it. This very one! My brother paid him a handsome reward for it so all ends happily there.

Kamil spoke with certainty, -A successful day, Princess. We have moved on apace in the Red Man's absence.

-The mice have run free, Kamil.

Their eyes fixed upon the cream vessel and the grey slate that lay beside it on the table.

Chapter Ten

Abandon what you have lost before you carry it forever

Her father was waiting for her. She used to enjoy these occasions whenever he permitted them. Though he was a loving father he considered affairs of state to be his priority at all times. What she wanted always was to be a child to him. Yet most of the time she had to draw herself up, look suitably austere and deal with him as though she was just another man. He was still dressed in his sleeping attire of a long blue silk gown and he looked haggard after the hunting and heavy drinking. In his early sixties he still maintained a younger man's figure though his hair and cropped beard were white.

She, meanwhile, had risen early and was the perfect picture of royal loveliness, a lavish combination of gold and silver silks and flashing jewellery. Her hair was festooned with multi-coloured needles sprouting fine tresses. Between the girl and her father were bowls of yoghurt and fruit, breads and thinly sliced meats. A small group of musicians were seated out of earshot behind a wide pillar, their low melodious morning music just reaching them.

-To think I spawned such a creature, exclaimed her father, -The empire has its greatest jewel yet to come. You will be an Empress, famed throughout history for your perfect beauty.

Princess Sabiya often heard her father talk like this. While it pleased her, it often seemed more court rhetoric than an intimate fatherly overture. She wished her father could show something more, some greater proof of his love. An embrace or a kiss, perhaps, or the soft words that a parent bestows on a child when hardly knowing what he is saying, so besotted is he. It should drop from the lips like the cooing of a dove.

-You look tired, my father, she scolded him, -Is it the hunt or the nightly carousing?

-Don't talk like your mother - may God please that she be enjoying Heaven! he glanced upwards. He rubbed his chin, sorrowfully, -I wish she was still here. I miss her counsel. He wiped a tear away. His daughter stared at him, uncomfortably. This was not the behaviour of the commander of all armies. Something was badly amiss.

-I am sorry Father, I did not intend to be stern. It is just a loving daughter's wish to see her father well. She reached forward and patted his arm, looking as contrite as she could whilst her mind pondered on whether his vulnerability provided her with an opportunity to question him about the Red Man.

-My child, my child! he murmured, tearfully, laying his hand on hers, -I am the victim of feelings I have not experienced for such a time. You are right. Hard days at the hunt followed by wild excesses as we drowned in wine. It has left me with a thin skin. I am bruising too easily.

-Was it so excessive? she asked, innocently, now adding her other hand to his.

-It was. That red fellow knows a dervish dance or two. We were spinning like tops, the lot of us. What nights! We finished lying on the ground like corpses.

-He seems a mad one that one, she offered, slyly.

-Yes, it's true. Yet he has knowledge far beyond one such as I, even with all my scientists, artists and libraries. He sees the future. He can penetrate the hearts of men. He leads the way with ease through the labyrinth we call fate. His gaze transfixes one and all. And he is such a bull of a man. Her father's eyes glittered suddenly as he remembered something, -We had surrounded a boar in a thicket of small trees and scrub, a real tusker. While we sat on our horses waiting for beaters to drive the creature out, bows and guns raised, the Red Man lifted his arm to make us desist, dropped from his mount and threw himself into the bushes. There was a screeching and bellowing followed by a loud crack and silence. A minute later, the giant strode out of the thicket carrying the beast across his shoulders, blood from the creatures claw marks dripping from his chest and arms. Its neck had been broken by his bare hands. No-one spoke. It was unearthly.

-Is he a danger to the throne? Princess Sabiya said this with as much fear in her voice as she could counterfeit.

-No child. Despite his wild ways, he has a gentle heart. Have no fear.

-I do fear. Where is he now?

-He will return this night. He left our party as we journeyed here because he said he had business on the river. She felt a pang go through her body when she heard this and did her best to shorten the meal but her father continued in the same unaccountably sentimental mood for some time.

Eventually it was over and the Emperor dismissed her and went to dress for court business while she hurried to her room to have a message sent to Baligha.

*

Later that morning she was visited by a handsome young man, a noble dressed stylishly in the silks of the day, his burnished hair made up into a topknot, -Your wig is a work of art, she giggled, -Was it taken from the living?

-In truth, yes. It is a woman's head of hair which I purchased and had made up, so. It cost silver. When my normal hair grows enough after my interlude as a scribe, I will store it until I have use for it, again. His eyes were mischievous and bold and there had been moments when Princess Sabiya felt that she might make him her first lover but, somehow, the feeling always passed. Perhaps it was because they had been inseparable as children she could not see him as anyone other than a brother. On his part Raashid felt fortunate that he could sometimes look at the most beautiful woman in the world. She was so beautiful in fact that he never considered that she would be interested in him in this life. He always told himself that when they came back in the next one she might allow him to offer himself.

-You have a new errand for me, Sabiya? Only Raashid was allowed to use her name unadorned and only then when a certain closeness settled upon them.

-I do. You know the apothecary who has special gardens to the south of the city, in the grounds of the old broken temple?

-Of course, we used to play there as children.

-We did. I had forgotten. We go back to the beginning of life, you and I, Raashid. It seems a long age. She blew a kiss at him, -Well, take this phial to him and have him test it for me. Tell him it is said to reduce men to bestial behaviour. Invent a tale. It must not be traced back to me.

-Your Highness, he bowed, taking it from her, -As always it is my pleasure to serve you. He adopted a fey air and talked to the imaginary

461

fellow as though he was actually at his counter, -You may wish to know that I came across this pot of poison when playing at cards with a strange crew in the dens down by the river. My noble friend and I were fleeced of all our gold, even our caps and trousers. Can you imagine the ignominy? We woke, semi-naked from a stupor after the game and –

She was laughing helplessly by this time and shook his shoulders to stop him, -Enough! Enough! You could convince a dead man that he was alive again.

*

Raashid returned in the late afternoon with the news she had been expecting.

*

While Princess Sabiya was sharing a meal with her father, Kamil was nested in the Great Library, documents strewn around him. He had been there since cock crow wanting to investigate the writing on the slate before his assistant arrived. First, so that the original evidence could be removed from sight, he had traced its engraved message on fine paper. Satisfied that every detail of its words was caught clearly, he had put the slate in a velvet wallet Baligha had given him and hid it in a pocket. Next he had taken out the notes he had made when the river cook translated its message. He had laid them side by side. Finally he began to collect from the shelves all that was written in the same northern script.

There were translations of sagas in which the originals were annotated down their margins in his own tongue. There were one or two glossaries and, best of all, a book wherein each page of northern script was balanced by another in a language he had learned when he was young. It took most of the day but by diligent cross-referencing he had, according to his own stringent standards, interpreted the slate's true meaning.

The only break in his labour came when a messenger brought him a note from Baligha.

*

At their evening meeting the Princess was not prepared to wait until the next Tale was read. She had not changed clothes since the morning and Kamil was blinded by her magnificence. So much so that he would have acquiesced to any suggestion that she made. In a few breathless minutes she had recounted Raashid's story. The pot contained a mixture of dried fungus and herbs which would indeed bring a halt to a man's critical faculties and moral awareness. Wild, untamed belligerent behaviour would take possession of his mind, succeeded by a torpor that could last hours.

-It explains the banquet, as we surmised, she said, -No doubt the other phial contained a drug to induce forgetfulness. She narrowed her gaze, -I shall keep it safe. Who knows, we may have need of it some day. So what have you discovered, my man of letters?

Kamil drew out the three slips of paper that he had made ready. The first was the tracing of the words on the slate. The second was Lazim's translation. The third was his own, painstaking rendition. The Princess stopped him in sudden alarm, -The River Cook!

-Have no fear, I think she is safe. Baligha let me know that she had sent a message to her but she had already gone. She left immediately after I met with her. I am sure the Red Man would not have arrived in time to find her if that, indeed, was his intent. Princess Sabiya forced her anxiety to subside, though her fears would only be truly stilled by absolute proof that Lazim had escaped the giant's clutches.

-On then, Kamil. What were you saying? She stared at the three leaves of paper.

-It was about my own interpretation of the message on the slate. Look, here is the original which we do not comprehend, here is the interpretation I took from the lips of Lazim and here is my own. I would wager that each word in my translation took a half hour to decipher, using texts from the Great Library to cross reference.

She interposed, -Let me read them out. First, Lazim's:

Brother, know that I have been and gone, causing you the sleep of the dead. Fear me, brother. Next time your eyes will remain closed.

She paused and cocked her head and then nodded as though she had committed it to memory. before she pulled Kamil's translation towards her:

Brother, know that I am still here. Our next sleep will be the sleep of death. I fear for us, Brother.

-This is not unlike the first but there are important differences! she cried, -Does this not suggest that she is close to him rather than his enemy? Will this not double his strength against us?

Kamil moved to pacify her, -I think not, your Highness. Look, she may say that she fears for them both but she also may be saying that they are both facing a final reckoning. I do not think it suggests love between them but a shared fate.

-I bow to your superior skill in such matters but I am not fully pacified. It frightens me. They are both products of sorcery. I thought in the sister we had an ally we might call upon. Calm me with a Tale, quickly. I do not want to think further about this.

-They stay with me, she complained, -All those clansfolk with but one face! She patted her roan's neck

-I have not seen such innocence before, he replied, -Even among young children. Perhaps they are a sign of what is possible if we follow the Right Path, then we might embody all that is good. His eye caught something at the furthest reaches of his vision. A tiny splash of white on black but it disappeared again and he stored it in his memory without really noticing.

-I think not. Without their feathered man to care for them they could not live as villagers, even. They have no guile, no way with weapons. Even their husbandry of the land is by rote and slackens off if they are not guided daily by their protector. As you see they are not even children in their ways and yet they become parents. She shook her head in amusement, -Infants caring for infants, it is a miracle that they survive like this. She stopped talking and looked over her horse's shoulder. It had slowed to a careful walk, finally stopping on a grassy sward. Before them was the sharp edge of a cliff that dropped away to a thundering torrent, thrashing its way over rocks. There was no immediate way down to it and even then, crossing it would be a hazard they would not care to undertake. The main trail turned north although a less distinct one ran south along the cliff's edge. North would lead them to where the channel was narrow and might have a bridge, south to where the cliff would give way to banks and the river might be forded.

-Which way beckons you, he asked, raising his voice but deep in thought.

-North, she shouted, pressing her roan that way, her pack horse following obediently. But she stopped after a few paces when she saw that he had not moved, -What is it?

-The horses are unwilling. It was true, she had had to push her mount a little against its will.

-What then? She returned to his side. He dismounted and walked forward to the edge of the precipice, looking up and down the river. His eyes focused at length on a large, flat rock that remained dry owing to its height above the water. She followed his gaze but could not observe what interested him, -What have you seen, son?

-The rock. Examine it. She did so and, as though her eyes had been restored by his shamanic spell, she saw the faint outline of drying footprints on its surface.

-How can that be? There is no way down for man or woman. Perhaps it is a relative of our feathered man who flew there to perch. She giggled

Her son grimaced, -That would solve the conundrum, Mother, but it is more likely that there is some earthbound way to reach the rock. I can only think of one manner of access. I would not have thought of it at all had I not lived in the City in the Mountain for such a time. Curious, for an image of the city came to me as we approached the river.

-And what manner is that? she asked, scratching her nose and staring about her. As often happened with her son, he did not respond immediately but walked away from the cliff, inland, his eyes fixed on a cluster of rocks. There seemed nothing unusual about them but he scrambled under the overhang of the largest and disappeared from sight leaving her sitting dutifully on her roan, waiting for him to return. She had no notion why he was doing this or where it might lead. After some moments his powerful, tailed head reappeared again and he beckoned her to him. He was standing among the hard white boulders. Behind him was the shadow of a natural vault, concealed from passing eyes. Beside him on one face of the boulder, hidden from all views except one, a single point on the trail that had led them to the river, was a small, black square with a white serpent painted on it. He pointed to his feet and waited as her eyes became accustomed to the dark. In the ground was a wooden stake, like a large needle, the ring at its end providing a securing place for a rope. This in turn was connected to the top of a ladder which dropped away into the darkness.

-It is as if we are at an entrance to the City in the Mountain, said the Warrior in a whisper. He touched the emblem, -This is their sign.

-How far away are we from that place?

466

-Not more than one month. He looked at her. Only now was he completing a picture in his mind. The ropes, the shaft into the earth and the protection of the water could only have been designed by someone from that city, -We have been drawn to this place by someone who knows me, he said.

-An enemy?

-No. But all the signs are that whoever resides here has waited for some time.

-Like the old warrior in his mountain lair?

-Just so. Whoever it is has hung out a hook and we are ensnared upon it. It is very appealing. He allowed his face to soften into something approaching contentment, -I wonder whether we have met? I think not. This is a subtle design, one that wishes to promote a mystery, as though asking a question of me and challenging me to find an answer even before we meet our host. Let us descend.

He led the way, carrying just his knife. She followed, once the rope ladder gave her the space she needed. The rungs dropped gently at first, over a bend and then straight down into the shaft. A faint light was just visible below. As they stepped down from the last rung, they found that the illumination came from a passage whose end was a small hole. They crawled towards it and found themselves peering out at the river, an average man's height below them. Their eyes narrowed and their ears began to reach beyond the besieging sound of the pounding water.

There on a rock facing them was a seated woman. She wore the garb of the City in the Mountain. She had long hair as black as the blackest bird, a hooked nose and light skin. Her eyes were pale grey, almost white. She acknowledged them with a hand on her heart.

-Welcome Father. Welcome Grandmother.

Later that day they were camped near the north crossing of the river, a log bridge that straddled it as it thrust its way down the gorge. All three generations lay back on their skins, their feet towards the fire, their bellies full and touches of wonderment still softening the edges of their eyes. For the grandmother it was yet another example of the unexpected events that attended her journey with her son. She had heard the story of his strange act of fatherhood but she assumed, like everyone else, that the child that issued from that union would never be known, nor would she have any clue as to her father's real identity. Wasn't it the chief's and the mother's promise that this would be so? They had overlooked the power in the blood of her father, the Warrior. But it did not matter, her heart was full. Another granddaughter! For the father consternation had quickly given way to loving acceptance. She was a little like his other daughter, tall and dark with his eyes and hair and a serious manner, a little detached from the world. For the daughter, this was all that she had wished for herself. Her father was noble and wise, a true Warrior and shaman who had offered her his love, immediately and without reserve.

As they lay there, warmed by the fire but also heated by their extraordinary coming together, father and grandmother heard her story again and again in their minds. Her upbringing was special as it became known that in her ran the Warrior's blood. It was a secret that could never be hidden. His act with her mother had been to ensure that their tribe would have a seer. Without his gift the tribe would have lost the strength of their religion, the binding power of their ties and their gift for trade in metals. A woman had always led them but their spiritual guide had not been able to provide them with an heir from her own body.

When she was just five she had had a dream that she was inside a bird and flew across mountains and seas. She saw a battle below her, a single man against many and, sweeping closer, something told her that this was her father. She challenged the chief who promised to tell her all when she became a woman. As she grew to that age, she discovered other gifts. She could foretell tribal events, she could enter the minds of all creatures and she knew, without being told, about all matters of healing.

On the first day of her thirteenth year, the chief took her away to an isolated place and recounted the story of her conception and birth. Though she loved the man she called father, she resolved in that moment that she would find the Warrior, her blood father. To secure the bloodline of the clan she conceived twins with a noble from a different tribe with whom they traded. The chief was satisfied that the twins held the secrets of the Warrior's bloodline, too and took them as her own, to raise and educate them, releasing her to journey to find her father. Now in womanhood she crossed the northern mountains and laid her plans for this meeting. It was easy to track the movements of her father for everywhere he went, he and his mother left signs and stories of their passing. She had time to prepare. Her dreams led her to this place, an ancient hideaway. She lived in the cave by the water for half a year. There were fish and wild creatures in plenty and she knew every leaf, fruit and root that might sustain her. She saw not one human being during all this time, lost in the daily round of tending to her needs, and meditation. In that time she dreamed of the Warrior's past as though it was a book being read to her but of his future she could discover little for it was written each day and only its covers had been assigned by fate, itself.

Yet what made her story burn in their minds was her final pronouncement, delivered with the authority of a priestess and which brooked no argument.

-It is my destiny to travel with you to meet with the General. I, too, have business to conclude where east meets west.

-**That was a** shorter story but it changes my expectations of the entire book! I had got used to the Warrior being accompanied by his mother and now a daughter arrives to add complication. You are a wily writer, Kamil. And we know nothing of her. Will she be help or hindrance? You have pushed a stick into a hornet's nest, lord of history, have you not?

-I try to please, your Highness, bowed Kamil, a touch too pleased with himself.

Chapter Eleven

Do not equate strength with the size but with the will

The first indication that the Red Man had returned to the palace felt like a faint breeze sighing in her head. Kamil experienced it at the same moment. While the historian took a first line of defence and barricaded his mind by focusing on his work, her royal Highness went one step further. Shutting out all but her favoured maid, standing demurely before her, she questioned her less obliquely than she might have wished, -Tazmeen, tell me, is the Red Man back in court?

-Yes Princess.

-Someone has told you this?

-No Princess. I know.

-How do you know? She looked softly at the girl who smiled and dipped her head.

-I know it in here. She patted her stomach and looked coy, -I can feel him, she said, a little too breathlessly from her mistress's point of view.

-Feel him? How?

-Oh Princess, I cannot describe it. I just feel a tingling. And if I shut my eyes, I can feel his gaze upon me.

-Does he ask questions inside your head, like you are the doll of a ventriloquist?

-Certainly not, my Princess. And if he did I would ask him to remove himself and tell him nothing.

-Good, Tazmeen. That will be all.

When Princess Sabiya asked the question of her other servants, their replies were very similar. It did not seem that the Red Man was interrogating all and sundry. But she could not be certain. She would need to be careful what her servants knew about this whole affair.

*

Later the Princess asked Raashid but his answer was different.

471

-No, Sabiya. He is not in here. I feel nothing though I have heard many discussing it.

-What do they say?

-As you have guessed already. It is as if they are not the sole occupants of their thoughts, as if they are sharing their heads with him, though it is unequal. They don't seem able to enter his mind. It frightens some of them. I gather it got worse after the great banquet. Perhaps I am lucky. I was not there. I was far away.

-Thank you dear Raashid. Report on all you hear and stay prepared. There may be more for you to do. And be careful. I would not want his ugly thoughts inside your handsome head.

*

Kamil had had enough of warding off the insistent probing of the Red Man's mind. Every time he became distracted from his work he felt the return of the whispering echoes in his thoughts. He, too, resolved to experiment just as the Princess had done but in his case he thought to test exactly the furthest limits of the Red Man's influence. At first he was going to take a horse but he disliked such exercise in the hot sun and so used his royal warrant to borrow one of the Princess's single carriages. It took a short while for the request to be granted. A messenger had run to the Princess with his sealed note and the boy returned with another one from her.

Your request is granted, historian.

She would have liked to have asked him about his need for it but decided it would be imprudent to commit such words to paper.

Kamil sat in the curtained box, now and then peering between the swaying crack but most of the time concentrating on what was happening inside his skull. He had ordered the coachman to walk the horse slowly out of the first set of palace gates and afterwards take a route that ran along the west bank of the river. He was encouraged to discover that the Red Man's power waned as soon as they were clear of the inner palace walls. This meant that Baligha and the children were outside his occult orbit. Nevertheless, the strictest security would be needed. As for his meeting with the Princess that evening - they must be careful, very careful.

It was a scorching day and Kamil had no intention of returning straight away. He ordered his driver to pick up pace and opened the curtains fully. The river rolled past, a glassy brown from the earth it was carrying from the north. When they reached a landing stage of rocks and roughly laid logs, he ordered a halt. Several river boats were tied up and there was much sailor attendance to their maintenance with vats of hot pitch. He took one step down, gingerly, his portly, perspiring frame not up to the drop from that step to the ground but the coachman came to his aid with an obliging knee and a strong pair of arms.

He walked over to a large fire where several boat galley cooks sat gossiping while their pots bubbled. They were all women, wild looking figures, their heads under scarves, their bronzed bare arms muscular and glistening with perspiration. They fell silent at his approach. It was rare that they would ever see one such as he, with only a coachman as guard, standing at a distance.

-May I trouble you with a question? he asked. No one moved. He continued, -Lazim, who cooks and owns her own boat, was here yesterday. She is a friend of my wife, Baligha, mistress of the palace of the senses. She visited us yesterday, also. Has she left?

A short, broad woman spoke up, -She is my cousin. She was not here when we moored, yesterday evening.

-Ah. And I have another question for you. Were any of you visited by a giant of a man with red hair and beard? I hear he was searching for her. All eyes focused suddenly on the fire as though some strange chemical event was happening in the flames. Finally, the squat woman looked up.

-He has not been here, she said, dully. The others nodded in agreement.

-You know of whom I speak?

-We hear the stories.

-Were any of you here just after midday? There was something in their manner which troubled him, almost as though they didn't really hear his question. They shook their heads. But, as they did so, a new arrival, listening in to the latter part of the interrogation, raised her arm. She was from the far south, black skinned and covered in layers of brightly dyed muslin.

-I not here, she interjected, -My boat comes up river. I see Lazim as we pass. The woman hesitated, suddenly self-conscious with everyone's eyes upon her, -She is behaving strange. I know her as good as her cousin here. Many times our boats stop together. I wave to her but she not speak me. Like she do not know me.

Kamil turned to go, -Thank you. The gossip began again behind him. As he reached the coach his driver gestured that someone was behind him. It was the woman in muslin.

-Yes? he asked.

-Your pardon sir but the cooks is lying. They is all here yesterday all time. They is here for city business.

He nodded thoughtfully, not surprised, -Here, for your trouble. He dropped a coin into her hand.

*

On his return he had enough time to call on Baligha and the children, persuading her to stay away from the city at his sister's home.

*

Their stories told, Kamil and Princess Sabiya summed up what their latest discoveries meant for their campaign. There was the indisputable feeling that their battle against their adversary was becoming more dangerous. The Red Man had gone to the river, they were sure. It sounded as though he had cast his familiar spell on the boat people and Lazim alike.

-Raashid will organise a guard for your family.

-Good, he responded, gratefully, -They are beyond the Red Man's immediate influence but it is better to be sure.

-What does he know of us do you think?

-He may suspect. If he entered the mind of Lazim he might know about the slate and about Baligha. I am not sure.

-He seems to enter and then leave the mind clean of the memory of his stay so that people have no answer to questions about him. And some victims he may find easier to penetrate than others. Or perhaps it is that he must distinguish them from others and ply his power in increased strength. She stretched her white silken trousered legs in a manner less than appropriate for a princess.

474

-We must act as though you are right, suggested Kamil, earnestly, - They are a tight clan these river cooks. Lazim would never have passed a close friend without acknowledging her unless she was bewitched or ill.

The Princess tugged fretfully at the white lace cuff of her gown, -So, we have a picture of his powers. He can reach the minds of all within the palace walls but whether he can enter and seize information from all at the same time is doubtful. As I have said, I think it likely that he must focus on one person at a time for this. There is nothing in your research to suggest that he might do more.

-You are probably right, Princess. He has ways of swaying the crowd but not of the crowd speaking to him, as one.

She continued in her self-absorbed, analytical way, -What else? We have his drug and we have his slate. We know something of his history such as the strange relations he enjoys with his twin sister and his repeated returns to the world of the living to fulfil some obscure purpose but whatever his motive, he brings destruction with him. Is that the picture?

-A fine summing up, Princess.

-Then let us see if the next Tale can teach us more?

It was a completely unexpected and befuddling pleasure to have his daughter with him. She brought grace and beauty, humour and loving warmth to their travelling. She touched and stroked them both often, murmuring endearments as if she felt guilty that they had not enjoyed her company all the years of her growing up, rather than she, herself, having been neglected by them!

She was no warrior princess. She carried no weapons and would not fight nor learn how to. But there seemed to be no weakness in her, no expressions of fear or jealousy or anger. She cooked, made fires, hunted with snares and mended their garments. Her father and grandmother found flowers and fruit by their beds when they awoke though neither was disturbed by her rising before them. She saw to the animals and had as many potions for keeping them healthy as the Warrior had. The Warrior's pack horse had been converted into her mount and it doted on her like a dog.

She was much taller than her grandmother, slim, lithe and perfectly balanced. Her dress was more feminine than most women would wear, except in the courts and she cared for her hair as though it was a priceless gift. She transferred this devotion to her grandmother's grey locks and the pigtailed black snake hanging from her father's head.

Whereas before they had followed a route determined by their own instincts and those of the roans, now she led them on her massive horse, the other beasts accepting her lead like their riders, without question. On occasion, when she was in doubt as to where they should point their mounts next, she would sit still in her saddle and close her eyes. The Warrior could follow dimly what she was doing, casting her mind forward in time or seeking a bird on which to ride and view the land from the clouds.

They were seated by the fire one night, the air cold, the moon absent

476

and the silence broken only by owls and wild dogs when the mother said to her granddaughter, -Fate took my son, your father, away from both of us yet now here we are as though we had never been parted. It demonstrates that if you keep hope alive, all that is lost may return again. And when this happens it can mean more than if there had been no parting and such a possibility had not been thought about. I knew that I might die before my son was returned to me but I never lost hope. She lay back on her sheepskin and smiled contentedly.

-I was determined to bend fate to my will, said the young woman, - And make it bring my father to me. Thus it happened but it brought you, my Grandmother, too! A double blessing. She giggled quietly and infectiously.

The Warrior did not say anything. While he did not entertain the possibility that fate might be responsible for this confluence of life paths, it was nevertheless startling to find himself with these two women. It was a joy of a kind he had never imagined and he was learning quickly to embrace it with an open heart. It also introduced an increase in another emotion that he had hardly suffered since childhood. Anxiety. He was burdened with the safety of two others on his wanderings.

This anxiety was put to its first test when they arrived at a small town which had grown up at a cross roads of major mountain trails running from north to south and east to west. It was in a bowl in the hills and was almost unavoidable for travellers given that there were no other easy paths through the terrain.

Rather than try to slip through the little town at night, they decided to be bold and walk casually down the main thoroughfare in mid-morning when the market was in full swing. There were numerous blankets laid out with villagers selling animals, birds, meat, vegetables and bread, as well as pots, weapons and tools. They were conspicuous on their horses, a sign of wealth in a region where donkeys and hill ponies were luxuries. The locals would imagine that they were traders but for the quality of the weapons at their sides and sheathed on their horses. It was a noisy and good natured gathering but the volume of chattering, calling and laughing became subdued as the three riders threaded their way through the hubbub. Eyes took in the tall, weathered warrior, the wiry, grey-haired fighting woman and the lissom young beauty. Curious eyes, troubled eyes, greedy eyes.

At the edge of the market was a well. They allowed for their horses to be watered. While they waited, their own gazes abstracted, trying not to draw attention, a man approached in fine leathers and a short-brimmed hat banded with snakeskin. Behind him were four roughly dressed, armed men, their swords in their hands.

-You are the Warrior? asked the man, formally.

-I am a warrior, he nodded, non-committedly.

-And this your mother?

-I am, said the older woman, tensely, -What of it?

-And this flower, is she from your harem?

The three stared at the man, not enamoured by his attention.

The young woman spoke, -Why should it be of interest to you?

He drew himself up and curled his lips in a patronising smile, -This is my land and you cannot cross it without my permission. I make it my interest.

-The land may be owned by you, admitted the Warrior's mother, grudgingly, -But the trail remains free. Even the General acknowledges that.

He sniggered, -I pay my duty to the General, have no fear. And in return I rule my kingdom as I wish. He turned to the tall man, -The woman interests me, Warrior. I will pay a good price.

Before the Warrior could reply, his daughter stepped between them.

-What is a good price, landlord? she asked, -Gold? Cows? A palace? She looked up at him and laughed coldly, -If you had the wealth of the General himself, it would not be enough. I cannot be bought and sold.

-You are a woman. You are as I will have you. And I will have you. He stepped forward and made to place his hand on her arm. At the same moment her grandmother's hand leapt to her sword handle but the Warrior stayed it in the same instant. He had seen his daughter's hand enter and leave a pouch at her side. He followed the speed with which she placed a tube to her lips and blew. As the local lord's fingers reached to touch her, a jet of powder covered his face. He fell back, scrabbling and blinded. His guards stood motionless as they looked into the Warrior's eyes and then glimpsed his bow tighten, while his mother's hand now balanced a throwing knife.

-Save me! screamed the sightless one.

-Only I can save you, hissed the young woman, -Call off your dogs or you will never see another flower as long as you live.

-Go! he cried, -Leave me with her. The men drew back and the trembling crowd pulled away from this demonstration of sorcery.

No-one stopped them as they rode on through the town, their hapless victim stumbling behind them, holding on to a rope tied to the young woman's saddle. Indeed, there were many who smiled behind their hands.

The prince was slumped on a boulder, his body wrapped in his arms, rocking to and fro, his face scarlet, his eyes tight shut and tears streaming down his cheeks. The three travellers eyed him patiently. They stood in a half circle around him. Even their horses faced his way, as though life had stopped still and nothing could happen until the prince had been judged and a sentence passed. Just out of bowshot, his four man guard waited dutifully but fearfully.

-I will reduce your suffering if you agree to certain conditions when we let you return to your people, advised the young woman, touching the Warrior on the arm and nodding to him, knowingly, -What do you say?

The prince nodded, fervently.

-If I hear that you have broken your vow, your punishment will be permanent darkness. You will be as you are now, forever. The pain will return, also. Imagine, a blind man who still wishes to tear out his useless eyes!

-I will give my oath, moaned his cracked and tear-ridden voice.

-Let me deal with your pain. She took a tiny stoppered jar from another of her belt pouches and a small pad of dried moss. Then she poured a few droplets onto the pad and dabbed it into his eyes. The screwed lines from his pain and the waterfall of tears gradually decreased.

The Warrior observed his daughter with a sense of another awakening. It was a new aspect to her that had not been visible until now. She was completely in control. Her eyes never ventured to meet his own or his mother's. Her voice was clear, commanding and the natural music in its tones was now edged with underlying menace. She leant forward so that the prince could sense her from her breath.

-Are you ready to do this? she asked. He nodded, -Then call to one of your men. They are a bow shot away. The prince raised his blind face and shouted. There was silence as the man approached, nervously tugging at his beard while studiously keeping his other hand well away from any weapon. She commanded, -Bring me as many heads of families as you can find in the market. Now! Tell them that if they come armed, they will not walk away from this place. Tell them that their clans will be rewarded. The man lumbered away and they watched as he joined his comrades and they trudged off back into the settlement.

☥

An hour later found the prince still on the rock but now, facing him, was the black-haired female with a line of elders standing behind her. They were weather-beaten, hard muscled mountain shepherds. Behind them stood the Warrior and his mother, impassive, unmoving.

-Name yourselves so that he knows you, she ordered. Each elder did so, -Now you know who are your witnesses. He nodded, -You will enforce four laws in your land. These my father will shortly announce. Her eyes never strayed from his subsiding face. The Warrior was half-prepared by her earlier glance and had been shuffling through his thoughts, distilling the wisdom that he had gathered on his travels. At the same time he was exhilarated by the confidence with which his daughter had assumed he would be able to announce the laws, simply and with the impact she desired. The prince spat and touched his forehead to show his acquiescence.

The Warrior spoke, -First you will set up a clan council of elders and it will settle all disputes. The prince repeated his gesture, -Second, you and the council will protect, upon your very lives, all women, children, the old, the sick and those who travel on these routes through your land. They will not pay a levy. The prince again showed his compliance, -Third, the clan will feed its people first and set stores for the winter before paying tithes to you and the General. There was a mutter of agreement from the elders. The prince concurred, -Fourth, neither you nor the elders will conscript young men into the General's army against their will.

The prince cried plaintively, -How can I refuse the General's decree? I must give up five young men each spring after lambing.

-Our laws overrule those of the General, interceded the Warrior's daughter, sharply.

-And we are travelling to the General's fortress to bring to an end this unfair conscription by his recruiting captains, added the mother, fiercely.

-He will not listen to you. Many have pleaded with him in these last months. His army commanders rule in his place now while he spends his days locked away in reading and prayer. The man is now a monk, whined the prince, dolefully.

-Then he has returned to his beginnings, replied the Warrior, thoughtfully, -And this being so, he may wish to seek advice from one who set him on the course to become our supreme leader.

-And who was responsible for that? asked the prince.

-Me.

The prince and his guard had returned to their town, his sight slowly recovering and a warning resounding in his ears that the three travellers would return should a message reach them that he had broken any of the laws that he had vowed to uphold. The elders had followed him at a respectful distance, happy at the turn of events and having sworn to the Warrior that they would send a message along the trade routes if the prince returned to his old ways.

It was some time before they spoke. Their horses were moving slowly, picking their way around a fresh fall of boulders. As usually happened it was the mother who broke the silence, -You have ways of defending yourself, Granddaughter. Sorcery, I would guess.

-I mind not that people think me a witch. It keeps most at bay. How else did I travel those long months to meet with you? A witch's curse outweighs the desire in men's loins when they are faced with the choice. And I fear there are few reasons other than base desire for them to hinder my journeys.

-You use your powers well, murmured her father, -We did not need our blades. No-one died. And yet the best outcome was achieved. This is surely an example of a better path.

-Even so, I would wager that the General is not as likely to fall for her magic as an ignorant mountain prince, warned his mother, -All we have heard on our journey conspires to make me think that he is no longer the boy who travelled with you. Your cub has grown fangs and claws and has forgotten any lessons he learned from you, my Son.

-Perhaps, puckered the Warrior, pensively, -But I think it unlikely. Anyway, he taught me as much as he learned from me in these matters.

-I still believe so, said his mother, firmly, -What say you, sorceress?

-We will be prepared to act as the occasion demands of us. But it is not an immediate concern. It will be some time before we set eyes on the General, even if the distance to him is not so far. There is as much for us to overcome as we have all already encountered on this quest. That much I can foresee.

-As much to come! moaned her grandmother, -I thought we would be face to face with the man any day now. Ah well, if it prolongs the precious time I am spending with my son and granddaughter, there is much to recommend it! She waved her arm in the air and laughed.

-**Do you see**, historian, how the sorcerous craft carries your Tale forward? Here we are, I don't know how many hundreds of years later and we are still in the grip of these same ancient forces. The Warrior's daughter is a self-confessed witch and did not need her father's shamanic powers to subdue the prince.

-I think of her more as a doctor than a witch, if I may disagree with your Highness. But you are right about how the Tale and our lives proceed down similar paths. The Red Man and the daughter both know how to make a man a puppet of medicinal plants, both to control him and to learn his secrets.

-You are right to disagree. I must remind myself that the tricks of the Red Man are nothing but that! This is not witchcraft or wizardry beyond our power to repel. There are strange forces at his disposal, it is true but we are stronger than we at first imagined, Kamil, because it seems we are the only ones who know him for what he is and, if we judge it right, he is not fully aware that we know it. If he had been he might have already acted against us.

-He is suspicious. He showed it by his trip to the river and when he seemed aware of you at the banquet.

-It could be more serious than I think, replied a defiant Princess Sabiya, -But my instinct says not. And it has never been wrong, remember, even when I was a little girl. It is my best shamanic gift.

-I have utter confidence in it too, murmured Kamil, bowing.

-Let us leave it at that for the moment. I feel stronger, suddenly. She looked down at the pack of tarot cards, -The Wheel of Fortune has brought them all together again. The granddaughter impresses me. I feel I am like her. I can see her adding much to the quest to find the General, however remote he still is from them.

-It is a long venture. Remember that however long it is, only some of the events of the Warrior's history are included here. It discounts events that might eat up too much of the author's time! He shook his head as though it was all beyond him which made Princess Sabiya laugh.

-Kamil, you wrote this book and behave as if you controlled nothing within its pages!

He protested, -It is true in some ways only, Princess. To read is different than to write. I am now a reader and it feels new. Also, the events that are shaping our lives here in court are such that the stories take on different meanings than the ones I envisaged. I hardly know what comes next, except in generalities. He spoke so passionately that she accepted it without further comment. He went on, -The whole journey takes years and each year inevitably ages them.

-Though the daughter is young enough.

-Even she. She will soon be a mature woman making decisions that change the whole course of great empires.

She grimaced at him, -On this count, the Warrior may end up as old as my father and the grandmother a frail burden on them!

-We shall see. I have poked my pen into a wasp's nest, as you made mention, earlier. There are stings ahead.

-Hm and what can that mean, I may ask? She sat up straight, suddenly and clenched her fist, the victory gesture she had copied from Raashid and other boys when they were children and she had grown old enough to conquer them. -The daughter never doubted she had control. It is a good lesson to us. We must not fear our enemy because it slows us down and makes us defensive. We must instead construct a leash to contain him and reduce his power over events, just as the daughter did when she used her father's wisdom to constrain the prince's indulgent ways. We will gather more and more evidence and use what we glean with what we already know to spin a web to keep him anchored and thrashing and impotent.

Kamil pretended to be caught up in her sudden infectious confidence but wondered exactly how they might combat so fearsome a foe.

Chapter Twelve

Even the purest heart can have evil as its companion

It was a far from happy Princess Sabiya who sat in front of Kamil the historian that evening. She had had an unnerving encounter with the Red Man and it had disturbed her greatly. The sudden proximity of the giant had been unexpected. Her father had commanded her to join him for the first meal of the day, as sometimes happened. She had dressed specially because she knew her father took such pleasure in her beauty and was wont to brag about it to all and sundry, particularly suitors who were as one in his opinion, not worthy of her. Actually, she knew that she would be allowed her head in all matters of marriage. Her father had sworn to her mother on her deathbed that this would be so. Today she adopted a more child-like presentation of her undoubted charms for her father's delectation. She was dressed simply but prettily for the meal. She did not want there to be any evidence that she might be in the remotest bit interested in any man but her father. Over her pink tunic and trousers she wore a full length garment of shimmering silver lace, with an attached headscarf, which floated around her like a cloud, now revealing her face and now obscuring it, tantalisingly. A tiny posy of white flowers was pinned to her bosom and she carried a girl-doll, dressed to match herself perfectly. It had been a gift from her father when she was barely old enough to speak and it bore no marks from her child's love for she had treated it like a fragile sister.

Her father was dressed for the day's work which was unusual. He normally received her in his night attire but here he was, groomed and oiled, shaved so that his grey beard stood out sharply against his face. Her eyes took in the detail in an instant and she surmised that this was not to be an intimate family occasion. The meal, laid out on the low table was much richer than usual. As well as nuts, fruit and yoghurt there was a huge oval silver platter piled high with a great assortment of meats and a mound of still warm flatbreads. It seemed big enough for a royal delegation from a neighbouring state which disheartened her for she had no voice at such events and was only present as a symbol of her father's virility and vanity in producing such a wondrous beauty from his loins.

-Sabiya, he chuckled, -Heaven must be grieving in allowing you to leave its angels for your father's meal table! She could not help but smile at the laboured compliment.

-I see we have guests, was her polite rejoinder, -I am glad I took care with my dressing, this morning. Look, even Walidah is clothed for the occasion.

He nodded, humouring her, -I can see. That doll is almost alive. Do you know, Sabiya, I can never predict when I meet you whether it is going to be a girl or a woman who appears before me. But I am a mere male and unlike your dear mother am not given to understanding the subtler aspects of a woman leaving childhood. His daughter smiled but said nothing, settling herself cross-legged on his right. She was puzzled because court decorum dictated that guests should be seated before the entrance of the Emperor.

-Whose company are we to enjoy? she asked.

His smile intensified to almost beatific proportions and he pointed to the doorway where a giant of a man was framed. It was the Red Man. He bowed gracelessly as though in mere condescension to their royal blood and stepped forward into the chamber, -Enter my friend! Enter! cried her father, -Come and sit here on my left and partake of the gifts of our much esteemed kitchen. I know your appetite and have had the meal prepared accordingly. He waved a hand at the food but the Red Man was not following the gesture. His eyes were on Princess Sabiya. They were burning with such intensity that it was all she could do to break their engagement and stare down at her lap, twisting the rings on her fingers and focusing on nothing else but the glitter of the stones and the burnished shine of the gold and silver.

-I am honoured to meet with you personally, for the first time, he said, his deep, foreign voice rumbling so that his words were half lost. Sabiya maintained her downward gaze but managed to raise a palm in acknowledgement. She did not see the burst of irritation pass over the Red Man's face.

-Is she not the finest gem in my treasure chest? gurgled her father, sounding almost drunk with the pleasure of the occasion.

-In all the treasure chests of the world, replied the bass voice, altering his gaze slightly. Princess Sabiya could see his reflection in the rim of

486

the meat dish. Only his eyes were visible in the tangle of hair that covered his face and head.

A mouth opened in the luxurious red forest and he asked, -Is she promised? Sabiya was deeply affronted. It was a question too far. Only a royal equal was allowed such a courtesy. Yet her father just smiled. Obviously the two men had built a bond that made such a protocol redundant.

-No! laughed her father, -And it will not be by my order either when such a day dawns. The last thing I promised her dearly departed mother was that Sabiya will choose freely. He leant forward and patted her on the arm, causing her to look up at him with a child's smile, even though she felt like withdrawing her arm.

-Thank you Father, she said, -I hope that when I choose I will bring great joy to your heart and pride to the empire. Then she made herself blush and looked down again timidly.

-To be so beautiful and not promised to a man is a rarity, indeed. Your fame is everywhere, far beyond the borders of your father's lands. I imagined you to be a woman in her twenties, such is the fascination people have with you. Yet you are a girl, still with her doll! The man gave a disbelieving, caustic laugh.

-Do not insult my Mistress, you ogre! cried out a tiny, piping voice, indignantly. Sabiya stroked Walidah the doll as if to calm it, for the voice had undoubtedly issued from its lips.

-Stop your witchcraft, Daughter! interjected her father hurriedly but laughing to show their guest that it was just an amusing deception.

-Do not laugh, Emperor, retorted the tiny, shrill figure, its mouth opening and closing, -I am protesting on behalf of your daughter. She is dismayed that this giant should be allowed such impertinence.

-Sabiya! began her father angrily, -This must stop-

-I apologise unreservedly, thundered the Red Man, drowning him out, -I am still not well-versed in the etiquette of this court.

-Apology accepted, responded a subsiding Emperor Haidar but he glared at Sabiya.

There followed a meal, begun in near silence. Sabiya shut herself off and did not speak. Any questions directed her way were answered by Walidah in monosyllables. Quickly, the men appeared to forget that she was there. Nor did the Red Man attempt to enter her mind. It was only when they had finished eating and were sipping mint tea that

487

attention returned once again to the Emperor's daughter. The Red Man put down his glass noisily and focused his eyes upon her bowed head, - I think that your daughter does not enjoy my company, Emperor Haidar.

-True! snapped the doll.

-O come! began Sabiya's father, trying to douse the flames..

The Red Man continued, unperturbed, -She fears that my friendship with you threatens her succession to your throne. This time Haidar did not speak. He and his daughter avoided each other's eyes. The great brute continued, -I will make it my honour and duty to put her mind at rest.

-Good, good! blustered the Emperor.

-Yes, very good! came the shrill voice of the doll. But this time it caused the Princess, herself, to gasp and cover her mouth in shocked wonder with one hand while the other tried to subdue the suddenly writhing little mannequin.

*

-What happened next, asked Kamil, infected by this latest twist in the horror of Princess Sabiya's account.

-I felt sick! He had somehow taken control of Walidah and it felt as though he had desecrated some intimate part of me. It was far worse than him entering my mind. I managed to excuse myself before the beast tried more of his tricks. And do you know, Kamil, she continued angrily, -I heard them laughing like conspirators as I left the chamber. He has such power over my father. What shall we do? Now her voice betrayed despondency.

Kamil considered the question as he watched her. His mind was suddenly very clear and he thought he had an answer, -I think there is but one strategy but it is extremely hazardous, he whispered, softly.

*

When he had told her what she might undertake next and the sweat had dried on their foreheads, they settled themselves for the next Tale. It was like a balm to Sabiya.

The plains stretched everywhere so that the line between land and sky was a perfect circle around them. Spring had not yet arrived so the grasses were a mix of browns and yellows and crackled underfoot or swished with the passage of horses' legs. The sun afforded the riders a little comfort but it would be another month before it would lead them to roll up and put away their riding coats.

They would have cut across the flat earth directly to the east but the Warrior's daughter had counselled against it. She had stood on her own, bleached grass to her knees, staring into the distance. Her meditation came to a halt when her body gave a twitch and her eyes opened, -There is trouble, she said, -We may avoid it if we take a northerly path for a while before returning again to this one. The Warrior had watched her silent, still form with a contented smile. To have fallen into such an easy, loving friendship was a gift indeed. She had not harboured bitter thoughts at her tribe's dispassionate decision to draw from him the blood they needed. If she had been chief she would have ordered the same. And, as soon as she was able, she had conceived the next in line so that the Warrior's blood filled the arteries of her twins. The signs were there for all to see. They too had light grey eyes, almost white, just as her father and she herself had. Her husband was now with another woman for she had rejected him upon the children's birth.

The Warrior was surprised, also, at how she had become the leader of this odd, travelling trio. Her decisions ruled their journey. She trapped meat and cooked it at least as well as he did. Meanwhile, her grandmother did little but bask in being cosseted by her son and his daughter.

-What kind of trouble? asked the older woman as her granddaughter swung easily up on to her heavy-chested mount.

She spoke slowly, recalling her experience, -A falling out between brothers. A dead father... weapons raised but none have struck yet ... each, strengthening a small army. She said all this in a quiet, distant voice and then her eyes focused again and she nodded across to her grandmother. They turned the horses to the north and cantered for a while in silence until, suddenly, the daughter signalled a halt, looking to the south east, quickly followed by her two companions. The roans' ears were flicking as they, too, gazed in that direction.

-It looks as though my advice had better be ignored, said the daughter. The Warrior and his mother could just make out two riders converging on them at high speed but from different directions. They were racing but not as part of a game. It was obviously more serious than that. First one and then the other brought their horses to a thunderous stop, their mounts rearing in front of the roans who stared unmovingly at them, establishing immediate dominance.

-I was first, shouted the one who had arrived momentarily before the other, patting his sword hilt, -So it is my right to put my case.

-It is, said the other, -Yet I implore the great Warrior, who even the General acknowledges as a sage and lawmaker, to keep his mind open until I have also spoken. They glared at each other. There was no love lost. They were dressed much like the prince who had recently suffered at the daughter's hands. Each wore a short brimmed hat with a snakeskin band and a double peak. One wore mostly red clothing and the other wore mostly green. Their jackets were heavy leather and reached to below their waists. Below them were thick, woollen, embroidered trousers.

The two brothers were still facing each other angrily, -We will hear you both, said the Warrior in a reassuringly kind but imperious voice, breaking the deadlock. He gestured to the first man to follow him and they walked a small distance until they were beyond hearing. They settled, facing each other and the first rider began speaking, nervously tugging at an ear and rubbing his jowls in turn.

-We are brothers, he began, jabbing in the direction of his green-clad rival.

-There is likeness in your faces, replied the Warrior, stifling a smile.

-We are both like our father. The truth, great Warrior, is that we are at war. Our blessed father died in a fall while hunting. By all known law I should take his place for I am the elder son. Yet before he died, witnesses say that he decreed that the land should be divided between my brother and I. He broke it up into small parcels and we were to choose areas in turn until all had been apportioned. I have first choice as I am the elder son. But it is wrong, my father cannot overturn our customs like this. Any clan chief would agree with me.

The Warrior questioned him, -What use is the land?

-It is as you see. Grazing land.

-Why do you want it all?

-Because, great Warrior, it is mine by right.

-Have you sons?

-I have a son. My brother has three. He stared into the dark-skinned face of the Warrior but could not hold the deep gaze of his light grey eyes.

-And when you die, you wish that the land will pass to your son?

-By law! said the man, vehemently.

-Your brother was your father's favourite?

-It might be said but what of it?

-Why was this so? The grey eyes pierced him.

The man shifted from foot to foot before answering, -I went to fight in the General's army. While I was gone those four years, my brother whispered against me in my father's ear and turned him.

-If you become prince of this land, the Warrior's hand swept a complete circle for emphasis, -How will you rule it?

Again the man shifted his feet and looked doubtfully at his questioner, -I do not understand. I will be its lord. The will kneel to me and pay their dues. I will in return keep the laws, settle disputes, choose each year's conscripts for the General's army and preside over marriages and funerals. The Warrior nodded. It was the same here as in the last prince's territory. In truth, it was the same in most lands. What was unusual was a father insisting on the sharing of land between his sons. Why?

-Do you wish your brother harm?

-Only if he continues to claim my land.

-Half your father's land, insisted the Warrior, -It is not all yours. There was a mean spiritedness in the man's demeanour and the way he answered questions which did not endear him to his listener, -Let me speak with your brother now. The man bowed, put his hand to his heart and marched away to where his brother and the women waited. The two crossed without a word or glance and soon the younger one was standing before the Warrior. His face was open and confident. He was asked the same questions. Yet when the Warrior asked him why his father had rejected tradition and named him as an heir to half his land, he answered thus.

-It is because my brother is not liked. Many think he is not fit to rule. He was never interested in the land or the people except what the tithes might bring and these he would take from them by force if they were not forthcoming, regardless of what the land is able to produce in the bad years. He knows nothing of growing corn or grazing animals. He wants the tithes to feed his treasury so that he can wager at the races with other nobles, clothe the young women who take his fancy and indulge in drinking bouts with his cronies. This behaviour angered my father who, as a penalty, had him conscripted against his will in the General's army. But there, I hear, he did not fight but rampaged with fellow officers among the General's own people, taking what was not his. On hearing of our father's death, he returned to claim this land.

The man in green sat back, expecting the Warrior's verdict, his young face serious and focused on the fighting man's features but a response was not forthcoming. Instead, the Warrior reflected for some time before gesturing that the others join them. The brother in red strode towards them, flanked by his mother and his daughter. The Warrior made the brothers stand side by side in the high grasses, - Whoever becomes lord of all this land or half of it must agree to follow rules I shall lay down, he told them, soberly. -I call these rules, the Right Path. As he said it he was surprised how readily it issued from his tongue and with what certainty. At last he was clearer about what it was that had been germinating over the years in his mind. His daughter had known it without him having to tell her. It had come to the surface now and then when he had made his last great journey with his father-not-of blood. These ideas were an alternative to blind religious faith, a guide that anyone might follow and one which, if pursued with zeal, would help make life better for the each and everyone in clan and tribe.

-What is this Right Path? asked the suspicious brother in red, -Is it the sacrifice to the fire bird of the sun? We have all pledged to do that..

-No. It is the virtuous way for princes, warriors and generals to conduct themselves; everyone, in truth, including farmers and those who follow trades, merchants and beggars.

-You are suggesting that princes and generals must obey the same commandments as beggars and the ordinary men of the clans? spat out an outraged brother in red, -A prince needs no rule except to exercise the rights that his blood bestows on him.

-Nevertheless, you have asked for my judgment on your conflict as do many that I meet on my journey. Since you have asked you must accept the consequences. The man glowered and said nothing.

-What are the rules of the Right Path, asked his brother in green, seriously. He did not show the same frustration and anger.

Now, after one rehearsal with the blinded prince, the Warrior was clearer in his thought. In the last few hours he had reflected for some time on the Four Rules that he had imposed so recently and he had refined and simplified them. He cleared grass from the ground at his feet and scored four lines in the soil with the point of his dagger, -Let these four lines represent Four Rules. He indicated the first, -A council of all the elders will oversee this land. You will ensure that the laws they make and the decisions they come to, are upheld.

The red-robed brother was shocked and his mouth twisted in a snarl, -The clan elders cannot usurp the power of their lord! he growled with an outstretched gesture of his arm, -Do you not agree, brother?

It is a strange idea, said his brother thoughtfully, -It may stop the fighting within the clan. Let us hear what else the Warrior wishes from us.

The Warrior went on, unsmiling, -As a lord you must ensure the safety of all of your people and all who would travel peacefully through your lands. This brought no response from either of the brothers. He then continued in his deep, measured voice, -The council will decide what tithes the people must pay each year according to the success or failure of their labours in the fields and grazing lands. Again he paused and then went on, -The last Rule is that all recruitment to the clan's own army or to that of the General, must be voluntary.

-This is against all reason, shouted the elder brother, -First, our father breaks the old laws and now the Warrior inflicts new ones upon us! What point is there in being a prince?

His brother put out a restraining hand, -It is the Warrior's verdict. We called upon his wisdom and must accept his judgment. He has the General's ear. Whichever of us becomes lord must obey the four rules.

-Or risk the wrath of the Warrior and the General, cut in the mother, sharply, unable to remain silent and exasperated at the slow pace of proceedings.

-How can this be? cried the elder brother in his rage, -I cannot accept it. It will demean me before my subjects and in the eyes of my forefathers. I would die rather than accept this stain upon my bloodline. Let us settle this the old way. He stepped back and unleashed his sword, making to stab his younger brother. But his intended victim was long practised in his deceits. He dodged the lunge, causing him to spin completely and lose his balance. Instinct then led the younger brother's sword to thrust and cut into him, penetrating him deeply.

-Hold, brother, said the younger one, immediately distressed that he had stabbed him, -Accept the verdict and share the land!

-Never shall I do this, cried his wounded foe, rushing forward, his sword held high but his wound already slowing him and the younger man's blade's second thrust caught him at the throat. He slumped to the ground, brother at the foot of brother.

Shocked at what he had done, the younger one kneeled and turned his brother's body gently so that his head rested on the crook of his arm.

-May your spirit return to the sun, he blessed him, before the tears blurred his sight and his body shook in grief.

The three witnesses to this act of fratricide glanced over their shoulders impassively as they urged their horses into a trot. When at last the younger brother could see, he found that he was alone. Next to him were the four marks that the Warrior had scratched into the earth. He ran his fingers along each one and bowed his head in acceptance, an obedient palm on his heart.

It seemed to the Warrior that the journey upon which they found themselves was sucking venom from the peoples they encountered, as if the three travellers were poultices on the arm of one bitten by a snake. It had been like this on his last great journey too. He, his mother and his daughter had become travelling judges in lands that suffered because there were few champions to protect ordinary people. Tyrants and victims alike drew the three of them into their conflicts for he was now known everywhere as a shaman. In the past the General had often spoken warmly of his growing wisdom and fighting prowess saying that all must hear and obey him. But the General was not to know that of late the Warrior preferred wise judgment only, wishing not to exercise his blade. When they met again there would be much to discuss. Would the General accept the Right Path and its Rules or would he see it as a heresy? Would he recognise now, as he had done once, that all must rule with the acceptance and loyalty of their peoples rather than forcing them to bow before weapons. Otherwise they would live in fear of the assassin's knife or bloody revolution. Nor could rulers invoke a snake god or god of fire or any other deity to maintain their dynasties and increase their empires in reigns of terror. These gods were created by men to ease the fears of the abyss at the end of life. But they must not be used to keep credulous people in bondage.

It was not his intention to challenge people to face the gap between their fears and their gods. Instead he would teach all who were prepared to listen, how to live a daily life of fulfilment and purpose. To do this he must hone the principles of the Right Path and scatter its seeds everywhere.

As the last syllable of the story left his lips, Kamil was shocked almost into paralysis by his Princess's sudden theatricality. From under her satin cloak of fur-edged silk she produced Walidah. Its small face snapped at him, -What kind of heretic are you old historian? He didn't know whether to laugh or keep a sober face.

-Pardon ...er...er...baby Walidah?

-This story does not fit well with the ruling of our empire, does it Mistress?

-Indeed not, replied Princess Sabiya, shortly.

Kamil looked slightly fearfully at the doll. It was dressed as in the Princess's account of the morning's events, though her mistress was now in white. Its round, black cheeks were highlighted with pale pink rouge and its exaggerated ruby lips opened and closed only in approximation to the words that appeared to come from its mouth. It went on in squeaky tones, -It is all too much like that radical Jew's teachings, though the shaman professes not to believe in any religion. What say you, scribbler?

Kamil decided to humour the doll, -The life of the Magus shows us the beginnings of civilisation. It is the birth of modern thought. I asked Emperor Haidar when he commissioned the first volume of the Tales about this aspect and he insisted I write all as it happened. He said it was better to be forewarned and thus forearmed.

-Good enough, chirruped the doll, a little happier and it dived out of sight into the folds of Princess Sabiya's coat.

-Ha ha, Kamil, you should see your face, laughed his Princess, -She is good, is she not? She says things that sometimes even I cannot say! Have no fear. I am not disturbed by your Tale. If my people adopt the Right Path then the empire will be a more peaceful place, as long as they accept the royal throne.

Kamil frowned nervously, -She has a strong character, it is true, he said.

She giggled, -Would I have a timid little girlish creature for a doll? I don't think so. But Kamil, from that horrible meal something has arisen to our advantage. Her voice returned to normal, -Although the Red Man controlled Walidah for those few moments, I regained command of her when I left and he could not stop me, I could tell. I could shut him out by speaking through her, only. I will carry her with me everywhere. The Princess became still more serious, -And I will proceed cautiously with the plan you have devised. It is the right way forward. It is our Right Path!

Chapter Thirteen

Split a hair an infinite number of times and still you may not achieve justice

Kamil and Princess Sabiya were seated in his anteroom staring distractedly at each other. Kamil had only just managed to arrive first and was glad he had done so when his eyes took in Princess Sabiya's heaving bosom, following her running down the corridors of the palace, her strained features, damp with tears and her red eyes. Kamil was unsure what to do next. He had a little morsel of discovery to place before her but it obviously could not compare with whatever had happened to her. He also felt terrible pangs of worry that his suggestion to her, when they last met, might have led to this. He reached a hand forward with splayed fingers, not to touch of course but in supplication. He held her gaze with a questioning furrow over his eyebrows but she shrank back, making her lips exaggeratedly mum by pointing at them. Next she gestured to the tarot pack. Next she mopped her face with her sleeve and twisted herself as deeply as she could into her chair.

Kamil had no option but to read the next Tale. He turned over the card, revealing a man hanging by his leg from a gibbet. Yet his hands were not tied so he was able to escape if he so wished.

His mother was a wild woman more in tune with the creatures they hunted or rode than his daughter who had a developed sensibility about people and their ways. The older woman was blunt and reactive, not displaying too much reflection while the younger woman's mind weighed and measured, sometimes at a speed which left him a little in its wake. They were like the far ends of what was possible. At this moment the two were discussing the events of the last day, side by side with an easy familiarity while he and his roan trailed a little behind, allowing him to drop in and out of their conversation.

-Do you know what I find so impossible about death? asked his daughter, patting her horse's neck as though including it in her remarks, -It is that when a person dies they can no longer grow and change in your thoughts. They are stuck where they were when you left them behind. The horse gave a tiny whinny of approval.

-It is certain, replied his mother, -The dead cannot change your opinion of them, only others that knew them differently and that not often. The dead do not speak from under the earth. All that can be said must be said while their lips can still move.

His daughter smiled, secretly. She and her father often exchanged amused glances at his mother's pronouncements. At times the older woman talked incessantly, remarking on everything around them or any thought that strayed into her mind such as her present anxiety about the future. Her quest was solely to challenge the General and all their adventures on the way were at last becoming irritating distractions. The daughter said gently, -It may be true of your lips and mine but not of your son's, my father's. He writes and what is written will be read long after he is gone.

-And so much he throws away. It is a waste. So what of it? His mind is stretched by thoughts I do not begin to understand. What is this writing to do? I have not been instructed to use the skill so I do not know.

-It is a collection of wisdom. The words are exactly those he has spoken aloud as well as thoughts he may not yet have spoken. These can be copied and learned and spread throughout the land, forever. She laughed, -And so his lips will move after death.

Her grandmother snorted disbelievingly, -If people do not take happily to his preaching about the Right Path when he stands before them with his great strength and his unblinking eyes then what influence will his writing have?

-That is a good question, came a deep voice, a little behind them, -Words are not enough in themselves. They must be arranged in stories so that the reader is carried along as though by someone at the fireside recounting adventures. The Warrior pushed his mount forward to join them, -It is a task almost beyond me. It is easy to write 'it is wrong to kill' but it is a daunting challenge to demonstrate this in a short tale which is caught by the wind in a person's mind, bursting into flame so that it is felt to be true.

His daughter turned in her saddle, squinting at him, -Yet it is possible. There are many manuscripts that lie in temples and monasteries with just such knowledge. Someone wrote them just as you do. The General carries divine papers in his box does he not? He believes them to be the words of the god of the sun, himself! This has always been the work of seers. They capture the counsel of the gods so that future generations can read them and learn from them. It is a gift known only to the most learned to say so much in but a few pages. When I was waiting for you both, in my underground palace of rock and water, I saw scratching on the walls. At first I did not look too closely for I imagined them to be the marks of creatures or stones once carried that way by tumbling water. Yet one day I saw a horse and I then made out the figures of men with bows, pictures of fires and of fish and birds. Why did the engraver make these marks except for others to learn? He must have lived hundreds of years before the men who copied the divine words in the General's box, yet, if we knew how to read his inscriptions, we might learn new things.

-Your thoughts are my thoughts, agreed her father, -It is not enough to talk and persuade only those we meet. The lessons of the Right Path must find their way to all those who know nothing of me so that they can learn from them, tell others, copy the lessons, spread the word. It is my challenge. Words must be dressed in such a way that both a simple mind and a learned mind find persuasion there. Only then can the Right Path be a force that will alter people's lives.

-This is a cruel place, murmured the daughter, sniffing the air, -It is full of the laments of frightened victims and those that have lost them to an unknown fate.

-I hear it, too, said her father, -Yet I can conjure up no pictures of the cause...

They had paused half way down a rock-strewn incline, the roans showing signs of fret with their ears flattened and overhead there were wheeling birds, screeching dolefully.

-There is no dwelling place, said the mother, her eyes roving over the land below them, -Yet I sense something human here. I smell it. Ah, burning wood! They caught the scent as one.

The Warrior shaded his eyes, -I can see it but it is cleverly concealed. He pointed. -See those bushes? They are breathing a faint mist. Somehow the smoke is spread through them. I can tell from the scent that only well dried hard wood is used in the fire. A hidden chimney makes it difficult to keep a fire alight.

-And chokes those who sit before it to cook on it, added the mother.

Each pictured the underground habitation in his or her own way. The mother saw a large vaulted room with beams and supporting timbers, covered with sods and a step ladder reaching up to a trapdoor in the bushes. The Warrior imagined a small bandit's hole, perfectly concealed should its owner become the quarry of a vigilant pack of angry villagers or a military troop. Who else would want such camouflage? But it was his granddaughter who divined the true nature of what lay beneath the earth's surface. After all she was born and raised under a mountain and tunnels and caves were her natural world. She had instincts that enabled her to move freely in the dark, know every direction, feel how thick was the roof of rock between her and the air above ground and how to survive on just the moisture dripping down the walls, the mosses and lichens and the insects and leather winged creatures that inhabited that world. Indeed it took her many hours each time she entered the land of sun and sky to become at home in it.

Her images were of a long tunnel leading from an entrance concealed by a boulder to a room in which the creator of this prison lived and a further short tunnel to the cells in which he held his prey. She did not see in her mind an image of the captor or those he kept at bay but she sensed them there.

She described what she felt to her companions, gesturing here and there to illustrate what her instinct was informing her, -The rock we are standing on is the same as envelops my city. Water will have run in underground streams, making long tunnels. But see how the grass begins to grow where the rock ends, showing there is deeper soil which also sustains those plants and trees. She pointed, -Now take a line from the bushes where my father saw the smoke and join it to where that blasted tree stands. The grass along the line is a different hue, showing where the tunnel runs underneath. The Warrior could follow now that it was pointed out but his mother was no wiser. His daughter continued, -Among the roots of that tree are cells holding people. The captor lives beneath the smoking bushes. A further tunnel runs from the bushes to this hillside. See? Again the grass is paler so there must be an entrance over there. She indicated to their left.

-Then let us search for it and drag them out by their tails, grunted her grandmother, taking hold of her reins.

-No! her granddaughter stopped her, -If we begin a search for the entrance we might fall foul of snares that have been laid to warn those that hold the prisoners. I cannot be sure of their nature nor of what they might do with their captives. There may even be another exit that I cannot yet see. We must wait and watch. Our quarry will emerge in time but only at night when all is silent and even the lightest footfall from the smallest creature will carry a message under the earth. We must retrace our steps and camp at a more distant point of good vantage.

The Warrior was musing on the nature of travelling and how time sometimes stretched into an indeterminate void or could become concentrated into rapid clumps of action, events and people that blurred into each other. This was their seventh night of waiting and he had been woken by the touch of his daughter. It was she who slept by day and watched by night while he and his mother kept to their natural cycle. His daughter lay on a rock in her skins, now and then pressing her ear to it. She had ascertained that there were two captors, a male and a female and that they held five children in separate cells.

-More like tombs, growled her grandmother, angrily, -Child traders! I will sever their heads. Any parent would.

He and his mother had been woken before morning broke because his daughter had caught the unmistakable sounds of movement along the tunnel to the hillside, -The man is coming, she whispered, -He is close to the entrance, leading his horse. And with a child. Look! They saw no boulder move but a man on horseback with a child before him, began to pick his way through the darkness down towards the trail.

-I will follow him, said the Warrior, -You stay with the children. Find the entrance. We will finish this business before the end of the day. He moved off silently, leading his roan, hidden just below the long ridge.

The child trader with his victim, his mouth bandaged, stood in the centre of the village, haggling over the price of his goods with the local shaman. He was listing the virtues of his boy captive, his plump flesh, his young years, his all white eyes and his fine white hair showing pink skin beneath. The shaman nodded greedily and tried to barter horses, cattle, sheep and women for the child but the trader would only accept gold or silver for wasn't the child perfect? Wouldn't his sacrifice on the altar excite the gods and bring years of plenty, thus multiplying the clan's outlay many fold? The village elders clapped their agreement and cajoled the shaman to pay the price.

No-one saw the shadowy figure in the brown robe approach until he stood among them as if he had dropped from the sky. One powerful arm held the child to his chest.

-The Warrior! came the shocked and frightened cries of the crowd as they fell back. A silvery blade arced in the sunlight, touching the child trader's throat and then the village shaman's with the faintest of kisses, drawing a fine line of blood on each. In an instant he and the child were gone.

The child trader returned to the entrance of his tunnel like the prey of a chasing beast. His eyes searched everywhere and he jerked this way and that as if expecting a blow from any quarter. His wife was waiting for him, her own body shivering. He began to gabble his story to her but she forestalled him with a hand over his mouth and a sweep of her arm. He followed the direction. There, where the tunnel had been, was now a trench and where the smoking bush had stood, there was a crater and where there had been a blasted tree, now there was both a hole and a broken pile of boughs and trunk. Beyond the destruction they were being observed by a warrior, two women and five distressed children. Then, as one, the silent group turned away.

They left the children with a gift of jewellery in a friendly village, instilling in the villagers a fear that, should the children be harmed, they would return full of wrath. Messages were sent along the trade routes to their families. The mother could not clear her mind of the strange spectacle of these pale, defenceless creatures, made even paler by their stay under the soil.

-I would have liked to have flayed the child merchants, since skin is their disgusting trade, she informed them through taut lips, -I know the art and have had occasion to practise it.

-We all would, replied her son, -But we cannot be seen to be made of the same rank flesh as they. This may be a better punishment.

-Better than death? Pictures! I do not think so, replied his disbelieving mother.

-Better. The pictures mean that they will live in the perpetual agony of being discovered.

-It is a threat that will pass as they make themselves invisible. The pictures will be lost or forgotten.

-No, said the daughter. They will live their lives in torment, such is the fear in their bones.

-It was our sentence and punishment, concluded the Warrior, - Casting my mind to where they are, even now, I can see them following a trail like headless birds not knowing whither they go or if they will be safe. They have no desire other than to find anonymity, fearing the vengeance of those they have wronged. It will never cease. They know that one day an albino warrior will chase them down and their sins will be washed from their bodies in a waterfall of blood.

-I hope it is true, grumbled his mother grudgingly, -But I like my vengeance to be immediate. It did not seem possible to her that the drawings made of the child traders by her granddaughter, with paint on silk, even though they were as like them as their reflections in water, could carry such potency.

Her granddaughter pressed her arm, -Grandmother, the power of words and pictures can travel everywhere, believe me. Each growing child will carry the traders' likenesses in his or her pocket, showing them to all they meet and repeating their dreadful tale. Such is the power of inscription.

Calmed by the Tale, Princess Sabiya gazed at her historian. In the course of his reading she had gradually eased herself forward, dabbed her eyes several times and massaged cream into her hot skin. She was still pale but her breathing was normal.

-That was a terrible Tale Kamil. Those poor children. Do you know that the same unspeakable practice can be found in my mother's homeland, even today? My father issued an edict there, at my mother's behest, saying that anyone who sacrifices a child, particularly a ghost child, which is our name for a white skinned one, will be hung upside down and slit until every last drop of blood has leaked so that they become blanched in a public square. It is a great deterrent. Is that what is going to happen to the man on the card? We have a painter in the court who also constructs wonderful images like the daughter in your Tale. He is hairless and has no tint of any kind in his eyes or skin. People are fearful of him but they know he is a protected creature.

Kamil let her talk, waiting for her to be composed enough to recount what had happened. Eventually she sat up straight and smoothed her garments in that familiar way.

-After we last spoke I considered more deeply your advice as to how I should proceed. Although I could see that I would be in greater danger, I resolved to follow your guidance. I reasoned to myself that I was in enough danger already and if I was one day going to become Empress then I had little choice but to go forward.

Later that evening I attended the usual meal. It was nothing special, just my father, close friends and family - and the Red Man. My father, like the blind fool he can sometimes be, placed me next to the beast. Do you know Kamil, he is loathsomely crude in his eating and his gigantic body hung over me, filling the air so that I felt squeezed under it. But, remembering my role, I did not shift on my cushion, accepting the occasional brush of his clumsy arm and the constant, sweaty heat of his unwashed body.

We did not speak for a while and I did not feel him prying into my thoughts. There came a pause in the meal and the dwarf entered to entertain us. He is allowed to poke fun at all and sundry whatever their station, except me. After my mother died I took on the mantle of seeing to his well-being. Even as a young child when I played with him I felt sorry for his stumpy arms and legs and his oversized head. But he was always a gentle soul. Anyway, he wandered round the room, asking rude questions and making naughty comments, pointing out who wore ill-fitting or inappropriate clothing, wigs and so on, who seemed lacking in sexual comforts, who were still virgins like my young cousins and whom he deemed to be liars. He is always severe on my father but the Emperor takes it well. "Ah, Emperor Haidar the Great!" he called out in his husky old man's voice, "Yes, my evil fellow," replied my father, expecting the worst. "I hear you have fallen in love. Again". The dwarf's sigh of boredom made us all laugh. It is true that since my mother died and he recovered from the loss and that of my despicable stepmother, my father has satisfied his male urges with young women brought in from the city. Not the best families but not the worst, either. He treats them well enough and they are amply rewarded for their charms. It is innocent enough as these things go and none succumbs against her will. Then the dwarf said, "But this time it is no sweet-buttocked girl, is it my Lord? It is a beast as big as I am short, as red as I am black, as crude as I am suave." This last remark brought more laughter for suave is not a word to associate with the little fellow. But there were also a few worried glances in my general direction since I was at the ogre's elbow. The Dwarf went on, "How has he stolen your heart, my Lord? Why are you lost in those big bad eyes? It is a conundrum. The man mountain comes out of the north like a cold wind with his strange powers and soon he sits like a lover at your table. He can do no wrong - except drug everyone at a banquet!" I could feel the giant stiffen at my side. I think only I, gripping Walidah under my coat, understood what happened next. The dwarf went suddenly into a fidgety, slobbering dance, his mouth agape. He careered around the room, beating his breast and barking, grunting, mewing, neighing and clucking like a farmyard. Everyone laughed thinking this was his best performance for a long time but I saw his eyes rolling under his lids. He danced out of the chamber to great applause. "An insulting little rat, don't you think?" growled the Red Man's voice next to me, half under his breath. "Of course, my Lord," I agreed, almost biting my lip on the title I was bestowing on him, "He is our conscience and well paid to stop us from taking ourselves too seriously." I looked up at him with fluttering lashes but could see that he did not understand. "Vermin!" was his retort.

I was able to excuse myself shortly after and attended to my business. Never once did I feel the pressure of the Red Man's mind.

Today passed by and when I had a moment, before I was to come here, I thought I'd pay a visit to the little fellow to make sure he had recovered and to hear his recollections of the evening's events. He lives in the compound outside the main palace walls so I took my guard and Raashid with me.

The guard knocked but there was no response so we entered as the door was not locked. Raashid tried to prevent my gaze but I saw everything in one clear picture. My naughty, rumbustious little friend was bent into a tiny ball, his neck broken so that his head appeared on the wrong side of his body and on the floor tiles beside him someone had daubed in the red powder he used to colour his face, "Ha Ha".

We called the palace guard, sent a message to the Emperor and as soon as all was secure, I rushed straight here. Raashid went back into the palace to uncover the movements of the Red Man after he left the meal and up to the point of our entry into the dwarf's chamber.

It is worsening, dear Kamil. The creature is exerting his evil power. I fear that terrible forces are locked in that man and he does not know how to control them otherwise he would not have killed the dwarf, for what was he to him but a fly buzzing around his head?

Kamil stood and began walking round the room, his plump face frowning in concentration, -He is undoubtedly the murderer, either with his own hand or by manipulating another. You must ensure that Doctor Aziz examines the body. He has a way of building past events from the place of death. And you, my Princess, must think again about the wisdom of my counsel. As you say, the danger grows.

-I will keep to our course, Kamil, and enamour the Red Man with my charms, as you suggested, I am both his greatest obstacle and his greatest fascination. By offering myself as the prize we may reveal a way through his invulnerability.

*

It was after she had gone that Kamil realised that he had not relayed to her his small reward for another day's laborious research in the Great Library.

Chapter Fourteen

Is the moment of death this one - or the next?

What Kamil had discovered in the Great Library the day before, was this. In a reference in a footnote to yet another treatise on the strange reappearances of the Red Man at the courts of empires from north to south and east to west, the writer proclaimed that his invincibility remained intact unless that which was hidden within him was brought into the open. There was a brief description of how this might happen though it did little more than whet the appetite. Kamil had copied out the full footnote in his scholarly hand to show to his Princess.

*

During the day, as he laboured with his researches, he received a letter from the Princess, rolled and sealed several times along its edge. It commanded him to represent her that afternoon at a meeting with the High Priestess in her caves beneath his very feet for she had sent a missive to the Princess that she had dire news to report. Kamil burnt the roll and prepared himself. On his belt he hung the insignia of the Princess to add to the badge of the royal historian already pinned to his belt. They were symbols of power and would gain him entry to all but the chambers of royalty. They were necessary because, despite his status, he was unknown in the palace except to the Princess and the Emperor. He had always preferred the Great Library to the court and had no ambition to become even a junior minister.

*

The reason why Princess Sabiya could not respond to the High Priestess's request to meet with her, was that the day was to be spent on the royal barge. Each year it floated down and back up through the city decked with flowers and banners and with musicians on its roof playing joyful tunes to make the people dance. It was called the

Festival of Ten in memory of the ten heroes who liberated the city more than a hundred years before. Ten oxen would be roasted and the meat distributed along the river banks as the barge passed by, a hundred pouches, each containing ten coins would be thrown into its waters for the children to dive and find, ten prisoners would be released from the dungeons and ten couples would be married by the Emperor. It was an occasion that the Princess never missed for, in truth, it paraded her ever increasing beauty to the public eye, spreading her fame and encouraging suitors from near and far.

Today would have the added attraction of the Red Man.

*

Kamil descended the dismal, damp mossy steps to the underground cavern, as had been described to him by the Princess. One of the guards who had accompanied her before, led the way with a lighted torch.

He was made to wait, as the Princess had been, before being taken down the final steps to the deepest chamber. The only detail to catch his attention was the grill on the floor that covered the shaft from which issued the wailings of the oracle and which the High Priestess translated for those who came for guidance. The stench that dredged up from the hole in the floor sickened him and the howling noises unnerved him. He was thankful for the security of the torch for without it he would quickly have become demented.

*

There were three thrones, one for the Emperor, one for her and one for the Red Man. They sat on the top deck, directly below the roof with its musicians and the rhythmic pounding of their feet. They were sufficiently high up for everyone on the banks to have a full view. She and her father waved generously but the Red Man seemed surly and irritated by his exposure. Indeed, it was clear that he was not a popular guest in the Emperor's entourage. There were shouts of Beast! Guard your children! Foreigner! Sorcerer! Yet her father seemed oblivious to them, now and then clapping the Red Man on the shoulder and pointing out this and that in the crowd.

-You must forgive some of our people, she said demurely to him, -They are not used to such as you.

He made a great effort to be civil, -I would conjecture that it is my red hair. They see little like it in these parts.

-Or your magnificent size!

-Perhaps, he smiled, his yellow teeth gleaming.

-And all the tales of your magic!

He said nothing for a moment but stared at her slightly open mouth with its pretty, full red lips, -What magic? he asked, finally composing himself. But she was unable to answer him because her father had grasped his arm once again to direct his attention to some naked children, garlanded in flowers, hanging over the rail of a footbridge under which they were about to pass. The Red Man looked up and smiled, his eyes becoming unnaturally bright and narrowed, then suddenly a young girl fell from the jostling crowd towards the front of the barge. With reactions unexpectedly fast for a man who seemed usually so clumsy, the Red Man leapt forward, reaching out from under the roof with his long arms and caught the child as though she was but a pomegranate.

Within seconds the news of his act was everywhere and the cries of disgust and hate were replaced by cheers and chants of his name.

*

-So what, asked an intrigued Kamil, -Happened next? The Red Man has become a hero and you must sit beside him for the entire return journey? She was back to her spritely self, full of youthful exuberance.

-I will tell you but first you must tell me what the High Priestess wanted to tell us!

He laughed, responding to her impishness, -Let me read the Tale first for no matter how difficult our stories of the day might be, the Tale may trump them. She thought he joked but her face fell when she saw the card.

The three travellers were lying in the mid-morning sun watching their horses sporting in the river. It was just warm enough for them to have dipped themselves and washed days of travel from their bodies but too cold to linger in the mountain-fed waters. His mother had been the most fastidious. The experience in the underground tunnel had unnerved her, particularly the fine trickles of earth from its ceiling penetrating her clothes to her skin. She felt she was washing away all the sins of that abysmal place. She had dreamed about it for nights, an experience which also caused her distress, since, in her entire life, dreaming had hardly ever occurred.

-You are troubled, Grandmother?

-I am, child, she replied grimly, -The horrors of the tombs are still with me. Then she told the story once more, as she had done each day, as though trying to talk it out of her mind, -I could see nothing but felt the wet darkness around me, my hand holding on to your belt as you led me, relying on your powers of seeing in such places. Then I was blinded by the sudden lighted room when we burst in on the wife in all her jewellery and silks bought with the flesh of young children. I could have killed her there and then but you restrained me and we shackled her moaning body. Then we went into the next tunnel and the torch we carried lighted up the long grey hairs on tree roots and the small wooden doors that barricaded the tombs. We unbarred each one to reveal mute children too frightened to speak, sure that death had entered their grim world. Their little faces and big eyes stared at us and each had a leg tied to prevent escape. The unclean smell of those holes still fills my nose.

Her granddaughter came close and hugged her and stroked her until the tortured expression on her face began to fade once more.

The world, ruminated the Warrior to himself, is a shameful place. How can it be that, faced with all possibilities, a human being can choose to harm another whether from envy, desire, vengeance or pleasure? We are worse than beasts, he concluded, for they have no choice but to act in accordance with their natures. He was more than ever certain there should be a book of lessons to help people conduct their lives. He had made a start. It would be known as the way of the Right Path and it would not carry his name nor that of any other for it would be a collection of wisdom culled from all he met, as well as his own meditations.

He thought back to their saving of the children and his decision to release the child traders. Should he have allowed his mother's instinct to prevail? Once there would have been no second thoughts. Summary justice must have its day, too. Someone must take the responsibility to kill when there is no alternative. If human beings choose to cause injury and death to others, then they were inviting punishment. His thoughts meandered on. But there must be a difference between killing in the heat of action to prevent the spread of further evil and killing in retribution while the mind is cold and calculating.

He was trying to find new ways of resolving this conflict, new sentences that could be interposed, new ways of coming to judgments. These had been his first awkward steps when he began to inscribe thoughts on parchment. It would be hard because he was aware that there would always be circumstances where one such as he, with his almost invincible power, would find death dancing, involuntarily, at the end of his sword.

Days later they had left the mountains. Now villages and towns seemed less given to their own strange traditions. They were in the prosperous region where the General kept his main residence. The people here wore the same brightly coloured wool tunics and stockings with cross garters, leather and wood sandals and rough canvass hats with woollen ear flaps. As it was early spring, herders were everywhere, driving calves and lambs to market. There was much evidence of the symbol of the bird of the sun in their clothes, on flags and on their buildings. The little they could glean from the villagers was that the General was highly regarded here for hadn't he slain the princes who had persecuted them and grown rich on their backs? The General's tithes did not leave them in poverty.

-It is obviously one thing being the generous lord to those near and dear and another to those of us on the edge of his empire, commented his mother, sourly, -And who has even seen him in recent times? The stories we have heard that he has become a hermit, need testing.

Behind them the mountains had disappeared into a blue-black cloud. A wind was rising and everywhere people had begun preparing for the storm, -We will discover more of the habits of the General by staying in this place among people than pitching camp under our skins, suggested the Warrior. They agreed. Before the rains arrived, the horses were with hay in a travellers' barn, they had stowed their bags and the daughter was preparing a meal. His mother, who regarded herself as the most unobtrusive spy, left them for a few minutes and made her way to the great drinking hall to discover what she could about the General. It was becoming very dark from the blackening sky, the falling light and the heavy rain. The Warrior lay back and slipped into sleep.

They were disturbed by the mother's roan suddenly snorting and stamping and kicking at the sliding door.

-Go! shouted his daughter, as they both leapt to their feet at the warning. With controlled speed the Warrior was armed and running in his brown cloak, thrusting the great door aside. He threw himself out into the lashing rain and ran to the hostelry. His first attempt to burst open the door was met with rigid resistance but he would not be denied. He slid his sword between door and jamb and forced the bar up, entering in the same moment. What he saw brought ice to his heart. His mother was pinned to the log wall with a sword through her stomach. At her feet were three dead soldiers and more were ringing her but wary of the blade she held defiantly above her head. Her eyes caught his and her arm dropped and she sagged. Warnings were shouted and the ring of men began to turn but he had already borne down upon them, slicing limbs and leaving them prostrate. With a brutal tug, he plucked the sword from her, bearing her up on his arm and wheeling to face her assailants. A space had cleared around him. Villagers and soldiers were tumbling through the door and into the rain.

He followed them as they scattered, carrying his limp and unconscious burden to the barn. His daughter was waiting with her medicinal bag open and mosses and herbs spread on silk. The mother's roan came and stood over her, nuzzling and licking her neck. Father and granddaughter worked to staunch the blood and clean the wound. She was utterly white from what she had already lost.

They no sooner had her bound and still with straw and skins warming her when the lips of both roans pulled back and they pranced and reared towards the door. The Warrior unsheathed his sword and slid it ajar, letting them out. In the dim light and cascading water was a small army of the General's soldiers, bows strung, spears and swords ready. He pushed from his mind the shock that this was happening to him, the General's friend, he whom the General had visited many times in his retreat in the wild, seeking counsel, the teacher of the boy novice. Instead, his eyes took in the disciplined rows of soldiers and the cask of oil and the fire being brought. They were going to burn them in their sanctuary!

Successive arrows from his desert bow left the cask rolling in a pool of water, followed quickly by the fire bearers' bodies. There was darkness again and the sound of armoured men slithering backwards in the mud and suddenly screaming as they were caught by the lashing hooves of vengeful beasts.

His daughter, behind him, could see more than he and shouted, -They are preparing more arrows!

-Then I will douse them at source! He slipped through the half-open door in a fast twisting run, his cloak roped at his waist. Ahead their horses were causing more chaos, allowing his shadowy figure to pounce, drawn by wherever there was flame. Moments passed and the discipline emptied from the army and they retreated in disorder and fear, scrambling to get away from the lethal assassin, away from the shadows of buildings where he might lurk, away from the village. The moans of pain, the clumsy falls and the oaths faded until there was left only the noise of pounding rain.

She already had the returned horses ready when he came back, his sword cleared of blood and his anger a little satiated. Picking his mother up like a stook of hay, he mounted his roan and followed his daughter as she led them where only she could discern, deep into the unrelenting darkness.

Safe for the moment and sheltered from the wind in a copse of trees with skins stretched above them and a fire by his mother's side, they ministered to her. Though he had held her so that his arms took most of the jarring of the ride and his roan had chosen the smoothest route, she was much worse. Neither father nor daughter could fashion a future for her in their thoughts but, sitting in the rain, his back to a tree, they could see the reason why. There, motionless, was a gentle-faced, white-haired old man. They recognised what he was. He was her life-taker.

They looked away, as one.
-What do you think? asked the son.
-She has a strong heart but the body does not contain it. The daughter was dipping a straw into a gourd of clear liquid, placing a finger over its end and transferring tiny drop by tiny drop into the mother's mouth, -All the elements are in this elixir that might forestall her last breath. She will not die for the moment. There is a balance in her. If it dips towards death, even then it will take hours.
-If this is so, I can be of more use seeking an answer to why they have attacked us. I will not be gone long.
-Be careful Father, I do not wish to have to tend to two of you.

The soldiers, like them, were sheltering in a wood. They had a circle of sentries around its perimeter facing outwards, wet, disconsolate and fearful. A captain stood under a skin canopy. He was plainly anxious. Knots of soldiers surrounded him, protecting themselves as well as they could from the water dripping heavily from the trees.

None challenged the Warrior as he marched through their ranks. None expected him to be so brazen and the cloak made him indistinct so none saw him for what he was. He ducked his head and stepped under the covering, pressing a finger to the captain's mouth. The man's lips opened and then closed under his hand. Looking round he saw that none of his men were aware of the stranger. It was as if he was alone.

-Sit! whispered the Warrior. They sat on the log stretched between crossed and tied stakes.

-Who gave the order that we must be killed? In his hand the Warrior balanced a knife.

-My commander. Not killed. Captured

-Where is he? The knife twisted in the stranger's fingers like a live thing.

-At the main camp. The captain indicated the direction, -North. Less than an hour's ride.

-Was he acting on orders from the General?

-I do not know. The man appeared to be telling the truth, -The General does not bother himself with the army any more, it is said.

-Tell me what happened in the hostelry.

-We were returning to camp and the rains came so we sheltered in the village where there is welcome drink and warmth. Your mother, though I did not know it immediately for I expected her to be with you and your daughter, entered. At first none took notice of an old woman but then someone saw her sword and laughed. She was asking questions about the General as if she was an assassin seeking his whereabouts. One of my men told her to hold her meddling tongue or he would cut it out. This angered her and she threatened to slit his throat. All could hear this now and everyone laughed. It seemed absurd. The soldier, a big-bellied rough type, stood up and made to hit her with the flat of his sword but his arm met nothing for she was quick. Instead it was she who slapped him. He slashed at her with his blade and I shouted for them to stop but the noise was too great with the cheering of the crowd. It was his last act before her point was driven into his belly. All went still and quiet. None had seen an old woman so skilled. It dawned upon the crowd that this was the Warrior's mother. I ordered her to stay her weapon and two soldiers jumped forward to hold her but she cut them down with a smile, like butchering two lambs. Then, my finest swordsman leapt forward, throwing wine in her face and in the same act had her pinned to the wall with his blade. Again I ordered my men to stop for I had been commanded to take you all alive and she was sorely wounded. That was when you arrived and quickly routed us.

-I could kill you.

-You have already spared my life. The captain gulped, tears in his eyes.

-Tell your commander that I am coming to talk with him. If anyone stands in my way, they will not live.

The captain nodded, then spoke, -You have spared me. In return I should say that I cannot vouch that the commander will accept your terms.

The brown robed Warrior stared at him. Then he nodded and left. No one saw him go.

They each held a hand as the mother drew her last breath. The three horses stood stiff and silent for her leaving of them. Both daughter and her father saw the same image in their sorrowing minds. She was standing, smiling before them with her hands outstretched, holding theirs. That was all. Then a final blackness. They looked to where her life-taker had been waiting for her and saw the last of him dissolve into the rain.

-**Kamil! she cried,** -How could you have done this? It makes me weep! I am reminded dreadfully of the loss of my own mother. She dabbed herself.

He was taken aback but defended himself as well as he could, -In truth, Princess, these are the facts. I may have dressed them to raise the audience's sorrow, it is true, but it is exactly as it happened on the Magus' second great journey. It was an experience that coloured his later years and his teachings.

-I liked, nay loved, the mother. She was wilful like me and cared little for whomsoever spoke against her. Her granddaughter was right. She was a warrior. There is much in her that I would emulate. To be an empress requires guile and tenacity and bravery such as she possessed though, perhaps, a little caution too. You have shown me that more than amply! Come Sabiya, she reprimanded herself out loud, -We shall consider more the meaning of this Tale, later. Kamil, tell me of the High Priestess.

Kamil responded immediately, grateful for this switch in attention, - She would have you know that events have occurred which render her impotent. She has all but lost the battle with the Red Man, one that has been raging but invisible to the mortal eye. She can no longer be of much assistance to the court. She said that whereas before she was able to channel the voices from the depths of the caves so that supplicants could hear the words of the oracle, the Red Man has, through his wizardry, placed a psychic barrier between her and the depths. It happened the day after you visited her and she tried to tear it down but she had to admit failure. The Red Man was too late to prevent her transmit the oracle to you but there will be no more. You must act upon it. It is your salvation. She must recover her strength for, she insists, the final battle cannot be won without her. Her words were strangely prophetic in their nuances. Kamil delivered the news earnestly. He had been impressed by the High Priestess, despite his misgivings.

-You have the words? I cannot remember the detail.

-Yes, your Highness. They are here, together with the little I extracted from the Great Library, yesterday. He described the work, then slid the two pieces of writing towards her. She read on the first sheet:

Find the she-worm and feed his flesh to her as he sleeps the sleep of truth.

and nodded. Yes, it seems more cryptic than ever! Then she read on the second:

In pursuance of such action that might avail thee when malign fate, in the shape of the Red Man, erupts like a pestilence in your court, corrupting its goodly ways, hear this. That which comprises the beast has two heads, one inside the other. Scrape away the outer and the inner becomes as docile as a well fed cow. This is what I have heard, though the weaponry for bringing about such a separation is not within my grasp. Only those charged with the skills of alchemy can sever the two.

-I think this is of the same ilk! Impossible! It fogs me. Let us hope that clarity is at hand when we most need it. She pushed the papers back across the table, -As for me and the second half of my voyage, I kept up my act with the red brute, pretending that he was the most eligible male to have ever crossed my path though I took comfort that Raashid was nearby, even if he would have been powerless before the Red Man's strength and anger.

When we alighted from the barge to the cheers of the crowd, he lifted up the little girl to her waiting parents. Then he offered me his great hair-backed hand and I tripped down the ramp on to the quay like a schoolgirl. As I passed him he whispered in my ear, "It will not be long before you are mine". Oh Kamil, the disgust that wracked me! Yet I played the coquette until the very end and curtseyed before taking Raashid's hand and departing.

Chapter Fifteen

You may lose if you see all but the detail

The card was upside down and Kamil could not understand how this might have occurred. It had happened once before with the kind of consequences for which the tarot was famed. Sabiya remembered immediately, -This is a reversed card, she called out, gleefully, -All is on its head. Does that mean that I now have the upper hand with the Red Man? What is it called? she clucked, not waiting for an answer from the historian and staring at it, -Ah, I see the name. Temperance! What you wished I had more of last time you read it to me. Is that not so, Kamil? Now it speaks of intemperance, eh? Much more my style. She paused and thought, before saying, -I would guess that the card represents the dead mother.

He nodded in agreement, pleased that she had learned some of the basic rules of interpretation, -You are right about the meaning of a reversed card. Sometimes it signifies the opposite meaning to its import when it is upright and sometimes it suggests a blockage in a person's progress. It depends upon the querent. And it can represent the dead mother. You have a skill worth developing, my Princess.

She clapped her hands, -I do, don't I? Read, my spymaster.

He prepared to do so while his mind recalled the details of their conversation during the last half hour and the difficulty he had had in keeping his questioning objective and reasonable in the face of a Princess who was almost giddy in her elation. He also remembered, anxiously, that she had not seemed to hear his strictures on being careful. She was like a lovesick child. It was extremely troubling.

He realized that he was not fitted for what must follow. He had overseen the last rites of his enemies and friends many times and had even managed to find words of sufficient eloquence to satisfy the bereaved that the need for honour and respect had been served. His own preference for the disposal of his body was to be left on a mountain peak for the birds of carrion to feast upon, a desire that had not been shared by his mother. She had scorned it just as she had the notion of being weighted and slipped into the sea. For her, fire was only just permissible but burial was the heart of the family tradition. And now her final resting place was to be in an isolated tomb, far from her village and far from those who loved her.

His daughter sensed his strained feelings towards what they were about to do and took command. They seated her body, her head bowed, on her roan, holding her there from either side and walked slowly to the nearest high ground, a small, exposed cliff of brittle red stone. They laid her along its base and the Warrior took powders from saddle bags and mixed them before working them into a crack in the vertical face just above her prone form.

Whatever she had been before her death was no longer evident no matter how much he reached his mind out to her, -May your spirit go where you have always wished it, he said in a soft, caressing tone, -And may further life spring from your decay.

-Goodbye my Grandmother, whispered his daughter in a breaking voice, bending to straighten the dead woman's hair, so that her tears fell upon the lined face. She and her father looked down upon what seemed too tiny a form for so powerful a woman, dressed as always in a warrior's garb, knife in her belt and sword in her hand.

The fuse was short. He lit it. Then they retreated, pulling the reluctant roan towards its waiting kind, watching the body until the crack of the explosion brought the rock fall from the cliff, leaving a small mound of rubble.

The daughter stripped her grandmother's roan of all its leathers save the strap around its head and ears. She tied a pouch of oiled leather to it, containing a lock of hair and a ring. The son spoke quietly in the beast's ear. It whinnied briefly to its fellows and then cantered towards the setting sun on the long trek back to the valleys.

-I fear she died because of her intemperate anger, he said.

-It was so.

He continued sadly, -She could not purge herself of the feelings she had about the child traders. If she had killed them, there and then, all may have been different. Her emotions would not have besieged her and spilled out in the hostelry. It was her way, an absolute belief in instant justice.

-You are right. She was a warrior. It is fitting.

He said slowly, -My desire to find another way of meting out punishment contributed to her end.

She replied, -The Right Path shows how to live according to virtuous principles. Even so, the consequences cannot be guaranteed.

The absence of the mother affected them as powerfully as if she had still been with them. It was to her son as though a hole in the air had been created where she would have been and this hole accompanied them now on their journey. He and his daughter retired, silently, into the routine of looking after each other and their horses, who showed signs of distress at the absence of their erstwhile companion, particularly the roan. During the following day they spoke little but prepared themselves for their visit to the commander and his garrison. They hunted, ate, rested and saw to their weapons; the Warrior to his sword, knife and bow and his daughter to her belt of many pouches. They took to their sheepskin beds as soon as the sun had left the horizon and, with the fire well banked with short dry logs, they had their first conversation since they buried the mother.

-It is as if she is still with us, said his daughter, -Though there is no sense of her presence that I can muster with my inner eye.

-No, I cannot reach her either. She has gone just as the bough is taken by the axe. But as you say, we can still take pleasure in her life in our ordinary thoughts. He tapped his head, -She is there, yet does not exist in any other way. She is not in a world beyond ours, eating at the table of a god but exists in our memories, only.

-I feel as you do, she responded, -As you know, my tribe's snake god seems to serve them well enough. Perhaps I do not share their faith because your sceptical blood runs through my veins. Or perhaps it is because our leader opened her heart to me before I left. She told me that the shape and the name of the god does not matter, as long as people believe in a supernatural being that will punish their sins and reward their good nature when they come to judgment. She said that belief holds people together and if it is strong and benign it outweighs the differences between them which are the main causes of conflict among tribes.

He nodded, -She is a wise woman and taught me that lesson also, she and my father-not-of-blood, together. He instilled in me a respect for the power of religion to forge bonds between peoples. He grew irritated with me when I questioned his reasoning, saying that I was imprudent and forever unrepentant. He was right to teach me to hold my counsel in the face of people's faith. I struggle with this even now as I try to build the foundations of the Right Path. It must not cast doubt upon their beliefs, thereby inflaming them but augment their religions so that they are guided to live in peace with their neighbours.

-Grandmother was simple in her religion, recalled his daughter.

-She was. She disliked anything that did not conform to the rituals in the valleys. She was bemused on this journey to come across religious practices that were unlike any she had encountered before. In her own land there seem as many gods as there are things in the world, yet the observances of birth, becoming an adult, marriage and death are much the same everywhere, the name and shape of the god that is invoked remaining the only difference. She was cut from the same stone and soil as everyone in the valleys. Suspicious and stubborn. You saw how she took against the General's desire to have all his peoples worship the god of the sun? Her lips curled and her nose wrinkled as though there was a bad smell. She did not need to say it aloud! They laughed.

His mind jumped from memory to memory, his mother at the centre of all of them. He saw her in the egg house with the man to which she might have returned. He saw her at the diseased long house of the clan that wished to live forever and he saw her at the house of skulls in the village where the women were Watchers and cared for their dead. He began to conjure up images of the underground world of the child traders but the face of the Watcher, kept returning, her lips moving as if she was still passing on messages from the departed. Then, with shock and a horrible sense of foreboding, he focused his mind fully so that he could recall the Watcher's words.

His daughter had been observing him closely. She hadn't seen his feelings displayed so clearly. He was normally inscrutable. She saw the sorrow, the amusement, the tender love and the pride walk across his face in turn and then the sudden halt as his eyes widened in surprise, followed quickly by anger.

-I am a traitor! he cried, -I was warned yet I quickly forgot because I had become too arrogant to make myself remember.

-Forgot? she asked, drawing her knees up and gripping them in her arms, alarmed at his outpouring.

-Do you remember we told you about our visit to the village of the Watchers where they keep the skulls of their ancestors in a special temple?

She remembered vaguely the adventure but could not encompass all the details, -Not with great clarity, she was forced to admit.

-I was warned of a great loss.

She stiffened, -Surely they did not foresee the death of your mother? Surely?

He went on sorrowfully, -I fear so, though I did not realise it then or until after the dreadful event. These were the words the Watcher used. I must beware, 'the child, the sleeping man, the mistaken sword and the fire of god'. He stroked his forehead, thinking aloud. The child must have been the boy that I saved from the trader. And the sleeping man? This could only be I, the Warrior, the arrogant son who dozes as his mother ventures into the death trap of the hostelry on her own. The mistaken sword must be hers, the one she held in her hand when she struck out in anger instead of appealing to the reason that would have cautioned her arm. The fire of god rules the land we have entered, land where the General, himself, abides. And it was the self-same religious fire with which the soldiers ignited their arrows in their desire to take us prisoners. All the elements of the warning were there yet I did not see them.

-You were too close to events to see that they were upon you and, to add to your lack of sight, the warning was given some time ago. It is also the case that the prediction did not seem likely to come to pass, she said, soberly, -You were not arrogantly blind but blindfolded by events, she stroked his arm, -None could have loved and protected her as much as you.

He ignored her comforting, -I did not believe in the Watcher because my mind was blinkered. You are right. I had determined that here was yet another strange god-game that human beings played. I was cynical about the Watcher's so-called powers. Yet do I not have visions and see some things that come to pass? Like you? I know not what this power of foresight is with which I am gifted. Some would assume such an occult force must stem from a god or fate but I have always denied it. I am godless. There must be an explanation for it but it is not to be placed at the door of a deity. It is a paradox that I, the disbeliever, am able to do uncanny things which conflict with my scepticism. Whatever the reason, and arrogance seems as likely a cause as any, I did not heed it. I was both deaf and a fool, wrapped up in my meditations on the Right Path. I would have saved her if it had been I who had had the vision and the self-same words of warning had issued from my own lips. I would have remained ever aware of the danger. But because the prophecy came from the mouth of a woman of a clan which was nothing but a fascination to me, another example of the foolishness of humanity's belief in the supernatural and a life hereafter, I took little notice, so sure was I of my superiority over their superstitious ways.

As he was finishing reading, Kamil could see that the Tale had doused some of the heady spiritedness of the Princess. But even though she had become a little more reflective she could not disguise completely the excitement which she had displayed when arriving at his quarters.

-It was as much as they could do, she said, finally.

-Princess?

-To bury her in this way. They could not take the body back with their quarry, the General, so close. The Warrior owes it to his mother to stop the abduction of the young men in her valleys. But why is it that the Magus was unaware that the conditions of the Watcher's prophecy had come to pass.

The historian thought carefully before replying, -Only God is infallible and even the Warrior suffers what all humanity suffers. It is his struggle to understand his own mortality that drives him on his quest for purpose. Kamil had adopted his teacherly air which the Princess recognised immediately and which usually amused her. He was a deeply religious man, and yet remained open minded, even if, as a historian, he might uncover truths that conflicted with his beliefs. She liked this in him, the appeal to evidence whether it fitted his scheme of things or not. Kamil accepted that paradox must occur in the imperfect world of human affairs.

He continued, drawing himself up and striking a pose with an arm outstretched, -Though the Magus was self-avowedly godless, his toil was, in its outcome, as spiritual as any religious prophet. How can anyone believe in the goodness of God and at the same time behave as a base creature without thought, in an act of evil, and still pray at the altar? The Magus offered us a way to live. If we follow his principles then our hearts become purer and more able to witness divine purpose in all things.

She laughed, as much at his pose as at the import of his words, -Poor Warrior, he tries to be an atheist yet he drives people to their gods! He tries to be a man of peace yet he needs his sword to save him. It is true that he is a paradox. She sighed, feigning tiredness, -But I am afraid I must draw this delightful discourse to an end, my most favoured counsellor. I will remember your advice and concerns, do not fear. She smiled, rose and started to leave the room before saying over her shoulder, provocatively, -The next encounter with the Red Man awaits!

*

Kamil felt abandoned it was true, he had to admit it. Despite the flowery flattery as she was leaving he could plainly see the youthful exuberance and almost breathless anticipation in her manner. It had been worse when she had entered his ante-room, her head in the clouds and recounted the following.

After her trip the day before on the river which had apparently caused her so much disgust, she had spent the next morning with her close female retinue, immersing herself in the serious work of making her radiance even more dazzling. In the midst of this happy indulgence a maid brought her a note. She was lying in a thick, creamy bath of skin-rejuvenating extracts from desert plants, perfumed with rose essence when the missive arrived.

She took the folded sheet and called for a knife to cut the seal. When she had first seen it she had had pulled back at the alien symbol on the wax. There was a single head with two profiles, one looking left and the other right. The image was disturbing. What did it tell her about the ogre? Was it his dual nature? she wondered. Good and evil? Yet when had he evidenced good? Catching that falling child? No! She felt sure he had made the child fall with one of his spells. He tried to appear unthreatening but he was plotting the downfall of the Emperor and she should always remember it.

His writing was bold but he had a child's hand. Some of the letters were reversed and one was upside down. All were comprised of simple sticks with no hooks anywhere. The gist of it was; "a beast may change under the spell of perfect beauty - take tea with me in my garden".

She could sense there was some oddness in the paper and ink and on a whim dropped the paper in her bath and crumpled it under the water, watching the inky cloud disperse, then she drew it out into the air again. The words re-formed. She had to repeat this cleansing act three times before she was sure that the message was banished. Meanwhile her heart was pounding and she was experiencing a slight dizziness.

She ordered her maid to take a reply by word of mouth, -Tell the Red Man that the Princess is happy to attend his table for tea at four o'clock. She will bring her own leaf. Thus satisfied that she had progressed with Kamil's strategy of engaging more closely with the ogre she also surmised that she had more than hinted that she did not entirely trust him. Certainly not enough to swallow his potions.

*

She had billowed into the small, internal courtyard, led by a servant and accompanied by her guard who had then retired to the entrance. For some unaccountable reason she had felt strong and purposeful, confident in her task and assured of the impact of her incomparable beauty. But what her eyes had encountered had dissolved her firm intent like a saffron stick suddenly immersed in hot water.

-Good day Princess, had rumbled that unmistakable voice, somewhat clearer and more refined than she had remembered, as the Red Man turned to greet her. He was dressed in long, white flowing cotton with a golden rope tied round his waist and a thick, silver chain adorning his neck. But atop all this refinement what had so unmoored the Princess was the ogre's head. Gone were his beard and his bushy eyebrows and gone were the tangled, dirty locks that had hung to his shoulders. His red hair was short and lustrous, his eyebrows clipped and his northern pale face, smooth and oiled.

He was much younger than she had thought.

Sabiya had been overcome. His eyes burned as before but somehow they seemed less malign and more flattering in their intensity, more like the eyes of a handsome suitor than a crazed madman. She had contrived to sit gracefully, despite the weakness of her legs, -My Lord, she had managed to murmur, -You are much changed.

-For the better I hope, had come the strangely pleasing, rumbling voice.

-Indeed, it is a transformation. You look-

-Human? He had laughed and suddenly she had heard echoes of the old Red Man in his barking. It had steadied her but did not entirely unhook her from him.

They had talked for a while as she sipped her tea, though when it came to telling Kamil about it later the content of their conversation had completely left her head. All she could remember was him suddenly standing over her, bowing, his red hair gloriously reflecting the slanting sun, so large that he seemed to shut out the entire world.

-We must meet again soon, had growled his deep, soft voice.

-I should like that, she had replied, less than hesitantly.

Then he had taken her hand to help her to her feet and brushed the back of her palm with his mouth. She had turned away quickly and joined her guard, almost fainting from the strange sensations engulfing her body. Where his lips had touched, there had been an instant, wondrous, fiery pain which coursed through the rest of her body, leaving her helplessly palpitating while she struggled to her room and she was able to fall upon her bed. She had looked again at the source. There, as plain as any mole, was the outline of his lips on her skin.

*

She had begun her meeting with Kamil by showing him the marks, as evidence of her success in entering the den of the creature, but also, despite herself, aware that somehow she found the pink imprints of lips, enticing.

When Kamil ventured to say that he could see nothing on her skin she was askance and said that he must be able to see it. But when she realised that he was telling the truth she laughed and said that she may have been mistaken and quickly changed the subject, encouraging him to talk about the reversed Temperance card and the latest Tale of the Warrior.

Kamil was not deceived.

Chapter Sixteen

Life is a dream from which there is but one awakening.

To say that he was concerned about Princess Sabiya's safety was an understatement. Kamil suffered as waves of sweat washed over his body leaving him hot and cold in turn. His stomach was heaving with the turmoil he was feeling. There seemed to be very little he could do but wait until he saw her that evening. He had by now scoured every last scrap of information in the Great Library for clues to combating the power of the Red Man. The Princess was trying to lure the monster into a trap they had yet to devise and at the same time the Red Man was doing the same to her.

By way of distraction he decided to walk in the orange orchard in the palace gardens. The sweet smell of ripening fruit might calm him. When he reached it the gardeners had not yet removed the fallen fruit from under the trees. Wasps and beetles and myriads of tiny flies were everywhere gorging themselves, the air thick with the heavy scent of rotting, combined with a constant buzzing and whining. He had to step carefully and walk slowly to avoid angering the more vicious insects. He wished his darling wife was waiting for him on a bench as she once had when they were falling in love but the orchard was empty of humankind. He sat and tested for the Red Man's presence in his thoughts but it seemed the beast was elsewhere in his machinations. Kamil leant back and rested, his eyes closed and almost instantly fell into a dream so lucid he felt as though he had walked through a doorway from one world to another.

He seemed to be outside, in a territory far north of the empire. As far as his eye could see, it was wild, unruly land with no roads or tracks or paths, only hills and rocky outcrops and dark swathes of trees. It seemed as ancient as time itself. Not knowing why, he forced his way through trees and bushes, being scratched and his clothes torn as he went. Then he came into a small clearing in the foliage. Above his head were both sun and moon, unnaturally shining with equal brilliance. Their mirror images were projected in silver and gold on to the centre of a circular table of rock at his feet. Strange markings were carved around its edge. As he watched, two wraiths of smoke seemed to flow down from the heavens, one from the moon, a female djinn and one from the sun, a male djinn. The she had black tresses and was wild, naked and sensuous. The he was red haired and immensely muscular, his body covered in fighting leather. The eyes of the she-djinn sparked and exuded evil while the eyes of the red haired warrior were calm and self-possessed and seemed to have no ill intent. The two landed lightly on the table, unaware that Kamil was watching them.

Then the he spoke, "So, I have come at your bidding, sister mine, what do you wish of me?" He spoke softly and with some affection but received none such in return.

"I have called you to bind our agreement once and for ever; that which was made at our joint birth. You have dominion over the day and I over the night. In the course of each year you will influence the ways of man more at some times and I more at others but our effects shall be equal when the final count is made."

"It was the agreement."

"Yet you break it by upturning the vessels of my influence."

"And you mine."

"Do not stray into my preserves".

"Nor you into mine."

The she-djinn rose into a towering giant of smoke and white flame, "Keep your love of humanity in check, brother and leave me to plant discord and chaos in their midst."

"Or?"

"Or I will prepare myself for our final battle - and I will be the victor! You will be thrown into the pit and reside there forever and only those creatures who can move in darkness will inhabit the land."

Her brother laughed, his red beard shaking with his mirth, "We shall see. You cannot murder me for am I not you? Are we not one?" Then the she-djinn screamed and flew at him and they wrestled in a long coil of gold and silver, reaching to the sky before suddenly vanishing upwards as though sucked by a god's breath.

Kamil found himself awake in the orchard. The gardeners had arrived.

*

He had no time to say anything about his hallucinations to the Princess when she had seated herself for she was almost hysterically troubled and insisted he read to her to calm her. This was now a pattern and, although he wished fervently to know of her plight, he began the next Tale.

The man and his daughter seemed to be the only moving figures on the landscape. Even the sky was grey, unmoving and silent as if it was too heavy for the air to breathe below it. It was as though a day from the depths of winter had strayed into spring, imposing its will. They were travelling towards the garrison, north of the settlement were the mother had been killed. The two were considering what faced them. The captain had been right, the commander had no intention of receiving them peacefully. Lookouts were posted around the entire perimeter of their camp. Archers were in position and horsemen were stationed by their steeds, ready for instant battle. Because the commander was only too aware of the Warrior's exploits and his victories against impossible odds, his own quarters were protected by his elite troops. It seemed that an entire army was waiting for the Magus to arrive.

The roan led them to a watering hole where they had to sieve the brown, sluggish liquid through a perforated pot full of dried leaves. While the horses drank, the two sat and discussed what was about to happen.

-You see the soldiers' camp as I do, she said, referring to the images both were able to cast within their minds, -They have made it impregnable to mortal man.

-I am a mortal man, he said bitterly, thinking of his mother's death.

-It is true. There is a picture of you behind every pair of eyes in the garrison.

He was unwilling to accept what she was thinking even if he had come to much the same conclusion. Neither of them could cast their thoughts forward to see the outcome of the day's events but both had located the weakness in the commander's defensive logic. Finally she spoke, -I am a mortal woman, she said softly, emphasising the last word.

He laid a hand on her shoulder, -I have just lost my mother in this sad train of affairs, I cannot lose you. I fear that such a blow would be more than I could survive.

-Yet, if you are with me, the risk would be greater for both of us. And if we were discovered or I was harmed, the killing spree that would result would be more than you could bear for the rest of your days. There is no other way save leaving the commander unmolested and seeking the General without his help. Yet there is nothing in me to suggest that such a course is the better one.

-Nor me, he said, -It is unfinished business here. My mother's death remains unanswered by acts of mine and the commander holds the knowledge of what has happened to the General. No one else. Is he hidden in a sanctuary to continue his meditations? Is he imprisoned? Is he dead but the commander and his circle of military men pretend his continued life for their own ends? Whatever the reason, they are fearful of our arrival for it upsets their plans.

-All your thoughts are equally possible, she said, -He appears to have retreated from the world for some time and is now just a ghostly presence. She took his hand in a loving gesture, stroking his fingers as though to persuade him, -Father, let us use the advantage we have. They hardly know that I am here. There are few tales abroad of my adventures or my blood connection to you and they did not see me in the battle that took my grandmother from us. If I had been a warrior like you both, it would be different.

He spoke heavily despite knowing what she was about to suggest, - What would you us do? His mind recoiled at the prospect of her inside the garrison on her own, at the mercy of hundreds of brutish soldiers.

-This is my plan, she said and described it to him, -I see it coming to pass.

The lookouts saw the small caravan wending its way up the incline to the camp and were instantly on their guard. Was the great Warrior secreted on board one of the wagons? It was more likely than him arriving on his fabled beast in broad daylight, though they even entertained that possibility. Most felt that he would come in the night like a demon but there was no subterfuge of which the man was incapable. This fear and expectation made the men jittery.

The three wagons were bringing much needed provisions of flour and oil, vegetables and meat and barrels of that soldiers' delight, grain spirit. The carts were attended by an old woman and six local village boys, hardly into manhood. Soldiers searched every one thoroughly, knocking on barrels, looking under sacks and even checking under the floors and around the axles, before waving them in.

They were not allowed to stay more than a few minutes. Their goods were unloaded, immediately. The old woman was paid and they were turned back from whence they came. It was a sharp-eyed guard who raised the alarm. It had come to him as he sat on the bough of a tree, long after the carts had rumbled off down the hill towards the settlement, that there had been no sign of the old woman. He checked with others around him and they scratched their heads and shook them. He ran to the captain with his news.

☥

-We have searched the camp, the captain told a sweating commander, -We cannot find her.

-It could not be the Warrior, disguised? asked his agitated superior.

-No, he is a giant of a man and could not squeeze himself into such a frail frame. Although he appears occult there are no stories of him shape-changing. I saw the old woman briefly. She had little strength and did not help with the unloading. She stood to one side, tapping her stick and grumbling like any old hag, though she was clear enough when she bargained the price.

-Then we know who she is! The commander had gone even paler, - She is the infernal Warrior's daughter. She is among us. Invisible. Search again. Get every man to examine whoever is next to him. Find her! Who knows of her powers?

This second search unnerved the battalion. If they were fearful of the Warrior's arrival before, this was all the greater for the man's daughter was somewhere in their midst, preparing to do his bidding. Men were leaping at their own shadows, trembling at the sounds of twigs breaking, challenging their neighbours and forgetting the basics of their training. A callow youth among them gave way to temptation and levered open a barrel, pouring spirit into his mouth indiscriminately so that it ran down his jaw. Others followed. Barrels were rolled out and transported to secluded places where the captain could not see them and the men drank away their fears.

Soon they became happily at their ease, languid and amicable, clapping each other on the shoulder and joking and laughing. They forgot why they were positioned in these distant parts of the encampment and began to play games and some even started dancing, led by the youth who had opened the first vat.

A little later a monkish figure in a brown robe strolled among them much to their great amusement. The youth seemed to know him and the pair embraced and walked towards the commander's quarters where the two officers had just emerged, suddenly aware of the changes in the noise of the camp. They were standing, staring out through the trees.

-What is happening with the men? asked the commander of his captain, -Is that drunkenness I can hear? Where are my personal guards?

-I do not know, Commander. I will investigate-

The commander's imagination became wild, -Do not trust any of our men. She could be dressed as one of them... and his voice stopped as a young soldier and a giant, brown-cloaked hermit appeared before them.

The commander's hand went instinctively to the handle of his sword but his captain stayed it, -Do not, he said sharply, -The Warrior is beyond any powers we might possess.

-It is true, gasped the commander suddenly aware of his actions, his hand falling limply at his side, -I understand you are here to learn of the whereabouts of the General, Lord of all armies? The two strangers looked at him coldly but did not answer. In a lather of fear, the commander, with his captain aiding him, pulled a table out into the square and arranged four cut tree boles for them to sit. It was a strange sight. Around them, soldiers wandered in and out of the small, flattened square, ignoring them while the assorted quartet sat, two with military emblems on their clothing, one in a finely woven brown hooded cloak and the fourth in a simple soldier's tunic.

The daughter and her father gazed at the commander and saw a tall, thin man in his middle age, with greying temples and quick, cunning eyes. There was no doubting the calculating air and the lines of greed and ambition around his mouth.

-You are fortunate you are not dead, said the Warrior, -Not long ago nothing would have stayed my blade. Your men killed my mother. Even two months ago that would have led to your death and the death of every soldier that attacked us in the town.

-She is dead? That was not my wish, said the commander quickly, swallowing the fast running saliva in his mouth, -My orders were for you to be captured, as my captain told you.

-Your orders led to her death. Whose were they? Yours or the General's? The two pairs of eyes bore into him.

-Mine. I was acting on the General's behalf.

-Where is he?

-A day or two's ride from here. He is ill and must be looked after. We did not think it was wise for you to see him but knew we could only stop you by force. The man attempted to smile, persuasively.

-We?

-The five commanders.

-From what does he suffer?

The commander found it difficult to frame his answer, -Perhaps a form of madness. He is not able to shape his thought and cannot bring himself to make rulings.

-There is more. Tell us. This was spoken by the daughter who was studying the man's eyes.

-That is all I know. Neither the Warrior nor his daughter believed him but they realised it made little difference what they were told. It had become imperative to see the General and for better or worse that was what must happen.

-Then you will take us to him and we will see for ourselves, said the Warrior. The commander stood up in protest but the sword that suddenly appeared in the monk-warrior's hand, stopped him, -Captain, the Warrior continued, -Lead the troops with a greater care for the people of this region than this man has offered them. It is my command on behalf of my old friend, the General. Take this as your guide. He passed over a rectangle of thin reed paper with the first four Rules of the Right Path boldly inscribed in ink. The weight of his command impressed itself fully on the captain.

-I will, said the man, though he took care to avoid the commander's eyes.

538

They set off through the camp, soldiers watching them with beatific expressions on their faces, sometimes shouldering their way through platoons who showed no inclination to stop them. There were many calls of greeting to the commander, as though he was in his village among neighbours rather than in charge of an army. In passing they collected the commander's white horse, its handler grinning from ear to ear as he saddled it and soon they were putting a distance between them and the camp.

-They will make better soldiers if they remain so delirious, said the Warrior, a little humoured by events.

-It will wear off soon and they will not remember the detail, replied his daughter.

-Sorceress! snarled the commander, despite himself.

They travelled the rest of that day with the commander's horse leading, the Warrior next and his daughter at the rear. The roan had wasted no time in becoming acquainted with the white mare. It had laid its head on her neck, whinnying. She had immediately dropped her head in obedience and returned his call. Now, no matter what the commander ordered her to do, she would first seek permission from the Warrior's steed.

Finally, they stopped for the night. They were in a broad leafed wood though the canopy was not yet fully protective. Its leaves were pale and young. Here and there were mature, prickly evergreen trees which afforded better protection once their lowest branches were removed and the brown spiky carpet swept away from under them to provide a comfortable place for their blankets and skins. No one had spoken since they had left the garrison. The Warrior and his daughter made camp under one tree and the commander, reluctantly, with skins they gave him, under another, nearby. While the daughter prepared a fire, the Warrior hunted game. Both knew that this would be a temptation for the commander and were curious to see whether he would try to make his escape. So it proved. As she spread herbs and spices on a square of silk by the fire, he leapt up and with military precision vaulted on to his horse. But the mare reared and snorted and he was all but unseated. He kicked and slapped her but she would not move.

-I would return to your place, the daughter said, -The roan is now her rider. The commander screamed a volley of abuse at her and slid to the ground again. She could see that he wished to attack her but knew that he was fearful not only of her strange powers but of reprisal from her father. The Warrior returned minutes later with three plump birds. He had already drawn them and plucked them, away from the camp, leaving traces hidden. He was fastidious about this. No-one could follow his trail easily. His daughter took the birds, rubbed salt and oil into them, sprinkled a thick coating of hot spice and some herbs over their skins and set them on her father's magical spit above the flames. Her father cleaned his hands on leaves and a little water and while he crouched he studied the commander. The soldier was still bubbling with anger.

-We will eat soon, he said evenly to the man. -My daughter keeps the best kitchen you will ever be lucky enough to encounter.

-Except that of my father, she chuckled. The commander said nothing but lay back on his blanket and waited, his eyes closed. It was only when they were finishing their meal that he spoke.

-They say that you do not believe in the Sun God, Shaman. They say you do not believe in any god. How can this be? Do you worship devils and only pretend to do good to draw gullible people to you? Is your design so deep? Will it be revealed only when the entire world is in your thrall?

The Warrior studied his eyes for a moment or two, -I do not make war on people's beliefs. It is for them to choose. He continued to chew the mix of sharp berries and honey that his daughter had prepared.

-But you yourself, Warrior, the commander repeated, -You do not believe in anything, isn't that so? You are godless! As he said his he threw a handful of dried leaves on to the fire and they spurted into flame with a crackle of tiny explosions, emphasising his remarks.

-I do believe in something, replied the Warrior, firmly, -I believe in virtuous living. I believe in a code of good conduct, a true warrior code such as I gave to your captain. If all followed it, no matter which god they might be beholden to, then there would be greater harmony between peoples. He looked at his daughter who smiled to herself, nodding in agreement. Then he continued, -Gods are for the hearth and the temple, not the battlefield or the courts of princes and judges. No-one should have the right to impose a god upon others. The priests and the shamans may try to persuade but they, too, should not enforce. He stood up and the commander was shaken again at the size of him, -If I too, preach, it is for a better way of living between clans and tribes. It is true that I am godless but I see that people's gods bring them security and contentment if they are chosen by free will. For me, this life is all there is. I do not know from whence I came or to what destination I am bound. My existence seems but the flight of a firefly over a marsh, lighting up a tiny part of earth and air before its flame expires. I do not know whether this life is real or just a dream or whether it is a punishment or a reward. Since I do not know I feel all that I can do is make my presence here worthwhile and that I fulfil my purpose, whatever that might be.

-And what is this code of which you speak? growled the military man, -I hear it is only concerned with unseating princes and sharing their lands between their peoples!

The Warrior laughed, -Only if the princes behave with cruelty and greed. None should fear the Right Path for it is a code to protect both weak and strong, rich and poor, young and old.

The commander grunted, sarcastically, -A nobleman owns what he owns, according to the most ancient laws; land, rivers, crops, animals - and people. Their fate remains always in his hands to be discharged however he wishes.

-And if he visits hunger, thirst, poverty and death on his people, asked the daughter, sharply.

-It is their fate to be born under his rule.

-They did not choose to be born thus!

-Exactly. Suffering or pleasure are written in the blood and no Right Path can alter that. The lands are full of people for whom there is no choice but to live their lives as they find them. A few fortunate ones are born to rule and prosper. Beyond them there are an even smaller few who, through dint of their strength of mind or body, leap the boundary between the two. Such a man am I. I was a boot maker's son who now has the best leathers fashioned for him. He slapped a shin. No-one will take this privilege from me save by force of arms or God's will.

They took to their beds for the night, both Warrior and his daughter able to sleep and, at the same time, keep watch over the commander. They were both aware when he eased silently from his bed, shedding his skins. Their eyes opened and they watched him in the faint light, creep towards the daughter's steed which carried spare arms, taken from the child trader. They saw his hand reach out to grasp a sword and then witnessed the flying rear hooves of the roan connecting with his backside. Amusement shook them as he was lofted into the air by the force of the double blow and deposited winded, back upon his bed. He heard their quiet mirth and, in ignominy, crawled back under his skins.

Mounted and ready for another day's ride, the commander spoke, smoothly, -I swear I will make no further trouble for you before we meet with the General, if this will ease your minds.

The daughter laughed, -You are hardly a trouble to us, commander. Swear what you will. My father and I see every design in your thoughts before they reach your own ears. You are as trapped as a prisoner in a dungeon with iron braced doors and no key. I divine that we are only a day's ride from the General's fortress yet he seems not to be there. She stared at him, waiting for an answer.

-We can only ascertain where he is when we reach there, he replied, - His location is only known to the commander at the fortress. It is through these means we maintain his security.

Father and daughter looked deeply into his eyes and said nothing.

-Thank you Kamil, though I am not sure I heard all of it and one day I may ask you to read it again. The Devil card brings evil to the bosom and now the Warrior and his daughter travel with the commander. I would erase him from my life, I can tell you. I suspect the worst. But your Warrior is made of different flesh and I see his ways can teach us much about how easily we take up our weapons when diplomacy might prevail. Not much has changed in human history since the Magus sought to bring enlightenment to the world. The question lingers; will weapons or diplomacy make any difference in our engagement with our sworn enemy? Let me now tell you my tale, for you saw how distressed I was when I arrived at your rooms.

*

It appeared that at the same time that Kamil entered his reverie in the orange orchard, Princess Sabiya was breakfasting again with her father and the Red Man. If her father found the changes in the Red Man's appearance a surprise, he certainly had not shown it. It was unsettling for her to hear him babbling gaily like a child in front of his new friend, desperate to please him. Where was his famous gravity and authority? Where was the imperious father who stared at all and sundry in that haughty way? Every now and then the Red Man glanced at her with a half-smile, confidentially, as if the pair of them were on intimate terms and her father was the near-stranger. It both stimulated and disgusted her.

The inconsequential mumbling of the Emperor was suddenly broken when something he said made the ogre prick up his ears. It made the Princess's face flush.

-What did you say, my Lord? asked the guest.

Emperor Haidar repeated the sentence he had just uttered, word for word, without hesitation, -I said that Kamil the historian is my daughter's protector and teacher.

-Ah, now I have a name for him! murmured the Red Man, in his most oily fashion, -I sensed there was someone of that nature in the court. I would like to meet him. Academics interest me. So much learning locked in their heads, unable to find a practical consequence. What do you say, Most Beautiful Highness? He turned his handsome, cleansed face towards her with a faint smile, his now white teeth

543

gleaming, his eyes smouldering.

-I will arrange it, she said, after a moment or two. She had just managed to restrain herself from saying that Kamil was not available and that he was away from court, realising that the beast would have seen through the lie and she did not wish to provoke him.

-How has he protected you? asked her inquisitor, innocently. As she paused to frame the least informative answer, her father burst out with his own explanation.

-He uncovered a plot by my last wife and her nephew, Sabiya's half cousin, to take my throne and her inheritance! She calls him her master spy and none know of his role except the two of us and one or two favoured servants in Sabiya's retinue. Her father laughed, -He looks most unprepossessing, just like any well-stuffed librarian. Not remotely a man of action. But, the gods strike me down if I tell a lie, he has the most uncanny mind. He does not stray far from his family and the Great Library yet, in his work place among the shelves and boxes of manuscripts that would bore the hind legs off a donkey such as I, he finds illumination to questions and solutions to puzzles that would defeat an army of military commanders and court advisors.

The Red Man nodded sagely, -I have felt his intelligence abroad. I am looking forward to meeting your master spy, Princess. He laughed and once again it was only within its abrupt tones that she recalled the real person hidden in his new finery.

*

-So you see, Kamil, she said despondently, -I was exposed like an edible crab on its back in the sun by my own father. We have kept your role a secret from the world for all these years and in a few moments the Emperor revealed everything. I feel sick that I have told him so much about you. I was not aware that I had but over time I must have given him crumbs to build the cake even though I thought I was secretive in the extreme.

-Perhaps you were, replied Kamil, a far away expression in his eyes, -I have always sensed you have been close mouthed with your father.

-Then how? she asked, puzzled, -You think my father spies on me?

-Undoubtedly. But not from the usual source. You say he was babbling like a child? Perhaps the Red Man was using him as a puppet and has known about me for some time but not, until now, who I was. He may have felt my presence. He may have encountered my defence against his mental intrusions and known I was in the court from that very fact. He may have put thoughts into your father's mind. By encouraging your father to pour out his knowledge of your relationship with your master spy while you were there, he was setting in train the next phase of his campaign to usurp the throne. All he wanted from it was my name. And for you to know that he now knows.

His Princess shook her head in a mix of admiration for Kamil's cleverness and dismay at the Red Man's cunning.

-All this is enough for me to consider for now, Kamil. I will retire to my solitude and compose myself for the war ahead. I am drawing him to me - but at a cost to my self-esteem. Quickly, tell me of your news, we become waylaid by my distress. Is there anything to offer us a further chink in the ogre's armour? He told her in detail about his dream, even though it hardly seemed consequential now, as was so often the case with dreams but for both of them there lurked within it something valuable that they could not quite grasp. It was to do with how the Red Man was depicted in the hallucination. Why was he so benign? They put it aside in their minds for further reflection.

She stood and raised a hand in departure, -Prepare yourself Kamil. I cannot keep you from him now. I fear that when you meet, even though I trust your resourcefulness more than that of any man, he will overpower you, such is his trickery.

Kamil trembled inside but managed to appear calm, -It will be an honour to do battle face to face with him, for you and the future of the empire, he said bravely and bowed.

Chapter Seventeen

If life is a prison, those who are entranced by the window can become escapees

Later that same evening the court was to welcome seafaring travellers who had arrived the day before from the east. They had sailed in two ships from China, calling at ports in India and the east of Africa before coming north to the empire. It was ten years almost to the day that they had last visited. Sabiya had been a young child but still cared for the gifts that they had bestowed upon her. The most prized item was Walidah, her doll, which her father had bought at the auction. She was, even now, nestling in the pocket of her over-dress. Her hand stroked it for security as she made her way to the banqueting hall. She pushed her way through the heavy drapes of the royal entrance and was immediately deafened by the cacophony of furious dance music, loud laughter and shouted conversations. Below the Emperor's throne where Haidar sat, flushed and slightly drunk, was a pile of gifts. There were rugs, furniture, jewellery, ornate arms, painted screens, fans, embroidered silks, cosmetics and children's playthings.

Further away a table had been erected. On it stood a diminutive, dapper man in a sea-captain's hat and braided white jacket and long black boots, oiled and shining. He was a man of fame, having made many courageous journeys over the oceans and across lands, from his country in the west of the Mediterranean. This journey had seen him cross the great continent from west to east, trading constantly. In China he bought two vessels and crewed them with Chinamen to bring the spoils of trade back to southern Europe and auctions like these.

-Next item Lot 401! The noise decreased. One of the crew, another European, handed up to him a small, heavily gilded table, inlaid with ivory figures, -Emperor Haidar, my lords, ladies and gentlemen, this is a table fit for the most gracious of boudoirs. Can someone start me with a thousand? Princess Sabiya stood in the shadows by the curtains and watched as frenzied bidding drove prices higher and higher.

She was thrown into confusion when a voice by her ear whispered gruffly, -Tell me, most beautiful Princess, what do you desire from these thieves and vagabonds? Again, she was aghast at the Red Man's flouting of protocol. Only the Emperor and herself were allowed to enter from the drapes.

-My Lord, she managed to gasp, hiding her anger with fluttering eyelashes and putting a hand to her mouth, -You startled me! He was dressed in what had now become his uniform, a long white coat and white trousers with gold and silver adornments to his neck and wrists.

-I am glad, he rejoined with an exaggerated smile, -For the flush on your cheeks only enhances your perfection! And may I also congratulate you on your unsurpassed eye for dress? His eyes roved slowly down her body, causing her cheeks to flush even more. She had opted to mark the occasion with a short silk black jacket which boasted a high, gold-embroidered collar and cuffs over a tightly bodiced white dress with fine gold stripes that flared from her waist to her ankles. Her upturned gold slippers completed her decor.

-Thank you, my Lord.

-And in answer to my question? She looked uncertain at the request, forgetting what he had asked, -May I buy something for you in the auction, he persisted, nodding at the bustle and clamour across the hall, -A dress, perhaps?

-Ah, thank you from the depths of my heart, my Lord. She pretended to consider, even though she had made her mind up immediately, -I see they are coming to the jewellery. My father and I were given a preview, a little while ago. Among his treasures, she said, indicating the captain, -There is a gold locket and chain. It is a miracle of the metal worker's art. None in these territories can match such craftsmanship. It is a gift that will accompany me for the rest of my life, always caressing my throat... The locket opens and in it I can place the likeness of -, she paused dramatically, -Whomsoever I please.

-I will not rest until it is adorning your delicate neck, he muttered with a growl of heightened excitement, like that of a predator. Then he left her side to jostle his way through the crowd, though, as soon as they sensed his presence, courtiers and visitors alike drew back.

When the locket came up for sale, the Red Man matched the opening price and glared around the ranks of bidders. At once everything went quiet. The sea captain rested a hand on his hip dramatically and called out, -This is a low bid Ladies and Gentlemen. Low! It is theft. Then his eyes took in the Red Man standing in the space that people had afforded him, -Ah, I see our bidder now! He has cowed you all, -'Tis you with the red hair, is it not? His eyes narrowed, -Have we met, Sir? -No! snapped the ogre, -Never! The sea captain looked as though he was about to say more but swallowed his retort.

He turned away, -Take the man's coins and give him his prize, a bargain among bargains, Ladies and Gentleman. The Red Man has picked my pocket! There was a little covert laughter. So, on to our next item. It is a ring that adorned the finger of nobility in China, a queen's marriage finger...

Moments later the Red Man was at Princess Sabiya's side, clutching the flimsy gold chain with its flat, circular locket in his fur-backed hand. More like the paw of a wild creature, she thought, repulsed yet at the same moment being troubled by the tremors of excitement in the pit of her stomach.

*

-What did you do, asked Kamil agog, peering at her over his little table.

-I let him put it round my neck. It took some time and he does not bathe properly and his man's smell is overpowering. His great fingers could not manage the tiny clasp so I had to guide them and, in truth, fasten the locket myself. Ugh! Every finger has red hair along its back like the great moth caterpillar that used to frighten me as a child.

They had met as usual in the early evening. The fears and anxieties of their last meeting seemed to have subsided and Princess Sabiya appeared to have returned to the same girlish high spirits of recent times. Even in her tones of disgust and exclamations of revulsion, Kamil caught some undercurrents of delight at her escapades, -And Kamil, there is more! She laughed impetuously, -But I do not intend to divulge further secrets until after you have read to me or I will have nothing to offer afterwards and I like your stories to be the stuffing in the vine leaves of our adventures!

-If you wish me to offer a rendition of my day, Princess, it could be summed up in a word – void!

-I am not dismayed, she replied, -I have enough action to recount for two people. Even so, I am sure you practised for the meeting with the

Red Man, knowing your attention to the details of our campaign.

-It is true, Princess. I walked the corridors of the palace and tested my mind against invasion. The closer to the man, the stronger his presence but it is a general power that he has rather than precise and focused. I think he needs to see his victim and study his or her likeness before he can mount a true assault. Kamil looked at her, meaningfully. The Princess was truly vulnerable. And soon he would be, too.

-O Kamil, why does this danger not paralyse me? I feel the opposite. My blood runs fast and I feel ready for the confrontation. Read, read! Let us see how the Magus and his sorceress of a daughter keep the commander in the chains of their magic! Her eyes were flashing and her chin was pushed forward.

After another full day's ride they decided to camp the night within an hour of the General's fortress. Better to approach it fresh and in full daylight, signifying that they were not going to be a threat, than during the evening when soldiers would be returning from their tours of duty, watches were being changed and the guard at the gates tripled because their fear of the unknown would be heightened by the encroaching darkness.

Neither father nor daughter found anything agreeable in the commander's character. Never once did he utter a kind word, being ungracious and selfish in all matters. They had sensed his rising hopes as they drew nearer the fortress and had no doubt that his cunning mind was constantly working on plans to escape and then capture or kill them. Meanwhile he tried to be conciliatory but the deception was plain to the eye, never mind his audience's capacity to read his mind. His mood became darker when they announced their decision to stop for the night.

-The castle is known for its fine food and hospitality, he growled, settling into his skins and blankets.

-It may be, replied the daughter, -But there is something happening there. Some impending event that is difficult to foretell. I cannot read it clearly but I sense that there are large forces, armies moving. The General is not there, of that I am certain. She turned to their prisoner, -Someone loyal to you sent a bird ahead, without orders from the Captain. They were preparing to ambush us but something has changed their plans.

-It is not sinister. The General has taught many bird handlers how to train doves as messengers. They are bred in the castle and return there as sure as water travels down a hill, no matter how many days away we release them. They come and go. He spat in irritation, -This is the

General's land. Everything that moves is known to him. You cannot hide.

-We have never doubted it, murmured the daughter, -But just because we are known to the General's spies does not mean that they have ascendency over us. Nor does it mean that the General is aware of our approach to his home. Nor that you are disobeying his orders.

The man half sat up, -What orders?

-To see that we are unharmed and treated like family guests. He vowed it when he became General of the empire, for much of his success was owing to the advice he was given by my father. They are as close as brothers. She pulled her bedding up to her chin. The commander stared at them both. The Warrior did not appear to have followed the conversation, being deep in thought but the commander guessed that the daughter spoke for both of them and so there was no need.

-It may have been the case, once upon a time, snorted the commander, -But there have been changes, the General is no longer a novice monk. He has no need of a shaman.

-He has visited my father many times. As recently as two years ago. Did you know that commander? Did any of the General's lieutenants?

The commander could not hide his surprise but chose to scoff, -No doubt you were teaching him ways to parcel up land in squares of cloth to be shared among the peasants!

-No, spoke the Warrior at last, -I had not become coined the Right Path when last we talked though there were the green shoots of today's thought.

-Then what did you discuss with him, asked the commander brusquely and to the daughter's angry ear, uncivilly, but her father's untroubled face showed no irritation.

-We discussed how to command his army so that they keep discipline and serve the needs of the people as well as the nobles. He was troubled by the conflicts he was suffering between his desire for meditation and the demands of ruling the empire. I now see that my advice was in vain for it was the mutinous behaviour of your recruiting sergeants that brought us here.

The commander subsided into silence.

They reached the General's fortress the following morning just as the sun began to show on the horizon. They had ridden in the pearl dawn light, the commander in a brisk, almost light-hearted mood, sensing he would be free of his captors soon. Indeed he felt certain that once within the fortress the garrison would overcome the troublesome pair and place them in his custody. Then he would exact a painful revenge! They halted at the spidery path that led up to the General's bastion of impregnability. The road upon which they had been travelling carried on to the east. The father and his daughter stared at the ground. There was a jumble of signs of the recent passage of carts and horses which had descended from the fortress. Some had then turned to the east and some had journeyed straight on to the south.

-A large contingent left the castle, said the Warrior.

-That will not weaken the garrison here, retorted the commander, -It is too great.

The intimidating building was backed into a cliff, the preferred key position for the main defences of the empire. There could be no attack from the rear. The approach to it was steep and narrow with the cliff face on one side and no hiding place or a sheer drop on the other. There were sentry posts at intervals but they appeared empty, much to the anger of their companion as they laboured past them, upwards, -I will speak with my brother commander! This is not acceptable, he snorted.

The stones that had been used to build the castle were cut from the cliff behind it so that the edifice blended into the rocky face. A lowered draw-bridge over a deep cut provided the only access. Everywhere could be heard the sounds of the natural world but amid them there were no human voices.

When they stopped at the drawbridge, expecting a challenge from guards, no sentry cried out to them, -We will enter, said the Warrior and led the way over the wooden boards, their hooves rattling and echoing inside the open gates of the fortress. They walked their horses gingerly into the compound, certain now that no one was there.

The commander's spirits fell as fast as they had risen, -Where are the men? Where is my brother commander? Where are the servants? He raised his voice into a bellow, -Soldiers! Soldiers! but his desperate yells brought no response apart from the shrieking, rising colony of the castle's large black birds. The fortress was devoid of human presence.

A preliminary search of the ground floor showed that the occupants had left in such a hurry that there was still food on the table from the early morning's meal.

-We did not see them when we approached so they must have left before it was light, said the Warrior.

The commander sat and broke some bread and chewed it, saying, -I will make an example of those who have left their posts without their commander's orders.

-It was by his orders that they left, said the daughter softly, -But for what reason I cannot fathom.

-Hah! it is not possible, was all he would say.

-I will go up and search the General's chambers and see what story might be learned there, said the Warrior.

The commander leapt to his feet shouting in righteous anger, -You cannot! It is not allowed! The General's chambers may not be entered by anyone save his servants. He was thrown forcibly back into his chair by a hard, flat blow of the Warrior's sword on his thigh, delivered with such speed that he only knew afterwards who had dealt it. He moaned as pain slowly returned to his numbed leg and he laid his head upon his forearms.

-Blind him as you did the prince if he tries to stand, commanded her father, menacingly. The Warrior set off up the broad stone stair case and followed a trail of ever richer wall tapestries to the General's quarters. The door to them was ornately carved with images of the God of Fire among clouds, birds rising from flames and men bowing and offering gifts. There were two chambers, simply furnished, one a bedroom and another for private audiences with guests. He found no sign of the carved casket nor of the black sword. Impelled by some inner sense, allied to his rudimentary ability to forecast the outline of events, the Warrior moved to the window slit. It was still shuttered from the previous night, which further suggested that the evacuation of the fortress had been sudden and swift. He pressed back the shutters and fastened them. The room faced south west, across the abyss and to the fields through which they had recently ridden. It was only at the limits of his sight could he see a train of animals and people moving south. He could see nothing of the military convey from the fortress. As he stood there, waiting for something he felt certain was about to happen, he caught sight of what might be a scrap of linen falling through the air. As it dropped it took on the shape of a dove and flapped down to the sill of the slit. As he had guessed immediately there was, attached to a leg, a familiar tube of fine, stiff leather. He took it and uncorked one end. Out slid a piece of torn white silk. It bore the familiarity of the General's art of drawing and reminded him of one that he had received when meditating in the wilderness following his first great journey with his father-not-of-blood. In that message the General had been looking down on him in his Spice Merchants' brown robe and there were soldiers with weapons circling him either to protect him or to keep him prisoner, it had not been clear. In this one, a brown robed observer was looking down on the General, casket in hand and round him were the same soldiers! The Warrior picked up the unprotesting bird with its rapidly beating heart and stroked it as he returned to his companions. His daughter took it and caressed it and whispered commands to it. It cooed blissfully in her gentle hands. Meanwhile the Warrior drew in charcoal a sword severing a rope on the reverse of the silk and put it back in the tube, tying it again to the dove's leg. They watched as it took flight, turning direction in mid-air to the east. Both father and daughter willed themselves into the bird's mind, observing through its eyes until the vision faded and the bird was beyond their skill to accompany it.

-Now we know our first two days' journey is into the morning sun, nodded the daughter. The commander had been watching them, aware of their unearthly connection with the messenger for he had seen the General demonstrate just the same gift.

-East! he exclaimed, -The General is at eastern command? Why? It is too close to our enemies on the border. Then he swiftly added, unconvincingly, -I will lead you.

-It is not necessary, replied the Warrior, shrugging, -We know the way. You may remain here or return to your garrison. But you will have no horse, whichever you choose. This will slow you enough to prevent whatever ill you might wish to cause us.

They left him still seated at the long table breaking bread into pieces and then assembling them into small hills.

-I felt corrupted by his presence, said the daughter.

-And I. I sensed little good in him or capacity to change for the better. What should the great Warrior do with such as he? He scowled at his inadequacy.

-Return him to his beginnings, his daughter said sweetly, -Let him make boots for others. Perhaps if his life is long enough, he will learn from his experience. They looked at each quizzically. There was no need for them to voice the thought that the commander was an old dog which could not change its ways.

What had led the occupants to leave so dramatically with not a soul left to guard the fortress? This thought plagued them as they rode, the white mare now easing the burden of their goods and provisions. No matter how much they cast their minds back, no images appeared. It was certainly the case that the people from the fortress had passed this way a few hours before and signs were everywhere that they were trying to make speed, either to escape an enemy or to reach a destination. Even a child could see that.

The Warrior and his daughter had retraced their ride down to the crossroads at the bottom of the crags where the road to the fortress crossed the main east-west route and then continued south. Here was where the soldiers had separated from the rest of the castle's people.

-We will catch them up by midday, said his daughter looking at the signs, -Then we shall see what drove them from their nest. Perhaps it was news that the Warrior and his fearsome witch of a daughter were coming, seeking vengeance for the death of the mother.

-It is as likely a reason as any other, replied her father, -And not so far from the truth, though vengeance takes many forms. It could be that they knew of the General's message to me and decided that an entire army, encamped around the eastern barracks, is needed to protect the General from us, either as their prisoner or for some other reason. At least the bird proves that he has not changed his view of me. Whatever is happening is beyond his control.

The young woman tipped her head in agreement, -I sense we will have the whole story soon enough and it will be little different from our ruminations.

-It's a good Tale and we will return to its meanings but I am too full of my own events for the moment, historian! She pulled back the high collar of her jacket, revealing the gold chain and pendant, rubbing the latter between her thumb and forefinger, -So, to continue my own tale, I had this around my throat and it was as if the beast felt that he now possessed me more than ever. I had to rest my fingers on the hairy back of his proffered hand and be paraded by him to my seat at the banquet. He took no time in telling my father and all and sundry that I was wearing his gold. While we ate, the guest of honour, the noble sea captain, sat on my father's right. I was on his left and the Red Man was next to me on the other side. I intercepted many curious glances from the seaman, towards the ogre. He saw that I did and he raised eyebrows and laid a forefinger across his lips as if to prohibit public talk. I could do little but suffer in silence because the Red Man was paying me frequent attention which I received in the time honoured female way, with smiles and bows as though I found the whole event most agreeable. She laughed, -Luckily, as if offering recompense for his loose-tongued behaviour the day before, my father came to my rescue and insisted that he and I change places so that I could hear of the frightening exploits of the captain, first hand. In truth I think he was desperate for the attention of the Red Man, so besotted is he. So I sat on the chief seat that I must one day occupy and all around me people were nodding admiringly and complimenting me on my beauty. The captain was a worthy companion with the excellent manners of a noble and is capable of delivering a tale so that you feel you are there yourself. He is a Jew from Portugal. He eventually told me many stories that made him seem a little like the Merchant in that he is driven by the desire to trade and make even greater fortunes than those he already possesses. But this was later. As soon as I sat beside him he launched into a warning to me about our red headed intruder.

-He knew of him? asked Kamil.

-More than that. They had met. Kamil nodded, not surprised. Both men had travelled on the trade routes and could easily have crossed paths, -On his first great journey to the east, a decade ago, the captain found himself in Samarkand, that hub of all trades. It is the crossroads of the great routes that run north-south and east-west.

-I know of it, smiled Kamil.

-Of course you do! Pray forgive me. I am sure that the Spice

Merchants in the first book travelled through Samarkand for it has existed since the beginning of time. Anyway, our intrepid captain was busy with barter there when he heard of a monster caught by narrow-eyed Wolfmen from the far north. Curious, he arranged a viewing, for which he had to pay. He found the wild creature in a tent in chains and swears it was our own Red Man or his twin brother. The beast had two bowmen in constant attendance, their arrows dipped with poison and he was trussed between two staves, driven deep into the ground. Frequently the beast was ordered to roar and shake his chains so that visitors could be truly frightened and have stories to tell their friends and families. Some ran from the tent, so effective were these bellows. Not the sea captain. Instead he approached the creature and asked him where he was from, using all the tongues that he had acquired on his journeying. He gleaned a little from his interrogation of both beast and captors. They had found him on a floating island of ice in the middle of a great black lake. He had killed a bear and was eating it raw, stripping the fur with his teeth even though he appeared weak from the many arrows that now lay beside him, bloody. These he had plucked from himself, staunching the blood with handfuls of snow. They boated him to shore and treated him. Stories came to them from traders, passing by, that he suffered from a curious madness which made his moods swing like a pendulum from that of a civilised noble to a fiend. None could predict which of these extremes might face them. By use of his arts of detection, developed over the years in foreign countries where customs are different and confusing, the sea captain soon realised that the chains and the struggling and roaring were all a deception to attract audiences, conjured up by the Red Man himself in order to pay the Wolfmen for their nurture. Once his debt had been discharged they would go their different ways.

-So, it was an act!

-Only so far, I think. Remember the traders' tales of him? He was capable of great savagery. But whether he loses his mind in such acts... She paused and gave a slight convulsion of trepidation, -Anyway, when the sea captain was leaving he discovered something which adds to our knowledge of the beast.

Kamil leant forward because his Princess had that look on her face that he recognised too well, a mixture of teasing and enjoying the attention, -What Princess?

557

-Each night when the display in the tent was finished, the Red Man set off by himself into the wilderness. One such time, a Wolfman, out hunting for night creatures, saw him remove his clothes and dive into the icy waters of a river and swim to a small island at its centre.

-And? asked Kamil.

-When he emerged from the water, the Red Man was transformed. It was a little like your dream, Kamil. He raised himself from the water, a full-bodied woman, with long black hair. The Wolfman ran, shaking in fear. Shape-shifting djinn cause terror everywhere.

-It must be the same creature. There can be no doubt.

-Yes. He is a fearsome threat to us. They sat in silence for a while, until the Princess began to gather herself to go. But she stopped, waving a hand in the air, -I am remiss. The Tale. We have not discussed it! And it is intriguing. The fortress emptied of all save the black birds. I am glad the General is not the evil behind the commanders and their armies. It is always a danger to an empire. My father changes his generals regularly and rewards them with riches so that they have no need to try and usurp him. This general from the western command is a snake. In times gone by the Magus would have cut off his poisonous head.

-It is said in some legends that to do so would sprout a multitude of new ones. Better that he goes back to ignominy and poverty. The General, if he remains the man that the Magus once knew, will ensure he is not reinstated. It is a bitter lesson to all who would do as he did.

Chapter Eighteen

If hope is all you seem to possess then think again before it breaks your will

The daughter of Emperor Haidar once again prepared herself like a butterfly to attract a child, for that was how she now saw the Red Man, at least in his understanding of women. She had him firmly ensnared in her web of feminine ways, so much so that she could read, plainly, the obsession in his eyes. She was dressed in a long green gown with silver and gold threads that made it iridescent whenever the light caught it. Her hair was tied up with emerald headed pins revealing her long neck and the faintest hint of her bosoms bedecked by her new gold chain and pendant. The latter now encased, not an image but something that the Princess's instinct told her might protect her against the ogre's powers. She looked in the mirror that her chamber maid held for her and was almost unnerved by what she saw. Was she being too brazen in her attempts to lure the beast into a trap? But there was also a trembling delight in her body, a wilfulness to see what might ensue because the Red Man had some deep creature power that affected her senses whenever her defences were lowered. It pulled her towards him.

She had agreed to walk with him in the orange orchard, the very same place that Kamil had recently been assailed by his strange dream.

Flanked by her guard and ladies in waiting she walked under the stone arch and into the garden. Unlike during Kamil's visit the paths were crowded with courtiers taking in the sweet smells, acknowledging her beauty with decorous nods and smiles but carefully keeping their distance.

She saw him standing, waiting under an orange tree which had been pruned into a great parasol. He was a full head and shoulders taller than anyone else in the garden, his red hair aflame and his white tunic, brilliant. Yet, despite or because of his majestic appearance, none went near him. She approached demurely and was gratified by her effect upon him. He was almost struck down by the apparition in front of him.

-Princess! Princess! he gabbled in his throaty growl, -You are a

559

Goddess! A star dropped from heaven's firmament! A jewel dislodged from an immortal crown!

She bowed her head slightly, managing a degree of haughtiness, - Thank you my Lord, she laughed and her voice seemed to him to tinkle like exquisite bells or crystal water pouring from a gold vessel into a silver cup. -Shall we begin our promenade?

They walked together, her retinue at a small distance, discreetly out of earshot.

*

Kamil spent the day fretting again. Although it was certainly his idea to have the Princess hold her enemy closer than a friend, it put her in such danger that each hour was an agony for him. He sat in his chair, the tarot cards before him with The Star upmost, though turned face down, ready for the Princess to reveal it to herself. He liked these moments, watching her face register its possible import. In this case the motif was of a beautiful, naked woman, holding an urn in each hand, bent over tranquil water, seemingly pouring liquid from one container to the other. Kamil had always thought of the card as The Star of Hope but was now in deep doubt. There seemed little hope in their present circumstances! But the tarot cards, throughout his rendition of the Tales, seemed to offer connections, some obvious and some allusive, to the events that they were living through. Perhaps The Star of Hope was not at odds with current events. He checked again but the card was not reversed. It signified hope.

*

When the Princess did not arrive for their daily appointment at the prescribed time - and she was rarely late, Kamil called a servant to him.

-Go and talk with the Princess's guard, at her chambers and see if she is there. Find out what has obstructed her passage to my rooms. The young man nodded and raced off. The fact that everything the fellow did, he did at speed and with a desire to please, endeared him to Kamil.

It was not long before the flushed youth reappeared, -Please, Lord, she is indisposed in her chambers, as you thought. She has been thus for several hours.

-What do you mean indisposed?

-In a deep sleep, Lord. She dreams and calls out your name. Beyond that the guard would not say but he said that you can visit her. She had expressly ordered him always to let you come to her unless told otherwise.

Kamil dismissed the youth and prepared himself carefully with everything he might need before setting off along the corridors to the Princess's chambers. He had not been there since their battle to defeat the Emperor's second wife and nephew, nearly three years before.

The giant of a guard was standing as usual outside her door. He remained sternly unmoving at Kamil's approach, -How is she?

The man's face did not flicker, -Sleeping, my Lord Historian.

-I may enter?

-It was her wish.

-Has her father, the Emperor, visited?

-No my Lord. He has gone to watch the Red Man fish.

-Fish? asked Kamil, incredulously.

-Yes, Lord. There was a wager between them that the Red Man could not catch a fish in his bare hands while swimming.

-They are at the river, then?

-Yes Lord, replied the guard, -Outside the city.

Kamil entered. Amidst the fountains, the flowers, the pretty decorated tiles, the gossamer wall hangings, ceiling drapes and gilded furniture, Princess Sabiya lay, waxen-faced upon cushions, covered by a sheet of golden silk. Her eyes were closed but darting this way and that under their lids. Kamil knelt a little distance from her. Even if he reached to the full he would not be able to touch her.

-Princess, he called in as gentle a tone as he could muster, -Princess! But she did not stir. He waited. Then, as though from some other body, her little voice whispered.

He bent forward on to his hands so that he could hear, -Read to me, Kamil. Read. Read. Have you the Tale?

-I have, Your Highness. He laid out the sheaf of papers and the tarot card beside it. Her eyes were still but closed, -It is the Tale called The Star, Princess, he said and as persuasively as possible, -It represents hope!

There was a flat, featureless plain in front of them with no trees or bushes, just tall grasses and bands of lurid green marshland. The track they were following was spongy underfoot which excited the horses and they cantered in high spirits, only contained by the roan's authority. Everywhere there was the murmuring of insects, the fluttering of birds' wings as they hopped and flew from tussock to tussock and the whispering of grasses in the scented spring breeze.

-Do you think the Right Path will one day be so known that it will become a guide to every clan and tribe? she asked.

-What do you see? asked her father.

-It is hard to discern. It seems so but I cannot picture writing. I sense its influence on the behaviour of men and women but I do not see your actual words on parchments or scrolls such are said to be contained in the General's casket and which guide him in all matters.

-I feel as you do, he nodded, -Perhaps because these ideas have been voiced in the air, they then exist and cannot perish but travel ever on, persuading and influencing. It is as I have always hoped. They have a life.

Then, at the same moment both the Warrior and his daughter saw a vision, in absolute clarity in their minds. Something told them that this was a time long in the future. A man, both noble and yet dressed in simple garb, without any desire to hurt even the smallest creature, was meditating under a great tree whose roots seemed to exist mostly in the air and wrapped themselves around it as though cradling and protecting it. He owned nothing and begged for nothing, yet people fed him and sat before him, listening to his sermons. And he was telling them about the Right Path! The Warrior felt a surge of pure love pass between himself and this man, binding the two of them. It was as though this mysterious stranger was travelling back and inhabiting his mind even though he would be dead for generations before the stranger was born. And he could see that the stranger was no ordinary man but a great shaman who had taken the ideas of the Warrior as though they were the work of an infant and shaped them into a glorious, rich tract of endless lessons to challenge the minds of even the most sceptical of men, converting them to this great code of living.

His daughter stared at him, astonished at what they had just shared. As the vision departed she said, -It is proof. It will not be wasted, this purpose of yours.

They saw that there must be bodies on their path long before they came upon them. The birds of death were wheeling in the air and floating down to gorge themselves before, finally, they were forced to rise in slow flapping movements, almost too heavy to fly and shrieking their displeasure at the two riders. Already the fresh carcasses were mutilated beyond recognition, the bones protruding into the air, the skin hanging in torn strips. The Warrior offered his father-not-of-blood's prayer that they might enrich the great cycle of constant renewal then bent over one of them to discover the cause of their deaths. The body belonged to an officer, judging by his garb and his weapons. An arrow had entered his left side and was lodged between his ribs. The white, flecked flights of the missile were unusual in design and he had not seen their like before. Each feather was thin and long and tapered to a point. Further feathers were notched into the side of the long, hard shaft like the fins of fish. He pulled it free and saw that the tip was a sliver of finely crafted iron. It was the arrow of a professional marksman.

Puzzled, his gaze swept the north of the track and then stood and shaded his eyes before striding towards what he had seen. His daughter watched as he grew smaller in the distance until she saw him stop and cast about, nodding his head as though his suppositions had been confirmed.

When he returned and they had mounted their horses again, he delivered his verdict, -One man was responsible for these deaths. He ambushed the convoy. All five are his victims. He will not have gone far for the arrows are too well crafted to be lost to his quiver. I warrant there will be more corpses on our route. His bow is unusual for it kills at a distance beyond any that I have encountered. There may be more assassins like him. We must beware.

-They are from the Eastern Empire?

-If the commander is to be believed. Whoever is taking their lives, it is causing fear and disarray in the convoy for, rather than sending troops to deal with their ambushers they have hurried on, accepting the brutal culling of their ranks.

As they cantered relentlessly on the pair came across many such scenes of carnage. Small groups of bodies lay, the blood only just congealed, abandoned by the moving convoy. The pair kept their eyes turned to the north of the route, for all the arrows had come from that side. Every possible tall clump of grass might hide an ambusher. The roan's ears flicked and cocked as it cast around for danger.

-You think there may be some who still lie in wait, though the convoy is far ahead? she asked.

-I agree it is unlikely but we must maintain vigilance, even so. The only occasion an arrow entered my back was when I assumed that it could not happen and that I was alone. Reading the traces of their presence, I believe that the assassins were glimpsed and the sight of them disturbed the convoy greatly and further disarrayed their senses. There is evidence that they moved in continual arcs to the north of this track, to ambush again and again. They are accomplished mercenaries. There are few unsuccessful arrows in the earth beyond the bodies. I thought at first to catch up with the convoy but now I feel we should lay at a distance until we have ascertained our safety.

She looked at him grimly; here was the great Warrior, his long black tail, his dark, sun-lined face, his hooked nose and his pale grey eyes the same as her own, with his weapons of destruction, now preaching caution. He had developed a self-effacing demeanour, unwilling to ride into the enemy's camp as he might once have done. Had the death of his mother so changed him or had his preoccupation with the Right Path taken hold of his spirit? It certainly wasn't fear, more an unwillingness to cast death's dice for it.

The plateau was ending. They had slowed to a walk to keep their distance from the military train which was now driving dust into the air as it left the marshlands for harder earth. Then the roan stopped still suddenly, its tail swishing fretfully, its ears flattened and its lips bared. The daughter reached a hand and tugged at her father's arm, pointing. At last his eyes caught what she had seen. There, threading its way among the rich grasses across their line of sight, was a figure, almost lost in the shimmering veil of mist rising from the last band of wetland. The Warrior dismounted and removed outer clothing. He stood with his strongly muscled limbs gleaming and taut and then, unarmed save for his throwing knife, he doubled to grass height and loped forward. For some this would have been impossibly strenuous but it was not so with her father. Soon he was just a small bobbing black dot disappearing into the mist.

She lay in the grass and waited for his return, not suffering the least anxiety. She was fortunate, she thought, that she was the daughter of such a man. He was a great warrior, so extraordinary that another like him might not be born to this world for a hundred generations. Their journey together, even despite the terrible loss of her grandmother, was everything she had hoped and wished for, discovering who her father was and growing close to him. Now the bond between them was strong and unshakable. It was a miracle that they seemed to share so much of what they believed and how they saw life. She was born with it, perhaps as a legacy of his blood, while he had learned it through the forge of experience and the wisdom of his father-not-of-blood.

His purpose overlapped with her purpose.

She heard the hissing of grass as he strode through it but no footfalls. He moved like a cat.

She sat up as his shadow fell across her and she looked up. Within the moment of seeing she realised that it wasn't him. It was a wild creature like a night djinn covered in fluttering strips of white cloth and whose face was hidden inside a white hood with slits for its eyes and mouth. It was plunging a sword at her body but her reflexes were those of her father and she rolled so that the point embedded itself in the moist earth beside her neck. Her assailant pulled and thrust again but now she was ready for the battle and with one hand tore the mask away from its face while the other leapt to her belt and a silver tube pouched there. She glimpsed a face as black as a moonless night, the whites of the eyes gone yellow and rheumy and the pupils dilated. On his back was a long bow and on his belt was a quiver of arrows with black stems and white flights flecked with grey.

All this she saw in a moment as he came at her a second time, slicing the air in silvery sweeps of his sword. She bent easily under the arc of his attack and put the tube to her lips and blew. The sword changed direction and swung down to cut her in two but she was not there. The man grunted and lifted it again and then laughed at the irritation of the innocuous, tiny arrow embedded in his cheek, attempting to brush it away before tottering and falling at her feet.

Her father returned minutes later carrying a fluttering white figure over his shoulder. His astonishment at seeing an identical killer lying on the grass before his daughter caused an eruption of laughter from her, -I see I need not have bothered myself with this burden, he exclaimed, you have your own specimen! He dropped the ragged assassin on the ground beside the other. She pulled away the white mask to reveal another black face.

-I have never seen men such as these, she ventured, touching the nearest man's still features.

Her father looked down, -I have met some in circuses for they are great travellers. They come from the south where the sun never gives way to cold but I have never encountered them as mercenaries, though I have heard much about them. These are contract killers and I hear that once they agree who is their quarry and take half payment, nothing will make them desist from their course until they secure the final half. They are much prized by those who can afford their services. I would hazard from the flattened grasses that there may be just the two, preying like wild dogs on the weak stragglers of the herd of military men. From what we have seen they must have taken at least thirty lives.

-They are dressed as night djinn.

-There is method in it. It would take a brave soldier to chase after them for they waken deep dread in all who fear ghosts and ghouls.

The man he had carried there began to waken. As he stirred his eyes opened and he saw, leaning over him the biggest warrior he had ever encountered, pigtailed and harsh-eyed. Beside him stood a beautiful slim young woman as stern in face as the man, -Who are you, she asked but he did not understand her. The Warrior repeated the question in his father-not-of-blood's local tongue. The man replied in a halting, child-like version of that speech.

-Fighter man. From far. He indicated south. -Pay-kill.

-Your Masters?

He pointed east.

-Who do you kill? The Warrior touched his sword for emphasis.

The man touched the ground, -Men here. He turned his head when he heard a sleepy groan and saw his companion for the first time, the arrow still in the man's cheek and a tiny trickle of blood below it. It seemed to make him more fearful.

-How many? the Warrior asked, pointing at them both. The prone man held up two fingers and indicated them both

The Warrior and his daughter walked a little way off and conferred and then returned with their judgment. The father had a sword in his hand now and pressed its point into the man's throat, enough for blood to seep around it.

The man did not flinch, -You kill. My gods wait me.

-What gods?

-Gods take spirit.

The Warrior allowed his preoccupations to take over, -You have seen them? The man did not understand and the Warrior realised that the question was too difficult to communicate. Nor would the answer help them.

She tried, -What do men in the east want? The Warrior translated. A torrent of broken words came from the man, the Warrior understanding only some of it but he was able to piece some sense together.

He muttered to his daughter, -The Lord of the Eastern Empire wants his western lands back. They were taken not long ago by the General's commanders by force. The Lord of those lands was fighting far away on his own eastern borders. Now he has won that war he has come to take back what is his. His armies are near.

This was all that the Warrior needed from the man. He took away the black fighters' weapons, -Go back to your lands, he ordered.

-No, came the reply. -East Lord owe half.

-How much? The man appeared to understand.

He held up ten fingers, -Horses me. Him. He pointed at his companion.

The Warrior went to the white horse and took a bag from it. Inside he located a small purse and from it he rolled two uncut stones into the palm of his hand. He held one up, -Five horses, he said showing the fingers on the other hand. Then he held up the other, -Five horses, he repeated and pointed to the man's sleeping comrade, -Go home now.

There was silence. The sword point had returned to the man's throat. The man thought for a long time, then nodded, -It good, he said.

A little later the Warrior and his daughter reached the end of the marsh and grasses. They now could see the convoy from the garrison in the far distance on rising ground, moving quickly for such a large body of men.

-It is a bad time, he said.

-War leaves everyone a loser, she replied, -The dead, the vanquished and the victorious. The weight of death is a burden for all whether they know it or not.

He looked at her, -You say what is in my mind, he said.

-Is that such a surprise? They laughed soberly. Then she asked, -What should we do now?

-Once, replied the Warrior, -When I was young, I left my valley just as my clan was being attacked by neighbours. I felt it was not my destiny to become involved. I felt no remorse. I was growing to be a Warrior as the tradition demands. All I was concerned about was my fate, my purpose in carrying arms. I see now how much has changed. I have not killed despite the opportunity to blood my weapons on these last stages of our journey. Not since the blind letting of blood at my mother's killing.

He put a hand on her shoulder and looked into her eyes for

confirmation, -It will be the greatest test to bring these armies to a table of bread and wine. A test of the Right Path.

-Be careful Father that you do not become the nut between the teeth of these opposing forces. It is sometimes the fate of the peacemaker.

-It would be a noble death, he replied.

While he was reading the Tale to her, the grey pallor gradually left her dark cheeks and they returned to their warmth and beauty. Her eyes opened and she smiled, -Ah, my old historian, what better sight for my waking eyes? I cannot think of many that would delight me as you do!

Kamil blinked back his tears and waited.

-I heard it all, Kamil. It was like a magic spell calling me back to myself from that dangerous world of fog and ghosts, as dangerous as the assassins in your Tale. Do you know, we employ such killers still. They are in our elite guard. They are from my own country. The best warriors, she whispered, -They would die for me, I know. So where is the hope in this Tale?

-The Warrior finds ways of not killing the two assassins. They are not his enemies. And he believes the Right Path may bring an end to this desire for war that is bent on killing thousands and for what purpose? A strip of land between two empires whose inhabitants care not who their lord or emperor is, as long as they are left to pay fair taxes.

-It is true. I would only wage war to be certain of my throne. But I shall try to rule according to the Right Path. She lay in her half-stupor, thinking for a while and then roused herself and smiled.

-It was terrible, I knew that I was sleeping and had a vague idea that I was here in my rooms but could not wake. My limbs were too heavy and my eyelids were glued shut and I had no knowledge of what brought me here. But the antidote of your reassuring voice and the events of The Star were what I needed to save me or else I would still be in that torpor. It was as if a light was being shone into my empty head and with it came back my memories, both good and bad Kamil. Her voice wavered.

-You do not need to tell me if the effort distresses you, Princess.

-No, it is important. Time is everything in this war. And tonight you are a guest in his quarters for the evening meal! I fear that this is the beginning of his actual move against me. A watershed. Before this it is as if he has been playing with me and preparing the ground. Give me your arm. I am still sluggish. He edged forward to her side, on his knees and offered an arm, his palm turned down so that she could not touch it. She slowly pulled herself up and he pressed cushions into her back for support, then retreated again.

She continued, -We walked together along the avenue of orange trees, Kamil. Curious, don't you think since that is where you had the dream about him? When we started there were people everywhere but such is the power of our foe that they were soon gone and we were alone. It was as though he had wiped them off the path with a cloth! It was both repulsive and attractive at one and the same time. I can see the horror on your face and so it is with me as I hear these words falling from my lips! We began talking about you and he made me agree that you should dine with him, as I have said. Then he reached up into a tree and plucked three oranges. Laughing like a courting youth he began to juggle them in the air like a circus man. Stop me when you wish and you shall have the orange in my right hand, he called. The oranges were spinning and I shouted, excitedly, stop! He held out the orange in his right hand and somehow the others disappeared. As I watched, its skin curled back in strips as if cut by a knife and peeled by an invisible hand. Choose a piece, he said and I pointed at one of the segments and the others fell away, leaving it standing on its own. I took it and ate it Kamil, like Eve in Paradise taking the apple. Kamil, if any food be thought a love potion this was it. A river of burning lust ran through my body, stimulating my limbs. I wanted to consummate my terrible hunger there and then. She stopped, shocked at what she had just said, -Never repeat this to anyone Kamil, not even your wife or on your deathbed! Kamil had gone icy cold with embarrassment and looked away.

-I must continue to the end, she cried, -I do not know how it happened but he drew me behind a tree and placed his hands on my shoulders, on my very skin! But his fingers inadvertently touched my locket and it was as if he was suddenly burnt. Neither he nor I understood it. I was in thrall and desired him more than anything I have ever wanted. But I could see that he believed some sorcery protected me for his face changed momentarily into a female's, hissing and venomous. He screamed for my retinue to come and left me there, dazed. I think I fainted and must have been carried by my guard to these chambers.

-O Princess! Thank God on high that you were not subjected ..., he could not finish the awful sentence but his copious tears spoke for him.

-Calm yourself, Kamil. I am safe and more protected than I could have thought.

-How Princess?

-The locket. I did not place a picture in it. I followed the example of the General in your Tales and put a square of silk there.

-Your Highness? he asked, puzzled.

-I wrote on it the words of the High Priestess's prophecy. Do you remember them, Kamil? She undid the clasp of the locket that lay on her bosom. It flicked open and a small, white square of material floated from it. It revealed the words:

Find the she-worm and feed his flesh to her as he sleeps the sleep of truth.

Chapter Nineteen

Illusion relies upon deception and deception, in its turn, upon gullibility

Be prepared! **Kamil** told himself over and over again. After Princess Sabiya left him he had two hours to make ready for his meal with the Red Man. Heart, mind and body he chided himself. Was that all? No, there was magic too. He must try to be totally protected.

The Red Man was already reaching out towards him for he could feel the brush of the ogre's thoughts on the back of his mind. The beast now had his name and it helped him focus but he had not yet seen him in the flesh. Once that occurred Kamil knew that this vague probing of his thoughts would give way to something more direct and difficult to resist. It would take every sinew of his body, staunchness of his heart and blockade of his mind to survive future onslaughts. And more besides.

Yet, perhaps buoyed up by his Princess's victory over the Red Man's advances, he did not quail at the prospect of the encounter. Instead, he meditated. He brought to his mind a complete silence, blankness and calm. His body relaxed and it was as though he floated above the cushion upon which he sat, in his favoured half-lotus posture.

*

While Kamil withdrew from his senses and thereby erased all emotion from his being, Princess Sabiya lay on her bed as though it was an uneasy, rolling sea. Waves raised and dropped her without pattern or rhythm. Her very soul was being fought over in a conflict between her heart and her mind. Thoughts showered her with all the evil aspects of the ogre, his monstrous history, his occult powers, his hairy touch, his odious lack of sensibility. And his ambition to take the Court as his own.

Yet her heart acted differently. It sent tremors that thrilled her body

573

from finger tip to toe, submerging her in a delightful longing, far more intense and extreme than the untamed and capricious lust of a young creature, just reaching womanhood. It was as though her heart was a bell at the top of a temple borne away in the floods of a black ocean, pealing out melodies of love as well as craving.

*

The first thing that Kamil noticed when the door was opened by a servant, was the faint scent in the room. Kamil had a good nose and recognised some of the elements in it. He was fed with pictures of roots, flowers and herbs, spices and minerals, pounded to a mixed pulp and dried before being added to melted wax and fashioned into a candle. But there was something else. While he was considering, he saw the source, one simple brown candle at the far end of the room on a plain altar beneath the portrait of the Emperor, wreathing it in a pale brown haze. He forgot what had made him suspicious. The Red Man must still be in his bedroom, Kamil conjectured and walked further into the room. There was a square table with a chair at either side and a large bowl of fruit that he did not recognise. Other than that the room was empty with its cream stone walls and white marble floor.

He sat at the table.

*

The next morning found Kamil awaiting the arrival of the Princess. As usual the door swung back revealing the great frame of her guard, filling the opening. He stood aside and a flushed and feverish Princess stepped hesitantly inside.

He started to his feet, -Princess! Are you unwell?

-It is a mild affliction, only. I had a turbulent, nightmarish sleep. I think it was the lasting effects of the drug our enemy gave me. But I could not wait any longer to hear what befell you last night. I could not! she laughed roughly, -After my sleep with the demons of the night I needed to hear your voice of reason and, perhaps, some success in our campaign. She said the last with a little confidence now that she could see that Kamil looked well and untroubled.

Kamil bowed and sat again, -I was delighted at your command that we should meet this morning. I too was concerned about you and the consequences of your meeting with the Red Man. The passing of a full day before seeing you would have caused me too much anxiety. But in truth on my side there is little to report.

-Little? How can you say that? She sat up in shock, -It cannot be, Kamil. Explain!

-Yet true. He was bemused by her startled face and shaking head but tried to ignore it, describing his reaction on entering the ogre's chamber. He finished his story, saying, -I managed to resist trying the strange fruit in case it had some sinister purpose. After a short while, the servant returned to offer the Red Man's apologies but that he had been called away on a whole night's business and would have to postpone our meeting. That ended my visit. I left immediately and came here. Though still early I took to my bed and slept like one dead! I was woken by your messenger and command to be here to receive you.

-Aiyee, Kamil! muttered the Princess, rising unsteadily from her chair, -What has happened? He has moved against us and we are oblivious. I fear it, Kamil, his evil embraces us. She walked in a circle around him as if in a trance.

Kamil was bewildered. It seemed to him that nothing much had happened to change how things had been the night before. Were her fears merely evidence of the fever? He stood up, intending to offer some conciliatory words, following her round the table but unable to find the right moment..

At length she stopped her circling and motioned to him to sit with her again. There was a long silence as he gazed, curious, taking in her plain oatmeal gown and black hair tied in a tail with no adornments. Her face was girlish, reddened by the drug and without any creams or paints. Her eyes were heavy lidded and hardly opened any further as she spoke.

-Kamil, read to me. Fill my thoughts with the adventures of the Magus and his daughter. Fill my heart with the delights of their love for each other and their success against their foes for I am heavy with foreboding. I fear the Red Man may now know what we know and he took this knowledge from our very lips though we were unaware.

-Princess? Kamil shook his head at her wild words, -Fear not, he said gently, -All is not as you see it.

-You are wrong, dear historian. Read! Read! Then, when you have eased my heart of its burden, I will tell you of that which has escaped you. What is the card? She reached forward and turned it over, forcing him to follow her cue, despite himself, -The Moon! How appropriate. It was a full moon last night Kamil, filling my bedroom with its duplicitous glow and under it evil fluttered around my head like a moth seeking entrance. Read!

They camped under an overhang of white, powdery rock, chosen so that none might approach without being discovered. With the roan on guard, the night was their fortress and the heavy cloud wrapped them in invisibility. Though it was cold they built no fire, taking dried meat and fruit. While they ate, swaddled in skins, they discussed their tactics. In strategy, he marvelled, she was more than an equal. Her mind moved quickly down different tracks. She was never satisfied with one answer but piled more and more in front of her like arrows, picking them up, turning them over and testing them to determine which would travel the furthest for the task in hand. Having established a quiver full of ideas she considered for a while and then said, -We can only resolve the conflict between these great armies by separation. You must go one way and I another.

He agreed with more than a pang of concern. Despite the ease with which she had helped bring about the downfall of the commander, first disguised as an old peasant woman and then as a young soldier, he was still afraid for her safety. It was something he would suppress but it was yet another change in him. Once, he would have trusted his invincibility and the seeming way he could bend the path of fate to bring about what he felt was right. He imagined that those who stood at his side like his father-not-of-blood, his mother and the travellers, sages and shamans he had met on his journeys, would be protected by the strange powers that swirled around him like a cloud. But that had been the thinking of a novice. Hadn't he nearly died after being struck by an invisible arrow? Hadn't his mother died while under his vaunted protection? If he had become the Warrior he had projected when leaving his village with his father-not-of-blood on that first great journey, he would not now have had this fear of losing his daughter. It was something he would have to deal with, since bringing about peace between two massive armies must be the outcome even at the cost of both their lives. If they should be successful, with this journey complete and having returned to the valleys, the City in the Mountain and the desert, he would withdraw from the life of the Warrior and gather his families around him and listen to the truths that his children and grandchildren brought him. They had his occult blood pulsing through them and it appeared to bestow gifts, some of which were not part of his own armoury. Just as with his daughter, here. She had been made partly by him and also by a mother he did not know. She carried no weapons but was powerful in many ways. Something in her slim, wild haired beauty, in the cool appraisal of her white-grey eyes distinguished her from all around. She was fearsome despite the charm of her outer form.

Her final plan, once all the others had been shown to have weaknesses over which they would lack control, was one he himself would never have thought of, no matter how much he may have mulled over possibilities. In fact, the truth was that until she accompanied him he had usually acted on instinct, reacting to what was before him. It was his daughter who had used her more refined gift for seeing an outline in the future then, marrying it to practical steps that would take them to her preferred destination.

It was the best strategy but for it to succeed would require father and daughter to be at the height of their powers. And beyond that, events would have to fall in such a way that they did not increase the dangers before them to a point where their efforts would perish, unfulfilled.

As usual she was on her feet before he had raised his head. By the time he had stowed his skins on the spare, white horse, food and water were ready. There was just enough light to see as the clouds had begun to break and the first birds were announcing the day. They ate in silence. All had been decided. When they were done they mounted and rode due east, into the rocky hills. After two hours their paths separated. Overlooking and marking this division was a tree which had been blasted by lightning, yet out of its split bole grew a young sapling. It was an omen. He turned north and she continued east towards the army of the Lord of the Eastern Empire. They touched fingertips once and smiled lovingly and then turned their backs on one another.

The track was not churned up or rutted. That would be her father's discomfort as he followed the army from the garrison. Few had passed this way in numbers so she could just discern the narrow outline of its direction among grasses and bushes as she travelled. Her horse was an obedient, sturdy creature but had none of the wiles of the roan and so she had to be vigilant always. They would each reach the opposing armies at much the same time, as night fell. While her father sought a way to the General, she must insinuate herself into the presence of the Lord of the Eastern Empire.

It seemed to her that she had two possible tactics. She could allow herself to be captured by guards and hope to persuade them to take her to their lord or she could seek, through subterfuge and sorcery, to present herself as if out of thin air, to his lordship. The problem with the former was that the more lowly the soldier, the less imagination and the greater the likelihood that he would seek to detain her for his own pleasures. She was aware of the power her female attraction seemed to have over men and often tried to subdue it but something in her nature captivated them. It both entertained and alarmed her. If she chose the latter course then her sudden appearance might be seen as the work of a witch and they might still try to kill her.

Her father had no such dilemma. He was dressed in his brown cloak, shimmering and floating in the sun, he was fully armed and he allowed the roan to pick its way slowly along a little trail used by sheepherders. He had left the route that the garrison had taken and was aiming to circle to find a vantage point over the army of the General before deciding on his next steps. He would not make any move until he had discovered where the General was secreted, whether it be from his own volition or from the insubordination of his commanders.

He met a group of five children, aged around six or seven years, wandering down the path towards him. On seeing him they clambered swiftly on to a large boulder, rocks in their hands and small knives waving in the air.

-Go away, child trader! called one, -Or we will kill you! The others joined in chanting that he should go away.

-I am no child trader.

There was no spokesman and so their voices fell upon him in a babble, -Keep away, whatever you are. What is that brown cloak? You carry weapons like a warrior. Are you the General's man or do you obey the Lord of the Eastern Empire? Our fathers will hunt you if you try to touch us!

-I will do you no harm. He drew the white mare alongside and pulled open a leather buckle, -I offer you a gift of peace if you will let me pass peacefully. He spoke as though he was talking to the armed guard of the General himself and the children puffed up their little chests and looked round, nodding to each other. Their arms dropped to their sides but they held on to their weapons. In his hand he revealed a drinking horn which would hold enough liquid for five thirsty mouths. Into it he poured a powder and then water. He pressed the stopper back in place and then shook the horn vigorously.

-Is that poison? asked a child.

-My mother said we should not take gifts from travellers, said another.

The Warrior pulled out the stopper and drank a little, -See, it is safe. He smacked his lips, -A taste you will never have tried, all the way from the far east, beyond the Lord's lands. It is like all the sweetest fruits mixed into one. It makes your mouth tingle with delight and little bubbles break on your tongue so you laugh and smile whether you want to or not! See, is there anyone who will try it? My wager is that you will not be able to keep a stern face such as you now are showing me once you try a little of my concoction. He took another sip, -Be quick now or I shall have it all to myself.

A girl among them, a little older and the headman's child, spoke up shrilly, -You cannot make me smile with such a brew unless it is wizardry!

-It is not. On my heart. He clapped a hand to his breast and leant forward and put the stoppered horn on a ledge on the boulder's face below them, making the roan retreat a little. The girl climbed down and then scampered back to the others. She drew the wooden stopper and allowed a couple of drops on to her tongue. Immediately she convulsed in shock and then laughter as the mixture frothed in her mouth. She only managed to take one more gulp before it was wrenched from her by the others. The horn passed quickly between them until it was finished and they were sitting, blissfully at peace on the rock.

-Have you more, warrior? called one.

-Perhaps. But I won my wager! Return the horn. One of them threw it to him and he caught it by swivelling in the saddle and bending low, -Now are you going to let me go?

The girl spoke, -You can go after we have asked you some questions. The group stood up in a line like they had seen their clan elders do when interrogating a thief.

-Ask, replied the Warrior, his face serious and attentive.

-Where are you going?

-To see the General.

-Do you wish to kill him?

-He is my friend. No.

-That is sad, said the girl, -Once he was the tribe's friend. No more. His soldiers do not follow the laws he set down. He should be killed.

-He is a coward, said another, -He hides behind thick walls and never comes to us as he once did. Our fathers will pay you to kill him.

The Warrior shook his head, -I come in peace and to stop the great war between the General and the forces from the east.

-On your own? The older girl laughed, -There are more men than grass stalks in our valley. It will be the greatest battle ever seen. The elders say that it will take a hundred years for the dead to be replaced. It is not the work of one man. Even the great Warrior would find it a task beyond him to tame such armies. He stared at her and drew her gaze deep into his mind. She threw her hands up and clapped them, her mouth forming a perfect circle and her eyes bright with excitement, -It is him! I know it. Look, the brown robe, the weapons! He has come here for the General. It is the Warrior! The children whooped and danced, as one. They had all heard tales by the fireside of this man's exploits and how he was not favoured by the princes and clan chiefs who treated their people badly. He was the hero of their dreams and he was here! They dropped from the boulder and he slipped from the roan. There was much touching of hearts and finger tips during which he was able to ask them about what lay before him. The girl proved resourceful and intelligent. With the help of the others she drew a map in the sand of the way ahead. Two mountainous ridges, then on the last great arm before the hills dropped away to the central plains and lands of the eastern lord, was the redoubt of the General, his most eastern fort. Her father had said that thousands of men had been marching there for weeks in preparation for the great battle. They had taken conscripts from every village leaving only the elderly, women and children.

-My father and brothers are there, she said sadly, -They have to fight and are not trained. They will die because the army of the eastern lord is like no other. Its men are born with a knife in each hand, my father told me and they cut their way out of their mothers' bodies, ready to fight. Please make them release our fathers and brothers, she said, her voice pleading, young and vulnerable again.

He took some more powder and twisted it up in a dried, resinous leaf, tying it tight, -Take this and mix a little with water. It will bring you happy dreams. I will try to do as you wish.

Almost at the same time his daughter caught up with an old woman and her donkey, carrying a great bundle of firewood so that it could hardly be seen beneath its burden. The old peasant stopped and screwed her eyes up at the graceful young female, perched above her on her broad-chested mount. She was too old to be frightened. She had seen so much in her life.

-What are you, she asked, much as the children had done of her father, -Witch? Djinn? You are a noble woman of a kind, I can see.

-Just a traveller, replied the daughter, -I am seeking the Lord of the Eastern Empire. I have business with him.

The old woman chortled quietly, -You have, have you? You will not get to within an hour's ride of him before you are cut down like a reed. The men of the east take no prisoners and allow no ambassadors. They know their borders and guard them with the force of wild dogs though they are trained in obedience to their lord. See, I am taking them wood. It will be paid for and I will not see one soldier, only a man who barters for them on the edge of their lands. The General was a fool to steal earth that was not his. It will be our dark destiny if the Lord of the East decides to double his empire.

The daughter nodded and gave the old woman some salt before cantering away from her.

It was hard going. The herder's path was slow and wound its way up and down the steep inclines of the sharp pointed hills. Frequently he had to dismount and take the lead rope of the white horse, following the roan by grasping its tail. The sun had reached full strength and then waned as he came to the second ridge. As he reached a high point he saw the eastern most fort of the General, stuck like a tiny block on the steepest and highest land, two hours ride away. Not far from it was the convoy from the garrison. His path would keep him clear of the main trails though he had no doubt that soon it would be guarded. Night would have fallen by the time he reached the fortress. He watered the horses and rested, chewing more dried meat and fruit, trying to visualise what he would have to do. He had already a half-lit picture in his mind of the defences of the fortress. To reach the castle, itself he would have to penetrate lines of soldiers camped in the shelter of rocks or positioned behind wooden defences of angled, sharp pointed staves. Already he could see the pillars of smoke from the fires along the General's battle front. It was almost comforting to picture what was before him. He had no fear. Moving at night through the outer defences would prove simple. He would stay in the shadows and alert no-one. He did not want a hue and cry before he reached the General. And beyond that he did not want to kill anyone, even the worst offender among the soldiers.

She could see the first of the outlying forces, spread out in a large arc across the plain. Smoke from fires was rising in the evening air. Birds were wheeling above looking for the remnants of the meals. She could go no further until it became dark. If she was to find herself inside the rings of heavily armed soldiers and ready to enter the tent of the lord then darkness would be a necessary friend. She rested and ate just as her father had done.

When the light had faded to a deep grey she resumed her journey, now dressed so that none would be in any doubt that she was the daughter of a noble family. She wore a long ankle-length, black silk hooded coat over wide white trousers, black sandals with thick, hard wooden soles and she had added a jet jewel pin to hold her hair up in a twisted bun. Her earrings were white, cloudy spheres, clasped in silver. She sat side-saddle and demurely approached the first lookout post, a square wooden hut with straw for the roof.

The solitary soldier stared at her as though he was seeing a ghost. It was not possible for such a woman to be travelling alone unless she was a witch or a djinn; And at night! He raised his bow, peering at her in the gloom. She stopped and pursed her lips in a kiss. The bow lowered, raised and then lowered again. The man turned as if to tell his comrades around the fire inside, but stopped, a smile on his lips.

-I see you are a sweet girl from a rich family, he said in his peasant's broken tongue.

She inclined her head and smiled.

-Are you looking to lie with a brave soldier? he asked, his bow wavering in his fingers.

-Only with the Lord of the Eastern Empire, she replied, -I hear he is brave. And he is expecting me. Will you slow my path to him or let me pass? Her eyes and his became fixed on each other, -I think you will let me pass, she whispered, -Let me pass. Her voice was soft and insistent and he began to nod, his bow unstrung, -Remember me not, she said, -Good soldier! The man stood there long after she had cantered on, staring into the darkness with a smile on his face but not knowing what had caused it. The next post was a further hour along the trail. Again there was a hut and a guard of several soldiers. Again, only one stood beside the track. This time he called to his comrades and now six men stood before her. They held a torch up to her to see her more clearly.

-What is the purpose of your journey? asked their leader, courteously. All of them carried swords and the lone guard, a bow.

-I am travelling to meet with the Lord of the Eastern Empire.

The man laughed, -You are either brave or mad, he said, -I see from your clothes that you are from the west. My Lord will kill you and eat you! The other men laughed, -Anyway, we cannot let you pass or it will be us he eats. Again there was laughter. Again the men began to look at her with desire in their eyes. They had been here in the wild land between the two great armies for too long, far away from their women, -Why don't you join us by the fire in our post? She smiled and dropped lightly to the ground, entering the hut before they did, hearing their heavy breaths behind her and the lust in their grunting. With a sweep of her arm she showered the fire with crumbled leaves that flashed and sparked and whined and gave off a thick white smoke. Across her mouth and nose she had pressed a cloth soaked in a clear, sticky sap from a tree that draws water from even a desert's soil. As she breathed, it caught the white fog before it entered her, turning it into a grey glue that perfectly outlined her lips and nostrils on the fabric. The men were staggering and fast becoming helpless. Soon they were sprawled by the fire, subdued like farm dogs before their master, in charge of their minds but not their bodies.

-How far until I reach your lord, she asked.

-Another hour, witch, said the leader.

She thought for a moment and then said, -I need you to be my messenger.

-Hah! I cannot move.

-I have a potion to loosen your limbs.

He tried to smile but his face would not obey him, -Give it to me then!

-Hear my order, first. Listen carefully, you must go to your Lord and tell him that the daughter of the Warrior is come to meet with him. She wishes to save his life and that of every soldier in his army. She knows this for she is a seer even more powerful than her father, the Warrior, the greatest fighting man who has ever lived. Tell him that she will appear in his tent before the night is done with its darkness. Tell him that she is more beautiful than an ordinary man like yourself could ever describe. Now, repeat to me what I have said. The man responded with a word for word rendition of what she had just told him, with a look of surprise in his eyes for he could not stop himself saying it. -Good! Now, in a few moments you will gain control of your limbs and ride to your lord. She took a paste from a small pot that had been hidden in a pocket and spread it on his lips. And then was gone.

From her hiding place not far from the post she saw him stagger unsteadily out and climb on to a horse, spurring it down the trail to the east. A little later, she followed.

Her father, shrouded by the night and his hooded brown cloak, was making his way through the encampment of boisterous men. They were eating and drinking, full of false bravery, aware that no battle was likely for several days. No one looked at him twice for he was more shadow than flesh and blood and he walked purposefully, like a high ranking military man, so nothing about him courted curiosity.

The General's soldiers occupied much of the tilted plain below the fortress with thousands of men and their horses carefully deployed in a series of arcs, facing towards their enemy from the east. The Warrior made his way up the gentle slope towards the iron studded gates. Entry for all but horses, carts and carriages was through a small wooden door, set into the wall at one side. On either edge of the final approach were torches. Guards were standing between them, examining every individual that wished to enter and everyone who wished to leave. The Warrior noted that each visitor carried as a right of entry, a red disc when they entered and a yellow disc when they exited. In a half-hidden corner behind a kitchen tent he watched the soldiers come and go with their discs held above their heads as they passed the sentries. He slipped between tents, moving away from the fortress's entrance to see where the soldiers were collecting their discs. He found it quickly enough, a rough table with a senior officer sitting at it, a pile of red and yellow tokens before him. Soldiers, messengers and the occasional citizen arrived, discussed their business, showed seals and other means of identification, visitors leaving their weapons in a nearby tent and continued on foot up to the doors.

The Warrior could have stormed the entrance and fought his way to the rooms of the General but that would have endangered the tactics that he had conceived with his daughter. He had to be less a Warrior and more a shaman so that the two aspects of their carefully thought out plan came to fruition at the right moment. He took off all his weapons save his throwing knife which he had holstered in a boot and hid them under the edge of the tent. Positioning himself in a deep shadow, he waited until a large, bulky soldier picked up his red disc. Craning his ears he caught enough of the conversation between the man and the officer to be of use and then hung back until the soldier walked past him. Moments later the man was lying bound and gagged, asleep. The Warrior had secreted his brown cloak in his belt and now forced his way into the man's leather and metal helmet and the iron plaited shoulder harness that could deflect the slicing blows of a sword. He hung the man's blade and knife on his belt and thus complete strode commandingly up towards the sentries holding a red disc above his head.

-Rank? asked the officer in charge, dressed much as the Warrior was.

-Sergeant, he replied.

-Your business?

-To bring the latest positions of the enemy to the attention of the fiv ... four commanders. The Warrior hoped his deliberate slip-up made him more authentic.

-Yes, four! snorted the officer, -We now know that the Warrior paid a visit to the fifth. Our missing comrade is presumed dead. His garrison is here. The Warrior may not be far behind, God help us. The enemy's armies are threat enough without this half-man, half-djinn seeking we know not what.

-The Warrior is so powerful? asked the heavily built sergeant.

-I would not wish to face him with a hundred men at my side, replied the officer, stepping back, -On your way. The sergeant smiled thinly and was soon through the small door, set into the wall.

He was in a vaulted chamber that could take several carts in a line, side by side. Stables, store rooms and barracks led off it. Men were moving to and fro, carrying weapons, equipment, carcasses, bread, spirits and fruit. Another officer sat beside a table with yellow and red discs in piles before him. The Warrior dropped his red disc and picked up a yellow one, nodded to the man and then followed a boy into the kitchens and soon had balanced a board on his head upon which he had laid bread, fruit, dried meat and a jug of fermented apple.

-Where are you going with that? shouted a cook over the noise, -Can you manage it? It's the work of two men. His eyes were streaming from the onions and peppers he was dicing. The Warrior grunted and pointed upwards with his forefinger.

-The commanders, eh? You better take this leg, that offal is for the men. The cook removed the joints of fatty meat from the board and replaced them with a large, freshly roasted shoulder of pig. If they like it tell them Isaak cooked it. If they complain, tell them nothing! The big soldier nodded and set off across the entrance hall to the stairs. They led up to a wide, stone-flagged chamber, built on top of the barrel roof of the entrance hall, with double doors at the centre and other doors at regular intervals down each side. Guards stood by the double doors and one single door. The two by the double doors looked at him curiously. He balanced the board with one hand and showed his disc with the other.

-Cook got a new helper? sneered one of them. Sweating in the kitchens was the least privileged work in any castle.

-Doubling up, snapped the Warrior, -Captain's orders. I've news of the enemy positions. Captain said I should bring food at the same time.

-Bloody captain. Changes orders all the time. The fellow rapped on one of the doors with his fist, listened closely and then nodded and opened it. The Warrior entered and heard the door shut behind him, his eyes recording everything in the room. No-one looked up. There were four men in rich armour seated at a table, a knot of captains standing a little way off. A rough map, inked on to skin was stretched out before the commanders. They were arguing about whether to attack or wait for the enemy to make the first move. The Warrior stood obediently by the table until one glanced up and then pulled the map to one side.

-Good, food, I am hungry, he grunted. Small expressions of expectation flitted across his fellow officers' faces, already reaching for the jug and bread on the board, -You can go down and eat with the men, the chief commander called sharply to the captains and they trooped out as the Warrior took his time unloading the board so that all four commanders could stretch for everything without rising. He heard the door close heavily and stood straight.

-That'll be all, said the chief commander and waved a hand of dismissal, again without looking. The Warrior left the room, pausing with the two guards once the door was fastened shut.

-Greedy aren't they? he grinned.

-Nothing but the best for them. What was your news about the enemy?

-They've horsemen gathering to the north and south, on their right and left flanks and only a platoon or two in the middle. Looks like they are going to try to draw us out and then cut us off. He made a pincer movement with his thumb and forefinger. -Pity the General isn't in charge. He would know how to win this war.

-Sshh! the man put a finger to his lips, -Don't you care for your head? His name is not to be mentioned. Where have you been?

-Doing real soldiering, he glared back, -Scouting. Fighting. Weeks of it. Anyway, that's what I think and they can discipline me for it if they want, he added, snorting.

-Well, you should know better than to open your mouth or you won't stay a sergeant for much longer. His voice became a whisper, - The General does not exist now as far as those four are concerned even though everyone knows he is kept a prisoner in there. He nodded across to the door where the other two soldiers stood guard, -But whether he knows his own mind still, only the commanders could tell you. No-one else is allowed to enter.

-I wish him well, grunted the big sergeant and set off back down the stairs.

His daughter's eyes followed the officer from the lookout post as he jumped from his sweating horse, leaving it with a groom, and made his way hurriedly to the biggest tent in the encampment. It had the most ornamental canvas, covered with brightly painted scenes of war. Wondering as to her next move, the daughter saw something that made up her mind for her. From the back of the Lord's pavilion, a small flap opened and she saw that the officer that she had followed was being bundled away by guards. It appeared that they were protecting him for they looked around constantly and he seemed at ease. They took him to a small, unadorned circular tent among many of the same size and shape. He waited a moment while requests were made and then was taken inside.

The daughter tightened her lips, hid herself in her dark coat and hood and floated easily from shadow to shadow. Unlike the big ceremonial pavilion this was standard military battle equipment, erected for four or five soldiers. She saw that it was a clever ruse. Assassins would be attracted to the big, colourful royal construction while the lord played at foot soldier. However, it was guarded by a dozen men standing stiffly, facing outwards, swords unsheathed, helmeted in flat metal rings that had been wired together in a bowl shape to cover the head and ears and then fastened under their chins. Armour plates were fixed to shoulders, elbows and knees. The guards carried shields of iron spiked wood. She had no doubt that these were the eastern lord's elite troops. She observed them for a while. Their eyes moved constantly. Everywhere immediately around the tent was lit by torches. The lord had well-established security. Finally, the officer she had sent as messenger left the tent. Soldiers parted to let him through and then reformed.

A little while later a dark-skinned man with a small white round hat without a brim and wearing a long white tunic, stepped into the torchlight. The flames lit up his gold earrings and bangles. He was tall and slim and carried himself just as she thought a lord of such an empire, should.

He stopped behind his guards and ordered them in a voice that carried unquestionable authority, -Sheath your swords! As one they did so. The Lord of the Eastern Empire called out, his eyes on her hiding place, -Daughter of the Warrior, come inside. It is cold! His gaze followed her as she left the shadows and walked towards him, becoming transfixed when he saw her face, her silk clothing and her straight backed, graceful walk.

The men parted for a moment as she followed him into the tent.

Her father had adopted an unusual strategy. Instead of trying to avoid being seen he did the opposite. He managed, within a short time, to have passed greetings and a few words with most of the more senior soldiers in and just outside the fortress. Whenever he talked to someone, others saw him conversing and thus everyone assumed that he was a trusted soldier and had important business in there. Indeed, already his exploits as a spy behind the enemy lines had grown to legendary proportions. He made sure he came and went several times through the small door at the entrance, exchanging red discs for yellow and vice versa. By now the guards felt they knew him and they exchanged pleasantries instead of questioning or searching him. Later, when all but the guards on watch were asleep, he mounted the stairs. There were no soldiers at the double doors as the commanders were in their beds now. Only the guards at the General's door remained. The two men were sleepy but perked up when they saw him. He carried a jug of spirit and some sweet biscuits. They laughed and clapped him on the shoulder before eating and drinking. It had been too easy. One of the first things he had learned from his father-not-of-blood was to make a sleeping potion. It was by a similar drug that he had once released a wild cat from captivity. Like his daughter, he always carried some with him, though she had an entire belt of powders to make concoctions for this and other purposes. The men stood, leaning against the wall on either side of the door, their eyes open but their rigid bodies fast asleep. He searched them but neither had the key. He set off stealthily for the chambers of the four commanders. A short while later the Warrior returned, None of the commanders had woken before he had administered cloth soaked with potions to their faces. He now carried a small ornate box and a black sword, as well as a collection of keys. He did not take long to find the right one from the many that he had stolen.

He walked into the General's room, locking the door behind him, his eyes taking in everything in a moment. It was within minutes of his daughter entering the tent of the Lord of the Eastern Empire.

Princess Sabiya stared at him, -You do not mean to tell me that that is the end of the Tale!

-Princess, he protested, I –

-The other Tales all end as they should. They are complete. Here you have left me hanging in the air at the end like Scheherazade tantalising the sultan. Each of them, father and daughter, are at the point of utmost danger, hoping to change events, prevent a war. And you ... stop! Just like that. It is neither fair nor acceptable.

-I am sorry Princess, said Kamil meekly, -It is a storyteller's trickery to keep up the interest of the reader. The Moon -

She shook her head impatiently, -No! Now I hate the Moon. I cannot allow it to dominate me for a whole day. What is the next card? He pushed the pile towards her and she turned it over, -Be praised, it is the Sun! she exclaimed on twisting its face to the light, -We have the morning. Read it to me, my faithful writer. Drive away the deceits of the Moon and bring me the glories that bask beneath the Sun.

Kamil smiled to himself and continued straightway to read the next Tale.

The Lord of the Eastern Empire was an intelligent and cultivated man in his fortieth year. While able to wage war with speed and devastating power when the occasion merited it he preferred the life of the court, cultivating the arts. But the balladeers and musicians, the jewellers and painters, the architects and philosophers were far away to the east and here he was in a nondescript tent about to engage in a second war within one year. The lands on the eastern borders of his empire were now in subjection. Perhaps once he had routed this western general in the coming battle then the all the territories would be at peace again but it would be a bloody and terrible affair. Never had two such armies faced each other, not even among the warring gods.

Then, out of nowhere, he had had a report from the lieutenant of the one of the furthest watch-posts. He had brought surprising news. The daughter of the famed Warrior was about to materialise in the middle of his camped troops. He knew nothing of her but if she had some of the powers of her father then she would be a redoubtable foe - or a worthy friend. She had humiliated but not actually harmed any of his men and her desire to meet with him in this way did not suggest the strategy of an enemy. In truth, if she had intended to take his life it was likely she would have done it already and his body would have come to light long after she had vanished into fire smoke like her father had often done, though more recent accounts of his exploits did not portray him as quite the assassin he once was.

Once he had digested the messenger's news he sent him away to be fed and watered and then removed his helmet and armour and changed into court clothes. He washed, brushed his short black hair and long moustaches and put on a cap. It took minutes only but inside he felt the preferred character of the courtier taking over from that of the soldier.

When he was ready he stepped outside and ordered his men to stand at ease. Then he called out in her tongue, -Daughter of the Warrior, come inside. It is cold! Instinctively he looked where he thought she was and saw her emerge from the shadows. Something burst inside him, a sense of a future that he had long held suppressed. As her image imprinted itself on his mind and everything about it made him tingle with a delightful sense of awakening, he turned and re-entered his tent trying not to show his anxiety that she might not follow.

He gestured to cushions and they sat, facing each other. Her beauty to his eye was greater than any that had been brought to, or voluntarily visited, his court. The pale eyes that watched him from that warm-skinned, oval face, her bearing and the laughter lines at the edge of her soft, full lips, mesmerised him. And yet all these feminine traits were somehow contained within an invisible cage of strength and purpose that made her as worrying as she was beautiful.

-Welcome, daughter of the Warrior. My camp is at your disposal.

-Thank you my Lord.

-Yet you are only safe for a short time. My men have orders to save me from djinn and witches! I have insisted that they kill any woman who seems to have seduced my brain. He smiled, amused, -And I fear that this order cannot be undone for what would be the point of that in ensuring my safety? Here I am in the middle of preparations for a war that could result in the deaths of thousands, a hundred days journey from my court and you appear out of the thin air. It does not look good! How could I make them believe that I am not the victim of a sorceress?

She liked his voice. It mixed experience with a childish impatience for adventure, a soldier's toughness with something much more cultured, -I will not be long in your tent.

-That would be even more distressing, he smiled, -I could wish for you to be much longer at my side.

-What will come to pass will soon be our history, she replied cryptically, -Let us make decisions.

-Decisions?

-Yes, decisions that will change the lives of clans and tribes. Change the course of this war. She looked at him and her pale grey eyes seemed luminous and large, tugging him into her inner world. She continued, whispering low and urgently, -We have met, as we both knew must happen and now you must trust me, the witch who has captured your senses!

He knew that she was not using sorcery to command him for his mind was clear and able to observe the emotions that flooded through his heart and limbs. He accepted it. Suddenly the life he had lived until now seemed a game, a way of filling time until something meaningful entered it. His love of the arts was a way of making ready for this moment, tuning his sensibilities, opening his awareness of what was possible.

-I will do anything you wish, he said, -Even should you command me to abdicate from my empire.

The man lying on a litter looked nothing like his old friend, the General. He was emaciated and his eyes were rolling behind their lids. His wrists and ankles were tied to the wooden frame of the bed and he wore just a rough sacking gown. His finger nails and toe nails had not been cut and so were long and hooked and his hair was wild and unbrushed. A small fire stayed the cold. With his knife the Warrior freed the man, rubbed ointment into the places where the rope had chafed it raw and dripped water into his mouth. The General coughed and spat but he managed to swallow some of the liquid but as yet his eyes did not open. Then the Warrior placed the black sword across the General's breast, clamping its haft into one of his hands. He took the casket and laid it beside the General's head and put one hand on the poor fellow's forehead and the other on the flat, wooden box with its intricate carvings. Almost at once the General's eyes stopped rolling and the twitches and jerks left his body. If the sword had become alive in the man's hand or the man's hand had become alive at the touch of the sword, the Warrior could not tell but as he watched, the thin, wasted arm of the General seemed to gain strength and muscle. Yet still he did not wake.

Pursing his lips, the Warrior took the sword and hooked it into his own belt. The flat casket he slipped against his chest, under his coat. He cloaked himself in the long brown silk of his hooded habit so that his face could not be seen. Then he unlocked the door, picking up the sleeping General in his arms and made his way across the chamber to the stairs.

The guards outside the Lord of the Eastern empire's battle tent at last decided to take the law into their own hands. Hadn't their Lord told them that they must allow only a short time to pass before enquiring as to his health? Wasn't this a short time? They felt uncomfortable. The Lord had invited a beauty into his tent. But where had she come from? Was she what he had warned them against? They did not want to stumble across his passion, if that was what was now in full spate. Listening close they could hear nothing inside. Finally their captain coughed loudly. There was no response, -My Lord? he called. Then, even louder, -My Lord! Nothing issued from its interior. He tugged at a little of the tent fastening and peered inside. It was empty!

Within moments he had raised the alarm and soldiers were waking, grabbing weapons and hurrying to their stations. This was the most orderly army ever trained and assembled by an emperor. The lord's most trusted commander stood above his officers and barked out orders. They had to stop the witch in her flight with her captive. She would be going to the west to deliver their lord to the opposing forces. But take care, not a hair on their lord's head must be harmed.

Two servants came across the great figure of a hooded monk walking down the stone stairs, causing them fear and alarm. He was massively built and a brown cloak wavered around him. In his arms he carried a burden but they could not determine what it was for it was hidden beneath the folds of cloth. They feared he had taken human prey and was a phantom or a life-taker. They wished to consort with neither and ran to their rooms.

The Warrior opened the small door beside the fortress's main entrance. Outside, everything was quiet save for the distant snores and rustlings as men and horses turned or moved in their sleep. The guards on either side stared at him as he came out into the torchlight, -Who goes there? one of them asked in a quavering voice.

-The Warrior, said the monk's deep voice, -Back to your posts if you value your lives. The men stiffened straight and turned their gazes away like well trained soldiers should. They had heard all the stories. They knew that the Warrior had sworn that he would come for the General and would kill an entire army if it stood in his way. How many throats had he slit already to enter the fortress? If that bulky shape under his cloak was the General then they would say nothing for the Warrior had the power of a djinn and would return to their midst and they would succumb to his savagery. Anyway, the General was no longer in charge. He was mad or worse. The commanders would thank them for letting the Warrior take him away to die.

There was no-one to cross his path as the Warrior made his way back to where he had left his weapons. He removed the soldier's armour and, feeling lighter and more agile, swung the General over his shoulders. Something was stirring in the man because he was able to clutch his hands around the Warrior's neck. Moving like his daughter from shadow to shadow, the Warrior and the General eased silently and secretively through the camp of sleeping men. When, after a long, furtive trek they had slipped by the last outpost of guards, the Warrior whistled. The roan appeared almost instantly, trailed by the white mare. He sat the General on the mare's saddle, tying his feet but some instinct for riding had entered the sleeping man's mind and he balanced himself clumsily, his head bent forward at a drunken angle.

It was in this fashion that the two riders made their escape into the grey of the morning.

Under the lightning-blasted tree, in a safe haven between rocks, the Warrior tended to the General. The sleeper was warmly wrapped in skins and beside him was a small fire with sticks so dry that they gave little smoke though they crackled noisily. The Warrior was spooning a rich soup into the man's mouth which he swallowed, seemingly without any problem. He must be close to a return to consciousness thought the Warrior for all the signs were that, despite his condition, something in the General knew what was happening to him and the rebellion in his body had been mastered enough to aid the Warrior in their escape.

As soon as he was fed and had fallen into what seemed an even deeper sleep, the Warrior climbed up to the tree. He watched the trail by which they had come. Below him the roan showed signs of excitement. Then, a tiny smudge in the dawn gloom came into view, becoming larger with the passing moments. Finally he could make out the shape of his daughter, riding in front of a man. The Warrior knew who he must be for this was yet another enactment of the plan they had devised to halt this calamitous war. But there was something in the way that the stranger held his daughter before him that caused a shiver of apprehension to pass through the Warrior's body.

As her horse halted, the Warrior pulled her down and embraced her. The Lord of the Eastern Empire dropped to the ground beside them. He looked the Warrior in the eye and bowed, his hand on heart. The Warrior did the same.

The four commanders ordered their army to battle readiness as soon as dawn broke. The Warrior, for it could have been no other, had come and taken the General from under their noses. They should have killed the General as they had often discussed. Now, he may have woken and their insurrection could be exposed. They must first win this war and then deal with the Warrior.

Their men were not as well drilled as the enemy. It would take several hours before they could be deployed for the conflict. The huge encampment, spread as far as the eyes could see, was noisy and chaotic with men running this way and that, horses being pulled in spite of their rearing and bucking, carts trapped in soft sand and weapons clashing on metal as soldiers suddenly began practising for a battle they had thought was still some time away.

The most esteemed commander of the Lord of the Eastern Empire's army called his captains together. Since their lord was missing, presumed to be abducted by the witch daughter of the Warrior, it was likely he must have been taken to the fortress above the plain. They would move the army forward first and then barter for his release. He gave his orders and the men and horses and carts began to move in tight formations up the inclined plain towards the ridge with its fortress.

Later in the day, with a sun beginning to force its way through cloud, the two armies were close enough to make out the faces of opposing soldiers. It was a terrifying sight for both, the numbers were so great and the fear of death was everywhere. Soldiers on one side prayed to the god of the sun and on the other side to the god of war. Bows were notched, swords were in hand and horsemen were sitting still on their champing mounts. Both the commanders from the west and the most esteemed commander from the east knew that this would be a battle that would leave their armies in ruin. But honour was all. Neither could withdraw. Nothing could prevent it now. Life-takers would be massing to lead the dead to the next world.

It was then that it happened. It was as if the two armies had taken a half step towards each other, all sense of individual goodness suppressed by a desperate kill-or-be-killed obsession. It was the moment that the Warrior became famed beyond the borders of even the two great empires. The eyes of all the soldiers in the massed hordes became aware of a man on a horse galloping at speed between the front ranks of the opposing forces. He was dropping small bags tied to each other by lengths of string in a line behind him. When he had done his horse reared to a halt in a cloud of dust. He leapt from it and set a flame to a taper affixed to the nearest bag and then mounted and galloped a distance away, wheeling to watch. There was the sound of an enormous thunder crack and smoke billowed in the air. Even the orderly troops from the east fell back in fear. Horses were rearing on both sides. They saw flame run like the wind, down to the next bag and another clap rent the air but already the flame was coursing onwards. Bag after bag exploded and by now the two armies were cowed and utterly fearful. As if fulfilling the exacting demands of a history, already written, four riders appeared out of the dwindling smoke in the middle of no-man's land, creating a silent tableau. Stretching away from them in a perfect line were a number of craters in the ground. The silence from the facing masses was sudden, bred of their confusion. Who was the frail, skin and bone creature on the big white mare, the idolised horse that belonged to that jumped-up general from the garrison west of here? And was that not the Lord of the Eastern Empire, hugging a woman to his chest? And their hearts shook when they saw the third rider who had laid the thunder from hell. He was the great Warrior on his fabled roan. The weak, thin General turned to the west and raised his arms wide to his armies. The Lord of the Eastern Empire turned to the east and raised his arms wide to his armies. Each, simultaneously, drew their swords and dropped them to the ground. Instantly, this signal given and understood, the two armies sheathed their weapons, the horse soldiers dismounted and the bowmen replaced their arrows in their quivers.

The Warrior raised an arm and there was a sudden deep cheer, taken up by more and more men until the plain and the battlements rang with the tumult of relief.

-Ah Kamil, you see I knew the Tales would revive my purpose! I had become all but resigned to the Red Man being victorious over our puny efforts to resist him. It was his drug that made me languish so but your Tales are the antidote yet again, and it has left my body. I am myself once more. Like the General I am able to see the world again, though in better condition! It was true, the fever was gone and back on her face was that familiar haughtiness and determined jut of the jaw. She was ready to return to battle.

-Isn't it always so that the moon and the sun are opposites yet must be taken together? Just as in your Tales, each is an unfinished story that needs the other to complete it. The sun is all honesty and hope while the moon is all fever and despair. The sun is what we know of ourselves and the moon is what we don't know. One is the good in us and the other is what might be if we do not control our instincts. In these two is the lesson that you have been teaching me through your readings. Better to wait and watch, plan and employ tactics than to rush in, imagining your instinct will prevail. That is what the great Magus learned, too. Never believe that events are final for something that you had never imagined can overthrow even your worst enemy's seeming power over you. She laughed, pleased with herself and full of vigour at her return to health, -Now your Tales are almost joined to the one thing that the world remembers of this man. He, almost single-handedly, brought peace to the greatest empires of that time and without shedding a drop of blood, though in the fables he is supposed to bring thunder and lightning upon the earth and not gunpowder. Is that historian's licence or a matter of research? Kamil smiled and said nothing. She gazed at him, almost maternally, before saying, -Is it time that I should tell you what you do not know?

Kamil narrowed his eyes, suddenly disturbed, certain that the tone in her voice presaged something awful and threatening. He blurted out, - What happened to you last night, Princess, that has changed everything so?

She laughed, a little triumphantly, -Me? No Kamil, not me. What happened to you? While I suffered those nightmares it was you who bore the brunt of the Red Man's invasion.

-But Princess, he did not appear, I told you... but he was stopped by her raised, flat palm.

-Kamil, know you this, I always have someone watching over you. I would never allow it otherwise, you are so dear to me. My spymaster. My historian. I owe you so much.

-Thank you, Princess, he bowed, confused and emotional. She was rarely so direct about their friendship.

-Enough! Listen! My spy had orders to do nothing but wait outside the Red Man's chambers for you to come out. You were inside for three hours! And the Red Man was there, too. I have the proof. He must have drugged you. Perhaps with that little brown candle. Then he had all the time he needed to rob your mind of we know not what. She drifted into silence and then looked up suddenly, -Yet I have an idea, Kamil. A possible answer to our plight, if her sorcery be strong enough.

Kamil hardly heard her. The shock of discovering that he had been the unsuspecting victim of the Red Man's pillaging of his mind had blotted out everything.

Chapter Twenty

Reflect upon yourself before others do and there will be less despair at their judgment

Kamil had tossed and turned through the night. He had woken several times, strange imaginings plaguing his brain. It seemed that his room was infested with the grim odours of the Red Man and that the ogre's shadow passed back and forth across his half-seeing eyes as he tried to make sense of his sleeping chamber. The knowledge that he had been held captive for three hours without knowing it was so disturbing he could not erase it from his mind. What had the Red Man discovered? Certainly he was now aware of Kamil's role in the Princess's campaign against him. Occasionally, Kamil had heard the sounds of the two guards outside his room, positioned there on Princess Sabiya's insistence. They both knew that if the Red Man so desired he could enter the room without them being aware and Kamil might be found with his throat slit and no-one would have seen his assassin come and go. But having the two men there at least ensured that, if the terrible crime was executed, people would know that a malevolent sorcerer must have committed it. And that could only mean the Red Man. It might even be enough to persuade the Emperor Haidar that their guest was plotting against his blood line.

Finally he woke up properly. Dawn was about to arrive, the first bird was shrieking a long, single note over and over, as much a warning as a welcome to the day. He sent off a servant to bring him fruit and milk and dressed slowly. When the food arrived he sat at the little table, the tarot cards on one side and began drawing. It was something he had instructed the Princess to do, once before. She had drawn a picture of the court in the form of a map with colours showing enemies and alliances. Kamil made do with a newly sharpened quill. As he chewed pieces of coconut and fresh figs and sipped the cream off the warm, frothing milk, he recalled pertinent facts about the Red Man that he and the Princess had gleaned, one way or another. The Red Man had a mysterious twin sister and they still did not know if she might turn out to be a danger or an aid to them. The words remained clear in his memory:

On your awakening, brother, know that I am still here. Our next sleep will be the sleep of death. I fear for us, brother.

It was confusing because had not the Red Man turned into a woman when swimming to the island? Had he assumed the shape of his sister or had she taken over his body? The explanation was beyond immediate reasoning.

The Red Man returned every hundred years but, as the Princess had wisely asked, why? Did he return because this was his fate throughout existence or had he not yet found what he was bound to look for? In his many visits to the land of the living he appeared to have gathered the powers of a malevolent shaman. His mind entered others and forced them to act, sometimes against the very essence of their characters. He used potent drugs to bring about mass hysteria. He had superhuman physical powers and could withstand extremes of heat and cold, fight armies or crazed beasts with his bare hands or change his own nature from wild man to courtier, almost seducing the stubborn and wary Princess on the way. There was no doubt that he entertained little compassion for his enemies since his history was one of chaos, death and destruction. Kamil guessed that this was the consequence of him not finding what he was searching for, the childish anger at being frustrated spilling into a frenzy of hate. Whatever the ogre sought, Kamil's ploy to have the Princess apparently offer herself willingly to him, seemed to have worked. The creature's desire for her must be closely entwined with whatever secret purpose drove him. History showed that it might not be the royal court itself which was the likely focus of his interest but something within it. He resolved to go back to the library and scrutinise again the texts he had gathered if only to rid himself of the gnawing suspicion that he had missed something obvious and important.

The two guards fell in behind him as he began the walk down the corridors. It was still early and he moved slowly, deep in thought, his head down when he was startled by a wizened figure gesticulating in his face. He recognised her immediately though they had never met. She was the deaf mute, Khawlah, the Princess's long-lived servant.

With a strong claw-like grip she began pulling him in the direction of her mistress's chambers. He needed no tugging for he was already rushing with her, panting from the exertion, the two guards protecting him at the rear.

The door was open revealing a room in broken pieces. At its centre, among the upturned shards of marble basins and fountain jets, lay the Princess's guard, blood spreading from his neck, his body almost bent double, his hands palm upwards as though trying to ward off an attacker. Behind his hands his face was contorted into a grimace of such fear that Kamil's heart nearly seized. He shouted to the two guards to bring the elite soldiers of the Emperor. With the deaf mute making strangulated wails that barely broke the silence, Kamil searched the room for a clue as to where Princess Sabiya had been taken, though he was certain as to the cause of her disappearance. Within moments he had the locket with its broken chain in one hand and had lifted a cream silk pillow with the other. There were shivers running down his sweating body as, beneath the pillow, he found her doll and, under its skirt, the little slate with the message from the Red Man's twin. He looked around for a last time and saw, among the tiny containers of creams and powders before her mirror, the tiny, stoppered ceramic pot, stolen by the fat cook.

*

A little later and the full, frightening picture had made itself clear to Kamil. He had returned to his rooms and sat in his chair as though expecting his Princess to enter and sit before him. Not only Princess Sabiya but the Emperor himself, was missing! It seemed he had been taken during the early hours like his daughter, while his guards had had their throats torn out as if by a ferocious beast and there were signs of further frenzied madness in the royal chamber. Nothing remained intact.

He was roused from his despairing meditation when a soldier ran in through his open door with the news that the Red Man's rooms were abandoned and empty. No-one had seen him leave and there were no reports of him on any of the roads out of the city.

Rouse yourself and act, Kamil told himself as the man had departed, you are the only person in the court who has even the faintest chance of influencing fate at this time. Everything would be in chaos. Already there would be those who would see this as an opportunity to plot against the royal blood-line. The Emperor's brother would act as regent but he was much older and preferred his hookah and the scent of flowers in the gardens to the hurly burly of the court. He, Kamil, would be overlooked because few knew that he was the Princess's secret weapon, her spymaster, her confidant. It would take too long to persuade her uncle that his voice should be heard. He had only one ally and that was Raashid, Princess Sabiya's life-long friend. He sent a servant to fetch him and while he waited he cut the full tarot pack and turned over the card that was uppermost in the bottom half of the split. He had focused on one question. Why had the Red Man taken the Princess and her father at this time? Why now? It must have something to do with what the Red Man had learnt from him while he was under his spell for those three hours. He, Kamil, must have divulged something that had precipitated the Red Man's actions. Something that made him need to take the Emperor a prisoner, too. The card was the Ace of Swords. Kamil nodded to himself. The card gave hope. It was the card of decisiveness. And it was Kamil who might bring resolution to the events that had erupted but the way was perilous, even more so for a man who was unused to action.

He was interrupted by the arrival of Raashid. The man looked dark eyed and weary, his fulsome night with a young woman of the court being interrupted by the clamour of the early morning lamenting and the need to help the regent gain control over the purposeless charging to and fro of courtiers, servants and guards. But above the bags his eyes glittered with anger and the desire for instant revenge.

Quickly, Kamil sketched in those parts of the history of their conflict with the Red Man of which Raashid knew nothing. He spoke assertively and with authority so that the young man found himself accepting his leadership without question as Kamil moved on to what he felt they must do, -See that the army is ringed around the city and all the roads guarded!

-I will do it.

-Let us hope he has not fled beyond our grasp.

-If he has both the Emperor and Sabiya it would be difficult even with his strength and evil stealth. I think not.

-The river?

-I will have the landing stages guarded.

-Good, said Kamil, -Now, if they are in the palace, where are they? It was at this moment that he felt a slight brushing of that familiar incursion into his thoughts. If he had been talking he would have missed it. The moment he sensed it, it withdrew instantly.

-He is in the palace! Kamil exclaimed, leaping up, -I sensed him. I know it!

-A flea will not escape our search, every room and corridor, from the highest to the lowest. Unless there is some secret chamber of which only the Emperor is aware... I will keep the search raging until they are found. Kamil clapped him on the shoulder and nodded. Raashid made for the door.

-Do not fail us, called Kamil as Raashid left.

*

The historian sat back and allowed his mind to enter inner darkness. There were no signs of intrusion from the Red Man as he returned to his reflections and deliberations on what he might have revealed to the beast which had caused him to panic, for the signs of wanton destruction in the royal quarters suggested terrible anger or fear. He could think of nothing. Finally, when there seemed no way forward, his memory recovered his last conversation with the Princess. By not concentrating on what she had said, somehow her words came back to him, alive and clear, as though he was hearing her for the first time! "Yet I have an idea, Kamil. A possible answer to our plight, if her sorcery be strong enough".

It caused a sick shudder. When he had been interrogating his mind to deduce what he might have told the ogre, he had assumed he must be able to recall something that was significant enough to cause the beast to act so decisively, something that truly threatened the Red Man. He had sifted through everything he knew about the invader, the entire history of what he had teased from the Library, from tales along the trade routes and from Princess Sabiya's discoveries at close quarters. But his rational memory was not the place where the vital clue had been lurking! Instead it was in a hidden retreat in his thoughts, waiting for its door to be opened. Until this moment he had not been able to recall what she had told him during their parting the evening before.

But, under the influence of the Red Man's probing eyes, he must have revealed it, without even knowing.

He knew now why Raashid would not find the Red Man and his captives.

*

In the early hours of that morning while Kamil tossed and turned, Princess Sabiya was wakened from her slumbers. She did not know what had caused it and nestled herself deeper into her pillows to go back to sleep. As she was falling back into a daydream in which a magnificent young warlord from the south had come to seek her hand in marriage, she heard a scuffle and then a dull thump in the corridor. Some instinct made her push Walidah under her pillow and the slate under its dress and almost at the same moment the door burst open and the mountainous figure of her guard flew through the air and thudded on to the marble tiles by her bed. Following, like a djinn intent on the kill, was the salivating, wild-eyed figure of the Red Man. Princess Sabiya tried to scream but no sound came from her paralysed throat. The Red Man fixed his eyes upon her and began destroying everything that came to hand, never breaking his terrible gaze. Fragments of marble and crystal showered her, pricking her skin and making her cover her eyes. Water was gushing from broken pipes and flowers lay strewn everywhere.

She felt a sharp wrench at her neck and then became aware that the noise had stopped and, lowering her arm, she saw the beast standing over her, his face subdued and his eyes having lost their lurid glitter. In his hand he held the locket. He threw it across the room with a snarl.

-Come, he offered her a hand.

-My coat. I can't-

A brief twist of rage crossed his face and he tore the sheet from her and gathered her up in one arm and bounded from the room, uncaring about her lack of modesty. She found herself being bumped and shaken so badly that the breath was knocked out of her as he loped to Emperor Haidar's bedchamber. There were no guards in the corridors but as he carried her through the doorway she glimpsed two dead sentries on the floor. As if she was no heavier than Walidah, he turned her and tucked her over his shoulder before bending over the royal bed. Haidar was drugged, with his eyes open, his enlarged pupils staring and a deep snore issuing from his slack mouth. Sabiya clung to his furry red neck as the Red Man released his grip on her and picked up the Emperor like a child. With the ease of a circus strongman he strode from the room, carrying them both. Within a minute he had put the Emperor down and was dragging aside the heavy drapes that concealed the door to the steps that led down past the walls that enclosed the Great Library and into the vaporous vaults of the Oracle. His madness did not blur his judgment for he was careful to return the drapes and shut the door before carrying his two victims down the slimy wet flights of stone steps.

The rank smell screwed up Princess Sabiya's nostrils but she could not reach to her gown to cover her face. Sure-footed and with boundless energy, the Red Man's legs danced ever deeper into the subterranean chambers. Finally they were on the flat stone floor outside the vaults of the High Priestess and she was being put down, trying desperately to straighten her simple nightdress. The Emperor was laid beside her. Then the Red Man took out a small phial and allowed a few drops to fall between the Emperor's parted lips. Immediately, he began to stir.

-Come, my Hag Sister! shouted their captor at the arras that curtained off the High Priestess's rooms, -I have business for you. I know you are expecting me. It is what we have both scried, eh? The High Priestess appeared, alone, in her long black gown, her painted white visage, her coal-black eyebrows and lashes, her white hair in long, luxuriant tresses.

-This is the final monstrous act, Devil! She stood, looking up at him triumphantly.

-It is, She-hag. Prepare yourself.

-She is headstrong. She will refuse.

-Then I will break her father's neck in front of her, grunted the Red Man as Emperor Haidar was being helped to sit up by his daughter.

-What do you want of me? cried the Princess, -I have never done you harm.

-It is true, he smiled grimly, -But only because you could not find the means. You and your historian. He has a cunning mind but I made him feel as safe as a child and tell me all I needed to know. I am aware you planned to lure me down here and with the help of this she-witch, rid the world of me. Well, here we are but not as you imagined it! Look around you, Princess-mine. Is this not the ideal place for marriage? Below, the gases rise from hell. Beyond those drapes, the sacred chambers of the High Priestess where our holy bed awaits. What better, eh? To be conjoined by a witch to a wizard! He leaned forward and smiled victoriously, -It is something you have contemplated in your daydreams, is it not?

-No! screamed Princess Sabiya, -Please - no! It was obscene. Her idle wishes had turned upon her with venom. It was true what he said and she suddenly despised her wilful mind. There had been a strange attraction even when he was unshaven and most animal-like. But to be faced with real events here in this grim cavern of dank growths and poisonous fumes, to be touched by his hands and lay beside his naked hairy form, to be unable to stop him from... She threw her terrified arms around her father, seeking solace.

-You cannot do this to my daughter, Emperor Haidar spoke, in a trembling, half-incoherent voice, -Even an evil creature like you could not seek to rob her of her purity. She is but a child. Have pity. Take my life and my throne but do not touch one blessed hair on her head.

The Red Man stared down at him implacably, -No-one can slow the haste of fate, Haidar. These events have been ordained. Ask our witch here. At last there will be the consummation for which we have striven on all our sad visits to the courts of the living. His chest puffed out and his fingers turned his fists into lumpen balls. Then he reached down and grasped the Emperor by the neck of his night shirt and pulled him roughly to his feet, forcing Sabiya to fall back on to the stone, -Stand, Father, for you must give your daughter to her suitor! He bent again and pulled Princess Sabiya up. His voice trembled with emotion, - There we are, father and daughter with a High Priestess to officiate, sanctifying the union, a solemn bond that can never be undone. Who else but only this witch can unite a creature such as I with a woman of this earthly world. Let us conclude.

Princess Sabiya stared round desperately, expecting some intervention to stop this gruesome charade but none came. She half-heard through her sobs and attempts to block out sight and sound, the High Priestess incanting the runes for marriage. Her gaze swung drunkenly around the damp walls. She had no control over her voice. She felt the beast's fingers pressing a ring on to her finger. She heard herself agree to his proposal and, thereby, accept him as her husband. Yes, it was her own mouth moving and it was her own voice yet the words did not come from her mind but were inveigled there by the sorcerer standing in front of her. Lastly, and in shocked revulsion, she felt strange woman-soft lips pressing against hers, tenderly and then, as he picked her up and pushed his way through the drapes, she lost consciousness.

*

Kamil had felt like this when he had served the Princess years before and her fate then had also been resting upon his shoulders. His blood was racing and he was sweating but some inner exhilaration had taken hold of him and with his jaw stubbornly strong and his pace measured and determined he forced back the drape that covered the secret door to the High Priestess's lair.

Every step he took with caution, his rotund figure balanced upon legs made increasingly infirm by fear and horror. He tried not to touch the green, slithery walls to keep his balance but instead paused on each slippery step until he felt secure. The flame from his torch lit up each bend of the circular flight. Apart from the sounds he was making he could hear only the dripping of water and a low murmuring from the depths below which gradually increased as he approached the base of the last stairs. Once he rounded the final bend of the last flight and had a full view of the cavern he saw a woman's body lying over the grill that enabled the sounds to reach up from the depths, as though drinking in the gases that carried the macabre noise. It was the High Priestess. She was lying on her stomach, her legs splayed out, her robes revealing bare, veined skin and her fingers grasping the iron bars of the vent. He ran to her and dropped to his knees, placing his ear against her back. There was no doubt, she was still alive. At his touch she started to move, using her hands to lever her upper body from the metal work. She twisted into a sitting position and smoothed down her clothing.

-Where is she? he whispered. Her eyes indicated the stairs up to her quarters and he started to rise but her fingers held his sleeve.

-It is too late! she said, a strange laugh bursting from her lips, -He has fulfilled his destiny at last. She pulled him closer, -But I shall be the cause of his final peace, once and for all. Help me rise and we will,

611

together, prepare to release him. It is as fate has prescribed. I have conserved the last of my mortal energy for this. She leant on his arm and pulled herself to her feet, then led him up the steps, into the cavern and through the thick curtains to a small ante-room from which one door led to the Priestess's sleeping quarters. They stood, facing each other. Then, with an uncanny smile she said, -You have brought the doll, the slate, the locket and the ceramic pot?

He nodded, fearful at the look on her features but unsurprised at anything she might know. There was enough of a respect for the old ways still lurking in Kamil's breast.

-Then do as I will tell you, no matter how hard it is for you and how contrary to your heart. They are drugged by magic. I had enough power left in me to augment the drowsiness that follows a union. But only for a short time. We must be quick.

*

They entered the bedroom. It tore at Kamil's already distressed heart to see the scene before him. The Emperor lay, plainly sleeping, on the tiles in the corner of the room. His eyes were flickering and his chest heaved up and down. On the bed, locked in each other's arms were the Red Man and his Princess. They were half-covered by a white cotton sheet. Princess Sabiya seemed to be in a stupor rather than sleep for her eyes were open. Kamil steeled himself and moved closer, following the High Priestess whose lips were incanting silently. Now Kamil could see that the Princess's eyes were cloudy and her pupils wide. But there was a greater shock in store. Perhaps because he was half-awakened by their entry, the Red Man turned over so that they could see his face. No longer was he the groomed suitor for the Princess's royal hand. His visage was as it had been when he arrived at the court with its long, wild red hair, bushy eyebrows and beard and little of his features visible.

With a finger to her lips, the High Priestess bade Kamil to help her. She lifted the arm of the Red Man which had lain across the breast of the sleeping Princess to let Kamil pull the Princess away. He kept his eyes averted from her blue-black, naked form, immediately eliminating from his memory any glimpse of what he should not have seen. The Priestess tugged the sheet from the Red Man's limbs and they wound it round the young woman, before easing her from the bed and carrying her to rest, next to her father. Then the High Priestess continued her chant, walking round the bed and laying her hands on the air above the beast. Finally she turned to Kamil and motioned for him to put on the bed where Princess Sabiya had lain, the doll, the little pot, the locket and the slate. Their sudden proximity to the creature seemed to agitate him for he began to moan and twitch. Next, the High Priestess indicated to Kamil that he should put the locket and chain around Walida, the doll's neck. Kamil did so, winding it several times before fixing the clasp to an intact link in the chain. The High Priestess placed the doll on the pillow and lifted the Red Man's arm so that it rested across its little bosom. Next she took the slate, murmuring the message over and over that were inscribed upon it, changing only the last words:

Brother, know that I am still here. Our next sleep will be the sleep of death. I do not fear for us, Brother,

before insinuating it between the Red Man's fingers on his other hand. His moans became louder and his feet began to thrash.

Her last act was to unscrew the lid from the ceramic pot and dip her forefinger into the cream that it contained. With infinite patience she spread it on his eyelids. The thrashing stopped and his eyes stilled, their lid-covered, blind gaze towards Walidah.

-What is this? he asked in a strange falsetto, his fingers tracing her face.

-I am the Princess's creature, came a voice from the doll, its lips moving.

-Ah, moaned the Red Man, -What have we done? He tried to move but his body seemed paralysed. His head was fixed, as though staring at Walidah, whose lips moved again.

-Tell me why you coveted the Princess Sabiya, daughter of Emperor Haidar and from the royal line of Ethiopian kings and queens?

The Red Man could not lie. Words fell from his lips in a high-pitched rush that contained none of his deep timbre, -She is the one for whom I have taken this shape. Countless times I have had to build the strength to leave my prison beneath the ice and give a final spirit to this body. I wandered, searching for her, my spirit extinguished just as the end seemed near. Arrows, fire, blades and sorcery always drove me back. Court after court, royal princess after royal princess. We could never conjoin. The moment slipped from us and the pain started again. His high voice paused, -Until now! Is this not true? he asked, turning his blind face towards the High Priestess.

-It is so, she replied, placing a hand on his arm.

-Tell the historian why you are thus! commanded the shrill voice of Walidah.

In his slow, ghostly woman's voice, the Red Man told the tale, -Near the beginning, when the world was all but water, we were the first-born male and female children of Woman. She had wilfully rejected Man and taken exile from the sacred bower to consort with a demon that flew the skies and never rested its claws, save once, upon the flesh of her form. We were as babes found and taken back into the perfect bower and given protection and nurture. It was expected that we would, in time, begin our separate bloodlines in the newly created World. But we resisted, pretending we were not of sufficient maturity. It came to pass that our love for each other was too plain for all to see and we took to exile just as our mother had, among the djinn and outcasts. In punishment we were cursed to seek a virgin daughter of the first and only unbroken earthly line, one who might take us into her loins.

-Is this so? questioned Walidah, dementedly.

-It is so. Otherwise it could not have happened.

The doll shrieked and struggled inside the sudden grip of the Red Man's hand. In the struggle, the ogre's fingers touched the clasp of the locket and it fell open and the small scrap of white that it contained, fell upon the back of his hand, bursting into flame and causing the skin and hair to hiss and sizzle. It was the Red Man's turn to scream for there, inflamed, as if it had been inscribed by a craftsman's miniature hand, was the message:

Find the she-worm and feed his flesh to her as he sleeps the sleep of truth.

The Red Man's eyes opened, seeing the High Priestess and Kamil for the first time. He lifted a hand to wipe his brow, unknowingly pressing

614

the slate against his forehead. As he did so, the High Priestess called out the words, inscribed upon it, in a commanding voice:

Brother, know that I am still here. Our next sleep will be the sleep of death. I do not fear for us, Brother.

Whereupon, she laid herself upon the prone figure, holding the slate against the creature's forehead. He groaned loudly and went still. Kamil stepped forward to give her aid but was stopped, mid-movement, as an eerie change began to unfold, leaving him transfixed.

The High Priestess's form slowly sank into the body of the Red Man as if into quicksand. While Kamil watched, her tortured expression, ravaged by the gases of the Oracle, peeled away revealing a younger face while her hair darkened to a shining, raven black. Below her, the Red Man's features changed, too, so that only half of it remained his as, magically, the other half took on the countenance of the now young, High Priestess, radiant and beautiful. Together, the lips of the creature spoke to their conjoined owner.

-Sister! they murmured softly, -It is done.

-Brother, mine! came the reply.

The half brother, half sister smiled and gently diffused into a mist. As its outline spread through the air and vanished, Kamil heard a sound behind him. It was the Princess, propped on an elbow, eyes wide, irises filling them, crying. Beside her, his arm around her, was her father, Emperor Haidar. They had both witnessed the occult demise.

Chapter Twenty One

Know that, as a man, you are all men and as a woman, you are all women

Ten years later, Kamil, only a little more portly but with hair turned grey, was reading, at the behest of the Empress Sabiya, the last two Tales of his book about the great Magus, father of the Right Path, to her beautiful, coffee-skinned daughter. They had spent two months together at the same time each early evening. It was a pleasure beyond measure for Kamil. The child's wide eyes, blue and as piercing as her mother's could be, framed by deep, lustrous red hair, never left his face as he read.

-I would like you to read the final two Tales together, had cried the young one, laughing. -It is like a pot of honey. Why leave just a little at the bottom when you can have your fill?

Kamil always obeyed his princesses!

The General and his four commanders faced each other across the table in the war room of the fortress. Around them stood the Warrior, his daughter and the Lord of the Eastern Empire. The commanders looked fearful and defeated, the General straight-backed and dominating, despite his weak body. It was his pride that drove him for his skin was so fine that his bones were visible to them all. In front of him lay his black sword. Beside it was the thin wooden casket with the ancient scrolls of his religion.

-You took me while I was ill and imprisoned me, he said to them. They did not speak but stared straight ahead, -You wanted my empire.

The leader among them said, -You had withdrawn to your retreat. You refused to meet with us. We felt that the empire needed governing. We found you dying. What else could we do?

-I was ill and knew not where I was but my last orders were that all my people should be treated well and no war should be entered into. Was that not my decree? He did not wait for their response and continued, -Yet you disobeyed my wishes and took land that belongs to this lord, he motioned to the Lord of the Eastern Empire, because it is rich in gold and when you saw that he would come with his army, after conquering the rebellious hordes on his eastern borders, you began to conscript young men, taking them from their clans and splintering their villages, cruelly. That is what brought my brother, the Warrior and his mother and daughter on their great journey to me. But, worse than all of this, despite even the children of my empire knowing that the Warrior must never be harmed, you attacked him and murdered his mother. What do you say?

The leader of the commanders looked up, -It was not our doing. It was the work of the fifth commander.

-Did you not discuss together that you would try to prevent the

Warrior from reaching me and finding me a prisoner in my own fortress? The captain from the garrison of the fifth commander has sworn that those were his orders and that he had received them after a council meeting between all of you. The man looked down and said nothing.

The General bent forward across the table, slowly and painfully. No-one tried to help him for his face was determined. He put his hand on the handle of the black sword. Then, it was as if a whirling wind had entered the room, for the sword, which even the Warrior had thought too unwieldy for battle, swung with a whisper through the air, dragging the General to his feet. It circled in four rapid arcs and the throats of the commanders were severed so that they lay upon the floor.

-Judgment, said the General. The moment he said this, the sword fell from his fingers, inert, back to where it had lain upon the table, -Look, he said wearily, -It is mine no longer. I never had need of it until this moment. I took it from a man high in the mountains when it was done with him. It has some spell on it which gives it potency. It becomes alive if it is in the right hands. Someone must take it. Warrior, you must try, for who else deserves such a blade?

The Warrior picked it up but it was a heavy, clumsy piece of useless metal. The Lord of the Eastern Empire tried and it was also inert in his hands, -You must try, Daughter, said the General.

-But I have no need of a weapon, she said.

-Try, nevertheless. It may have a different purpose for you. She frowned and leant forward. Her hand grasped the handle as it lay before her on the table and the short sword leapt into life, rising lightly into the air, its surface transformed into a dull sheen.

-You are a warrior now, laughed the Lord of the Eastern Empire, seeing her animated face, -Will you cut off my head? Are we still enemies? But he spoke in jest and smiled at her with his new-found adoration.

Some time before he had laid the trail of explosions between the two armies and before the General had enacted his final judgment upon the four commanders, the Warrior, his daughter and the Lord of the Eastern Empire had eased the sleeping figure of the General onto the ground in the hollow between the rocks, beneath the blasted tree. The daughter had felt his pulse, eased open his eyelids, forced his mouth wide to look at his tongue, pressed her knuckles repeatedly into the soles of his feet and then placed her ear against his chest.

-He will recover soon, she said.

-Has he been poisoned? asked her father.

-I thought so at first but now I do not know. It is a strange illness and it was not helped by the treatment of his commanders. They were keeping him weak but alive.

-Why did they not kill him and be done? asked the eastern lord.

-I think they felt they might need to parade him before the army if they wished to make a decision that was not popular. Better a General so weak that he could not countermand their orders, yet strong enough to be carried out in front of them on a litter. She stroked the sleeping man's forehead, -It is good that he sleeps. When his eyes open I will administer this elixir but not before. She held up a thin, reed phial. She stood and faced the two other men, -Father, may I present to you the Lord of the Eastern Empire? My Lord, may I present to you my father. The men touched their hearts and bowed.

-It is my honour to meet the famed Warrior, said the man from the east.

-And mine to meet such an esteemed lord and general, replied her father, courteously, -I hope that this meeting will bring peace among our warring armies.

-As do I, replied the Lord, -It is a simple matter to resolve in the mind but to bring it to a practical fruition may require the deepest thought. The General's armies marched across my western territory while I was engaged in a war in the east against a similar intruder. In one year his men stole all the gold from my mines, conscripted young men from my villages and made free with my young women. How could I overlook such crimes? I could not. My army is camped in readiness for battle and requires just one word from me or my trusted commander if he thinks I have been abducted by the enemy.

-I can predict his thoughts on your disappearance! said the Warrior. He liked this lord. He was intelligent and had none of the brutal ways of many chiefs and princes he had met.

-It is simple. He will be preparing for battle. The last he saw of me I was entering my tent to rest. Then he will have received news that a beautiful witch appeared in our camp and soon after she must have clouded my senses because I invited her into my sanctuary. When, later, the men would have checked inside, as I instructed them always to do, they would have found her gone, taking me with her. I think my men will be ready for battle by the time the sun has half-descended.

-We have opportunity then, said the Warrior, -And I have a way of averting this war, taught me by the General, himself, when he was but a novice monk.

-You were a good student, came a voice from the ground, with a pained laugh. The General opened his eyes. The three standing figures smiled as one, the Warrior kneeling instantly and holding up his old friend's head in the crook of his arm while his daughter passed him a reed tube, stopper already removed.

-This will give you strength, said the Warrior, soothingly and dripped the liquid into the sick man's mouth. It was as though a sudden fire was lit inside for his eyes grew bright and the old vitality returned to his face.

-My casket! he ordered.

-It is here, beside you. And your sword. He took the General's hand and laid it on the casket, watching as the man's reawakening fingers moved over the carvings on its lid and sides.

Not long after this the General was well enough to be propped up against a boulder. It was then that the Warrior and his daughter were able to hear the events that had led him to the pitiful state in which they had found and rescued him.

-Until two years ago, not much longer than a week after my last visit to you, Magus, in your solitary meditations in the mountains, I was in my full prime and, I believe, ruling the empire with some wisdom. It had taken me many years to gain the right balance between the rule of law and the rule of tolerance. During the course of this time I had to eradicate the most despotic of the princes and nobles and quell insurrections in my territories. Perhaps I was too severe but lessons had to be learned. A calm had settled on my empire, if not a happy peace. During my last visit we discussed your thoughts on what laws might bring about greater harmony in my lands. We also discussed what was and is for both of us, a never ending puzzle, the purpose of our lives. While I always believed fervently in the God of the Sun, you have been the doubter, the critic and the sceptic. But, like blades on

sharpening stones, the two of us gained from our hot disputes!
They smiled at each other in recognition of that time.

-As I said, since all seemed well in the lands under my leadership, I turned more and more to these eternal questions. If you remember, I carried away from the tower of my education, some ancient writing in this very casket, the earliest testaments that founded my religion. I meditated on their import. I sent out emissaries to discover and bring to me the most venerable scripts that could be found in lands along all the trade routes, whatever the god they purported to venerate. I became known as a collector of the old and the arcane. I paid well. Most, at best, were mere copies of ancient texts. Some were faked to separate me from my riches! Occasionally, a trader would bring me a treasure, some scrap of luminance from the darkness of history and I would store them here. He patted the flat box, -As you can easily see from the size of this casket, there is little in the world that can tell us anything about existence before and after we die! But I persevered.

Then, a man from the lands furthest to the east, far beyond your empire my Lord, visited. He glanced at the Lord of the Eastern Empire. -He was a beggar in rags, his face as gaunt as mine is now but with eyes that glittered with some deadly knowledge, I now think. He carried a thin skin, rolled in an old leather tube. On it was drawn pictures and symbols in columns brushed there in black ink but dotted with gold, silver and many coloured flourishes. It smelled of the most ancient of days. The man did not want to trade with my riches. He was but a messenger from an emperor who had heard about my desire for the oldest knowledge, still surviving from the beginnings of the world. Or so he said. I fed him and clothed him and the next day he was gone.

There was not one person in my empire who could translate the strange messages on the skin so all I could do was sit with it in my hands and close my eyes, running my fingers over the raised marks, hoping that it would infuse my being with new knowledge. It became an obsession. Soon, I could not allow an hour to pass without touching it. I withdrew from the affairs of my state, appointing commanders to each part of the empire, meeting with them less and less and working alone in a cell, separate from my fortress. I often refused food and took water only. With the symbols and pictures under my fingers I began to see strange sights, seemingly outside my head, though I was in a small room in the cliff rock. It was wild and uncontrolled. I saw wars between the golden giants of the sun and the silver demons of the moon. I saw great spears flying through the air, across mountains and seas, mounted by an insane god's naked creatures, carrying weapons that shot boulders of fire upon the earth. I saw volcanoes erupt out of water, throwing a thousand djinn into the air, released from deep dungeons and watched them scramble from where they landed to terrorise the living. Parchments floated in front of my eyes with all the knowledge that ever was and ever would be inscribed upon them but as I tried to focus on a key message it would burst into flame. I saw the births and deaths of nobles and peasants and their lives in between but all in one instant as if a second was a year and an hour a lifetime. It was as though all things were being stirred together in a vast pot and I had no way of separating what was important from what was madness but found myself in it, half-swimming, half-drowning in this nightmarish place. As the days passed I realised that I was experiencing all the worlds presided over by all the gods who ever existed and who would ever exist. Yet it became apparent that all these gods lived and died as we did. Then your words came to me, Warrior-Magus, that it is we who create them and also all the djinn, the phantoms, the ghosts, the life-takers and all the unseen and ghoulish things that we believe in, in our credulity. If the truth be known we only see them when we are fevered and never when we are sane.

It was a terrible moment for me. All that I had believed in burst into flame like the parchments of my nightmares. I was like you, Warrior, stripped and naked of trust in a god. I collapsed into a deep well of sickness. Time must have passed because at some point I heard your voice in my prison in the eastern castle and felt myself bound by ankles and wrists and covered in coarse cloth, though not before I was able to pass word to you by the bird and receive your reply. And now you have saved me from myself and my commanders!

He lifted the casket and touched a secret mechanism in its intricate carvings so that the lid opened, -Here is the skin that took me to the verge of insanity. I will not touch it again. The daughter took the box and sat with it on her lap. They watched her as first she sniffed at it. She prepared a small pot of liquid, then wetted a tiny brush from her pouch and touched the ink with it before dipping the end in the pot. She did the same with every colour on the skin, cleaning its hairs each time. It was the silver that stayed her experiments. As the brush touched the liquid in the pot the liquid frothed slightly.

-It is a poison, she said, -Each silver dot contains it.

-Why? asked the General.

It was the Warrior who spoke, for it came to him immediately in one of his unpredictable shafts of clarity, -The poison protects the knowledge in the symbols. I hear a voice in my mind saying that it is a most ancient text, forecasting the end of the time of gods. You saw this in your nightmares and hallucinations, my General, for you also have an inner eye for such things. It speaks of a time when men and women watch upon their own lives and bring judgment to their every breath and no longer wait until their deaths for their god to do so.

-I think it is so, said his daughter, -For the same message came to my own mind. The silver points are not from the ancient authors rest of the inscriptions. They have been added later like eternal watchmen over this cryptic well of knowledge. The intention was clear. Such a testament should not be allowed to flourish for what would happen to shaman, witches, priests and priestesses with the end of the belief in gods? How would emperors, generals, kings and queens control their peoples? So much is invested in human gullibility. She took her knife and sharpened it before slowly and painstakingly scraping away every silver dot.

They left the room of the dead commanders. The General carried his casket, the daughter the short black sword and the Warrior the ancient skin, now missing its silver. They rode together to the edge of the battle arena. It was then the Magus performed his magical feat of thunder and lightning.

The General appointed five captains to take the place of the five commanders and they sat as part of a ring, alongside the commanders of the army from the east. The General, The Lord of the Eastern Empire, the daughter and the Warrior completed the circle. The cooks from the fortress above them and the cooks from the eastern army worked together to lay food and drink upon the silk-covered floor in the centre of the cushions. Beyond the pavilion there were other tents, filled equally with soldiers from both armies. Bands of musicians moved between them, playing melodies to soothe the most bitter breast. The war was over before it had begun.

-More! cried Princess Shahrazad, twisting violently on his knee and running a hand down his face, -More! The last one, please, Uncle Kamil. She has the same impulsive charm that her mother had, smiled Kamil to himself and began to read the final Tale.

-And so it is agreed, said the Lord of the Eastern Empire, -Let us drink upon our pact! He raised his vessel to his mouth and all followed. Even the Warrior who had long refused spirits of any kind, allowed a droplet or two to wet his lips. It had not taken long. The General had begun the council meeting with a heartfelt apology and offered immediate reconciliation by decreeing that the lord's lands should be returned to him with immediate effect, together with every grain of gold that had been stolen. All soldiers who had committed crimes against men, women and children would be tried by the highest court and the punishment would befit the crime. The following day a captain would be dispatched with a large cohort of men to ride to the camps that guarded the sequestered land and command their return to the eastern fortress. He had asked what other retribution he might make for the injustices of his commanders. But the eastern lord refused any such penalty. It was enough to have his lands restored and for it to have happened without bloodshed. He had lost enough brave men in the last year. Now they could return to their villages and towns and rest. So it was that he asked them to drink to peace between their states. Then he ordered his commanders to organise the dismantling of the camp of war and the return to their homeland. When they had left the pavilion, the lord, the Warrior, the General and the daughter remained behind, stretching and relaxing their limbs. They were fatigued by events but the energy that comes with accomplishing a great task still flowed through them.

-It is good to have ended this train of events thus, the General exclaimed, -No war! No imprisonment! It is thanks to the Magus and his daughter that it has turned out so well. I drink to you both! He was joined by the lord from the east, -And now, he continued, -It is time for further change. What is borne home to me is that I have no more stomach for the responsibilities of ruling the empire. I am tired. My body has been flayed by recent trials. I have not the physical appetite for it any longer. Yet I have thought long and hard these last few hours as to what should happen next. I have no growing child to accept my mantle, not that I believe in such dynasties and I have not groomed a successor. Here I am, a frail man dressed in the clothes the Warrior has given me, like a child in his father's garments, so capacious are they. They laughed, for it was, indeed, comical; he was dwarfed by the tunic and trousers, -Time reveals truths to each of us. The clothes tell a tale. I am a lesser man than my friend, the Magus, here. I exist inside his shadow.

-General, it is not so... began the Warrior.

But he was stopped by a raised hand as his friend continued, bullishly, -I have much to learn before I die. And since I do not now imagine my spirit rising as a bird to the sun, I would like to focus, in these remaining years, upon what will happen after my last breath and I enter oblivion, if that is what it is. Not that I am yet able to relinquish my casket and its contents for they have provided protection and succour for so long! When I am well enough I will go to the camp in the mountains that guard your childhood's valleys, Warrior and share my thoughts with you. By then I may have new illuminations with which to test you!

-We shall go together, said the Warrior softly, laying a hand on his shoulder but even as he said it he became aware that the General had much more to say to them.

-That would be a fine journey! First you travelled with your father-not-of-blood, then your blessed mother and your daughter and next you will share adventures with the General, no longer emperor of these lands but a worthy friend and fellow hunter after truth. No doubt new Tales will be told about you around the firesides of these lands, Magus. He patted the hand of the Warrior, still on his shoulder. Then he paused and looked round at their watching eyes. They were waiting, sensing an announcement.

-I said, a moment or two ago that I was vexed by the question of giving up the burden of the empire for I could not leave it to chance that a successor would follow the code that you have begun to construct with the Right Path, Magus. I have learned that if a leader leaves a hole in his departing then there is always conflict and pain as ambitious lords and generals seek to fill it, such as neighbours like the lord here, were he an evil man which, fortune being on our side, is not the case. No, I had a flash of inspiration, a glimpse of the future such as sometimes attends you and your daughter, Magus and the moment I had it I was at peace with myself and the future of these lands.

Only the daughter did not look at him in puzzlement. She was sitting with pursed lips as though already weighing up what he was about to say.

-This is the thought that burst like one of your explosions upon my struggling mind, my friend. I will put the empire in the hands of your daughter!

There was little reaction. Sometimes news, though unexpected, seems to carry an irrevocable rightness and so it was here, -It came to me when I thought about the sword and how it had left me for her hand. It has had an age-long journey and we only know of its more recent history but for the time being at least it is in her care. And she knows of all your thoughts Magus. She, herself, displays the conduct of one who follows the Right Path. She is wise beyond her years and has gifts that make her a fearsome enemy to those who would try to depose her. What do you say, daughter of the Warrior?

Her words were simple, -It is why I am here. Her father nodded as though a hidden truth was revealed to him. Without realising it he had always been aware that his daughter was independent of him. She had been following her own course in life, even while accompanying him on his journey. She had seen their joint events and circumstances from another vantage point. She had been fulfilling her own destiny and had long-glimpsed the role she would now play.

-And there is more. I may have not the gift of seeing, said the Lord of the Eastern Empire -But I am a man who feels in his heart what must be true. Though it seems we have not known each other for more than a day, it is as if we have always been together across time and place. As soon as I saw her, I was lost to my former life. I told her that I would give up my empire to be with her if that was her command. He touched her arm and she placed a hand on it.

The Warrior and the General smiled sagely. It was not a surprise to them and indeed the General could have been even more presumptuous in his speech about the future of his lands and those of his neighbour's but had desisted for he felt it was not from his mouth that such a suggestion should issue.

-I saw this too, said the daughter, her face calm and untroubled. She took up the sword as lightly as if it was a quill and held it point upwards before her mouth, kissing the handle where it joined the blade, -I swear on this ancient blade that my Lord and I shall from this moment be together as one and rule all the lands that once were his and the General's, as a united empire, according to the codes that these shamans have begun to fashion. And we will seek their constant counsel in discharging the duties of our one great state.

With embraces and soft words of encouragement, the four stood close together, hopeful that in their lifetimes there would be peace in the great empire.

-**O Uncle, cried** Shahrazad, it is over. You are a great writer. Will you write a book for me too? After all you wrote TWO books for my mother!

-If it is your command, Kamil looked down at her upturned face.

-It is! she shouted, deafening him, -And it has to be about what comes next. The Warrior Magus has to have more adventures and he has not finished working on the Right Path, has he?

-It is true, he laughed, despite himself.

-And I shall tell you how it must start!

-Oh, I see.

-Do I begin with The Magician again, she asked, looking down at the scattered tarot cards with which she had been idly playing as she listened.

-You can but it is usual to start with The Fool because each time we begin another great adventure in life, we should empty ourselves and be ready to fill our beings with new understanding.

The Princess gritted her teeth and nodded, pulling a sheet of stiff paper towards her and picking up a red crayon. Carefully, she wrote, The Fool and, without any help from Kamil, began inscribing the first sentence as he placed card before her:

The Warrior went to his retreat in the mountains to gather his sword, bow and throwing knife because his daughter, now the Lady of the United Empire, had requested his help....

Book 3

Chapter One

Not knowing can be a great strength for those who live each moment

The ageing historian had a surprise for his pupil. It had taken six years of toil in the Great Library, as well as innumerable hours crossing out words and infelicitous sentences, replacing them with improvements and all the while sharpening goose quills and mixing inks. But, at the very moment he was about to announce his gift, her question stalled him.

-Am I like my mother when she was sixteen? The question caused a feathery walk of anxiety down Kamil's spine as disturbing as being woken by a night spider. He had always tried to avoid having to make royal comparisons. Nothing but trouble. He raised his eyes and looked at the exotic creature sitting in front of him with her sandalwood skin, her rich red hair and her sparkling blue eyes. Unlike her mother, the Empress Sabiya, she wore no jewellery or feminine clothes but sat in a plain, oatmeal tunic over robust white twill trousers. Around her waist was a deep mahogany-coloured leather belt with an ornamental knife handle protruding from its sheath, hung at her left side.

-I never thought another could match your mother in her beauty, he replied, -Though you seem to be flowers from different plants. It does not surprise me that you command the eye of the onlooker as you do. One could not expect anything less from a daughter of the Empress. Like her, you will have suitors drawn from the far reaches of the world to pay homage and ask for your hand.

Shahrazad sighed and lounged back in the chair, her legs splayed in front of her, -They started long ago, she grumbled, -Princes have attended the court since I was eight or nine, a mere child! They visit on all sorts of pretexts but actually all they want to do is to size me up like any girl in a slave market. How easy on the eye, how big my bosoms and my buttocks, how narrow my waist, ankles and wrists. Well, it is always a shock for them to find that I already tower over them with a body as well-hardened as a boy's and teats no bigger! She laughed as she saw his face, -My mother told me not to speak of such things in front of you Uncle Kamil unless it be to amuse myself. I see why. Her laughter tinkled on for a while.

Kamil had learned to hide some of his discomfort at the language of a precociously naughty young woman during the times that he had served her mother but he could still be found out, as he was now. Despite all the dangerous and sometimes less than proper escapades he had endured for the Empress in her battles to succeed her father, the Emperor Haidar, all those hours they had plotted together or shared the Tales of the Magus, he was still, at heart, a simple, devout man and easily embarrassed by impropriety. The royal daughter, slumped nonchalantly in front of him was no different from her mother in her ribald amusement at his vulnerability.

-I am pleased you think me a fine young beauty Uncle but that was not what I meant. In character am I as she was at this age? She dropped her head slightly to give him her full, earnest stare.

Kamil often reached the point with Shahrazad when the normal courtesies dropped away and they behaved towards each other like close blood relatives, despite the gulf between them in social standing. He had been her companion since she was born, entrusted with her education by her mother. Now she was at an age when he must adopt the protocols of respect owing to a royal Princess until such time as some signal from her drew him back into easy informality. He spoke frankly, -Your mother played a woman's game from girlhood. She knew how to twist a man around her finger like a loose ring. You have always been more interested in –

-Boy's pursuits! She grinned impishly at him, -It is true, I hardly feel that I am in a woman's body most of the time. I only have one doll, Walidah, who was my mother's treasured baby when she was young. There will be time enough to grow into a woman's ways and so I will enjoy what I am for as long as I can make it last. And you will continue to teach me my lessons, as always. What have you brought me?

She looked down at a simple wooden box on the table between them, the playing cards beside it, their faces hidden and smiled in jubilation, - Today is the day! she cried, -How long has it taken?

-Six years, he bowed.

-Six years too long! she frowned, in pretend irritation, -But now, in my sixteenth year, you give me equal standing with my mother. You will read me new Tales of the Magus, ones that she has never heard. Your first two books are now read everywhere are they not? And my mother was the first to hear them.

-She was very kind to have copies made for the people. It has given me a fame of which I did not dream.

-And both of those books have an inscription in them so that the world knows that they are dedicated to her Highness.

By now he knew where her thoughts were leading her. Without further preamble she leant forward and raised the lid of the box. First, the title made her smile:

Tales of the Magus
The Final Journey

And then she lifted the following page and her face broke into an even broader smile, -You have not forgotten that it was I who asked you to write the third book! She read aloud, "This book is dedicated to Her Highness Princess Shahrazad, daughter of Empress Sabiya and heir to the empire." Uncle Kamil, this is so exciting. Will you read me the first Tale, just as you did for my mother? Beginning now?

-If it is your wish, your Highness.

-It is! It is! She clapped her hands and lay back again, a look of contentment on her face, -I am ready.

-Then you must turn over the first card. He pushed the deck towards her.

-Of course! She remembered how she had done just this when he had read her the first two volumes, as her mother had done before her. But that was six years ago when she was ten. No wonder she had forgotten. Images came flooding back to her of the major Arcana cards in the tarot, their almost impenetrable meanings and the magical tales of the Warrior who became a legend, a Magus whose adventures and philosophy had helped shape the destinies of empires. And now it was going to happen again. Just for her. She turned over the first card and exclaimed, happily, -The Fool!

Kamil half-smiled and said before he began reading, -The first sentence was written by you.

-Me? What do you mean, Uncle?

-Do you not remember? When I finished the last Tale of the second book you were so excited that you demanded I wrote a book about the rest of the Magus' life. In fact you were so entranced that you wrote the first words there and then. Here! Kamil took a roll of stiff paper from beside him and placed it before her. She unfurled it and laughed.

-It is my writing but not very elegant. So those were my words, I had completely forgotten. Then follow my lead, fellow Author!

The Warrior went to his retreat in the mountains to gather his sword, bow and throwing knife because his daughter, now the Lady of the United Empire, had requested his help....His long hair was twisted into a single grey tail that stretched down his back, his skin showed that time had inched its way across him, cutting deep lines in his sun-blackened skin. Only his eyes remained bleached grey and glittering as they had done all his life. His limbs were a little stiffened but his gait remained strong and what he may have lost in fluid grace, was made up in heavy muscle.

Secretly he would have liked to have undertaken the long journey to the eastern half of the united empire on his own but the blood that flowed through him also flowed through his first daughter and he had promised his wife, after his last great journey, never to leave her side again. Although his first daughter never spoke of it, he knew that she felt her life was incomplete. Hadn't her grandmother and her half-sister, his second daughter, adventured with him, crossing rivers and mountains, unending plains both wild and tilled and crossing the paths of clans and tribes who were as unlike them as beasts to birds?

It was only their intention to be his companions that made him seek his old weapons. He had not fought for many years and in that time had not practised or even taught young men the arts of fighting. But, despite his confidence in the two women and their capacity to defend themselves, something too deep inside him to relinquish, forced him to arm himself for their protection. He sat outside the small wooden stockade with the woodcutter and his wife, who tended this precious hideaway for him, eating the morning stew he had prepared from the traps they had set. The thick morass of meat and plant roots aided by the woman's coarse grey bread, was comforting. It would keep him from hunger on his day's ride. He would miss it.

-You are to be gone again, Master? asked the woodcutter.

-It is to be.

-Will we still walk this forest on your return?

-No. Your son and his wife will take your place. They ate for a while in silence and the Magus's thoughts took their own course, without guidance. The woodcutter interrupted him again with a flat, determined statement.

-We will keep to the Right Path, Master.

-I know you will. And I know that you will see to it that your son and his wife do, too.

They had made his weapons ready. His desert dwellers' bone and wood bow shone from repeated waxing, fresh strings were coiled in a pouch. His sword and throwing knife and their sheaths had now been unwrapped from the tightly folded oilskin that had kept them free of any spots of rust. Clay pots containing the ingredients of thunder and lightning, medicines, cooking herbs and spices and face paints were already stowed in his roan's saddlebags. The horse stood nearby, occasionally cropping grass but never taking its eyes off him. It was the great grandson of his mother's roan, the horse his grandfather had found as a solitary foal in the wild.

-Win all your battles and come back safely to this place and our children, Master, entreated the woodcutter's wife, her head bowed, not wishing to gaze into his eyes. He had never managed to rid her of her deep reverence and fear of him. Once, he had lifted her head up by touching her gently under the chin but when their eyes met, she began to shake and flecks of white saliva bubbled on her lips.

-If these tools of my Warrior-past remain as unused as they have been these last few years, then I will be a happy man, replied the sage as he mounted and wheeled the roan round and on to the path that led back to the valleys of his forefathers. The right hands of all three touched their hearts and then the roan cantered down the hill, through the fine gauzy tracery of the spring leaves.

He passed through small settlements with a raised hand of acknowledgement, speaking briefly to herders and farmers as he came across them and stopping to talk to children, enquiring after their knowledge of the lessons of the Right Path. All knew him and he knew all. What each one he met, grown up or small, noticed with a shudder of pride and fearful excitement, were the weapons of war that he carried. They knew the tales about this man but many only half believed them because he was ageing and was devoted to peace. They had not seen him so prepared.

At last, with the sun losing its strength and the air cooling, he rode up to the rough log and thatch building that had been in his mother's family for generations - except when she had fled from those wishing to wreak vengeance for her killing of his father. Villagers began to gather as he dismounted but, even those who normally would reach to touch and greet him, stood a little apart from him in his warrior's attire. Instead he smiled and went to each of them, listening to their news and occasional requests for help, then entered his family house.

His first daughter was waiting for him and once he had closed the door, she bowed to him. His two grandchildren by this daughter came for their hugs and were sent away happy with a small clay pot of sugary particles that bubbled and frothed when laid on their tongues

-They know you and I are leaving? he asked.

She nodded soberly, -Your son's wife will care for them. His son, her brother, was a farmer and had none of his father's prowess or spirit of curiosity.

He could see that she was ready for the journey. She had always had a wanderlust and had travelled with his father-not-of-blood on his last long journey, before his death, to the far south, the place of his birth and the centre of his thriving merchant business. Like his other daughter she had taken, early in womanhood, a good husband to give her clan children whose blood issued from the Magus, her father. Now that they did not need her breasts she felt free to leave and desired above all to meet and know her half-sister.

Whereas her unmet sister never carried weapons, yet possessed knowledge and powers that protected her in other ways, this daughter had a likeness to both her grandmother and mother. She had been born, it was said, with a knife between her teeth and a quiver of arrows on her back. She had fought and killed, adventured without fear across the mountains of her father's people and the deserts of her mother's and was now a mature woman, subtle in her arguments, kind to all except her enemies and respected, if not truly loved, by any except her family. She was tall and tautly muscled, though slim. Her hair was braided in a long tail like her father's, her skin was dark and hardened by weathering and her pale grey eyes were searching and impossible to outstare. She was dressed as a warrior, even to the metal strips on her shoulders. Her helmet, built of hoops of iron on a bed of leather, hung by the door. A jerkin sewn with metal discs like flattened petals was hooked beside it and below it rested a scabbarded sword.

-Let us eat, she said.

The journey would take many days and they were sparing of their mounts, riding in the mornings and evenings when the sun was lower. She trapped and he cooked and most of their time was spent in silence for, though he had not seen her grow up under the guidance of his wife of the deserts, she had forced him later to know her as well as his other daughter, to assuage the abandonment she had felt in those early years.

With little riding left before the desert sands carpeted the land, they were camped, hidden in a small clump of trees beside a spring. She had shot a rodent, large enough to fill their stomachs and he had turned it on the metal spit he carried everywhere. They munched the long tapering white roots of plants he had dug up nearby and pulled the hot meat from the bone with their fingers.

-I sense a storm brewing, she said in a low voice, as though not wishing to bring it closer.

-Something is coming but it may not only be disquiet in the clouds, he replied. Both watched the roan stiffen and offer its muzzle to the breeze. Gradually it turned towards the barren lands to the south. His daughter stood and checked her sword and armour before notching an arrow to her bow. Her father stayed as he was, seemingly unperturbed by the approaching threat. As they waited, the wind began to whip sand and dust towards them so that their horses were forced to turn their backs and droop their heads.

Out of the dimming light and thick, driving air came an apparition, unlike any seen before by father or daughter. The giant was riding a broad warhorse and both were covered in dull, black armour. A metal gauze covered the features of the rider so that they could make out no detail of its character. The mount stopped a little way off and the veiled head bent forward. It spoke in a man's deep, strange accent, each word separate and carefully wrought.

-Magus, we take your only wife hostage. She now on road to our lands. You and your daughter come, or you never see her again. Then the stranger turned his horse back towards the desert and waited. At the same moment, as though by command, the wind dropped.

☥

They followed him without a word on a trail that shirked the worst of the sands, edging round the desert and camping where there was water. The stranger never showed his face or spoke again. When they camped he took off by himself, only returning when it was time to continue. What he ate or how he slept remained a mystery. The roan and the daughter's grey could not befriend the warhorse. It seemed impervious to their whinnies or pawing of the ground. While they travelled he led by some distance, out of earshot and never once looking back to see of they followed.

It was several days before the daughter began a conversation about their silent guides, -Are they djinn?

-They seem like flesh and blood, no less than you or I.

-You believe that his countrymen have my mother, your wife?

-It would appear so. He has not asked for our weapons. It is an act of faith.

-It would be hard to find any part of his body in that armour. She sniffed and ran a sleeve across her mouth, -I have never seen the like. Have you?

-I thought not but his voice reminded me of a warrior who travelled along the trade routes from the east to kill me.

-Why?

-He had heard of me and could not sleep thinking that I might be the greater in battle. I could not dissuade him and so he died.

-You saw his face?

-I did. His eyes were narrow and raised at the corners. He had high cheek bones, a little like the spice traders of whom I have spoken. He had black hair that shone with oil and lay in a double, twisted tail to the belt at his back. His eyes were black, too. There was no warmth in them. He had killed since he was a young man, protecting his mother and from that point he had a lust for it like the creature that kills without the desire to eat. This man is like him though I feel that his lands are not of that warrior's birthplace.

His daughter's face was grim, -If you are right, and when were you ever wrong O Father, this journey will take us further than even the lands of your other daughter, my half-sister. I will become as old as my mother was when she travelled with you, should we ever return. She turned and stared at him, angrily, -We know so little. Is my mother safe? Why have they taken her? Where have they taken her? Is her kidnap a ruse merely to draw you to their lands? If so, why? Is it that they want to have sport in an arena, the fabled Warrior in a contest with abducted slaves or with beasts that are beyond even our dreaming? Why else? She slapped the pommel on her saddle angrily.

-I cannot see the end of it either, he replied softly, -But my instinct tells me that we should allow events to flow through us. Let us be passive. Resistance will only slow the progress of our knowing.

It was now that their nostrils caught the first unmistakeable smell of water. Shortly they could hear it too. Not too long after that they breasted the low, hilly embankment that kept the river in check and there before them was a great expanse of slowly moving current, the far side of which was protected by another low ridge. But their gaze was transfixed, not by the river and its banks but by what was roped to the shore, directly below them. They trotted behind the warhorse and its rider down the incline to a levelled jetty of pebbles and sand, increasingly aware that the boat that waited for them was big for these waters, though much smaller than the sailing ship that had once taken the Magus and his father-not-of-blood to the island of a hermit, across salt water far to the south. Sailors stood silently along the deck rails, watching them.

As if everything had been foretold, the moment their hooves clattered on the shingle a wide gangplank began to extend outwards from its hanging place at the boat's side. Ingenious ropes and pulley wheels drew it into position. Their guide drove his horse up it and disappeared through a rectangular opening in its deck housing and out of sight. Without a glance at each other the two followed. Their mounts took them into the darkness of the boat's interior while behind them they heard the gangplank being cranked back to its hanging position.

The realisation struck both of them that they were now properly captive and they were at the mercy of their silent companions.

As he completed the last sentence with a low and sinister inflection, the Princess Shahrazad leapt up and clapped her hands, her eyes showing a little pretend fear, -O Uncle, that was a good start. Another daughter to travel and fight with him and a mystery already. What a frightening stranger! And we don't know what he looks like. And a ship with silent seamen to sail it. Perhaps they are djinn! She looked down at the Fool card, -The Fool is having his bottom bitten by a dog, she nodded sagely, -I think I remember what this card means. He is journeying into the unknown and appreciates little of what is going to befall him. The biting mongrel represents thoughts at the back of his mind that give him anxieties but he can't work out what they might be. That is exactly the case with the Magus and his daughter. What do you think?

-You have even greater wisdom than your mother possessed at your age, replied Kamil, -I am astonished. Few are able to remember the symbolism and you have done much more. You have retained your learning and added a deeper colouring of meaning.

-Greater than her! Shahrazad's blue eyes flashed. Kamil caught an oddness in her countenance but it was like a momentary veil that lifted instantly. It confirmed her continual competition with her mother but other than that he was not able to say. She went on, -I like this beginning because it feels different than the first two books, I don't know why. Perhaps it is that the Magus and his daughter are falling helplessly into the unknown, into mysteries beyond normal understanding. If there are ghosts, spectres, djinn and occult happenings then it will transport me even more than the earlier Tales.

He laughed, -You must remember that the Magus is not one for the supernatural. It is possible that he was the first human being ever to consider a world without gods and he always sought an explanation for whatever appeared to be magical or mysterious.

Shahrazad wrapped her arms around her body and looked down at him, sternly, -Mother said you were a paradox! God-fearing to a fault but obsessed with the Magus and his anti-religious behaviour.

-I do not see him as anti-religious. He has already learned to leave well alone, to live and let live. I admire him because he was driven to understand and communicate the practicalities of living a good life. After him, religions began to include his teaching among their rules of adherence. For example, before him it was the practice for people to kill in their war-god's name. I have read that in the east, peoples were once of two kinds, farmers and hunters. The hunters were warlike and took what they wished from the farmers, be it cattle, crops or women, for they fashioned themselves after a god of war. The farmers, meanwhile, were gentle and giving and could do nothing to withstand the raiders, choosing a god of the harvest and plants and the weather. The farmers became, in time, more warlike which meant that the raiders could not pillage so easily and so they began to farm a little, too. Soon it was impossible to tell them apart as both were now worshipping two gods! The Magus seems to have lived in this time of conjunction.

-It happened as you say, she nodded, sagely, her eyes turning inward, -Something in my bones tells me it was so. Then her expression changed and she gave a twirl around his little room, -It is good we have started. Because I am the first listener, the Tales seem as though they are happening as you read them even though the events are far in the past. She paused and snorted, impishly, -Which reminds me Uncle, we have adventures of our own to undertake. In two days we leave!

-We?

-Yes, just you and I. Well, if truth be told we must be accompanied by a cohort of the elite guard but even so it will be exciting.

Kamil smiled indulgently, imagining this to be a little foray into the interior, -And where are we going? he asked.

-Far away to the north end of our borders.

-And what does the Empress Sabiya say to that? he laughed, indulgently.

-O, my mother... she does not know of all of my plans. With an inscrutable glance she turned to leave the room but then whispered over her shoulder, -And you are instructed not to talk about this with her. You have plenty of time to say your goodbyes to your wife and children.

Chapter Two

The rush of the fool may reveal more than the caution of the sage

-**Ah, my dearest** historian, faithful servant of the state and entrusted guardian of my wayward child! purred the Empress Sabiya in the ornate language she had picked up from her late father, the Emperor Haidar, -How are you faring? While there was warmth in her words, he was aware that her cool eyes were appraising him, looking for evidence of something.

They were sitting in her lavish reception chamber, normally reserved for private meetings with visiting royalty. The pale blue walls with their gold, stencilled friezes, were festooned with hanging silk drapes, paintings, ivory-framed mirrors and silver lamps. Tables and chairs, carved and inlaid by the finest craftsmen were positioned around the room to afford each its magnificent due. The white marble floor was covered in a circle of rugs, intricately recounting the story of the long war that gave birth to the empire. All the emperors were featured, from Empress Sabiya's oldest forebears who had forced the tribes into unity, to her father, the Emperor Haidar. Light suffused the room, percolating through the screens of gold and silver tracery etched into the windows and, as though floating upon it, the scent of jasmine and rose wafted across the seated couple. Kamil had ventured into this royal retreat many times over the last few years since Sabiya had become Empress, but he still found it difficult to keep his mind clear. In truth, he preferred utter simplicity and would far rather have been in a rough, monastic cell than in this besieging of his senses.

-I am well, your Highness, at least as well as my aching bones and over-zealous eating, allow.

-Yes, your esteemed wife indulges you too much! And I expect you exercise little more than the walk between your quarters and the Great Library. I should send you on more adventures for they did wonders for your physique, as I remember.

-I fear I am too old for a return to that world, he laughed.

-Not your brain. It is still a scimitar among bludgeons. She lifted a crystal glass to her lips and sipped the pomegranate juice. He followed suit. -I hear from my ruffian of a child that you have begun reading the third book to her. It was at moments like this that Kamil congratulated himself upon his deep-seated caution. He had informed the Empress that the book was done, not wishing the news to be conveyed to her by the lips of Princess Shahrazad. He loved the girl but knew that she would have used the knowledge to exact a gleeful emotional victory over her mother, -I am glad, the Empress went on, -She has a difficult example to follow. She sees me as a great heroine, a female conqueror who stands out even among my male ancestors. It is good that you can give her this special time. It redresses the balance a little. She put the glass down with a sharp clink on the table between them. He immediately followed her lead.

-Too true, your Highness. She loves to … compete with you.

The Empress Sabiya laughed, -You are doing fine work, educating her. Every day I see some refinement of thought, some insight, some clever machination and plotting that bode well for her future as the royal empress. It is very pleasing for she is an extraordinary child. From the moment she forced her way out of my body, all rush and screech, little hands and feet kicking wildly, she has been in a hurry to get somewhere, a place she probably only barely discerns. But you calm her, make her think before acting, consider alternatives, just as you did with me.

Like daughter, like mother, thought Kamil wryly, aware that the Empress was leading up to something. He fidgeted uncomfortably.

-And now she tells me that she wants to visit her cousin in the Second City with you as her companion. Two days by horse and three by carriage. Looking at you, I wonder whether you are made of willing enough flesh for such a journey.

-I was surprised …

-I am sure, Sabiya interrupted, -Like me she makes wilful decisions and it is then that her heart rules her head, no matter what sense you might have pounded into it. But if she is to go then your constant cautionary admonishments would be no bad thing. There is much that bubbles under the soup with that girl and we know from where it issues, do we not?

Kamil maintained an expressionless face and waited. The looming subject was one they had discussed rarely and was taboo throughout the empire. It was probable that only he had been the audience to the Empress when she felt disposed to talk about it.

-Her father, who took me just as the Magus' mother was taken, a rape under the influence of his magic, caused her to take root within me. Yet when she emerged her blue eyes bewitched me and within seconds her screeches had become coos, as though she had an intelligence in the art of managing a mother. And so it has been ever since. I can be taken aback by her, even fearful sometimes but I become molten wax whenever she wishes it.

-She is precocious.

-She has gifts, some of which have still to be unearthed, Empress Sabiya paused reflectively and then continued, -Do you remember my talent at that age?

-You had an instinct for who might be your enemy, suggested Kamil.

-Indeed I did. And do. She also has it. But I used to reveal my disquiet too readily. I have noticed that, even though she can blurt out many a derogatory remark without thinking, she conceals her appraisal of even the most obvious conniver in the court. As yet she has built up no stock of enemies. She is everyone's favourite tomboy, from scullery maid to the lord treasurer. Take care of her well, Kamil. Allow her her head whenever possible even when there is seeming danger. She is your future empress. She is a gem beyond measure. Raashid and his inner guard will accompany you.

Raashid was the Empress's closest friend from childhood and Kamil was suddenly reassured that they would be in safe hands.

*

Fulfilling the command of Shahrazad in this one instance, was a pleasure. Here he was, sitting cross-legged on a cushion facing his wife, Baligha. Since he had met her, admittedly as a consequence of the Empress's demands upon him to undertake assignments for her, life had changed forever. She was an ever loving companion, a devoted mother and a wise counsel. Indeed, she had helped him uncover the first great plot against Princess Sabiya and her knowledge of the world beyond the empire had aided in the battle to bring down the Red Man. She knew Shahrazad well. It was the Empress's indulgence and desire to broaden the child's experience of the world beyond the court that allowed the girl to spend so much time with Kamil's family. For many years their children had shown no deference towards the royal girl but once she had begun the transition to maidenhood, the natural order returned and they saw her rarely in the family's modest quarters inside the palace's external walls.

-My wife, my wife, murmured Kamil resignedly, as if everything in existence was quite beyond him.

-It is a conundrum, Baligha replied, -If you are to be gone for a few days then that's an end to it. You could hardly complain. It might even be a pleasure to see some of the countryside after the months you spend in the vaults of that library. But if, as you imagine, Shahrazad has some plot buzzing in her head that might turn it into weeks then I will be desolate. I see you little enough and your children are at an age when they need your guiding wisdom. Perhaps you should tell the Empress.

He took up yet another piece of honeycomb and dipped it in the yoghurt, letting it roll around his mouth with closed eyes, lost for a moment in the reverie of this paradise, -I do not think I can. The Empress once told me that I must never betray the confidence of her child, even to her. It was important that Shahrazad should trust me absolutely. And the girl was with us at the time so there could be no mistake about the contract. That is why when Shahrazad told me not to tell her mother I was bound to silence by both of them. I am sure that if I disclosed what the Princess plans, the Empress would be furious and that would be the end of the royal historian. I would lose the confidence and friendship of both. No, he said, his hand unconsciously sneaking towards the bowl of sweetness, -I am on a hook and the more I struggle, the deeper it bites into me. I must just go along with it. She may be playing games and testing me as she sometimes does. You remember when I had to extricate her from your old workplace, the palace of the senses? The Empress had told her of how she had caused you and I to meet there and the naughty tyke wanted to see for herself what men will pay for. I was ordered by her never to mention it to her mother. I am sure I saved her young body from molestation beyond imagination.

-Perhaps, but since she is the best known young creature in the empire, it is more likely that everyone in the palace of the senses was humouring her.

-It would only have taken one man to have transgressed...

Baligha laughed, -But none did, so let it go from your mind. We cannot carry what-ifs in our thoughts for ever. Let us concentrate on the present. That is difficult enough. You leave in the morning and tonight you have the last reading before you return?

-Yes we leave but it is not the last reading. I must take the book with me. She wants all her pleasures on the journey. He looked glumly at his wife, suddenly taking in her white hair and patrician features, her elegant grey tunic and silver bangles as if he hadn't seen them for months, -I will miss you, you are so extraordinarily beautiful.

A tear or two found their way to the corners of Baligha's eyes and she rose and came to him, -Let us enjoy each other's comforts for an hour while this house is ours alone, she said and helped him to his feet and led him to their bedroom.

*

-You had a meeting with my mother, giggled the Princess Shahrazad as she dumped herself noisily in the chair in front of him. She was wearing her usual outfit and had managed to turn her hair, upon which her chambermaid had lavished so much attention, into a bristling, unkempt red stook of hay.

Kamil was not seduced by the giggle. He saw the glint in her eye under the fluttering lids, -I did, Princess. And, in case you are anxious about it, I told her nothing of your plans.

She sat up in a pretence at indignation, -I was not anxious! I am amazed you should think so. You are my confidant, Uncle. All my secrets are safe with you. Then, as if nothing had passed between them, she continued, -She has appointed Uncle Raashid to accompany us.

-She told me.

-That should not be a problem. She pursed her lips, -What do you think?

-He is a fine man. There is none finer and he would die for you or your mother. There have been times-

She broke in roughly, -I know, I know! You do not have to lecture me on the qualities of my Uncle. He is a darling. I love every fibre of his body. Yes, yes, yes! But that is exactly the problem I was talking about. It will be like having my mother's long arm constantly around my shoulders. Or worse, hugging me so tightly that I cannot breathe. Kamil kept quiet. Secretly he thought it was a good thing that Raashid was accompanying them. This might mean an end to her fantasies, whatever they were.

-I have a plan to douse his flame, don't worry Uncle. And you can do your duty by my mother. But remember, you are my spymaster now! She stood a little and wrestled her clothes into some sort of order, before alighting boyishly back on the chair, -Come on, Uncle. Read! You can sleep on our problem. We have time enough later for our solution.

-Is this ship housing two fools and a dozen ghosts?? asked his daughter. They had found a stable ready and waiting for the horses with fresh straw. A seaman led them to a communal table laid with bread and goat's cheese, a pitcher of fresh water, dried fruit and salted fish wrapped in broad green leaves, the latter plant unknown to either of them. Of their other companions there was no sign though their horses stood in the next stalls, relieved of armour and munching hay reflectively. The Magus had tried to enter their minds but, as he had surmised, it was to no avail. He had been met by an opaque wall. In the end, they had stowed their weapons, eaten and returned to the deck to view the land from which they had come.

-Every one of us is a fool some of the time, replied her father, - Particularly when we try to guard against it most. But here? No. We came on board, knowing the risk but anxious for a positive outcome. It seemed the only course and we have not been bewitched or beleaguered and we have been treated courteously, albeit by an inscrutable foe. Then they felt the ship stir. -Now our journey is beginning. They both turned and saw their fellow traveller at the giant tiller at the rear of the craft. Elsewhere, men pulled ropes, climbed the single mast and stowed the anchor. An expansive red sail caught the wind and bowed taut above them and they were moving quickly into the centre of the gently flowing water, pushing against its force but seemingly unfettered by its pressure. Their enticer, too, had shed his armour and clearly was not from any tribe from these parts. He was naked to the waist and his body and arms were painted in swirling blue snakes. His black hair was coiled upon his head, its ends held in a topknot tuft and his face had a yellow-brown tinge, framing black eyes and a chin-beard, pointed like that of a goat. They marvelled at his skill and strength and once or twice during the next hours they tried to talk with him but he appeared deaf to every entreaty, as did his comrades.

The first day's journey came to a slow halt as the sun dropped from sight. The sail was drawn in and the anchor was weighed so that they became stationery, like a tiny island with each bank far in the distance. Their companion of so many days appeared to be the ship's captain, going about his business methodically and without any suggestion of fatigue. They watched as he organised men to unhook a long wooden spar, swinging it out over the water. A rope ran through an eye of metal at its end and back to them. They pulled on it, drawing a silk net like a giant's stocking, along its length. As it reached the end, they allowed it to fall into the water. The Magus estimated that it must have sunk to twice his own height. For a while the sailor-fishermen watched and then, satisfied by circles of bubbles and a gathering pool of oiliness on the surface, they retracted the apparatus. As the jerking net came to the side of the ship, they could see several fish of different sizes, flapping in the silk. Men took those that were too small and dropped them back into the waters, saving several large silver bellied creatures with red streaks down their sides and mottled green and blue backs. They struck their heads with a small wooden cudgel and placed three on the deck, nodding to the Magus and his daughter and pointing to each in turn and then at their captain. It was the first and only communication of that day. The Magus cooked them on a brazier on the deck, their shallow-scored sides and inner cavities stuffed with herbs he took from his saddle while the sailors secretly watched his alien arts. The moment he finished, the captain arrived to take one of the fish away to eat on his own somewhere, leaving the pair to each other's company.

The fish were big with dense flakes and proved wholesome enough to satisfy their hunger when supported by a little dried fruit and afterwards, in the blackness of a moonless night, they arranged their skins beside their recumbent horses and slept on their straw.

Over the next week their strange companions showed that they understood that the horses required time on land each day. Though they did not display signs of distress, they were very subdued when the boat was under sail. A canter along the river bank and a splashing swim in the shallows rejuvenated them. Since there was no conversation possible with the sailors, they spent most of the time in silent thought. In the Magus' case this involved intense meditation and in his daughter's, reflections upon her life thus far, from childhood to the present. She felt few pangs in leaving her two children behind. They would be happy enough in the extensive family setting in the valleys. There were cousins and half cousins everywhere and their aunt was a better parent to them than she could ever be. She had left them many times as the urge to travel came upon her, once for nearly a year, so it was not unusual for her to be away like this. In fact, when her father received the message from her half sister requesting he come immediately, she followed her mother's lead and insisted she travel with him. Yet this was only partially because she wanted to see new lands and people with gods and behaviours unlike her own, it was also because her father was no longer the invincible man that he had been in his prime. There might be few who could outwit or outfight him still but he had separated himself from his weapons for such a long time, he must be vulnerable in a way that even he did not appreciate. These days together would be full of precious time and she would truly feel that she had taken every opportunity to fulfil her desire to know him through and through.

She asked him once again, -You still have no knowledge of what your other daughter wants of us?

He emerged from his thoughts, -No. I suspect that war is imminent with the empire to the north. He looked at the crew, -And now that events have overtaken us so strangely and we are captives, even if it is of our own volition, I would hazard that all is connected in a pattern that will be revealed to us.

She grunted, -It seems so to me also, now that you say it. The tides of war are more common in the east. She paused and looked over to the man at the tiller, -And it is true that we are captives even without chains and with a jailor who seems unconcerned about whether we flee or not. Then she looked at the passing hills and said, -Still, we are moving somewhere with purpose. It is better than sitting in a dungeon such as the one your father-not-of-blood and I endured on his final trip to his homeland.

-Tell me again. He wasn't humouring her, there were questions he wanted to ask her. It was odd that he had not sought to know more than she had already told him. Perhaps it was because a great many members of the clan had been there to greet her return and she had recounted her adventures without interruption from any of her listeners. She had sat by the fireside, her face joyful at her safe return and the stories had poured out of her as they all ate and the hours drifted past. So when she had finished it was as though a full and true account had been furnished, one that everyone had heard and one that would be part of the clan's history to be told and memorised and retold by succeeding generations. There was no demand from her listeners to know more. But, for the Magus, there could always be a search for more.

-You know the story, she said, puzzled.

-I know you were captured by rival merchants and entombed in an underground cell. I know how you escaped. But I do not know what you felt during all those weeks in darkness. How did you stay prepared for the moment of liberation?

She frowned as she dragged back her experience, -It was a little like what is happening to us now, save we have the shores with its shapes and plants and birds to keep our interest. Every day was like the last, we could tell their passing by the sounds in the fortress. Your father told me your whole life story as he knew it and that of your mother. And his own. I recounted mine, though it was much shorter! I remember that he had to work harder to keep my mind bathed in optimism than I his. We ended up talking about fate and religion and the gods. He was not happy with your denial of forces outside man's knowledge and felt that I had been a little poisoned by you since I too have no fixed sense of occult powers that might toy with humans. We talked thus and we argued for hours, this way and that, much of the time not really believing our arguments but happy to keep the blade's edge of our thinking, sharp. All the while, as you know, he used a metal spike we found secreted between stones by some other prisoner to scrape further at the top of one wall where our predecessor had begun to gouge at softer rock. It was in this manner that he brought a little light into our hole and it was a great relief to me for I have none of my sister's upbringing in caverns and tunnels. Nor do I want to be buried when I die. I always wished to be burned on a pyre, though, she added hastily, -I seek no great comfort in the God of Fire.

The Magus asked softly, -And by this time were his faculties still strong?

-If you mean his mind, yes, it was as strong as ever. But his physical prowess was declining. We were given water and a little bread each day but it was not enough to sustain such a man. When we broke free he had waned to half his size. Though I regained strength very quickly in the home of our friends, it took him some time. His hair was streaked with white, his eyes had turned pink and wept constantly and his face had lost its lean, leathery vigour, becoming round and almost womanly. There was a rash upon him that scourged his skin and, despite his medicinal arts he could not rid himself of it. It was but a few weeks travel to his home and his other son-not-of-blood but we had to make our way slowly. I think we both knew he would not live to make another journey.

-An unfitting end for such a man. I will always regret not being beside him when he died but I am grateful for the twist of life's course that had you there with him. You ensured my blood's warmth comforted him. The Magus stared sternly at the passing water, watching the reflection of their silhouettes bend and twist on its surface.

-He died at peace, I to one side and his other son, your brother, at the other. His eyes remained open until the last and when the spirit left them, they stayed clear until your brother stroked them shut. As I have told you, his last words were of his love for you and your brother and those of us within whom your blood flows.

The final two days of sailing against the currents were more arduous. The river was narrower and the hills higher on either side. The sailors seemed to be losing their power over the wind which blew across the boat now, necessitating constant tacking to maintain momentum. At last they had to yield to the forces that were stalling them and turned the vessel with the wind to force a landing among reeds, in a small tributary. The flat keel grumbled and screeched as they became grounded. Minutes later they were on spongy grass, the horses jubilantly aware that there would be no more rocking and pitching. The Magus and his daughter trekked a little way with their bows and returned with a tusked creature that was so heavy they had to drag it back on a litter.

It was while they were eating on the shore, a little distance from the crew and the sun was casting its last long tree shadows across the water below them, that they heard the distant splash of oars. The seamen rose as one and stood in bowed salute as into view came a long, slim rowing boat, carved from a single tree and carrying a standing woman and three oarsmen. Even at the briefest of glances, it was obvious that they were of the same stock as the waiting sailors.

It was also clear that the imperious woman, dressed in a long white silk coat emblazoned with dragons, her feet planted apart for balance, was their leader.

-**A warrior woman!** Your books are full of them, Uncle. Now the Magus and his daughter are firmly on their journey and soon we will be on ours. The two journeys will reflect each other just as some of the events of the Tales mirrored what was happening to my mother! I wonder what this woman has in store for them? What race are they? The descriptions suggest Chinamen but the Magus seemed to think not. He hints that they come from the northern borders and are the cause of his second daughter's fears. She was wandering around his ante-room, her fingers twisting in and out of each other, oblivious except for her thoughts about the Tale.

-They are not of China, as you have guessed, replied Kamil, -But a kindred race to the north of those lands and stretching further east and west than we can imagine. That is what the ancient manuscripts tell us.

-Then why are they so far south I wonder? It is a plot! She pouted at him.

-That is for you to uncover in my readings, replied Kamil amusedly.

-O Uncle! She stamped a foot and snorted but then gave way to laughing, -The book will be a good diversion on our own journey, don't you think? Once we have loosened Raashid's grip on our destiny, you and I will travel as fast and light as the Magus and his daughter! Before he could venture any protest at such an outlandish notion she sat down again and changed the subject, -I liked the part in your Tale when the Magus questions his daughter about the details of her imprisonment with his father. My mother often says to me when I am lying to her, detail, I want detail! She knows my story won't stand up to scrutiny. She must have learned this from you. The pair survived because each tells the other the finest detail of their lives and their deepest beliefs. The Magus is curious about what this detail is. God and religion. Fears and beliefs. They are in the most hidden part of us, are they not? What we fear and what we believe? Learn this about someone and you have control over him, I think. The heart becomes a portal and you can reach through it and take his heart away from him and make him your disciple. That is why prophets are so powerful. Shahrazad was staring at him with unblinking eyes and it made him shiver a little. It was not the import of what she said, which was cause enough but the words she chose and the way she spoke them. He had noticed this trait more and more in recent times. It was as though the Princess could switch personalities and assume the character of someone much older and more cunning than the young girl she presented to the world most of the time.

Chapter Three

The impossible is an offspring of the unimaginative

Raashid arrived at the first lightening of the sky. Kamil had just risen and was sending off a servant to bring him yoghurt and fruit which Raashid then requested should be doubled. He had not eaten but had come a little early hoping for a brief conversation and breakfast with the historian before they made their way to the Princess's rooms. They exchanged pleasantries until the food arrived. As they did so, Kamil observed his companion. He was tall and broad and had a handsome, if slightly effeminate, face, the conspiracy of full lips and long eyelashes. His hair fell to his shoulders and was combed into shiny ringlets. He fought as well as the best in his troop but was more noted for his love of the arts. He acted in his own plays for the court, producing them with great flair and always in flamboyant costume. He was a fine musician wherever fingers and strings were involved and he was happily married with several children. Kamil felt that he had aged since they had last met, having the heavier muscles of a mature man and a less swaggering air than he had assumed in his twenties.

It was Raashid who broached the subject of his early arrival, -So the Empress has us on child protection duty! Kamil laughed at the expression, -She is still a child, do you not think? went on Raashid, -I see her now and then and she is full of mischief and breaks more rules in a day than I did in a week at that age. And I was difficult, so I am told. She fights boys with her fists, is better with a sword than many a man and can shoot straighter than her mother who I helped train, myself. When she finally turns and becomes a woman with a woman's desires, I fear for all the men in the empire, young and old for they will be dazzled to distraction by her beauty.

-She is unique, replied Kamil.

-She was a miracle birth. Her colouring, her hair, her eyes and her tall body mark her as someone from a far off place, no-one from this kingdom has ever visited. Even Sabiya is a little frightened of her potential to create mayhem in the empire. Raashid, as far as Kamil knew, was the only person who could address the Empress by her first name in this way. Although Raashid was talking in a jocular, informal way Kamil could sense tension in him, nonetheless. This was confirmed when Raashid put down the rind of an orange he had been sucking dry and said, -Sabiya thinks her daughter might try to trick us in some way but we should humour her wherever possible. This means treating her as the future Empress and acceding to her wishes. I think Sabiya is anxious that she grows up quickly. She senses that there is an undercurrent in her daughter but would like to see it exposed through events. She must be watched carefully, particularly in the Second City. Sabiya is suspicious because Shahrazad saw her cousin not a month ago so why this sudden rush to visit her when she could demand that her relative visits the royal court? Yet, even so, Sabiya was adamant about one thing, Shahrazad must make whatever decision she wishes and we must accept it, if she disagrees with our counsel. No matter how dangerous it seems to us. I don't like it. I feel fettered. He sighed and changed tack, -At least Shahrazad will not complain if her cousin's chambers are not up to royal standard. She likes to rough it with the best.

Kamil thought about his promise to the Princess. He decided he could give Raashid no hint of her plans to travel further than the Second City. Instead he said, -I am glad you will be with us. Surely she won't try any of her little treacheries with you there.

-Little do you know her, then! I have suffered many a public humiliation at her young hands. I think only you seem to be sacrosanct. She values your role in saving her mother.

-No more than yours.

-You are being too kind, mine was a small contribution while yours was the lynchpin of her victories over her stepmother and the Red Man. These words gave Kamil a warm current of pride. While it was true, he never voiced it, even to Baligha and only the Empress, herself, ever alluded to it. Raashid continued, -Which is why she thought it best that you, too, accompany the Princess.

Kamil looked puzzled, -It was the Princess who desired my company.

-Hardly! The Empress insisted. At first Shahrazad sulked but suddenly she seemed to come round and agree. She became excited that you would have the book ready for her and wanted it to be read on the journey.

*

An hour later they were leaving the gate through the outer wall of the palace. Kamil sat with the Princess and her maid in a speedy carriage, despite her wish to ride horse with Raashid's elite corps. There was nothing to indicate from its exterior that a royal personage was travelling in it. It was simply constructed with hard leather seats, shutters on the windows and not intended for comfort. Raashid preferred to ride in front, his mount between the lead scout and the cavalcade, his eyes watching for any sign of danger.

They had agreed to make regular stops to ease the punishment of the bouncing seats. The sand roads made for a comfortable passage for short periods but potholes and rocks would suddenly throw everything a kilter. Nevertheless they were making good progress. At their first stop, an oasis of sorts with low clay houses, palm trees and a growing population which lived off camel herding and the north south trade, their escort of soldiers formed a phalanx around the carriage, keeping the local people well away. Shahrazad dropped lightly on to the sand and went to the edge of the water where she removed her shoes and began bathing her feet. Kamil and Raashid joined her, sitting either side.

-You can wash your feet, too, she laughed, -I have not polluted the water. They smiled at her but stayed shod. Lemon and mint drinks were brought for them by the coachman in a locked wooden container packed with ice bags. Only the Princess held the key. Despite her popularity no-one could guarantee that plots were not simmering somewhere to usurp her place as rightful heir to the empire. Already clansfolk were gathering beyond the line of soldiers rushing forward and clapping their hands excitedly above their heads, chanting her name. She finished her drink and stood up to wave to them but almost immediately dropped to her knees. At the same moment Kamil saw clearly a man with a gun pointing at them. The sound of the gunshot followed a moment later and there was a flash of white spume as the bullet hit the water wide of the Princess. Immediately there were screams of alarm, rushing bodies and soldiers waving weapons while Raashid threw himself over a struggling Princess to protect her from further attack. Kamil was now flat on his stomach, his eyes lifted to follow the scenes of chaos. He could no longer see the assassin. The main troop of soldiers were yelling and marshalling the crowd into order while the scout and two others mounted their horses and galloped off to check the roads that led from the encampment.

-Get off me Raashid! stormed the Princess, her bent knees straightening and kicking him to one side, -The danger is over. Put all the villagers in a line and Uncle Kamil and I will question them. Now! Her voice was sharp and authoritative, the other voice that Kamil had begun to hear, the older voice. Her face had paled but remained stern and intense. Raashid pursed his lips and then nodded and got up. What she was asking he would have done anyway. He was dismayed. He was here to protect the Princess and she had saved her own life! Kamil rolled to a sitting position beside her. He realised that she must have seen something to have avoided the bullet.

-You saw the assassin? she asked.

-I did, said Kamil.

The Princess looked at him swiftly, -And?

-Bearded. Bald.

-I did not see the face, she said, -But I sensed something in the crowd, an unusual movement out of the corner of my eye. The arms were all raised and this one was suddenly pointing at me. It happened very quickly. I was in real danger, she said, wonderingly, -You heard the shot? It was a new pistol. They can be very accurate in trained hands. There are not many guns of that kind in the empire, outside the royal household. They come to us in strong boxes from the gunmaker. He and the Chinaman who crafts the weapons are guarded every second of the day. Each weapon must be accounted for and branded. Let us do our investigation.

They stood up and slowly walked towards the waiting clansfolk. There was a silence that, it seemed, nothing would interrupt. Everyone knew that, if the Princess so wished, lives could end that day and they almost felt they deserved it for hadn't they harboured an assassin in their own ranks? Shahrazad could see the conflicting emotions on their faces, the desire to smile and reach out in supplication but also the dread at what might happen next. She stood before them, tall and imposing, despite her young years. The sun made her hair flame in a halo and her blue eyes glittered. Close up, she was terrifying.

-My Uncle will ask the first question, she stated coldly. Kamil somehow knew that she would say this. Her thoughts seemed to pass to him before she spoke.

To the puzzlement of the crowd, it was the portly figure of the historian, standing only to her shoulder, who spoke, -The shot came from the middle of you all? he asked. There were nods, -Then whose ears were deafened by the sound of the gunshot, right next to them? Hands went up, -Show me how you were standing. Next to each other? In front? Behind? This seemed a difficult question and with furrowed brows, four men arranged themselves, looking at each other and nodding and gesticulating. -Then where was the person holding the gun? They pointed at the space between them, -So who was standing there, do you remember? As if shutters had dropped from his eyes, one of them spoke urgently, -I remember! He is not from the village but he is here, often. He is a traveller. I did not see his gun. When it exploded near my head I shut my eyes and covered my ears. When I looked again, he was not there, I think.

-Describe him! The description tumbled out of them. Bald and bearded. The man that Kamil had seen.

Princess Shahrazad nodded and came to stand beside Kamil, -Put you hands up in front of you, palms towards me. They stood in a long straight line for her inspection. She walked past them, eyes sharp and focused, her nose wrinkling. Seemingly satisfied, she drew Kamil and Raashid away, out of hearing, -I wanted to check. The assassin is not among them. I smelled no fired gun on any of them, nor were there marks on their hands or clothes from its smoke. She said to Raashid, - Get the traveller's description from as many as can give it, where he comes from, how often he visits, his connections, his clan, his religion, his dress. Details are everything Raashid. Only an hour into our trip and already we are assaulted, she giggled, -This is going to be even more exciting than I had planned!

-I think we should return to the court, immediately, growled Raashid, shortly, -I cannot vouchsafe your protection, it appears. I promised the Empress to return with you should there be any attempt to molest you. I thought she meant unwanted attentions from men, not this!

-An assassin would have to be very skilful to take my life, Raashid and even more so, a man with a beast's intentions. I can catch the scent of an enemy as clearly as you can see that carriage. It enters my mind, almost as though I can suddenly hear the thoughts of one who would do me harm. It is strange indeed. Her words, particularly the reference to a beast, affected Kamil greatly. The times that he and Shahrazad's mother had referred to the girl's eventual father, the Red Man, as the beast. It was uncanny that this grown child was using the same term, blithely and innocent of that history. And her premonition about her enemy's intentions seemed as though they had been cultivated in the blood of her father, -Oversee the interrogation, Raashid, please. Be quick. I want to be back on our journey. Then she added, -And have no concern about my mother's anxieties over what has just happened. She has a way of understanding these things.

Raashid stared at her glumly. Whatever had happened to the child he had known who would take his advice with a skip and a smile? He had to obey her. The Empress had been explicit that he could not overrule the Princess even though, if she had known that her daughter was close to being the victim of an assassin she must surely have changed her mind. In fact this trip would never have taken place. With any normal mother and child, his duty to her would have been to take her back to court but while he escorted her his duty was to obey her every command. Disturbed, he strode off to vent his anger on the witnesses.

-Good, said Shahrazad to Kamil, -We shall soon be on our way.

*

That evening, at the end of a long journey lacking any of the alarms of their first halt at the oasis and having eaten, the Princess and Kamil retired to the coach so that he might read to her. Her orders to Raashid were to keep everyone away from them, the reading of the Tales meant so much to her. Kamil lifted a hinged tray that hung from the inside of the door of the carriage and propped it in position. He lay a silk square over it and placed the remaining Major Arcana upon it. Next to this he put the box that contained the Tales of the Magus.

Without further ado she turned over the next card, -The High Priestess! she exclaimed, -She is the one who is wise in all things except earthly passion, is she not? I have no affinity for her. Women who give themselves to their gods are traitors to their flesh. They are incomplete and yet they pontificate on everything that breathes under the sun. Still, the Magus seems to find enough examples of such creatures even if I have never met any of their ilk in this world! Perhaps this is another one. That is the pleasure of stories, Uncle. They fabricate falsehoods. She settled back and closed her eyes.

The woman stepped lightly from the canoe, the white silk of her long dress coat rippling and making the red dragons dance. The Magus and his daughter stood, almost to attention, such was the effect of her bearing. The daughter looked at the woman curiously. Here they were in a wilderness of crags, forest and strongly rushing river, face to face with a mysterious female who, in dress and appearance, seemed like an occult visitation. It was as though she had been cut out of the land of gods and heroes and glued against the trees and water.

She spoke the tongue that could be found everywhere in the empire in one bastardised dialect or another, with a crackling deep timbre and in an accent that forced her listeners to concentrate on each word, - Welcome! She bowed to them with her hands, palms together at her midriff and pointing down. They responded with bows and right hands on heart, -I sorry we bring you like cattle, she went on, -But you not come otherwise.

-It is true, said the Magus, -Whatever your reason, it would not have been enough. Only the capture of my wife keeps us here.

-So. She looked at them, -Here. We talk? Neither answered her, though, if there had been a lingering sense of danger, it now disappeared. She did not seem duplicitous and her smile appeared engaging, if cool. She indicated a grass-covered bank and sat, gesturing that they sit beside her. She pointed to herself and her men, -We travelling people of north ice deserts. You, western mountain valleys. You Magus and you his daughter. We hear about you many times. We let traders pass our lands. Stories always about you. Whatever scent she was wearing blew across them. It was heavy but not sweet and it made both of them a little light headed, -Famous warrior. Kill, kill, kill. Always more stories. Scholar guru, also. Many scriptures. Emperor want you meet. She paused, collecting herself, not used to speaking at such length in this tongue, -Man who warrior and write. Rare man.

-We are not mercenaries, snapped the daughter, coldly.

-Please?

-We do not fight for reward.

She pointed at the daughter, -Reward, your mother. She turned to the Magus for emphasis, -Your wife also. We go Emperor and her. Much way. River. Land. Many nights. First make boat fly! she laughed, - Then win war.

They all slept on board, though the horses remained on shore to graze and exercise their legs. Before they went to sleep, father and daughter had a quiet conversation. There were other sleeping berths along the bulkhead.

-Will you fight for them?

-No.

-Even to save your wife?

-It will not come to that.

-She is not a bad person. The daughter was referring to the newcomer.

-Beware one who laughs yet who permits no change in her eyes. She can use a sword.

-How can you tell? The daughter's forehead ruckled as she thought back to her memories of the woman.

-She prefers the left hand. It is bigger and stronger than the other. There is hard skin between the thumb and the forefinger. She is balanced like a fighter. Her feet were always rocking on their toes. She was careful when we met and was ready to defend if she felt we might attack her. She hides a sword under the coat.

-Oh, said the daughter, -I saw none of this. I saw her smile and her dress was not for battle. I must be more wary.

-Hah! said the Magus, -You are always wary inside. If she had moved against us, she would not have caught you unprepared. I am just speaking aloud what your body knows but you have not yet thought about. These people are not like any I have met. They have not extolled a god, nor have they shown any signs of worship. They have travelled far over land and water to find us and planned it so your mother would be the lure of a smaller fish to catch bigger. I have heard that their armies are spreading and grasping more territories. She is to be watched for if the emperor of that hungry empire has chosen her to bring us to him, his confidence in her must be absolute. But it is confusing. She wears the dress of the spice trader. It may mean that unbeknownst to me, during my time away from the world, events have overtaken the great empires to the east, perhaps threatening even your sister, my daughter, who then sent for me. It may be that all is conjoined in the one mystery. When we find your mother, we may aid your sister at the same time. We shall discover all soon enough. Meanwhile, sleep will not harm us.

-Yes Father, she replied, submissively and they pressed themselves down into their skins, their noses capturing the smells of the passing river, damp wood, waxed ropes, bilge water and stable straw as they drifted to sleep.

They woke to the sounds of trees being logged. It was barely light. Arriving on deck they could make out a line of long tree trunks, scalped of their branches and bark, neatly laid out on the shore. The female chief of the industrious workers sat at a table further along the deck with food before her. She gestured for them to join her. In the chill of early morning, she had covered her long garment of red dragons with an extra black woollen overcoat, held tight with hoops of cord and wooden pegs.

-You eat, she declared, indicating the bowls of fruit and flat bread while she chewed a rind of fat, -Soon all work! They took stools and joined her, eating silently. The day was gaining its full light when the men had gathered and prepared enough wood to match the length of the boat. There were heavy ropes in coils, balls of twine, pulleys and large metal hooks beside the white, sap-glistening logs. The crew stopped work and came up the gang plank to eat, quickly disappearing below.

The daughter remembered the words last spoken by the female chief when they retired for sleep, -Did you not say that the boat is to fly? she asked, more curious about the choice of phrase than any suggestion that her adversary might actually mean it.

-True word. Soon we start, the woman laughed in her crackling voice, -Fly from one river to other.

By midday they had moved the boat some distance over land. It defied the expectations of father and daughter that so much progress could be made so quickly. Only in the circus had the Magus seen such a heavy load being transported by the hands of men. Using the tree boles as rollers and attaching pulleys fixed at the other end to trees, to the sides of the boat with ropes, they moved it slowly uphill. As rollers became redundant at the rear they were carried to the front again to smooth the bark's forward progress. Pulleys were constantly unhooked and moved on to succeeding trees while thick rope hawsers, stretching from the bow to a wooden harness, enabled the crew's horses to add their considerable strength to the momentum. The roan and the grey were spared this hardship. While this synchronised activity kept the vessel moving through the forest, two men with scythes cut a path before them. The Magus quickly realised that the entire crew was being rotated constantly so that the labour for each man was equal and that they must have used this route regularly and recently for there were no trees blocking their narrow passage, just straggling plants and grasses.

They stopped at midday and the head woman came to eat with them, - One week, she exclaimed, -End fly. Take new water north. She pointed vaguely and then started eating. The daughter was determined to find out more of this woman's country and she stretched out a hand and touched the dragon dress.

-From your land? she asked.

The woman smiled and shook her head, -Me trade in south east war. Good! She pointed to a dragon and made a gesture of flames coming from her mouth, -Fire! We search this animal. No see anywhere. And she laughed at what appeared to be a joke. The daughter looked at the Magus and he nodded as if what the woman had said confirmed something for him.

By dusk they had doubled the distance of the morning. The father and daughter had gone hunting during the afternoon and between them now built a large fire and spit to cook their catch. They had a collection of animals of varying sizes and some plump birds. There were plant roots and leaves. They skinned and plucked, drew innards and slashed through the fat on the sides of beast and fowl, stuffing them with herbs and spices from their saddles. They made a great aromatic broth with the birds and roasted the animals. Once again the crew, this time with their chief, chose to eat on their own while the two cooks chewed reflectively a small distance away.

-They do not like the vegetables!

-So I see, said her father, -It is true that they must come from the far north, as she says. My father once told me that, in those icy wastelands, the people know nothing of plants for they are nomads and live off meat and fish only. They love the fat on creatures and carry it in their bags on their journeys. You saw her this morning.

-And her dress is not from her own land.

-No. She is unlike the spice traders who wore such garments. She said that there was a war with those from the south east. Her dress is a trophy.

The daughter shook her head perplexedly, -Why? I cannot conceive that I would wear clothes of another people except for deceit or some other necessity. She is proud of it.

-Different tribes have different traditions and behaviour. Some wear the teeth of their vanquished on a thread around their necks, some take the skin and hair from their victim's heads and sew them into fighting coats, some skin the entire body to make pouches and bags...

-Then this is only mild disrespect! she laughed, truculently.

-So I believe. We do not know if she killed for it. She said it was from trade. Let us believe her unless we come to know more. He lay back, his stomach full, -I sense no desire to hurt us in her thoughts. He paused and then he changed the subject, -This is the longest I have been with the people of another tribe and neither heard nor seen prayers, invocations, dances, songs or other rituals. They have not made any small offering of their food as is the custom elsewhere, they do not pour their tea three times back and forth between cups and pot, which I have seen everywhere and there is no sharing of food once each has his portion. They eat with either hand, having cleansed both in water. It is hard to understand them, so different are they from any I have met.

The chief came over to them, -Good food, she said, smacking her lips loudly in a gesture of appreciation, -Hot spice. We find in south. You learn this where?

-Travelling, he replied, -Spice traders. Many places.

-Ah, you, too? she asked his daughter.

-A little. Mostly from him, she touched her father's sleeve.

-Night comes, she said abruptly, -Sleep there. She pointed upwards. This time, the horses were all taken on board and the gangplank removed, the boat being trussed in position with ropes. The head woman did not explain her reasons but they were happy enough to share the straw with their horses. In the night, the Magus heard the roars of a pack of hunting creatures close to them but nothing came of it.

The evening before they would arrive at the new river, they had their first lengthy conversation with the northern woman. Although they had gathered some details during the days of hauling the vessel through the trees, it was too insubstantial to gain a picture of what her tribe was like, how its lands were governed and what role she played when in her emperor's court.

They had finished eating and were seated in a large clearing, The boat was propped in its centre. All afternoon the men had been attending to its hull, scraping and then daubing a thick black liquid on it. The smell was pungent and they sat at a distance from it. There was still some light which was augmented by the flames of a bright fire. The Magus and his daughter had prepared all the meals on the journey and, as far as they could judge, they were appreciated though no-one said much in thanks. At any event, everything was eaten except the vegetables.

-How long until I see my mother? asked the daughter.

-Long time. River, one moon. Horse two moons.

-No ice when we get there?

-No. Small hot. Change quick. She sighed, -Pretty! Many flowers.

-Tell us about your lands, the daughter said, solicitously, then in a rush she asked? -What homes have you? What do you grow? Have you a man? Have you children? Is your Emperor a good ruler?

The woman stared at her stonily and then said in a low, menacing voice, -No-one talk about Emperor. Not possible. Wrong. Bad. He God. She wrung her fingers as though washing them.

-I am sorry, said the daughter and touched a hand on her heart.

The woman's face softened, -You not know. Land not like here. My land like this. She pointed at the flattened earth. I General. Emperor make ten generals, she put up all her fingers and waggled them, -I am hunter. Go after enemy. Kill or take home.

Somehow this started her talking. They did not interrupt with questions, recognising that this might well remind her that she had other business but kept their faces fixed on hers and listened attentively. It seemed that she was a wife of the Emperor, one of many. She had a son who was cared for by servants along with all the other Emperor's children. The Emperor had a castle that the tribe had captured when they had taken bordering lands for they were not builders and lived, for the most part, in skin tents like the Magus' wife's desert people. They herded cattle and horses and never stopped moving. Even the Emperor. He came to his castle three or four times every year and met his generals and ambassadors from other lands there. Every man and woman was a warrior and was expected to spend time on conquests in far off territories. If they met with resistance, they left and came back with an army. They were pitiless in their vengeance, massacring everyone in a rebellious settlement or town. If one of her warriors was killed she took a hundred lives in return. While she was telling them this, the general was smiling unconcernedly. There was no hint that she might think it questionable to take lives on such a scale or that women and children should be spared. She was proud that she had been asked to find and bring back the Magus. First she and one other warrior, the one that had ridden to find them and bring them to the boat, had taken his wife at night and handed her on to a cohort of soldiers who would take her north and east to the Emperor's castle. In fact, they had joined this very same route a half a month before. This was why the passage through the forest was so clear.

If the Magus found her matter of fact, calculating attitude to killing at odds with his own beliefs, he did not show it. He had encountered much the same, everywhere. It had become his mission in life to teach people to understand that killing was an evil act. But the times were turbulent. Very few areas of their own empire were untouched by great upheavals. The General had introduced the god of the sun to all his people and had forced every clan to convert from many gods to him alone. Most clans found the rituals of serving a single god difficult to accept. He had also passed a decree that every clan should train its young to fight, whether they be sheep herders, fishermen or farmers and to obey the universal tithe that two young men be conscripted to the Emperor's army for five year tours of duty.

The General had also sent his monks on journeys around his empire to teach reading and writing to sages in every region. This meant that his people's minds were being opened to new ideas, new stories and the new ways that the General wanted them to live. He had blended, like honey and vinegar, the principles that the Magus had discussed with him concerning the Right Path and those of the demands of the empire. Now, all tribes were expected to put the empire first and their tribes and clans second. When he had become ill it was the Magus and his second daughter from the City in the Mountain who had saved him and the empire from internal strife and destruction. Order and the respect for law were restored. But the Magus was under no illusion that people had actually accepted the new word. The difference between the attitudes of the female general, sitting beside him and the tribes of his own empire was no more than a hair's breadth.

When the Magus's second daughter and her husband, The Lord of the Eastern Empire united the two empires, they changed very little. Both had become followers of the God of the Sun and were trying to build on the foundations that the General had left them. They sought peace with neighbouring lands and encouraged trade between their own peoples and those from afar. But this partial harmony was seemingly so threatened that the Magus had been called upon this journey. He was certain that he would cross many more clans who shared this ice-general's unequivocal view of killing, as they travelled to her lands.

It was the Magus who framed a question which took a little while for her to fully understand.

-Have you a god or have you many gods? She looked puzzled. -Do you know the God of Fire? She nodded her head but scowled, -Any

God? Again there was confusion, -Do you pray? That was met with a blank expression. Finally, he asked, -If you die, what next?

Her face cleared, -Next, we join water again.

-Water? he asked.

-Water is start and end. Water is most most strong. No water no plant no animal no man no woman. Baby live in water in mother. Follow water out. Put in big water. If live long life possible. When we die, go on water in dead boat. Words say on top of body. Put in water with stone. Deep. Come back some time again. Animal. Plant. Baby. No know. Then, something seemed to make a connection in her mind, -Ah God! Yes. Fire God. Thunder God. Tree God. Many animal God. She tapped her head, -Before not understand. Water is God. We please water, it watch us. We angry water, it leave us to die or kill us. Then, as though the strain was too great for her, she stood up, -We wake and go to most big water. Tears came to her eyes, -It is the water of my land.

Kamil put the leaf of finely wrought paper down and looked at Shahrazad, -And that is the end of the chapter, he said, quietly. She opened her eyes and tightened her lips.

-I like it. Perhaps we might also go on a river to the north, Uncle Kamil, -Later, you and I.

-Some day, he said thoughtlessly, forgetting their recent conversation.

-Very soon, she glared at him, -When this adventure is over. Then she looked down at The High Priestess card, -Was the woman general the High Priestess? I don't think so. She has not developed civilised understanding, Uncle. She is still a primitive. She worships water and kills. Admittedly, she is another strong woman and we should be grateful for that. But she is not the fount of wisdom, is she?

-Perhaps it seems not but do not be deceived by her. There is much to come. She conceals a store of knowledge and, so far, it is hard for the Magus and his daughter to make her tell them all she knows. But she is a powerful general and high in the court of the northern empire and well versed in the lore of that land. When she meets the Magus she shows no arms for she wants to make an impression upon him. She wants him to see her as an ally. She has heard of his writings and knows enough of them to be certain that even if he bears arms he does not wish to use them. She has heard the tales about him and is a little fearful, too. But at the same time the Magus recognises she is a warrior and as powerful as any he has met. He is curious about what she knows of life and death and of the temporary existence we enjoy in this world. The card also suggests that wisdom can vanquish war. This is why the Magus waits to see all the outcomes.

-I think that a little fanciful! She is more like The Empress than The High Priestess but if what you say follows then I will be fulfilled I am sure. She is like some of the emperors before Haidar, my grandfather. The empire was not built on love and harmony, Uncle, as you know but in much the same way as hers. Men only give up their power at the point of a sword or after they are threatened with the blood of their children. How far are we from the Second City?

-We have made good progress. Less than two days.

-Then tomorrow you must find me a pretty young girl, Uncle. We must disappear before we enter the Second City for it is like a spider's web and our wings will thrash but we will never be able to fly out. We must dissolve like ghosts into the darkness and when we are visible again we must be far away from that place.

Kamil's face filled with consternation at her words but as his mouth opened, she placed a finger on them. This act froze him and he went mute. All he saw were the pools of her blue eyes, the pupils so large that he floundered in them. Where had he experienced this sensation before? Even as he asked himself the question, the answer seemed to drift into insignificance, his fear drained away and he felt at one with his Princess's plans.

Chapter Four

In your deepest self you will find the treasure of knowing others

All the next day, Kamil was wracked with conflicting emotions. Somehow he felt closer to Princess Shahrazad than ever and an obstinate force deep within him was determined to please her in whatever way she desired just as had been the case when he was a child and about to disobey his parents' wishes. But he also felt dismay at his determination to give her his unqualified support. Even though he felt his duty to her was paramount he also had a duty to the empire and its ruler. Should the Empress be told of their impending break from what had been agreed with her? In truth it would be better if she heard it from him before Raashid was forced to offer up his head in guilt at having lost them. At least then Raashid might be spared the worst of her anger. Poor fellow, he did not deserve any criticism, even over the attempted assassination. He knew that he, Kamil, would not be spared the lash of the Empress Sabiya's tongue when they met again even with the Princess safe and well after her mad escapade. Then, gradually, everything would return to normal. It did not occur to him that the Princess might never return.

In the event, he determined to send a messenger to the Empress as soon as they had broken away from the convoy of carriage and troops. This decision calmed him and he promptly forgot his misgivings.

*

That evening, after a very fast day's travel, they rested and ate cold meat, fruit and bread. Kamil, Raashid and the Princess sat in the carriage with the victuals on the little table between them while the accompanying cohort put up tents and made fires. Raashid was still on edge, the frightening events of the previous morning not yet put to one side. He had wanted to send a message to the Empress, telling her the news that her daughter was safe but when he had voiced this the Princess had prevented him with a curt look and a hand on his arm.

679

-Raashid! Do you wish my mother to be thrown into a fit of anxiety for the entire period that I will be away from her? Your duty is to keep her happy and see to it that no further attempts are made on my life.

-That is true, he mumbled, still disconsolate.

-You can send her a messenger with all the news when I am safely tucked up in bed in my room in my cousin's house. There, will that make you happy? She softened and smiled fully and warmly. He nodded, grudgingly, -How far away are we from the Second City? she asked, -From previous visits I would think we should arrive early tomorrow, is that so?

-It is so, he agreed, -We will be there before mid morning.

-So, what is it, a couple of hours' ride on horseback, without the carriage?

-For most! For me, perhaps an hour, he replied, not too humbly.

-Only an hour? Hmm… She looked at him pensively.

-What Princess, does something bother you?

-Only a small thing.

-Yes?

-I do have a little anxiety after yesterday's drama that my cousin's house may not be totally secure. I worry that we might arrive and before we know it, another attempt will be made upon my life. What do you think? She feigned the tiniest distress.

-I understand completely. I shall send a couple of men to check that all has been done to keep you safe. Raashid smiled happily.

-Men? I do not trust men, Raashid. Only you have the intelligence and experience to ensure my safety. Raashid is like the Magus in your books, Uncle, is he not? Only the sage had the imagination to see obscure sources of threat. She looked at Kamil with a sweet smile and then at Raashid.

-I could go now and be back in three hours, he muttered, thinking through what was involved. But it means leaving you here without my protection and I am not sure I can…

-Raashid! Three hours? In that time, I will be comfortably settled with Uncle here, listening to the next Tale of the Magus. The troops will be all around us. The fires will keep away snakes and wild beasts. I shall be no less safe than if you were here. And it is for such a short time! It is better that I spend this night not tossing and turning and unable to sleep for fear at what might greet me at my cousin's, don't you think?

*

They were in a low house, built from clay with a palm leaf roof. A central oven was alight so that the flames cast flickers over Kamil and the Princess. At either side of Kamil, oil lamps threw their illumination on the pack of cards and the box that contained the third book about the Magus. Shahrazad seemed content that they were now some distance from the Second City and was entirely focused on Kamil's prospective reading. So he began.

In the morning light the Magus and his daughter were asked to vacate the boat and prepare the morning's meal in the clearing. When all was done they carried their own food with them and walked along the path that lay ahead of the vessel. Rollers were already in place and hawsers attached. They took the narrow track for a short while and found that it came to an abrupt end on the edge of a cliff. A little way ahead and below, a river rolled placidly to the north but first the crew would have to lower the heavy vessel a distance many times a man's height to the banks of the water. Rope ladders were attached to trees and dropped to the earth below and some of the men climbed down. Guide ropes were fixed to the prow and to pulley wheels mounted on stakes driven into the shore. Now the hawsers that had been used to drag the vessel were detached from the front and taken to the rear where they were fixed as before but this time the trees and horses held all of the weight of the boat as the remaining crew tipped it delicately over the edge of the precipice. With consummate skill and timing, the boat descended gracefully through the air, angled away from the cliff face by the guide ropes, slowing only at the end of its descent to allow its flat hull to engage with more rollers. In no time at all, it seemed to the Magus and his daughter, the boat was afloat, all the ropes and ladders and pulleys stowed away and they were ready for departure.

-They are engineers indeed, remarked the daughter, -It is true that they can make boats fly!

The Magus considered what they had just seen, -The ingenuity of a nomad tribe to overcome every obstacle as it travels, he replied, -Makes it a frightening enemy. It expands its empire because nothing can slow the swift progress of its army. It arrives for battle long before it seems humanly possible and always catches its opponents unprepared.

They were made to wait before boarding while a religious ceremony was conducted by the general. She chanted verses while her men stood in a line along the shore, their heads bowed, their hands together at their waists, fingers pointing down. While she was finishing her supplication to the waters, she took a cup on a pole, filled it from the river and poured the contents on to the deck of the boat. Then she and her men knelt and gathered water in their hands and anointed themselves with it. The ritual satisfied the Magus that there was not yet a people in his experience who were bereft of a god.

-I have not heard of two such great waters abiding so close to each other, yet flowing in opposite directions, said the Magus. -If you can carry your boat on your backs then you can cross the entire world in this manner! They were sailing at speed, the river widening all the time, -Now we are heading north and east.

-It must be a true giant of a river as she told us. It is already wide and she said that we will be tied to this floating home for some time to come. You are right, Father, I have been watching her and she is a harsh task master. She only has smiles for us. The men fear her. She will not give way to them on any matter. If they even raise their eyebrows, she taps the sword at her side, under her fire-eater's dress.

The time seemed to pass slowly on the whispering currents. The Magus found it easier to withstand the monotonous sameness than his daughter. For him it was a time when he could descend, like the boat had done, to deep waters inside himself. She, meanwhile, wandered constantly about the deck, watching the crew at work and fishing. She asked for more shore time for the horses but was only granted one docking, in the later part of each day. When ashore she hunted on her own, relishing the hard physical activity of chasing prey and dragging it back to the boat. For the rest of the time she shared the duty of cooking for everyone with her father. At night the general ordered the vessel to be anchored in the centre of the waters. They could still see the banks though they were at some distance from them. When the daughter asked why, the general pointed to each shore and said, -Enemy! She mimicked the rowing of oars and the loosing of arrows. -Bad, she said, frowning, -Very bad! See? She pointed again and they saw a thin wisp of smoke curling above the trees on one shore. She gave orders to the crew and weapons were brought on to the deck, the anchor was weighed and they moved forward again.

The Magus found a place where he could sit by himself, his legs crossed and his palms on his knees. He closed his eyes and concentrated on listening to the new world in which they had found themselves. Gradually he focused on tiny sounds and shut out everything else. First he could hear the beat of feathers as birds crossed the waters. Then he could hear the faint plopping as tiny fish broke the water's surface. Next he could hear the chewing of beetles somewhere in the woodwork of the boat. As he sank deeper he could hear his own heart beating and the blood hissing as it flowed around his body. He heard the air deep in his chest whispering and then the crackling and rustling of his skin, peeling and dropping from his body. The very bones inside him vibrated like drums to the sounds of his living being reverberating through him. Then it was as though everything, the flesh, the blood, the bones, the air became a single distant hum and he was no longer held together in the shape of a man but was spreading, without boundaries, floating in a light whose quality he had never encountered. A silence followed that was so profound, he was lost. The light was mystifying. It was bright but not blinding, it was translucent but revealed nothing, only its own reality. In it he ceased to be. Became the light. Was no-thing, not-being.

What dragged him upwards and out of his submergence in this perfect delirium to an awareness of himself again, was a hail of arrows slicing through the sail, smacking into the woodwork and deflecting off metal. With the effortless ease of a lifetime of facing danger, he rolled over and over along the deck and came to rest where he could just see over the side of the vessel without the fear of a stray missile striking him. It was as the general had prophesied, a number of long, fast boats, fast approaching from a hidden tributary, driven by rowers and with archers standing four to a craft. He looked for his daughter and saw her sheltering behind the mast, her bow already knocked. Along the deck there were two men lying dead or wounded. Despite the general's anxieties they had not been well enough prepared. She herself was holding the great tiller, a man either side of her protecting her with shields, the remaining crew pulling ropes to change the angle of the sail or firing back while trying to dodge the deadly barrage. She made the sailing boat slew this way and that, creating a wash that unsettled some of the racing oarsmen so that their craft fell back in its wake. His daughter's arrows were deadly and one after another archer fell into the water. Only the lead rowing boat reached the side of their vessel so that its bowmen could now throw ropes with grappling hooks upwards and begin to clamber on board. The Magus ran bent double to where the first head appeared over the side and knocked the man into the water with the heel of his hand. His sword cut the rope and the rest tumbled away to be left floundering in the boat's wake. In that moment the chase was over and the attack had been repulsed. The distance between sailing vessel and ambushers lengthened by the moment until soon they were out of sight.

A cry of dismay from one of the crew brought him quickly to the general. She was slumped over the tiller, blood spreading across her breasts from the feathered shaft to blend with the red of the dragons, her body wracked by juddering breaths. Her crew at first tried to stop him but a look from his light grey eyes was enough and they fell back, allowing him to ease her to the floor. His daughter appeared with his bag of medicines moments later and he set to work.

It took the general two days to come out of the sleep that the Magus induced. She was pale and fragile. The wound had to be dressed every few hours, its cavity filled with a mulch that stopped poison forming. As the Magus was tending to her towards the end of the second day, her eyes opened and she stared at him, -You doctor.

-It is good to be able to heal, he nodded, -Better to heal than make the wound.

She let him swab the hole for a few moments and then said, -Not change.

-The dressing must be changed every day. He had misunderstood her.

-No. Nothing change. I owe nothing.

-It is true.

-I Emperor warrior. He own me.

-I am sure, he said in agreement.

-Take you him. Say you doctor me. Him decide. Nothing change here.

-I come with you to take my wife home, was all he said. When he had finished with the medication, he helped to prop her up on the straw-covered pallet. She waved away the two crew members that always guarded her.

-You say, better doctor than warrior?

It was true, that was the gist of what he had said, -I did.

-You no warrior now. Same as farmer. No fight. Make corn. Sheep. Cow. Easy for Emperor. Take land. Kill few. Keep rest quiet. Make food for Emperor people.

-Why kill? He watched her steadily. She did not look away.

She frowned, -No know you mean.

He pointed to himself, -I wrong to kill. Man, woman, child. Wrong. Live side by side with each other.

-Water God say war. Water fall big. Fill river. She pointed to the sky, -Send boom boom and fire. Water take land. Fire take tree and grass. All village die. We make Water God happy. We fight. It Emperor way, always.

He leant forward, -What do you feel when you kill your enemy? He patted his heart for emphasis.

-Good kill! She seemed mystified by the question.

-You are not sorry for making a person die?

-Sorry? What mean?

-To kill a man. Is it not the same as killing your brother?

She laughed, -How? No. We people of Water God. Not kill people of Water God. Kill people believe god of sun, forest, corn... They not Water people. Just animals. Good kill them. They not return to water when kill them.

It emphasised to the Magus that tribes must learn how to feel the hurt of others before they could even begin to follow the Right Path. If a man kills and feels nothing then the first step on to the Right Path might be too far. Only by entering the heart of another, not of his own blood, was it possible to begin the long road to enlightenment.

Princess Shahrazad watched him put down the last sheet of the story with puckered lips, -I see that the Magus is now more a seeker of peace and less and less the Warrior of this world. But has he met his match in this northern general? She is like the mother of the empire and a she-cat. She will fight to protect everything in her tribe. She is why the card is affixed to this Tale.

-I think so, replied Kamil, -Though she is not a lover of anything beyond her tribe, you are right to think of her as offering worldly love to her own.

She shrugged and stroked her red hair, -It is said that the lion may only lie in peace with the lamb if he is frightened his acts might bring retribution and death. Each to his own. The Magus is not like this female general, is he? His ideas are beyond her understanding. He wants peace and harmony, compassion and justice. He is also the card. Yet they were not saved by his beliefs but by his fist. His daughter also helped to save them with her acts of war for she killed many enemy archers. The general helped save them, too, because she guided the boat even though she was near to dying, a truly protective act. Her crew fought the pirates with them. So, your story says to me that you can only adopt the Magus' Right Path, if you are at peace. In war it is a luxury that we don't have. Do unto others as you would have them do unto you only works in harmonious times. Being kind to others did not stand my forebears in good stead. It was unkindness that brought them their empire.

Kamil floundered a little at this challenge. What she said had more than a dash of truth but that was not the point of the Tale. He tried to explain, -I agree, Princess, but the Tale is about the Magus and his development of a way of living a good life in a difficult world. That is all. It cannot be black and white. If every emperor begins with the desire for peace and harmony, then the chance of war decreases.

-I agree with that! Who wouldn't? It is logical. But wars come about from the gut and not the head. Greed drives reason. Or vengeance. Or madness. I am not sure how I will feel when I have to kill someone. Will I be like the Magus or will I be like the general? Have you ever killed someone, Kamil?

He looked distressed at the very thought, -No, Princess!

-I wonder if our journey may allow that opportunity to cross your path. She laughed, wickedly, -We are in unpredictable times now, are we not? We have become separated from reason, for our planned visit to the Second City was always a sham and now we are cast into the wild where tomorrow brings we know not what. It is good. It makes me feel alive. Her face was alight with excitement.

What she said frightened him but her eyes kept his fear at bay, as though she had caged it. She talked like her mother, full of certainty and authority, a woman's words from a child's lips. Already her rebellion had smuggled them easily through the cordon of protection that the Empress had devised with Raashid and now there was no cohort of troops, just a sixteen year old girl with uncanny power, her henchman and a fat, ageing man and three horses.

*

Their escape from their guard had happened very quickly. So fast that Kamil, who was most instrumental to the plot, remembered it as a blur. As soon as Raashid had instructed his captain to guard her, on pain of life and departed, galloping full tilt towards the Second City, Princess Shahrazad tugged at Kamil's sleeve. He bent forward and she poured words into his ear. Despite knowing that what she was planning was devilish and wrong, he found he could do little but listen intently and nod like her lap dog. It seemed as though his heart was trying to revolt but his head was dictating what he must do. He did as he was bid.

He pulled down the shutter at the side of the carriage, -Captain, he called, -Are the tents ready?

-Soon, my Lord.

Kamil replaced the wooden cover and then climbed down, pulling the door closed behind him. He walked several paces away from the carriage, gesturing that the captain follow him, -I have a request.

-My Lord?

-We passed through a village a few minutes past.

-Yes, my Lord.

-I caught sight of a girl there. Perhaps sixteen years. A beauty. Did you see her? Slim. Standing in a doorway. The hair and skin of an albino.

-I did my Lord. Everyone saw her. The captain kept a straight face.

-Bring her to my tent, I… need company this night.

-Is it wise my Lord? Who knows… The man looked nervous.

Immediately the shutter came down in the carriage and the Princess's face appeared, scowling, -Do as my Uncle requests, captain. He has my permission. If he wants to quench his ardour between the thighs of a village girl, obey him. He is my chaperone, on the orders of the Empress and he must be entertained. Hurry, I want to rest in my tent. The shutter went up. The captain's eyes were wide with shock at her coarse words but he acted immediately and sent two men off to find the girl.

By the time they returned, Kamil was in his tent with a linen bag belonging to the Princess. The girl was thrust into the tent and the flap tied shut. She stood before him, terrified, her eyes downcast. He came over to her and whispered, -Do not be afraid, I shall not hurt you. Tears fell from her eyes. She had heard such words before and they meant something disgusting and painful, -No, said Kamil, -Stop crying, I do not desire to take you to my bed. If you do as I say you will be well rewarded and no harm will come to you. He tipped up her head by the chin and smiled, -I have a wife and children and have no wish for another woman's body. Will you do as I command?

She spoke at last, -I cannot disobey a Lord.

-Good. Now take off your shirt. The words shook her again but, trembling, she obeyed, -Now, spread this dye on your arms and face. We are to make you look like the Princess. He handed her a pot of black nut cream. When she was done, he beckoned her forward, -Now, put on this tunic, he smiled, handing her one of the Princess's plain garments. This calmed her a little, -Give me your head. She bent forward. Quickly he massaged another dye, red as a cockerel's comb, into her hair. It took some time but finally he was happy with the effect, -Now – wait here.

He went outside and signalled to the Princess who was watching from her tent. Then he returned to his own and went to its rear and lifted its bottom edge, motioning the bemused girl to crawl out. He followed and, in the shadows, they slipped swiftly to the back of the Princess's tent which she had already raised for them. When they were inside, Shahrazad stepped out into a night lit only by the flames of a nearby fire, -Bring my coach to the door of my tent, she called the driver. The guards made way as the coach drew up, -Now leave me to eat my meal in solitude and more comfort than there is in this insect-ridden piece of canvass! The guards moved away some distance.

The Princess ducked inside her tent again, -Quick, she said to the girl, -This note is for Lord Raashid on his return. It will demonstrate to him your innocence. It has my seal. And here is a gold coin as a reward. You are a good girl. She slid them into the pocket of the coat and opened the tent flap, -Climb into the coach and shut the door. Once you are there, you must wait for a while and then open the shutter on the far side so that you can just be seen. If anyone speaks to you, wave a hand to silence them and say nothing. Understand?

The girl nodded, blanching with fear.

-When I return I will take you to the palace as my favourite serving maid. You are very pretty. Yes? That's a good girl. Her eyes stared into those of the girl and their hypnotic gaze calmed her. The girl smiled and bowed her head, then pulled back the flap and climbed quickly into the coach.

-Now Kamil, follow me out of the back. We have a man waiting, with horses, a few of our clothes and your book in its box and the cards. She laughed quietly against his ear. He followed her under the canvass and they stole past other tents. Finally, stepping past two unconscious guards, they met with her accomplice who was holding the bridles of four horses, one already loaded with what they might need for their journey. Kamil stared in dismay at his bald head and beard.

Chapter Five

The more you wish to dominate the less independent you become

The Princess was kind to him and kept their first ride to less than two hours but even so he was saddle sore after the first half hour and in a state of tearful exhaustion when they finally dismounted. They had cantered in the moonlight while they could and then later picked their way across wilder country where there was no trail. It was only the arms of the bald man with the beard that prevented him from collapsing from horseback to soil. Through blurry eyes he saw the Princess leap nimbly to the ground and, like the veteran horsewoman that she was, remove saddle and bags, immediately. Unceremoniously, they left him to lie while they secured their camp. The bodyguard, for that was what he evidently was, tied the horses and took from them canvass and telescopic poles of light metal, from which he quickly constructed a shelter for the young royal. Then he threw a rolled up, oiled skin on to the ground next to Kamil who was now beginning to shiver as the sweat dried on him and the fatigue stiffened his muscles. With every inch of his body screaming in protest, he managed to lever himself into a sitting position and arrange the skin on the hard ground before wrapping himself up in it, prone, with his head and one hand visible. Food and drink were placed beside him and, dimly aware that his royal companion had disappeared into the canvass to sleep, his eyes closed. Now and then he jerked awake, saw the horses standing nearby and the bodyguard sitting vigilantly at the entrance to the tent.

As soon as it was streaking with dawn he was shaken roughly awake, more food put in his hands, a balm for his sores set beside him and then the bodyguard repeated in reverse his toil of the previous night. The Princess sat beside him, wrapped in a thick wool blanket, chewing the cold meat with relish, her face content and her eyes half-closed as she pondered deeply.

-A good beginning, Uncle, she said, eventually, -But we must be on our way. If I know Raashid, he will have sent a messenger to the Empress and set out in pursuit of us in this early light. We have two hours on him and can quickly multiply that when my guard works his skill at covering our tracks. Another day and my mother will send out a search party, too. In many ways I worry more about her deviousness than Raashid's proximity. She knows my mind and will take short cuts to catch me that Raashid could never conjure up. More riding, Uncle. Soon we will have you like the lithe young man you once were.

Kamil managed to joke, covering the internal groans he felt at the thought of mounting a horse again, -Sadly Princess, I was never, ever lithe.

This made her laugh, -Very good Uncle Kamil. And even better that you have not questioned me about our escape and my plans for the journey ahead. As your Magus would have it, everything comes to he who waits.

*

It was gruelling. At first Kamil felt that he would die from being dashed on rocks when his thighs eventually gave way. Although the soreness and cramps had not got worse, the inside of his legs were chapped and blistered and his hands were raw from holding the slippery sweat-slicked leather of the reins. His back was constantly hunched unlike the postures of the other two who sat, ramrod straight in the saddle, balanced upon the rhythmic swaying of their mounts. They were now far from any trail, as far as he could discern. More than once he reflected upon his descriptions of the Magus and his family members, travelling over just such terrain and cursed himself for including so much detail of journeying across the wilds. It was as though his self-indulgent prose had brought this upon himself, that his words were magically predicting the events of his own life so that he was destined to suffer a parody of the reality of the Tales. It would not have caused him so much distress if he had been younger but he was approaching an age when no normal man wanted to test himself in these ways.

He had a general idea of where they were because they were pointing north and calculating upon the time they had spent travelling and his knowledge of the topography of the empire, he felt sure that they were at the beginning of the mountain range that marked the northern edge of the Empress's lands. As far as he knew, the further they travelled the more inhospitable the land would become. The mountains were the highest in all these lands and snow capped them all the year round. Tribesmen here bore allegiance only to their kin. There were no known routes to ease the hardship; no rivers, no north-south valleys. All the while the Princess kept her thoughts to herself and her guard remained impassive. Kamil could see that the man was puzzled why he, Kamil, should be brought along, for did he not slow them down and what use would he be in the event of a skirmish with some enemy?

-We will rest here for an hour, she suddenly said, pulling up and casting her gaze about, -We can enjoy the flowers and the horses can enjoy the grass. How are we with the food, Murabbi? she asked the guard.

The man shrugged, -Two more days.

-And the house of the Chief Justice?

-Midnight or, if we rest, mid-morning.

-We cannot overtax my Uncle. We will rest this evening. You have an idea where? Again the man nodded. They had dismounted while they were speaking and the Princess Shahrazad led the battered Kamil to a flat rock surrounded by mounds of yellow flowers shaped like stars, - Bring his things, she called to her man, -The box and the cards. He can give me a reading, as we eat. What better place than this to synchronise our journey to that of the Magus.

The tarot pack and the wooden box duly appeared and Kamil sucked and licked his sore and bleeding fingers before laying out the square of silk and preparing himself. Constantly eating away at the edge of his mind was a chaotic whirl of questions and fears. It was a terrifying nightmare that he had come to inhabit and he wished it would end suddenly and he would be back in the arms of Baligha. He could not believe that he was actually in this vast wilderness with the rebellious Princess and not attempting to block her headstrong plans. Indeed, he was conspiring with her by his silence and acting directly against the Empress Sabiya, his absolute ruler and the one to whom he owed total loyalty.

Over the next few days the general visibly returned to health. She supervised their journey with caution, only permitting landings for the horses to exercise and forage when she was sure that there were no enemies about. But the Magus sensed that her watchfulness was the result of previous experience of these waters and the roaming warrior clans.

-You think they will come back? he asked, once again catching her furrowed brow and sweeping gaze.

-We no far from them. Send message with bird to other. See? She pointed away across the trees and he could just make out the same tell-tale spiral of smoke, far from the river but a distance a horse could cover in an hour. She pointed downstream, -They wait. Once again weapons were being made ready and she was keeping the boat at the very centre of the current with the sail full and billowing tautly.

They remained on alert for the rest of the day and she would allow no landing. The daughter spent time comforting the horses and feeding them while the Magus perched above, mimicking the general. His eyes were not as sharp as they once were, so again the general saw the movement before him. A canoe was pushing its way upstream towards them, hugging the bank on their left side. There were two oarsmen and one passenger. He carried a small, thin pole from which a flag fluttered. As it came further into view, the Magus saw its design. He had not seen the like before. On a white background was the emblem of a red circle like the sun but it was decorated with white dots. There did not seem to be arms on board but they could not yet see into the bottom of the boat.

-Ah, she said, -He trade us. Her men relaxed and they eased the sail and put a brake on their progress but they did not drop anchor. The canoe switched to the middle of the river and turned downstream in

694

front of them as the rowers picked up a rhythm. Soon they were paddling alongside. A rope was thrown down, followed by a ladder. The seated occupant rose and grasped a rung and levered himself up. Then the rope which held the canoe was payed out so that it fell back into the slow wash behind the big vessel and the two rowers shipped their oars and lay back to rest.

After a moment or two, the man became fully visible as he vaulted over the side, just as the daughter came to stand next to the Magus. He was dressed as though from their homeland, though they were now far beyond its northern boundaries. His hair was black and pigtailed and his skin the same colour as the daughter's. He wore a jerkin and cross-roped, sacking trousers and heavy short leather boots. Over his shoulder was a small bag, also made from sack cloth. When he spoke, it was in a dialect not too different from the Magus' childhood valleys.

-I greet the people of the God of Water, spoke the man, his hand on his heart, -May you pass through these lands in peace. His eyes were only for the general.

-Welcome, trade of dream. The general indicated for him to sit by her on the cover of a hatch to the hold. She said no more and waited as the man took the sack and opened it in front of her. Removing the contents, one by one, he placed them on the surface between them. They were rich green leaves, rolled and tied with thin cord. She took her knife and opened one. Inside, like a jewel perfectly preserved, was a plant with a cream stalk and a bright red hat, spotted with white. The Magus now knew the meaning of the symbol on the flag. The general picked it up delicately and sniffed it. Apparently it was good for she nodded and called something out to one of the crew. He darted off and returned with a shallow metal dish, supported on four feet. The stranger placed it on the deck. Inside it was a small heap of broken, blackened wood, which he lighted expertly by striking two stones together against a handful of dry moss, the flame quickly igniting the wood. Over it he stood a tripod upon which he placed a clay pot filled with a little water and waited for it to boil. As the bubbles rose he dropped two red-topped plants in it. The general raised her hand and began to intone a prayer, picked up by her crew. It seemed to have few words and flowed through the air like a deep moan, falling away eventually into silence. The trader took out a tiny wooden pestle and gently crushed the concoction until it became a thick cream before removing it from the heat. When it had cooled the general hooked her forefinger in it and tasted it. She closed her eyes and nodded, then gathered herself and stood up. The man followed. At this moment he saw the Magus and his daughter with a start. He had not expected to see southern people here.

-Who are they? he asked the general.

-They come with me to Emperor. She looked at him and he nodded and looked away, apparently disinterested. She called to the same man who had brought the dish and once again he raced off, returning with some pebbles that glittered in the late evening light, -Choose, she commanded. He pointed to the biggest one and she shook her head. Then the next largest and again she declined. At last he pointed to one that she felt was appropriate and she indicated that he could take it. They bowed to each other, his hand on his heart, her palms flat together, pointing down from her waist. Then he made the universal gesture of grouping his fingers to mouth and she nodded vigorously, -You make food, she said to the daughter.

Nothing was said for a while as they ate. The light was lessening and deep shadows were spreading from the river banks. The trader complimented the daughter on her food and her good looks, using terms that were gracious and courteous. He ate his vegetables with relish. By now the daughter did not serve them to the general and her men. At last he looked up and spoke, -You are the Warrior. And you are his daughter. We speak of you often. The Magus bowed silently and continued to eat, -Yet not so much in recent days. Nothing since you stemmed the certainty of war with the Eastern Empire when your daughter became the wife of the lord of those lands. Now you are here on this boat as a guest of the feared manhunter general, cherished wife of the Emperor of the Ice Lands. He glanced round and saw her talking to her men along the deck, -It is a curious turn of affairs, is it not? I could not have predicted it. Then he lowered his voice, -Are you a prisoner?

-Of our own making. The Emperor has taken my wife as a hostage. I know not why but I seek to bring her back with us.

-Hah! This is not the first such ploy. The general is well versed in kidnaps, barters and exchanges. It is you they want and they have come a long way to achieve their ends. You witnessed them carry the boat over the forest ridge?

-We did. And then we were attacked by a clan in long canoes. We fought them off.

-I know them. And trade with them. They worship a war god. They can not help themselves, they are slaves to the old ways and will not change. But they like the dream plant and bear no enmity towards traders like myself. They use it to raise their mad desire for blood.

-Is that why the general trades for it? asked the daughter.

-No. It helps bring them close to their god of waters. Each opens his own door with the plant. It will liberate for one what it will not for another and also in reverse.

-And what door does it open for you? asked the Magus.

-I have no use for it. I am older and wiser. I do not need the visitations of gods, ghouls or life-takers in my sleep, like some. But it seems true that whatever god you worship will look upon you more favourably once you have imbibed the dream plant. That is why my trade is good to me! He laughed but neither the Magus nor his daughter laughed with him. Something cunning and self-serving slithered deep in his eyes, -You will be asked to share the plant with them shortly. As will I. But I pretend so as not to insult her. She is not to be crossed. He changed the conversation, looking sideways at the daughter, -You have a man? She did not answer but stared coldly at him, -No matter! And he looked away in exaggerated disinterest just as he had done earlier with the general. The Magus and his daughter knew that he was feigning.

The general chose this moment to rejoin them, -We take plant? Good. Like this. She clasped her two hands together, interweaving her fingers and looking at them with a smile. The trader looked on knowingly. She clapped and her man appeared with the small pot and a hard flat spoon. The general bowed to the vessel and murmured words of praise before dipping the implement in it, taking a small amount and spreading it on her tongue. The trader followed suit but her eyes were closed and she did not see him put the cream back. He passed the spoon to the daughter, raising his eyebrows complicitly. She mimed taking the substance just as he had and then passed it to her father. The general's eyes opened and she sighed in contentment as she caught sight of the spoon in the Magus' mouth. The trader and his daughter stared with impassive faces but each was dismayed that he had taken it on his tongue.

-You go now, she managed to say to the trader, -Trade finish. She raised a limp hand and two of the crew came along the deck. The trader rose and bowed. Father and daughter said nothing but each touched a hand to heart and allowed their eyes to engage with his, one last time. They heard the oars approaching and saw him slide over the edge of the deck with the sounds of the rope ladder stretching and his booted toes knocking against the hull. Then he was gone.

As they lay that night beside the horses, his daughter whispered to him, -You took some! Are you ready for a night of peril?

-I am.

-Why?

-I was given such a potion once by a woman sage and learnt to fly by its use. If there are secrets that it can reveal, I would unlock them. I have controlled it until now. Keep watch until I return from the dream world. I suspect our parting with the trader is not for long. Then he closed his eyes and she was left alone beside him, so, much disturbed, she got up and went to sit on the deck.

The Magus dropped instantly into a sleep so dark and cavernous that he ceased to be aware of even himself. It was not the sleep of the mystical light that he had experienced in recent meditations which seemed as though it was the effluvia of life itself but a deathly absence of everything. He did not know this at the time but when the potion percolated his deepest mind so that what lay there began to bubble and boil to the surface, he became aware that he had been in a darkness without end.

The first inhabitant of these deep recesses was familiar and, therefore, easeful. He was still in a limbo that had no geography; there was no sense of up or down, sitting, standing or lying. He could not touch himself or sense himself breathing yet his life-taker was there, whether inside him or beside him. He first apprehended her as two faded pinpricks of light, gradually coalescing in the blackness. These became her eyes and soon after her face slowly took shape, followed by the brown habit and cowl. It wasn't that he could look at her and see her but more that she just existed in her usual form and he was aware in a way that was beyond his normal senses.

-You have changed, he thought.

-That is because you have changed, she thought back to him, -You are older, a little wiser but no less demanding.

-I have not progressed much in wisdom, he thought, -I still know little of the meaning of my existence.

-You know death, for you experienced it just now before you fashioned me again in your thoughts. You know life because your meditation has flooded you in its essence. You have learned as much as the great sages will ever come to understand; being dead, being alive. These are the twin states that all is built upon. From their union comes everything that you are, the world that you inhabit, all you experience in your imagination, the illusion of the real. There is no being dead. There is no being alive.

-Then my life is purposeless.

-Of course! But your imagination is a forge and its sole imperative is to give meaning to your world. Just as you fashion me now, you fashion your entire world in all its infinite detail. It is what you do. It is what you are. All living things build their unique worlds in forges like yours. Together, the universal world is created. Between birth and death they share it with each other. One of the ancient allegories for this transitory state is that of the old woman and her broom. When asked how old it is, she replies that it is as old as time. How come? It was here at the beginning and it is here now, she replies. But it still seems a worthy tool for its job! exclaims the questioner. Of course, she says. Every time the handle breaks, it is replaced. Every time the brush wears out, it is replaced. That is its nature. His life-taker went on, - Singular lives forge themselves for a while but are constantly replenished like the broom. There is only the illusion of being a separate entity. All is flux. The shape of his life-taker began to fade again. The last thing she thought to him was; -Do not exist from any one standpoint, imagine from every one possible. Seek the infinite. The twin fading points of light disappeared. There was darkness again but not the profound emptiness of nothingness. The Magus felt that he was existing in something palpable just as, when asleep, danger wakes you up though there are no signs or clues as to what it might be.

There then followed the series of nightmares that he had expected. In them he died over and over again, from blade and arrow, from drowning and burning, from garrotting and decapitation, from disease and poison. It went on and on and it was physical and real. Throughout these hours he was at first wracked by its extreme horror and then he came to terms with it; he learned that silence and acceptance drew the terror from each event and he was able to experience them as though he was an observer, outside himself, devoid of sympathy but curious and disinterested. It was then that the realisation dawned upon him that each death was inflicted upon him by the same agent. Even though he understood this the assailant remained nameless and formless, never spoke and never wavered in the desire one day to become his assassin.

As the dream plant lost its potency, he was left with a single thought in his mind. This person existed somewhere within the orbit of his future life, they would meet and he would recognise his killer in the first instant of seeing, whether it be a man, woman or other creature.

-A very **interesting** plant, Uncle! I believe some take it in the court though the Empress does not encourage it. She says that men are wilful enough without the extra charge given by such a drug. We all have battles between our emotions and our reason, do we not? If such a plant makes our common sense so thin-skinned that it gives way to the volcano beneath then we erupt. I can not understand why those that partake cannot achieve the same effects by will alone. I am sure I could.

Kamil looked at her quickly and saw that she was serious. He did not doubt her belief in herself. In truth, he felt that this young woman was capable of anything, whether good or evil and it was not a comforting thought. His mind cast back to the Red Man and his use of just such plants to bring about mass madness at a banquet. Did this girl, the ogre's daughter know everything about her father? Sometimes she talked as though he never existed and at others there seemed to be inflections in her voice to suggest far more than she would ever make public.

-Do we understand from this that the Magus must die on this, his final journey?

-I will not give any clue to the story. It would spoil all my efforts to make it hold the reader in a tight embrace. Kamil showed his most resolute face which caused a familiar giggle.

-Good enough, Uncle! So, the card tells us what? I cannot fathom the hidden meanings sometimes. Here we have the male ruler, a symbol of force. Someone who gets his own way and steps on people in his path. That is how I see it but I suspect you have some other ideas. She tightened her mouth and looked at him quizzically, an expression she had inherited from her mother.

-It is true that the card can represent a person and the person could be male. But it could also represent a powerful female. Kamil bent forward and tapped the image -But we should not look beyond the card representing power, itself. This may be someone the Magus meets or merely some aspect of himself. Time will tell. I am not one who can use cards to foretell the future as some claim but as signposts that show where a person has been. They make the path clearer and record for posterity what may easily be forgotten. When I wrote these Tales, I was privy to the whole and could then use each card in turn to help seduce my readers with clues as to what might happen next.

-So the card could be the cold-blooded general or the drug trafficker or the Magus, himself. It could also be the killer in his dreams! And this killer might also be the drug trafficker or the general or some other whom we have still to encounter. He nodded, smiling, caught up in her infectious train of thought. She reflected further and stated amusedly, - It is a kind of game, a maze of possibilities. You lay down trails everywhere and only one will take me to the last full stop of the last sentence.

-Is this not true of life, he asked, -Only at its very end can all our choices be connected by one thread. All others will have proven to be roads leading nowhere.

-Unless you are a djinn, she exclaimed in triumph, -Then you can live all the threads at the same time and follow each one to a different conclusion. She saw his face contort in incomprehension, -You see Uncle, it is possible that this adventure is your only adventure, yet for me - if I was a djinn - it might be one of many. Djinn do not experience time as we do. It does not fetter them. They can split into infinite parts and each is equal to the whole and thus they can grasp every thread that exists around them. And on these threads they can proceed forwards and backwards at will. Her eyes were bright with that strange fervour that made him feel like a toy in her hands. He could hear her words clearly but the meaning in them was too crazed for him to comprehend.

Chapter Six

What is the bridge between two minds? Word or flesh?

Kamil awoke surprisingly refreshed. Not one dream inhabited his mind. His sight revealed a world where every colour had been painted anew and his less sore thighs and hands showed the efficacy of the cream that Princess Shahrazad's bodyguard had found for him. He looked across at the muscled fellow, seeing blind obedience to his mistress, fastidious attention to feeding the three of them and their horses and the toil of striking camp. In all this while he hardly spoke. When the Princess gave him orders he bowed curtly and moved swiftly, his gun and sword always at his side. Kamil pondered on the Princess asking how far it was to the house of the Chief Justice. So that was where they were going. He scratched at his memories of the man but nothing significant came to mind. The Chief Justice had never been on the Empress's red list of enemies but neither had he been on her green list of supporters. He carried out his duties as one might expect; fair to those who had not fallen foul of royalty but ensuring that those who had done so, received a maximum punishment regardless of the virtues of their cases. Whatever the reason for using the man's village as a stop on their route, Kamil knew better than to enquire. He and the Princess had, it seems, a tacit agreement. Ask no questions Kamil and all will be revealed in due course, he told himself.

So, dumbly, he was helped back on his horse, his muscles aching with cramping pains, but the soreness almost gone from his raw skin.

*

For the last hour of the ride, Princess Shahrazad covered her hair. The red tangle was too glorious a fire in the sunlight and it was famed throughout the empire. The path they were on was barely more than a rabbit track and they had not seen or met anyone but caution suggested that they might be observed from a hidden, distant vantage point. Then word would be spread and the Empress's hawks informed. The bodyguard's horse picked its way carefully at the front, the girl's in the middle and Kamil's at the rear, leading the pack horse. The slow progress suited the older man with his physical travails. It allowed his mind to focus on his role in this bizarre train of events. Whichever way he looked at it, he could not understand why Princess Shahrazad was determined to bring him along. Even though she had promised her mother that Kamil would remain at her side, she had broken all her other vows, so why keep this one? Her inflated pride might mean that she wanted to hear out the Tales, as they had been written for her but it seemed a lunacy to have them read in such inhospitable circumstances. Why not wait until they returned? No, there must be something else. Kamil would have a role to play and the Princess knew what this would be but she would not disclose it until the moment of her need of it.

Meanwhile, the Empress would be in a cold fury, sending out search parties and cursing her erstwhile historian. Kamil tried to find solace in the possibility that, when all was weighed and measured, the Empress Sabiya would at least be consoled that he was accompanying her rebellious child. Maybe that was it! Princess Shahrazad was taking him with her to ease her mother's anxieties! He pursed his lips and shook his head. Was it a credible reason? Though he had never been able to deduce the full extent of the schemes that simmered deep in the Empress's mind, he felt sure that the events that now entrapped him were probably less obscure to her than they were to him. She had an uncanny gift of awareness of what drove those around her to do the things they did and used this knowledge to her best advantage. Even traitors and sworn enemies would jerk and twist, ignorant of her manipulation of their puppet strings, fulfilling roles she had elaborately constructed for them. As Princess Shahrazad said, if anyone had a sense of what she was planning it was her mother, no matter how devious her daughter's attempts to deceive her.

*

They stood in the shade of a clump of tall, spiky bushes watching Murabbi ride down into the village. It consisted of a few meagre homes in a circle around a more ostentatious pink, plaster-walled house which looked out across a small lake. There seemed few people about.

An old woman scraping vegetable by the doorway of a clay and wood shack, a couple of children playing on the shore of the water at sword fighting with sticks, a herder with his oxen approaching along the trail from the opposite direction. Above the gate to the big house they caught some movement as a watchman leaned out of a slit to look at the stranger. They observed gesticulations of arms, nodding and shaking of heads and, finally, the bodyguard retreating the way he had come. A little while later he was beside them.

-Neither the son nor his Lordship are here, said Murabbi, -The boy is at the Second City this very day, on business and will be for some time. The father is at the royal court.

She was pleased, -Good, just as I planned. And neither are aware that their house is known to me. How is the place guarded?

-Only the old man I talked to and his wife. It is locked up. The doors are fortified with heavy iron bolsters. It is as you thought.

-It will serve us well. You did as I asked?

-Yes, your Highness. I said a lady, who wished not to be known, would arrive soon. He was plainly terrified, saying that he could not make it ready and fit for you. It is only used by the lordship and his son as a hunting lodge and to collect tithes, once a year. The rooms are not suitable for a woman, never mind a lady.

-He does not know my ways! Let us rejoin him.

*

The sun was overhead and those locals who remained in the village during the day had retreated inside their homes when the bodyguard rapped his sword's pommel against the door. It opened immediately into the yard designed for horse and carriage. Not waiting for the old man to shut it, the bodyguard leapt down, pulled the doors too and bolted them. It was a plain and unadorned area. Weeds fought for space with broken stones and clay earth. The door to the living area was ajar and so blistered that only the faintest smears of ochre showed the original colour. In an attempt to force out the musty air from the interior, the caretaker had opened up all its orifices. A window hung at an angle because its top hinge had broken. The chimney stack was cracked with deep fissures, blackened by smoke. The three riders could smell the decay of the interior as the air was flushed past them.

Bowing, the wife of the watchmen waddled past the hooded royal, carrying mounds of sheets to be washed and dried for that night. The Princess did not forestall her. She slipped gracefully from her horse as Murabbi helped Kamil down, too.

Inside, there was a moderately spacious banqueting room stacked with trestle tables and benches which might hold up to fifty guests and radiating from it were the sleeping quarters. The old man performed his most genteel bow and indicated to the Princess which was hers. She went inside and nodded. A slatted wooden bed, a stand with an unchipped, coarsely fired ewer and a poorly constructed mirror were all it contained.

-This will do, she said, pulling the cloak further down over her shoulders and hair, -Stable the horses, she said to him and he bumbled away happily, -Food? she requested of her man and he too disappeared. They heard the bolts being pulled on the outer door. Then she smiled at Kamil, -Uncle, you look like you are a child, waiting for orders! It is still as musty as a rarely used cellar in here. Let us pull a bench into the courtyard and sit in the shadows together. There is time for you to entertain me before we eat. She grasped one end of the bench while Kamil took the other and they carried it to the most shaded wall of the compound. Then she brought the jug from her bedroom and began pumping water while he watched like some elderly and much respected relative. After she was satisfied that the ewer and its contents were clean enough she went through an arch into the stables and returned with Kamil's box and the little calfskin wallet containing the tarot cards and their square of silk.

She grimaced when she saw the image, -Ah, Uncle, yet another of our chief priests, divine representatives, sages and religious madmen! Which is it going to be? If it is the Magus again then I will be sorely disappointed if he becomes a pillar of the temple to the gods of fire or water or war.

-We shall see, replied Kamil, -As you now know, it could be all of those things or none of them.

Having survived the nightmares inflicted upon his mind by the dream plant, the Magus found he had an urge to repeat the experience. He wondered where this urge came from. Had the plant cast its spores into his blood and did they nestle there, an insidious poison gathering his thoughts like white of egg on a twirling stick, thickening and slowing the movement of his mind? He pushed the desire away from him and threw himself into physical labour, helping the crew with the boat and his daughter with the hunt and the preparation of food. Even so his time was not fully consumed and he sat for hours at the rear of the boat watching the silvery wash, the swooping birds and jumping fish. For most of this time of contemplation he explored the basic principles of the Right Path, meditating on each one, looking for circumstances which might confound its efficacy or for examples to show why it was fundamental to harmony between peoples. At such times he would fall into reveries, close enough to dreams but subtly different.

It was in one of these strange casts of mind that he felt himself transported to a territory far to the south and of a time long before. His father-not-of-blood had traded with its descendents but had imparted little to him of its customs and practices save its ancient adherence to animal gods. He wandered among its men and women in their swathes of white cloth, their bandaged heads, their hands clutching scrolls of poetry, their multitude of slaves drawn from every territory they had captured. He saw the edifices to their dead kings, teeming with construction workers, that took a lifetime to build, so massive were they, with tunnels and caves built under them. He watched as the royal dead were massaged with unctions to preserve them so that their spirits were freed to exist in the next life. Somehow he was able to read the lines etched in the stone of their death-boxes, though they were in a language unlike anything he had ever imagined. He tried to memorise what he read but it was a truncated and distorted copy that remained in his mind when he awoke. All he could be sure of was that the lines were protestations that the dead had not committed certain sins during their lives. But there was some resemblance to his suggestions for the Right Path. Studiously, he wrote what he could remember of the revelations in ink upon sun-bleached paper, made from hammered reeds:

I have never spoken against God or his shapes on earth
I have not forced my desire upon child, woman or man, against their will
I have nor shortened the life of another
I have not taken what is not mine

He was staring at his dream-captured words when the shadow of the general fell upon him as she settled beside him. She took the stiff card from him without a word of apology and also studied it. It seemed she could read better than she could speak.

-Where this come? she asked.

-The dream plant.

-Hah! Good! We same and not same. And more.

He understood, -How do you observe the wishes of the Water God? he asked. She bowed and touched her finger tips together.

-This true for Water God, she said, tapping the words, -Not true for other tribe. We say, only Water God, no other. We say, no man make God or picture. He water everywhere. We say no work on day of Water. Kill beasts for God of Water. We say fight for family, kill enemy who do not bend knee. Always speak with open eye to friend. Share - belong all. Tribe is family.

The Magus nodded, gathering much of the meaning. He had seen such laws everywhere. What governed behaviour inside a tribe, did not shape behaviour outside it. Was it possible that only he, the Magus, could see that all clans in all tribes that ever had been and ever would be, were children as if from a single womb?

708

The river continued its languid progress to the north, slowly widening and erasing its boundaries as if it was determined to be a sea. The danger of attack was both greater and lesser for the wind had dropped, slowing them and making them more vulnerable to oars but also giving them plenty of time to see an enemy approaching. Decisions to anchor at a shore to let the horses exercise became fewer and seemed to depend upon the general's instinct. While both the Magus and his daughter could read the flight of birds and knew whether a hazard was near or far, she had no trust in their knowledge. What also bothered both of them was that their inactivity was taking its toll on their physical prowess. So much so that the daughter suddenly said, one day, -We must practise arms! We are becoming like old women! The sudden injunction lifted the Magus out of his meditative torpor with a lurch. It was true, he had succumbed to a constant diet of dreaming and reflection. While this was where his purpose was always focused, he knew that he would be of little use in the recovery of his wife if his flair for battle was so blunted that he could not defend her even though he had no intention of ever killing an enemy, abductor or not.

So they cleared a part of the deck and gestured back the sailors who were resting there so that they became intrigued spectators as the two began their mimicry of battle. The clash of their swords brought the general running but as soon as her eyes took in the flowing beauty of their weapons and limbs she stopped, impressed and intent. Father and daughter danced round each other, he more heavily but physically strong and athletic, she a wraith of shadow and light always mere inches away from his blade yet never in danger. Both were breathing heavily from their exertions when they stopped, proof of their need of them.

The general raised a hand and said to the daughter, - Tomorrow. You me.

At exactly the same time on the following two days, the general practised first with the daughter and then with the father. For the crew it seemed like clashes between immortals. Having seen the blur of their blades, not one of them would now dare to raise a weapon against any of the three. But for the protagonists a different plot unfolded. While each became certain of the sublime arts of their opponents, each also knew that all three of them were holding something back. Great swordsmen could sense another's thoughts through the points and edges of their weapons, thus each knew that there was much still hidden from thrust and counter thrust.

The practice swordplay between the Magus and the general marked the last memorable event on board ship. Mid way through the next morning, at the point at which the great river of the general's God turned to the northwest, she ordered the ship to shore. A light-headedness descended on the father and daughter as they were infected by the joy of the horses charging up the shallows, spraying water everywhere and eager to have their hooves in contact with solid earth. They looked about them and once again it was obvious to them that this was part of an established route. A well-beaten, wide track led off into the low hills down which a group of armoured soldiers came down to meet them and escort them to an encampment not far away, where a small army seemed to have been deployed.

-Leave tomorrow! Here, safe with men, said the general, curtly, -No fighters attack. She made a gesture of rowing while shaking her head. Rapid orders found them in their own tent, horses tethered outside. It was also made clear to them that it was too dangerous to hunt.

-Well, we must make the most of our pallets, daughter, murmured the Magus stretching out, -There will be a time when there is no time. Here, we have it to use. Wasting it would be a sin.

-Is that a law of the Right Path? she smiled.

-I had not thought it until you remarked upon it. Time is allotted us by the boundaries of birth and death. It would be an injustice, at least, to act as though each moment is not the most valuable. As death approaches, time becomes more precious. Who could not value the last hour? Even in the greatest pain? For is not that pain the last signal of the body's existence? It encloses the last beat of the heart. The last breath in the chest. The last picture in the mind. The last feeling. Yet when we are young, death appears so distant we cannot focus on it. We are sad when others die but even then the lesson is not borne home to us. The death of a parent or child does not presage our own death. Yet death accompanies us in all we do. We should seek to be aware of it at all times. Then we might understand what it is to be alive.

-I see you have thought long about this, said his daughter as she, too, stretched out, -So how shall we spend the time we have been given in our enemy's tent?

-Perhaps you should choose, he said quietly, -For I have often sensed that you wished me to speak about events that trouble you but the occasion forestalled it or the mood between us was not fit for it. Perhaps it is that such subjects are not the meat and drink of talk between father and daughter? I cannot be certain which of these may apply.

-It is true. Fathers and daughters do not talk of anything except her prospective marriage or what he expects of her in the house and kitchen until the day she leaves for another family. But you are not a father. You are the Magus. And I am the daughter of the Magus. Much more should be expected of us. You must remember that you left me in my mother's womb when you continued your journey with your father-not-of-blood. I was passing monthly blood by the time you returned. Your son, my brother, hardly knows you and the weight of your fame is so great he does not wish a closer tie. But I am different. Your blood lives more strongly in me than my mother's, much as I have the greatest love for her. I feel sometimes that if I knew you better I would understand myself more.

I have tried in many ways. I have sat in solitude in the hills. I have studied religious tracts. I have undertaken long journeys. I have fought and killed. I can cook. I can cure ailments, I can hunt with just my bare hands and I have little fear. But even as I know that I am your daughter, for who else is so like you in her thoughts and deeds, why is it that I do not feel I know you as I would wish? We are together yet always apart.

-We are not each other. He said it with a certain finality as though the conversation could not deliver the meaning she wanted.

-Of that I am also certain! she laughed, -It is not that I wish to be more like you. I want to know what it is that I am and must do.

He turned his head to her, -You want to know your purpose?

-It makes me seem even more like you when you use those words.

-It has driven me since I was a boy, like the vision in the desert that

711

never comes close. I did not realise that you also felt this way.

-Your essence is strong within me as I told you. I gave birth to my children and there was meaning. But I also felt that that meaning was lost in the waters of birth for what else could lie ahead? Was not my purpose complete now? Nothing before or since has been so...so...full. I had passed on the blood of the Magus to the next generation. I had been a mother-bridge between you and them. But once they had survived and taken my milk, what else was there for me? Other women do not ask such questions I know. They cannot fix their minds upon such a subject. For them it is enough to have achieved this one thing. All else is a passing of time until a life-taker comes for them. It is as you said when you began this debate. Time is more precious than that. How do I fill it with meaning, Father? It is in this way that I wish to know you better.

The Magus allowed silence to extend before he answered. Looking up he could see the fibres of the brown canvass roof, the corded seams, the stains of travel on the walls. His thought seemed to know nothing else but the infinite detail of what sheltered and surrounded him. Then, as though his mind was speaking equally to both him and his daughter, he began.

-I cannot say what I have learned on my journeying. If I measure it in words and deeds it is, without doubt, great. But if I measure it in its universal meaning then I do not have an estimation. It seems so little. After all I have seen and done, I have less feeling than ever that there is a god or gods. Indeed, the greater a tribe's belief in a god, the more it seems intent on dying for it rather than living in its honour. Gods do not have the power to feed their worshippers, to defend them against plagues, or famine or their own worst desires. Show me a god who brings harmony to the land. I have not yet met the people of such a god. Yet it is to gods that people ascribe their purpose. As long as their belief is that their gods are waiting with rewards for them after death in some version of paradise, then they seem to enquire no further. They attend their rituals, rise to a fervour, propitiate with their sacrifices and then return to their ways in forest and field or the Emperor's army. Is there a god? I do not know. But I feel that we must act and forget whether there is or there is not. We must live as humanely as we can, treating others well and being an enemy to no other. My sense of purpose is that at all times we are faced with a choice. Choose one way and someone suffers. Choose another and someone benefits. Whether we be farmers, hunters or soldiers, by following the Right Path there will be greater harmony around us. Even if, like you and I my daughter, people seek to understand purpose through great journeys and adventures, within every moment there is this single choice to be made.

She had listened with her eyes closed but now opened them and reached over to him, -Hold my hand Father. He did so, -Do you know that you have rarely touched your own daughter and taken her to your breast? If you had stayed as I grew, I would have known you better as my father for I have seen how much you embrace my children and how close you are with them. We learn through the touch of flesh what words can never convey.

The Magus held his daughter's hand with his eyes closed and a new feeling crept over him at the same time that an insight was born in him.

Both of them were so involved in the import of the Tale that it was a little shock to return to the reality of sitting on a hard bench in a decaying old courtyard. They had not heard the bodyguard come back but they could now hear him working with the old woman in the kitchen. Indeed, Kamil was surprised to catch the man's low laughter and apparent ease with the servant.

-The Magus is the Hierophant! Princess Shahrazad exclaimed, -But there is no religion in his preaching. I see why my grandfather thought it so important for you to educate my mother through the man's history. He does not preach for conversion to what can never be known but has an eye only for what we can experience with our senses. If that is all that life has to offer then why not make it as rich and fulfilling as possible? The flaw with this belief is that there are those who deny a god but would be rich and fulfilled, also. Those who live in harmony and peace are ripe plums for their plundering.

Kamil nodded. He had also found his mind chasing this thread, -It is true. Goodness is not a prize sought by all. Some seem willingly to ignite their desires with evil. Only emperors and sages can take the throat of a whole population and shake sense into it. Then, by living according to these principles, an empire's children and children's children come to know no other than the demonstration of daily goodness.

She stood up and looked into the afternoon blue, -It is the stuff of wars, Uncle, if it is the emperor's task! Of the power of seers I know as much as any who have had some historical schooling. There have been divine prophets in most lands but they have brought war not peace. Yet you may convince me I am wrong as your Tales proceed. My grandfather, the Emperor Haidar, told my mother that the only future for prosperity in our lands was to return to the teachings of the Magus and draw enough from them to make a contract with our people so that they seek no change in our authority. It is too costly to keep the lid of military power clamped upon them and it leaves them with but one bitter resort, to overthrow our dynasty. She twisted to look down at him, -But, dear Uncle, though this excites our intellects for it seems to point to a better world for all, it is not the most significant part of your Tale for Princess Shahrazad. Kamil tried to keep the perplexity out of his expression for he could not think what else might be more important to her. She considered her words carefully, standing before him like a boy, her feet spaced and her bearing, combative.

-I sense, she said, -That the daughter is teaching the Magus a great truth. He is too rational in his Right Path and needs to remember the times his heart has been touched by others and what was to be learned from this. Even as I stand here, a disloyal and rebellious daughter, the love of my mother means more than anything. Nothing else has such a strong effect upon me. Perhaps because it is so strong, I am led to this temporary sundering. When the daughter reminded him that he was her father, I was thrown into a moment of inner sickness for I never knew my father, the Red Man. Just like the daughter, I was implanted by him in my mother's womb, at the moment of his passing. So I must have been made by him as much as by her. The daughter knows she is more Magus than her mother. Perhaps it is so with me, too. Only by leaving the stifling air of the court and my mother's never-ending concern for me, can I establish what ingredients are mixed in my blood too. You see Uncle Kamil, it is your Tales that have led to this escape from my childhood. Did my mother know what she was doing when she insisted you read me the first two books? Did she know that I would request a third and final book? Did this all happen in the mixing bowl of her heart rather than her head so that she was only dimly aware of the cake that might then be baked? I suspect so, for she is surely part sorceress and part goddess! If so, what does that make me? She touched her tangled red hair as she looked at him steadily.

Chapter Seven

A child can understand anything - it is all in the telling

That same afternoon, Princess Shahrazad ordered the old woman and Murabbi to prepare a meal for ten or so people. The bodyguard took some local men and they hunted in the hills and fished in the lake. They garnered enough for the meal and distributed the what remained to villagers. While Kamil rested in his room a couple of girls arrived to help the old woman and the bodyguard light up a large stove in the courtyard. He could hear their laughter as they joked with the guard, cleaned dishes, gutted and descaled fish and prepared flesh. Later, as the sun left the courtyard, they started peeling vegetables and washing rice. Only when there was a hullabaloo at the gates and the sound of hooves and a wagon's wheels, did the cooking start. He raised himself from his bed and went out to see the cause of the commotion.

The heavy doors had been opened. Outside them there were mounted men. Inside there was a cart with its two horses still in harness. The carter had dropped to the ground and was walking round to the rear. The old man held the horses' bridles. On the back of the cart was what seemed to be a large box covered with a heavy canvass. Princess Shahrazad had a brief word with the obsequious carter and he began yelling orders. Four men dropped from their horses outside and came into the yard. Poles were locked into place along the base of the covered box and along its top. The men lifted it from the floor of the cart and, following the Princess, disappeared into the house. Kamil thought he heard a noise from under the cloth covering but could not be too sure. It sounded like an animal mewling. Feeling of little use, Kamil started towards his room but on second thoughts he accosted one of the men at the gate.

-What was that they took inside? The man shook his head.

-I do not know, Lord. On pain of death we were warned not even to touch the shroud. Not even the carter or our captain knows. We took delivery of it just as you see it now and were ordered to bring it here.

Kamil re-entered his room and sat on the hard bed. The world was passing him by as if he was merely a witness. He had become an observer like a servant at court who, while ever-present, must give no indication of seeing or understanding events, no matter how disturbing or exotic. It was not a role for which he was fitted. His face had always been a moving echo of his emotions. Even when he tried to be inscrutable he felt he was liable to suffer from some little tic or movement of his eye that gave away his feelings. But his sense of uselessness proved short lived. There was a knock at his door and a soldier stood there, the captain of the platoon.

-The Lady says you must come.

Kamil followed the fellow across the courtyard and through the stables. At their rear was a battered wooden staircase, covered in bits of straw, bird droppings and dirt. He trudged up them leaning slightly against the wall as there was no banister. A short corridor gave way to a tackle room. Horses' leathers, weapons, tent canvass, bottles covered in grime and sundry other oddments were scattered round its edges. It had not been cleaned for years. Momentarily, Kamil wondered whether the Chief Justice treated court cases in the same slack manner. Being naturally fastidious about his possessions, Kamil judged others accordingly.

In the centre of the room was the covered box. No sound came from it. Princess Shahrazad motioned the captain to stand to one side and gestured Kamil forward. She was excited and a little agitated.

-Uncle, you will now begin to understand why we have come here and why you are so important to my plans! She took out her knife and cut the first rope that held the canvass. The captain stepped forward to do the rest for her. He could not allow the Princess to do menial work but her raised hand and fierce eye made him step back just as quickly. She continued cutting her way around the tied ropes until the canvass hung free. Then she nodded to Kamil and he walked forward and took one corner of the canvass while she took the other. They pulled and withdrew at the same moment. All who were in the room were shaken by what had been revealed though the Princess recovered quickly. The captain covered his face as though he had seen a demon. Kamil lurched back, his eyes starting and his hands held up, warding off the vision. But Princess Shahrazad stood, shadowed by her hood, motionless, her face grave but her eyes gleaming. And the fourth member of the tableau, the creature inside the cage, blinked in terror with the sudden

717

extra light, huddled as he was on its floor. After all the hours of lonely travel in his cage he was face to face with his captors.

What the three outside the cage saw was more lizard than human. He was completely naked and his flesh was covered in the palest green markings, like scales, though they were not raised as in a fish but were as if drawn by a brush tip on the surface. His manhood was a dark green stem hanging in front of large globules. His feet and hands were partially webbed and their nails pointed into claws. Atop this djinn-like manifestation, his red and yellow eyes viewed them in obvious fear from a head which was elongated from back to front so that his nostrils protruded furthest with the mouth recessed below them. The latter had no lips and opened and closed constantly, allowing a pale red tongue to be glimpsed. His ears were long slits, half-hidden by flaps of skin. Whereas in a man there might be hair, in his case there were deep furrows that ran transversely over his skull. He was much the same height as the Princess, taller than Kamil and the captain.

In an act of bravery the creature shambled forward to the cage bars and gripped them with his hands. He had stopped searching the room for more detail that might unseat his mind and was now focused only on the half-hidden face of the Princess, his orange irises receding to pinpricks in his stare.

-Lady! warned Kamil as she moved slightly towards the cage. He had nearly said, 'Princess' and it left him trembling.

Again she raised a hand to desist help, -He will not hurt me. He recognises something about me. Don't you? The creature went still, - You see? She turned away, -Is his room ready as I requested? Check with the men. The captain did not want to leave her with just Kamil, - Quickly! Look at his soiled prison. It was only then that Kamil was aware of the grey dung on the floor and the putrid smell. They heard the man's retreating feet on the wooden stairs. The Princess looked at Kamil, -He will not harm you or I, have no fear. Then she faced the creature again and said, -Soon you will be cleansed and fed. Just one more small journey in this cell! She smiled and reached out and touched a pointed fingernail. The creature drew back, puzzled but less fearful and watched them as Princess Shahrazad led Kamil out of the room.

They passed the four carriers with their poles in the courtyard, entered the main living quarters and thence to the chamber created for the creature. It was little different from Kamil's except that a tub sat on its terracotta-tiled centre, filled with water. There was a bed, a pile of linen for drying, a ewer and on a stand, a white gown and loose white trousers. A pot with a linen cover stood in one corner for the lizard-man's toilet and on another stand, a large flat plate with raw fish, doused in sweet vinegar and some bread. The only window was high and barred. They left the room as the men approached, grunting from their exertions. She stopped them at the entrance, -Turn the cage round so that its door faces into the room. They did so and pulled out the poles. She bent forward to unbolt the cage door, pushing it open. The creature left its little prison to walk slowly into the bigger one, -You are safe here, whispered the Princess softly and persuasively, -I am going to close and lock the door for tonight. Eat and sleep well. Tomorrow we will meet and talk. Do you understand? It turned towards her and then moved quickly to the covered pot. Princess Shahrazad motioned the men to take away the cage and closed and locked the door, taking the key. It was as much to protect her captive, as to prevent his escape.

*

Later, after they had eaten, Princess Shahrazad commanded Kamil to read the next chapter of his third book. He still had not asked her a single question about the journey and its purpose even though this latest twist had, beyond all reason, introduced a demon into their midst. A demon! One that she was expecting! He had thought such visitations were the stuff of fiction.

She was calm and at peace with herself. They sat together on his bed and he laid the cards and the box on the sheet between them. Nor did her eyes raise to his when she saw that the next card was The Lovers.

It was many years since the Magus had travelled with such a large group of horsemen. He did not like it. Riding alone or with his daughter who rarely talked in the saddle, allowed him to be part of the earth and the air. There was also an immediate and powerful communication between the roan and himself which was not bedevilled as now by the flying hooves all round him, the grim faces of his armoured companions and their guttural snarls and commands. All was dust and concentration on the withers of the mounts in front. Beside him rode his daughter, equally stern, her eyes also narrowed and focused in front of her. They were galloping on the orders of the general who felt that it was best not to linger in the present territory where kidnaps and attacks were common. Even though she managed to convey to them that her men had hunted and killed whole clans here, the battles had not ceased. So they charged on for some time until the sandy track through the straight, soldier trees came to an end and they were able to canter across grassland. The path was just discernible, almost covered by fast growing plants.

The Magus spoke for the first time in hours, -The roan senses misadventure. As do I.

-Perhaps I do, too, replied his daughter, -But I have not your horse's keen nose for the future. Danger has to be so close that I can touch it. Should I tell the general?

He nodded and she called out immediately, -General! The woman slowed her mount so that they could come alongside, -My father senses that there is an enemy near us. With a cursory look at the Magus' serious face, the chief spurred her horse forward and began shouting orders at her troop. They were well advanced on the plain now and attacks had never occurred here before. They pulled to a halt and formed a circle, facing out. All eyes roved around the horizon in every direction but nothing could be seen.

The general shrugged, -Not there? she asked but the Magus pointed to the roan, who was staring fixedly a few hundred strides ahead as if something was in the air but invisible to them. Its ears were flicking back and forward and its nostrils were dilated but all they could see was tall, waving grass, its tips a riot of white flowers and early seeds. It was the daughter who tuned to the horse's gaze and detected something.

-There! she pointed. They could not see where she was indicating. The grass, it changes in the wind! At last they saw it, a shadowy line, not a man's stride wide, ragged, as though disturbed by an animal crossing the track. The daughter pointed again. -There and there! At either end of this line and a little beyond it appeared to be a number of small, darkened circles, just discernible. The Magus was able to picture immediately what had been prepared for them.

-An ambush, he said calmly to the general, -They have laid a trip rope across our path and are hiding on either side.

She nodded, -We attack. She gave orders and raised her hand. The cavalry moved into formation, facing forward. Cautiously they cantered, the general's hand still raised. Then, when they had halved the distance, her hand dropped and the horses broke into a controlled gallop, separating into two zigzagging groups, aiming towards the ends of the trip rope.

Moments later, it was the chaos of battle. The immediate enemy rose from its hiding, firing arrows at the metal clad north men. At first most of these flicked off the armour but here and there metal tips began to break through the joints at knee or elbow, bringing down riders. Two of the general's men fell to arrows in the throat. Mounted warriors dropped to the ground to engage in hand to hand fighting. The toll of deaths rose. The Magus and his daughter stayed back, watching impassively. It was none of their affair. Then, far in the distance, they saw more men being disgorged from the earth, this time dragging horses from their hidden beds in the deep grasses. The daughter shouted another warning to the general, pointing urgently. The general saw and knew immediately that the battle was lost. With a fusillade of orders her remaining soldiers remounted and reformed a circle around her and the father and daughter, setting off at full gallop back towards the woods. Behind them there were screams as injured comrades were being mutilated. But, as the long, dark horizon of trees came into view, the predicament of the galloping cohort, now less than half its original size, became suddenly worse. From the foliage emerged a whole phalanx of archers. They were now trapped between the north and south arms of the enemy's small army. At some distant command, further platoons of bowmen appeared from hiding, on either side, their bows taut. They were boxed in. The general waved her men to veer towards the north, braving the cocked arrows before them while to their rear the rest of the enemy converged in pursuit. She and her two voluntary prisoners, their heads flat against their horses' manes, galloped behind a single armoured line. When a man was unseated in front of them, the line shortened as the empty space was filled by the line contracting. Then they were upon the archers, slashing and cutting their way through, suffering more casualties than they were inflicting. With a handful of men, the three galloped into the clear. It was now a race to any kind of safety but the grassland that stretched before them allowed no possibility of shelter and their horses were tiring. The enemy was slowly gaining.

Their only hope was to make for the forest again now that they had created a precious distance between themselves and the gathering storm stretched behind them. They crashed through the first line of saplings at the wood's edges and drove forward, deeper and deeper, the roan in the lead with its uncanny sense for safe passage through danger. They could not hear any sound above the thud of their own hooves and the crackling of snapping branches but it was increasingly difficult to maintain speed for the roan was taking them into the most hazardous terrain. The trees became almost impenetrable with low boughs and the earth littered with rotting branches and scatterings of hand-sized rocks. They were reduced to walking slowly, in single file, the ground rising beneath them. Then, as if this was what it had intended, the roan led them out of the warren and on to a path that once again would take them north. The Magus dropped his mount back, letting the fighting men take the lead again, the general and his daughter following.

-We not long, said the general in a low voice, -It only road here. They find quick.

-You know it? asked the daughter.

-I hear. No use. Bad.

-Isn't everywhere? smiled the daughter. They heard the first signs of

722

their pursuers not too far away to the south. They galloped on, leaving hoof marks on the needle-covered floor until a black rock cliff reared up on one side and along its base, a narrow stream.

-You up, gestured the general at the rock face, -We go small water. God watch us. Meet with Emperor next. Without further word she led the remaining few of her guard into the stream to work their way north west and back once again to the river that they had only recently left. The Warrior and his daughter also set their mounts into the stream, following it in the opposite direction for a short while, then dismounting and scrambling on to a shelf of rock and leading their horses upwards.

The roan quickly found a route up what had seemed like a sheer incline, following the narrow ledges used by nimble grazing animals. The daughter's horse followed obediently, almost like a frightened human, not looking down. Within a short while they had reached the top and were able to conceal themselves from view beneath. It was an odd outcrop of hard, pock-marked stone, a single finger poking up from the always green canopy. Here they rested their horses and ate food from their saddle bags. It was not long before they heard the sound of cantering hooves and men shouting to each other below them. From their hidden vantage point they saw dozens of tribesmen approaching, following the path north. They heard them stop at the point where their quarry had entered the stream and then the splashing of a horse in the water. Gradually the sounds receded.

-They have a scout watching to see where the general leaves the stream, murmured the Magus, -I cannot hear any of them doubling back this way.

-Why did the general make us go separately?

-She is drawing her enemy away from us. She would rather die than prevent us reaching the emperor. She knows our skills as warriors, they are at least the equal of her own. We will make our way though it will be difficult. Who may we ask? This seems to be a land full of those who would do all they can to kill the north men. The tribesmen are well armed and they have drowned their differences in their shared hatred of the common enemy. It is as though someone has found a way to harness them. He paused and thought for a while. She watched her father, waiting for the thinking to end. She recognised the signs. Some new door had opened in his mind. When he spoke again he was nodding in affirmation of just such a revelation, -There is another explanation. It is not the general that they seek. It is us.

-Us? Why?

-I cannot think but if it is so, it will still be connected to the men from the north. Are they trying to stop us reaching their enemy? What reward would there be in that?

They were still lying on grass at the edge of the top sheet of black rock when they heard a single dismounted rider and his horse approach, tracking their route from the stream. Whoever it was had no wish to hide his passage and deceive them. There was much grunting and heavy breathing and the journey seemed tortuous in comparison with the speed that the roan had drawn from them. The daughter took her bow and nocked an arrow.

A head came into view, just as it had when the man climbed over the side of the boat. His hair was black and pigtailed and he wore a jerkin and cross-roped, sacking trousers and heavy short leather boots. It was the purveyor of dream plants.

-Greetings Magus! called the red-faced, sweating trader, -And my warmest felicitations to you, the Magus's daughter!

-**I don't trust** him! exclaimed the Princess, he's only interested in the daughter. It is the way you have written it. I like your hints about the characters of people. We gradually find out what they are truly like through their actions. I hate it when the author tells you at the start what sort of person someone is. For most people life is not like that. Only time can show what plant grows from what seed. Most people, when they first meet someone, form an opinion. Sometimes they are right and sometimes they are wrong. Only those with a gift, like my mother, sense what is being harboured below the skin.

-And you, too. She told me, said Kamil.

-Ah, she told you, did she? Yes, I have yet to be proven wrong. Even so, I gain much pleasure in testing my instinct against events. The Lovers is a good card for a young girl, don't you think, she said, changing tack, -Does it have any other meaning than two people being attracted to each other?

-Strictly, no. But the attraction can be pure friendship, or father to daughter, or brother to sister. It denotes a bond.

-Can it be one-way or must both feel it?

Kamil looked at her and thought for a moment, -I do not know the answer. I expect not. The title is plural. Lovers. I should think one of the other cards will be more prominent if the feeling is only entertained by one.

-I have said before, there are many that have professed love for me despite my fledgling years but I have always been left cold. How dare they, I think. What have I done to deserve their interest apart from being the Empress's daughter?

-And very beautiful! Her hood was down and he could have stared forever at her rich red hair and translucent amber skin.

-It is true Uncle, though I would not allow anyone but you and my mother to say it. She looked hard at the card, -So it is unlikely that the card refers to the drug procurer and the daughter. Good. It must be the father and the daughter. There are no other suspects! I do not think the general and the Magus...?

-Perhaps not, he replied non-committedly. She gave him a small slap on the knee in pretend exasperation at his refusal to give her a clue. -Remember, she loves her Emperor, he said.

-That is true but I prefer the love between father and daughter. Perhaps it is because I have not known it. She fell into a reverie, her eyes closed. Kamil looked at her, lounging beside him, far less self-conscious than her mother had ever been. Her boyish clothes disguised her growing womanhood. She was not a typical beauty for there was no soft roundness in those parts of the body that attracted most males. Yet her long, supple and lightly muscled figure gave her beauty the same dominating power that he had pictured when he had described the daughter of the Magus.

-What about the new arrival, Uncle, she asked suddenly, -Is he one of two? Does some girl love him and he, her?

Kamil flinched at the very thought. The demon creature was beyond human understanding. -All must have their admirers, he managed to say.

-I hope so. He is a sad one. When I discovered his whereabouts, I had to free him from a travelling show that displays all the freaks of human nature. I paid to own him even though my men could have taken him by force. Indeed, I wished to have killed all his captors except that such an action would have caused too much speculation in the land. No-one knew that I was his buyer. Kamil wanted to ask how she had come to hear of the predicament of the creature but dared not. -They were advertising him as half-man-half-lizard and he spent much of his time crawling in and out of a tank of water on all fours. The crowds were encouraged to throw coins for him which he dived for and were collected at the end of each performance. No doubt you are wondering why I have had him brought here? Kamil stayed silent. -That is for later, Uncle. You see, I am as adept as you are in building mystery. Her belly laugh made him smile.

*

Kamil washed himself in the lake before breakfast the next morning. Though the water was cold, which speeded his ablutions, his body began to tingle with heat once he had attired himself with clean clothes. He handed his journey-soiled garments to the old lady and went to eat fruit and cold meat in his room. No sooner had he sat on the bed than the Princess entered, hooded, finishing segments of orange. He stood and bowed and she flapped a hand to make him sit again, -Sit and eat, Uncle. Embarrassed by her lack of formality, he lowered himself and took the last few mouthfuls of meat. Meanwhile, she stood by the window and looked out over the lake, -I saw you bathing in the lake. Very hardy of you Uncle. It is fed from the snows I hear and rarely becomes warm like the river by the palace. Kamil was glad he had been fastidious in keeping himself covered throughout his washing. It proved that his natural caution could be a blessing. To be seen by the Princess, naked, was not something to which he could ever come to terms. He finished his orange and placed the peel in a neat pyramid beside him on the plate.

-Good! she said, -Now we can converse with our lizard man, together. He will have eaten, too. Let us see. She led the way to the creature's room where two guards stood to attention, tapped on the door and unlocked it. Then she stood back and motioned Kamil to open it. He did so with more fear than confidence but the lizard man was not waiting to pounce. They entered and she closed the door behind them so that the guards could not see or hear.

The creature was in his tub of water. It was barely big enough. He had to sit in it with crossed legs and tight arms so that the water could come to his chin. It had turned greenish so they could not see his flesh. He had soap in one hand and a washing stone in the other and was busily abrading his body under the water in the little space allowed. He seemed unconcerned that they were present. The Princess made Kamil sit with her on the lizard's bed.

-You will talk with us while you wash, she said kindly. He did not look at her but lowered his head in acquiescence, -Good. What is your name?

-Ull, he said softly, rubbing away beneath the water.

-Not a name I know. You, Uncle?

Kamil shook his head, -It is not from any near language. It sounds like ones I have seen from the north-most lands.

-What, where the general's Emperor lives? She laughed, -Has our friend, here, crept off your pages Uncle? Are you a magician? There are some in court who believe that words once written can invoke creatures from other worlds. Remember the ancient text at the end of your second book. Drawing them from the lands of gods and demons. Does it not say in the Bible, in the beginning was the word...

-True Princess. What we write may come to pass.

She turned again to watch the scrubbing. The creature's eyes were absorbed, staring down into the ever greener water, -Are you from such a place?

-I do not know.

-What is your earliest memory?

-Fishing on rivers.

-How old?

-I do not know. Always.

Kamil and the Princess looked at him, -Are you sure? asked the Princess.

-There is nothing else. Just a boat with a man and a woman. They were kind. I swam and chased the fish into the nets. They fed me.

-You could talk? asked Kamil, -From the beginning?

-Yes. Always. The frantic scrubbing was slowing down. They did not know whether it was because they were distracting him or that he was now satisfied with the results.

-Why did you leave the boat?

He raised his eyes to look at them both, -Men came. They saw my hands and feet. He showed them the webbing on the green hand that held the soap, -They paid for me. Gold. I did not know what they would do but I went with them because the man and the woman said that I would be looked after well. It was not true. I was put in a cage. Every day I was painted. I had to swim in a pool, catching fish and collecting coins with my hands. They threw money. The men took it.

-Painted? asked Kamil.

The creature's head tilted back so they could see him smile, -I am not a lizard, he laughed in a light rumble. He unwound his legs under the water and sat straight. It was incongruous. His unwashed, green head now sat upon a perfectly pink body.

Chapter Eight

Only excess teaches how much is enough

-**He is not** the only one, said Princess Shahrazad when they were alone again in Kamil's room. She had released the prisoner once he had removed all the green dye. He had given his oath that he would remain with her until she wished it otherwise and so was already swimming in the lake seemingly oblivious to the cold.
-Your Highness?
-My spies told me of others. They were looked for and are coming here, as we speak. She sat in her hardy trousers and strong woollen jacket, elbows on spread knees like any soldier in a barracks.
-More lizard-like men?
-No, she smiled, -Just creatures that are not wholly human. I have located six more, I think. My men had coins enough to buy them where it was necessary but two lived normally and must be persuaded to come. Kamil desisted from asking the purpose of this creature-hunt. He avoided any questions that were deeper than those seeking clarification over what she was ready and willing to talk about. It was a complex web and one that she had been building over time for how else would she have gathered tales of strange half-beings from distant parts, tracked them to their source and elicited their circumstances? Once this information was in her hands and she was satisfied that the creatures were of a kind that she hunted then she must have charged her men to bring them to her, -I will talk more with our no longer green man later today, alone, for there are questions I must ask that are for no-one else's ears. Even yours, esteemed Uncle.
-Of course, Your Highness.

*

Shahrazad preferred to eat before he read her a tale so it was much later that evening when she came into his room. She was pensive. Kamil had brought in a chair so that he could sit opposite her while she half sat, half lay upon his bed. It was not appropriate to be sharing a seat on the bed so late in the evening. It intruded upon his thinking. She did not comment on the change but slumped on her back with her knees up and the soles of her feet resting on the sheet, -I will tell you of this afternoon's engagement with the webbed man when you have read to me Uncle. Your stories help me to relax from the tensions I feel, here.

Kamil thought that this was something he could question, -Tensions, Princess?

-It is my word for them. My mother will have begun the search for me. Her agents will have scattered everywhere, seeking sightings. I have laid three false trails but she will assume they are false. Nevertheless she will have them explored in case I am double bluffing. Raashid will have been scolded for his gullibility but no more than that. She knows his value to both of us. She will let him devise his own search party. I must have this business completed by the time they uncover my whereabouts. Please read!

It was the custom in every empire to feed a stranger. The Magus and his daughter offered the drug peddler food and water which he gratefully received. No sooner had his teeth sunk into meat and dried fruit than he raised a quizzical eye, -How did I get here, eh? Seems impossible doesn't it? The battle, the chase, the ride through the woods, the stream, the rocks and yet here I am. There is no mystery in it. Nothing supernatural. The dream plant once moved my mind to another place far away but not my flesh and blood! He paused to eat.

The daughter stared at him stonily, -So how?

His eyes followed a route down her body with a slight nodding of his head to show he liked what he was seeing, -Simple prediction. Once you are off the plain and into the woods, every entry leads to the one path and you were only ever going to go north with the general. Given the circumstances, you had to separate. This is the only place you could hide your passage. When I left you on the boat, I rode to where your enemy waited in the trees. I heard the battle and then saw you retreat and break through the northern cordon. The moment you were free, I set off and took to the path. It was easy to stay out of sight of your pursuers. They weren't looking behind them. When the trail ended at the stream I saw that you had split from the general. You are the treasure that they all seek. You could only be here.

-My father had already deduced that, said the daughter, -But what is the value of the treasure and who wants it?

The man smiled, -Isn't that obvious? The Emperor who sent the general to bring you to him. It is well known that your wife has been taken as a barter. The tribes here are at war with the Emperor and would die rather than let his armies cross this land, no matter how savage his retribution. They have learned to disappear into the wilds and yet form an army in a day if the opportunity arises to attack his

731

forces. Then it became known that you and your daughter were being escorted north. Your fame, Magus, is greater than any emperor's. If the tribe was to capture you, then you would be a treasure indeed. The ransom would be great and they would also force closure of this passage south through their land.

-They would ransom us for gold? asked the daughter dubiously.

-Gold, prisoners taken from these lands who are now slaves in the ice, weapons... who knows what else?

The Magus scrutinised the man's face, looking for lies, -You have told us how you came to be here so soon after our enemy passed by but not why.

-I know the Emperor. He does not trust me but he does business with me. My dream plants are much sought after by his people as you saw. If I take you to him, the reward will be great. And Magus, I will take you there faster than even the general. I know these lands and its peoples. I have a route which will evade their attempts to capture you.

The Magus did not hesitate, -We will do it, he said, -But you know the perils attached to any agreement with us.

The drug trader did not smile but touched his heart, -You are superhuman, Magus and your daughter is a famed fighter. You will kill me as surely as you did the beast I am now eating if I do not carry out my side of our bargain.

First they returned to the stream and made their way north along it. They passed the point where the general had left it, followed by the small army that chased her and then they forced their way on to its banks where the bushes were thick and thorny. Beyond them lay the path north again. They crossed it directly and into an equally dense barrier on the other side but not until after the drug trader had swept it where they had left a churn of hoof prints. The sheer denseness of the foliage gave way after a while and they were back among the soldier trees and able to remount. There was just enough room to ride among the shiny grey trunks as their boughs did not begin until much higher than a man on horseback. Above, the branches grew into each other in a ceiling of deep shade. The sky was not visible and the wind did not reach down to the grey-green silence, yet the trader seemed able to read enough signs to be sure of their direction.

When they stopped for the night it was very dark under the foliage. They had to raid saddlebags yet again because game was too scarce here. This time however the trader shared what he had brought. They lit no fire and the evening was already cold as they settled in their skins and found comfort on the bed of needles between the trees. There was not enough room for the daughter to lie close enough to her father to talk privately so they allowed sleep to take them.

Another day's travelling took them much further to the north. The trees were more spaced and where there were silver barks among the shiny grey there was occasional grass underfoot. Here and there they could see the sky and bird song, which had seemed almost a thing of the past, had returned.

A three man hunt brought a mixed bag of beast and fowl. It was now that the Magus lit a fire and to add to their invisibility he constructed it in a hole and draped it all round with a skin. The wood was dry and what smoke there was disappeared in the dusk. When he saw the folding metal spit, the trader clicked his tongue admiringly. Three whole birds were roasted on it. The animal was big enough for the next day's midday meal so it was gutted and skinned, wrapped in leaves that the Magus carried with him and buried to cook slowly under the ashes. They would unearth it in the morning.

-I know as much about you as my brother, said the trader, lying back, satisfied, -You must be the best known man in the world. I have even been read some things that you have written. The shaman in the village can read. Many go to him to listen. The Right Way!

-The Right Path! interjected the daughter, testily.

-Is it? Well, much the same, is it not? Be good to everyone. Be peaceful. Don't steal. You see, I remember most of it. But...

-What? she asked.

-I meet people all the time. Some would cut me down as soon as look at me if I did not possess a sword and a willingness to kill. It has been my salvation, I think. People see it in my eyes. Do not try me, my eyes say. Better to forestall them. There are many who weigh up a man and would be willing to strike the first blow if they felt there was any weakness.

This unsettled the daughter. On her long journeys she had adopted exactly the same reasoning and it had protected her, too, she felt sure. She looked uncertainly at her father for an answer.

The Magus poked the fire with a long twig, -There is truth in what you say, he answered, -But there is a line to be drawn. If you use your eyes to prevent battle and thus the death of yourself or another then I see no wrong in it. If you become like your enemy and seek to take advantage of another's weak eyes then you are disgraced by your acts. We must seek to be noble wherever possible. In time, the Right Path should appeal to all. It will sheath the sword and protect the weak. Great change does not come with one sunrise.

The man nodded, -I see no issue between us on this. He considered his next question. While he lay with his eyes shut, comfortable in the heat of the fire, the daughter observed him, trying to gain a better picture of his character. She saw a man, slightly older than herself, strong and intelligent with a warrior's face but wilful and scarcely trustworthy. He shared with her the desire for travel and adventure and did so through his trade. Her feelings towards him had become a little less antagonistic which was usually the way when you must travel with someone. Those you dislike can become a little more acceptable. Those you like can become a little more irritating. Friendships and antagonisms were best managed by how much time is spent with the other and in what circumstances. For every person it was different. She no longer saw much of the father of her children whereas once they had been inseparable. She screwed up her face when she thought about her family and put it from her. But she realised that she found the trader worthy of a little more good nature than she had shown so far.

-They say you have no god, Magus, the fellow stated.

-Not as yet.

-Why? I thought everyone had a god. Some have many. The tribe that seeks you here have a god for everything; sun, moon, stars, plants, war, peace...

-Have you? cut in the daughter.

-Once I believed in the gods of the valleys from which we, all three of us, have sprung. But when the will to leave the valleys took my heart, I also left the gods behind. I became for a period a sun god believer under the rule of our own General, your friend, Magus but I had not travelled outside the empire. When I did, on the great roads of trade, I came upon lands, years to the east, where the dream plant helps people to see, touch, hear and smell their gods. They make their slaves eat it and then collect their urine for drinking. Many are sick when swallowing the raw plant but feel no ill when consuming it through the waters of others. Over time I trained myself to take the plant into me with only good effects. Wherever I was I fed myself enough to open my thoughts and I become close to the gods of that place.

-You saw these gods? asked the Magus.

-Inside. Visions. But they were as real as anything that may be disclosed by the eyes. It was a reward for leaving our valleys. All who knew me said that I was foolish. What good could come of it? But, I said, one of us became the famed Warrior and he did not do so by sitting at home. If I had not escaped the shackles of the valleys I would have learned little. And I would not be lying here in the company of that warrior, now the great Magus.

The Magus nodded. It was a tale that resonated with him. It also made him more curious about the trader's experience of these visions, - Do you believe that all these gods in your visions exist?

-There are two answers, One is yes and one is no. If I say yes, it is because my senses tell me so in my visions. If I say no, it is because I think they are all offspring of the One who began all things. The One, as I think of this father or mother of all gods, can not be seen or felt. The One is beyond all understanding and we only know of such a being by its absence. It is like watching a person die and seeing them suddenly without life. What has left them? We call it many things but we only know of it because it is now absent. It seems to me that behind everything that exists there is an invisible god, a creator of other gods and the other gods are there for people to touch in some way. They are channels to the One. He turned his head towards the Magus. -I have not taken the plant for a long time. It gave me too much to reflect upon.

The Magus spoke slowly, -This is what the plant taught me, -When I took it I found no god in my head or heart. It was the absence of any god that burned in me. Then, in a later revelation, I was aware of the many deaths I might suffer and the assassin who would kill me.

-You saw his face?

-His, hers – no. But I knew that when I met my assassin I would know, immediately.

735

The trader laughed, -The power of the plant. But it must settle your mind to know that you are travelling with someone who will not be your killer!

-**Very good Uncle**. The Chariot is a powerful card, is it not. It is about the will to reach beyond what might tie you down. It is the card that represents my own escape from shackles, just like the trader and the Magus and his daughter. You see the chariot has horses that would try to pull it apart but the charioteer is strong and harnesses their power and energy. I am riding my chariot. Being a princess pulls me in one direction and being the daughter of the Red Man pulls me in another. I must wrestle with these opposing forces and find my destiny.

Once again Kamil was in awe of her precocious maturity. She had a philosopher's mind in the body of a girl. Where had she learned these things? He had helped educate her over the years and there were moments when he had an insight into her intelligence but there had been nothing like this. She seemed able to pluck thoughts out of the cosmos itself. "Being the daughter of the Red Man pulls me in another." They were choice words and they were potent. He bedded them in his mind. They gave him some slight inkling of why she and the Empress had ensured that he accompany her.

-As to god or gods, she went on, -They are necessary features of life but cannot be seen to impede the workings of the state. Isn't that what my mother always says? He nodded. -Then that deals with this card, I think. Shall I tell you some of what happened in my conversation with the webbed guest? She assembled her limbs in a more prepossessed posture.

-Please, Your Highness. Kamil involuntarily leant back to maintain the space between them.

-I asked him many questions but will not divulge them here for they give too much away concerning my enterprise. He is happy for the moment. Life has been very hard on him. To be different from other men leads to danger at the hands of those who do not countenance such differences, as you described in one of the Tales concerning the albino children. Do you remember? Again he nodded. -Anyway, I gleaned certain things from him. Ull talks and understands perfectly well though his accent is from the north like his name. But he has no knowledge of it. Everything began in his memory on board that boat. There may be ways of opening up his past. It made me think of the trader's dream plant, the red mushroom. That is supposed to unhinge doors that have stayed shut resolutely, but they do not grow here and the royal apothecary is beyond my reach for the moment. I feel that

737

something may jerk him awake over the next few days when others come with similar tales of isolation and pain. We shall see. Anyway, he has a gift. Do you know what it is? She did not wait for an answer, - He can swim for hours under water. Is that not miraculous? His ears are like a fish's gills. They are slits only and he closes his mouth and nose and the slits afford him enough air, drawn from the water itself!

-That is astonishing. Kamil was certain that the creature was a demon, now. A djinn in their midst! It truly disturbed him but the Princess seemed to feel no such fear.

-The other event of note in our conversation was when I let him see my hair. He began to shake with an emotion. He put one hand over his mouth and pointed with the other and then bent his head and cried. I stroked his hand and he gradually became calm. I think it might be the first time that anyone has shown him affection since those days on the boat. But they ended in treachery when he was sold. I wonder whether what they did to him then caused the loss of his memories. I know it can happen. There were other aspects to him that became revealed but I have told you enough. What do you say, Uncle Kamil?

-You are able to draw blood from stone. You are your mother's child, all right - and more!

-Very true, Uncle. I have much more than she could ever have given me.

Chapter Nine

Thought is the sibling of action. Weigh it for purity in the same way.

The second part-human had arrived in the night, the Princess informed him over a shared breakfast. Whether she could have been said to have a gift or not, the fact was that she had scaled the walls of the house, though Kamil could not see how. She must have been able to insinuate her finger ends and toes in the tiniest cracks, despite the lack of illumination. What particularly terrorised Kamil's thoughts was to discover that she had found a room to sleep in and had curled up on a wooden pallet. She could easily have attacked her Royal Highness. In any event, Princess Shahrazad had woken, knew by instinct that someone had arrived and investigated to find her still asleep. The Princess told Kamil that her first words to the intruder were, -You are the second. Welcome.

*

Later in the morning he was required by Princess Shahrazad to meet with the newcomer in a room now cleaned and prepared. For reasons beyond his understanding, the Princess couched the request in a cryptic announcement, -This will be my first proper meeting with our new visitor. I have to decide, on the merits of each case, whether you can be present throughout or just at certain points.

The creature was sitting on her bed and was tiny, as small as a ten year old but obviously beyond adolescence. She wore work clothes comprising a rough brown woollen jacket and tightly fitted fawn sacking trousers. She was barefoot and Kamil could see that his surmise about her toes and fingers had been correct. They were horny and calloused and seemed big in proportion to her tiny frame. Her black hair had been cut to prevent lice and was shorter than most boys' but overall her face was regularly featured and even attractive, if unnaturally pale. When she spoke it was slow, as though she was inexperienced at answering questions.

-Your name, little one?

-Vatisha, Lady.

-Born in a storm, yes?

-I think so, Lady.

-My men found you? asked the Princess.

-Yes, Lady. The girl looked her in the eye. It was obvious that she did not yet know to whom she was speaking.

-What did they say?

-If I come I will get a reward. A Lady wants to see me. The Princess looked to the door to make sure it was closed and then dropped her hood. Slowly the girl's eyes opened wide as she struggled to accept that the coffee skin and red hair meant that this must be the Empress's daughter. She blurted out, -Lady is the Princess?

-I am.

The girl's eyes became tearful. As an afterthought she realised where she was and dropped off the bed on to her knees, -I want no reward, she exclaimed.

-There will be rewards, responded the Princess, kindly. -Sit! Now tell me where they found you. Was it among the builders, as I had heard?

-Yes, La – Princess.

-Good. You can call me Princess or Princess Shahrazad or your Highness. Yes?

-Yes, please. Your Princess.

-So tell me. The Princess and Kamil were standing. There was nowhere for them to sit but the Princess obviously felt that the girl would talk more if they did not remind her of her station.

-Yes Princess. Building a spike on a temple. Very high. Northern territory.

-How old are you?

-Nineteen, Princess.

-How long have you been with the builders?

The girl shrugged, -All the time. My mother is a builder.

-And your father? The Princess looked at her narrowly.

-I have no father.

-So your mother can climb like you?

The girl laughed, -No, Princess, my mother is too fat. She is the builders' cook and money
dealer.

-Have you always climbed?

-Yes Princess. And crawled. Everyone says I can pass through a needle.

-You have become well known!

-Yes, Princess. They come for me to take rope to the highest points if there is no other way.
It pays well. It is quicker than making a scaffold.

-Is your family from the north territory?

-No, Princess. Beyond. Further north. My mother was a cook where the boats tied up. But the river washed away everything. Mother came south to the north territory.

-Do you have any idea why you are here?

-Yes, Princess. You want me to work on the palace roof.

-No, not that but I do want you to work for me. But not yet. You will stay here until I am ready. Yes?

The girl bowed gracefully, -Thank you, Princess. For ever.

-What did your mother say when you left?

-Your man gave her money. Much money. She was happy. He wanted to bring me here himself but I did not like the way he stared at me so I came on my own. I walked, ran and got lifts on wagons and carts. Her voice was very matter of fact.

-Was my man rude to you? Did he touch you?

-No, he did not. But I saw inside him. She screwed up her nose and sniffed, -Not good. I did not like him, she moved her head in the direction of Kamil, -He is a good man.

-He is, indeed. I could ask for no better, said the Princess, -Now you are free to go where you will. But do not tell local people that I am the Princess, that is all. I hide my hair so nobody knows I am here. Do you understand? On pain of life.

-Yes Princess. The girl beamed.

*

Kamil spent the day in his room. Looking out over the lake he occasionally caught sight of the webbed man who seemed to prefer the water to the house. As a gesture of good will the strange fellow had brought several big fish to the kitchen, caught by hand and his underwater guile. He also saw the girl sitting on the shore, dangling her feet in the water. At one point the two of them seemed to be in conversation, his head just above the water and hers bent towards him. Much of the time Kamil's brain was challenged by trying to figure what the Princess might be concocting but it always came to nothing. Why come here and attract these part-humans to her? She could have done that in the palace, couldn't she? Except her mother would have interfered with her plans. Whatever she was up to, it was bound to be against the Empress's wishes. Perhaps she was collecting these creatures because they were, like herself, of mixed demon and human parentage? Was that it? She had begun to mention the Red Man more often and had talked about not knowing her father. She could only know the public history of his short time and death at the court. That would not be truly knowing. If she was desperate to know more, Kamil could not really empathise. His own father died when he was too young to have known him but he had no desire to find out the man's earlier history or his character. He supposed that he must have inherited a lot from him but what difference did it make? If he had still been alive it might be different. After all, hadn't he, Kamil, written that the Magus' daughter and mother wanted to spend time with the great man to know him better having not seen him when the former was a child and when the latter was fleeing assassins? They wanted to grow closer to him to love him properly! But the Princess had never known and would never meet her father.

*

Trying to deduce her motives caused Kamil to fall asleep. He woke up when there was a rap at the door and the old man announced in his rough dialect that the lady would visit shortly for her story. He sluiced his face and straightened his clothing, then flattened out the ruckles in the sheet and placed the chair ready. The next card was Justice and it was ready to be turned over by the Princess.

She strode in looking happy, hood already falling as she closed the door. Before she had even sat beside him she was asking about his impressions of the little climber, -Isn't it a paradox that she is smaller than me, looks younger and yet is older? I must admit I took to her immediately. I like her innocence. The first creature is deeper and, on the surface, stranger. What lies below we will only discover over time.

What do you say?

Kamil was sitting upright in his most obedient pose, -I am sure you are right, Princess. They are a little strange but you have their undying loyalty already.

-On the surface. My trust is only in you and my mother. And perhaps, Raashid. She returned to her theme, -She shares a gift with me, don't you think?

Kamil recollected the details of their conversation, -Ah Princess, you are right, It did not strike me immediately. She can measure a person's worth on a first meeting. That may be a greater gift than the skills in her fingers and toes.

-It is excellent for survival in a world where men would do as they wish. I do not know if the webbed man shares it also. It appears not so but he has settled well and seems to trust me, as you said. Perhaps the events which turned him from a happy boatman into a circus act blunted this acute sense. There will be much to glean from him if we can pull back the curtain that has been drawn across his history. What is our next symbol? She turned the card over, -Justice eh? Many of the Tales focus on justice, don't they Uncle? The Right Path is based on moral judgment. Decisions must be made between good and evil as in the Ten Commandments. Life for most people is full of Dos and Don'ts which have to be measured and interpreted. It is a hierarchy, you might say. At the top is the Empress and there are very few dos and don'ts for her because she can do as she wishes. But then you descend through the princes and lords and officials until you arrive at the bottom with the palace cleaner or the labourer in the fields and the list meanwhile has become longer and longer.

-The Magus was looking for a common creed for everyone, no matter how important in the eyes of others, said Kamil, -Such a moral outlook hardly existed among the tribes before his life and work.

-Is it any different today? she asked, -It certainly is not universal, -I have that to face when I become Empress. Let us read.

They were travelling through the mists risen over a massacre in a broken, gruesome countryside. Fields and copses were smouldering with villages torched or torn down and bodies decomposing where they had fallen to blade and bow. It had been like this for settlement after settlement. Their horses were distressed by the constant spectre of death, walking stiffly on their toes with their heads high and eyes rolling. The macabre desolation affected the three riders differently.

For the daughter it brought a shrug. She had seen similar scenes in the past even in her own valleys. This is what people did to each other. She had no connection with the dead and so had no feelings one way or another. If it was a local dispute then all the better. If these deeds were the evidence of some greater force which may one day turn out to be their enemy, she would deal with that when forced to face it.

The Magus was severely disturbed by what he saw. There was a time when he would have reacted much as his daughter but those days were long past. Something had so changed inside him that he saw, beside all the decaying villagers, seated life-takers tugging at the feeble spirits still clinging to the burnt flesh. Though he knew this was his own delusion, it was the personification of the sorrow in his heart. He mourned the dead and he mourned their pitiful last thoughts, still echoing from those moments when they had closed their eyes on the world for the last time.

-The first time I saw such a sight, said the trader, -I was lost in my heart. I swear I cried tears of blood. Even now I suffer. I passed this way some years ago. These rotting bodies were people I knew. They never fought, preferring the contest of earth against plough. The armies of the general's Emperor have been this way like a plague that allows no recovery. If you look more closely the hands are missing on every corpse. They will have been placed in a heap on a hand-raft and left to float down the river to the ice covered seas where the land ends in the north, as an offering to their god of water.

-This is the work of the Emperor? He must be, as you have said, a cruel tyrant. And it is with him that we must deal. The daughter spoke matter of factly.

-Do not speak such things aloud, even in the absence of listeners! Such words would be enough for him to have you killed. The trader gave his horse a nudge with his heels and they cantered away from the obscenities.

-I would like to know how this came about, said the Magus, -It will inform my meeting with the man.

The trader halted, -One thing we learn from tyrants is that when they seek to eliminate all who live and might rise against them, they fail. The flame of revenge will find and burn in even a single remaining heart and it will be passed on through generations if need be. One day this Emperor, like those before him, or his children or children's children, will be called to the knife point of account for acts such as these. Even if his armies have carried out his commands and murdered every member of this clan, it will still not be enough. The crime will be inflicted on sleepers far and wide, as nightmares and thus a knowledge of the killings will be spread. You have experienced such events yourself, Magus, I would surmise. He looked at the older man, curiously.

-It is true that I have sometimes travelled further in the mind than I could have done in my body. Without your plant.

-Indeed, but whether the plant or some other sorcery carries you back through time to witness these terrible events, be prepared, for such a journey is often worse than being there. To be a helpless spectator who can do nothing to change the march of horror is, for a man like you Magus, a burden few would wish to carry.

By the end of that day they were far enough away from the fat-laden air and wood smoke to be able to breathe cleanly. The breeze was in their faces too, bringing with it the scents of drying grasses and evergreen trees. They stopped by a stream which had formed a large pool and soon father and daughter had caught three slithering snake-like creatures, as long as their forearms, while the trader prepared the fire. The snake fish were covered with a sticky slime and had to be rolled in dry leaves and trussed. Using the Magus's spit and sweet-smelling wood, they smoked them while they prepared camp. It was a satisfying meal and it left them lying by the fire, in their skins, staring up at a sky crammed with the stars that swept with a line of white mist across its centre.

The trader spoke softly, -It is said that the mist is snow that never falls. It is a bracelet around the earth. The sun cannot melt it and the moon lights it like a lantern.

-That is true, said the daughter, -The story is one I heard as a child. We are protected by sun, moon and stars. They are the eyes of the gods. It is comforting.

The Magus treated her thoughts with his usual courtesy, neither condemning them nor encouraging them. Instead he said, -I stayed with a shaman who showed the stars on the roof of his egg house. By acts of dexterity with metals and stone as clear as water, he showed me the patterns in the night sky at the touch of his hand. The seasons of stars appeared, one after another. He said that there was more in the sky than we could ever understand or see.

The trader smacked his thigh and laughed, -I met him! He lives on a small island in the greatest river in the empire though I was never invited into the egg house. He is a wizard indeed and has more secrets in his head than the shamans of a dozen tribes. I exchanged with him a sack of dream plants for this. The trader took out a flat circle of clear stone. It magicks fire but only under the sun. The moon has no heat. Let the sun shine through it on dried fire-moss and it becomes alight in an instant.

With a smile, the Magus said, -I have the same and he pulled from his belted pouch a similar circle, wrapped in silk. He unrolled it and there was a disc, though more ornate than the trader's, for it was set in a carved horn frame. The trader took it in his hands, -It is fine workmanship, he said, -To be housed in horn might have cost me many sacks! He handed it back, -You use it?

-No. In truth I had all but forgotten I had it. It does not mean that I won't use it but I make a fire without thought. The old ways are deep in me. There is something in the smell of twisting, burning wood and its waiting moss that comforts me as much as the stars do my daughter.

746

The scientist, for that is what he called himself, then described how, by using the disc, tiny creatures could be seen on decaying food. The wizard had not told the trader this and he resolved to test his magic eye in this way as soon as he could. -If it is true what you say then much time could be spent looking at such things. I have often thought that if I can see, depending on the quality of the light, tiny forms, then there may be many that are there that I never see. As when I have an itch but cannot see the cause. The trader looked at his disc with new eyes, -I cannot wait to try it. The man's face was lit with pleasure. The Magus was warmed by his open curiosity, despite not trusting him in the affairs of barter.

-It does not seem possible! The daughter's face was, unlike the trader's, quite indignant, -How can there be tiny creatures that exist beyond our sight? Is it not the magic of the disc that gives them birth?

-There is much that is beyond our senses. Why not these? You will see, said the Magus.

-I do not follow, Father.

-Do we not use animals to find prey or the roots of plants? They smell them and we do not. Does not the roan sense oncoming danger when we are innocent of the knowledge? Have I not travelled in the sky and seen through a bird's eyes? The world is not fixed, it is not the same for everyone. Each knows it in his own way. There may be creatures and plants and rocks that lie below the sight of all men's eyes, even wizards with their magic discs. Our scientist on the island, using his instruments, says that through them he can see a multitude more stars than he can without them. It is obvious to me that we do not know everything that exists about us. We see what we expect to see. It is more difficult to train ourselves to seek what we have never seen and yet has always been in front of us.

Earlier, while they were catching the snake fish, father and daughter had an opportunity to talk about their companion for the first time since he had joined them on their journey. Both had changed their opinion of him but even so their present views were different. The daughter thought him more agreeable than when they had met him on the boat but his trade was not one she could countenance. She did not like the possibility that a person's mind could be invaded by the poisons in a plant. It frightened her. She wanted to stay as she was. Adventures and journeys were different. They were challenges of the real. She sought them because they made her feel more in control of her destiny than if she had stayed at home in her village. They did not change her, rather she became truly herself. Nothing she had seen or done, no matter how strange or unworldly, altered her view of herself as the warrior daughter of the Magus. This was what she had always been and what she would always be.

When the Magus spoke of his feelings towards the trader, he was divided. There was something that he had sensed on the boat which did not lead to trust. The sale of the dream plant was more than a simple barter. There were undercurrents. The real trader hid behind courtesies and gifts. He was polite and gregarious yet it was all a cover for deeper intentions. Even his curiosity and delight in new things stemmed from the realisation that one day they could bring him advantage. The Magus had fought to gain insights into his own purpose in life and he thought he knew something of his daughter's but what drove the trader was hidden below the well-rehearsed surface of his face.

The divides between them became more apparent when they came upon an old man, dying in the woods. The roan had snickered as they were forcing their way through low bushes. The Magus allowed it to pull off to one side and it led them to a small clearing of deep grass and blue trumpet-like flowers. Lying among them with his eyes closed in a blissful smile was an ancient one in a clean white robe. He had white skin and white straggly hair and beard. He could have been a benevolent djinn.

The sound of their snorting mounts stirred him, -Ah, it is the Magus. Am I already dead among gods and immortals?

The Magus dismounted and laid a hand on the fellow's brow, -No, he chuckled, -You are still among the living. He sat beside the reclining figure, -How did you know me? His voice was deeply respectful.

-Who does not? Warrior. Magus. The Right Path. I have feasted like a drunkard at a barrel of root spirit on tales of your great journeys, your feats of strength in battle, your wisdom and your shamanic powers. His voice was still strong, despite his failing body. -Who is this with you? He put a hand across his eyes and looked up at the two riders, -Your daughter I see from the look of her, as beautiful as any I have loved in these long years. A good heart and a steady mind, though not sharing your search for the ineffable, eh? His gaze turned to her companion, - And the peddler, just as I expected, bringer of truth and deceit, rage and humiliation, sickness and strength. You barter the red cap for gold and have little thought of the consequences.

The trader smiled uncertainly and made a gesture with his hands as if to say that he was talking senile nonsense.

-No, said the old man, -Do not pretend confusion. All we do has consequences for others. Even if we entomb ourselves like hermits, something of us spills into the world. We cannot think without the thought taking on a life of its own and wandering in search of a new home. You believe that, don't you, peddler? It was true and the trader knew it. It was little different from what he had said about the Emperor's desire to silence a whole tribe being futile for such acts, once committed, would inhabit the dreams of others.

The Magus reflected that if everything a person said and thought, even when alone in the wilderness, remained forever in the air to influence others, then the Right Path must include much more than being judged on one's actions. One must be judged on one's thoughts, too. To follow the Right Path a person must cleanse the mind of all bad thoughts so that, in time, the purification became so thorough that no unwanted act would ever follow. He looked down at the soft, unwrinkled face of the old fellow and reached out his mind to him. There was a brief, intense contact but he encountered no pain or fear, just a peaceful contentment at what was now to come. The man was a shaman and the wisdom he had gained throughout his life was guiding his last few hours. He turned to look up at the mounted trader.

-You have been judged, he said, -How do you now judge yourself?

-I take no responsibility for others. I do not force the dream plant on them. It is not for me to say whether a man is good or evil and therefore may use the plant for good or ill, he said. But when the Magus and the daughter looked into his eyes, they saw that he did not believe this.

With his lids closed, the dying man spoke again, -All the corpses in all the villages are your brothers and sisters. They have died at the hands of the general's men. His army travelled to this land on the wings of the red cap. It took from them any nobility of thought and left them without their senses, slaughtering for the pleasure in seeing the blood spill and the congregating life-takers everywhere. Every man must face severe judgment if his acts are not gauged to improve the lot of others. Even to be silent does not absolve us from crimes committed by those we have never met and will never meet. A malignant mind does evil by its thoughts. He stopped talking for a while. The daughter and the trader dismounted and sat on the other side of the recumbent figure. The air in the little clearing was rich and heady with the sweet scent from the blue flowers. There was a soft drone of flying insects flashing vibrantly in the golden light that filtered down upon the silent face.

-Take my hands and make a circle, said the ancient one, firmly. The Magus' left hand enclosed his right. The man's right hand held the daughter's left and the trader completed the circle. As it became closed, the man's eyes opened and gazed into those of the Magus, - You were called to administer my final rites. Burn my body on the sweetest wood, bury my bones where here I lie for it is safe from sorcery and throw my ashes upon a stream that they be carried to an ocean. Then his eyes closed.

A vision appeared to the Magus. The shaman's life-taker appeared at the dead man's head. It was his own female hermit in brown cowl and robes. She intoned, -Your life has led you to this man. He staved off death until your arrival. What he has been has now passed to you. Do not neglect it. Then, as before, she diffused into a mist in the rich, golden light.

-I have heard people say, stated a pensive Princess, that someone had a good death but usually they mean that the person either died while sleeping or engaged in whatever was his lifetime's work. For example, warriors falling in battle or farmers lying, like your Ancient in the Tale, in the fields on the grass beside their flocks. But your story adds something almost mystical. I have never heard of someone preparing to die at a chosen time and with the right person in attendance, fully prepared for the final journey of all, his life weighed and measured. She held the card of justice between thumb and forefinger and stared closely at the detail, -She is blindfolded. She cannot be from the royal court, Uncle! The eyes of our agents of justice are always open wide to see whether pleasure or displeasure rules the countenance of the Empress. I am better than my mother at excluding the heart when it comes to guilt before the law but also better than her in allowing the heart to speak for those unfortunates who find themselves in trouble for no other reason than they are poor. I think that the sentence should not add unduly to the pain already inflicted upon them by life. The greater the wealth, the greater the sin is my creed. The noble who has everything and commits a crime deserves a far greater punishment than the peasant who has nothing.

-That is very far-sighted of you Princess. Kamil meant it. He had not seen too much evidence of the Princess's famed and much feared tantrums so far on this adventure. She had behaved with great restraint and shown that she possessed a warm and humane side to her character. Her comments on the card displayed her uncanny maturity.

-Thank you Uncle. It is another reason why I have you with me. Talking to you as a result of the Tales, helps me think more clearly what it is I must do. It is always fertile and as easy as I could have imagined though, I have to say, there may be far greater tests of our friendship and quite soon. She stood up and went to the window, - Look, the webbed man is in the water and the climbing girl is with him. He is teaching her to swim. Kamil joined her. He saw the man standing to his waist and holding the woman under the stomach as she thrashed her arms and legs in a froth of white spume. In the midst of it she suddenly stood up, coughing and spluttering. The man laughed and put his arm around her shoulder but she pulled away, though little more than a pace and then ducked her shoulders for another try, -He likes her, said the Princess. -Good. Soon there will be five more.

-Five? queried Kamil uncertainly.

-In time but not in one arrival, she replied, her tone happy and light, - They come from different points and even beyond our empire. The furthest will have taken a whole year to reach us but I had the sense to explore all the maps in the Great Library and from them I drew up my stratagem for bringing them here, one after another, according to the distance they must travel. Only when I knew when the distant ones were likely to arrive did I seek to include the closer ones in my web. I am hopeful that they will all be here within the week. One day I will show you my map and how I drew it up. It is the equal of those you advised my mother to construct when she calculated the poison in the court.

*

The day was fast disappearing. Princess Shahrazad held further interviews with her two guests without Kamil being present, after which they retired to their rooms to eat alone. When he was finished his own meal he set out for a walk around the small courtyard to help his food descend in his stomach. The misgivings he had about his role here had diminished as he became aware of his importance to the Princess's plans, whatever they might be. He no longer worried about what sort of retribution the Empress might exact for his conduct. He had convinced himself that in some strange way she was colluding in her daughter's defiance, even if she would apparently be doing everything she could to return her to the court.

As so often happens in a person's life, the moment he felt least troubled by these events, his reasoning became subject to severe undermining. The Princess joined him and linked an arm in his, the sign of a very close family relationship and one that made his heart brim.

-Did you hear the messenger? she asked. He thought for a moment and then nodded, there had been the sounds of the gate being opened when he was eating but he had paid no attention to them, -News from the court, she stated. His stomach churned immediately. She squeezed his arm and said, -Raashid is nearest among our main pursuers. He has a body of ten riders and they are west of these hills. None has supposed we might make for this lap on the snowy peaks. They are checking all

752

the noble residences, imagining that their Princess will want to sleep and dine in state, but, she paused, -As I have said, my mother does not dwell on logic when she imagines what her daughter might be up to. Besides the spread of her search parties, each one following a different spoke from the royal hub, she has enlisted a manhunter to find me. Once he has tracked me down he will bring the nearest platoon of troops. I know him. He is ingenious and has found many an enemy singlehanded. She will have given him special instructions to which my messenger was not privy but I do not doubt that he is somewhere in the foothills, already. Let us hope he will meet his match in my guard who I have sent to head him off. Whatever happens Uncle, no barrier will block the fruition of my plans.

-Could someone have followed your messenger? Kamil asked; though he felt a little foolish at the obviousness of it.

-I hope not. My messenger is not one person but a combination of ordinary citizens, unknown to the court, each with the simple task of handing on a sealed document to the next person. To open it would be death. To talk of it would be death. The Princess's eyes became narrow and intense, -And I would exercise the right to take such a traitor's life with my own weapon.

Kamil was taken by surprise again. He had been entirely oblivious of the network she had established throughout the empire among her subjects. He realised with a pang of fear, the full import of it. She had become a threat even to her own mother!

Chapter Ten

The greatest adventure is the journey to the centre of your self

It was mid-morning the next day when two more visitors passed through the gates. They were a little older than both the webbed man and the climbing girl. At first Kamil thought that they were man and wife or lovers for they held hands continually and were never far from each other's side. It turned out that they were unalike twins. They had come unaccompanied and on horseback though the saddles and leathers were simple affairs and the beasts no longer young. They were well enough dressed in the practical riding garb of the well-to-do from the adjacent lands north of the empire. Both were fair skinned with rich coppery hair and wide, full mouths that smiled pleasingly. They did not lack confidence, despite their need of each other, walking purposefully across the courtyard to the hooded figure of Princess Shahrazad and giving her curt bows as they should to a lady. She nodded to them and said welcome and then crooked a finger at Kamil to come and join them. A table was got ready in the shady side of the courtyard and the four sat down. The Princess's clothes might have been changed every day but were always in the same casual male style she preferred. Kamil was in his uniform of white suit with buttoned robe and wide trousers. It was warm in the courtyard by now after the chill of the night.

Food and juice were brought and a pitcher of water. As Kamil and the Princess watched, the two began to eat and drink, displaying surprisingly cultivated manners.

-Your names are Zemfira and Timur? They nodded politely, after all the Lady must have known their names to have sent for them.

-How long has it taken you to reach this place? she asked.

Timur spoke, -More than a half year since your man came to us with your proposition. Three exchanges of mounts. It was not the reward that brought us here but what else you offered. We could not leave until our business was done.

-We will discuss the reason for your coming, later, said the Princess swiftly, avoiding Kamil's eye. The twins caught the inflection in her

754

tone, looked across at Kamil and then studied their food.

-What is it that you do? asked Kamil, in all apparent innocence to smooth over any disquiet. He was quite taken by their countenances. They seemed to have little untoward about them, unlike the first two guests.

-We are gold panners and teeth doctors, said Zemfira, -It is a good profession, if you know where to look for the ore. My brother has the scent. I have the eye. There is gold in this lake, though not enough to make one ingot. It would take too long to sieve out. There are easier pickings in our country.

Kamil was intrigued. There was something about gold that had always stirred him. He loved its constant lustre and heavy softness. He had sometimes dreamt of a banquet in which bowls were filled with gold dust and plates were piled with soft gold sweetmeats. He had two gold teeth and hoped to have more, -You leach your own gold to make teeth? he asked.

Zemfira smiled her full smile, -The profits are high. Gold bought from a smith would make a full mouth worth more than all but the very rich could afford and many need most of God's gift of thirty two teeth filling or replacing once they are in middle age. It would be a rare individual who does not need some treatment, however slight, some time in life. We wire loose teeth to hold them but then, as they begin to ripen and blacken they must have the canker drilled out and the gold insinuated. We have devised a way to do this. Afterwards the teeth may last many years with no pain.

-Your secret…? asked the Princess.

- …is our secret, Lady, said Zemfira.

-A fair answer. Princess Shahrazad waited a moment and then continued her questioning, -Were you born on our northern borders?

It was Timur who replied, looking confused, -In truth Lady we know not. That is what we thought you might reveal to us. His companion nudged him and once again they both looked down, this time at empty plates, -I mean, my Lady, he went on hurriedly, -Our first knowledge of life saw us as child servants in a merchant's household. He told us later that he took us in from a passing caravan. Our mother had disappeared from the company during the journey and the caravan master had no kindness in him and would have left us to die in the desert. We kept the yards clean and helped the cook and gardeners where we were able. The merchant was stern but fair. One day we were brought to his trading room and told to polish gold articles that he was taking to the market; candlesticks, cups, plates... I made a discovery. When I picked them up I was able to smell the differences between them though I did not know what it meant as far as value was concerned as I was too young. Something told me that pure gold was special, I do not know what. Being a child, I put the pure gold to one side, then the articles that had a high proportion of gold next and so on. The Master came in and saw immediately that I had a gift for divining the quality of the metal. He asked how I had done it, for even he found it difficult to tell apart the pure from near purity. It was then that I realised that I could detect one from another by my nose. He made me accompany him then in his trade and Zemfira came too, as we were inseparable. He was able to bargain for the best pieces and no-one knew that he did not gamble on their quality but relied upon my gift.

Zemfira took up the tale, -We went on many caravans with him and helped him to become rich. One day we were camped by a river and I said to Timur that there was gold there. We said nothing to the merchant but pretended to play by the shore. Timur picked up a pebble and sniffed it. It did not look like gold but he knew that there was some hid within it. We were at the furthest edge of childhood and so were able to plan what we might do. We decided to stay with the merchant until such time as we could fend for ourselves properly, then leave and return to the river for the gold, though I think it was much later on a visit to panners with the merchant that we saw how to separate it from stone. Then one day with terrible toothache, he engaged a doctor to cure him. We watched what the surgeon did and asked children's questions. He was happy enough to tell us. We followed him round the caravan because there were many with tooth problems. Both of us remembered in clear detail everything. We practised with bits of broken silver in the merchant's trading room, making wire, mending holes, replacing worn handles. The merchant liked our work and gave us free rein. He was able to profit very well from our labours. Finally, he retired and gave us his blessing and a bag of coins to keep us in comfort for a while. But we bought horses and tools with them and went back to the river. As with everything, our memories had allowed nothing to slip away. We found the river quickly. There was a good horde there. It was the beginning.

Princess Shahrazad cut in, -So you have two gifts between you? Knowing where gold will be and knowing its strength, through its scent?

-Not just gold, Lady, said a smiling Timur, -I can tell whether anything is pure. Gold, silver, copper, iron…

-And people! cried Zemfira, -We can tell a person's worth.

-Indeed? How do you measure my friend here, Kamil?

-He is almost wholly good, said Zemfira looking at her brother for corroboration and finding him nodding.

-And myself? asked Princess Shahrazad, impishly.

The pair looked at her and seemed to have difficulty in replying. It was Timur who spoke for them both with the naïve innocence that seemed to attend their every utterance , -We have not met one like you. Much is hidden from us. What we can see is kind and without malice but it is like the rind of a strange fruit. What flesh lies beneath, poisonous or wholesome, we cannot as yet tell.

*

-Kamil, what do you think of our newcomers? An interesting pair? They were as shocked as the climbing one when they saw my red hair. It seems that I am known even in empires beyond this one! She was seated beside him on his bed and it was late afternoon. The cards were stacked between them and Kamil held the first page of the next Tale.

-Everyone on earth must know of you, Princess, he said, his voice full of sugar, -Most pleasing, they are. One cannot help smiling when they talk. They are fresh and without guile.

-Are they not! I saw you smile to yourself when the man, Timur, said that they could not vouch for my total goodness. Kamil's face paled for a moment until she laughed, -I am jesting, though your reaction suggests some truth in my barb!

-No your Highness, I assure you!

-Very well. Let us continue with the Tales before discussing the twins and what unusual qualities they possess. She turned over the card, -It is the Hermit. I hope this Tale is not full of grim accounts of the fasting and praying and flagellation which some renouncers seem to imagine is the way to God.

The death of the ancient one left all three with a miraculous sense of calm. His leaving of life had been so full of grace that it had passed from him to them through their clasped hands, bringing a serenity not even the Magus had experienced before. While the daughter and the trader built a platform half a man's height above the ground, the Magus prepared the pyre, collecting the driest, sweetest wood from thinnest twigs to boughs the thickness of his thighs. The latter he cut into small logs and he arranged his collection in tiers from thin to thick upon the sods his two companions had laid upon the platform to prevent it becoming alight and collapsing too early in the cremation.

They raised the Ancient's body above their heads, finding it light and insubstantial as though the burdens of life had already slipped from it, and placed it on the logs. With conspiratorial smiles, the Magus and the trader pressed fire moss around the base of the pyre and took out their discs and offered them to the sun. They walked slowly around it, lighting it as they went. Soon, the heat was so intense they had to retire to the edge of the clearing. The body of the ancient shaman dissolved in a fire that seemed more liquid than air and with a scent that elevated the thoughts as it invaded their senses. When it had lost its human shape, the daughter said, -I will hunt while the fire dies.

-There are plants here. I will gather them in his memory, said the trader.

They left the Magus seated among the blue flowers, lost in contemplation on the shaman and his wish for a ritual to mark his leaving of life.

He lay back, agreeably released from the feeling of his own body enclosing him. It was a state wherein his mind became acute as he meditated on the Right Path. He thought about what he had written and taught. Already it seemed to him that his extolling of human acts that are good in themselves was too superficial. He had been looking at the symptoms of humankind's ill-endeavours and not the causes. At the same time he had to accept the fact that it would be difficult to change the widespread desire for gods. It seemed to swim in the flow of human blood. There was so much that could not be understood by any living person that it was inevitable that people should gather these mysteries under the omniscient robes of invisible and untouchable forces. Why should people choose to be like him, the Magus, striving for purpose and understanding in a fearsome world without the comfort of gods? It had become a dominating, almost oppressive focus of his life. It was far easier to believe in something great and powerful, make sacrifices and engage in rituals and then be released by those rituals to concentrate on filling days with work and survival. What the Right Path had established was a set of commandments for living in harmony with those around. The most important Rule spoke against acts of violence which were not in self-defence or the defence of the vulnerable. These were wrong in every sense. They led to suffering and they encouraged greater acts in retaliation. Stealing should not be countenanced because it destroyed the security of clan life. A family who works to build a flock or a dwelling or a store of corn should not have it taken away by another who has not the will to persevere and build for himself. Life was harsh for most clans. If they were not confident that their fellow men would respect their endeavours why undertake them in the first place? Just so with lying. Heart must speak to heart. If we cannot believe another speaks the truth and holds by his word then all disintegrates when times are hard. The Magus had become certain that violence, stealing and lying were the principle evils in human behaviour. All else seemed to be born of them. But in truth they were symptoms and he had not uncovered the causes. When the Ancient had clasped him at the moment of death, his mind had become fallow, ready to accept new thoughts and the teachings of others. The latest of these jostled in his mind now.

The Ancient had said that a malignant mind was no less evil than a bad deed. His daughter had spoken of love when their hands had touched and he had felt the sudden force of her words. Everything, it seemed to the Magus, in his state of heightened understanding, flowed from thoughts and feelings. Not the thoughts and feelings that could be spoken of easily but the thoughts and feelings which lay in the very depths of being and which influence the nature of a person, forming character and purpose. The challenge for the Right Path was how to reach these depths so that they may be influenced at their core, to embrace selflessness rather than selfishness.

His illumination was the consequence of a living touch in an act of love. The hands of his daughter and those of the Ancient had reached inside him, life communicating with life and alchemy following. Such loving acts open the portal to self-awareness. Another route was through meditation. The Right Path had come into being during solitude and reflection but it was not complete. He must also wrestle with the practices he was using to seek self-knowledge.

His eyes were shut and his breathing was regular which, as he considered it, became deeper so that he had a new awareness of it filling his body with the world around him. It was as momentous as his daughter's hand. He was touching the world with his breath and it was touching him. As he breathed, the air that he drew into himself became richer, laden with all things, the earth, the plants, the air, the sky, the sun and moon and the stars that could not yet be seen. It was what his father-not-of-blood had believed and had tried to teach him. There could be no division between him and what was around him. The existence of all things could be found in the existence of the self. A person in meditation could take the first step to purifying the essence of his being by excluding all but his own breathing. It was this that proclaimed that he was truly alive. It was the primary evidence of the wholeness of which he was but a part. The ancient shaman had communicated this to him. A pure being could not commit acts that the Rules sought to forbid. The water from the deepest well does not poison if, as it rises through the earth, it is cleansed on its journey. Meditation was the earth, itself. It provided a filter of goodness that cleansed the bubbling waters.

The Magus knew then that he must teach breathing to help others begin the journey to knowing the self. Afterwards he would teach meditations on the nature of selflessness to enable them to escape the shackles of behaviours that were so ingrained they were unaware of their pernicious effects. It was the way forward in the challenge that had beset him all his life. Meditation would be a ritual as powerful as the prayers and sacrifices of any religion. Preach its value and people would learn to overcome even their fear of the mystery of death. They would not need to invent or adhere to a god for an explanation of existence. The power to understand purpose would be found deep within themselves.

-I like the sentiments of the Magus. They chime well with my dislike of rituals that have grown over time to increase the power of priests of whatever hue, to the detriment of their deities. There are many faiths in the empire, all of which are free under our rule. When I am invited to their places of worship it takes me further from a god, not nearer! At least the Magus sees salvation from the trials of life as an individual's responsibility. Quite so. Do you know that my grandfather did not believe in any of today's gods?

Kamil shook his head, though he had little doubt that this had been the case. -I never heard him speak of such things.

-His was an older faith, a bit like the Merchant's, set at the very beginning of time, if faith you could call it. It was before the emergence of all the gods we know now, as well as those we have long forgotten. This is another reason why he wanted a history written about the Magus. No doubt, long after we have graced the world Kamil, a new god will emerge to whom everyone will bow and scrape and offer incense and sacrifices. It is the way of things. Yet, despite this never-ending cycle, your Magus began a tradition of dissension which lives with us even today, though, erroneously, it is to those who followed him that we ascribe the most significance. Yet the Magus influenced my grandfather and mother and led finally to the commissioning of your Tales. He tells us much about the ways of men and this knowledge can only help to moderate our rule of law. Whether they have a belief in a god is one of the questions I have asked our new friends. Do you know that none so far does so? I find that very illuminating!

-They are idiosyncratic in every way, murmured Kamil.

-Of course! How else did I discover where they were? So, since we are now talking about them, what do you think? She looked at him, impassively.

Kamil shifted a little uneasily, -As I no doubt showed, I liked them at first sight. They seem open and child-like yet they must have heads for business. Gold is a magnet for those who would rob or worse. Its value only increases. Anyone who configures gold has great standing in my eyes. This made her laugh.

-Gold is the eternal measure, is it not? The Empress has more gold than any, while the peasant has least, if any. Only the Empress can license miners, by law, to take gold from the rivers and the mountain rocks. If thieves do then it is at their peril. What else do you have to say about the twins?

He considered a moment, -As we discovered, they share with you and the girl climber, the gift of weighing the good in a person. And Timur's ability to know the purity of all metals is strange indeed. However, their history remains a reed, separated from its root, which is a condition they share with the webbed man, Ull.

-Only for the moment. I lured them here with promises that their beginnings will be revealed and so they shall be. Meanwhile, do you remember the locket and chain that my father bought at auction and presented to my mother?

-Clearly.

-She gave it me when I showed the first blood of womanhood. I have carried it everywhere, for there are few mementos of his visitation. I showed them to Timur and Zemfira and they were in awe of the workmanship. Timur lifted them to his nose and pronounced them nearly pure. They have an ingredient to harden them otherwise they would fall out of shape, even when being worn round a royal neck. But then he became agitated. Princess Shahrazad put her head in her hands, propping them with her elbows on her knees.

-Distressed? asked Kamil.

-It seems he senses gold's history and when I questioned him he said he could not divine what events had attached themselves to the jewellery but they contained something he could not discern and it was not good for the wearer. Her face darkened, -It seems my father may have bought a cursed jewel from the east. Kamil said nothing but wondered whether the Princess had entertained the possibility that the Red Man himself had contaminated the locket and chain. It did not seem as if she had. There was a far away, longing look in her eyes whenever she mentioned the ogre or his deeds just as one might find in any devoted but orphaned daughter, -I asked him what would happen if I wished it to be melted down and made anew. He said he could not be sure but it was likely that fire would release the curse from it. He has it now and I have instructed the pair to mould it into a new form of my design. She stood up, -I shall go now. I am expecting Murabbi with news of the manhunter. They will have been chasing each other's tails like dogs in the wild though I would wager that my man has had the better of it.

Chapter Eleven

Self-knowledge does not come with age. There are old fools and young sages.

Murabbi's tale was relayed by the Princess to Kamil with great relish. Like her mother, she could act out a narrative with waving arms, gyrations and thrusts of the body and wild cadences of her voice. It was the next morning. Her loyal bodyguard had arrived late in the evening and had been ensconced immediately with the Princess in her room. Kamil had not seen him arrive. When the historian had settled for sleep he could still hear the muffled sounds of the man briefing her. Now, she stood before him as he sat on his bed and gave full vent to her theatricality.

-It seems that my man set off at speed for the road we ourselves followed when we managed to deceive Raashid. It took perhaps three hours and he was careful to ensure that he approached it from a direction which did not point to this hiding place. Once he was on the road he followed it some way towards the Second City, asking questions everywhere. He wore a soldier's helmet to disguise his hairless head and had already removed his beard. Gradually he picked up the scent of his prey which led him to double back and then take to the hills. It was a shepherd who told him that the manhunter had ridden that way. He was on a grey horse with white dapples and was like a warrior but without arms, so the man said. Murabbi picked up his trail soon afterwards, crisscrossing through the hills as he searched for signs of our earlier passing. He was still far to the west of the route we took. Murabbi made for higher land so that he might look down on his prey, working his way along ridges but careful never to expose himself on any summit. The land was barren, even for shepherding. He saw just a few goats and one goatherd. But then, as night began to fall, he picked out the tiny gleam of a fire in the gloom. He approached carefully, leaving his horse when it was necessary to be stealthy. It was all but dark as he lay upon a mound of sandy earth, high above the fire. Below him was a strange sight indeed.

He recognised the manhunter in the flames from the descriptions given him by me. He was stocky, heavy-shouldered and seemed to have little neck as his head squatted directly on to his body. He had fair hair which he tied in a knot at the back of his head. He wore a heavy green wool jacket and trousers with a broad belt and no weapons other than a throwing knife, belted above one of his boots. He sat immobile, staring at the heart of the embers. The Princess dropped on to Kamil's bed and adopted a frozen solidity to emphasise the point. Sitting opposite the hunter was a human being with black hair so long it flowed on to the ground all round where the person sat. It was impossible to tell whether it was a man or a woman. The face was painted in black bars, edged with fine red lines. The eyes looked out of sooty circles, again picked out in red. Long ear rings reached to the shoulders, flickering in the firelight as it played across cascades of stones embedded in silver wires. On the knuckles were silver rings, two or three per finger and there were broad silver bangles around the ankles. Even in the rapidly cooling night, it wore no shoes. Its garb was a long gold shirt.

Murabbi nearly fell from his perch when the jewelled one looked up and smiled at him, his teeth long and white. It raised an arm and beckoned to him. Princess Shahrazad put out a stiff arm towards Kamil and curled her fingers under his nose as if he were her guard and she was the stranger, -My protector got up slowly and walked down the bank to the fire. The manhunter still did not move. His eyes were open, unblinking. Fearful that this was a ploy, my man pulled out his sword but the strange being waved it away, -He is in a sleep and will only wake when I snap my fingers. Sit down. You are the Princess's special guard so now that you know I know, let us finish this business here and go together to her nest. My man sat down, disorientated. The Princess rolled her eyes for emphasis. -He now knew that the stranger was likely to be a man but of a kind of which he had never seen nor heard. He was not like those men who dress as women and provide pleasures in the whore houses, of the kind your wife used to run. Kamil flinched. It was true but Baligha's brothel had been no sordid establishment. The Princess went on, oblivious that she had upset him, -The stranger spoke with intelligence and his voice was soothing and persuasive. A thought popped into the mind of my man as if from nowhere, demanding that he must submit to the creature's authority. Then, do you know what the stranger said?

765

-No, said Kamil.

-If the Princess wishes this hunter dead, then kill him now, he will not resist. Princess Shahrazad's eyes were even brighter, -Such power! For good or ill my man resisted the temptation, if only because the manhunter is a favourite of the Empress and he wished not to deepen even more the enmity she might feel towards this expedition of mine. So my man said that he could not do it. The stranger laughed but my man found the sound chilling. He said that the one kind of person worse than a killer who enjoys his work is a killer who has no feelings at all about such acts.

Kamil nodded. There was much truth in what her bodyguard had said, -What did they do with the manhunter?

-The stranger put a hand on his forehead and said that he must wake up in an hour and go back to the Empress and tell her that to pursue her daughter at this time would endanger her life. She must leave me alone until I am done with my business. Then all might turn out well.

-I can imagine Empress Sabiya's reaction to that! muttered Kamil.

-She will be angry but it will forestall any precipitous action, replied the Princess, -She will become canny and try to find me and keep me in view but it is unlikely she will do any more than that. I am happy with the outcome.

-And the stranger is here?

-He is. He accepted a ride behind Murabbi otherwise he would still be walking! I saw him briefly but sent him to bed straight away It is a good time for my next card, then we shall see if our newcomer is awake. She smiled unconcernedly.

Of the three, only the Magus remained at peace. The trader was still suffering disquiet from the words of the Ancient. It was not that the accusation of blame for the effects of his dream plants on soldiers' behaviour was new to him. It wasn't, but he had always been able to deny the link and place responsibility for consequent actions on his plant users. He had convinced himself that he was just a messenger, an agent. His buyers had the choice to use the plant or not. The daughter focused on her bow and arrows, single-mindedly following the spoors of creatures, edging closer and closer but then deliberately making a noise to frighten them. She did not want to kill for the moment. Even the death of an animal was unsettling after the passing of the spirit of the Ancient. She did not want to hear the squeal of pain and watch the thrashing of an animal's limbs. It would be a time before she was composed enough to creep so close to a large, rooting creature which was grunting and snorting so much that it didn't hear her nor the swish of her sword as it sliced through its neck.

They buried the bones where they had found the ancient shaman lying and the daughter wove a tight basket from broad leaved grasses, spreading a thin layer of clay on its inside to repel the water. She stuck a flat splint of wood into its base to act as a keel and make it stay upright and they gathered the ashes and poured them into the tiny bark. She carried them before her as they rode, until the track forded a stream and there they set the vessel floating, watching it speed towards the river that would carry it to the sea.

Many weeks of watchful journeying took them to the edge of the northern Emperor's lands. The forests had been an endless green and grim covering of the earth with few breaks for settlements and cultivation but now they had emerged into the beginning of the icy plains where the summers were so short that the lives of plants were momentary before they were covered again with snow and most animals wore white to avoid being detected. The trio had had very few conversations of depth during their travel but there was, at least, an amnesty regarding the thoughts they might have about one another. The trader spent a great deal of time looking at the daughter with guarded eyes which she viewed with an indifference bordering on irritation. She was capable of losing herself in the daily round of riding, hunting and cooking, shut off from what was immediately about her. Now and then she embraced her father to encourage his love for her and he responded by holding her to him. Meanwhile, he had his ceaseless, tumbling thoughts, raining through his brain and constantly needing reordering so that he could understand them.

The trader led them to the lea of a hill where a cliff had been formed by wind and rain washing away soft sand and leaving a horizontal, striped surface of white and red rock in thicknesses greater than the Magus' height. There were holes in it drilled by the beaks of birds and wheeling around them were carrion eaters. Here, the icy breeze abated and father and daughter put up their tent. They had enough cold meat for several days following the daughter's hunting but there was no wood for a long-lived fire. Gathering dried grasses and bundling them gave a short respite from the cold and they made hot drinks with preserved fruit and herbs. Once he had eaten, the trader bade them farewell and set off, even as it was becoming dark, to make contact with the Emperor's people.

-It is a relief he has gone, grumbled the daughter.

Her father agreed, -Even silent, he presses himself into my mind.

-Do you think he is a bad man?

-To whom would you compare him? Perhaps against the Emperor we will soon meet, he is a good man. Perhaps against the ancient one whose ashes are now sailing to the edge of the sea, he has much to do to redeem himself.

-Am I good?

-My daughter, you are a woman of the valleys who has not yet woken. It can take a lifetime, as you can see in this father before you. It is hard to be severe in judgment on those like you who have not opened their minds as if to view themselves from afar. They are where they are and must be judged accordingly. Each time a man reaches out to understand the world and his place in it, it raises the good in him. To burrow inside another's skin and remake the world through such a stranger's eyes, feeds goodness. To remain cut off from others does nothing to deepen an understanding of the rightful place of goodness. The words fell from the Magus' lips easily because these were the very thoughts that he had been putting into order on their journey through the shadowy forests.

They lay side by side inside the simple tent, an angled square of skin, pegged to the ground at one end and elevated by the Magus' extendable poles at the other. From here, looking out with the cliff behind them, the stars were piercingly sharp, as though covered by ice formed by the bitter wind.

-Be there Gods, these must be their eyes, murmured the daughter.

-It could be so, replied the Magus, -Who can tell unless we meet with them? If they remain in the heavens then we shall never know for how can we reach up to their world? As yet we have no evidence that they have ever come down to visit with us. Just because men desire it to be so does not mean that it is. The blackness in the heavens is the same nothingness that existed before birth and returns after death. Is it any wonder that people try to fill the blackness with the eyes of gods?

-Father, have you no answer to the mystery of death? she asked, sadly.

-I have no answer to the mystery of life! If my place in the scheme of things could be made a little clearer then the mystery of death might recede. With that, they closed their eyes and as was their habit, sleep took them to its own within the instant.

Both were woken by the roan pawing the ground near their heads. The first splinters of grey were splitting the sky when they felt the faint tremors in the earth of approaching horses. They were armed and mounted and waiting, a short distance from the tent as the group of riders arrived, just silhouetted in the birth of the day.

-Magus it is me, hold your weapons! came the trader's voice, -We are seven and all our swords are sheathed. Slowly the father and daughter edged towards the platoon of Emperor's soldiers, the daughter holding her bow with an arrow nocked. They stopped a few paces away, able to discern men armed like those they had met when they had disembarked from the boat. Even their horses wore armoured hoods and protective, metalled leathers across their backs.

-Take your men down the track we must follow and wait, said the Magus, -While we put away our tent and eat. The trader conveyed this in a mixture of gestures and stilted words and the group set off back the way they had come. In a moment the trader had returned and the three cleared the camp and took food and water.

-I do not trust them, grimaced the daughter, -They do not have the minds of which you spoke, Father. No warmth reaches out from them. We are no better than animals to them.

-She is right, whispered the trader, -From this moment there will be nothing but danger. They would normally contrive to kill either of you immediately they suspect the slightest ill intention but they are bound by the Emperor's edict that you should be given safe passage on pain of death for any who might attempt to impede you. And they are fighting men who uphold the Emperor's rule and would die happily for him.

-Such loyalty to one who is so evil can only be because he treats them harshly They must fear him more than their own deaths!

-Not so, daughter of the Magus, -The Emperor has made his empire the greatest in the northern lands and he has brought wealth to his tribe as they extend their frontiers and pillage the lands of peoples whose armies are rabble compared to his. They have a savage pride and love him for his victories. He has skirted the eastern territories of your half-sister and her lord for he knows that the war with our own new, united empire would cost his armies dear. He is biding his time but he is not a man to allow this uneasy state to last for long.

-Is this why he took my wife? asked the Magus, -First he draws me to him using her as the prize and then he holds us hostage so that the united empire bows to him? My son-in-law will not submit to this. He will put the lives of all his people before ours. We began this journey following a request to come to their aid. We did not know why. Perhaps the war between the two empires is closer than you imagine.

-It may be so but I think there is more to his plans than bargaining with your lives to increase his lands. Your fame attracts him. You are the Warrior, the greatest ever to have warred on the battlefield and you are also the Magus who teaches. What emperor would not want to see with his own eyes such a man and even match himself against him?

The daughter snorted, -Of such a contest there could only be one victor!

-I did not mean through the wielding of swords, said the trader quietly, -I meant in all things. The Emperor is a scholar. He paints as well as any of his artists. He gathers philosophers and musicians, historians and writers to his ever-moving court. He is especially obsessed with those sages who teach the pathways to the gods of the hereafter. Most emperors who become unrivalled in this life wish to find a way to repeat their success in the next! He put a finger to his lips and said, -We must go. They are waiting for us and I would keep them sweet now that I have delivered you to the border of their land.

It was a fearsome, dark cavalcade of galloping, armoured riders that was protecting the three strangers from the valleys, which made its way across the rolling terrain. They were in the Emperor's true territory now and as they clattered through the nomadic settlements of skin and pole, they drew nods of approval from the inhabitants. They were heading for the fortress which was his seat of government at this time of the year, the very first he had captured in his long history of violent conquests. The route would take them two days of hard riding and the first night was to be spent in a semi-permanent barracks of wood and straw long houses.

When they arrived, the trader explained that they would sleep in one of the long buildings with the rest of the convoy. The daughter grimaced at her father and then refused for both of them, -We will not sleep out of sight of our horses and bags, she said tersely, -We will set up our tent. This led to a violent torrent of abuse from the captain of the barracks who did not expect the slightest of his orders to be countermanded. He marched over belligerently to the Magus and stood, glowering up at him, his hair at the level of the Magus' eyes, swearing and pointing inside the building. The Magus looked him in the eye, unaffected, so the man, snarling, grasped him by the throat of his jacket and tried to jerk his head down to butt him but he could not move him even a fraction. Instead his own head was suddenly pulled back and he felt the edge of a knife at his throat. The Magus had not moved. It was the woman who had grasped him by his hair. Attracted by the violent movement, men appeared, dragging out their swords. They witnessed the daughter twist their captain over a thigh and drop him on to the ground before leaping astride him with her knife point pressing his throat. The Magus still had not moved. The soldiers began to shuffle but the trader shouted at them and they stopped, confused.

-Please let him go, pleaded the trader, an edge of desperation in his request. The daughter leaned forward and put her hard and predatory eyes close to the captain's before, with a lithe bound, she was back on her feet. Again the trader called out in a loud, commanding but broken accent. The captain scrambled up and touched his sword menacingly. The trader shouted again. Everyone stopped. As his words sank in the tension slowly eased and arms went to sides, away from the pommels of their weapons. The captain spat viciously on the ground at the daughter's feet, turned on his heel and marched away stiffly pursued by the trader, still remonstrating but in a quieter tone.

As if nothing had happened the Magus and his daughter took their horses to a point away from the barracks and began putting up their tent. They refused the food that was brought to them, eating more of their rations and waiting for the trader to return.

When he finally arrived, he looked at them grimly, -You have made a great enemy.

-He has made the greater, smiled the daughter coldly.

-It was only my reminder to them that you had been guaranteed safe passage by the Emperor that stayed the battle.

-Then they should be grateful to you that their lives were spared. Tell them that! She looked at him in disgust, -I do not trust you. You play only one game and that is your own.

-Magus, this is not true! he yelped, pretending his pride was wounded, -I saved your lives.

-You may have saved your own but not ours. I am telling you, she added angrily, -Not only would the captain have had his throat opened to the air but his men's too. Do you think my father would not have stood beside me? Do you think that we would be unequal to soldiers such as these? Even had they been trained in all the warrior's arts they would have fallen before us like grass before a scythe. She looked across at four soldiers, standing, watching them and ran her knife across her throat and smiled grimly. They dropped their gaze uneasily and slowly walked away.

-They will come for us in the night, said her father in a soft voice as they lay down, -I sense the captain's thoughts. He is of that kind whose pride stands in death's embrace. Rob him of one and he reaches for the other, gladly.

-Then let us rid the world of him and whomever lines up with him. I am a warrior and my blood is ready. She touched his forehead, -To die beside my father in battle is no bad thing, though it will not be here in this empty, cold land.

-No, it will not.

The Magus heard the clash of battle from his bed but did not move. What was happening around the tent had been revealed to him in a vision just as had the skirmish with the captain. These living dreams foretold what would come to pass but they obeyed their own laws. Sometimes he was as blind as anyone to the future. He could not call it to heel. He went to sleep when he felt his daughter settle quietly beside him and stroke his arm.

In the morning they rose to begin the next stage of their journey. They ate and drank and loaded their mounts, finally setting out to wind their way among the bodies of the dead. The captain's corpse was half-hanging from the wall of the long building, pinned there by his own sword. Neither then nor at any time afterwards did the Magus question his daughter about the events of that night or the fate of the trader.

-**In truth, that** was the Wheel of Fortune!

-On the surface, Princess, said Kamil, -It was unpredictable but the card is more than the surface pretends to show. The two are in limbo now, in a hostile land. They have neither their scout, the trader, nor their convoy of guards. They have no contact with the daughter's half-sister and they do not really know the motives of the Emperor in drawing them to his court. And it must have been hard for the Magus to accept his daughter's bloody reaction which invokes an age-old right. It is always painful for a parent to watch his child act in ways he cannot condone in his own behaviour! I hope I never have to face such a dilemma.

-My mother does, every day! She was never as wayward as me, was she Uncle?

-No, her heart was always in tune with political consequences, even as a child. Kamil said this without reservation. Something inside him told him it was right and that he did not need to add his usual apologies for overstepping his status.

-Good, Uncle. Your frankness is unusual for you but it is sincere and I can only gain from it. Be more so. We are approaching a time when I will need you more and you will fulfil your destiny at my side. Though I am the child of my mother, I am in many ways from a different lineage. She and I will accept our differences one day soon, even after what I do now drives a wedge between us and we reach a point when we imagine we have no further use for each other. All the while you will be the bridge between us. Do not collapse for it will partially be through you that we will find each other again.

Kamil heard her words but they did not truly sink home. Was this his purpose on this adventure? He hadn't remotely understood why he had been brought here and although he still had little notion of the practical nature of his role, what she said made the beginnings of sense. It was in accord with his hope that he would always have equal standing before mother and daughter, more so even than Raashid. The old historian was their confidant and of no threat at all to either of them.

She interrupted his thoughts as she pushed on, wanting to deal with the next step of her undisclosed plans, -Thank you for the Tale, Uncle. Our own Wheel of Fortune is smiling upon us. All is change but it is the change that I'd hoped for. The daughter in your Tale is admirable in some ways but as the Magus told her, she is naïve concerning the ways of men. I have grown past that stage just as my mother did. It is not enough for a woman to equal men in battle, they must outfox them in all other ways. Let us meet with the long-haired newcomer who, as I intimated, may conjure up powers we have not before encountered.

They made their way to the room that had been allocated to the man. It was as crude as every other chamber, again looking out over the lake. He was waiting for them, completely at ease. On his lap was a scroll, the parchment covered in tiny pictures. The Princess dropped her hooded cloak by the door, -I see you can read.

-Of course.

She rose to the challenge, -Why, 'of course'?

-It would be expected of me. I am not of low caste. I am not a village peasant. My blood is as rare as yours, Princess. He put the parchment down, -But I should say welcome to my humble chamber and the chairs you had the forethought to have placed here for our audience. He looked sharply at Kamil, -And you are -?

-He is my historian, Princess Shahrazad grinned at him, just like a boy, -This is my Uncle Kamil. The men nodded to each other briefly, all the while Kamil measuring the creature. However he had been ornamented in the Princess's account, now he was not. The paint like that on the webbed man, had been washed away. The hair was coiled at the back of his head and all the rings and embellishments were now piled beside the pitcher on his little table.

-Historian? A weaver of the past. What is the difference between a historian and a storyteller, Uncle Kamil?

-Evidence, replied Kamil, testily. He did not like the man's familiar confidence and refusal to honour them with due respect.

The man laughed, -Evidence! Is there any such thing? I understood that every man's eyes sees a different story. How then is evidence conspired? By mixing all the tales into one? Kamil found his opinion of the creature swinging to and fro. He was too clever by half. He saw a long, thin, sallow face with a pronounced aquiline nose and hard unforgiving lips. The fellow's eyes were grey, flecked with gold. His wrists and ankles were bony and his unshod feet ended in long toes, more like fingers.

Princess Shahrazad flopped on a chair, -Enough of this contest. I need to ask you some questions. Her tone was more imperious than it had been with the other visitors.

-Princess? said the man agreeably, turning off his challenge to Kamil like a tap, who, as a consequence, sat down and waited.

-Let me begin as I did with the others, she said. A glint came and went from the man's eyes, -You are?

-Chaksu. He smiled in obvious amusement.

She ignored him, -You were born where?

-In a reed basket on a river far far away, safe from the harm intended me.

-Your mother?

-I never knew her.

-Your father?

-I never knew him.

-How did you come there?

-By sorcery. Someone must have seen my future and decided it was worth saving but that is my intimation, only. I was found and passed around like a coin of ill-omen from one family to another, never settling with anyone. I think each of them probably wanted to put an end to my young life but dared not for fear that a curse would befall them for the story of my arrival suggested the work of demons. I was a strange child and was always able to look at people and make them do what I wished. It was a gift. It is now very refined.

-Where did my men discover you?

-They didn't. Even before you sent your men to search me out, I began my journey to you. Why should I need someone to find me? I have the eye. Chaksu looked at each of them in turn, his pupils glowing with a light that simmered in their depths. It was hard for Kamil to break his gaze.

Chapter Twelve

Be ready to be stung by the Past when you try to grasp the Future

While he awaited the Princess for her next reading, Kamil's mind reclaimed from his memory the story that the Princess had told him about Chaksu.

All five arrivals could be seen from the window of his chamber on the shore of the lake. Chaksu appeared to be holding court but it did not seem too conspiratorial. The Princess had visited Kamil earlier in the day to relay to him more about this latest addition to her collection once she had spent a further hour in the new man's company.

It appeared that after being passed around different families, eventually he was taken in by a rich Prince. In much the same way that the twins had been recognised for their affinity for gold, Chaksu had come to the attention of the Nawab of a large province far to the north east. The family had profited from east-west trade and the Nawab ran the affairs of his state with great humanity and tolerance but it was always difficult to reconcile the different clans and tribes. There were those who were war-like and those who were peaceful, there were hunters and farmers and there was a caste system among the majority but equality only among a rich minority from whom the Nawab, himself, had sprung. This noble held a court of justice every month which sometimes lasted several days because his people used litigation to solve all their conflicts. It was he who had taught them this way to reconcile their differences but their expectations of justice were now so high that it needed the intelligence and second sight of a seer to be the judge and jury in the courts. It was not long before Chaksu came to prominence. Once he had been taken in by the Nawab, he showed he had a gift for learning and was quickly able to read and write. Soon he had exhausted the house library and turned to reading the scribes' accounts of law suits. These he mastered quickly but not only that, he soon developed a shorter way of making judgments. By comparing the essence of each case he demonstrated how a judge could be seen to be fair by relating the judgment to those of previous crimes. Gone were the arbitrary decisions of the Nawab and his court officers, treating each case as though it was unique. From the stealing of possessions to the murder of another, each crime had a fixed sentence. And the final lance in the flesh of the guilty was often the appearance in court of Chaksu himself. He had merely to stare at the accused and out would pour their confessions, if guilty they were. His fame became so widespread that, even if he was not present, no-one would come to the Nawab's court without just cause in case he made an unexpected appearance. The Nawab grew to be very fond of him and named him as his heir. After this journey to see the Princess, he would return to claim his rights.

-What of his strange face painting when your protector found him? Kamil had asked.

-I wanted to know that, of course. He said that since people thought he was protected by demons then he would present himself as the occult agent of a god. It became a ritual to cover his face in that way and it made people even more in awe of him. It was because of this painted visage that no-one hindered his passage here, most averting their eyes the moment they encountered him.

The historian had been satisfied, -He has the same gift of knowing the hearts of others but seems even more skilled than his new companions, here. I fear him in a way I do not fear them. He has little respect for you or anyone. His arrogance may be founded on a power that is hard to resist.

-It is true Uncle but do not underestimate the forces that reside in your Princess! She had leant forward for emphasis, -I tell you, Chaksu does not and I am one of very few who can look without fear into his eyes.

*

She entered the room in her usual, non-conformist way, hitching up her trousers and splaying herself on his bed beside the cards and the sheaf that made up the Tales. Without demur she raised a hand and launched into the latest news. First, her mother had left the royal city bound for the Second City with a small army, This had followed the return of the manhunter. Raashid had been recalled to lead her

778

cavalcade of troops. And the last piece of news was that the final two creatures were close by and should arrive shortly, -Everything is on the move as your last card proposed, she said, -And what of the next? She turned over the card, -The Will! It is my card is it not? At least it feels like it at this moment. It is only by exercising the desire to have things turn out the way that you want them to that you are victorious in anything out of the ordinary! People around you will always try to steer you to do the expected. What does history say about this, Uncle?

-It tends to follow your reasoning, Princess. Those that change the ways of the world are rarely like other people. They plough a separate furrow, as in the saying. Sometimes they are ostracised for their beliefs. Even killed. The forces of tradition are difficult to overthrow for many owe their power and recognition to upholding and championing the past. But where would we be if nothing had changed since before the time of the Magus? Would people such as you and I exist with our thoughts and feelings? It is a good question. What we ask about right and wrong can be traced back to his day. The single idea of harmony between peoples was his. Kamil was ready to expound further his thoughts about the lineage of thought but stopped when he saw that her attention was wavering. She looked carefully at the card as though something hidden might be revealed to her.

-What is the beast whose jaws she grips in her hands?

-It is a symbol only. It represents the forces that we must control both inside and out. Some see the jaws being held shut to prevent the forces destroying the individual. Others see the jaws being held apart by sheer strength so that something new might result.

-I like the latter, said the Princess, reflectively, -It seems to me that I am holding all the forces apart so that they cannot converge upon me. Let us hear where the Magus and his implacable daughter are to lead us. She settled back, a woman in all but body, capable of thought that would stretch any scholar. Kamil realised fleetingly that of all the gifts that might be hers, this was one which it would be by far the most dangerous to overlook.

Instead of the headlong charge to the fortress of the Emperor, father and daughter left the obvious trail and rode a parallel course to it. The way was not too hazardous, the land being covered mostly by grasses, dried and whitened by wind and low sun. There was a continuous shower of seeds and dust around them that covered their garb and their mounts. Half way through that day both they and their horses sensed an impending event ahead. Was it a storm? Was it an enemy, an ambush? Undoubtedly something or someone waited for them. They slowed, following the rolling ups and downs of the earth, sometimes able to see ahead and sometimes not as they dropped into steep declines. In any one of these dips their fate might be hidden. Now and then, far to their right, they could just observe parts of the well-beaten track that they would have followed with the convoy but nothing seemed to be travelling along it. Then, two or three pale, straw covered ridges before them, they glimpsed a flash of red and white. At length, facing them as they climbed over yet another brow, fluttering in one of her dragon robes like an exotic bird attended by three soldiers, her hand upraised in salute, was the general. Far beyond, on a shadowy hill on the horizon, was a fortress.

-You escape, she grunted, as they came together, greeting each other with hands on heart and dipped palms, -Track you long time. Dead men. Dead captain. She showed no sign of emotion in her announcement but turned her mount and led the way down the shallow valley and back on to the main route.

The unassailable structure that faced them was on a man-built mound around which there were layered, deep gulleys to defend against any attack. It was built from soldier tree timber and in-filled with a clay and small stone mix. Its height was impressive, rising sheer with arrow slits only at its top. The spread of its interior was equally enormous, there being enough space for a city. It could be seen from every direction, imperiously commanding the rumpled landscape, dark and troubling, even in the noonday sun. The general's approach led to the double doors being swung open immediately and they rode slowly inside. From the relatively muted sounds on the outside to the cacophony of noise inside was a sudden blow to the ears and the horses reared a little. It was a carefully designed habitation. Hundreds upon hundreds of wooden cabins, all the same size, were backed against the interior of its walls and at its centre was the palace, built of white brick made from baked clay and straw and covered in brightly painted scenes from the Emperor's victorious marches. There were people milling everywhere with markets, workshops of every description, military training and eating houses. Adjacent to the palace was the only other construction larger than a big cabin. It was a circular earth dish, paved inside with dressed, polished stone and blinding when it caught the low, glancing sun. Above its centre was a long arm, like the bough of a hanging tree, braced to remain firm and attached to a wooden tower which could be ascended by a flight of steps. The horses neighed and skittered to one side as they passed it and they halted at the palace entrance where they were made to dismount.

-Horses safe. You leave here. Weapons. Take bags only, ordered their guide, doing the same with her own mount. Thus, with servants carrying their saddle bags, they entered the dark, cold interior. There was little allowance for daylight to enter save through the high arrow slits. Enormous wooden pillars in long rows reached to hold up the distant roof so that everywhere they looked their sight was stopped as the pillars appeared to close upon each other. The daughter estimated that there must be at least a thousand of them, creating a labyrinth for any intruder. It was as disorientating as in the forest that they had recently left and impossible to tell where might be the Emperor's quarters for, at the tops of the heavy poles, chambers were perched like nests, none accessible except by ladder. The walk took some time as they weaved a path at a diagonal through the maze. Then, before them, trundling on wheels, a wooden staircase appeared which was then affixed to a balcony above. They followed the general. As soon as they had reached the wide platform the steps were pulled away. A door led them into a sumptuous interior, much better lit and reddened in the failing sun. Everywhere there were the spoils of campaigns; drapes, sculptures in wood and stone, ornaments of every kind in gold and silver, embossed with jewels. A panoply of gods, demons and half-breed winged or walking creatures grimaced, howled or smiled benignly at them from every side and among their still forms, courtiers stood rigidly to attention, as though in reverence to the general. Behind the courtiers in their black iron, stood rows of soldiers. The air was heavy with incense from candles and lamps. They processed along the wide, carpeted aisle, meeting sets of steps every twenty or so paces so that gradually they rose towards the throne.

Before and above them sat the Emperor in fine gold armour, veiled, shoulder to toe in a gauze of black silk. They could see that it was not for protection because the metal was finely wrought and any spear or sword would have impaled him easily. The general kneeled and her two companions stood behind her, heads slightly bowed, hands on hearts.

She spoke and they caught a word which sounded like Magus as she indicated them with a hand.

-Stand, said the Emperor in the common tongue of the valleys of the Magus and his daughter and the general stood, -You are the greatest daughter of the empire and my most favoured wife! Tonight we will consummate your mission. His voice was a growl but there was little accent. His hair-free features were the essence of iceland flesh and blood with black, slanting eyes, high jutting cheekbones and wide, thin lips set in a pale ivory skin. He stood and they could see he was tall for his race, strongly built and supple, in age somewhere mid way between the daughter and her father.

-Let me welcome the Magus and his daughter, he proclaimed, -While in our palace, keep them safe and show them our hospitality, unless the Emperor orders it otherwise! He clapped his hand against his breast with a loud grunt of Ay! and everyone in the hall did the same so that the building reverberated with the sound. -Bring them to my chamber. His acknowledgement of their tongue raised their hopes of him. They could see that it was both a matter of respect to them but also a demonstration of his superiority among his fellows, few of whom knew any other than their nomadic language.

They were seated before the Emperor on a row of cushions covered in the same fire-breathing creatures that adorned the clothing of the general. His was placed on a low stool so that he was raised above their eye line. Throughout their conversation he never smiled. Later the daughter said that he had been carved from stone since his face never gave any indication as to his thought or feelings. His questions were short and abrupt and in this, their first meeting, he hardly entered into debate over their answers or offered any information or explanation. It could have been unnerving but the Magus saw him for what he was, a powerful man, mortal, proud, merciless and obsessed with the domination of people and territories. The daughter shared this view but she also caught in his gaze a desire to possess any woman who might withstand him. She did not miss the way his eyes glittered briefly when she answered his question about the battle at the barracks.

-It was kill or be killed, she said, simply, -They may have determined to spare my father but I had spurned the captain and he took it upon himself to take vengeance. He came at night with his men. That was his mistake.

-Your father did not help you? Again his eyes showed his greedy interest.

-He does not wish to kill. Anyway it was not necessary.

-I pardon you, he half-snorted, half-guffawed, -The captain was always a fool. Hear that? he called over his shoulder. A clerk, sitting in the shadows, nodded and recorded it, -How many owe their deaths to you? he asked looking at them in turn.

-I have not counted, replied the daughter.

-I do not wish to count, said the Magus.

-A thousand? the Emperor suggested. Neither spoke.

-You are here to take back your mother and your wife, he stated, changing he subject. They stared at him without speaking, -We shall discuss that tomorrow but first, tonight, you will witness the will of the Emperor! Enough. I have seen you.

The Emperor prided himself on the luxuries he offered to those he had invited to his court. He provided rich chambers with the best food and drink, wool mattresses and guards at the door to protect them. Both the Magus and his daughter would ignore the soft beds and sleep on the floor with just a blanket beneath them. They were not royalty. Now, they washed from pitchers and changed into the multi-coloured, flowing silk robes brought for them.

-You look like a preening bird, she said, chuckling.

-As do you, my warrior daughter though it suits you more. Does it make us different from our old selves? These rainbows last a few moments only. They laughed and remained in good humour until a servant came for them. He led them down the wheeled staircase and through the pathways between the pillars and then up another set of steps and on to a long balcony which overlooked the great dish with its sombre scaffolding. It was the unending northern dusk and flares were lit all round its edge. The flames were caught and reflected off the already-filled dish onto people's faces. Crowds had gathered to stand on the tops of cabins and they were led by black-robed priests in singsong prayers to their god. The eyes of the Magus and his daughter scanned the far-off figures. They saw something that tightened their stomachs though neither showed it. The praying masses had begun dancing, carrying vessels filled with holy water and each time their voices rose in unison to a climax, they sprinkled themselves and each other with it.

The Emperor lowered himself on to his seat between them. As soon as they were settled, the chanting grew to a mad fervour and while the Emperor looked on implacably, prisoners were carried one by one up the steps on to the scaffolding, their hands tied behind their backs and their legs strapped together. Each was hooked and hung upside down before being lowered into the waiting waters. As they entered, the chant stopped for a few heartbeats and then continued when the victims were fully immersed. There was no struggling. It was as if each one gave up his or her spirit freely and without hesitation. Upon being drowned the hook was released leaving each to bob to the surface like a log. Perhaps twenty were floating as the ritual ended with the priest on the scaffolding bowing to the royal balcony. The Emperor stood and raised his arms. Instantly the hymning stopped and the circling rooftop hordes went still. Without further word or gesture the Emperor turned, walking in front of the Magus and his daughter until they were parted from him and were taken up again to their chamber.

-You saw her?
He nodded.
-We could go now.
-No. It is a test.
She thought for a while, -You think the Emperor placed her there for us to see?
-We would not be the Magus and his warrior daughter if we had not seen her, even in that short moment. He knew. It was to demonstrate his control over us. There is nothing he does not engineer to see how he might extract the most from it. In this he is different from any I have met, whether kings or princes, military men or cruel queens. All of them carried a frailty. When I looked into their eyes there was something, a weakness which they could not hide. It fermented inside them and drove them into thoughtless action. I even felt pity for them because they were subject to forces beyond their knowing. His voice was far away.
-What kind of forces? she asked.
-Greed, envy, lust, anger or revenge - all the obvious...
-And yet they did not know it in themselves? How is that?
-Perhaps they sensed it but it had become such a dominating part of them that they could no longer contest it. It had become an intoxication. As I have said, we must guard against unthinking acts for they lead to disregard for others. They are barriers to what we can achieve on the path to goodness. They lay in silence for some time and, as is often the way, both, at the same point, recollected the drowning prisoners.
-I assume they were prisoners of war, she said flatly.
-At best they have angered the Emperor, whether through battle or through disobedience. At worst it was a lottery and he chose them at random to feed his need for the theatre of blood. It was a glorious spectacle for his people but it was not so for me. I suffered a terrible sorrow at those lives being extinguished. His deep voice betrayed emotion.
-Sorrow? she asked, puzzled, -Why is that?

-It was as if they were my children and I had done nothing to prevent their massacre.

-But they were not, she said and turned over to prepare for sleep, - Save your concerns for your wife, Magus. These are not people like us. They are little better than animals. But sleep would not come to her and after a number of tosses and turns she asked him, -Do you mean that he has no weakness at all?

-None of the kind I described. He is like a demon in a story, created for the express purpose of frightening the listener. There is nothing rounded in the picture I carry of him. His evil accepts no frail bedfellows.

She considered for a while, -The task then is so much the greater. That is why we are here Father, for fate always plays the game of opposites. Here there is evil on the one side and on the other... she paused, -Whatever we bring to battle with it.

-The Right Path.

That was always his answer and all it did was make her purse her lips and shake her head. Unlike her half-sister, she barely understood his preoccupations, much as she loved him. If the Emperor was such a monster why had not her father killed him already?

-**Can someone be** wholly evil, I suppose they can, said Shahrazad, asking and answering her own question in one swoop. -There have been tyrants, big and small, ruling their empires or even just their families, usually men but sometimes women, single-mindedly bent on destruction. Do we all have evil lying in wait in some deep part of us, Uncle? Is there evil in me? Sometimes one must act in a way that cannot be condoned in any other circumstance. The Magus grapples with the puzzle, does he not? She put her strong index finger on the paste board, -What is the card then? Does it represent the Emperor who can stifle all forces? Or does it represent the Magus and his daughter who have the strength to wait, even though they have seen the mother and wife, almost within reach? Or is it me, Uncle, composed and confident in the face of an approaching storm? She looked at him in pretend confusion.

-You have all the possible answers and more, Princess!

-I do but which is the one most suited, I wonder? This Emperor is the greatest villain in history. We know it. We are taught it at school. We also know that the daughter is right. Fate throws up both the poison and the antidote. Though you are going over well trodden ground in the meeting of the Magus and the Emperor you have become such an astute storyteller that I am waiting the outcome with excitement, though I already know it.

Kamil's chest puffed, despite himself, -Thank you, Princess!

-It is true. Now, Uncle, it is time to begin earning your praise. You were my mother's spymaster, she never tired of telling me, -The man with the velvet tongue. So let us employ you in that role. You are to ride out with Murabbi, first thing and persuade the last two of my quarry to come to me. They are like timid wild creatures, afraid of flame and lingering beyond where the firelight falls, yet wishing to be near the warmth. But first we must have a meeting with Chaksu.

Chapter Thirteen

Beware the self-wrought chains that prevent your liberation

Kamil did not like Murabbi. The first sight of him in the crowd, pointing the gun at the Princess could not be dispelled from his mind, even though it was a deceit conjured up by her. It was the look of an assassin's undisguised bloodlust on his face which suggested he would have loved to have killed the Princess had not his role been otherwise prescribed. Yet, in everything he had done since the man had shown loyalty and even servility. So, Kamil ruminated, shouldn't he ignore his instincts and show a little warmth and friendship to the man? The Princess, whose gift made her an expert compared to him, obviously trusted Murabbi. Yet she did not trust him enough to bring in the last two creatures on his own. Perhaps he was too rough-tongued to tempt them? Anyway, the Princess had said to Murabbi, as they left through the courtyard door, that Kamil was the chief and Murabbi must follow his orders and instincts without question. Had he seen an indignant flash in the bodyguard's eye despite his bow of acquiescence?

Well here they were riding one behind the other along rabbit paths in the hills with Kamil staring at the man's broad back. The Princess had given them directions, visual clues involving the shapes of hilltops, ridges and slopes, blasted trees and protruding rocks. Up above them there was snow at the highest points where the sun never reached. She had said that they would come across the pair in time to bring them back before nightfall but only if Kamil could persuade them that there was no danger waiting for them. He hardly took sightings of where they were going which was always the way when his companion appeared to be confident of the path. Instead he considered what his ploy might be to lure them to her. All she had said was that they were man and wife and, of all the creatures they were the ones who had been living nearest the house on the lake. He had gained the impression that she had chosen the house for her hideaway after careful plotting of the routes the seven must take and it represented the most central point for all her journeying quarry. She had used the word, quarry, as if they were her prey rather than creatures to comfort her! How typical. But, like prey, they seemed distrustful of her intentions.

They halted by an icy stream to water the horses and eat bread. Murabbi had chosen the spot because it was blessed by a full, though low, watery sun and there was some protection from the wind. Kamil pulled the hunting fur that the old lady had insisted he would need, round his shoulders and began munching. Just like the Magus, he groaned to himself, a traveller in the wild. He rubbed his thighs and the insides of his calves.

-Why are you here? Murabbi's question cut through his self-pity.

-Here?

-With the Princess. Murabbi stared at him angrily. The man was aggrieved.

-She has her plans for me. Kamil felt an unusual anger rising in him. The man was insolent.

-You are fat and old and you ride like a sack of camel dung. Murabbi thought the jibe funny and laughed coarsely. A cloud crossed the sun and the air chilled for a moment, -I would not be able to stop you falling from your mount and breaking your aged neck. Kamil caught the threat, not too hidden, in the voice. He said nothing, kept his eyes down and continued eating his bread, -Can you use a sword? Kamil shook his head. -Any weapon? Kamil repeated the gesture. -I thought there might have been some enjoyment even with one as gone to seed as you but it is not the case. The manner in which he said enjoyment made the word reach through the air like a poison vapour. Murabbi took out his sole weapon, a twin-edged hunting knife, pushed the remaining crust of bread on to its point and stood its haft on his palm, twiddling it.

-What are you going to do? asked Kamil querulously, the bread sticking in his throat.

-Kill you, smiled Murabbi.

-Why?

Murabbi's face clouded in fury, -The Princess does not need you. She has me.

-She will know the moment your knife enters my body. She has sorcery in her blood. Kamil's voice was strangulated but he managed to rise and stand defiantly in front of the assassin, his hands clenched in fists before him.

-She will forgive me. Murabbi stepped forward but as he moved closer he slowed or Kamil quickened, he was unsure which. Kamil was aware that the knife wavered in Murabbi's clumsy fingers. Somehow he snatched it and in the same moment turned it and plunged it into the man's chest. With a sigh and blood bubbling from his mouth, Murabbi fell at his feet.

Kamil stared at the dripping blade in his hand and a coldness swept his body followed by a momentary exultation which later he could not fathom. Was it the relief at his survival or the fact that he had killed for the first time? He dropped the weapon and took several steps back, his mind chaotic. What would the Princess say? How could he explain this act to her? What would Baligha think of her husband whom she had always extolled for his passive, loving nature? How could he have done this thing, a mere sack of cow dung?

☥

He was seated on a boulder some minutes later still staring at the body when something distracted him at the corner of his vision. He turned and looked into the shade cast by a jutting arm of the hill. A man and a woman stood there, dressed in white tunics and trousers. The male was bearded with a white skullcap and a sleeveless jacket in green, heavy wool while she had a thick robe in deep blue with a hood. Kamil adjudged them to be a little older than the Princess but the youngest doctors he had ever encountered.

As they walked down the incline towards him, he stuttered, -I have killed him. They reached the body and the man felt Murabbi's neck. It took only a moment.

-It is true. He is dead.

-He was going to kill me, he said in anguish.

-We saw, said the woman, -You were defending yourself. We are witnesses. They stood solicitously before him.

-Thank you. It was true, if they had not been there to corroborate....how would he have explained it? -I have never killed before. I never thought I could ever have done such a thing.

-We know. We could see. We also have sworn never to kill but sometimes even the deepest devotion to preserving life is overruled by fate, said the woman softly, -Compose yourself. All is well. The man you have killed took his own life. It may have been your hand on his dagger but it was his thought that impelled it.

Her husband continued for them both, -If you had seen through our eyes, you would be more at peace with yourself. This man, he looked at the body, -Came at you with his knife. Then, as though he entered a dream wherein he had little control of his will, his limbs became heavy and clumsy. You were able to take the knife from him and stab him even though you, yourself, hardly moved more quickly than he. But your grip and plunge were exact and strong! It was as if all was foretold and you were but an agent of fate.

The historian stood in silence, digesting what had been said, before the husband spoke again, -We knew him.

Kamil looked at them both in turn, startled, -How?

-The Princess sent him to us some time ago with the command that we come to her at this time. He entered our hospital without respect for us or our sick and demanded arrogantly that we come to her. We knew this was not how she wished us to be asked. We can see inside people. The man was not what he seemed. Why we know not but he was plotting against her, of that we were sure. Unless you had not removed him from our path we could not have made the assignation with her Highness.

Kamil felt weak. His mind was cast back to the days when he had been the Empress Sabiya's closest ally. He had done many things that he had thought were acts of courage for such a timid man, independently driven by his love for her, despite his fears. Then, when all was over and her safety assured, he had discovered that she had used him as her puppet, much as she proclaimed her devotion to him. Now here with her daughter, the Princess Shahrazad, he felt the same sense of being used. He knew for certain that the death of Murabbi was in the script the Princess had written for him. Immediately, with an even greater clutch of horror he remembered her smiling at him with that woman's hardness she could sometimes adopt, "Have you ever killed someone, Kamil?". "No, Princess!" he had answered. Then she had mused, "I wonder if our journey may allow that opportunity to cross your path."

*

791

Accompanied and aided by his new companions, Maat and her husband Darwishi, Kamil took the body back to the house, reaching it at nightfall, the doors opening for them as they approached as if all the portals of the world had been waiting for this moment. Princess Shahrazad put up an imperious hand to him as he attempted to speak and led his two companions away.

*

When they finally came to talk about his journey and its shocking event, what she had to say engendered in him an even deeper sense of abject helplessness at his role in her machinations. He was stunned and incapable of raising a single word of protest when she finally asked him to read, not that she would have listened if he had. She exuded a harsh confidence and was in complete command over his every action.

They woke with the dawn and the sounds of fowl crowing all over the hilltop and the turning of wooden wheels on wooden floors below them. Both felt refreshed and ready for whatever lay in waiting. Servants appeared. Their travelling clothes had been either washed or otherwise cleaned of sweat and dust and they exchanged their borrowed robes for them. A small flame inside a pot with a circle of holes was placed nearby, heating a fish broth and two eating bowls sat beside it with a ladle. There was a pitcher of water and rough grey bread.

-This is the life, said his daughter, in bitter amusement, -I feel like a chick up here in these trees being fed by a mother bird!

-It is true. We would need wings to carry us safely down to the floor. It is the work of a clever man. This fortress is safe from all but fire and perhaps even that. He rubbed his hand on the boards of wood and sniffed. Then he took a loose splint from a plank's edge and held it in the pot's flame but it would not light, -He has dipped the wood in some juice that might pacify an inferno. I would know the secret.

-Ask him when we meet, she said angrily.

-What is it, daughter? he viewed her frown, stoically.

-I woke up many times in the night with just one thought tumbling like a leaf in the wind. Why did we not kill him? There were opportunities enough.

-It is true and that thought passed my mind, too. But your mother could have died at the vengeance of his troop's hands for I am not the invincible warrior I once was. Also have not I vowed not to kill if I have any choice in the matter? It was not the answer, even to the oppression such as we have seen here. There will be another way.

-It may be a time when we act without thinking, she said stubbornly

-I hope that I have trained my mind so that my actions are as they would have been if I had had the luxury of thought and that you are able to follow my lead.

They finished their meal and as soon as they had pushed their bowls away, the ladder again rumbled below them and the general's head appeared at their feet, -I show you round city, she said, -Miracle of Emperor.

☥

Walking with her through the busy populace brought home to them what a feat of man's inventiveness the city was. Towns and cities were usually higgledy piggledy collections of buildings of all shapes and sizes, grown over the years. It was left to the rich to raise splendid edifices to themselves or their courts. Such planned, stately constructions normally stood, watching imperiously over a jumbled mess of housing and business premises. But here everything had been built of a piece from the grand to the humble. There was no stone laid which did not seem to be part of a pattern.

-It is all in lines, said the daughter.

-Emperor train in building numbers, was their escort's reply. The general seemed much more relaxed now that she had achieved the mission of bringing them to her Emperor. Or perhaps it was the result of her reward of a night with him. She wore her dragon's motif coat over warmer clothes now that they were so far north, -Build city in two years. Many thousand slaves. Many forest. Bring our people far away to stop travel. Live all time here.

-It is like one big house, she nodded appreciatively.

-Not bad for animals, murmured her father, out of earshot of the general. He looked at her to drive the lesson home. She tightened her eyes in affirmation that she understood. Their promenade took some time and led them back to the palace, leaving them with the realisation that sheer force married to imagination could bring to fruition the most fantastic dreams of a single man.

She led them to a waiting staircase below his rooms and gestured that they should ascend, before turning on her heel and disappearing into the labyrinth of pillars. They sat on cushions and waited the Emperor's arrival. He entered the chamber dressed in black robes, edged with gold and sat opposite them. A sweep of his arm sent everyone scurrying from the room. They were alone.

-What do you think of my city? There is not another like it! His eyes were gleaming mirrors.

-It is the work of a great mind, said the Magus, truthfully.

-I am glad you see it. I had a good teacher. We brought him from the east where he designed shrines for the gods that could shelter a thousand worshippers. I built it in two years. Five thousand slaves.

-Where are they now? asked the daughter, scornfully, flaunting her disregard for the man's achievement.

-You think I am cruel, he smiled at her, -So? We all have our uses and fate prescribes what these are. But in answer, some died, others still labour or fight for my people and a few are free men with thriving businesses within our very walls. We do not kill the source if it can bring us good.

-You drowned those men last night. Her face retained its coldness.

-That was their fate. My people need to have proof that we are invincible and that the God of Water nurtures us daily. They knew themselves that their final gift was to God and were happy to offer themselves. The dream plant opens the doors to such purposes. He smiled again, his lips drawn into thin lines, his eyes penetrating, -You have the courage of a warrior. Few speak to me as you do and most of them are now dead. The daughter shrugged, maintaining eye to eye contact. The man turned his gaze to her father, -Let us talk about other things. You are not here to question my rule even if, as my guests, you have that licence. My God allowed me a vision when I was about to succeed my father. Take your father's life and be an emperor like no other. Learn from the wise. Close not your mind to the new or the strange. Do not destroy a source of knowledge whether it be a territory or a person. The Ice Lands can become the greatest empire ever known but only if you remain true to these words.

-How did he speak to you? Did you see the God of Water? asked the Magus.

-It was in a dream. In it I walked under a waterfall and was swept away into a great lake. As I sank in the lightless waters, spirit hands, white with long fingers, caught hold of me and held me like a baby in the depths. There I floated and His commands entered my thought. I awoke full of sadness when I found that I had been ejected from the holy waters of God but I was truly inspired by His words. I was a boy only but straightway I went to where my father slept and cut his throat. He did not know what I did for he was in thrall to the dream plant. He was too weak for our people. I mounted the throne and demanded a full court be wakened to attend me. Within an hour all the great warriors of our nation that resided in the palace at that time were arrayed before me. I showed my bloody hands. See this blood, I shouted. It is my father's and has been spilled to make our people great. I made a cut in my forearm so that blood ran down into the blood on my hand. You see, I roared, the blood is one blood. I am my father's son. I have all that was strong in him and none of his weakness. Bow to me, warriors and uphold your Emperor! None dissented. All fell to their knees. Their belief in me has not wavered since that day.

From that moment I have tried to learn all that there is to make me feared and invincible. I train my armies using the methods of your own empire builders, Magus. I bring here all the best artists, craftsmen and philosophers. Here have visited the holiest of men from every land. The God of Water is not too proud to admit that His powers can benefit from the ways of other gods.

-Did you bring my father here as a holy man or a warrior? she demanded.

-Both. I was attracted by the stories of him. He seemed to be what I want to be. Great in many ways. A man among men with powers beyond most people's understanding.

-In exchange for the life of his wife, my mother? she said, quietly.

-Indeed. Your mother is making ready to be taken back to her sands. She will be safe, he paused and then said coldly, -No matter what happens next. You have my word. He made the promise sound mysterious and full of foreboding as though even he was ignorant of the consequences of his decision to let her go. -She was a fascinating visitor. We talked many times. Proud. A fine leader of her tribe. I could have taken her to my bed but I prefer women who give after only a little resistance. Why bite into a bitter, withering fruit when there is so much else on the branch that is blushing to be picked?

-I am happy that you let her go, said the Magus, ignoring the goading, -I realise that there is a barter between us, even though we did not sit down and talk of it beforehand. But the general said enough for me to understand that I would owe you whatever it was that you wished if my wife was allowed to go free. I will stand by the contract.

Tell me what it is you want of me though it must not include my child, here. Their eyes held their gaze for a long time.

When the Emperor spoke, it was insistent and low, -Your daughter would be a worthwhile addition to my women's chamber and in other circumstances I would ensure her stay here until such time that she pleaded to share my bed and bring me a warrior son with your blood in its veins, Magus. But even that is snow in the high sun when compared to my reason for bringing you here. No, she will leave with her mother. I have no need of the distraction of this beautiful snake.

The daughter's shocked eyes met those of her father and knew immediately that protest would be useless.

There was a long pause as the pair of them sat side by side on his bed, enclosed by the peeling walls and crude furnishings. The only fresh, replenishing vision in the tired chambers was the view of the sky and white mountain tops beyond. Shahrazad said thoughtfully, -He has nothing to commend him, this Emperor. I am beginning to form a picture from your words, Uncle. At first I thought he was like all successful warlords. There has to be something unyielding in their characters or they would quickly succumb to the plotting inside their territories or from beyond their borders. That is how they hold on to their lands. And if they are ambitious to conquer more of the world it is even more the case, is it not? But this man has sinews of cruelty none of my own family have displayed in their long history. He is a monster for whom killing is either a sport or a conspicuous means to frighten his friends and foes alike. He does not even have the excuse of those predators whose blood boils at the sight of a death. She grimaced at him, -When I have to bring down my talons upon my enemy, Uncle, I do so after much contemplation. My mother taught me this. And she learned it from you. It was the final act for Murabbi. I did not mind the stealing of small locks of hair which he could sell to those who wished some part of me. But he was ignorant and crude. He thought I did not know that he was about to double deal and send intelligence to my mother via Raashid for reward. Chaksu confirmed it. At least she will come to realise soon enough that I did not have him removed until I was absolutely certain he might threaten this adventure and therefore my life. He watched her turn the tarot card slowly between her fingers, -The Hanged Man! Tell me about him. I have forgotten much of his import except that he appears in the midst of a voluntary hanging.

Kamil swallowed his reaction to her calm dismissal of Murabbi's end, opened his palms and smiled grudgingly, -That is the clue. Whenever we place ourselves willingly in a situation whose circumstance make it ill for us or whenever we find ourselves a victim in events over which we have control but do nothing, then we are represented by this card.

She viewed it and said mockingly, -So the card may represent Murabbi for one. He knew he was going to die but could not extract himself from fate's flow. And you, of course! You have no control over your life, staying beside me through thick and thin. The Princess Shahrazad laughed out loud but not to his ear, melodiously. -And of course you intended the card to signify how the Magus and his daughter place themselves in danger in order to rescue his wife. I see it. It is a clever card. Of all the cards you have shown me this one represents most what it is to be alive in these times, Uncle. Everyone seems subject to forces beyond them. Even the Empress cannot say she is fully in command of fate.

Kamil felt emboldened to ask, shocked, -Murabbi knew he was to die?

Her eyes focused sharply upon him, -In a sense. He went to his death as I had planned. Chaksu was my first instrument and you were my second. You remember we sat and talked with the young seer the evening before you travelled to kill Murabbi? Kamil flinched involuntarily. -He told us more about his strange powers? How he could see into the hearts of people? How he could make them do what he wanted? All those tales of how he persuaded his master and others to dote on him and give him gifts and bequeath him their possessions. How he had to be careful because it would have been easy to outstrip his master in wealth and create envy and become the target of every rich man's wrath rather than the object of their intrigue? I was struck by how cleverly he spreads his ambition over time so as not to make unnecessary enemies.

-It is true, said Kamil, the picture of the haughty Chaksu relishing in recounting more of his history, fresh in his thoughts. Chaksu was powerful, of that Kamil had no doubt. Was he a threat to the Princess? Kamil almost wished it were so.

-When I asked you to leave us for private conversation, I enjoined him to hypnotise Murabbi. We had him come to us and our young wizard put his hand on my bodyguard's forehead and spoke gently to him and asked what he might tell us. It all spilled out. The Empress Sabiya had foisted him on me years ago and though I saw through his snakery I thought it better to keep him close and say nothing for the while. He proved useful in many ways and there were certain matters I wished to convey via him to my mother if only to muddy the pool we share. I disclosed nothing of my real plans but took him along with me like a dog, only letting him know minutes before, what I wanted of him. Anyway, under the hex of Chaksu, his drugged voice repeated my mother's command. There will come a time, she had told him, when I will ask a lot of you. Until then be my daughter's closest ally. But never forget to whom you owe your allegiance. The words rang true to Kamil. She had said the same to him when she discovered his love for Baligha. The Empress jealously held her subjects in absolute loyalty to her, above everything. The Princess continued with her tale, -So I said nothing but waited until I could no longer be assured of my safety. That was when we arrived here. I could see he was plotting how he might use this situation to his advantage. He said, under Chaksu's influence, that he intended to barter with me so that I would reward him more than my mother! He was cunning enough to deceive most mortals but not one such as I. A true double dealer, don't you think?

Kamil put his hands together and bowed his head judiciously, then told her what Maat and Darwishi, the doctors, had said about Murabbi and his visit to them. They had seen through his deceptions, too.

-We shall probably never know the extent of his subterfuges but I knew enough to muzzle him, eh? Thank you Kamil. As you are now aware, you are at the heart of events. She stood up with a soft smile but her words brooked no argument, -I wish you to talk with all my strange crew of creatures without me being present. I fear that my questioning is occasionally too direct. I may be asking questions to bring me the answers I desire, not those I need.

Kamil didn't understand. He asked, -With respect, Princess, am I allowed to know what questions you have been asking?

-No! The vehemence startled him, -That is the point! I do not want you to have any notion as to what I hope to glean from them or want them to do. Just talk to them and see what comes out, spymaster. She got up to leave, -I will have them assemble here in your room in half an hour. Arrange for cushions, will you? Kamil bowed as she strode from the room. Then she stepped back for a moment, -What is it that the Emperor from the lands of ice and snow wants so much to strike such a bargain with the Magus? It will hang in my head until you read again.

Chapter Fourteen

Those who would be gods are either devils or fools

The seven new residents of the house by the lake sat in a horseshoe around the quiet historian. He tried to look confident and certain of what he wanted from them though he was fumbling in the dark. The Princess had offered him nothing except the demand that he discover what she could not. Then he had a tiny illumination. This was just the same as searching in the Great Library for a book or a manuscript without any coordinates, clues or even questions from previous experience that might give rise to a train of enquiry. In that sense he was very experienced in facing the unknown and digging something worthwhile out of its solid featureless wall. Had not al-Khwarizmi, that great conjuror of numbers, shown how to approach the unknown blindly, step by step, so that gradually its topography became visible? There had been times when he had walked, his eyes unseeing, around the circular walls of books and, for no accountable reason, found himself taking down a volume without even registering its title until it was open in his hands! And such was the way of things that books found by this method had proven invaluable, taking his mind to places where it would never have visited. This protracted avenue of thought was interrupted by a question from Chaksu who seemed to have asserted himself as the natural leader of the group.

-So Uncle Kamil, what is it you want of us?

-It is a chance to talk and for me to find out more about you all, replied Kamil benignly.

-We have done a lot of the former already, remarked the seer, -But if the Princess has asked you to quiz us then how can we say no?

Kamil covered his consternation and looked at them in turn; the webbed man, the climbing girl, the gold finders, the doctors and the seer. It was difficult to contain them in one group, so strange and unalike they seemed to be. The only conformity between them was their strangeness. It was this that seemed to have drawn them together in a familiarity and comradely ease which, at the same time, excluded outsiders such as himself. Finally, he spoke, -Of course the Princess Shahrazad will come to know what we discuss. I am her servant.

-Then why should we speak through an intermediary? Chaksu cocked his head.

-Who knows? replied Kamil, -The ways of conversation can not be predicted. Sometimes it is not what is said but the way it is said. Or what has not been said. Or again, what connects the words that have been said. Or it can be that a different ear can construct something new even from those who seem merely to repeat themselves. He had to admit to himself that his labyrinthine reasoning, though suddenly forced upon him by Chaksu's challenge, had an authentic ring to it.

-We will talk, said Ull suddenly, -Uncle is not an enemy of mine.

-Or mine, chimed in other voices. Chaksu smiled tolerantly and with a long gesture of his arm, requested Kamil to proceed.

Kamil took out the twenty two major Arcana of the tarot pack. To use it was the only ploy he could think of that might draw something hidden from them that the Princess had not been able to uncover, - Have any of you seen such cards? he asked, spreading them in a fan before him on their protective silk square on the floor. Bodies leaned forward but none touched the gilt-edged highly coloured images. Nevertheless they were transfixed. Kamil tidied the cards again and then shuffled them and fanned them in his right hand with the pictures face down, -Will one of you choose a card for everyone? he asked. Their heads pulled back and their eyes circled round each other.

Ull spoke again, -Let the twins choose. If they can find gold in a desert or lake they can find the winning card for us, he added triumphantly. Kamil guessed that Ull must have seen gambling with cards and assumed that this was much the same. He thought that Chaksu was going to intervene but the man closed his mouth and drew back. The twins looked round at the nodding heads and encouraging gestures and bent forward with Zemfira's palm atop the back of Timur's hand. Without any tremble, deviation or other sign of conflict between them, Timur's forefinger and thumb drew a card from the splayed pack. Slowly they turned it over and placed it so that all could see.

With puzzled looks they sat in silence until, gradually, most eyes turned to Kamil. Except those of Chaksu whose face was stern and intense.

-What is he? whispered Vatisha, her fingers clenching and unclenching.

-What do you see? asked Kamil. This seemed to melt their suspicion.

-He suffers from innocence, said Maat, -We see such holy fools in the hospital.

-They do not lack intelligence, said her husband, -But somehow their knowledge of the affairs of men is missing. They play when others work. They fall into danger and hurt themselves. Others abuse them. The two doctors nodded to each other as though they had pronounced an unequivocal diagnosis.

-What do others think? asked Kamil, -Zemfira?

She screwed up her face, -I see a young man, old enough to leave his parents, beginning an adventure, making his first steps in life.

Her twin agreed, -He could be a boy or a girl. He is like we were once as we began to fend for ourselves. Life truly begins only when you leave the protection of your elders.

Ull spoke in his guttural accent from the north, -To me he is lonely and seeks new companions in the world. His past is not shown but he is trying to leave it behind though it is hard. Yet even the dog of his village is holding on to his breeches to prevent him from going.

Kamil's eyes continued round the watching group. He knew that Chaksu would be last to speak so he caught the gaze of Vatisha.

-He is brave to be on his own, carrying everything he possesses, she said, -I do not know what the others here see but I feel it is someone who seeks to know what he can become even in the face of great danger. He has the makings of a hero or a leader. Silence descended as they waited for Chaksu's pronouncement, as though his judgment would tilt the balance of suggestions towards the truest interpretation.

Finally Chaksu spoke and brought to them yet another illumination of his uncanny powers, -When Uncle Kamil spread the cards so that we could glimpse their finery my mind recorded them all and held them like a tapestry here, he tapped his head, -There were twenty two cards, each with a number except this one. He looked around quizzically, -We chose the only card without a number. All the other cards must come after this one and they speak of the trials and tribulations of life. They show death and love, strength and weakness, thoughtfulness, disaster, evil, adventure and success. I can see them all as I speak to you, although Uncle knows them as a scholar and might tell us more about their meanings. So, this card is the beginning card and we have each of us given it a true facet of its import. But we must ask why Uncle began our discussion with the cards? He paused for dramatic emphasis, -I suggest that by using them he helps us look deeper into our selves than by using mere words. So he has been proven right. Each of us interpreted the card according to his or her experience but together we have built a picture that represents all of us as one. We all have roots to our lives that cannot yet be understood or shown. We are all now at the true start of an adventure. We came because the Princess called across the lands and we heeded her. We did not come to serve her but to find an answer to what is missing in our history that only she can provide. It is this that connects us. Which then leads to a question that I asked myself even before I ventured here. What is it that we must do for her? Why us? We know what is the connection we have with each other but what is our connection to her? If this is the beginning of a great adventure, where will it lead and what lies at the end of it?

Kamil was shaken by the man's words. He had said what Kamil thought but much more coherently. This strange group did share a longing for how their lives had begun. Without this knowledge they were like the Fool card, ever searching.

*

Early the next morning, Kamil and the Princess took tea together while breakfast was being prepared. The sun was just up and making the snow caps far away and above them shimmer pinkly. Kamil was not exactly articulate when he repeated his experience with the creatures to the Princess. Although he managed to recount much of what had happened he stumbled in his words when trying to convey the strange air of mystery and suspense that had attended the card reading. It was probably because he found Chaksu so threatening. Even more so than he did the Princess! He reminded him of someone he had met who had had a similar effect upon him but for some reason it would not come to him. Chaksu created a distance between them which, coupled with his natural arrogance and his strange gifts, beleaguered Kamil. But he did not want to explore these feelings with her and so his words were more halting than he would have liked.

When he had done, she sipped her tea in silence. Then she looked up and said, -Chaksu truly frightens you?

Kamil found himself blustering, -I am sorry, Princess, I know you have a high opinion of the creature. His hands made involuntary movements in the air.

-It is not something that worries me, Uncle Kamil. Have no fear. It is true that in obvious ways he is the most powerful of the newcomers but his gifts are for us to use to our advantage as proved to be the case with Murabbi. She tightened her lips. -He did more than gain a door to Murabbi's thoughts and plans, Uncle. Kamil knew what she was going to say though he had not thought it until now, -He transfixed him like a rabbit before a fox. He told Murabbi that you had become more important to me than him which, it was plain to see, enraged him. Then he implanted the command that when you were alone together and far away from here, he must try to kill you but as he took the knife in his hand his anger must leave him and he must allow you to take it and use it against him. It was fascinating to see the Chaksu's dominance up close. It filled me with unusual feelings of excitement. My plans are going well Kamil and I feel closer to accomplishing everything I desire. Take out your cards again! See how they have become the instruments of fate? Chaksu was right. We see through them what we often cannot with our ordinary eyes.

She flicked over the top card and raised an eyebrow, -Look, I speak of Murabbi's end and here we have the card of the end of his days. It had to be so. Then she raised her eyes, -Or does the card represent you, Kamil, my Grim Reaper?

Again she showed how easily she manipulated his feelings. The

horror of being a murderer washed through him. He struggled to say, -
It was an end for Murabbi, my Princess, -But the card may mean far
more. Visibly shaking, he began to read.

The warlord from the Ice Lands commanded that the Magus' wife be brought to meet with them by the main gate to the fortress city. The daughter had packed her things and her horse was ready, looking well fed and eager for exercise, its saddle bags stuffed with food and her weapons buckled. The Magus stood at the horse's head, stroking its muzzle and giving it quiet advice about how to care for its owner. Then, approaching along the straight road between the orderly lines of houses they saw his wife, the daughter's mother. She rode, straight-backed, a guard either side holding her horse's bridle. To his eye she was the same woman he had met when just out of boyhood and he had first taken for a man, staring down at him from a camel and later giving her body to him in a tent. The intervening years seemed as nothing except something inside him was now different. He knew her intention was to be cool and distant and give nothing away to these northern captors. She glanced briefly at him and then she looked ahead. In the past this would have been the end of the exchange. Each would have put aside their years together and their feelings for each other to show the world that they were chiefs, leaders of their clans, even if death itself might come between them before they could ever again acknowledge each other.

But, for the first time, the Magus strode forward and with a warrior's glance made the guards fall back. He gestured to her to dismount and after a slight hesitation she dropped to the ground in front of him. Then he embraced her, his eyes shut, feeling the length of her against him. Nor did he let go for some moments.

-Go to our home, he whispered close to her ear, -And wait for me. I will return. Even as he said it he knew that his returning self might be nothing more than his carcass or his ashes. And she knew it, too.

She looked at him in wonder and gave him a rare, intimate, public smile, -You are my husband, she said and turned and remounted briskly. The daughter trotted up to her and they touched fingertips and then, without once looking back, joined the waiting cohort of troops.

The Magus stayed until the enormous doors closed behind them and then turned to face the palace. Even at this distance he could see the Emperor watching him part from his women, his face as impassive as ever.

♀
☥

The two men faced each other, seated on cushions. There was a thickening of the air between them as if their wills had formed a storm cloud of oppositions. When their eyes met neither blinked nor looked away until some implicit agreement in their words allowed them relief.

-You would do anything for those women, mused the warlord.

-It is our way.

-Not mine.

-Your sons and daughters might expect more of you, said the Magus.

-They know what I am, father of all, not just those of my own blood. Their lives are of little value when I weigh them thus. Do you know, Magus, there is no one strong enough to sit astride the empire if I die? So I do not intend to. That is why you are here. He looked at the warrior shaman with motionless eyes. For many, this remark would have proven confounding, hiding a meaning that could not be pinned to reason yet the Magus understood instantly.

-You wish to conquer death. It was a statement not a question.

-It is my destiny but I must have someone with me whose presence I can trust. A warrior. A seer. The Magus himself.

-I have no wish to evade the final oblivion.

The Emperor permitted his eyes to widen almost imperceptibly, -And this is your greatest gift to my mission. There will be no conflict between us should there be salvation for but one of us, one immortal hand to grasp, one elixir to swallow. Your word is immutable. You will never betray me. It is the barter you struck when I agreed to let your females return.

-So what is next...?

-We start this very night. My soldiers will ride with us to a point in the great wastes where we will disappear from them in the ice fog. Once gone we will travel alone, wrapped in white furs, no longer

Emperor and Magus but warriors facing the one challenge that no one has ever survived. The Emperor stood as though parading his fine, gold-rimmed earthly robes for the last time and the Magus stood before him in his battered, robust warrior garb. They bowed curtly to each other and the Emperor walked swiftly from the chamber, leaving the Magus to find his own way to his belongings.

They were far across the frozen flatness as the Emperor at last told the Magus of the Great Convocation, how he had brought together in a captured golden temple at the eastern extreme of his empire, the wisest men, the shamans, the soothsayers and the guardians of the oracles. To these he had added those who swore they had adventured where none had dared to the lands beyond life itself, either below the earth or above it and through fantasies or nightmares by using dream plants or the disciplines of meditation.

His voice was low and muffled so it did not carry to the wide circle of protective horsemen. The convoy made little sound in the shallow snow and threw up a constant haze of fine icy flakes that forced their eyes to smart and constantly formed a thick white crust on the scarves wound round their faces, -I became good at interrogation. I was not impatient. They told their stories time and again and I distilled each telling for consistency and truth. Then I compared one against the next. Slowly, for it took many months, I reduced what I sought to those that offered the most likelihood; three holy destinations. They are months apart Magus. We will take them in order of their distance and hope that the first and nearest satisfies my imperial desire. If not that, then we will investigate the second and finally the third.

-What if there is no channel to immortality at any of them? asked the Magus.

-Then, no matter how wise my oracles suppose themselves to be, I shall send assassins to demonstrate that when I ask for immortality, it is a mortal sin to lie to me. And I will begin again. He continued in his humourless, flat tone, -The first is a person, the second is a river beneath the earth and the third is the temple of a sect who cross a waterless desert in the manner of your wife.

-How far to the first?

-Two months. We will come to know each other well in this journey of mine, Magus!

Shahrazad gave the card of Death a questioning look, -I see it has yet another meaning, Uncle. It hangs over the story in a different way. It does not necessarily signify a person so much as the question we all face. The Magus is always preoccupied by what happens after life and he has been searching for answers through all your Tales but this warlord is demented in his desire to be immortal and for him this can only be an unending life on earth, not in some unproven hereafter. Just like that mad creature the Magus encountered, the one who consigned her flock to pestilence, remember? I can still see a picture of her lying half in and half out of her sect's long stockade, dying but refusing to admit to blame. She sighed, -It would be too easy to lose oneself in such an obsession. Only a djinn has mastery over the two worlds.

-He is a despot and such men can imprint their will on the world, no matter how crazed their desire might appear to the rest of us. Kamil went on, reflectively, -We know this tyrant ruled one of the greatest empires ever seen. We know that he and the Magus met and some time later his grip loosened. It is here that my knowledge of the history of the two men is also loosened for there are no records to turn to. If my books thus far have contained a poetic sensibility to make them diverting for the reader, they have nevertheless been based on solid fact but from this point on I have relied upon my instinct to portray what may have ensued. Kamil made a familiar gesture of self-deprecation and raised his eyes to the Princess.

She smiled warmly, -Uncle Kamil, didn't Chaksu say that history is just a long line of stories? How else to we remember what has happened to our peoples over generations? It may be that in a hundred years your final book will be taken as the true final chapter of the Magus and his times! Amusing, don't you think? This might be amusing, thought Kamil but it was so counter to his discipline as a historian that he could never accept it in reality. However, that argument was not one he wished to pursue at this time and with the young woman sitting beside him, her red hair aflame and her child-like features suffused in warm contentment. He knew she was capable of mangling his arguments if she so wished. She may look like a girl crossing to womanhood but her reason, emotions and navigation of the affairs of life were like those of a fully mature and all conquering leader. She made him, the royal historian, seem the child!

She murmured sweetly, -Anyway, Uncle, you have conjured up a great ending to your Tales! We have the perfect representatives of Good and Evil travelling together. We know that there is nothing that the warlord would not do if he felt so disposed, whether lying, cheating, torturing or killing in order to gain his ends. Meanwhile the Magus is sworn to accompany him to the end of his adventure and will not entertain any such behaviour. Who will survive the other?

-I can give no hint of the outcome, rejoined Kamil, happily, bathed in her enthusiastic warmth.

*

Everywhere there was bustle. Pack horses were being loaded with sacks of grain, dried meat and fruit, spices and sweet delicacies. Weapons were being sharpened, oiled, tightened and housed. The seven half-humans, as Kamil thought of them, stood quietly talking in a circle in the courtyard. The Princess had not yet appeared from her preparations in her chamber. Meanwhile, Kamil packed his final treasure, the tarot cards, wrapped in silk in their cedar wood box and looked from the window of his room for the last time. The lake stretched away like glass, motionless except for the little eddies made by dipping birds. The early morning sky was a flat milk reminding him of a blank page on which the next episodes of his adventure were about to be written.

Chapter Fifteen

Plant a seed in the heart and watch the destruction of reason

Kamil did not ask the Princess about their destination because she left no doubt that everyone around her was there at her command and to do her service. They should be obedient and carry out whatever she required of them, be it a whim or deeply thought strategy. If she wanted advice she would ask for it and that, Kamil thought, was only likely to happen when they reached wherever they were going. What a strange crew the nine of them had become. It led him to conjecture that their combined gifts somehow created a whole, like the facets of a gem and only the Princess knew how it was cut and polished to make it into this potent entity. The analogy pleased him because he could picture the jewel sparkling on her little finger, as she wrapped them round it.

He shifted his position on his horse, feeling the soreness, aches and pains of the ride with Murabbi all over again. They were slowly climbing in a shallow arc with the icy peaks now and then in view over their left shoulders. If that is where we are going, he thought, it would take several days on this terrain. Yet he could think of no other end to their journey. They had ignored the only two paths that seemed to offer a route to passes over the high ridges and they were crossing from one faint animal track to another without apparent premeditation. It was noticeably colder and everyone had sealed themselves in their furs, tying the earpieces of their caps under their chins. Even Ull, who could withstand more cold than seemed possible, wore a jacket, though it hung loosely on him and the straps of his cap were not tied but dangled past his cheeks. No one was complaining. Indeed, Kamil could see from their eyes that there was a singular excitement at what was unravelling in their lives.

They stopped to rest where there was a little direct sunshine. Looking down they could no longer see the house by the lake because their trek had taken them round a long, falling limb of the mountain. Instead, there was the beginning of the tree line with dark forests spread below it and far in the distance, undulating waves of blue land. Somewhere beyond was the palace and the Empress Sabiya.

Choosing a rock to sit on, some little distance away from the others, Kamil chewed on over-cooked rabbit legs. His sudden thought of the Empress, no doubt beside herself with worry over her daughter, filled him with a longing. Of all those he had met in his life only the Empress and his wife, Baligha, could provoke such an emotion in him. He could see Empress Sabiya as clearly cut in his mind as if she was standing there before him, looking at him reproachfully and asking why he had betrayed her. Then he jerked out of the slight stupor and smiled to himself. How stupid, he thought, jocularly, the Empress would never submit herself to such sentimentality! He had momentarily forgotten that she knew precisely where he was and what he was doing. After all, she had helped engineer it.

-You are smiling. Is it a good joke? asked Vatisha, sitting silently down beside him. She was a quaint little thing. She had taken off her cap in the sunshine and her snow white face and short cropped black hair made her look like a sprite, never likely to grow up. He saw that she had shod her iron-hard feet with soft skin boots and pushed her hands into folds in her jacket.

Kamil was non-committal but widened his smile a little more, -I don't know what I was thinking, he lied, -But I find my spirits lifted by your sitting here. You have the loveliest face. He managed to say it with enough gallantry in his tone for her to accept it with a courteous bow.

-Thank you Uncle. Yours is wise and -, she faltered as she tried to think of a word, -There is no evil in it!

-Thank you, too. Did you come over for any reason other than my company? he asked.

-Yes. The cards. I saw them when you made a fan in your hand but not as well as Chaksu, I can not remember any clearly except one. It seemed to jump into my eyes and frightened me. She looked at him, her eyes wide and without guile.

-Which one? he asked.

-I saw it upside down but it was a tower. It was crashing down because of lightning. People were falling from it. I saw myself being shaken off it like an ant from a honey comb. I always descend before a storm hits. What does it mean? Am I to fall when next I climb? She put a pleading hand on his arm. Kamil patted it and shook his head.

-No Vatisha! The Tower is not to be taken as an actual building. The card means the end of a period of your life. If you see it the right way up it can mean bad trouble for you. But you saw it as I held it out and so it was reversed. It tells you that change is upon you and this will disturb you but it will be for your own good. The past is being shaken off you. Something new is beginning. His interpretation made her smile radiantly.

-Thank you Uncle. Thank you. I did not sleep for fear. All I could see was the breaking tower and my face on a falling woman. She embraced him gratefully and left as noiselessly as she had arrived.

It was true, thought Kamil, her card was also a card for the whole group, as significant as The Fool chosen by the twins. For everyone, as Chaksu had said, this was a time of rupture with the past. And that included the Princess and himself.

*

He was riding next to the Princess on a broad tract of upland shale when Chaksu steered his horse between them, -Your pardon, Princess. I have just had a mind picture which you may wish to know. Your mother and a small army have left the palace in pursuit of you. They will be at the house in two days.

The Princess raised a bunched fist, -It confirms what I thought. Thank you Chaksu, you are invaluable to me. The man nodded and his horse dropped back, -Three days behind us, Kamil. Enough time to see this through! She hopes to be there at my final reckoning. It cannot be ruled out. Without a pause she went on, -What is our card for today? He thought for a moment, visualising the pack in order.

-It is the card called Temperance.

-I cannot think its meaning, she muttered, trying to remember.

-It means harmony, making all things equal, finding the right balance between varying forces. It is a good sign for anyone wishing to hold the world still and consider what might happen next.

-Where is the book?

-In my bag here, he pointed in front of a thigh.

-Read it while we ride, it sounds timely. I will put up with any stumbling, she said, brusquely. Kamil did as she asked, though he was slow and clumsy about it. He looped the reins loosely in his belt and took out and balanced the box between his thighs, carefully withdrawing all the pages of the Temperance before locking and replacing the casket. Then, gripping the pages in both hands and holding them awkwardly as they bounced before his eyes, he began to read.

The coat he was wearing was made from long-haired, white fur and cut and stitched in such a way that the head of the beast with its great slashing teeth and black staring eyes was perched on his neck as though watching for any assassin approaching from the rear. It was very warm even in this extreme cold. A fleece also covered his roan with leggings that stretched to its hocks and a cover for all but its eyes and nostrils.

He had woken in the night as the Emperor entered his tent, a knife leaping to his hand and ready. If his visitor was troubled by what he saw he gave no sign but crooked his fingers and turned abruptly. Their horses stood, pawing the snow, held by a soldier. One pack horse was fully burdened. As he mounted his steed the Emperor leaned and clubbed the man to the ground with the pommel of his sword so suddenly that he uttered no sound. Immediately they were forging their way through the windy, moonlit darkness.

-They will try to follow but will not know our direction, he called out to the Magus above the whistling air, -That is why I silenced him. It will give us an hour to become lost even with my best tracker among them. A little later he shouted, -Wait! There was a mound of snow which he kicked revealing a clump of frozen, low growing bushes. He unsheathed his sword slashing at three spread branches. These, once freed, were tied to the saddles so that they trailed behind them, their tracks being partially erased. The fine blown snow in the high wind would do the rest. In a final dissembling act the Emperor led the Magus across a wide, sloped expanse of ice where nothing could lie because the wind made whatever fall race away to its furthest edge. They walked, holding the reins of their mounts and though they slipped and slid a little they followed its flat course downhill. Far beneath their feet, though muffled by the elements, the Magus was sure he could hear the rushing of water.

Only when they had left its creamy surface by ascending a small, frozen stream, did they untie the branches. It was light enough to see but for the Magus it was a featureless desert. Just as in his wife's territory of sand and wind, the snow here formed successive, low ruckles as could be found in a disturbed bed covering. He could not see where the land ended and the sky began for between them and the horizon there were scurrying clouds of snow which blended into the milky whiteness.

His companion drew his mount next to the roan, commenting, -We cannot stop just yet even though our horses must rest. It is possible to see your prey hours ahead when the snow devils cease their howling. But there, he pointed, -Is a shadow where we can drop from sight and feed them and ourselves.

It was some time before the Magus could discern what he had been talking about. People learn to read the invisible in their own lands, he thought. The peddler knew his way through forests, his wife across desert sands and this warlord across the snows. One could see variety where another could only see sameness. When they reached the shaded line it proved to be a deep gash in the earth, its sides steep enough to make them dismount and slowly work their way down. The Emperor had them pull up. The air was suddenly freed of wind and his voice seemed unnaturally loud, -We must stay at this level. To go down further is dangerous for the floor catches the snow and it can be three or four times the height of a man, with treacherous water below. I know where we are. It is called The Slash and runs for weeks from north to south. In the summer it fills with flowers on its sunlit sides and has a harmless stream at its centre. He looked up through the intermittent billows of white that scurried above them, waiting to catch a glimpse of the sky, -We have come a little south of our stopping point. With that he led the way north until an overhang offered security from view with a fine dust covering grey rock.

-When we are on the plains it would be easy to imagine that the snow and ice sink eternally, said the Magus, -And that the solid earth has withdrawn forever.

-There are places like that, said his companion, -So deep that you can build cities beneath the surface, so cold that you can light the hottest fires and they do not melt the walls, so hard that it taxes the best forgers of metal to make tools that will pierce and polish, cut and shape. If ever I am cornered, which can not happen unless I am pursued by an evil troop of djinn, the like of which no one has yet met, I have such a place. It is as big as the city wherein we met. Even those sorcerous devils would not be able to pass through its walls. The Magus was surprised at the man's credulity. It was a weakness he had not expected.

They began feeding their horses, the one whispering while rubbing the limbs of the pack horse's limbs beneath the furs that kept it warm while simultaneously cupping corn to its mouth, the other doing little other than place water in a leather bowl and throwing corn upon the ground. Next the Magus tended to his own horse. The Emperor slumped to a sitting position, his back against the wall of the shallow cave, watching the Magus intently, -Why feed the pack horse first?

-It is a willing brute. My horse could not eat until it's companion is satisfied.

The Emperor raised his eyebrows, -This is the roan of which everyone speaks? Is it as old as you?

-His blood is older. But he is young yet. He is the fourth of his line that I have accompanied and there was one before them who found my grandfather when he was alone in the hills.

-They all share the magical gifts?

-It is as if they are the same creature. Everything each learns is passed on to the next and so this one combines all that has gone before. He may now bestow upon a foal wisdom about snow and ice and how to find a way across it. When you were cutting the bush to hide our passage, your horse found food there and mine followed her. Nothing will be forgotten. The Magus held the leather pitcher of water to the roan's mouth. It drank slowly, steam issuing in plumes from its nose.

The Emperor changed the subject suddenly, -The great God of Water proclaims that only tribes who worship Him can live with him when they die. No other peoples can take that journey. As for animals... what does your god say?

The Magus answered him a little cryptically, -I have no god but if there are spirits inside any of us then it is likely there must be spirits inside all living things. My horse here is the equal of most men or women or so it seems to me. Even if there are spirits within us I can see no hope for another existence after this one. The Magus wanted to ask why the Emperor needed to travel to far off lands and unfamiliar gods if he believed so devoutly in his water deity but he could not because the subject of their discussion, the roan, suddenly began prancing and baring its teeth, its ears flat and its eyes large and troubled.

Moving like a white wraith up the steep incline a distance below them was what the Magus at first imagined was a man like himself. The snow flakes had become large as they dropped out of the wind and they made the spectre blurred but it seemed to be covered in the same long-haired furs as he and it was bigger. The Magus gestured to the Emperor and pointed down. His companion struggled to his feet and stepped forward to the overhang's entrance, staring where the Magus was pointing and trying to discern whatever had been seen in the falling curtain. An instant later he had caught it so that his eyes were attracted to nothing else but the clear shape of the heavy legged climber, -We are in danger! These animals are hunters and kill my people. It can smell a man in the wildest snow storm and attacks without warning. If you are not looking exactly where it is, then you never see it. Few are able. He looked at the Magus with greater respect.

-The roan knew it was there. He can catch the scent of an enemy like your beast can catch the scent of a man. It is closer now. They had taken out their bows during their hurried conversation, the Magus his favoured one from the desert and the Emperor a puzzling construction that later the Magus would discover to be a crossbow, -Do you eat it?

-No, said the warlord, -The meat is poisonous. Death is slow. It is kill or be killed. The fur is the only prize. The Emperor raised his weapon and slipped a small arrow into it. They stood at the mouth of their shelter covered in the white fur of the enemy below, their weapons pointing and primed. As if it had divined their intentions in their scent, the great creature rolled back on to its haunches, its black muzzle and small dark eyes seeking them out.

-Do not shoot yet, whispered the Emperor, we are too far away. We will only wound at this distance and it will be upon us before we can draw another dart. The Magus nodded. Then, concentrating, he reached out his mind towards the white man-killer. The beast shook its head violently to try to throw him out of its head but it could not. The Magus sent let-us-not-fight signals. His intuition was that if he threatened conflict then the predator would fight for that was its way.

Nor could he engage the creature with a show of respect for such an emotion did not exist within its essence. They stood like statues facing it, the Emperor's arms heavy with the weight of his weapon, the Magus's arms tiring from holding his bow taut and the creature confused at an experience that seemed to block its thoughts and leave it unable to move in the snow. Then the Magus conveyed a leave-here suggestion and, almost as soon as he focused upon it the creature stood up and roared a warning to them before dropping to its paws and ambling away along the side of the gorge.

-I have not seen or heard anything like that! exclaimed the Emperor through tight lips, -Was that the magic of your roan, too?

-No. It was mine alone.

Before they left their sanctuary, the Magus was able to ask the warlord his question. The answer was typically full of the contradictions of a devout believer, it seemed, -The Water God is our God and ours alone but he has never said that he is alone among gods. He protects us where we live and breathe but he knows our borders better than us for He made them for us. He can take all the forms there are, be they solid or as invisible as the air for He is water, ice, snow and steam and He brings us into the world and then ensures the leaving of it. When I find everlasting life I will bring it as a gift to Him, Magus. And like your roan, He will learn from it and fashion it and bestow it upon the ice peoples and I shall be his favoured son.

They stopped for a moment as Kamil carefully replaced the tale of Temperance in its box and in his saddle bag. As he did so he was aware that their companions were much closer than before and were staring at him in awe. Even Chaksu gave signs of being impressed by his reading. The Princess turned and smiled at them, -They like what they hear Kamil. Your stories will enthral generations to come. They are beginning to understand that you are more than a gentle old historian! They began pushing the horses forward again and the gap opened up between them and the following group, -I think the chapter is a perfect example of Temperance. The Magus and the Emperor enjoy an uneasy peace, despite their extreme differences. Our hero treats horses equally well. He will not kill the bear because the meat is poison and so prefers to live and let live. With this gift of entering the minds of animals he would easily fit into my little group, don't you think?

-He would be a little overwhelming!

-I prefer to say, a challenge. Kamil looked across at her with her baby skin but mature eyes, her tightened lips and firm chin and her strong male riding gait. He told himself that she was joking. Had there been anyone since the Magus to compare with him? Both great warrior and great shaman? Who else had undertaken adventures that later became the equal of those cherished myths of gods and heroes of poets' imaginations? And hadn't he written the first truly wise words about how people and tribes should live in harmony? He was the founding father of all spiritual thought even though he avoided any supplication to a god.

From behind him someone called, -Uncle?

-It seems you are wanted by our young physicians, said Princess Shahrazad, -Go back to them and tell Chaksu to come forward. I would spend a little more time discussing my mother's progress. Kamil slowed his mount until he was among the others and passed on her Highness's command to Chaksu who immediately forced his horse forward. Then he allowed his own steed to drop further back together with those of Maat and Darwishi. He liked the pair. They had a curious naivety as though they were hardly of this world. He had already learned enough about them to know that they used plants and herbs for medicines which they refined and concentrated until they could be kept as oils and pastes in small phials. They were amassing their knowledge in a hand-crafted book with chapters headed by ailments and all the efficacious remedies for them that one might find growing naturally in any part of the land. He knew how they had met as young creatures not even as old as the Princess. Both were orphans and had no knowledge of their parents and they had grown up in those early years with families who were kind and considerate but expected hard work in exchange. Maat helped her foster mother in her garden where they grew herbs and spices. From her she also learned to name all the wild plants that grew around as well as beginning to understand their uses. Her foster mother used to say that every plant was a poison, it was only a matter of how much passes your lips and that between having no effect upon you and killing you was a world of knowledge about potency. At the same time Darwishi grew up in the household of an apothecary, working in his foster father's shop. Like Maat he learned quickly and never forgot a lesson. The happiest moment of their uneventful but fulfilling young lives came about when the two families met. Darwishi's foster father and Maat's foster mother were brother and sister and the sister sold her produce to her brother. The two young creatures had fallen in love the moment they viewed each other, not old enough to marry and torn apart when the meeting between the two families ended after a few days and they returned to their homes. A year passed and they yearned for each other, knowing that the other would always wait. Finally, Darwishi was entrusted with a special assignment by his foster father involving buying new stock for his shop. Darwishi came back with far more than his foster father ever thought could be purchased with the silver he had given him. He asked him what wish he might grant him. Darwishi of course said the hand of Maat in marriage. There was much communication between the two families but a wedding was arranged and they became a very young husband and wife. As was customary they had to live for five years with Maat's foster mother during which time they began working at a small hospital in the nearby town. Their fame spread and the hospital grew, taking in patients from far and wide. Then Murabbi visited. Now they were here.

-What can I do for you? asked Kamil.

-We liked your story, smiled Maat, her translucent face peering up at him from her furs, -Are we right, there are many more tales such as that one?

-Many. There are sixty six tales spread over three books. The tale I read today...

-Temperance, interrupted Darwishi, -It is the card for us! We do not like conflict in any form.

Kamil was not surprised, -Yes, Temperance, It is the fifteenth tale of each book. I wrote the first two books for the Empress when she was young and this last one for Princess Shahrazad. They are all about the same man, the great Magus.

-Oh we have heard of him! said Darwishi in excitement, -He pacified two great armies by riding his horse between them and bringing lightning bolts from the sky. The man he is travelling with must be the evil tyrant from the north, the man who was half-god and conquered the world with his heartless army of icemen. I see! But you tell the tale differently Uncle. It feels more real than a child's fable. Will you read all the books to us?

Kamil laughed, -Of course, when our adventure is over and if the Princess is so disposed, I will read all three books to you. Oh - and if it is also the wish of the Empress.

Chapter Sixteen

Goodness is a prize of hard labour but evil is free

Chaksu was in a daze. He was riding perfectly safely yet his eyes were closed and his head lolling on his shoulders. Princess Shahrazad had just asked him to tell her about the disposition of her mother. It would be more than a day before she reached the house, then they would stay overnight and cast around for the trail left by her daughter and her cohort of companions, so Princess Shahrazad felt secure enough with their lead. Providing they, themselves, were not thwarted at the end of their journey, all that she wished to be accomplished would have come to pass.

-Tell me what you can read on my mother's face, she had demanded. Chaksu bowed his head in affirmation and closed his eyes. Then he had become transported into this idiot state, as though all his faculties had left him.

Moans and mutterings burbled from his mouth at first but suddenly he spoke quite clearly, -I can see her face. It is smiling but not with happiness. She is pleased to be chasing you at last. But ... but... she does not want to catch up with you until the very end of your mission.

-I knew it! My mother has something of the gift, too. Like me. But yours is the strongest, Chaksu. We can sense where someone is and sometimes if they are good or evil but you can see them as clearly as if they rode beside you and can even gain access to their thoughts. What else? What of Raashid?

Again he began by mumbling incoherent sounds but then his voice returned, -He is angry because you fooled him and the Empress was harsh with him. He has always loved her and so it is hard for him to take the wasp on her tongue.

-How many ride with her?

The pause and then the words, -About twenty.

-Is there anything else I should know?

This time there was a long silence and Chaksu's head stopped lolling but stayed stiff, lying upon one shoulder, -She has found one such as I,

825

though not so developed, a woman from the south with a skin as blue as it is black. This woman is the sight and is following us with her gift. Ah! This is why your mother is smiling. I see. She has been told about the seven of us and it has woken in her a strange excitement. I think she has been expecting these events for some time.

Princess Shahrazad laughed bitterly, -I know the seer she is using. She is her cousin from the village of our ancestors.

*

Princess Shahrazad had wanted another reading, -It is to calm me before the final thrust, Uncle. Listening to you helps my mind settle on your Tale rather than what is in front of me. They were sitting cross-legged inside her tent, a small embroidered circular canvass dome that could be erected in minutes and presented Kamil with a constant worry that he might inadvertently brush against some part of her body. A candle flickered near her head. Kamil had an unadorned version to himself while the others were crowded into a further two. They were perched high above a sheer cliff in the lea of the wind, not yet at the point where the ice remained undisturbed for most of the year. The night was clear and Kamil had already peered out of his tent and counted the constellations he knew. The stars were so sharp they had made his eyes blur when trying to accommodate them and he had had to blink every few seconds to encompass the panorama.

-So what is the next card? she asked, leaning back into her cushion, arranging her furs and straightening her legs. She hooked her arms behind her head and stared up at the curved tent ceiling.

-The Devil, he answered, arranging the card for viewing and placing the manuscript open at the beginning of the Tale.

-Ah! she cried softly, -Am I to be undone by occult forces? Who is the devil, here? Not one of us, surely? Not my mother nor Raashid. If it is not a person then what does it represent?

-It is nearly always a negative card. Anyway, he said, -It is the card of the Tale, even though my Princess would like to extrapolate from it to her own life.

-That's true but it has said as much about my difficulties and anxieties as it ever has about the Magus and his battles, don't you think? Tell me a little more.

Holding the card up so that she could see it without moving her position, the historian pointed to elements in its image, -The Devil has two slaves, two prisoners but they are there because they have not the will to escape. They are bound to a course of action which could bring their downfall and they know it. They know that what they do is wrong. The Devil is a powerful force that takes hold and propels us to our doom. But it is not inevitable. We can break free, the sooner the easier, the later the harder as our will gradually perishes over time.

-Perhaps you and I are the prisoners, victims of my unswerving flight to my goal. Soon you will find that the Devil is unmasked and the reason for this convoy of human curiosities will become apparent. Thank you for the explanation. Now I will close my eyes and imagine the world of the Magus and the tyrant as they ride their horses over the ice and snow, something we too are about to encounter.

They spent days pushing into a wind that came from the south. It was warmer than the land it crossed and carried with it billows of heavy, wet snowflakes that clung to their furs and blinded them, building skins of burdensome wet ice down their fronts. At night they were too exhausted to talk, crawling into ice shelters made by the Emperor. They were becoming low on rations when suddenly the wind relented, the skies cleared and pockets of green vegetation began to poke through the dissolving whiteness. The Emperor's horse led the pack animal and the roan to shoots of succulence whenever they came across them. That first afternoon of relative warmth saw the Emperor strip off all his clothes and roll in a drift of snow, vigorously rubbing himself all over. The Magus followed suit though it was something he had never done before. The cold handfuls burned him as he rubbed and the blood beneath his skin seemed to flow faster. He was aware of the small insects that had colonised his body under the furs dropping away and he beat his coat to dislodge the remainder. Finally he dressed in cleaner underclothes, pulling fur around him to keep his body heat intact. He had observed the Emperor's torso as he thrashed around in the drift. The man was well muscled and his life as the overlord of the ice people had not softened him. He had a big, animal swiftness with groupings of heavy muscle around his shoulders and thighs. The Magus saw the body of a warrior, no different to his own, though younger.

They were slowly descending from the ice plateau and it was not long before an animal was pinned to the ground by a crossbow dart. The Magus had not fully registered the bow's action, so fast did the Emperor raise and fire. He cooked the red haired creature on his spit, adding herbs and spice which he stuffed into its knife-scored carcass. Once it was bubbling its fats over the heat of the fire he asked to see the crossbow. It was a powerful construction of rods and animal gut which could only be cocked by turning a ratchet, so thick was the string. Once fully tense, the Magus could see that the power released was greater than a pulling arm.

-Best when you can see a man's eyes, said the Emperor, -Longer than that, the dart becomes aimless and a bow such as your own is favoured. Try it. The Magus aimed and shot at a stump of wood in the copse where they rested. The dart embedded itself so deep he could not retrieve it without much gouging and levering. He passed the weapon back.

-It is formidable, he said, -Where is it from?

-From my newest territories in the east. They are an inventive people and we have much to learn from them though they only divulge their secrets when their bodies are wracked in pain. They have small kingdoms but if an Emperor emerges from their loins, they will become a force to be feared. Their languages are many and their rivalries far greater than any I encountered in my birth land. Small payments will have them slaughter their neighbours. Unlike the Magus, he had not donned his furs as yet. They were hanging from a branch and drying there. He sat with his legs wide apart and his hands on this knees, embracing the warmth from the fire, absorbed in the cooking of the meat with his black, angled eyes mirroring the flames and his thin lips curled in his pale ivory features, -You too have some arts from the east. I smell their spices. My cooks have also begun to use them though most of my people prefer our ancient flavours. It is said that even spoiled meat is made fresh by lengthy cooking in their powders.

-They counter the poisons.

Soon they were stripping flesh from bone and chewing their first fresh food for days. The entire carcass became a pile of cream bones and all of these had been chewed and sucked for the last morsels of sustenance. Finally, the warlord donned his furs, -This evening we will rest away from the snow and it will not be too long before we arrive at our first destination. He made his horse ready and the Magus followed suit. They picked their way among the rough rocks, shale and heaps of small boulders that lay strewn at the end of the ice field and it was some time before they were clear and could trot. At last they could hold a conversation, each curious about the other, each seeking to discover where vulnerability or strength might lie.

-You have but one wife? asked the warlord.

-It is so. She is all I need.

-And I let her go! I did not believe my spies when they said you had just the one and would ride to the end of time to be reunited. I have many. I do not even know all their names but as evening draws in I go to my wife-chamber and choose whatever excites me as they are paraded before me. Breasts, eyes, buttocks, arms, legs, lips. It is always the case that a particular charm impresses itself upon me. Sometimes I take several with me for the night, putting the legs of one with the buttocks of another and the breasts and arms of yet others to make a seductive mixture that will stave off sleep until the early hours. He grunted, -Whereas you have a single body before you that is fixed in its charms and faults.

The Magus allowed some time to pass before saying, -It is true that they are fixed as you say but I see no faults, only delight in what is hers alone. He repeated, -She is all I need. This has made me free to pursue the answers to questions I have asked since a child. The constant search for women to share their bodies with you must suffocate other desires. What can be achieved in life if such passions eat daily at your flesh? How can you seek an enlightenment that transcends the greed of the body? Even you, Warlord, who can demand anything you wish, have left behind your kingdom and riches to seek the one thing you can not command, everlasting life. Even then you need me to accompany you. I do not think you will take it with your blade as you have all else.

The Emperor spoke angrily, -Magus, my kingdom and its riches are in here, he tapped his skull, -When we come upon that which I seek, whether it be in a person or a shrine, if it is not given me voluntarily, my sword will make it mine. My road has been built upon the skulls of my enemies. They have been my stepping stones. This will be no different.

The Magus said nothing.

Like spectres, the white furred pair rode into the first village they had encountered upon their path. It was evening when they pulled their horses to a halt beside the long stockade where the villagers gathered to eat. The Emperor strode into the building followed by his companion. The sight of the two tall warriors bending to enter the room created immediate fear and bewilderment and people stumbled towards the rear door.

-Wait! Do you flee your Emperor and the great Magus? roared the warlord, -The first man, woman or child who leaves this room will be left in two pieces by my sword. Immediately all movement stopped. The villagers prostrated themselves, moaning for forgiveness and praising their lord and master, -Food! their overlord snarled and sat himself among them. The Magus moved to one side and stayed quiet. He could see the fear everywhere, so much terror that the villagers would never rise against the tyrant. A stew was brought in bowls for them both, the Emperor in the room's centre on a cushion and the Magus seated with his back to a wall. He saw the Emperor take a pinch of powder from his pouch and sprinkle it upon his broth. A slight scent of dream plant wafted across the room. They ate in complete silence until the royal bowl was empty and then the Emperor snapped, - Prepare a room for me and another for the Magus. I will need a young woman for the night. Untouched. Understand? The best. Anything less and someone dies. If she has a bastard son then your clan will be blessed indeed.

Soon he was being ushered to his place for the night and the Magus to another, a straw and clay hut attached to the long room. He made sure the horses were being well looked after and then retired to his pile of hair blankets and skins. He lay there and as he fell uneasily asleep he fancied he could hear the cries of a girl and the grunts and laughter of the Emperor.

The entire village stood in line as they departed, heads bowed and hands together and pointing to the earth. The Emperor showed no emotion, not even bothering to acknowledge their hospitality, -The girl was hardly better than an ox, he said, -And just about as shapely. She now carries my mark on her cheek so all will know that she has lain with me. It will give her power among her fellows. After that he was silent and they spent the rest of the day without conversation until finally they lay side by side under a makeshift skin cover, pegged to the ground on one side and tied to the branch of a tree on the other. Again it was the Magus who was being questioned.

-Your daughters are both worthy of an Emperor. One is already so tied I am told. Her husband stands between my armies and the south. Is she the equal of the one who accompanied you to my lands?

-In her way.

-Then it will be a great war! Give me the daughter who came with you and I will swear peace. The Emperor's voice was toneless and matter of fact.

-She is not mine to give. She has a husband and wants no other. Even if she was without a mate, I could not prevail upon her to do my bidding. My daughters are not my possessions.

-They should do as they are bid. It is just that you will not exercise a father's privilege.

-Perhaps it is so, said the Magus quietly.

-I am sure of it. Magus, I know what you have written but you cannot have a passive voice in a noisy world. If you do not shout, none will hear. If you do not chastise with a blade none will obey. If you do not impose your will, nothing will be yours. I tell you, everything that lives obeys these laws.

-Then why did you want me to come with you?

-I do not lack vision. We will meet many who will bow to the great Magus and not to me. You are the face of their dreams of peace. Many will not suspect that you harbour one such as I. I will hide in your skirts, ready to leap out and show my fangs and claws and take my prize. And you will do nothing to stop me for you have a debt to settle. The Magus listened to his harshly voiced calculation and again said nothing. He stilled his anger at its source and replaced it with an emptiness that gave no indication of what he might think or do.

-**Did you all** hear that? called the Princess. There was a chorus of acknowledgements from outside. -What do you think of the Emperor? There were hisses and shouts of disgust and anger. Kamil heard Ull's gravelly voice say that he would break the man's neck if they ever met. He was uplifted by the response that these creatures had given. They loved being read to. Such was their capacity for suspension of disbelief, it was as real as anything else they might encounter on this mission for the Princess.

-Well, said the Princess, -We must whisper for they have the ears of hounds! Chaksu says my mother is within a day of the house and has her cousin with her who can follow our journey like a seer. We will not have as much time as I had hoped to bring this enterprise to its fateful end. It seemed as though she was going to say more but after a moment's hesitation, she withdrew into herself, -How do you think my company of creatures is coping with this physical test?

Kamil said, -They are of good spirit. Ull finds riding the hardest.

-His feet and hands are made for sea horses not those of the land, she laughed.

-Maat and Darwishi are tending to him with their potent medications. And me, too! The soreness has nearly gone. Yes, we are all fit and well. It is amusing to watch Zemfira and Timur. They ride with their noses waving this way and that. Then they have little private discussions to confirm whatever metals we are passing by, hidden from the rest of us in the earth.

She patted him on the arm, -They all have their place in the scheme of things. Each will play a part, though they do not yet know what that might be. I am certain they understand that much will be revealed to their benefit as they strive to ensure I succeed in my own intentions. There was a pause that might have become awkward had not Kamil stirred himself to go, -Yes, I am sleepy, good friend. What are the next two cards? I think we will manage them both tomorrow!

He answered instantly, -The Tower and The Star.

-Ruin followed by hope! It seems likely. Tomorrow, we face danger. Kamil did not interject with his usual disclaiming of such a one-sided interpretation. Her certainty about what they might be facing was all his mind could embrace.

Chapter Seventeen

The moment can be stilled, entered and become your ally

The danger foreseen by the Princess was somewhere ahead of them but Kamil did not know whether it was physical such as a mountain hazard or human like marauding bandits or occult like djinn. He had never believed in the latter but his experience of the Red Man had opened his mind to that possibility. And here he was surrounded by half-earthly creatures. They had risen early to leave with the first light and were fed and watered. After two hours of uphill climbing along a small animal path scattered with pellets they arrived on an upturned bowl of land. From its highest point they could see the white jagged outline of mountain peaks before them like the lower jaw of a beast and by turning round, how far they had travelled.

-It is high, called Vatisha in satisfaction.

-I fear it, said Ull.

-If you fear this, then in the next few days you will be frightened indeed, laughed the Princess but her tone was warm and comforting and everyone smiled. The wind was unrelenting, they were very exposed and so they pushed on down the far side and on to a ridge that acted like a bridge between them and the slopes of the nearest mountain. It was a long time before the rearing cliffs above them gave them any shelter. Their faces, hidden in muffling fur, showed only their eyes. But their mounts seemed to be at peace with the world. They were small, long-haired ponies and they put their heads down into the wind and trudged onwards without complaint.

They finally stopped to rest even though they were on a northern slope and there was no sun. But the wind here was little more than a biting breeze. Princess Shahrazad beckoned Kamil to a cleft in the rocks and they ate together, looking down on the other seven who were huddled for warmth and comfort, chewing on their food, silently. When they had had their fill of cold meat and dry bread, the Princess slipped a hand inside her furs and pulled out a small rectangle of fine paper. She spread it on a knee so that Kamil could see it. It appeared to be a map of some kind but not one he had ever seen before. Everywhere there were strange signs, curious lines and small representations. She indicated a black square at its lower end with wavy lines below it, -The house and its lake, she said, intently. Her fingers were spread over it as if it was a musical instrument, each digit feeling its surface and tracing the many paths upon it, -Here is where we are. We have taken an obscure route which will slow us down. My mother will know nothing of it and be more direct. A finger lifted in the middle of a group of symbols revealing a mark, -And this is where we are going, the mountain water, she breathed, quietly. Kamil considered the picture of their trek. There were scatterings of snow and ice around them already so the mountain water would be frozen. Why, therefore, was it their destiny?

The Princess was oblivious of Kamil's focus upon their destination. Her finger denoting where they were now lifted from the map again revealing a curious sign, -This puzzles me, Uncle. I sense it means danger as I told you last night but what form it takes I cannot translate. Kamil had to bend close to see what she was indicating. There were three wavy parallel lines like those denoting the lake beside the house, close together, crossing their path and beside them a tiny, crude face with dots for eyes and an open mouth with a protruding tongue, -It is a face, is it not? But why here, in this desolation? I see no water ahead. Not even a goatherd would venture up here for there is nothing for his animals to feed upon. And look, there are more such obstacles further on.

-Why not ask Chaksu, said Kamil, despite his misgivings about the man.

-I will ask them all, though to draw them into the mystery now is earlier than I would wish. She folded the map and stowed it away again. The pair clambered down towards the upturned faces of their crew massed together in a sea of furs that gave no clue regarding where one creature ended and another began.

-Is Uncle going to read to us? called out Zemfira and Timur, in unison. The Princess began to say that he wasn't but she had a change of mind and turned to Kamil.

-A good idea, I think. We need a little more rest before we face whatever it is that awaits us. She suddenly exclaimed, -Catch me! and threw herself down onto the pile of bodies as though it was a bed, making them all giggle and struggle before forming a nest for her. Kamil went to his horse and gathered his artefacts in their two boxes. He sat with his back to a boulder, placing the silk wrapping on the ground, weighing it on four corners with stones and then adding the tarot cards. He gripped the next chapter in his left hand while preventing its pages from fluttering with his right.

-Why did you not undertake this mission with your army? asked the Magus. They were now in lush grassland that rose and fell under their horses' hooves.

The warlord frowned, -Understand this, Magus, I will go back to my people with the prize won by my own hands as a sole warrior. Then I will be known thereafter by all the world's peoples because I, alone, will have conquered death! The Water God and I will share the same table. I will have surpassed even you, Magus. The less my army sees of these events, the more exalted they will appear to them. I will ride back without escort and everyone who looks upon me will know that I have become part-god. There was a long pause between them until he looked out of the corner of his eyes at the Magus and said in his unemotional voice, -We know there must be an accounting at the end between us. Just you and I. How can I fear it? By then I will have become immortal.

The Magus flexed his shoulders as though in anticipation of those final moments, -If it be so then I am ready.

They had continued their ride without any more conversation about what end might await them. Anyone observing them who did not comprehend the intricate nature of their contract and what had brought it about, might have assumed that a harmony existed between them. They worked as a team, hunting, preparing camp, cooking and seeing to their horses, though the Emperor was cursory with the latter. What they did not do, which was customary for two warriors on such a long mission, was practise their swords upon each other. Each would go off to play with shadows, exercising their movements, their feints and parries, their crouching and leaping, their twists and turns, all in silence and isolation from the other. Neither wished to give any indication of what stratagems he might bring to the battle.

They were approaching their first and, so the Emperor wished, only engagement with a supernatural force that might make him immortal. The momentousness of it filled both their minds for each knew that once the warlord became convinced that he had achieved immortality then he would seek the death of the Magus in order to return alone, in glory, to the Ice Lands. Certain that this entire venture would lead to failure, the Magus pondered on the man's likely reaction when he discovered he was no less mortal than the next man.

All those they now encountered spoke in hushed voices about a recluse in an earth house in the hills. They all wore ribbons of yellow in their belts in homage to him. The people here were the Emperor's subjects, having been conquered by him long ago but were of little value to his empire and were left mostly to their own devices. They were farmers and bore no arms. The tithe they paid to his local governor was no more nor less than they paid to whomsoever controlled their territory and consisted only of an annual offering of grain and meat. They wore long robes and wound cloth around their skulls and painted their faces with lines and dots. The tribe comprised many layers of status from those at their head believed closest to the gods to those who were so humble that all could spit upon them. They believed that the recluse conversed with their deities and could even influence fate, so their very lives might depend upon maintaining his benevolence. Worshippers from their land and beyond paid visits to the sacred soil outside his retreat and left gifts there. A few were permitted to see him. Others prayed on the track leading to his domain, prostrate upon the ground, foreheads touching it and eyes closed. In what manner the shaman took the gifts and where he stored them none knew for audiences with him ended as darkness fell and he let it be known that terrible consequences would befall any visitor, should his privacy be disturbed during the night.

No one suspected that one of the two strangers who rode among them was the Emperor, their overlord but the Magus was a different matter. The two travellers were of equal stature and both carried the bearing of fighting men but there the similarity ended. The beat of the

Emperor's cold heart made people uncertain and fearful and they did not look at him in case it might attract his wrath whereas, in contradiction, the Magus engendered feelings of instant warmth. Calmness radiated from him and everyone who gazed upon him experienced an unusual peace in his presence and the feeling that they would be protected from harm. The stories about him, though they contained descriptions of his physical being and prowess, also told of his inner strength, his wisdom and the hope he gave the poor and the oppressed. The Right Path was widely read by shamans and spread by tongue ever onwards.

It followed that as soon as they appeared among them, everyone was plunged into a terrible conflict. Eyes were drawn to the one and repelled by the other. None could comprehend how two such men might share the same journey. Even if they did not recognise him at first, intuitively they soon knew that they were in the presence of the great Magus. Horrifyingly they also sensed that his shadowy, evil companion was capable of bringing despair and destruction to their lives and land.

☥

Dismounting, the Magus and the Emperor led their horses along the last part of the stony track to the shaman's dwelling. Poles marked the way with small, fluttering yellow ribbons attached to them. Small shrines built from loose stones were set at intervals and these contained the remains of offerings of grain from those too overcome to approach any further. By each shrine sat a monk, shorn of hair and wound about in a plain yellow sheet. These followers did not beg nor did they once relinquish their uniform meditative posture, sitting cross-legged and straight backed, their eyes wide open but unseeing and unblinking, their hands folded on their laps.

When almost upon the place of the recluse there was a stone trough of water for their horses and another for them. A group of bowing monks stood beside them and gestured what they must do. They removed their boots to have their feet and hands washed and then water was sprinkled on their bowed heads. When they were ready, each chose a flat splint from a bowl with an indecipherable symbol burnt upon it. The Magus was told in a whisper that his represented two hundred and the Emperor's three hundred and fifty. They were instructed to bow exactly the number they were given and their prayers would reach their gods. The path led under a crude stone arch made from rocks neatly balanced upon each other with a long boulder placed across the top. Through it they could see pilgrims on their knees, repeatedly bending to the yellow, petal-covered earth to touch it with their foreheads. Beyond them was a rough clay and straw dwelling such as one might build for beasts in winter. The rough hewn wooden door was closed. Monks stood either side of it. They took their places in turn and began bowing despite neither being at ease with it. When they were finished the Magus rose, waiting for his cue from the Emperor who did not stand but changed to sitting, cross-legged.

-I wish to have an audience with the shaman, he said.

-It is not possible, said one of the monks.

-Tell him that the great Magus has come to pay his respects to him.

-It does not matter… the monk's words were halted in mid-flow by unintelligible sounds from a voice inside, -You may enter, retracted the monk, meekly, bowing obediently.

The door creaked open and the Emperor gestured that the Magus enter first. They were in a single room with dry cracked clay walls, a ragged straw ceiling above them, a floor with brightly embroidered yellow cushions and a pitcher of water. Sitting on the earth, ignoring the need for soft support, was an extremely old man, entirely hairless except for a few straggling goat-like hairs clinging to his chin. It did not feel to the disappointed Emperor that his quest would end here. Nor did it to the Magus though his heart opened to the ancient fellow's demeanour, the soft and gentle sun-blackened face, the lively brown eyes, the erect back and the yellow robes and splayed bare toes. They sat before him.

-You are here, said the recluse in a light, amused tone, -You are here at long last. I have waited. All eventually come; emperors, generals, the rich and the poor but today is the day of all days because here I receive both evil and good in their ultimate human forms, one the bringer of endless suffering from the north and the other the bringer of hope for humankind from the west.

-Brave words! murmured the Emperor, coldly, -Be careful old man.

-I have no need. You did not come here for lies and so must allow the truth an entry into your ears. The shaman stared through him as if everything was made visible in the Emperor's heart and mind and then said, -I have lived two hundred years and have seen many like you though none so confirmed in evil. He turned to the Magus, -And you, Magus, were worth my waiting. To have shared breath with you before I die brings me peace and joy. You have begun to braid a rope that will forever join one to another, the hearts of people. Where once there were just vain words, music and dances among god-worshipping tribes, you have settled the ground beneath their feet and shown them a way to seek what is good. You have demonstrated that to take the Right Path is the only way to build a relationship with a god. I have tried to do the same in my limited way here. The shaman laughed delightedly causing the Magus to follow suit but the Emperor was not pleased with their talk.

-Two hundred, you say. I heard reports that you had lived over a thousand years. That was why I came here. I wanted your secret.

-And what did you think the secret would be? asked the shaman, -A potion? A sacrifice? A flame you must walk through? A stream below the earth in which you must bathe? A magical jewel to slip upon your finger? The old man continued, thoughtfully, -There is a secret but even knowing it will not help you. Its heat will crack your body as surely as if it was formed from untutored clay.

-What is it, demanded the Emperor angrily, -Tell me before I draw my blade and put an end to your talking. At these words, the Magus coiled himself to act in the recluse's defence but the old man laughed loudly making him relax again.

-You cannot hurt me with your sword, overlord. If that were possible I would have died before I reached my twentieth year. Try me! The Emperor leapt up and swung his sword at the old man's foot but it impaled itself in the earthen floor. Shocked at missing such an easy target he tried to withdraw it but it seemed to have taken root, -What, no strength in your arm? The shaman smiled, -Settle yourself and I will tell you what you have come to hear. The furious warlord slowly lowered himself on a cushion, eyes narrow, hand on his knife hilt. The Magus followed suit. The old shaman looked at the nearly closed eyes and twisting lips of the tyrant and nodded, -Even if I bring you truths, you may not have the gift of hearing, he said, -But you have brought with you a gift beyond reckoning, he gestured towards the Magus, -So I will try. He paused to emphasise the drama of his first statement, -I am both a thousand years old and also two hundred. The former are true years and the latter are my actual years. Anyone who would have aged beside me - and sadly none have accompanied me for the entirety - would have witnessed my body becoming what you see today. But this is the existence of the flesh. Inside there is a spirit which may age more quickly or more slowly than the vessel which carries it. It can be trained and with dedication and discipline it may allow its bearer to slow time so that much more can be experienced within it. I observed your sword in this inner time, moved my foot and put it back when the sword had passed. You did not see it for you know only the time of the flesh. Unlike you, Warlord, my spirit can extend the boundaries of being so that I am free to seek the kind of knowledge the Magus also desires.

The Emperor again rose to his feet, -Your desire is not my desire. It is a deception of the mind, only. You have nothing of value for me. I am leaving before I take my knife to your throat! He turned away towards the door.

-Do not forget your sword, called the shaman, -You do not need it here but you will need it on your journey to your second destination of despair. He stretched his foot forward and pulled the sword from the floor between his big toe and the next before flicking it, haft first, into the Emperor's hand, -Magus, you are worthy of that name. There has been none greater. I am grateful for the immeasurable time we have spent together.

-None greater? Not even you, old man? snarled the tyrant, not registering the meaningful stress that the shaman had placed on his last words.

-I have only conquered the vagaries of time, replied the Ancient, -Yet I am the only one who has truly benefited from my actions - and a very few who have visited me here. The Magus will bring the seeds of enlightenment to all who live after him.

Kamil looked over his shoulder at the closed eyes of his listeners. Gradually, one by one, they opened them. The profound pleasure of being read to had sent them into a rapture. Inevitably it was the quick-witted Chaksu who spoke first, though he should have remained silent until the Princess opened the dialogue.

-The ruined tower. The others looked at him. They had completely forgotten the nature of the card, -The picture, he went on, -The tower of the gods, falling! I see what Uncle is trying to show in this tale. The Emperor's mission is crumbling. Forces outside him are too great. They will destroy him. The tower represents his earthly body and it will crack just as the shaman told him. There was some slow nodding of heads as they tried to digest his suggestion. Then there was an unbridled shout from one of the miners.

-We love yellow! exclaimed Zemfira, thinking of gold and its power over Timur and herself.

-The shaman could easily have come from my own territories, said Chaksu, ignoring her, -For every village has someone who professes to be a seer like him. They gather their supporters mostly to ease them of their wealth, or if they are true and good priests they may believe they have found the answer to life and wish to have disciples follow them. He turned to Zemfira, smiling, -Most of them wear yellow robes.

The Princess spoke, -The gift of stretching time is a boon indeed. Perhaps we all can find it in ourselves. I have often thought that most of each day is wasted upon matters of no consequence. It is only now, as I face this challenge, that I sense the true nature of being alive. Everything around me seems vibrant and the blood races and the things I must do materialise sharply in my mind. I feel I can achieve so much more in only a little time. Her tone changed to one of reflection, -The tower card seems to me to be my past. It crashes to the ground as I become something else. They listened to her in reverence though they could divine no meaning in what she said. Only Kamil had some small inkling and this might have been fanciful. To have left the court on this mysterious and fanatical mission might well have an outcome that would reduce her past to rubble. And she was doing this with such a fine calculation that whatever it was that she pursued must be accomplished at the moment her mother reached her.

She struggled to rise and willing hands pushed her lightly on to her feet, -It is time to face the first danger. Chaksu, what can you and your friends intimate from this? Be careful, it is fragile. She took the map out again and handed it to be held between them. She showed them where she thought they were and the first apparent barrier to their further progress. Surprisingly, it was Ull who spoke.

-I have seen the sign before. It is a water demon. It has the head of a man and a body of many sprouting arms.

-But where is the water? she asked casting her gaze about.

-It is before us, under the rock, said Ull knowingly, -I can hear it far below but it will rise up to meet us as we climb.

They pressed on as the day became colder. The path turned into a corridor between high rocks which slowly cut deeper and only allowed the passage of a single beast at a time. Ull had taken the lead and now and then he stopped and put the side of his head to the ground. Finally he held a hand up, -We are close. See the tunnel? Their corridor would enter a mouth in the side of the mountain shortly. They prepared torches and moved on cautiously. The cold dry stone on either side was giving way to a slippery silver wetness that shone in the darkness, glistening in the torches' light. They had not gone far when he stopped them again. The passage had widened slightly allowing all but Vatisha to squeeze past their mounts and join him. She remained beside the rear horse, preventing the beasts from bolting backwards. What they saw across their path was a trench of water from wall to wall. It was narrow enough to jump without too much difficulty but there was something ominous about it. On its surface were oily bubbles that caught the light of the torches and slithered this way and that, lapping like animals' tongues on the walls. Ull stared down into the dark mirror and then dropped to his knees and slowly put his head into the water. He pulled back suddenly with a cry of warning, gesturing them to drop back, simultaneously throwing off his furs and boots. Then, like the half-fish he was, he slid head first out of sight leaving only small circles of ripples.

Chapter Eighteen

The strongest will can forge the greatest blindness

They waited and waited, their fears growing but there was no sign of
Ull. The troop of half-humans began showing visible signs of distress.
They could only see the back of the Princess as she stood still looking
down into the forbidding water. Kamil turned, made a placating
gesture with his palms and smiled at them in the light of the flame.
This calmed them a little but all of them continued to stare fixedly,
willing that Ull's head would break the surface of the water. They
waited for the Princess to make a decision. At last she said, resignedly,
- It is long enough. Let us venture on.

With difficulty they crossed the trough. Their horses had to be pulled
to make the little leap, their eyes rolling. Not long after this they
crossed another water channel that was identical. Then, following a
bend in the tunnel, their flares sputtering and casting inconsistent light,
they heard a booming, echoing voice. It was directly ahead.

-Is that Ull? exclaimed Chaksu.

-Ull! the others chorused, -Ull, where are you? Then Ull came into
view, water still cascading from his body. He was sitting on the other
side of the third trench, his webbed feet and calves in the water and
beside him, staring at them through sightless eyes was the giant head
of a water demon with its grey-green hair and its grisly black
protruding tongue. Beside it was Ull's knife, stained with the demon's
black blood.

-Ull, said Princess Shahrazad calmly, -You are not injured?

-No Princess, his reply rumbled, -I am well! Then he laughed in his
characteristic bass crackling way which made everyone's spirits lift.
He stood and helped them and the horses across the final water, picked
up the head and without explanation led them quickly out of the tunnel
into the open air. Here they gathered excitedly around him, helping
him on with his furs, desperate to hear his story.

-Well, Ull? Tell us what happened, said the Princess quietly.

-It is short, he said.

-Make it longer! cried Vatisha, -Like a card-tale from Uncle. They laughed, shivering with fear. Ull, unused to speaking at any length, dropped his head and gathered his wits before looking at them again.

-I put my head in the water and saw the demon coming fast. I dived in and caught him by a limb. He is strong and can capture a horse and its rider with his many arms by jumping clean out of the water. He is fast and can take his victims at each of the three traps, one after another, if the group is many, drowning them swiftly. Each of the troughs is like a sky over his watery home. The thought of it made his listeners recoiled in horror, -He is like me. He stays under for a long time but then he must have air. We fought. We went down down down. It is black as black below and there seems no bottom to it. I kept my grip on a limb and sank with him, dragging him after me. He tried to push fingers into my eyes while I searched for his neck. He always had more arms to stop me. But I am as strong. I cut off every limb as it came. Each started to grow again but not fast enough. He fought and fought, arms around me like thick ropes. Hold him, hold him, I said to myself. Cut cut! He got weak. He wanted to breathe. At last I found his skinny neck and chopped at it. It was hard like old leather. He struggled to free himself but I chopped faster. Then he stopped fighting. I came up for air. My breath was used up. I was faint. I floated for a time until I could climb out. But here I am, alive. Ull held up the head victoriously. The listeners whooped with admiration and clapped but also drew away from the grotesque trophy. -I will bury him in rocks far from the water or he will find his way back too soon. He cannot die. He examined the head, closely, -There are other scars on his neck. Others have done what I have done. One day the rocks will break open and free him again and he will return to his killing waters but it will be beyond our present lives. Ull nodded to them and set off with his conquest dangling at his side.

-Ull is our protector! cried Vatisha.

-Our warrior! added Maat.

-You are all warriors and protectors, said the Princess, softly, -That is why I chose you. They looked at each other in confusion but there was a swelling pride, nonetheless. They had come through this danger together, thanks to Ull. Who might be their next saviour?

*

They were now well above the snow line, clinging together as usual to eat. It was bright and they had found one small windbreak in the rocks that allowed the sun to slip through. There was a united demand for Kamil to read another tale. Ull had been welcomed back with much stroking and patting and knew for the first time what it was like to be everyone's hero. They settled themselves, the Princess indistinguishably just one of them and waited for the first lines of the next episode. Kamil showed them the card and identified it as The Star to intent nods and stares.

-He was lucky I did not take my sword to his neck, complained the Emperor, denying the recluse's power over his blade. -I gained nothing from him. If I had known that he was an imposter we could have saved weeks by going directly into the morning sun. The Magus did not deign to answer and so the usual silence descended upon them, allowing him to cast his mind back over their audience with the shaman. Unlike the Emperor he had found the assignation both rich and fulfilling. He had been elevated by the recluse to an almost mystical plane beyond the presence of his body.

When they entered the shaman's dwelling, the man was standing before them with arms open ready to embrace him. As they came together the ancient one had whispered in his ear, "This is a joyful time for me. You will illuminate your understanding of existence". "And you have much to teach me," he had replied. His eyes had taken in the single room, its walls of dry cracked clay, straw from the roof ragged above them, a floor with brightly embroidered yellow cushions and a pitcher of water. He had still been standing and embracing his host when he also saw him across the chamber, sitting on the earth, ignoring the need for soft support, a gentle faced old man, entirely hairless except for a few straggling goat-like strands clinging to his chin. He saw that the recluse enjoyed two bodies at once! His heart opened to the ancient fellow's demeanour, his sun-blackened face, the lively brown eyes, the erect back and the yellow robes and splayed bare toes. Next he watched as a seemingly identical figure to himself sat with the Emperor while his original self, more spirit and dream-like, continued to be held in the recluse's arms! "Let us talk outside in the hills," said the shaman, letting him go but taking his hand. Immediately they were walking together on soft pale grass and around them were trees, flowers and sky all slightly bleached of colour and wavering as though seen through a fine spray of rain. "Why are you with this terrible creature?" asked the holy man. It took him hours, it seemed, to tell him his story but he ended it by saying, almost fervently, that although he would not have wished it to have come about this way, there was much to be gained from it. The three destinations the warlord had chosen would each present some new illumination to him, he was certain, though none would provide the warlord with the prize he sought. "His prize exists in some form at all three destinations if he only had the eyes," was the old man's reply.

Meanwhile, back in the dwelling, the shaman was saying to his visitors, -You are here. At long last. I have waited. All eventually come; emperors, generals, the rich and the poor but today is the day of all days because here I receive both evil and good in their ultimate human forms, one the bringer of endless suffering from the north and the other the bringer of hope for humankind from the west, -Brave words! had murmured the Emperor, coldly, -Be careful old man.

"Enrich me with your own history," he had asked the recluse as they strolled together and he heard how the man had been born a wandering mystic who had travelled all his life on far off lands and across waters, searching for illumination among seers and witchdoctors, shamans, oracles, priests and even the insane, much as the Emperor had instructed his agents to do. Gradually he had come to realise that everywhere there was a universal longing for a way to be at peace with the awful shortness of life and the eternity of death. This longing led, he was certain, to the institution of gods, djinn, life-takers, paradises, hells; everything that was beyond the immediate flesh and blood. "It has been my experience, too," he had replied. "All my life I have sought answers though not as purposefully as you. My journeys took me where they wished and I learned to discard purposefulness and let the answers come to me, if they would. Yet all that I have experienced has filled me with little more than further questions." He described his life, his great journeys, his meetings with emperors, lords, warriors, seers and ordinary folk. In particular he spoke of his life-taker and how he had discovered his self-deception in imagining that this agent of death existed as an entity outside himself. He had realised that everything that humankind sought beyond the flesh was hidden inside each and everyone. There was nothing without. If this was so then humankind must heed practical laws devised to enforce goodness in their behaviour and rejecting evil. He had begun to construct such laws in the Right Path. "What you have created is already a great achievement," said the holy man, laying a hand on his arm, "My own labour pales by comparison. I searched and could find no answers that satisfied my desire to know. I had no skill in writing but I believed I might discover enough to teach others in the time left to me. This was the beginning of my own right path! I wandered lands where few found sustenance and practised the discipline needed to slow the march of flesh towards death. I learned enough to train others to lengthen their days and transform their beings into vessels that might, over their lengthened lives, add further fragments of illumination. Finally I came here and attracted disciples to me.

In his flesh he heard the shaman say, in reply to the Emperor, -I have no need. You did not come here for lies and so must allow the truth an entry into your ears. He heard him talk of being alive for two hundred and a thousand years, equally. He listened in detachment to the praise being heaped upon his seated self by the shaman, concerning the importance to posterity of the Right Path. He saw the recluse smile and his lips quiver with silent laughter and how this had made him smile too. And he saw that the Emperor was not pleased with their talk. All the while they continued their rarefied communion. The recluse said, "There was another constant in my discoveries. This was that people need dress and rituals to become faithful to their gods. My disciples and I wear yellow for it is the colour of the spirit in each of us and we spend every day following the practices I have been refining to open the doors to understanding. I have composed and collected songs that can be sung about what is beyond this life. Songs about goodness. Songs about love. Songs about going to meet death without fear. And I have devised what food should be eaten, how it should be killed or harvested and when and why, for I learned in the wilderness what can sustain the body and what can sustain the spirit. I also learned what poisons both."

In the dwelling the Emperor's voice was being raised, -Two hundred, you say? I heard reports that you had lived over a thousand years. This is why I have come here. I wanted your secret. He heard the reply of the recluse, -And what did you think the secret would be? A potion? A sacrifice? A flame you must walk through? A stream below the earth in which you must bathe? A magical jewel to slip upon your finger? The old man continued, with persuasive force, -There is a secret but even knowing it will not help you. Its heat will crack your body as surely as if it was formed from untutored clay. This retort by the holy man inflamed the Emperor and it prompted the Emperor's sword attack and the demonstration of the shaman's power. While he watched the battle of wills and felt his body tense itself to protect the shaman before relaxing he found himself back in the dream world where time passed as slowly as the stars moved.

"We have shared our lives," said the recluse, "Each has gained from the other and each is the wiser for it." And it was true! How long had they been together in this state of harmony? Time had stood still. He heard the shaman explain this altered state to the Emperor.

-Unlike you, warlord, my spirit can extend the boundaries of being, so that I am free to search for the kind of knowledge the Magus also seeks.

He saw the Emperor leap to his feet and shout, -This is not what I desire. It is a deception of the mind, only. You have nothing of value for me. I am leaving before I take my knife to your throat! He watched him turn away towards the door and the shaman exhort him not to forget his sword, magically plucking it from the ground with his toes and kicking it into the Emperor's hand.

Then, in both the dream world and in the world of flesh and blood, the recluse said to him, -Magus, you are worthy of that name. There has been none greater. I am grateful for the immeasurable time we have spent together.

They re-entered their bodies as the Emperor stormed out of the straw and clay hut snarling, -None greater? Not even you, Shaman? He had not caught the depth of meaning in the recluse's last phrase.

-I have conquered some of the vagaries of time, had replied the shaman, -But only I have truly benefited and a few of those who have visited me here. The Magus is bringing the seeds of enlightenment to all who live after him.

As the sun continued rising and falling, the two men became ghosts to each other. They rarely spoke save to indicate some act that needed combined effort. The weather was becoming warm and they rode in thin shirts, the pack horse carrying more as they wore less. Sometimes the Emperor was recognised and almost always the Magus but people were never sure of their eyes because together they formed a duality that none could believe. When they stayed in villages the Emperor insisted on his nightly pleasures and the Magus tried to sleep as far from the cries and growls as could be arranged. He did not intervene in the warlord's activities since it did not seem that the chosen females were maltreated beyond a robust satisfying of the Emperor's appetite. It was not behaviour that he felt pardonable but who was he to say? There was gratitude in every village that the Emperor of all these lands might place his seed in the belly of one of their own. He began writing his thoughts on the acts of gratification between men and women.

Yet it was just such a circumstance that nearly brought about conflict between them for a second time, the first being when the Emperor had grown angry with the recluse. They had ridden late into the evening for it was the season when the sun was loth to set. They found a farm with a stout building of logs and straw. There were beasts tethered nearby, a flock of fowl and a growling guard dog. A woman who turned out to be the farmer's wife, came to meet them. Behind her was a girl somewhat between child and adult. They wore long grey cotton dresses and sandals. The girl was like her mother in all other respects, too. Their hair was tied up and pinned with feathers, their skin was dark, their eyes brown and their features surprisingly becoming. With his prescience in matters of conflict the Magus saw immediately that there could be trouble.

-I am your Emperor! Do you know me? The warlord looked down at them both.

-Yes, lord. Their faces displayed fear.

-And do you know this man, too? They looked at the Magus and shook their heads, -We will stay the night. Prepare food. They were seated outside on crude benches with bowls of a heavy meat and corn stew on their laps and loaves of flat bread beside them, when the farmer arrived from tending beasts. He had seen their horses and his face showed his concern and anxiety. He sat opposite them. His wife and daughter returned inside once he had been given his food. The Magus liked the look of him. He was older than his wife with greying hair that was cut as close to the crown as a tool could achieve and he had grown a short beard. He was squarely built with large strong hands and his heavy working boots covered the ends of sacking trousers. His blue shirt was sleeveless and tied with wooden stays and cord. His brown eyes were steady and honest. To the Magus' eye he could have been a farming man from his own valleys.

As soon as they had eaten, the Emperor asked the inevitable question, -How old is your daughter? The farmer knew what was barely disguised in this question.

-Twelve years, Lord.

-Untouched?

-Yes, my Lord.

-Then she will be my pleasure tonight. And I hers. The farmer stared at the Emperor. On his face the Magus could see the distress and anger. How could the Emperor, known everywhere for his terrible acts arrive here, at his isolated dwelling where peace had reigned all of his adult life? If he showed any determination to protect his child, he would be cut down mercilessly and who would then protect her fouled body with him dead? But the alternative was almost as shameful, a pure daughter lost and in her place a corrupted woman, her natural course through life blighted. The farmer's eyes turned to fix on the Magus. Where else was there hope? This stranger was not like the Emperor, he could see that. His face was kindly despite his warrior bearing. The farmer's eyes pleaded for the stranger to intercede. As they did so, the Emperor was not ignorant of what was happening. A thin smile settled on his lips as he watched the Magus closely to see his reaction.

-My Lord, said the Magus, -Let us leave this family to their uncorrupted lives. He chose the word carefully knowing it would anger the Emperor, a tyrant who believed in his own divinity so that to be touched by him in any way should be regarded as a blessing.

-No! The Emperor leaned back but a tension had now taken hold of his limbs, -Our battle to the death is not to be written yet. Until then you are not free to stand between me and fate.

-It is so, said the Magus, -So do not press me to break my unsaid pledge to you. If we are to play out the story you have imagined for us, it cannot rest upon you alone. I have not stood between you and your nightly taking of women to satisfy your lust because those you have used have seen a purpose to it that brings them reward. There is no barter here. These are farmers. Their lives are set upon a path that you should not destroy for the sake of relieving your manhood on a young girl.

Slowly the Emperor rose. The farmer leapt to his feet and ran to his hut, pulling the door to behind him and locking it, his eyes at a peephole. The Emperor drew his sword as slowly as he had risen until it was held before him, pointing towards the Magus, -I could complete my quest without the great Magus! he snarled.

-That is for you to choose. I await your judgment. Not a flicker was there on the face of the Magus nor the tiniest tremor in his body. He was as still as the snake before its prey and the Emperor sensed it. The sword re-entered its sheath.

-We will not stay here. The warlord walked to his horse and mounted it, dragging the packhorse after him. The Magus stood and bowed to the peephole, a hand on his heart in thanks for the farmer's wife's hospitality.

The pile of furs stirred, eyes opened and the Princess sat up, the rest of her company remaining still and pondering on what they had heard, - Show us the card again, Uncle, she demanded. He lifted The Star so that they could all see it, -It is a lucky card for the daughter! The Star of Hope! If it had been the last card, The Tower, her life might have been spoiled forever.

Kamil was amused, -Except that I chose to construct the tales to follow the order of the Arcana. It helped me make sense of the Magus's life.

-I know! But there is a life to them that even you did not fathom when you construed the Tales around them. Can we be sure that one follows the other?

-Like the hen and its egg, called Chaksu, -We all know that there is no answer to which was first. There were noises of thoughtful agreement.

-Ull is our own Magus! murmured Vatisha, stroking his head, -He would not let the water demon swallow us in the depths. I am happy for the daughter. I was not so protected when I was at her age. Her tone suggested pain in her history but no-one asked what it was. Ull, though, squeezed her arm and she dropped her head on to his shoulder.

-We are lucky there is no emperor alive today like that one, said Zemfira, -Because then we would need more than Ull to protect us. We would need another Magus.

-There will come another, said Chaksu, -It is the way of humankind. Good and evil are always at war. The people of these lands are lucky to be here in the reign of the Empress Saibiya and before her, the Emperor Haidar for it has been a time of peace for all. There are no great enemies massing on the borders. All the tribes are happier trading goods than trading violence. But a seed is growing even now and it will bring poisonous blooms but not, we hope, in our time.

-Let us wish that it is as you say Chaksu, said the Princess, -And let us also hope that The Star is our guide. We may need a good omen. The Water Demon is not the last danger on our chosen route, according to the map. Timur lifted his head clear of the mound of pelts.

-Princess? She looked at him with an arch to her eyebrow, -Is this map taken from a djinn? Maps that we have seen have places and tracks upon them but not occult creatures that live and lie in wait. How can that be? The others, even Chaksu, were woken by his enquiry. It was true! Her map showed living danger and not just the fixed hazards of land and water.

She said carefully, -The Water Demon and all else described upon the map are eternally present on this mountain but only if this hidden path is followed. It has been thus since it was first piled high by the gods. It is known to be a sacred mountain though it is home to both good and evil in equal measure. Yet any innocent who climbs it unknowingly will not meet with anything other than the earth and the sky. I will tell you the story of how the map came to be in my hands after we are at the lake on its peak. That will be when I pull back the veil that covers the reason for this adventure. Let us prepare ourselves and press on. She stood and went to Kamil, taking the map from her coat, -Uncle, have you a notion of what may besiege us next? Her finger pointed first to what looked like a symbol for a snowstorm, a demon's face blowing flakes across their path, then traced a number of marks spread like a cloud. They were made of short, fine, valley-shaped lines which bulged slightly at the base. Kamil looked at them closely and then back at her face.

-The first shows wind and snow, does it not? she asked.

He nodded, -As for the second, I know the sign. It is found more and more in map drawings. Stand back. She did so, -Now look there. She stared at the mountain where he pointed and saw a flock of birds crossing its snows. She saw the similarity and nodded in agreement and looked down at the map again.

-I doubt that what is etched here will be as innocent as they, Uncle, or as ignorant of our presence.

Chapter Nineteen

Existence can never be as we imagine it for then there would be no uncertainty

They did not know where to camp. There was white all round and it was covered in a thin crust of ice so that when their horses' hooves trod on it, it crackled and their legs sank above their hocks. They battled on into a fierce, cutting wind with the light fading and no promise of a moon to shine through the thick cloud. If it snowed they would be in even greater trouble. None of them could remember experiencing this cold and this depth of snow before. It was the Princess who could claim the germ of the idea that saved them from greater hardship. The Princes and then Kamil.

-Did not the Emperor build houses in the snow, every night? she gasped.

He had to shout to make himself heard, -It is true. It can be done but when I wrote it I was unable to give detail. I remember reading about it in the Great Library when I was researching the history of the Red Man but did not take much notice of the practicalities. Your father was able to live in the snow for months on his own, I believe. He lived with people who knew no other world than this.

-Then we must teach ourselves quickly how to do it as no cave will present itself here. They were moving into the relentless gale on an upland plateau guided by Chaksu whose inner eye could see where the path lay beneath them. Stray either side and they were immediately half-submerged in drifts. She gestured them all to huddle round her. Above the wind her voice seemed faint, -We must build a shelter.

-But there is nothing to build with, cried Maat.

-There is, it is all around us. We must make snow bricks. In the dimming light they started patting and stamping. It took only moments for swords to appear and they began cutting the packed snow into blocks. With shouts of encouragement to each other and working in pairs they quickly created walls that rose about them. But there was nothing for the roof, nothing but more snow. Then it was Vatisha's turn to become a saviour.

-I know the answer! she screamed. They gathered inside their new walls to listen, freer of the tempest, -I have seen it in the domes of temples when I have climbed them! She knocked down some of the bricks from the wall and then placed them back but this time each brick overhung the one below by a small amount, thus beginning an inward curve. She mimed the curve sweeping over their heads to completion. They understood immediately and Vatisha, Kamil, the Princess and Chaksu took up positions within their shelter, placing the bricks as prescribed while the others made them and brought them. The shelter took shape and seemed as though it would be big enough for all of them but at a certain point bricks began to fall inside from their own weight, pulling others down with them. Even Vatisha was unable to find an answer. This pleasure, for he felt it as such, belonged to Kamil. He recalled clearly a drawing from a book on sacred constructions, the principle of the key stone of an arch. It was only a small step from this to imagining how their snow shelter must be completed. They were now well protected from the wind and could speak without bursting their lungs. They listened to him and then set about cutting bricks that tapered a little. Their work was clumsy and slow but with some of them pressing their backs into the walls to give them support, it allowed the others to add the final courses of bricks from outside, working as quickly as they could. The extreme cold came to their aid for the bricks fused immediately, making it easier to keep the growing dome from breaking up. When the final pieces of shaped snow were pushed into place they jumped about, hugging each other and yelling with laughter. Caught up in the frenzy of achievement they built further walls on to their home to give some shelter to the horses and then fed and haltered them before retiring for the night.

-We can light a torch, said Kamil.

-No, it will bring the roof down, said Zemfira, -The heat will turn it to water.

-Not so, cried Ull, sorrowfully, -It will not do this. They looked at him, confused and worried by his outburst. He was shaking his head and punching his temples, -Building this house has made me remember! My people made such shelters. I remember I was once a child beside a fire in a house like this. I can remember! he moaned out loud, for he saw his mother and sisters and brothers gathered about him, an image that was as painful as it was wonderful.

*

It was eerie under the glassy roof. They had had to make a small hole in it so that the smoke from their torches could be pulled out of their chamber by the howling wind. At first the heat of their fur-covered bodies and the surprising extra warmth of the torches made them heady with the feeling of achievement at overcoming such danger. But then they became affected by Ull's emotion at regaining his memories. It made them stare into the darkness of their own histories, trying to discover what might lurk there.

The Princess did not want this descent into maudlin sadness, -Kamil, she commanded, -I think we are all ready for another of your tales! Read to us while we eat. This drew them out of their reveries and their smiles began to reappear. He showed the next card, The Moon, and his soft, articulate voice began to fill their minds and calm them.

They were now far away from the place of their meeting with the reclusive shaman. They had crossed into an alien land, beyond the territories conquered by the Emperor's hordes. It was a little like the land of the Magus' father-not-of-blood in that it was never cold enough for snow and the people wore loose fitting robes, wide trousers and rope sandals. They sported head coverings of brightly coloured caps with a flap of material at the back to protect their necks. The people here herded, tended orchards for oil and fruit and carried weapons. The travellers did not come across one individual, male or female, beyond childhood who was not armed. This in itself was enough to make the Emperor desist from his normal nightly demands. Nor did they understand the language. Requests for food, shelter and directions were made by gesture and were often met with deep suspicion by those they encountered. Was it any wonder? Both of them had now grown beards, the Magus' almost white and bushy while the Emperor's was longer and like a black horse-tail. Their much mended garments were soiled by travel and faded from frequent washing and beating in rivers and it seemed as though their powerful frames were bursting out of them. They were head and shoulders taller than even the largest of the local people and carried all the trappings of warriors, identifiable anywhere by even the smallest child. The Magus broke a typical long silence between them as they left yet another village with bread, replenished water bags and dried fruit and nuts.

-What if this holy place boasts none who can speak with you? How will you then gain what you wish?

-My agents told me that all the languages of the world are understood there but only if needed. The priestesses know what is in your thoughts. Everything is conducted in a dumb show. I have a rising certainty that this will be the end of our adventure.

-May it prove to be so. Neither looked at the other. The day was already hot, the land was parched and their hooves kicked up little dust clouds. They had taken to wearing the local caps and their horses were now hooded with white veils and their backs with loose white sheets. By drawing in the sand and miming they knew that they must be coming close to the Emperor's second place of hope because those with whom they communicated seemed to understand their request much more readily. From what they could glean they were now on the final road and it would take two more days and nights of cantering and walking. This allowed them the luxury of finding somewhere to stay or setting up camp before the setting sun dropped from sight. The first of these nights found them with other nomads by a pool of water surrounded by fruit trees. A small payment to the local chief gave them a place to erect their tent. The plentiful green fruit being bartered were large and when sliced produced a sweet water which they drank and gave to their horses. The Magus, who had spent some of his life in the desert of his wife's tribe went in search of meat while the Emperor prayed to his god, facing the hardly moving water. They had eaten little flesh for days apart from tasteless dried strips they had managed to persuade villagers to give them. He returned some time later with a writhing bag of large sand grubs and a burrowing creature big enough to afford them one sizeable meal. He turned it on his spit and baked the grubs on a flat stone as his companion looked on, saying nothing. When they had eaten, they lay outside the covering of the canvass, their heads propped on their saddles while the three horses roamed the edge of the water. There were other travellers arriving all the time, setting up tents of all sizes until, by the time it was dark, the entire small lake was surrounded. Most were local traders and journeyers but there was a small caravan of distance travellers who camped in a circle a little way from the water's edge. It was one of this group who strode over to them, purposefully.

-Welcome brothers, he said, in the traditional greeting, -May I join you for a short while?

-It is our pleasure, smiled the Magus but the Emperor remained unmoving, his eyes closed. The stranger looked at them closely in the light afforded by the moon. He pursed his lips and nodded to himself.

-You are the Magus and you are travelling with the Emperor of the Ice Lands. There are stories everywhere about you. Everyone would like to catch sight of you but is fearful of the consequences! He laughed. From what he could discern, the Magus just made out a man in his twenties, confident and educated, curious about the world and a little like he had been at that age. His tongue was from the now conjoined territories of his daughter's husband and the General but the accent was from far to the east of his own valleys, -I think we are like two arrows aimed at the same target, the young man continued, -The shrine over the river of the dead. At this the Emperor raised his head.

-You are going there? he asked, brusquely.

-I am. It is my work. I am a wagon master and guide. I take people where they wish to go, protect them, feed them, entertain them. I have a band of warriors who would die for me - well, for the riches I pay! But they are not the usual mercenaries. I pick them for their good nature and wisdom as much as their skill at arms.

-Wisdom? snorted the Emperor in amusement.

-They can all read and write and so must be wiser than the majority, came the rejoinder. -They carry the writings of the Magus here and abide by the laws of the Right Path.

-Is your work concerned only with holy places? asked the Magus, refusing to appear flattered.

-Not so. It is more common that I take would-be brides to a foreign clan for marriage or craftsmen to far off markets or I attend the dead on their journeys back to the soil of their birth. I am known in all the courts. I have even been to your great fortress, Emperor, accompanying an astrologer who you wished to teach his arts there. You would not have seen me because my work ends at a city's gates.

-How many are you, asked the Magus, curious that this man's company could swear such protection.

-Around twenty. But my men are all skilled in battle, scouting and invisibility. What we cannot overcome we can evade. The man rose, -It would be an honour to accompany you to the underground waters, if you so wish. There are those among us who you might find pleasingly well informed and my men would feel that the fates had shone upon them if the great Magus was our guest.

-Accompany? You want payment, retorted the Emperor.

-Of course not, my Lord. Since we are going the same way, we both will benefit. Tomorrow you may see why. Like all such places, there is an attraction for thieves and robbers. We will be the safer for our union.

-We shall ride with you, said the Emperor, -Now leave us to sleep

The promised encounter with thieves and robbers did not take place the next day, it erupted that very night. As had often happened in the Magus's life, the roan woke them to warn them. Both men were out of the tent and swords were in their hands within an instant. Against the gleam of the moonlit water they could see a group of shadowy men surrounding the three horses. The packhorse was already captured and being forced away. The roan and the Emperor's horse were head to head, moving in a circle and kicking out with their back legs. Two men were already on the ground. Moments later it was all over. Several had run and the Emperor had dispatched the two that were prone. The noise attracted the chief's men who apologised profusely for the criminal abuse of the tradition of hospitality and dragged the bodies away.

-It was time we killed someone, muttered the Emperor, -Now we will be left alone. He returned to his bed and promptly slept. The Magus felt the horses all over for injury and satisfied that they were unharmed, stood for a while at the water's edge. At his feet was a reflection of the moon with its disc clearly showing its light and dark markings but magnified so that it seemed he could walk upon it. The thought amused him. Almost anything seemed possible under her deceptive reign whereas the sun allowed little such duplicity. The death of the two men disturbed him and served to show how apart he and the Emperor were. While he sought to frame justice according to the measuring of acts, for the Emperor death was a universal punishment for any who crossed him, no matter what the degree of injustice he had suffered. As he stood in contemplation, the chief himself approached. He spoke a little of a tongue known to the Magus.

-I give thanks you are well. Bad men.

-My thanks to you, also.

-We take bodies to fire at river of dead.

They joined the caravan as it set off. As predicted by the wagon master, his warriors were overawed but in raptures at the Magus' presence. Each one bowed to him and touched a hand to his heart with eyes full of wonder. They were cursory with the Emperor who affected not to notice but sat on his horse at the edge of proceedings. The commission for the caravan owner was to accompany three elderly devotees of a sect who worshipped oneness in all things. This, they explained to the Magus, meant the land beneath their feet, the skies, the sun, moon and stars, all animals and plants. In their belief everything that existed presented an aspect of the oneness to which they all belonged. They spoke a number of tongues and, as the wagon master had said, were well educated.

They were being taken in a carriage and after the brief conversation as they were setting off it was some time before they were able to continue to talk together. They did this at the first resting place, another halt by water, this time a deeply dug well. They were enthused at meeting the Magus. They had some knowledge of his writing and much of it chimed with their beliefs but like all followers of a creed, they wished to persuade him to extend his thinking to encompass their own which was somewhat like those of his father-not-of-blood. It seemed that they did not eat meat and felt it was sacrilege to kill knowingly even the tiniest creature. The Magus was not persuaded by their arguments for, he said, if all that existed was part of a oneness then surely that permitted all to feed on others whether you were predators, plant eaters or like himself someone who enjoyed both. But they were articulate and endearingly humble men and the Magus found himself much attracted to them.

The second stop for rest allowed him to ask them what they believed might happen after death. The answer was equivocal. Some part of a person's being continued to exist after death, a spark with no memory and this entered new life at its birth and gave it a sacred dimension. After many deaths and births, providing each succeeding life was tuned to acts of greater goodness than the last, it was possible to end the cycle and become part of the oneness which was existence, itself. The answer to his probing that he liked best of all came when he asked them about their gods.

-The matter of a god or gods is not for us to debate. We do not know what each other believes. It is enough to find shared meaning regarding the nature of life itself, was the reply. Wasn't that what he, himself, had come to believe? To aspire to goodness? To combat those base instincts that would have a man kill, rob, rape, speak ill, desire what is another's…. But the proposition that there was a repetition of deaths and births did not appeal to him.

-How do you know that such a cycle exists? was his question.

-When one of us has reached its end, he tells us, -That is it. The last Master of our order to do so lived more than three centuries ago. His final thoughts on the matter are still remembered, "And now I am gone. Through countless lives I have endured the pain of existence but now I am released and at one with all things." He died on uttering those words and his body was burned over sacred flowers whose scent was breathed in by his novices and he appeared afterwards to each one, smiling and beckoning. It replenished their resolve to continue the cycle as he had done, performing the rituals of meditation he had laid down until all might be revealed to them. And we are doing likewise. Each of us has seen many lives but we are not yet half way to enlightenment.

The third meeting between the Magus and the three monks was that evening, after having eaten. The Emperor lay half inside the tent while the Magus sat with them inside their carriage, a battle-worn, veteran warrior among three, white-garbed old men with faces so translucent that the spirit of existence seemed to glow through them.

-Why are you going to the shrine, he asked them.

-It is a place where that which one searches can be found, no matter what god engages your belief. It is here that a great Master, one of the first in our line of teachers, found his final peace and wisdom. He left us with guidance to follow. They chanted together with beatific smiles, "Where you find true emptiness, the search may begin."

Then one patted him on the arm, -For every god-worshipper and those like ourselves who only have interest in the essence of being, this place is holy beyond measure. I came here once as a novice, attending my then Master. There is a cave which some believe leads down to that place of monotony where the souls gather before they are revitalised in the fires of spiritual rebirth and transcend to the wondrous beauty of the land of the gods. There is an oracle which rarely utters its wisdom but each time it has done so, it has never failed the test of truth. There is a river as black as night. Should you submerge your hand, it disappears instantly from sight and when it returns to you it never again feels part of your body. It is said that it becomes separate, forever languishing between death and life. If you wholly submerge in this lifeless water then you may enter the empire of the god of death who might grant you one day each year among the living in exchange for the rest of time as his henchman.

-So you see, it is a shrine which is all things to all men. We do not hearken to any of these occult tales for we believe it to be a place where oneness may be touched more strongly than elsewhere and if you can find true emptiness in your meditation there, you can hasten the cycle to its conclusion and become flooded with the meaning of existence.

-But it is not yet likely for the three of us, laughed one and the other two joined in, merrily.

As they wakened from the dreamy state induced by Kamil's voice, the Princess spoke, intent on keeping their spirits up and not allowing them to return to introspection, -It sounds like a place of powerful forces, this shrine, she said, -Even if the Magus is ill-disposed to be influenced by the three wise men it seems as though something exceptionally eventful will meet him there.

-Is there such a place? asked Vatisha, -I would like to go there if there is. There were muted sounds of agreement, -Who would not? she added wistfully, -The shrine might have answers to questions that have plagued you as long as you can remember.

-And even ones you have yet to consider, suggested Chaksu.

Maat's voice was then raised, -We are going to such a place! The Princess said so. This is a sacred mountain and we are going to uncover its secrets! Her words stopped them in their flow. They waited for Princess Shahrazad to answer.

-I cannot be certain but Maat may be right. We are here to discover answers to questions I have had for a long time and, as Chaksu so wisely said, to ones that I have yet to ask. It will be the same for you.

-Can everlasting life be found in the lake? asked Zemfira, -If it was a metal then we would find it.

-And smelt it and everyone could wear a band of it, added Timur, seriously.

-One thing is certain, Uncle Kamil, said Vatisha, -The Emperor cannot succeed in his quest can he? Evil cannot conquer good. Is that not so?

Kamil presented them with his most impassive face, -That, dear Vatisha, you will have to wait to hear in a future tale! They groaned and shouted that he was teasing them and it was not fair and it was in the middle of the uproar that they were suddenly attacked.

Screeches like the noise of iron wheels skidding on stone erupted over their snowy shelter. They could just hear the horses whinnying pitifully and bucking and rearing above the furious wind. Then something inhuman tried to force a way inside their heads, yammering and wailing. Mute they pressed their hands over their ears, trying to squeeze it out. There were buffets against the ice walls from outside so that splinters cracked and fell upon them. Then there was silence.

-Do not move, ordered the Princess, -They will return. Kamil and I will face them! She twisted her body in the tight space to where the wall was weakest and pushed out some blocks. It was in the lea of the wind. She forced her way through and on to the wide expanse of shadowy whiteness. Kamil struggled behind, grunting and gasping, - Close up the hole! she ordered, -We must keep them safe. He helped her to push back the blocks. Then they stood and faced the night sky. It was undeniable, the marks that they had seen on the map were now transposed into the air beneath a fitful, yellow moon. There must have been a dozen air beasts wheeling to plummet towards them like arrowheads but much bigger than either could have imagined. They seemed as large as they were. Kamil was shaking but somehow straightened his stance next to the Princess, -Stay still! she ordered and raised an arm to point at the attackers while a hand sought his and gripped it. He felt her strength surge into his body. The noise began to build again inside his head, -Block it! she shouted. He knew what she meant. He had experienced this before when her father, the Red Man, had tried to take command of his thoughts. He forced his mind to go blank and pictured Baligha and his children and formed a shield with their images between the Princess and the curving beaks and yellow eyes that rushed down upon them. Just as their talons seemed set to rip them apart the Princess screamed an unearthly curse more occult than any mortal should ever hear and the sound of it echoed for an eternity, rising to a shriek that filled his brain with terror as it left her wide mouth and gleaming teeth and sped towards the demonic shapes. The images of his family faltered and tumbled but they had done what was needed as the awful power of the Princess's spell caught the enemy mid-air in a whirlwind simultaneously tearing each to shreds, their wings, heads and legs whipped away among clouds of feathers. In a bloody instant later they were all gone and Kamil was left leaning upon her with a terrible pain in the hand that she had gripped, his fingers stiff and bloodless.

*

-You vanquished them, Princess!
-Not I, we! Without your added strength and the shield you made, I might never have prevailed. They were not from the natural order but I expected it to be so from the map. Kamil took his weight from her arm and stood under his own strength. On the ground, its quill buried deep

in the crust of snow, was a long black feather. He bent to pluck it but her hand stopped him, -Do not take that thing into our shelter. Like the water demon, it will re-grow. Instead she stamped on it and forced it further into the snow until it was entirely covered, -You see Kamil, why you are with me? You were with my mother through her gravest times. You are like a precious amulet, warding off whatever might seek to do us evil.

A deep but still querulous voice came from inside the house of snow, -Princess, Uncle Kamil, are you both safe? It was Ull's voice and they could tell that he had waited long enough and was about to come out to try and defend them.

-We are well, she called, -Wait! Then she said to Kamil, -Before we enter I feel I must offer you the first of many explanations. She placed a hand on his shoulder, -Uncle, the map. It was left to me by my father. It was hidden in the doll, Walidah, so that no servant nor my mother might find it and destroy it. I discovered it when I removed its head as a wilful child will do. It was when I was first able to talk but I knew in my heart not to say anything. My first act of disobedience towards my mother! It has been my only link with my father other than what I have learned from my mother - and you. Though I have grown to know much more over the last days.

Chapter Twenty

Answers erect barriers to illumination. The way is lit by the unanswerable.

It was dark inside the snow dome but not pitch. The faintest of light filtered in. The Princess and Kamil had given a brief description of the battle with the night creatures before they all went to sleep, exhausted from the fear and panic. But now they were awake again, though it was not yet dawn, and nobody wanted to move until they heard the full story. The Princess took the role of narrator and, Kamil felt, rather overplayed his contribution to their victory. Now, as well as being liked and respected, he was the newest of the saviours among them!

-We were attacked under the moon, said Chaksu after they had digested the full horror of the previous night's events. It was a troubling card. There were nods as they remembered Kamil's reading, -What follows it, Uncle? I hope there are no more terrors in wait for us.

Kamil frowned, -The next card is the Sun and it is usually associated with happiness, it is true. Yet our quest is not over and there is more danger before us if I understand the map. Perhaps we are not yet out from under the moon's influence. He peered up through the hole in the dome, -It is still night for I can see a star.

-Light a torch, commanded the Princess, -And let us see what might be the danger of which Uncle Kamil speaks. She took out the map and spread it on Ull's stomach. Nine pairs of eyes tried to decode the tiny symbols. She showed them where they were now, beyond the three trenches of water and the killers in the night sky. Between them and the lake at the peak of the mountain lay a final barrier, -What do you think, Uncle? Kamil bent down with the torch close. Their further advance was blocked by jagged lines like tiny peaks which appeared to hang above a circular black mark. Above them were random, perpendicular scratches.

-They look like flames, he said, -But what the dark circle is, I know not. Zemfira and Timur stirred, excitedly.

-We have seen it before! exclaimed Timur.

-We use the sign on our maps, too, said Zemfira.

-It is a fire hole, said Timur, -The earth beneath this mountain is alive and breathes flames and disgorges vomit which turns to rock where it lands. Nothing can withstand its heat.

-Then let us prepare ourselves for earth and fire. We have conquered water and air so it will complete our trial by the four elements. She kicked at the walls of snow, re-opening the hole that she and Kamil had crawled through and they tumbled out one by one, -We will eat while we ride. To fulfil our destiny we must encounter whatever sits in wait before the moon leaves the sky. There can be no delays or diversions from its timescale. We are at a point of convergence. My mother is closing fast. We are nearing the peak. The last barrier to overcome is within reach. Her companions did not question how she might know this but they looked around in trepidation. They could see the blush of pink where the sun would soon rise on one side of the sky and the moon hanging high and imperious above, with, Kamil thought, a sour smile upon her face.

*

Timur was leading, followed by Zemfira. It seemed only right since they had some idea of what might lie ahead. The rest, including Kamil and the Princess, had only vague doom-laden pictures and as a consequence felt even greater apprehension. The gold miners were a resolute pair and seemed at home in this land of rearing mountain peaks, ice-scarred cliffs, silvery snow hollows and eruptions of black rock. They had left the flat snow field and the track was taking them through canyons, steepling ever higher. The wind had dropped to sudden gusts and below them, a half day's travel behind, were squalls of snow chasing each other on the lower slopes. Somewhere, hidden by them, was the pursuing pack led by the Empress Sabiya.

Timur raised his hand and they gathered next to him as well as the track would allow, -There is a path without impediment to the peak, he announced, pointing, -But if it is fire we want then we must go this way. Again he gestured, this time at an expanse of dark rock swept clean by the winds, a little less than a cliff and impossible for horses to undertake. As their gaze followed its line upwards they could see an almost invisible plume on its higher reaches, barely changing shape, like steam distorting the blue sky. Above the distortion was the moon.

The Princess attended to her map.

-I can just discern the safe way, she said, staring hard, -But that cannot be our fate. We must encounter this last great hazard to uncover the map's secret and understand why it was left to me. She looked up again at the far-off plume, -We will leave the horses here, feed them well and block their path back. If they wish to join us at the summit, then it is their will.

-How long will it take to complete the task you have set us, Princess? asked Vatisha.

-I hope within the day but we may need another moon. What do you say, Timur? He nodded. The thought made them tremble and they hurried arrangements for their departure. Timur and Zemfira levered a boulder to fall on the path behind them and they packed snow and ice around it. Vatisha removed her furs, handing them to Ull. As the others looked on, she began moving up the rock face, paying out twine behind her and keeping a steady, confident rhythm. Icy breaths attended her exertions. More than half way up, she disappeared from view and soon after there was a tug at the twine. Rope was attached to its end and slowly it, too, rose to the invisible climber. With the help of the rope's security they followed, one by one. Even so it was difficult. Their furs made climbing clumsy and the gusts of wind tried to dislodge them. Ull carried Kamil's boxes in their leather bag, over his shoulder. By the time that they were safe on the ledge she had found, Vatisha had already scaled the next passage of rock. Far to their left, the sun had risen, bloody against the blue, offering little warmth. The moon was dropping towards a lesser mountain peak. The hanging steam was much closer. In three stages they followed Vatisha to the end of the climb and on to another small ice field just below the summit, turned pink by the sun's low rays. Ull threw her furs around Vatisha and hugged her slim form for extra warmth. Though her body was hot, her fingertips were bulging with large, watery blisters and her face was chapped and red. Darwishi treated her with balm while the rest praised her skill and daring. But the reward of ointments, stroking and hugs was short lived as Zemfira pointed across the plateau to where the snow had melted, giving way to bare rock with a haze rising from a vent at its centre. As they watched a single white flame spurted momentarily from the hole together with a faint clap of thunder, before abating.

They approached as near as was safe. The hole was perfectly round, wide enough to swallow a horse and cart and its sides were smooth and shone like metal. Exhausted by the climb and worried by what it might be, they were happy to obey the Princess's gesture to sit. The ground around the vent produced a gentle heat beneath them that had them struggling from their furs as they stared, waiting for it to erupt again.

Princess Shahrazad sat at one end of the line of observers with Kamil, -What do you make of it? she asked.

-It looks like a shaft to the fiery depths, he replied, -Made by god or demon,. But what its purpose might be I cannot guess.

Timur stepped closer and peered into it for a moment before pulling back swiftly, -It is not a shaft, he said, -It is a crucible made from no metal Zemfira and I have encountered. And what is even more strange, he continued gazing along the line of troubled eyes, -Is that there is no fuel at its bottom. No wood. No peat. No coal. No fat. There is nothing to feed its flame. He was silent for a moment, thinking, before adding as an afterthought, -Nor is it any hotter than here.

-I thought the flame was occult, said Chaksu, -No flame can be that white. Nor does it give off smoke. If it does not burn, then what is it? Is there no clue on the map?

Princes Shahrazad produced the square of symbols and the sun made it shine pinkly in her hand, -I cannot see anything - except, she scratched her chin, -There is a dot, just after the fiery hole. I thought it was of no consequence. Who has the best eye, here? They looked at each other.

Then Darwishi said excitedly, -Maat has a doctor's tool that few have in our profession. With it we can observe the smallest detail in wounds and pestilences that cannot be seen with the naked eye. They handed her the map and she took out the magnifying lens.

-A glass! cried the Princess, -My brave courtiers have everything! Tell us what you see, Maat.

Maat held the paper so that it was most illuminated and moved the glass between it and her eye this way and that until she found a point where it was clearest, -It can only have been inscribed using a similar tool, she said, -Unless the maker had powers beyond any human. She studied it and then put the glass down, -Give me your flesh knife, she asked her husband. Darwishi handed her a fine surgeon's blade with a sharp point, -I will make the mark on the rock, here, exactly as it is drawn so you can judge its meaning, she said. Her audience watched, hardly breathing, as she scratched the surface. She drew a hand with a bangle around its wrist which seemed to be emitting fire, in accord with the marks that had been used to depict the flames above the pit. Maat then picked up the map again and examined their final destination., -Look, she said, -There is a repeat of this sign. It lies within the waters of the lake. It is on fire there, too. How can that be possible?

Princess Shahrazad spoke slowly, -This must be why we had to come this way up the mountain. Only by doing so will we arrive at the lake forearmed and able to uncover its secret. As we have seen, the route is guarded by demons and sorcery. My mother is taking the obvious way and will not have trodden anywhere where we have been so assailed. She stood up and faced them defiantly, -I think I know what I must do. Do not intervene. You must be brave and watch me to the end, whatever happens. Do you understand? It is my command. Their heads downcast, they nodded but their anxiety was manifest.

Without further pause, she stripped off all her clothes. Somehow even Kamil was untroubled by her action. It was if they saw her spirit and not her flesh. The tall, coffee-skinned, slimly muscled woman with her mass of red hair walked deliberately and imperiously to the pit, sat on its edge and then dropped inside on to its floor. They could just see a little of her hair blowing in the gusting breeze. There was a pause. No-one breathed. Then, as had happened when they first approached, there was a flash of white flame and the sound that might be made by a clap of thunder far in the distance. It forced gasps and cries from the watching troop but no-one made any move to help her. After what seemed to be an endless wait but measured only a few moments, her hands appeared on the edge and with a lithe swing she stood before them. Again they hardly registered her naked flesh but this time it was because what drew their eyes was the wrist of her right arm. It shone like silver and from it cascaded droplets of light.

*

They were sitting beside the vent, the Princess once again embedded in her nest of fur-covered comrades. She had been dressed by Maat and Vatisha. The bangle of silver had been covered with a winding of silk and all the while she had said nothing, though her face still showed that she had been transfigured by what she had undergone, -It was frightening but exhilarating, she murmured, -How did I know what to do? It was somehow written in my blood. When I stood in the middle of the metal bowl all fear left me. I became at peace as though you, my friends, were comforting me as now. This encouraged them to press even closer, -I shut my eyes and waited. There was a rush up my body like wind, from the soles of my feet to my head, lifting me into the air and a sudden heat burned everywhere inside me, cleansing me. For a moment everything went blank and it felt as though I was suspended in nothingness. Then, out of the darkness appeared my father. He smiled at me and reached out a powerful hand and gripped me by the wrist, - Be brave, blood of mine, he said, -And all will be as you wish. Then he was gone and the emptiness was filled by a surge of energy as I felt alive again and I was able to release myself from the magical pit, my wrist burning strangely but without pain. As she said this, their eyes automatically turned to the crucible and saw it quickly filling with snow. Within seconds it and the rock around it and their places upon the rock, were completely white and no sign was left of the crucible's presence. They could feel the cold in the air once again but it could not seep into their bodies, so heated had they become by the wonder of Princess's tale and the relief at her presence.

-Kamil! commanded the Princess, -See, the moon has left us, she pointed to the sky, -And the sun has sole control. It is time for your next tale. It was the right suggestion judging by the needy faces. Ull presented his leather bag to him.

The Magus found himself liking the young wagon master more and more. He was firm but courteous with everyone yet always sought the humour that lay beneath every situation. He took occasion to praise his men for acts that he considered beyond the call of duty, saw to their illnesses and advised them on their personal problems. He was fair haired, blue-eyed and had a north westerner's pale skin. After one or two attempts to engage the Emperor in conversation he studiously avoided him since the tyrant had now retreated into almost total silence. The Emperor was building up expectations about the outcome of their visit to the shrine and if he was to be disappointed the Magus knew that it was likely there would be an eruption of anger and a desire for vengeance.

-Do you gain spiritual rewards from accompanying your charges to these places? asked the Magus of the wagon master.

-Hardly, was the reply, -We have no time to indulge ourselves. There is always further work. Anyway, it is the old that come in search of help, not the young, unless they are so sickly their parents hope for a miracle. There will be a time when I have only a little life left in me and then I may indulge in the question of what happens beyond the end of my days.

-You will visit this shrine, at that time?

-It has a reputation greater than all but the desert tombs. I will come here or go there.

-Have you a god?

-Not to fill my mind and cause me to follow rituals. There are a few beliefs that jostle loosely in my head so that now and then I think there must be some greater power than we possess. Usually it is to the Sun God that I turn when I am skirmishing with death on the battlefield. I hear myself cry out, 'save me my God!' But, as the battle ceases so does my worship... The wagon master laughed, -I am no different from most. There are few like you Magus who make it a life quest. Or like the Emperor who wishes eternal life. If he finds it, no god can save us! But I am certain that even the sand tombs will thwart him. I have been to every shrine thought to have the eyes and ears of the gods and I always come to the same conclusion.

-What is that?

-If their supplicants have a successful homage it is because of what they bring to a holy place, not what they find there. Few, after an arduous journey to a shrine, want to go back to their land with nothing to show for it. So they imagine the enrichment they have received and tell the world of their fulfilment and thus the reputation of the shrine increases. The wagon master laughed again, -You must think me cynical.

-No, said the Magus, -It is unusual to come across one who speaks as he finds. If I had discovered evidence of a god, I would become a believer over night but I have found none so I must manage with what I have got.

-And that is?

-Three score years or more and a body that is a house for thoughts and feelings. I am trying to make the most of it.

-You are not unlike the three monks I am carrying, though you look younger.

-Closer to them than any god worshipper!

The sea rolled on to the sand to their right and they followed a line of high, hard white rock cliffs to their left. The Magus was in awe of the sea though his time spent upon it or beside it had not been great. Here it was translucently green at the shore turning blue further out. There were no clouds in the sky and the sun made the cliffs difficult to gaze upon, so dazzlingly white did they appear. It would be impossible to find a setting that seemed less occult than this. There was a steady procession of pilgrims walking along the beach towards the holy site and another returning. Beside their route, sellers sat beside their wares. There was everything a traveller might need, including stacks of fruit, elegantly balanced in seductive piles, dried and salted fish, meat, sandals, clothes and baskets. One merchant had erected a rough table on which he had placed carvings in wood, pottery and metal. The artefacts depicted monsters from the land of the dead and gods of every tribe as well as local goddesses of fertility and harvests.

-Carry your god through the portals of the shrine, the man called, -Heap blessings upon yourself and curses upon your enemies. I have every deity here! You, my lord, he singled out the Magus, -Tell me your god and you shall have his sacred resemblance to accompany you inside and protect you from harm.

The Emperor roared in vindictive pleasure, -He has no god. What kind of effigy do you have for him? Can you carve a likeness of nothing?

-No god? The man looked up at the Magus in horror, -Then may fate protect you when you enter the shrine. It is a place for believers, only.

They walked their horses the remaining distance through shallow waters. Set against the cliff and its honeycomb of passageways was a wooden frame made from stripped and bleached tree trunks as big as those used in the Emperor's city. It had massive doors which were swung inwards revealing a dark mouth half-lit by torches. In the entrance sat a bald fat monk, cross-legged in a white loin cloth. Beside him was a heap of gifts donated to his order from those who had come to gain solace within. The wagon master's men took care of the horses, offered alms and announced the arrival of the Emperor and the Magus. They made it plain that the Emperor would not venture inside on his own but that the Magus must accompany him… and that the Emperor carried great wealth. The two giants among men, in their warrior garb, waited for an escort while the three old monks in their white gowns and the wagon master joined the less esteemed worshippers in the queue for entry. The Magus caught the young fellow's eye, quizzically and stood close to him.

-This is an unusual occasion, whispered the young man, out of earshot of the tyrant, cocking an eyebrow, -The most infamous Emperor who has ever lived and the Magus visiting a famous shrine, together. This will be talked about for generations! I sense something memorable is about to happen.

A monk and a priestess hurried out to collect the Emperor and the Magus and they were ushered past the queue. They entered a large antechamber, hewn from the cliff. At its far end were openings to passages, signposted by torches attached to the walls. Each entrance had a monk on sentry duty. Everywhere the walls were green with a sheen of water dripping down them and the ceiling was blackened by the smoke from the flames. The floor had been covered in sand which was constantly being raked by monks. People milled about. As the wagon master had said, they were mostly old, dressed according to tribal customs or religious belief. In the centre of the space more monks gave directions, ushering people to one or other of the corridors. Everyone carried bags of gifts to barter their way to their destinations.

They pushed through the crowd, following the priestess in her black robes, headscarf and veiled face and were led into a wide passage. The Emperor grumbled in a loud voice, -It is said that through the practice of alchemy, immortality can be gained here. I have brought the gold that is needed for the rituals. Yet I do not favour this place. He plainly found the crude damp passages, the press of bodies and the stale air, distasteful.

They were not yet alone. Some worshippers were walking before them, some were coming back. Some chanted softly, some fingered the effigies they had acquired on their way in and others shuffled in silent prayer. Then, at a guarded side passage, the robed figure drew them away from the pilgrims. It was softly lit by regular flames and was much narrower than the main tunnels, sloping downhill. Again sand muffled their tread so that dripping water was all they could hear. The corridor ended in a roughly chiselled stone door. Their guide took out a wooden mallet and beat upon it. An eye appeared at a peephole and then the door slid slowly and noisily into a recess in the wall. They had arrived at an exclusive chamber that offered those with enough wealth, immortality. The door closed behind them.

What they had entered, lit by a hundred torches, was a temple, fashioned through years of constant labour. It had a vaulted ceiling and its walls, cut out of the white rock of the cliffs, reflected the orange and red flickers of the torches. Cloaked figures were moving this way and that. Food and water was brought to a stone table with four wooden stools and they were motioned to sit. Then they were left alone. The Magus absorbed the setting. There were two slabs of polished red stone, serving as dual altar pieces at the central point of the room, less than a pace apart. Their sides were inscribed with symbols of animal sacrifice, copulation, debauchery between demons and humankind, births and deaths, fevered dancing, the resurrection of the dead and the taking of potions. Above them, hanging from the ceiling, were flaming torches. To the Magus it seemed that here were represented those extremes of the human obsession to come to terms with the transiency of life. There was no evidence of the pursuit of goodness, only a submergence in venality. It was in total contradiction to everything in his writings, everything he had come to believe. The walls were bare. On them there was no marking, no decoration to distract from the excesses portrayed on the sacrificial slabs.

-You see the stone tables? asked the Emperor.

-I do.

-I would have some made like that. The carving is of a craftsmanship I have not before seen.

-What is shown is not to my liking.

The Emperor made a wolf smile, -I expect not, Magus. To me it is real. It is what humankind desires but is only within the grasp of kings and emperors! Why else would I want immortality? I have long feared the waning of my mind, my physical powers and desires. I have brought the greatest thinkers, craftsmen and artists to my court to feed me knowledge of what might be possible for me to achieve in a single life. But the lesson is brutal, life does not allow more than a brush with such understanding when what is needed is a thousand such lives and total immersion in the quest. He looked about him, -Four stools and only two of us? Let us eat! He reached a hand to take some bread but at that moment the swish of a long robe stilled him.

The tall, thin figure who entered the temple bounds could have been male or female. There was no hair upon a head or upon a face whose features seemed almost lifeless, without lines or blemishes. The eyes showed no whites and appeared as dark holes in the pale skin. Behind this priest or priestess was a young man, wearing only a cloth around his lower body. He was dark-skinned and black haired and had the look of the local people about him. His eyes were shut yet he seemed to know where he was. The strange pair joined them at the table, saying nothing. The only sounds to break the silence for some time were those of eating. Even the Emperor desisted from raising his eyes from his food. When the table had been emptied, they continued to sit in silence, heads bowed. Finally their host stood. They looked up at him, under his wordless spell. He clapped his hands and immediately cloaked acolytes began floating once again around the room. A long wooden table was brought and placed beyond the end of the slabs. Two stone receptacles were laid upon it. Fires were lit inside them and small platforms of metal were fitted to their rims. Two dishes were positioned over the heat and a liquid was poured into each of them which gave off a harsh odour as it bubbled. The scent from the torches over the altar slabs became more intense as heavy scented herbs were added to their oils, thickening the air to counteract the fumes from the boiling vessels.

When all was as their host wished, they were motioned to rise. The alchemist's hands became cupped and the creature's black orbs looked directly into the Emperor's. Without hesitation the tyrant drew out a bag from his belt and opened it, spilling stones of gold into the waiting palms. They were balanced there for a few moments and then, satisfied as to the weight, they were handed on. The gold was taken on a plate to one of the vessels and slowly, piece after piece was submerged in the fiery liquid. Another acolyte brought a pile of similar sized, grey, shapeless lumps of rock and submerged them in the second spitting dish.. All the lights except those above the red altar stones were doused. Finally, completely satisfied that the scene was ready, the alchemist laid a hand on the young man's shoulder and gestured to one of the slabs. As he approached it his final garment was removed and he mounted it to lie, still blind to the world, upon it. The Emperor's shoulder was touched in turn. Stern and determined, he took off his weapons and belt, removed his clothes and walked purposefully to the second red stone. There he lay and closed his eyes.

The tall, skeletal figure took up a position between the two recumbent bodies, facing the Magus. It placed a hand over the heart of each and began a silent incantation, its lips working and its eyes closed. From somewhere a breathy pulse started up from whispering reed pipes, making it seem as though the room itself had come alive. The breathing instruments grew louder and began to pound in a quickening rhythm, the boiling vessels throwing spurts of gold and grey into the air, the incense thickening and the torches casting bloody reflections over the lying men and the shamanic alchemist who held them by their hearts. Events slowed to a standstill even for the Magus and it was only with a great effort of will that he did not succumb to the heady event before him and close his eyes.

He watched as the alchemist's body began to shake and white saliva bubbled at the being's mouth. He saw the alchemist's eyes open and roll. He saw his hands sink into the chests of the men on the slabs, drawing a heart out of each and he watched the alchemist turn away from him, pressing the young man's heart into the Emperor's body and throwing the Emperor's old heart into a bowl on the table. He saw the alchemist close the hole in the Emperor's chest before he staggered to the boiling vessels, taking a wooden ladle and scooping the liquid that had once been gold and allowing it to fall in molten grey drops. Then he saw him do the same with the other vessel and the ladle now dripped gold.

Slowly the chamber began to quieten, the torches around it were re-lit, the breathy instruments faded to silence and the alchemist came to his senses and turned once again to the two bodies. He put his hand on the forehead of the Emperor, who woke slowly from his deathly state and then, remembering where he was, propped up his head to look across at the young man. The black skin had paled, the limbs were still, the eyes were still unseeing. He was dead. The dark cloaked acolytes returned to take away his body before clearing the table of its gold and base metal. And with them, as they took the last vestiges of the ceremony away, disappeared the alchemist.

They had been led out by their guide and were now in the sunshine, sitting on the sand beside the green waters. The Emperor looked content and calm. He said quietly to the Magus, -I was in two places. I could see myself asleep on the red stone and I could see the priest, if it was a he, follow his rituals! I felt my heart being wrenched away and another, younger and more alive, pressed in its place. A great wave of strength entered me. I saw the miracle of transposition of gold and worthless metal. And I saw that the young man was dead. He looked at the Magus, -Does this mean I have been transfigured as I have so long wished? He saw something in the Magus' eyes that brought a coldness to his breast, -What is it?

-I saw what you saw.

-Yet?

-Another part of me saw something else.

-Explain, Magus.

-I saw through the alchemist's mind as well as my own. He was assuming his mad, possessed state to deceive us. It was all a conjuring trick. My father-not-of-blood showed me many of this nature, as did magicians I met in a circus. The young man is not dead. He has an untouched heart, as you have. The metals were secretly exchanged and did not transmute. It was as clever a deception as any I have seen but the lights, the scented oil and his power of touch conspired to persuade you and the conscious part of me that it was real. But I was saved by my gift of scepticism. He finished speaking and the Emperor's face assumed a look of desperation. At the same instant the wagon master sat down beside them.

-I lost you both, he said, -Too many passages. Too dark. Where did you venture?

-The alchemist who promises eternal life, said the Magus, focused on the contorted features of his companion.

-Ah, the wagon master nodded, enjoying the moment and intent on causing the Emperor further pain, -They say that it is an overwhelming experience that can last until the victim one day realises that his body is ageing as fast as everyone else's. Some have gone back to take revenge but curiously it is said that the alchemist can never be visited twice, no matter how often the passageways are combed. It is also said-

-Enough, screamed the Emperor, erupting in rage and thrusting himself to his feet, -I will prove the deceiver can be found, and he ran into the shrine past the cowering fat sentry, his sword unsheathed.

-What is also said? asked the Magus, showing no emotion at the Emperor's loss of face.

-That the alchemist is the richest man in all the territories, so much gold has he accumulated from his temple of immortality!

The final words of Kamil's reading were no sooner from his lips than they became forgotten in a cacophony of laughter. The alchemist was quickly instituted as the group's new hero, so much hatred did they feel for the Emperor. It was some time before they were inclined to discuss the Tale's significance and by then they were climbing the last severe incline to the lake on the top of the mountain.

Chapter Twenty One

It is for you to judge whether your life has enhanced the greater good

As they climbed, roped again to Vatisha's regular secure mooring points, it was not surprising that the doctors dominated the early discussion of the Tale. Maat and Darwishi had encountered many a similar story of shamanic deceit where they had grown up.

-It is the old medicine, cried Darwishi.

-But it is still found everywhere. Patients are gullible. They will sooner buy a potion from a stranger passing through their land than from someone like us who is always there and tells the truth about what can be done, added Maat passionately, -It is important that a patient believes in the cure but charlatans find it easy to deceive them with their oils from snakes and scorpions and poisonous fruits and roots magically made safe, their powders from wild beasts' horns and their alchemical distillations from metals. The stranger the concoction the more gullible the victim.

Chaksu offered a story of his own, -I saw to it that a shaman was imprisoned for putting a curse on a pregnant woman. He told her she would grow a horned demon in her womb and that her child would gorge upon her entrails, from the inside. She was like to die of fear. I undid the curse by convincing her that the child was strong and healthy and would become a noble merchant and take care of her in her old age. Though a charlatan, the shaman was gifted with enough power to control the thoughts of his victims. With such a man, many things are possible. Kamil agreed, thinking back to how he had been the young Princess's puppet and how, under Chaksu's hypnotic will, he had killed her guard, Murabbi.

Then it was Ull's turn to break into the conversation from the end of the rope where he was seeing to it that no-one would fall any further than his strong webbed hands, -When I was a spectacle in the fairground there were many deceits. People paid to enter and brought their children to stare at us, half-djinn, animals with human bodies, two headed cows, bearded men with women's bodies. One of the fair's

886

biggest attractions was a shaman who cured the insane by removing their hearts like your alchemist, Uncle Kamil and washing them clean in front of the crowds, before replacing them. He used sheep hearts for the trick but had to find fresh ones frequently because they go rotten. I watched him many times from my tank and never saw how he did it.

They continued to yell at the tops of their voices to be audible in the scouring wind. Princess Shahrazad, climbing second to Vatisha was listening with only half an ear. Now and then the silk shifted on her wrist and a glitter broke through to catch her eye. She felt stronger than she could remember and if it wasn't for her friends and maintaining their need to feel they were protecting her, she felt she could have run up the slanted rock face as if it was a series of easy stairs. But she was their pride and joy. They felt they were guarding her even as they were also aware of her powerful nature and secret designs. And it was true to a degree. She needed them, she had searched and found them and what she hoped would transpire in a few hours time would be as life-changing for them as it would be for her. But to tell them what she knew before the very end of this adventure would disrupt their camaraderie and send them skittering back into themselves like frightened children. She had already witnessed a little of it when Ull tearfully remembered his family. Only Kamil knew a little. Dear Uncle, he didn't realise how important he was to her. He had been the only grown male in her childhood, a father, her teacher and friend. Poor fellow, he was torn between her and her mother, the Empress, whom he had sworn always to love and obey, even more than his wife Baligha. But he had sided with Shahrazad, the wilful child, because she needed him more and he had judged that he was being supremely loyal to the Empress by staying at her daughter's side. Who else could offer her that? There was no one.

She overheard more of the discussion below her as it turned to the Tale itself. The gold miners were talking.

-It can't be done, can it Zemfira? said Timur.

-It is not possible, she replied, -Or we would have done it. We have experimented with every substance we have found in the ground. We have discovered much that was not known before. We have smelted new metals and melded them together to make others that none have ever seen but nothing can be transmuted into gold, as the alchemists claim. Nothing! Even the most esteemed and wise members of that

887

brotherhood have failed in their attempts. It is as nonsensical as trying to turn the moon into the sun.

Her thoughts drifted back inside herself and the conversation became indistinct again. The sparkling circlet on her wrist continued to feed her blood, making it bubble excitedly and causing her mind to move swiftly over the pattern of fate to which they were now bound. It was a little like her mother's famous map which weighed up the dangers in her court, instigated by Uncle Kamil; the climb up the mountain, the occult threats from water and air, the magical crucible, the seven half-human creatures who travelled from distant points to be with her, the waiting depths of the lake with its secret locked under the ice, her mother quickly closing the distance between them and the last two Tales of Kamil's third book, written just for her, in its innocent way as supernatural as anything else in her life.

She joined Vatisha at the top of the peak and helped her steady the rope to ease the labour of those below. Here the wind was ferocious and was whipping flakes of ice and snow against their turned backs and the sun shone, making everything blindingly bright. When they were all together, standing braced against the elements, she at last looked down towards the lake. There, exactly as the map had foretold, was a circular, frozen water in a steeply shelving bowl of rock. She let out a long breath and asked Vatisha to lead them down to its surface. It was precipitous. Only when Vatisha was at the bottom was the rope made safe for the others to follow. The wind gradually lessened as they descended and the sun became a little warmer. No-one spoke for fear of breaking the spell that seemed to have taken hold of the Princess. She was smiling, her face radiant with success and anticipation of the last act of her quest.

They trudged like bears out onto the ice, so thick that an army could have camped there, -Let us sit together and be warm, she said and so they did, apprehension in their stomachs. -How long Chaksu, until my mother joins us?

-Not long, he said, his head lolling, his eyes closed, -Less than half a day. They will be here before the sun drops behind the rim. They are climbing the last section and they have our horses with them.

-And how is she?

-She only has pictures of you and another in her mind. She knows fear.

-The other?

-I feel I know him though I have never seen him. He is a giant with red hair like your own.

-Ah! she sighed, -It is nearly time. First we will hear what happens to the Magus and the Emperor when they come to the end of their great journey. If all goes well, Kamil will read his very last Tale when we are all safe, having survived the next hours. Are we ready? Let us cuddle. Once again they found child-like pleasure in the hillock of fur, this time with Kamil joining the Princess at its centre. It seemed like the perfect dream to Princess Shahrazad, here, hidden away from the world on a small platform of ice below a circle of dark rock with a deep blue sky everywhere beyond and the kindly sun trying to feed them its warmth. She had had a brilliant vision of this very moment, including even the book whose second last Tale Uncle Kamil was about to read, all those years ago. Only her mother was missing from that sudden burning picture which had come into her young mind when she had unscrewed the head of Walidah, her mother's doll. There she had found the map - and something else. A single sentence from her dead father. A request. A command. She could not let him down even if the effort ended in her own death.

For weeks the Emperor remained angry. The Emperor remained unfulfilled. Not only were they forced to travel the great distance to his third and final destination whose prize might be - must be - the secret to immortality but they had stayed fruitlessly at the shrine by the sea for two extra days while he wandered the passageways dementedly in search of the alchemist. He discovered that his authority meant nothing inside the honeycomb of rock, no matter how much he threatened with his sword and swore and grasped the throats of monks and acolytes. It had finally exhausted him, his will to punish seeping out of him with his increasing humiliation and the growing desire to escape the noxious corridors with their damp green walls.

Though his rage was entirely the result of his own fanatical determination to discover the secret of life itself, he did not see it that way. Instead he blamed the Magus. Why had he insisted on bringing this half-baked charlatan of a sage with him? What had the man done to aid his quest for the ultimate prize, except anger him constantly with his clever questions and long silences? Why had he to endure the fawning adulation of the Magus at every turn? Now and then he looked across at the ageing warrior, still strong and erect in his saddle and wished him malice - but he could not end it yet. Something brooded inside him, a nagging knowledge that without him, his quest would turn to dust, followed soon enough by his own mortal flesh.

The wagon master had given the Magus detailed instructions on how to reach the territory and discover the exact location of the tombs of the dead. At first they were simple enough, following obvious landmarks and not really needing the sun and stars. This was as it had always been for the Magus, travelling by night or day across unfamiliar terrain, with by-passers' directions and under the map of the heavens. Despite the poisonous presence of his companion, he felt at peace with it.

Movement towards the unknown made him optimistic, as though there was more likelihood of illumination where he had not yet been. But now the journey was more hazardous for they were crossing an endless wasteland of sand, far greater than the one to which his wife and sister had probably returned. Their horses had to be nurtured carefully. Water was sometimes days away. Their throats, despite their silk masks, were perpetually coarse and clogged. Sometimes they could not see the firmament above because of the rolling clouds of sand and had to wait for it to clear. Some way behind them, the Magus had become aware, a small caravan of travellers was following the same route.

They reached the valley that contained the tombs of the dead, almost bereft of water and food. They had just traversed the last ridge to look down on more desolate rolling sand but when their eyes adjusted they could discern, shimmering and never quite vanishing from sight, the familiar trees that always clung to the edge of water. The breeze was in their faces and upon its airborne dust, the horses caught the scent of life. Lifted by it, they broke into a canter and before too long their muzzles were deep in the clear liquid.

There was only one solitary occupant of the water's shore. He was no nomadic herder for he was wearing the robes of yet another religious order, white, cowled so that his features were hidden but instead of the usual rope his belt was of wide black leather and a curved sword was sheathed to it on one hip and a small horn on the other. They sat in shade and drank and waited as was the custom. He studied them for a while and then strode towards them. He carried bread, bowed and broke it into their grateful hands. To this he added dried fruit, taken from a pocket. Then he sat beside them and pulled back his hood. The Emperor saw a typical novice monk, serving yet another lesser god. The Magus saw a face that mixed the features of a fighting man with those of the devout believer, a redoubtable combination. It reminded him of his great friend, the childless General whom he had helped to educate and who had made the Magus's daughter heir to his lands. He had the same earnest expression though his eyes occasionally betrayed the mad shine of a fanatical follower.

It was the Emperor who broke the silence. Unlike the Magus he had not given any sign of thanks for the offering of food. He said, staring intently at the man's face, -We seek the tombs of the dead. They are here?

Putting his hand over his mouth and staring curiously back, the man replied in the general tongue, -Yes, my Lord. That is why I attend this place. They are not far but if you did not know this land from birth, you might not find them in the shifting earth. Here, we do not know them as the tombs of the dead. This is the temple to the God of the Underworld. Only He has the power to erase the prospect of death from the living. I will lead you there.

-You wish a reward, no doubt.

-If my service pleases you the Fellowship would be grateful.

-We shall see, muttered the tyrant and became lost in his own thoughts.

-I know who you are, smiled the man, turning expansively to the Magus, -Days ago we had travellers from the shrine you also visited. You are the Magus! This was a surprise to his listener. He felt that they had travelled as fast as any could have done, making no mistakes and using the moon as well as the sun, yet others had already reached here. Even accepting the delay while the Emperor sought revenge, they must have been hardy travellers, -I hope, the novice continued, -You are as enriched by your visit as we are by your presence.

-It is my wish, also.

-I see that someone also follows you, the man added. This made the Emperor look quickly at the Magus and see no surprise on his face.

-You knew this? he asked.

-Only when we reached the last high point, they are some way behind.

-A half day, said the novice, -I will send a guide back for them when we arrive.

-We do not need company, said the Emperor abruptly.

-Perhaps so, was the reply, -But we make all visitors welcome. We have few for it is a difficult and arduous journey, though fulfilling. For a moment it seemed as though the Emperor would argue but he had learned that those who proclaim their faith were not susceptible to his hostile bullying so he was reduced to lying back and glowering. After they had rested, the novice rose and they followed suit.

Their guide walked ahead, holding the packhorse's rein while they rode slowly behind. Sand billowed about them and their masks which they had washed clean, did little to prevent their occasional choking. When eventually he drew them to a halt in the middle of the desert hillocks and ridges, while clouds and eddies from its surface were being lifted by the breeze, they saw some way ahead, rising from the ground in the brown mists, the sand stone walls of the temple, its base softened and rounded by drifts, its flat roof heavy laden. As they reached it he indicated that they could dismount. Then he took the horn from his belt and blew a long, piercing note. Before them the sloping drift parted and fell away as a heavy wooden door opened inwards. They led their horses forward and the door shut out the desert behind them.

-At least we are not underground, muttered the Emperor, -Or is there a trapdoor to the afterlife here, yet another hole in the earth? The novice said nothing. A short passageway with steps took them up into a chamber. Unlike the shrine by the sea, the thick walls were dressed with blocks of yellow stone, quarried from nearby rocks by the shrine's first worshippers. Light filtered in from cunning slits under the overlapping roof which also kept the sand out. A contrivance of chutes and tubes directed water, piped from a spring down a spiral from a roof tank and into a decorated pool in the middle of the floor. As it did so it made a pleasing medley of sounds. A calming fragrance filled the air. Food and the juice of fruits was brought for them. They sat with their guide and ate properly for the first time for days, listening to the water music. It was a temple of peace and harmony.

Looking about him, even the Emperor was impressed by the effort to build such a place where few ventured and none lived. It made him think of his city fortress. The woven tapestries that hung from the walls, the massive wooden statue of a smiling, warrior god and the pottery with deep green glazes, made it seem like a palace for a living lord, not a shrine to the dead.

-It fills me with calm, he said at last, grudgingly, -It is a place of beauty. Why is it designed so?

-Do you think the door to eternity should be a place of gloom and sorrow? asked the novice with glittering eyes, -Look at God, the Father of Death, he gestured to the statue and put both hands on his breast, -He commands eternity, see how he smiles!

Gold was made to flow from the Emperor's pouch before he was allowed to proceed any further. Then he was taken for questioning and preparation for the rites that would bring him immortality. The Magus was not permitted into the chamber of sanctification. Instead he sat with the novice and asked what the Emperor might be undergoing. The man was not secretive about it. He spoke with the intense pride of an unquestioning devotee, -First he must satisfy the High Priestess that he is ready to become one with God. If she thinks he is an authentic seeker, his body is bathed in potions by handmaidens, unclothed virgins all. He drinks an elixir distilled from the dust of gold and the plant of everlasting emptiness. It brings dreamless sleep and total forgetfulness to him. Then the High Priestess spreads her fingers over his heart, slowing it, until there is no beat and his breath ceases. He is now ready. Verses are sung by the handmaidens to help protect and guide him in his battle to transcend the mortal realm. His body, neither alive nor dead, is carried below the temple and placed on a reed raft which is floated out upon the sacred river that divides this world from the next. Only God can wake him from this state. He will rest there until God decides. If God wills it in his favour, he will reward him by halting forever the march of time. When he wakes his heart will be bursting with joy and he will sing God's name in praise and be released to float to shore far from here where the waters leave the underworld for light and life. Thence he will be carried to the temple of reincarnation and he will regain his memories and know also what he has become. Immortal. Invincible.

The Magus showed no sign of disbelief but asked, -What if your God does not reward him?

-A glorious existence among God's chosen companions in His kingdom awaits him, as long as his body is protected and entombed here in the temple, against the ravages of decay.

-How does He choose those who will receive the gift?

-His will cannot be questioned. All who seek immortal life accept this.

-And the Emperor agreed to these conditions?

-The rites could not begin without such agreement.

-Do many come ashore at the temple of rebirth?

-How can we know? Our work is here.

-What of those whose rafts remain? The novice rose and beckoned the Magus to follow. They descended steps below the temple and, in chambers built and tiled with the same devotion shown in the building above, the novice revealed rows of bodies swaddled entirely in cloth. The Magus had seen the skill before, the coarse weave being soaked in a hardening powder obtained from a soft white rock which, as it dried, formed a thick shell that made the flesh inviolable.

-Their spirits roam in the delights of the Underworld, said the novice, -As long as their flesh remains undisturbed, here.

He did not know what to do next. The novice told him that none knew God's will and so he could not advise him on how long he should wait for the Emperor but he would find a bed for him and there would be meat and drink. At the same time he must not leave the temple, for the commandments forbade anyone entering twice. As soon as the fate of the Emperor was decided he would be informed.

The next morning it was a surprised and happier Magus who found the wagon master eating his morning meal in the main chamber of the temple. They greeted each other warmly.

-You have entered the doors of a second shrine, chided the older man.

-This land is inhospitable. I have visited many times and stayed at the door but I knew you were inside and thought to enter. We were to escort the three old men back to their monastery but a traveller arrived in search of the Emperor, missing your leaving by a day. He looked at the Magus conspiratorially, -I could not turn down his offer so I took my two best men and became his guide and protector to this place! The rest of my men are accompanying the old monks.

-Where is he now?

-When we arrived last night he talked at length with the novices. He wanted to know where the Emperor might be. I do not know what they told him but this morning he asked to be taken to visit the living dead, whatever that means.

-I have been to them, said the Magus, envisioning the wrapped bodies in his mind's eye, -Who is he?

-A northerner from the Ice Lands. He has been following you both since you left those territories. He hardly speaks, just like his Emperor. If you were to ask me to ascertain his purpose, he leant forward and spoke quietly, -All I would say is that he is a hardened warrior, though young, -But whether his mission is for good or ill I know not.

The older man rose, -If he is not a worshipper but a fighting man, then I must keep watch in case his intentions are to harm the Emperor. My promise to protect him has not ended yet. The wagon master followed him to his feet.

-I shall be your shadow. I brought him here. You may need my sword. Without further word the Magus led them along passageways to the steps that fell to the living dead. They began to run as the sounds of fighting echoed suddenly before them. A group of novices faced them with swords drawn, guarding the descent. Whatever was happening below, it had roused the entire brotherhood and they charged at the Magus and the wagon master, exhorting their god and screaming defiance. The pair had no time to do other than defend themselves with just enough room to stand shoulder to shoulder. Their enemy were no ordinary brethren, fighting like trained mercenaries but they had not met men such as these and fell quickly, wounded by carefully directed blows from the Magus or killed by the wagon master's less inhibited blade. Stepping over them the victors strode down the steps to find another bloody battle in progress. There were dead and dying novices filling the corridor and at the other end, the warrior from the land of ice dealing out blow after blow. Behind him, shredded by his blade, were the bandaged corpses of the dead, unbound skulls staring sightlessly, bodies sliced open and issuing a rotting stench that made the stomach retch. Now the brothers had twin enemies, before and behind. Some turned to face the newcomers while others pressed the desecrator of the dead. Their numbers decreased moment by moment until all lay on the stone floor, wounded or worse.

The intruder touched his blade to his forehead and nodded to them, then turned swiftly and took to a further flight of steps down to the underground waters. They were on his heels, still not knowing his intentions. Was he afraid for his Emperor and here to save him from his madness? Or was he an assassin, come to ensure that immortality would never be his prize? The steps led into a broad, dimly lit cavern with a rough stone floor and the black waters of the slow moving river beyond. Their eyes saw instantly a reed raft moored by a long rope, tied to a stake on shore. Another band of sword wielding men was guarding it. On the raft, just visible in the darkness, was the weakly struggling naked body of the Emperor. The northerner's sword took the first charging man's head from his shoulders with a single blow while his two fellow warriors ended resistance from the others and he grasped the end of the rope and faced them.

-He is mine, he growled.

The Magus's sword pointed towards him, -I cannot allow you to harm him. I swore to protect him until he met his destiny.

-I have come for him. He must not return to our lands alive. His time as Emperor is ended. I will take back his head upon my saddle.

-Who are you? A paid assassin? asked the wagon master.

-I am his son, he said, spitting.

The two were dismayed at the hatred in his announcement. The Magus remembered the Emperor's crazed boast of how he had taken the throne by slitting the throat of his sleeping father. This must be the cruel order in those lands. A dynasty steeped in blood. They heard moans from the raft, becoming louder as the Emperor gained awareness. He levered himself up and stared at the apparition pulling on the rope, not seeing either the wagon master or the Magus.

-My son? Am I dead? It cannot be you! The raft drifted closer but it was only held by a fixed loop to a hook at the back of the craft. Frantically the Emperor summoned the strength to unloose it and threw the rope into the water allowing the craft to drift again into the blackness. His heir threw off his jacket, belt and weapons and started removing his boots, his knife between his teeth. The Magus stepped forward to block his path when there was a hiss through the air and an arrow embedded itself in the man's bare neck. He fell forward, past the Magus and into the water. They twisted to one side and tried to locate the archer in the gloom. Above them on the steps stood a tall female in white and gold, fitting another arrow to her bow. The Magus's body bent and straightened and the knife from his belt flew to her chest so that her arrow fell harmlessly into the water. She tottered on the steps, her gown carrying a spreading stain.

The Magus felt a stab of horror in his heart. He had not killed another human being since before the war between the two great empires. And he had never attacked a woman. It was against every letter, every word, every sentence of the Right Path. He raced to her side, pulling his knife from her body and cradling her head on his forearm. She was dying but had some consciousness, -You are the Magus, she whispered, her blood gurgling in her throat, her pupils big.

-Yes.

-It should not have ended this way.

-No. It is wrong beyond forgiveness.

-Why did you kill my men?

-They attacked us.

-As did I. I was blind with hate. That man massacred my soldier monks and defiled and destroyed the bodies of those we are charged to protect. Their spirits have been extinguished for eternity, -Will you -? Her head lolled to one side.

-I will, he replied to her still form, envisioning her dying wish.

It had not happened before in the temple. He wrapped her body in bandages, soaked in cream from pounded white rock and they placed her on an unmoored raft and pushed her towards the centre of the hardly moving current. Each pressed a hand to his heart and waited until the raft disappeared from sight. The wagon master finally turned to him, -What will their god think of this? It is not in accord with their rites.

-She is the last of her faith. She died convinced that her god would take her in his embrace. The work of her faith ends here. Perhaps she will float undisturbed until the end of time, itself. Meanwhile, others will come with their own gods and their own practices and her sect will be forgotten.

The wagon master left in search of the Emperor. He set off with his two warriors following the downward tilt of the sands to find where the waters of the underground river might surface at a temple of reincarnation. Meanwhile, it took some days for the Magus and the handmaidens to treat the wounded. All weapons were removed and burned or thrown into the waters. Most of the novices who had survived and their sisters came to look upon the Magus as someone they might follow. He was a saviour to many of them with his skill at mending their injuries. It also had dawned on them that their god had done nothing to protect her holiness, the High Priestess and many of their comrades. He did not dissuade them, feeling that it was better for them to have his guidance than face the emptiness and desolation of their loss and the indifference of their god. All their lives they had been willing, unquestioning devotees, merely wanting certainty and security in their daily round. He taught them the rudiments of the Right Path and told them about the reclusive shaman who believed much as he did, meanwhile gaining for himself a kind of timeless existence. He convinced them that they should make a pilgrimage to him to see if he would accept them into his fold. When the wagon master returned, he would pay him to lead those who wished it to take the journey to the recluse's place of meditation and training.

He was relieved when he heard the great doors open and a young woman ran to tell him that the search party had arrived. They came into the central chamber, roughened by sand, beard growth on their faces, eyes narrowed from squinting. They were propping up a naked creature covered in a horse's cotton blanket, his hair thick with sand and neglect, his face bloated, his skin chapped and bleeding.

The Emperor was able to talk but only some of what he said made any sense. In the few days since he had disappeared on the raft, all he had swallowed was water from the river and an endless journey in complete blackness. The search party had come upon a herdsman who led them to the only point at which the waters broke the surface, far away from the temple. Here there was another tree edged pool fed from a hole in the rocks on one side and disappearing again into a deep hole on the other. It was a stream, broken free from the river and by great fortune the raft had drifted into it or the Emperor would have died in his small floating dark world. When he had seen light in front of him the raft became stuck and he half-crawled, half-floated out into the sunshine. He was tended by nomads who came and went each day until finally the wagon master arrived. He did not recognise him, his mind in disarray, mixing up the events of his survival.

His rescuers, on the instructions of the Magus, laid him on a soft litter in a small side chamber and he was bathed and given food and water while the Magus stayed by his side. When he was fully calm and had slept a little, he questioned him.

-Do you know who you are?

-Do you? came the reply and the Emperor's eyes narrowed, cunningly.

-I am the Magus. I travelled with you to this land.

-Not so. I am from the kingdom of the Lord of Death.

-This is the temple to that god, said the Magus, gesturing about him.

-It is not! There is no light in the Lord's temple, only darkness and water.

-That is below us. You came here in the search for immortality. You undertook rites led by the High Priestess. Do you remember? It was fruitless. The Emperor stared at him as if he were the mad one, -Do you remember your lands of ice and snow, your great city, your armies and the empire you built?

The Emperor replied in barely audible mutterings, his eyes staring wildly about, -I am an immortal spirit from the kingdom of death. I serve only its Lord. My body is preserved in white rock. There is a place where it is guarded for all time...somewhere..., he tried to picture it. Then his mutterings became mumblings and he fell asleep again. The Magus left him and joined the wagon master.

-I do not think he will ever recover, he said.

-I thought not. The madness is in his bones. He recognises very little around him and remembers even less. What is to be done for him?

The Magus was pensive for a while, -He cannot come with me and he cannot go with you to the shaman. I think he should stay here. I will reward the small band who wish to remain, to care for him. There is no evil in them. If they pledge it they will do it. He can live the rest of his time in the certainty that he has become an immortal spirit in the court of the god of the underworld. And the rest of the world is a better place for what has happened to him.

The fur on the ice, comfortable and content in the sheltered heat of the sun, came to life.

-We have a little time to talk, said the Princess like a teacher, -Who would like to start?

-So the Emperor achieved his immortality, said Chaksu, -But did not know he was mad. The price was high!

-You write well about non-believers for a man of god, Uncle, said Zemfira, -It is hard to comprehend how someone can exist, believing in nothing at all. How do you do it? Should you not be writing to persuade readers that only by believing in God are their souls to be saved?

-I am a believer, replied Kamil, seriously, -But I am also a historian. God is fully capable of understanding the difference. What kind of god would it be that was displeased about stories which show how belief in Him was partially shaped by a man like the Magus, no matter how irreligious he might seem. If God blesses the good then the Magus will be chosen for heaven. I wrote the books to serve the Empress and now her daughter, on the command of the Emperor Haidar. My orders were to show that religions are only dangerous to the empire if they fight over their beliefs. There is more similarity between faiths than differences so long as goodness is a state of being sought by all of them. Emperor Haidar wanted the tribes to understand that all religions were equal in his sight and none was more important than the next.

-The Magus is immortal, said Darwishi, struck by his insight, -Here we are, a thousand or more years later and he is still on our lips! But I did not know there were all these tales about him. I only remember he was a warrior and sage and the Right Path began with him…

-I did know he went to meet the tyrant of the Ice Lands, added Maat, -And prevented war between the lands of the General and the Lord of the Eastern Empire. But I was never taught anything else.

The Princess intervened, -You are right, Uncle Kamil has written a new kind of history for us all. In truth, no-one knows what happened to the Magus beyond his third great journey to the Ice Lands but our esteemed historian has guessed what might have happened next. Is that not so, Uncle? It is the art of making history speak to us.

-Thank you Princess for those kind words. I did as you say. The last we know of the Magus is his visit to the Ice Lands. At that time the Emperor had conquered most of the lands from east to west and was about to extend his boundaries even further. But something happened when the Magus stayed at the Emperor's court, a place of poets and philosophers, artists and craftsmen, sages and scientists. The man was cruel and evil, of that there is no doubt, his reason for drawing great minds to his place was to use the knowledge to further his empire. The Magus was by then a universal symbol of goodness. His writings were read everywhere. Something happened when they met. The Emperor's history ends suddenly, just as does that of the Magus. We do not know whether the Magus returned to his wife and daughter. We do not know how the tyrant met his end and who became emperor after his death and oversaw the gradual destruction of that vast empire. There is nothing in the records or even in the oral histories.

-The Emperor is immortal, too! said Darwishi, continuing in his vein of thought, -Evil can be immortal in memory, just as can goodness.

-I would have written that the Magus slayed the Emperor and returned to live out his days with his family, rumbled Ull, -I do not know where you find such strange tales in your head, Uncle. They all laughed boisterously and began offering different stories that Kamil might have written. Glancing up at the sun, the Princess finally stopped them.

-How long until my mother arrives, Chaksu? She paused while he arranged his mind.

-She is nearly here.

-It is time. The Princess clambered to her feet, -Timur and Zemfira, look below us. Can you sense gold? They stood and focused their gifts upon the bed below the water and ice. They walked this way and that and then pointed below.

-It is here, said Timur.

-It is small and already separated from the rock, said Zemfira.

-Sit in a circle, dear friends, ordered the Princess Shahrazad, -As large as you can with your fingers just touching. Slowly they did so, above the submerged gold, their excitement subsiding and the cold apprehension returning to their bellies. The Princess stood in the centre and once again undressed just as she had done for her entry into the crucible. Only Kamil carefully averted his eyes from her naked form, focusing on the circle of light that shone like a constellation of stars on her wrist. The rest looked at her in her entirety, the incandescent flame of hair, the tall, slim girl-woman with sandalwood skin, luminous blue eyes and with the bracelet that shimmered, -Uncle will tell you what you must do, she said to them gravely, -Follow his commands. Do not question them. Purpose flowed through Kamil's body. He was alert and ready, prepared to do what was needed. The rest stared from him to the Princess, hardly knowing what this might mean and watched as she knelt upon the ice. With her glittering arm she described a circle upon it, with her at its centre, her fingers lightly scoring the surface. At once it began to steam and as the circle became complete, it gave way and she sank swiftly into the depths below.

Her mother, the Empress Sabiya, had just surmounted the ridge of rock above them in time to see her daughter disappear. It seemed as though nothing could move. Everything and everyone was part of a frozen tableau. They waited, the circle of fur-clad followers, the Empress now standing framed among suspended flakes of snow as bubbles of air floated to the surface of the newly born pool of water. They waited as the sun slipped further towards the rim of the bowl of rock above them. They waited immobile for the commands that Kamil would give them. They waited without anxiety or fear.

The first command entered Kamil's head, -Ull, he called, -You! The webbed man pictured immediately what he must do, threw off his clothes and slipped without a ripple into the water, -Maat and Darwishi, prepare! The doctors moved swiftly, laying a bed of furs ready with their bags of medicines, -Vatisha, bring the Empress! The young woman scaled the rope to the Princess's mother who was waiting to descend and began helping her down, -Chaksu? Tell me! requested Kamil of the glazed and shaking seer.

-She is lying far below on her back on the lake bed but Ull is reaching her. He is lifting her. Make ready!

They waited and waited and then everything happened at the same time. The Empress Sabiya reached them, striding across the ice as the waters foamed in the small pool and the heads of Ull and the Princess broke the surface. Hands took her and laid her on the waiting bed, her fingers clutching a small solid sphere of gold to her breast while others dragged Ull out and on to the ice where he lay, gasping, furs wrapping him. The Empress dropped to her knees and took her daughter's head on her lap, stroking her red hair. Darwishi rubbed her body all over with fiery creams that made the flesh heat while Maat covered her mouth with her own and breathed life into her. Her eyes began to flutter and the fingers around the sphere twitched and then gripped it more tightly, the wrist circlet still glittering.

Her eyes opened, -Mother, she smiled with sly contentment, as she always did after she rebelled.

-Shahrazad! replied the Empress, impassively, seemingly unperturbed by her daughter's behaviour.

*

The Princess recovered quickly but refused to talk about what had happened under the ice. This would come later. Instead, she assembled them for the climb out of the rock bowl. Her manner was so precise and so full of certainty that no-one hesitated for a moment, not even the Empress. They reached the lip one by one and waited for her. She had insisted on bringing up the rear. The screaming wind buffeted them again and hard snow stung their exposed skin. Below them to one side was the Empress's cohort of guards led by Raashid. The Princess pointed another way to the route by which they had come. Vatisha again led the descent as each one moved slowly backwards, clinging to the rope. Ull was below the Empress, allowing her to use his broad shoulders for occasional support. At last all were again together on the small plateau of hard packed snow, collected around the spot where the crucible had appeared. As they stood Princess Shahrazad undressed and then held up the sphere and the circle of snow began to melt once more. The Empress watched as the strange metal vessel appeared in the ground, showing no surprise. This was Shahrazad's sorcery and she had been aware of it even as she grew inside her belly.

Once it was fully formed, the first pure white flame spurted high into the air and then died. All watched, spellbound, as she massaged the bracelet of lights down her wrist and off her hand and then positioned the sphere inside it. Immediately they seemed to attract each other and become fixed together. The Princess slid into the crucible, her red hair showing above its rim. She let the sphere and bracelet go and they hung, floating, beside her at the centre of the crucible. The golden sphere seemed to become ever more luminous, the bracelet almost blinding like a tiny sun surrounded by an aurora of silver. Then she climbed out to be wrapped in warmth and joined the silent observers. Time seemed to drift until a second flare of white flame pulsed into the air. It embraced the golden sphere and its ring of light and as it did it was transformed into a myriad colours that shimmered in a rainbow column that stretched up to the heavens. Then, as instantly as it appeared, it was doused. The land returned to how it had been. Snow re-covered the earth at their feet and the crucible quickly filled up until everywhere was level and white, except where it had been, resting on the snow, was a small solid sphere of plain grey metal.

Chapter Twenty Two

You face your end alone. Are you prepared for this, the ultimate moment of your life?

They met with Raashid and his men and their horses and took the speedier route down the mountain. All the while the Princess spoke little. She and her mother rode side by side, separate from the rest. Kamil rode on his own, his mind constantly turning over events. Vatisha and Ull rode together and Chaksu accompanied Raashid and regaled him with occult tales from his exotic life story. They stopped for camp and Raashid sent a couple of guards galloping ahead so that the house by the lake was ready the next morning in time for their arrival. It was good to be back. It seemed the safest place in the world. The Princess commanded everyone to relax and enjoy each other's company but they would meet together that evening in the courtyard for two events. There they would eat and drink and thank the gods for their safe return and they would hear Kamil's final Tale from the third book of the Magus' adventures. Everyone cheered. Finally she would unveil the mystery behind their journey together and they would finally know why all these strange events had come about. There was no cheering now, only a general nodding of serious satisfaction. As soon as she had made the announcement she disappeared for the rest of the day with her mother.

*

The servants ran to everyone with the order for them to gather. A big table had been prepared in the courtyard. Even as they were seating themselves on the benches, more and more food and drink were being brought to it. Torches were already lit and hung on the walls. They had all managed to find or borrow clothes befitting a celebratory feast so they made a colourful assembly far removed from the uniform brown furs of the last few days.

The Empress and her daughter came out from the house and

everyone stood, as much in awe as in respect. The Empress wore a full gold gown to her gold sandals and a narrow gold tiara on her tied up hair which made her skin blacker than seemed possible. At her side was Princess Shahrazad whom no-one had ever seen in anything other than boys' and young men's clothes, not even Kamil who had watched her grow from a baby. Her gown was cut like her mother's but it took everyone back to those final moments at the crucible. Every imaginable colour shimmered and wavered upon it and its edgings of silver sparkled in contrast to the glittering gold of her mother's. Her red hair was combed and plaited tight on her head, forming a bun at the back, pierced by an ornamental silver dagger. She carried a velvet pouch in the cupped palm of a hand and placed it on the table in front of her. The Empress and her daughter bowed to their guests and all sat. Then the Empress Sabiya rose again with a glass in her hand. There was immediate silence.

-I would like to drink a toast, said the Empress, -To my daughter the Princess Shahrazad, to Kamil whose loyalty is beyond measure, to the seven mysterious travellers who also accompanied her at her time of greatest need, to Raashid who did his best to protect everyone and to others who may have given of themselves but who cannot be here with us. My thanks to you all. What you have done is beyond repayment. She drank. With bows they, too, stood and drank the toast. The traditional formality over, they sat and began eating and talking boisterously.

When their hunger had abated, the Princess banged on the table, - Friends, what shall we do now?

-The Tale, the final Tale! they all called out, laughing.

-Yes, the Tale! she shouted. -Come Kamil, complete the story of the Magus

Kamil stood up and bowed to much applause. In truth he felt like a young man again, having spent so much time with them and having been through so much. He smiled benignly around, bowed to the Empress and the Princess and arranged his cards and the last chapter of his Tales before him.

-First, I must ask you all something, he said, -What was our last card? I am talking about the card I showed as we sat together on the ice and waited for the Princess to encounter her destiny at the bottom of the lake! They looked at each other, puzzled.

-You did not show it to us! called out Chaksu. He stood up, -Let me picture the pack. He closed his eyes and saw the cards fanned out by Kamil. -Next to the end was a card depicting an angel presiding over naked people coming out of the ground. I know it! he said, opening his eyes, -It is the Day of Judgment! Kamil clapped his hands in admiration and showed the card. There were cheers for Chaksu who sat, pleased with his endeavours as their minds recaptured the Emperor's last attempt to gain immortality. Darwishi summed up their thoughts.

-He was judged. His reward was madness. There was agreement from everyone. No-one, not even the Princess chose this time to connect the card to her own adventure. But what of the Magus? They leaned forward and became silent as Kamil prepared to read the last Tale. First, with a wry smile, he held up the last card.

-What is this card? he asked.

-The World, came a strong, firm voice. They turned and saw Empress Sabiya, smiling, -I have seen it twice already, she said, -It brings harmony and peace.

He said goodbye to the Emperor and the small band of novices and handmaidens who were to look after him. They were standing together in the main chamber of the temple. The once mighty tyrant did not understand, staring in puzzlement at the Magus's deep bow, hand on heart. He turned away and asked plaintively if someone would take him back to the temple of the underworld. This place was too light and unholy.

For all of that day the Magus travelled with the wagon master and the rest of the novices and handmaidens. But then, the next morning, they too parted as he struck out on his long journey back towards the desert lands of his wife, where she and his daughter would be waiting. The roan was not so strong now so they walked slowly across the sands, following the stars at night and the sun by day. Meanwhile, his thoughts criss-crossed the events of his life, great and small and it was borne home to him how much he had changed since leaving the valleys of his early years with his father-not-of-blood. He could not alter anything though he had done many things which he now found distressingly unacceptable. His last, terrible killing of the High Priestess, an ubearable scar that would never leave him, contained within it the same great lesson. No matter how disciplined you are in following the path of goodness, you exist among humankind and the force of other's trajectories through life will combine to try to force you off course. As the Spice Merchants had told him, purpose is not yours alone, it must vie and combine with those of everyone you meet. It must become the purpose of purposes.

They reached the edge of the wastes at last and rested awhile in greenery with plentiful water and game. The roan did not eat but stood close to him, whether he was sitting or sleeping, its muzzle grey, its eyes touched with a growing mistiness.

When they stopped in a remote but beautiful valley some nights later, it left him. He did not follow it. The roan did not question its end but went alone, without disquiet, to attend to that moment when its eyes would close for the last time.

He was now an island unto himself in a way he had never felt before, even during those weeks of solitude in self-imposed exile from men. There was no foal this time to take the roan's place. He was still an eternity from his wife and daughters. He had taken this last journey knowing he may never see them again. Did he have any desire to do so? He remembered the encounters with his brown-robed life-taker and the foretelling of this very time.

He slept peacefully and in the morning looked around. There was a perfection here. He had his tools, his traps, his dried plants from the east and his medicines. As for his weapons, he did not need them? With relief he buried all except his throwing knife which had its peaceful uses. That was it. Now he had time to remember, time to consider, time to wonder at his acts of kindness, his premeditated and unpremeditated crimes and his hardly changing, very human ignorance. Then, soon, like the roan, he would know what must come next and he would be prepared. How long it would take his assassin to find him had become meaningless. Time was his to command. He could stretch every second to become a minute and every day to become a week.

He began by beating reeds in water, then drying and bleaching the mulch in the sun to make his parchments, trapping a bird for its feathers to make quills and taking out a small pot of black dye that had been carefully stored in a bag, given to him so long ago by the Spice Twins.

The shortness of the final Tale took their breath away. It challenged their hopes and expectations, for the destiny of the Magus had been simmering below the surface of their thoughts. Kamil put down the last sheet and his eyes roved around the table. He saw confusion and even a little resentment. It was his little friend, Vatisha, who spoke.

-Your Majesties, she bowed, -If I may speak to Uncle Kamil? Both smiled and gestured that she or anyone else could speak. -Why does the Tale not bring the Magus home safe? Does he not deserve it? It was the question on all their lips, stemming from their own deep unrequited desire for a home where their families lived, their mothers and fathers and brothers and sisters waited. They had all been estranged from birth whether they had been brought up by loving foster parents or not. They wanted that feeling of hope to course through their veins. Now the roan and his line were dead and the Magus had chosen a final isolation from the world. They watched sadly as Kamil prepared to answer.

-He is home, he said and went silent, waiting for it to sink in, -But it is a different conception of home. That made them sadder. They looked around at each other and the ache only increased. Kamil was unwilling to say more but his dilemma was ended when the Princess stood and held her arms out, palm upwards. He sat.

-It is not the time to discuss this last Tale. It must hang with the rest of the book in our minds as good stories should. Then, when we have assimilated its import we can talk with Uncle Kamil about his intentions. No, now is the time for my own tale - and also, yours! Settle yourselves, it is not a simple story. Her words had the desired effect. They turned their eyes her way and became motionless.

*

-My story begins when I was two years old. Though I was so young I saw that I was not fully like my mother. Shahrazad touched the Empress's shoulder, -I had red hair and my skin was lighter. One day I was playing with a doll we call Walidah. She had been my mother's doll before me. A strange sensation came over me and I started to twist its head. How did I know that this was possible? It was the beginning of many such acts of wilfulness that suddenly commandeered my mind. Anyway, the doll's head unscrewed completely and my little fingers felt inside. They touched rolled up paper first. It was the map

911

that guided us to the little lake on the sacred mountain. There was indrawn breath from her listeners, -I shook the doll upside down but there seemed to be nothing else there. Yet I was stubborn, even then! Her mother smiled, -I forced my fingers to the very depths and found a scrap of paper stuck with a touch of glue. I pulled it out. I was too young to read it but there were words in a single sentence. My little mind somehow knew that these hidden treasures were for me alone. I put them back and never forgot about them. Meanwhile I grew older and was taught well by Uncle Kamil. I learned to read and write. He took me to the Great Library and showed me how to find stories and pictures and writings about every subject to which I became attracted.

By now I had learned who my father was though even my mother did not tell me what I really wanted to know. He was a wild, red haired and bearded stranger who arrived at court. It was much later that I discovered that he had taken my mother's body by force and put the entire court under his spell. Again there was shock on their faces. They looked at the Empress but she did not flicker an eyelid. -It seemed he was evil and I was tormented by the thought that I was the born of him. For many days, when Uncle Kamil was not present, I searched the Great Library. Finally, in a locked drawer in an anteroom, I found notes made by him. They contained all that was known about the Red Man, my father. It was Kamil's turn to look horrified. He had never suspected that his private writings had been uncovered, certainly not by the child Princess! -As you can imagine, I learned them by heart and so knew as much about the Red Man as anyone alive. I was nine years old but already I could think like an adult even if much of me was still a little girl. It was a true gift. It was then that I went back to the secrets hidden in Walidah. I remember feeling that the moment was right to read what was inside. I also knew with certainty that these messages were left me by my father.

I took out the map and it seemed alive in my hands. My fingers felt it stir beneath them. I located the mountain to which it referred but that was all I was able to do. It was trying to communicate with me but I did not understand its meaning. Next I drew out the slip of paper. It was a strangely terrifying moment to receive words from a long dead father who had raped my mother and caused destruction wherever he had gone. Yet I was his daughter and did not want to believe he could be so evil. I looked at myself and thought that I was not a bad person and if all was true about him, shouldn't I share and feel his demonic urges? What he wrote upon that piece of paper was this. She paused and looked round, heightening the drama:

Free me, daughter, free us all.

The request from my father never left my conscious thought from that moment until the events of the last days. I did not know what it meant but it gave me hope. It was a plea from the grave. I was convinced that whatever he had done, it was because he had no choice. I pored over Uncle's notes with even greater determination. I found the books, the scrolls and the inscribed tablets that he alluded to and re-read them, wondering if he had missed anything. I plagued my mother to tell me everything she knew about him and slowly I began to build a strange new picture, not of an evil man but of a tormented half-djinn, half-human who had been cursed to endure a cycle of living and dying, causing pain and suffering, despite himself, until the end of time. How had it begun? I know not. But there are clues, suggestions, vague allusions, stories twisted by time. They involve a world at the very beginnings of humankind. In it he may have been twinned with a sister. Perhaps they dishonoured or angered the gods. And so a curse may have condemned them to seek each other's destruction for, as I now believe, each time one of them came close to ending the terrible cycle, the other wrecked their hopes. Such was the spell.

Princess Shahrazad stopped and sipped wine. No one moved. They were drawn into her blue eyes and hypnotised by them.

-Now, aged ten, I began to have visions. I discovered that sometimes when my mind was calm and empty, by holding the slip of paper or the map, I could hear him. Not much. Words, fragments of sentences. I wrote them all down. It was painfully slow and it was not until I was twelve that I felt I knew enough of what I must do. What were in the visions? Well, dear friends, I saw each one of you! I saw you wherever you lived as clear as you are to me in this courtyard. I sent my spies out to find you and observe you. I made a map with each of you on it. I planted thoughts in your minds that when I sent for you, you must come. You see, I share this gift with Chaksu, though I use it sparingly, feeling that to exploit it would lead me into a darkness I may not be able to leave. Meanwhile, I foresaw the journey to the mountain and

913

knew what must happen upon it, though I could not read the dangers in the waters and the air. All the while I felt that I might burn up, that my soul would be extinguished by forces which did not want me to succeed. I had frightening nightmares and desires came into my mind urging me to commit awful deeds. I kept that world of evil to myself and often warded it off by listening to Uncle Kamil's Tales, Tales that I had asked him to write long before, knowing I would need them to protect me.

Finally, when all was ready, I sent for the seven of you in turn, beginning with Ull who was furthest away, my visions telling me that you would arrive at this house below the mountain within days of each other. The last to come were Maat and Darwishi who, because of their profession and constant contact with disease and death, were harder to draw to me. They were not so susceptible to the occult. I had to send Kamil for them with Murabbi, that tolerated snake in my bosom, except dear Uncle it was I, not Chaksu, who entered Murabbi's mind and commanded him to let your knife enter him. Only by having confirmation of the death of Murabbi would our doctors believe there was no threat to them. Even with his death, wicked Murabbi had an important part to play in the scheme of things. Kamil's head bowed to cover his distress, wiping tears from his cheeks, -Since I was a young child, Uncle Kamil, I have been able to enter your thoughts at will leaving no trace of my visit. Yet another gift from my father.

The Princess waited for him to compose himself again and then reassured him, -I could not have done this without you, Uncle Kamil, be certain of that. You have been at my very core. She turned again to face them all. -So now everything was in place. You were all here. My mother knew that I had planned to do something that might end in my death and that it involved my father but she also knew that only by my succeeding would there be a lifetime of peace and love between us. She could not intervene but she was determined to be there for the final act and I wished it, too. The rest you know but only in part. You saw me in the charmed metal bowl gain my amulet of pure light and then disappear under the waters to find and bring back the golden orb. You saw me return to the crucible and with what results. And here is what is left of that final act. She picked up the velvet pouch and weighed it in her hand.

-The gold orb had been transmuted and in its place in the snow was left another sphere, identical in size but of the same metal as comprised the crucible. This afternoon I prevailed upon our two friends, Timur and Zemfira to work their skills for me. All eyes gazed in momentary adoration on the embarrassed pair. -I had them make these gifts with a conjunction of that timeless metal sorcery, together with gold melted down from a locket and necklace given to my mother by my father, and then passed on to me. She untied the neck of the bag and rolled out eight rings of matt grey metal with spirals of gold insinuated into them, whirring softly as they spun and settled on the table top. She gathered them in her hands and walked round the table giving one to each of the travellers and holding up her own, -Are you ready? she asked, -Let us place them on our fingers. All did so. Each ring fitted its owner perfectly. Then, slowly, the rings began to glow with a deep silver and banded gold lustre. As they did so their owners experienced a feeling of all pervading contentment, warmth and belonging for the first time in their lives. They smiled uncertainly at each other, tears falling but on seeing the same emotion on everyone else's face, their expressions changed to something akin to rapture.

The Princess raised her ringed hand, -And now I will tell you what you must know and it will bind us together for all time. Her voice was so commanding that a circle of gripping hands formed and eyes once again trained upon her, waiting for the words they sensed would change their lives, -What I did on the mountain with your help, was release the Red Man from his timeless curse. His spirit and that of his twin sister were locked in that golden sphere from the time that humankind was first created. He was forced to suffer in a half-lit world between life and death, ever returning and causing mayhem and destruction, until such time as a child or children of his, retrieved the orb and placed it in the flame of its original making. I was the child who did this. But I was not alone. What I learned from my spies on the waterways, from Uncle's records and from my visions was that the Red Man, in this last life of his, had eight children. I found you all. I mapped you. We are all brothers and sisters of his blood. And together we freed him!

The revelation took hold of all the faces in the circle, shaping them into a single expression of wonderment. None more so than that of Kamil the historian, for whom this ending had never been better disguised in his own prose.

Acknowledgements

My deep felt gratitude to Helen, my wife, who saw me through the hazards of the final Book. Next to Hollie Etheridge for her magical rendition of the front cover. Grateful thanks also to Vanessa Ahlberg for her editing guidelines and Allan Ahlberg for his dialogue on all and sundry. Finally, there are the many friends and relationships that conspired over the ten years to feed my creative impulses. Thank you all.